CW01212931

Ghosts of Yorkshire

Three Novels Plus A Bonus Short Story:

The Haunting of Thores-Cross

Cursed

Knight of Betrayal

Parliament of Rooks

Karen Perkins

First published in Great Britain in 2017 by
LionheART Publishing House

Copyright © Karen Perkins 2017
ISBN: 978-1-912842-12-4

This book is copyright under the Berne Convention
No reproduction without permission
All rights reserved.

The right of Karen Perkins to be identified as the author of this work has been asserted by her in accordance with sections 77 and 78 of the Copyright, Designs and Patents Act 1988.

LionheART Publishing House
Harrogate, North Yorkshire, UK

www.lionheartgalleries.co.uk
www.facebook.com/lionheartpublishing
publishing@lionheartgalleries.co.uk

This book is a work of fiction. Names, characters and incidents are either a product of the author's imagination or are used fictitiously. Any resemblance to actual people, living or dead or events is entirely coincidental.

Classification: Historical, literary, biographical, horror, psychological, ghosts, suspense, thriller, British, haunted houses.

The Haunting of Thores-Cross: A Yorkshire Ghost Story   1

Cursed: A Ghosts of Thores-Cross Short Story   193

Knight of Betrayal: A Medieval Haunting   215

Parliament of Rooks: Haunting Brontë Country   373

The Haunting of Thores-Cross:
A Yorkshire Ghost Story

Ghosts of Thores-Cross (Book 1)

KAREN PERKINS

From the Back Cover

"One of my most captivating reads of the year."

"The ghost of a wronged young woman in the village of Thores-Cross waits 230 years to have her story told in Perkins's suspenseful and atmospheric first Yorkshire Ghost novel . . . This historical ghost story provides page-turning chills and sympathy for scorned women" - *BookLife by Publishers Weekly*

*

When a vulnerable young girl is ostracised within her community and accused of witchcraft, the descendants of her neighbours will suffer for centuries to come.

Emma Moorcroft is still grieving after a late miscarriage and moves to her dream house at Thruscross Reservoir with her husband, Dave. Both Emma and Dave hope that moving into their new home signifies a fresh start, but life is not that simple. Emma has nightmares about the reservoir and the drowned village that lies beneath the water, and is further disturbed by the sound of church bells - from a church that no longer exists.

Jennet is fifteen and lives in the isolated community of Thores-Cross, where life revolves about the sheep on which they depend. Following the sudden loss of both her parents, she is seduced by the local wool merchant, Richard Ramsgill. She becomes pregnant and is shunned not only by Ramsgill, but by the entire village. Lonely and embittered, Jennet's problems escalate, leading to tragic consequences which continue to have an effect through the centuries.

Emma becomes fixated on Jennet, neglecting herself, her beloved dogs and her husband to the point where her marriage may not survive. As Jennet and Emma's lives become further entwined, Emma's obsession deepens and she realises that the curse Jennet inflicted on the Ramsgill family over two hundred years ago is still claiming lives.

Emma is the only one who can stop Jennet killing again, but will her efforts be enough?

Prologue
26th April 1988

'I dare you to go up to the haunted house.'

I glared at my sister in annoyance, then up at the house. I'd been there plenty of times with Alice and my friends, but never on my own. I did not want to go on my own now.

'Double dare you.'

'You little—!' I lunged at her, but she danced out of my way. She might have been small, but she was quick.

She laughed. 'Scaredy-cat, scaredy-cat, Emma's a scaredy-cat!'

I eyed the house again, then frowned at Alice. But a double dare was a double dare. And I was not a scaredy-cat. At ten years old, I could do this. I took a deep breath, ignored the butterflies in my stomach and started walking up the hill. I didn't rush.

I scrambled through the gap in the crumbling dry stone wall that separated the house from the field, using both hands to steady myself. Something caught my eye and I stopped to have a closer look. Curious, I reached into the jumble of stones, and pulled it from the dark recess in the wall.

A little pot. Made of stone, it was rich brown in colour, roughly an inch high and two inches round with a small neck and lip. An old inkpot. I shook my head. How did I know that?

'My story.'

I froze, then spun round to check behind me. *Who said that?* I looked back at the house. There was nobody here. Although the stone walls still stood, there were no doors, windows, nor roof. Dark holes gaped in the walls and, I knew from earlier visits, it was knee deep in sheepshit inside. I must have imagined the voice. I glanced back at Alice, braced my shoulders and took a step towards the house.

'Write my story.'

My breath caught in my throat, then I sucked in a great lungful of air, turned and ran. Dashing past Alice, I didn't care that she was laughing at me, that I'd lost the dare. I was terrified, desperate to get away from that house, that voice. It was only when I'd stopped running that I realised I still clutched the inkpot.

Chapter 1 - Jennet
28th June 1776

Pa moaned and moved in his sleep. I groaned. I knew by now that meant he had shat himself again. I had only changed the heather and straw he lay on an hour ago – I would have to go through the whole thing again: wake him and force him to move so I could take the stinking bedding away and give him fresh. I cursed. Mam's body were laid out downstairs in the hall. She would be buried tomorrow, and instead of sitting over her, I were cleaning Pa's shite.

I sighed and got up to take care of the mess. I were being unfair. The bloody flux were because of his ducking in the sheep pit. But I had seen the bloody flux before, and it did not bring such a man to this so quickly, not in three days.

I were fifteen years old, had just lost my Mam, and Pa were leaving me too. It were his grief and guilt that had reduced him to this pitiful hulk. If he wanted to stay with me – take care of me – he would fight this. I heaved him over and recoiled from the stench of blood and shite; but gritted my teeth and gathered up the dirty bedding. Yet another stinking trip to the midden.

I picked up fresh from the dwindling pile downstairs – I would have to go out and pull more heather soon. I glanced over at Mam's body, then carried the bedding up and dumped it on the bed Pa had so recently shared with her. He rolled back over – without even a flicker of his eyes to show he were aware of what I were doing for him.

Tears dripped down my face. How could this have happened? I went back downstairs, took the pot of steaming water off the fire and poured some into the bowl of herbs. I had struggled to remember what Mam had used on Robert Grange at the Gate Inn when he had been struck down with this, and eventually recalled a tea of agrimony, peppermint and blackberry leaf, then as much crab apple, bilberry and raspberry mash as she could force down his neck.

The herbs needed to steep for a few minutes, and if he would not drink any of it, I would wash his face with the tea. At least the smell were fresh. I held my head over the bowl and breathed deeply, then carried it upstairs to Pa for him to breathe in the healing steam. He were too far gone for the mash.

Mam had taught me the cunning ways since I were old enough to walk and talk. She had showed me how to recognise the restorative plants and herbs, which ones helped fevers, which helped wounds, which helped women and childbirth – even preventing a child. I knew their names, where they grew, whether flowers, leaves or roots were best, and the best times to plant and pick them. I knew what she knew. Had known. But I were struggling to remember. My thoughts were as muddy as the sheep pit she had died in. I had racked my brains to think what to brew for Pa, and had had to take out Mam's journal to check. Even so, my remedies did not seem to be doing much good.

I dipped a clean cloth into the tea and wiped his brow. I did not know of any plant that healed grief. I only wish I did.

How could this happen? How could they leave me?

'Jennet?'

I started at the sound of my name being called and went downstairs to greet Mary Farmer.

'Thee's never alone here!'

I nodded, too worn out to respond with any enthusiasm.

'Ee, I thought that Susan Gill would be here with thee.'

'She were, she had to go help William with the sheep.'

'Oh aye, likely story, she's not a one for hard work, her. Happen the smell got to her.'

I glanced up at her, but she showed no embarrassment. I realised I had got used to all but the most pungent, and wondered how badly my home smelled.

'Go on, get out of here. Go get some fresh air, this is no job for a lass. Thee's done well, but let me stay with him for a bit. Go for a walk.'

I did not need telling twice. I grabbed my shawl and nodded my thanks. When I got to the door, Mary stopped me.

'Has thee put bees in mourning yet, lass?'

I shook my head.

'Well, do it now, if thee don't, they'll never do owt else for thee, thee knows that.'

I nodded and ran. I had never been so glad to get outside. The crisp June wind blew the fresh scent of heather into my face and hair, ridding me of the scent of sickness. Chickens scattering at my feet, I hurried to the beeboles in the wall bordering the garden to tell the bees of Mam's death, ensuring plenty of honey and beeswax to come, then walked up the track on to the moor and kept going – not in the direction of the sheep-ford, but the other way, uphill where there were just space. No walls, nowt constraining me; just wind and heather. I breathed deeply, trying to forget, but very aware I were now alone in the world.

Chapter 2 - Emma
4th August 2012

'Happy?'

I turned to my husband.

'Ecstatic.'

He wrapped his arms around me. 'It's finally finished. No more problems, no more arguments with builders. The movers have gone, it's just us and our dream home,' he said.

'Thank you.'

'What for?'

'The "our". This is my dream home, really. I was the one who wanted to build here, despite the problems with the planning permission. You'd have been happy anywhere.'

'It *is* my dream home, too, Emma. It's beautiful up here, we've done the designs ourselves, made all the decisions together: it's *our* home.' He kissed me, and I held him close in my excitement. This was our fresh start. 'Shall we go in?'

'Don't even think about carrying me over the threshold.' I laughed.

'I wouldn't dream of it.' He marched to the front door and left it open for me to follow him inside. I laughed again and followed him into our new home.

The downstairs was a huge open-plan living space with the front of the house mainly glass to make the most of the view. A large stone gothic fireplace on the north wall was the focal point for the three comfortable sofas.

Set out in a squat H, the kitchen-diner took up the south wing, while the centre and north wing were lounge, with a cosy reading corner in front of the most northwestern window. A wetroom/loo, utility and mudroom were hidden away in the eastern ends of the wings and a large entrance vestibule also served as the support for the staircase.

Upstairs, there was an office in the centre and four en suite bedrooms in the wings, ready for the family we didn't yet have – would maybe never have.

I loved it and had designed it myself. Admittedly, Dave had taken my designs, changed what wasn't possible or safe, then added some strange magic to make our dream home the showstopper it was. At times I had despaired that it would ever get built, and my encroaching on his expertise had led to the most serious fights we'd had yet, but it was worth it. Our marriage had survived and we both loved it. I hugged him and he squeezed me back. I hadn't been this happy for a very long time.

Dave let go of me and bent to take the bottle of champagne out of the cool box. He opened it, poured, then held out a full plastic "glass" to me – the real ones were still in a box somewhere. We touched our drinks together in a toast, both of us beaming.

'To us and our new life,' Dave said, and we drank. He led the way further into the lounge to the large windows in the opposite wall.

'Look at that view,' he said. 'We'll have that every day for the rest of our lives, if we want it.'

I stared out of the window at the expanse of water. The reservoir was half full, lined by a rocky shore and grassy banks. Pines hugged the rise of the hill until they gave way to the purple-blooming heather of moorland. From this side of the house we could not see another building and it seemed we were alone. I watched in delight as a flock of Canada Geese landed on the water. 'I know, we're lucky.'

'It's very isolated though. I'm worried about leaving you on your own when I go up to Scotland. I need to spend a fair bit of time up there over the next few months – at this stage in the project I have to supervise things personally.'

'I'll be fine, you don't need to worry. There's so much to do to get the house straight, I'll barely notice you're gone.' I waved my arm at the boxes behind us. 'And anyway, I love the solitude; I'll get loads of writing done, and it's not like the old days – I have a phone and a car and everything.' I laughed again.

'I know all that, but still . . . This is a big house, which makes it a target, and the thought of you being on your own concerns me.'

'I'm used to it, I lived alone for seven years before we met, and anyway, you went overboard on the security – no one will get through those windows or past all the locks.'

'Yes, but still . . .'

'Well then, don't go away so much!'

'You know I have to.'

'Yes, you have to get away regularly because you can't cope with me full time!'

He laughed at the old joke. 'Now Ems, you know that's not always true.'

'As long as you keep coming home.'

'You know I always will.' He smiled tenderly and refilled my glass. I took it, sipped, then surveyed the view again. I'd travelled extensively, but this was my favourite place in the world. I belonged here.

'The perfect place to raise a family,' Dave whispered in my ear.

'Please don't,' I said.

'I've seen you with your nieces and you'd be a wonderful mother.' He ignored my protest. 'I know you're scared after what's happened, but if we don't even try, we'll never have a family.'

'I'm not ready.'

'Em, it's been a year. You're the one who insisted on so many bedrooms, I thought that meant you were ready to fill them.'

'Not yet, and I know exactly how long it's been, Dave. One year, three months and eleven days, to be exact.' My breath hitched in my throat and I fought to keep control. 'I can't go through that again, I won't! I can't lose another baby!' I was losing my battle against my sobs.

He hugged me. 'Hush,' he said, kissing my temple and brushing away my tears with his thumbs. 'I know you're still grieving, I am too, but look out there. This is a new start, a new beginning. The miscarriage was bad luck, that's all, food poisoning – a bad piece of chicken. There's no reason we can't have a baby, we just need to keep trying. And this would be a wonderful place to grow up.'

'I know Thruscross is a wonderful place to grow up, but I can't risk it. I'd started to believe we would have a family, and then, then . . . It's too much. We had her name picked out, the nursery was almost ready . . . and she died, before she even lived. I can't lose another baby. I can't risk it happening again – I just can't.' I took a deep breath to calm myself.

He nodded and stroked my hair, then cocked his head at the sound of a car. 'That'll be your sister with the beasts.'

'And the nieces,' I said with a small smile and wiped my face clear of tears. Alice and the girls had babysat our three dogs while we moved house.

'Our family's big enough for the moment,' I said. 'If we don't try for a baby, we can't lose another.'

Dave nodded. 'Have you thought any more about adoption?'

'No, I've been too busy with the build. Let me go and greet Alice.'

He brushed my cheek with his thumb before letting go of me. 'Will you think about it now?'

I didn't answer but went outside to my family.

Chapter 3 - Jennet

1st July 1776

Pa groaned, but did not open his eyes. I had told him we were burying Mam today, but he could not hear me. She were in her box now – a simple thing, but I had used every penny of Pa's savings to buy it. I wiped the sweat from his face. It were chilly in the house, but the fever had a tight grip on him.

The front door banged and I went downstairs. Mary and John Farmer stood by Mam's coffin.

'Jennet.' John nodded at me, cap in hand. He would stay with Pa while I buried Mam.

'Here, lass, thee's never going dressed like that!' Mary said at the top of her voice as usual. I looked down at myself. Bodice stiffened with wood and reed, petticoats, collar of linen, apron and white forehead cloth and coif to cover long hair the colour of cooked mutton – all were the best I owned.

Mary led the way upstairs, showed John into Pa's room then strode to the chest against the wall and rummaged inside it. 'Here,' she said. 'Wear this.' She held up a long black skirt and shawl. 'Come on, lass, hurry up, they'll be here soon.'

I recoiled. 'They're Mam's,' I said. I could not wear Mam's clothes to Mam's funeral.

'Well, she don't need them now, do she?' Mary answered, impatient. 'They're thine now, Jennet. Quick, go and get changed.' She pushed me out the door, and I stood for a moment, then went to my room. It were easier than arguing with Mary Farmer.

'There, that's more like it! Just in time too, they're here.'

I could not look down at myself. I could not bear the sight of Mam's clothes on me. Both skirt and shawl itched. I knew I would be aware of every thread of wool on my skin all day. More noise at the door, and I followed Mary downstairs. Digger and his son, Edward, had arrived with the cart to take Mam to the church. I let Mary Farmer organise them. It were Mary who urged their care. Mary who gave instructions to John over Pa. Mary who pushed me through the door and out into bright sunlight. It were Mam's funeral, how could the sun shine? I looked back at the house and, for a moment, pity for Pa mixed with my despair. How long before Digger's cart came for *him*?

'Come on, lass, no dawdling!'

I turned back to the cart and started the long walk behind it down the hill, Mary Farmer at my side. After a few steps I stopped hearing her endless chatter. It became just another sound of the country, like the birdsong. Ever present but meaningless. We passed the smithy and William Smith joined us, then the Gate Inn and Robert and Martha Grange.

One by one, the village turned out, dressed in their best, and fell in behind us. Mary Farmer greeted them all. I hardly noticed. I felt as if my insides had frozen. My heart, my lungs, belly, everything. With each step, they splintered further. I wondered if I would make it as far as the church at the other side of Thores-Cross or whether I would be left on the side of the lane, a heap of cracked and broken ice.

'Here.' Mary Farmer nudged me and held out a handkerchief. 'Thought this might come in useful. John won't miss it. Not today.'

I took it. I had not realised I were crying, but when I wiped my face and eyed the scrap of cloth, it were sopping wet. My eyes and nose must have been streaming since we left the house.

I scratched my shoulder. Remembered I were wearing Mam's clothes and lost myself in sobs. Mary Farmer tried to put an ample arm around me, but I shrugged her off. I wondered if I would ever stop crying. The cart reached the bridge and turned right. I followed, walking alongside the river, the same walk I used to make every other Sunday with Mam and Pa. We shared a curate with Fewston and would have to make *that* walk twice a month, unless Robert Grange were making the trip in his dray cart and we could ride the two miles over the moor. I realised with a start that I would not have to do that any more – not if I did not want to. Less than half the village made the trip to Fewston, claiming a variety of ills, and we only went because Mam insisted. I cried harder at the jolt of relief I felt.

'Here we are, lass. Thee stick with me, I'll get thee through this.' Mary Farmer clung to my arm and I peered at the church. Digger and Edward lifted Mam down from the cart, ready for various men from the village to carry it inside. Robert Grange, William Smith, Thomas Fuller and George Weaver. Our closest neighbours. I took a deep breath and followed them into the plain single-storey stone building with the steps so worn they were more like a ramp. It were cold inside, despite the July sun. Or maybe that were me. Still ice, still cracking, but still in one piece.

I sat on the front pew, Mary Farmer beside me – mercifully quiet now – and sniffed. I used the sopping rag that had been a handkerchief, but it were not much use now. I could not bear to wipe my face on Mam's shawl. Did everyone know I were wearing her clothes? And what did they think of me if they did? Mam were not even in her grave yet.

The curate – a young dark-haired lad who had grown up in Fewston – started the service. I tried to listen, but I could not tear my attention away from the box in front of me. Mam.

Then I heard what he were saying, and the cracks widened. 'Merciful God? Merciful God? What kind of merciful God would drown Mam in the sheep pit?'

Mary Farmer tried to pull me back down on to the pew, shushing me. I had not realised I were stood, but I could not stop.

'What kind of merciful God would inflict the bloody flux on her husband? What kind of God would take Mam and Pa away? What kind of God is that?'

My sobs pierced the shocked silence that followed, and Mary Farmer finally managed to sit me down.

'She's distraught, poor lass – don't take no notice, she's distraught,' she told the congregation. 'Carry on, Curate, carry on.'

We moved to the graveyard and Mam were sunk into a great hole. Then Mary Farmer led me away as she were covered up.

At home, the stench hit me as we walked through the door. Pa were the same. My sobs tore the cracks inside me further apart. John Farmer went home. Mary Farmer stayed.

The next morning I were alone. I do not know when Mary Farmer had left – she must have waited until I slept. I dragged myself out of bed and went to clean Pa. It were for the last time. The bloody flux were not always a killer, but to survive it you needed strength, and Pa's strength had drowned in the sheep pit with Mam. There would be another funeral this week.

Chapter 4 - Emma
4th August 2012

My eldest niece, Chloe, was already out of the car when I opened the front door, and she ran to give me a hug. I grabbed her, spun her round and gave her a kiss, then gave her sister Natalie, three years younger at seven, the same treatment. Five-year-old Sophie needed help from her mother to get down from the Range Rover, then she ran over to join the scrum.

'Uncle David!' They abandoned me in their rush to greet Dave, and I laughed as three blonde angelic-looking terrors mobbed him.

I went to join Alice at the car and gave her a hug.

'How are you?' she asked.

'Great,' I replied. 'We're going to love it here.'

'I hope so.' She opened the boot and three equally excited balls of fur jumped down, then leaped up at me with their own enthusiastic greetings. I ruffled their heads before they bounded away to explore their new home.

'Come on in, you haven't seen the place since we finished it.'

'How's the unpacking going?'

'A complete mess.' I laughed. 'But at least we found the kettle. Coffee?'

'Would love one.'

I linked arms with my sister and we walked to the house. I whistled for the dogs and they came running.

'Thank you so much for looking after the beasts; I wouldn't have coped with them as well as the movers and everything.'

'My pleasure,' Alice said. 'The girls loved having them, and we've plenty of space. They were no bother.'

I smiled and felt ashamed for asking it of her. Alice had two dogs of her own, as well as a couple of horses, a flock of chickens and even a couple of goats. I didn't quite believe my three were "no bother".

'I'm very grateful, Alice, I don't know what we'd have done without you, I couldn't bear the thought of putting them in kennels.'

'Oh no, you couldn't do that! Don't worry about it, Ems, it was fine, honestly, we were pleased to help. You've had a hell of a time the last year or so, it was the least we could do.'

'Thanks, Sis. I know they couldn't have been in better hands.'

'Wow!' We had entered the lounge. 'It looks so different with furniture. Trust you to have unpacked your books first!'

I felt ashamed. 'Dave was furious when I started filling the bookshelves and left all the kitchen stuff in boxes,' I said. 'I couldn't even wait till the movers left, I just had to get them on the shelves.' I shrugged and smiled.

Alice laughed. 'I doubt he expected anything else of you, Em. Come on, I'll help you unpack the kitchen – Dave can amuse the kids, they adore him.'

'I know, he's great with them isn't he?'

Alice turned to me. 'Have you had any more thoughts . . . ?'

I shook my head. I'd already been through this with Dave, I couldn't do this conversation again. 'Don't.'

She nodded and stroked my upper arm. I turned from the pity I saw in her face, and led the way into the kitchen.

'Teatime,' I announced a couple of hours later. 'We'd like to treat you at the Stone House, a little thank you for having the beasts.'

'You don't have to do that, Ems, a sandwich here would be fine.'

'We want to. Anyway,' I surveyed the kitchen, 'I think we deserve it after all our hard work.'

'You have a point there. All right, that would be lovely. Kids!'

I jumped as she shouted the last word. The girls, Dave and the dogs ran in from outside.

'Wash your hands, we're going to the pub for tea.'

I chuckled when Dave obeyed Alice's instruction as well, then grabbed my coat.

Ten minutes later, we pulled into the car park, Alice and the girls behind us.

'Auntie Emma, Mummy said there's a haunted house.'

'Yes there is, though people live in it now, so I don't think it's haunted any more.'

'Bet it is!' said Natalie, and ran after Sophie making woo-woo noises.

Chloe stayed behind, looking thoughtful. 'Are ghosts real, Uncle Dave?'

'No, of course not. No such thing, it's just a way of explaining funny noises in the night. Now come on, help me find us a good table.'

They walked hand in hand to the pub entrance. Alice and I glanced at each other and laughed.

'I hope he's right.'

'About what?' I asked.

'No such thing as ghosts.'

I shrugged. I believed they did exist.

'Are you going to be ok, living out here? I'd forgotten how isolated it is.' She looked around. There was only a scattering of houses to break up the rolling expanse of moorland. 'There's not even a shop; and what if something happens, how would you get help?'

I shrugged. 'We'll make sure we keep plenty of supplies in. And there's always this place.' I laughed.

'Yes, but what if there's an accident? It would take ages for an ambulance or something to get here.'

'Not really, it's not like it used to be when we were kids. The doctors' surgery in one of the villages has a four-wheel drive, and there's always the air ambulance if something serious happens. We're not that cut off, you know, not the way it was,' I said.

'Yeah, ok, but what about winter? I can remember drifts up to our shoulders, and not being able to get to the sailing club.'

I shrugged again. 'I work from home and Dave is pretty flexible. This is still a farming community; I'm sure a local farmer will plough the lanes – he'd have to, to get to his livestock.' I nodded at the distant sheep and the field of Highland cattle nearby – only the hardiest breeds survived up here. 'And we'll make sure we have plenty of supplies,' I repeated. 'We'll be fine.'

'I hope so,' Alice replied. 'But I can't help worrying.'

I gave her a quick hug, then turned at a shout from Dave. 'Come on you two, the girls are hungry!'

I smiled and linked arms with Alice. 'Don't worry, Alice, please. I know it's isolated, but we have thought it through, and we'll prepare well for winter. Anyway, it'll be nice, the two of us snowed in, curled up in front of a roaring fire – romantic.'

She gave a small nod, and we followed Dave into the pub.

'Where's the menu?'

'Above the bar.'

We crowded round to read the blackboard.

'What does it say?' Sophie asked.

'Shepherd's pie with chips and peas, steak and ale pie with chips and peas, chicken pie with chips and peas.'

'Is there anything vegetarian?' Alice asked the barman.

'Aye,' he replied. 'Chips and peas.'

She stared at him and I burst out laughing at the expression on her face as she realised he was serious.

Chapter 5 - Jennet
9th July 1776

'Here, cut that pie up will thee, Jennet?' Mary Farmer called. I picked up the knife and sliced the large rabbit pie. The other women bustled around me, but for the most part they left me alone – apart from Mary Farmer.

It were the shearing. Two weeks after the sheep-washing and Mam's death, the whole village had gathered again. This were the last place I wanted to be the day after burying Pa. *How had I let Mary Farmer persuade me to come?*

I picked up the platter of pie slices and carried it into the shearing shed. The rest of the year it were Thomas Ramsgill's barn, but as the biggest in the valley (and Thomas having one of the largest flocks), everyone brought their animals here to be shorn each year. By pulling together like this, a thousand head of sheep could be bald by the end of the day. Somehow Thomas Ramsgill got his flock seen to without getting his own hands dirty, but it still worked out better like this than each farmer trying to deal with his own flock alone. Plus we had a party. Not that I felt much like partying this year.

The pie platter were cleared in five minutes flat and I went back for more. Thomas Ramsgill had taken the biggest slice and I scowled. It were supposed to be for the men and women doing the work – not only the clippers, but the wrappers, catchers and sharpeners, too.

The animals were sent in to the waiting clippers, who perched on their three-legged stools. The fastest clipper could take a fleece off in three and a half minutes – muscles bulging and sweat dripping as they worked the hand shears impossibly fast. I watched the ewes and wondered which one of them had killed Mam.

The clippers' wives and daughters chopped off the dirty locks around the tail before wrapping the wool into tight rolls. They had fleeces from up to twenty clippers each to lap like this and it were exhausting work. The catchers at the door dabbed the sheep with tar marks to distinguish each man's property and sent them off to their fold – one flock at a time. Add to that chaos William Smith sharpening countless pairs of shears, the bleating of the sheep, cursing of the clippers and wrappers, and the smell of sweating farmers and distressed animals, it were impossible to keep crying. I were soon swept up in the sheer busyness of the day and ran back and forth with pie and jugs of ale. I caught Mary Farmer watching me and smiled. She had been right to bully me out of the quiet empty house. It were good to be around people and forget – even if only for a few minutes at a time.

'How is thee, Jennet?'

I started at the deep voice, and turned to see Thomas and Richard Ramsgill. The Ramsgills were the most important family in the valley – Thomas the Forest Constable, Richard the wool merchant, Big Robert the miller and Alexander just getting his own farm established. There were three more brothers still working their father's farm.

Richard lived close to us. To me. Just down the hill at East Gate House, near the smithy and the Gate Inn. He were a stern man and had never spoken to me before today. Now he raised his eyebrows at my lack of response.

'Umm,' I said. It were the one question I never knew how to answer; I had no idea what to say to Richard Ramsgill.

'I remember thy mam when she were a young lass,' Richard Ramsgill carried on, ignoring my stammering. It's such a shame. If there's anything I can do for thee, thee only has to ask.'

Thomas laughed. 'Is thee gonna find her somewhere to live, then?'

'What does thee mean?' I said, panicked into forgetting my manners. *Were I being evicted?*

'Well, surely thee knew? Thee'll have to leave the farm, the tenure won't pass to a fifteen-year-old lass. Did thy pa write a will?'

'Umm, no, I don't think so,' I said.

Thomas Ramsgill seemed embarrassed.

'Don't worry theesen about it, lass,' his brother said. 'I'll look into it for thee, see if there's owt can be done. Thomas here is being a bit previous. Don't worry, thee won't have to leave farm.'

What to say to him? 'Umm.' I were dumbfounded.

'By the way, does thee know what the terms of thy folks' tenure of land was?'

'Umm.'

'Tell thee what, I realise this is probably a bit much for thee. Don't worry about a thing, lass, I'll pop round later this week. See thee again, lass.' He doffed his hat and they walked away.

I stared after him. Mary Farmer joined me. 'Ey up, lass, what did *they* want? Thee take care round likes of them, thee mark me words. Careful, lass. Now, grab this jug of ale, I reckon them in barn are getting a thirst on.'

Chapter 6 - Emma
12th August 2012

I whistled again. The beasts would stay out all night and day if they could. Cassie the Irish Setter came first. She was the eldest at nine and I'd had her since she was a puppy. The other two, both German Shepherds, would follow given time.

It was getting chilly now the sun was going down, and I was splashed head to foot with mud. I turned towards the house and smiled as I always did, unable to help myself. It had taken nearly two years and a great deal of determination to build.

From the big upstairs office window I could see the dam to the left – innocuous from this side but terrifying from the other. It had a massive drop, like a black run with no snow – or a ski jump that kept going down. Functional and massive, it hid nothing of its purpose and had given me nightmares as a child sailing here. I'd been terrified of getting swept up to its lip and having to stare down that chasm, knowing it was the only place for me to go.

I shivered and whistled again. Running up the slope after Cassie, I could hear Delly and Rodney following, and was laughing at them when we burst into the mudroom – cold, filthy and exhilarated from the fresh air. I towelled the dogs off and took off my coat, then walked into the kitchen for a hot chocolate. Dave already had the kettle steaming and handed me a mug, smiling and shaking his head.

'You're like a child out there with those dogs, Emma, a carefree little girl.'

I bit, hearing a reprimand in his words. 'You can't be surprised, surely?'

'I'm not complaining, relax. It's great to see, I wish I could do it.'

'You can, if you try. Just let go and enjoy the moment. That's how I write and that's what's built this house.' I was on my guard, expecting another lecture on responsibility, which was hardly fair. I had met most of the building costs as Dave had invested so heavily in his building project in Scotland.

'Oh calm down! Why do you have to be so defensive? I know things are a bit tight at the moment, but once this Edinburgh project is finished, there'll be a massive return – there's plenty of interest in the flats already, even the penthouses. In a year or two I might even be able to semi-retire.'

Silence. Most of our conversations had ended like this since the miscarriage, and had got worse with the challenge of building this place. Dave had thrown himself into his work, and I had tried to do the same with my books, but I had struggled to write so had concentrated on the house. I worried that we'd put our whole selves into building the perfect home, and had nothing left over for each other – or a future family. I couldn't bear it if that were the case.

I sipped my hot chocolate and waited for the atmosphere to clear. The dogs had become expert at this and jumped at us both, tongues lolling, whenever they sensed tension starting to build.

'What's for dinner?' he asked, trying again for domestic harmony.

'I stuck a chicken in the oven before I took the dogs out.'

'That sounds lovely. I'm going through to the lounge – I've lit a fire. Join me?'

'No, I've got another couple of chapters to edit, then I'll be done for the evening.' It wasn't the friendliest reply, and I felt ashamed at the downcast expression on his face. We seemed to be constantly sniping at each other at the moment, and I wanted to ease the atmosphere between us. 'I quite fancy dinner in front of the fire though, is there anything good on telly?'

'Probably not. We'll see.' He'd cooled again. 'You can't hide from life in your books, Emma. You need to face things, and live. You told me earlier to live in the moment, but you're still living in the past!'

'No, I'm not.' I was aware of my voice rising, but couldn't seem to stop it. 'I'm trying to enjoy each day, because life is precious, that's why I wanted to move here and build this house!' I didn't understand how he could have got over the miscarriage already, and he didn't seem to understand why I was still grieving.

'Is it? Are you sure about that? You threw yourself into building this place – negotiating with Yorkshire Water for the land, getting planning permission, then sorting out the utility companies so we'd have mains electricity and water. And then after we'd lost the baby you were here almost every day keeping an eye on the builders, it became an obsession. I think you did it to avoid thinking about what had happened. And now the house is finished, you're obsessing over your books.'

'That's not true!'

'Isn't it? You didn't use to work this hard. When we first met, you told me you had to stay relaxed, or you couldn't write, that you couldn't force the words to come.'

'I'm not forcing anything. I'm not obsessing. I'm just writing and earning a living,' I shouted.

He sighed and shrugged. 'Whatever you say, Emma.'

I stared at him for a moment, but there was nothing more to add. I went upstairs.

* * *

I hesitated before I switched the light on, wanting to take in the view for a moment. I'd wrestled with the design of this room. The forty-foot long west wall was all glass to give an unspoilt view of the water, and there'd been a very real fear that it would distract rather than inspire me, and I had a lot of books still to write – I hoped.

I thought of Dave and our argument. I didn't know how to tell him that my latest book was not going well. I was struggling to plot it and keep my characters consistent, and had barely written anything worth keeping for over a year.

Reluctantly, I switched the light on, hiding the reservoir in the glare. I looked up at the ceiling for inspiration. It had been carpentered in the same way as the old ships had been many years ago and, with keelson and struts laid out along the length of the house, I could imagine myself in an upturned hull of a leviathan square rigger.

I had a sofa and coffee table positioned in front of the large glass wall and balcony, while my desk was pushed against the left wall under a large noticeboard. Book shelves took up most of the remaining wall space as they did downstairs in the lounge. You could never have enough books. Well, Dave could, but I couldn't, and he loved to complain that they were breeding. Maybe I should turn one of the guest rooms into a library. *Now there's an idea.*

I walked to the desk and settled down in front of the computer.

I jumped and stared at the dark window. A flash had lit up the reservoir, followed by a crash of thunder. I sighed in frustration and put down my pen – I could not focus on my pirates and the tropics when I faced, literally, the raging nature of the moors. I switched off the light and stared out of the window – hurricane-rated to withstand the weather here. Lit up by bright flashes of lightning and surrounded by battered pines, the reservoir was a seething mass of waves and mini-waterspouts from the needles of rain.

My mind flew back over twenty years to when I had learned to sail here as a child. I remembered a storm like this and everyone streaming into the clubhouse, glad to get out of it. The instructor decided it would be a good day to do our capsize drill and, surprising the seasoned sailors, he gathered his little band of aspiring mariners to the water's edge where his oldest boat awaited, still rigged with a wooden mast.

Apart from the sheer madness of it, the thing I remembered most was how warm the reservoir had been after the rain, and how much I had enjoyed my swim, despite the water I swallowed through all the laughter.

I got up and grabbed a coat from the bedroom, then went back into the office and opened the balcony door. I struggled outside against the wind and cursed when papers flew off my desk, then shut the door behind me. The balcony was fairly sheltered, and if I stood close to the windows, I could just about manage to stay clear of the rain.

I stepped forward and grabbed hold of the rail, then lifted my face to the full power of the storm. Another flash of lightning and crash of thunder. I laughed at the majesty of it, exhilarated by the force of nature, then hushed. *What was that?* After the thunder had reverberated away, I'd thought I'd heard . . . *No.* I shook my head, *I can't have.* I stepped back into the shelter of the house, ran my hands over my now sodden hair, and listened.

Yes, I hadn't imagined it. In the wake of the next thunderclap, bells – church bells. But there was no church for miles, certainly none close enough to be able to hear their bells. I stared at the water, thinking of the village that rested beneath. The only church close enough was—

'I thought I'd find you out here,' Dave said, and I jumped.

'It's beautiful.'

He put his arms around me and I snuggled into his embrace to watch the rest of the storm, grateful and relieved that he'd made the first move to make up after our row.

'I'm sorry,' he said.

I stroked his arm. 'Me too, it's just . . .' I tailed off.

'I want a family so badly, but if you're not ready, you're not ready. There's no pressure.'

'I do want a family, you know that, I'm just scared.'

'I know, but we can adopt. You don't have to risk another pregnancy.'

'Yes, but if we adopt, we're giving up. And I want *our* baby – I'm not ready, not yet. And even if we do adopt, what if something happens? What if he or she gets ill or has an accident or something? There's so much that can go wrong – I can't lose another child.'

'Is it worth speaking to someone again?'

'What, like that counsellor? I don't know. How can talking help?'

'Isn't it worth trying? It helped me.'

'I did try! I spent three months talking to that grief counsellor. It was all right for you, but it didn't help me much, did it?'

'No, I don't suppose it did.' He squeezed and held me tighter. 'You're not on your own though, Em, remember that. You can always talk to me.'

'I know. I don't know what I'd have done without you.' I twisted to kiss him, then settled back into his embrace to watch the rest of the storm.

Chapter 7 - Jennet
15th July 1776

'Now then, Jennet, thee's got to eat, thee'll waste away.'

I sighed. Would Mary Farmer never leave me alone? I had been grateful for her help at first, but it were getting to be too much. She were here every day, fussing about me with non-stop advice and prattle. Even while she were forcing me to eat her soup, she stood at the table putting a large mutton pie together for later. I lifted the spoon to my mouth. The easiest thing were to do as she insisted. Maybe if she saw me eating, she'd leave me alone. Anyroad, I were hungry.

It had been a week since I'd buried Pa and I still felt as if made of ice. I did my chores, kept the house clean, fed the chickens – the sheep took care of themselves at this time of year and were loose on the moor behind the house. It were lambing season in February when they would need my attention, and I could not think that far ahead yet.

'By heck, summat smells good!'

I glanced up in surprise. Richard Ramsgill had walked through the open door unannounced. I stood in greeting.

'Mr Ramsgill! What's thee doing here?' Mary Farmer said at the top of her voice.

'Come to see young Jennet, Mary. Business.'

I smirked as Mary Farmer struggled to find words. He raised his eyebrows at her and glanced towards the door. Mary Farmer turned red as a rosehip and clapped the flour from her hands.

'Well . . . Well . . .' she muttered.

'Private business,' Mr Ramsgill stressed.

'Very well.'

I watched in amazement as Mary Farmer's nosiness battled against her deference to the man who controlled all our lives as the local wool merchant – and lost.

'It ain't seemly,' she muttered, just loud enough for us both to hear, as she picked up her shawl. 'Ain't seemly for a young lass to be alone with a grown man, not at all.'

Richard Ramsgill stared at her, waiting for her to leave, then closed the door. I shut my eyes for a moment in relief and opened them in surprise when he laughed.

'She can be a bit much, can't she?'

'She means well.' I leapt to her defence. 'She helped me all through Pa's illness, and every day since.'

'Oh, aye, I'm sure she has. Likes nowt else than to feel important, that one.'

I smirked at him. He pointed to the other stool in question and I nodded, embarrassed that I had not asked him to sit.

'Would thee like some soup?'

He shook his head. 'Not for me thanks, lass. A jug of posset wouldn't go amiss, though.'

I busied myself at the fire, pouring some of the curdled milk and ale that Mary Farmer had prepared earlier. 'There's not much spice in it I'm afraid, just some herbs from moor.'

He took a flask from his jacket and poured a little of the amber liquid into his jug, then took a sip. 'Mm, that hits the spot.'

I knew he were just being polite, but dipped my head at the compliment nonetheless. I sat back down in silence and studied my soup.

'I'll come straight to point,' Richard Ramsgill said after a short, awkward silence. 'I said at shearing that I'd look into thy situation for thee.'

I looked up at him. Would I be forced to leave the farm?

'Don't look so scared, lass.' He laughed and took another sip. 'I've been to London with our Thom since I last saw thee, to sort out enclosures.'

'Enclosures?'

'Aye, them new walls thee's seen going up? It's on King's orders, he's enclosing land and selling it. Our Thom's in charge of placing walls and allotting land, and me and me brothers are putting in to buy what we can. Anyroad, I had a word with land folk, and pleaded thy case. It took quite a bit of wrangling, but I finally got sight of papers and it seems farm belonged to thy mam – it were passed to her from thy grandpa and she had copyhold of inheritance on land.'

I did not react. What did that mean?

'It means thee can stay, lass. It means her tenure passed to thee on her death as her sole heir, even though neither of them made a will. And when these enclosures are done and land's awarded, it'll be thine for life.'

I sagged in relief. I had not realised until now how scared I had been that I would be turned out on to the moor – or on to Mary and John Farmer's hospitality. 'I can stay?'

'Aye, thee can stay, lass. Can thee manage farm does thee think?'

I thought of all the work involved in rearing the sheep, plus the haymaking and maintaining the farm. Pa had handled all that, with a little help from me and Mam. But the two of us had also been busy all year round with carding and spinning wool, gathering and drying our herbs, plus cutting peat and pulling heather, growing and gathering food and many more chores besides. How would I manage on my own? I were embarrassed anew to find tears in my eyes.

'Ey up, don't fret so, lass! Thee's not on thy own, thee knows. Mary Farmer's up road—' I cried harder '—and whole village'll pull together to see thee through first year till thee finds thy feet. And I'm sure one of young lads'll soon snap thee up – thee has thy own farm, lass, thee's quite a catch, thee knows, especially for a second son!'

'We struggled to manage with three of us, how can I do it all? I know village'll help, but they have their own farms and families to see to.' I sobbed harder. I ignored his comment about young men, I did not have my eye on anyone – although that Peter Stockdale always had a nice smile for me. Richard Ramsgill put down his posset and dragged his stool closer. He grasped my shoulder and I winced.

'Tell thee what, I'll let thee use one of me best tups in November, and send thee one of me best men for lambing. He'll see thee right, and he'll help thee with getting feed to them during winter, an'all.'

I cried harder at his kindness. It seemed my tears were unstoppable since Mam died. 'How can I ever thank thee?'

'Ahh, no need for thanks, lass. I told thee, thy Mam and me were great friends as nippers, it's least I can do.' He got up, poured more posset, then added a little of his own ingredient and passed the jug to me. I thanked him and sipped, gasping at the heat that slid down my throat into my stomach. I glanced up at him in surprise and he burst out laughing.

'Just a little whiskybae, lass, best thing for grief *and* tears in my experience!'

I took another sip, enjoying the heat now that I expected it, and smiled at him.

'See, that's better, lass. There's nowt wrong in't world that a little whiskybae don't put right.'

Chapter 8 - Emma
28th August 2012

There was only one problem writing about pirates in the Caribbean – I wanted to go sailing. Writing about the wind in my face and my ship slicing through the waves, the rigging singing, made me long to experience it myself. Trouble was, I didn't have a licence to sail on Thruscross and a white sail would hardly be inconspicuous – but what would they do? Charge me with trespass? What the hell.

Mind made up (let's face it, it didn't take much) I decided to go for it. After all the rain, Thruscross was full – a rarity in August – an hour drifting around free of the shore would do me good. I put my pirates away and went down to dig out my old wetsuit (a bit tight, but it still fitted) and lifejacket, then went to the garage to check the laser, *Guinevere*. A small singlehanded dinghy, it was pretty rugged and good fun in a blow, yet light enough that I could enjoy the meagre ten knots I estimated to be blowing out there. It was snug on its trailer and I hooked it up to the Discovery before driving down the old access road to the bottom. Just like old times.

It took some manoeuvring to separate the trolley and trailer, and more to get the mast up on my own, but a bit of frustration would be worth it. I felt guilty for a moment – I should be working really, but I consoled myself with the thought that I could justify this as research – what better way to plan a pirate attack than out on the water with the wind in my hair? Maybe this would cure my writer's block.

At last I was ready; *Guinevere* was in the water and I pushed off, then jumped in. It had been too long since I'd done this and I spent an age getting centre-board and rudder down, but at last I sheeted in, hooked my feet under the toe straps (a little optimistically) and made way.

Whilst I'd never left the water in my heart, I hadn't been in a dinghy for years. In my youth I'd sailed competitively, but life had got in the way. I'd never been able to bring myself to sell *Guinevere* though, and my return to a dinghy was long overdue. Perhaps alone wasn't the most sensible way of getting back into it, but hell, that had never stopped me before.

I felt my face stretch into a big grin, and relaxed. God, I'd missed this. Time to try a tack. Success. Gybe. Whoops, mainsheet caught round the transom. No problem, easily fixed. I unhooked it, sheeted in again and headed up towards the creek. How would my characters attack their rival? They needed to do something different, to take him by surprise. It wouldn't be easy, he'd been pirating for a long time. How would they get an advantage over him?

I was up at the creek already and running out of wind. It was shifty all over the reservoir – one of the reasons the sailing club had moved – and it had always been worse up here because of the high banks. I tried my hand at a roll tack – gently taking her through the wind whilst heeling sharply to help steer. Made it, not bad, apart from getting my arse wet, but that's sailing for you.

The wind was behind now and too light to run before, so I hardened up to a reach and practised gybing back and forth across the lake, heading southish towards the dam. I'd never been much of a light-weather sailor; I'd always preferred a blow, and now that the wind was dropping off I was getting bored. I turned my mind back to the Caribbean.

I grinned in triumph. I had my battle and knew how they'd fight. Now I had to get ashore and write it down before I forgot – I should have brought pen and paper out with me. Never mind, I'd remember next time. I had a brief image of me drifting around Thruscross, laid across the boat writing, then looked about me to get my bearings.

Oh no. Oh no. I looked wildly at the banks, but of course there were no transit poles to mark the danger – they'd gone with the sailing club. I looked at the dam again. It was far too close. I could see the water pouring over the outflow and hear it falling down the sheer drop on the other side. I pulled the sail in desperately, but there was even less wind than there had been earlier, and all I did was shake what little I had out of the sail in my panic. I knew in the depths of my mind that I had to stay calm and move carefully to get out of this, but calm was difficult to achieve this close to the dam.

I threw *Guinevere* into a tack, forgetting to roll her, and cursed when I got stuck. Head to wind and being pulled closer by the current of water flowing over the impossibly high dam, I had a flash memory of how the dam looked. On this side, a concrete wall with five overflows, blue sky shining through them. On the other, a concrete hell slide, one-hundred-and-twenty-feet long to a concrete sluice. Going over it would kill me.

I bit back my panic; I had to get the boat sailing. The closer I got, the harder it would be to get away. I remembered the nightmares I'd had as a child when I'd sailed on this reservoir every week, after I'd seen what was on the other side for the first time. They would not come true. They wouldn't. They couldn't.

I backed the mainsail across the wind so it could help the rudder turn me, and belatedly heeled the boat, but it wasn't enough. There was no wind, the water was glassy, and by the looks of it there were no gusts heading my way.

Why hadn't I paid more attention? I examined the banks. I was too close to the dam and the shore was too far away to swim for. If I didn't get out of the current, I'd be swept over and killed for sure. If I swam, I'd still have to get out of the pull of the middle opening, then two more. Even if I managed it, then what? Was that dead water beyond the overflows, or a swirling eddy that would keep the rocky shore beyond my reach and send me straight back into danger?

My best chance was in the boat; someone may see me and get help. There was a car park up there, people walked along the banks and they drove and walked across the dam itself, often pausing to peer over the sides. Surely someone would see I was in trouble and get help. Yes, my best chance was to stay in the boat. I started shouting in the still afternoon, knowing I should wait and save my voice until I knew someone was there to hear me, but unable to stop.

How could I have been so stupid? I grew up here knowing the dangers. I'd heard stories as a child of a boat going over for a dare, although I'd decided it wasn't true – nobody could be that foolish. I'd seen a boat rescued from the lip of the overflow. Twice. But there was no rescue boat here today. I took a deep breath and tried to calm down, but all I could think was: *it's getting closer, it's getting closer*. I remembered my phone, safe in a pouch hanging from my neck and fiddled with my lifejacket and wetsuit to get it out. I powered it up and nothing. No signal. Not a single bar – I should have thought of that; of course there wouldn't be a signal on the water, I was lucky to get one on the bank.

I yanked on the sail in desperation and was rewarded with a little spurt of speed – of course! I could pump my way out of this! But the current had dragged my bow round towards the dam; I was facing the wrong way. I thrust the tiller across again to harden back up, but nothing – no steerage.

I left the rudder hard over, stood, clambered forward to the mast and shoved the boom against what little wind there was, whilst heeling her sharply. Finally, I was turning. Not much, but the bows *were* coming round. It wasn't enough though, and I realised I would have to make my own wind.

I stepped up on to the foredeck and grabbed the mast in both hands, using my splayed legs to rock the boat from side to side as hard as I could, trying to build up a rhythm and force my way to starboard. It was working.

I kept going.

I was side on now and still going. I steadied a little and smoothed the rocking motion to go forwards. If I kept trying to turn her, I'd lose time and get pulled backwards; I needed to go for speed and get to the shore.

Is it getting easier?

Yes. I was out of the pull of the middle and strongest overflow. Two more to go. I kept pumping. My leg muscles, especially the inside of my thighs, were starting to burn, but I knew my only chance was to keep up the rhythm. I had to get more speed up and keep it going when the next current caught me. Then no stopping until I got past the third.

I glanced to my right, I could see only sky. There was nothing through that deadly concrete hole but air. Then I realised I *could* see more than sky, the wooded cliff face was coming into view. I was looking through the last one! I was nearly safe.

I took a deep breath and kept pumping. So much for a nice, gentle sail! I was exhausted. My legs were beyond protest, my back cramped in agony every time I shifted my weight from one leg to the other, and my arms felt like they'd done a full weights training programme as they pulled the mast over. But I couldn't stop. I had to find more strength. I had to keep going. The force of the current grabbed me again and threw me off balance. I tried to save myself, but my legs wouldn't respond. I was on my knees, mercifully still on the boat. I glanced round; my bow was being pulled back towards the dam.

'No!' I screeched. 'No! Not after all this! No fucking way! You're not getting me!'

I could almost see teeth around that square hole now; a concrete mouth waiting to chew me up and swallow me – although in this case it would swallow me then crush me. I was losing it. I had to pull myself together or I was dead. I pictured Dave; my sister and nieces; the dogs; my unfinished book.

I hauled myself back to my feet and hugged the mast, my legs shaking. I glanced over my right shoulder and my panic came back. *Good, it may save my life.*

I planted my feet as wide apart as I dared, gripped the mast hard and frenziedly rocked the boat. I was aware I was sobbing, but nothing would stop that now. *Left right, left right. Port starboard, port starboard.* What a time to start correcting my sailor speak. *Port starboard, port starboard.* I refused to look to my right, I didn't even let myself look behind for the shore, just stared at the sail and boom swinging across the boat and the uneven wake I was leaving – I could see the disturbed water being pulled towards the dam and over the drop. *Port, starboard. Port, starboard.* Can I look now? No not yet, keep going. *Port, starboard. Port, starboard.*

My sobs calmed in the monotony of the rhythm and I kept going. I thought running a marathon would be like this – *left right, left right, left right, port starboard, port starboard,* on and on and on. Forever and a day.

Aargh. Thrown off balance again, I fell, rolled off the deck and into the water. I put my feet down and felt rock. No wonder I'd fallen, I'd crashed into the bank! I sobbed again, this time in relief, and scrambled backwards, my shaking legs pushing against submerged rock. I'd made it! I was ok! I'd made it! I collapsed on the rock, my hands gripping it tightly, breaking every fingernail in my desperation to grasp terra firma. I'd never been so pleased to crash ashore.

I remembered *Guinevere* then, what had I broken on the rocks? Centre-board? Rudder? Hull? I turned back to the water to check for damage.

Horrified, I watched *Guinevere* drift towards the dam. I'd betrayed her – she'd got me to safety and I'd abandoned her. I had to watch her. I couldn't save her, but I wouldn't let her go all alone. I scrambled up the steps leading to the road, my legs still working, somehow, and staggered to the far side, realising that after the struggle with not a breath of breeze to help me, the wind was getting up.

Would she catch on the lip? No. Her mast was too short to save her, and I must have damaged her foils on the rocks: all they did was heel her over as she came sideways on, through the gaping jaws. I watched open-mouthed as she slid over the waterfall, the wind of her dive catching the sail and lifting her bows up as she surfed down the dam; then she heeled a little too far to starboard and capsized gracefully in mid-air, first her mast then her hull shattering on impact. No one would have survived that.

I sank to the ground, sobbing again, feeling as if I'd never stop, only now truly understanding how close death had come.

I stared at the wall, confused, how could I be in my bedroom? I switched on the bedside lamp, blinked a few times and, as my senses returned, realised it had been a dream. I sniffed and wiped tears from my face, then flinched. I'd scratched my cheek. I held my hands in front of me and examined them. Every fingernail was broken and dirty. I scraped the jagged remains of one nail under another, then held my finger up to the light. There was a small mound of peaty, brown dirt on my nail – the same colour as the mud of the reservoir's shoreline.

Chapter 9 - Jennet
19th August 1776

I opened my eyes and stared at the timbers above me, picturing scenes from my dreams – bright sunshine on the moors, heather in bloom . . . and Richard Ramsgill. Bathing in the beck . . . and Richard Ramsgill. I smiled, despite myself, and threw off the sheepskin I used as a blanket. Time to start the day.

'Ey up, lass, he's here again!'
I looked up from scrubbing the floor and stared at Mary Farmer standing at the open door. She had finished sweeping and had gone outside to knock the dust from the besom.
'Richard Ramsgill, he's only coming up lane again!'
I could not explain why my heart beat a little faster.
'Thee needs to watch him, lass. I don't trust him an inch. Just promise me thee'll take care with him.'
'Don't fret theesen, Mary, he's helping me sort tenure out so I can stay on here – for Mam's sake – they were friends when they were nippers.'
'Aye, I remember,' she said, paused, then turned back to me. 'Promise me thee'll take care. He offers a good bargain, but however much he gives with one hand, his other'll take back more. Whatever he's offering, he'll come out ahead on't bargain, thee mark me words!'
'Umm,' I said, threw my scrubbing brush into the bucket and stood, brushing off my skirts.
'I means it, lass, take care in thy dealings with him.'
I glanced up at her. She seemed serious. 'Aye, Mary, I'll take care.'
She watched me, then turned as Richard Ramsgill loomed behind her. 'Mr Ramsgill,' she said, in a completely different tone.
'Mary.' He nodded his greeting at her.
'What can we do for thee?'
'*Thee* can do nowt, Mary, though I'm heartened to see thee caring for Jennet like this.'
'Aye, well, her mam were a good friend, 'tis the least I can do.'
They stared at each other awhile, then Mary Farmer dropped her eyes. 'Aye, well, happen I'll be off now, John'll be wondering where I've got to.' She turned to stare at me. 'Think on what I said, Jennet.' She wrapped her shawl around her shoulders and hurried away.
I walked towards the fire, unsettled by Richard Ramsgill's company

again so soon, and offered him a posset. He laughed and took out his hip flask. 'Don't forget secret ingredient, Jennet!'

I smiled and took the flask from him. I raised my eyes to his when he kept his grip on it.

'I meant what I said other day, Jennet, if thee needs any help – owt at all – thee can come to me.'

I dropped my eyes, shy, and thanked him. Why were he being so nice to me? He let go of the flask and I poured a measure into our jugs, then filled them with posset from the bubbling pot.

'By heck, lass, thee's got an heavy hand there!' He laughed and I joined in. I passed him his jug, took a sip of my own and choked – I had enjoyed the heat of the drink before, but had not seen how much whiskybae he had added. This must be three times as strong. I tried to apologise, but could not get the words out for spluttering.

Richard Ramsgill took my jug off me, picked another off the shelf and poured half the thick liquid into it, then topped mine back up from the pot. He handed the diluted drink back to me and sipped his own. I noticed he had only diluted mine. I sipped the posset, tentative now, and smiled my thanks. Better. I sat down at the table, wondering what to say to him, reddening as I remembered my dreams.

'I thought a lot of thy mam when she were a lass.' He sat next to me. 'Might even have married her if thy pa hadn't turned up.'

I looked up at him in surprise. Mam had never said anything like this – she'd hardly ever mentioned Richard Ramsgill.

He chuckled to himself. 'Aye. Swept her off her feet, he did, and never left valley again. Her pa, thy grandpa, weren't best pleased, he'd have much rather seen her married to a Ramsgill than a poor journeyman from Scotland. But one thing thee could say about thy mam were that she knew her own mind. Not even thy grandpa could turn her head from a path she were set on following.'

I grimaced – I knew that all too well.

'Aye. Hated thy pa for a bit, I'm ashamed to say.'

I glanced at him again, this time in disgust.

'Oh, sorry lass, but he were a lucky bugger to have the love of Alice; and me . . . I had to marry Elizabeth Cartwright. Oh, don't get me wrong, lass, lovely woman, Elizabeth, but she ain't Alice.'

He lapsed into silence and I stared at my posset, touched. He had loved Mam. I took a deep drink then turned my attention back to him. 'What were she like? As a lass I mean, before I were born?'

'Ahh, Jennet, she were a lot like thee – really bonny, loved the moors. Out there all hours, she were, just walking and digging up plants. Always laughing, she were, never had a bad word to say about anyone. But, by heck, she could talk a lad into trouble.' He paused and shook his head, laughing.

'What does thee mean? What trouble?'

'Well, I remember one time, she had me and our Thom sneaking into Pa's cellar – for a jug of this actually.' He picked up the hip flask then put it back on the table. 'Pa's best whiskybae – guarded it something fierce, he did. Daft thing were, if me and our Thom had worked together, we'd have done it, no sweat, but we didn't. Scrapping with each other to be the one to bring it to her, we were. When Pa came down to see what all noise were about, jug were broke on't flags with me and our Thom rolling around in his whiskybae like a couple of fox cubs. By heck, we got such a whipping!'

I laughed, trying to imagine Mam sending two Ramsgills to get whiskybae for her. I took another drink.

'Thee remind me so much of her, thee knows.' He put his hand on mine and I glanced up at him, startled. 'Thee has her laugh. And her eyes. The most beautiful eyes in Yorkshire I've always thought.' He tightened his grip on my hand and leaned towards me. I felt his rough skin against my face, his whiskers on my chin and my lips forced apart by his tongue.

I froze. His other hand stroked my hair, then my back. He took his face from mine, held me tightly for a moment, then pushed his stool back hard enough for it to clatter to the floor.

'Sorry, lass,' he mumbled and rushed out of the door.

I stared after him, flabbergasted, but also disappointed. It had been nice to be held. I picked up the other posset and drank deeply, my breath shuddering, tears running down my face, wishing I knew why I were crying. Because he had kissed me? Or because he had fled?

Chapter 10 - Emma
29th August 2012

I looked across at Dave, fast asleep and oblivious of my distress, and my breathing calmed. It had seemed so real – I still wasn't sure if it had been a dream or a memory. I studied my fingernails again and gasped when I realised they were clean. Was I still dreaming?

I got out of bed and walked to my office. I kept a kettle in there for when I was too wrapped up in my writing to make it downstairs to the kitchen. I needed camomile tea. Well, no, I needed brandy, but I'd make do with camomile tea while I wrote the dream out – it would help me let go of it and you never knew, it might turn into a good story.

I left the light off – there was more than enough moonlight to work the kettle – and stood at the window, watching the water. I loved it here, always had, and adored this room with its view over the reservoir. But I didn't understand why the same water that calmed me; that made this place home and was the source of countless happy childhood memories should also be the source of my nightmares.

The silver light reflected off the water had a shine more beautiful than diamonds, and I felt myself relax as the kettle came to the boil. I made my drink and took it out on to the balcony. The shore and trees were black – made darker by the bright beauty of the water, even the rocky, muddy shore of the half-full reservoir added to the beauty; the uneven shapes and hint of old roads giving the place character. I smiled and sipped my tea – too hot. I put the mug down and touched my burnt lip. And froze.

What the hell?

It couldn't be.

I turned back to the reservoir in disbelief. But there it was again. Church bells. Deep and ... slow somehow, as if being rung underwater. I shook myself. I was being silly, my nightmare lingering. But no – I heard it again. Church bells, definitely.

'What are you doing?'

I screamed before realising the hand on my arm was Dave's.

'Sorry, Emma, I didn't mean to startle you.'

'No, it's all right – bad dream. And I thought I heard – there it is again! Did you hear that?'

'What?'

'Church bells! As clear as anything, didn't you hear them?'

He put his arm around me and hugged. 'No I didn't, and neither did you. You know as well as I do they took the bells away and knocked the church down before they flooded the village. They rebuilt the damn thing at Blubberhouses for God's sake! *You* told me that! You didn't hear any bells, it's just that writer's imagination of yours. Now bring your tea and come back to bed.'

I nodded in agreement. I *did* know there were no church bells ringing under that water. But I also knew what I'd heard, and it wasn't my imagination – that was Dave's rationalisation for anything I said that he didn't like. Nor was it the first time I'd heard the bells. I picked up my tea and followed him back inside; I'd lost the dream that had woken me – all I could remember was a sense of a black abyss and fear, and that could mean anything or nothing, I might as well try and go back to sleep.

I paused in the doorway and turned back to the view. Everything seemed peaceful out there, but I could have sworn I'd heard the bells again, just faintly, when I'd reached for the door.

I climbed into bed and curled up against my husband, grateful for his warmth.

'God, you're freezing, Emma, come here.' Dave pulled the covers up around my chin and pulled me closer to him. 'This has really got to you, hasn't it? It's just a bit of left over nightmare, that's all, nothing to worry about.'

'No, there were stories, as a kid. Hearing the bells meant something, something bad, but I can't remember what.'

'Shush, they were stories – you of all people know the power of those. The bells are in your imagination, they're not an omen. Nothing bad's going to happen, they were just stories.'

He stroked my face and I lifted it, ready for his kiss, but I couldn't shake the foreboding that gripped me. Dave's kisses grew more urgent and he moved on top of me, kissing my neck, then pushed my vest top up and kissed my breasts, my belly, then lower. I tangled my fingers in his hair, losing myself in the familiar sensations, in the feel of him, and gradually forgot my fears.

Later I lay in his arms listening to his gentle snores, but was still unable to settle myself. I thought back to the day I'd met him five years ago. I was still writing my first pirate novel and had been in my favourite coffee shop, scribbling away. I'd lost myself in those beautiful old sailing ships, and it had taken a while for me to realise someone was speaking to me.

When I looked up, I realised the coffee shop was full and this man wanted to sit at my table. I must have been ignoring him for some time because he seemed both embarrassed and cross, and I moved my bag and papers to give him room. I tried to get back to the Caribbean, but the spell had been broken. I smiled politely while inwardly cursing him for disturbing me.

'What are you writing about?'

'The *Zephyr*,' I answered. 'Pirates for girls.'

'What?'

'The *Zephyr* is my fictional pirate ship.'

'I see. Why the *Zephyr*?'

'It's named for Zephyrus, one of the Greek wind gods. Isn't it a wonderful word? I like how it looks on the page almost as much as how it sounds. Zephyr.'

He nodded. 'Pirates for girls? So – Johnny Depp?' He chuckled.

'No, not that kind of pirates for girls,' I answered, smiling back in spite of myself. 'Although they are in the Caribbean. I'm fascinated by those wonderful old sailing ships and the life they promised. Did you know the pirates of the Caribbean were the most democratic society of their time? And the cruellest – and greediest of course. There's a lesson in there,' I babbled, hardly aware of what I was saying.

'What, dictatorships are kinder?' he asked, his eyebrows raised.

'No, of course not, I just find it ironic, that's all. That the same men who prized freedom so highly wasted it so extravagantly.'

He smiled and held his right hand across the table. 'David Moorcroft,' he introduced himself.

'Emma Carter.' I shook his hand. He was quite good looking: dark hair, blue eyes, quite heavily built. He had a dimple on one side of his mouth – the right – a cleft chin and a slightly too heavy brow. He was clean shaven and wore a suit.

'What do you do?' I asked, nosey as ever – an essential attribute for a writer.

'Architect,' he replied. 'What do you do?'

I stared at him, then my manuscript in surprise. 'I'm a writer.' I laughed. 'Well, trying to be anyway – all I need is an agent and a publisher, and I'll have cracked it!'

He smiled. A year later I had a publishing deal and we were married.

Chapter 11 - Jennet
20th August 1776

I turned over on to my side, pulled the fleece tightly around me, and sighed in frustration. I had no idea what time it were, but I should have been asleep hours ago. I sighed again. Richard Ramsgill. I could not get him out of my head. Images of him pouring his whiskybae, holding my hand, the look on his face when he had talked of Mam, the feel of his whiskers on my face . . .

I turned on to my other side and hugged the memory of his kiss close to me, my body warming as I stroked my cheek with my fingers. He were the only person who were happy to talk to me about Mam and Pa. Oh Mary Farmer tried, but she were more interested in keeping me busy so that I did *not* talk about them – or even think about them. But how could I not? The house had always been filled with them – Mam's cooking and the strange smells of the healing preparations she made all day long. The nights filled with Pa's snores and grunts and . . . other sounds.

Nobody in the village mentioned them – some would not look at me and even walked away when they saw me coming. Frightened my bad luck would rub off on them, no doubt. *Cowards.* I scowled.

But I were not completely alone. Richard Ramsgill looked at me, talked to me, touched me . . .

I turned over again, this time with a grin. He had loved Mam; he had only married Elizabeth because he could not have Mam. And now he loved me. So what if he were over forty and I were fifteen? I were a woman, of marriageable age – and a catch now with my own farm. A small one, aye, nowt like the size of the Ramsgills' holdings, and plenty of women my age married older, wealthy men. I frowned, remembering Elizabeth – *she* were not much older. Well, so what if he were already married? He must know what he were doing. Perhaps Elizabeth were ill and he were thinking of the future – a future with me?

Even if Elizabeth were well, Richard Ramsgill could do what he liked in this valley – the only men who could stand up to him were his father and his brother, Thomas, or "our Thom" as Richard called him. If Richard Ramsgill wanted me, there were nowt his wife could do about it. And I needed him, I needed a friend and I needed a friend's help. I could have lost this farm if he had not stood up to Thomas and found out the truth of the inheritable tenancy and the rights it gave me with the enclosures. *And* he had offered to send a man to help on the farm – I would not be able to manage the sheep without that. It had taken all three of us to gather enough winter fodder for them last year – I would not be able to do that on my own this time. No, I were lucky – lucky to have such a good friend, whatever Mary Farmer said about him.

I rolled over again, then sat up with a start at a noise outside. I sat as still as I could, then jumped when someone hammered on the door. I dared not move.

'Jennet! Jennet, is thee there, lass? Quick, let me in before some bugger sees me!'

Richard Ramsgill! I jumped out of bed and ran downstairs to the door. I smoothed my old linen shift and my hair as best I could, knowing I must look a right sight after all my tossing and turning.

He banged on the door again. Called my name. My heart leaping, I opened the door.

He swayed in the doorway, framed by the feeble pre-dawn light. I stepped aside to let him in and poked the fire back into life, excitement shivering through me as I thought of Mary Farmer watching from her window and seeing a Ramsgill at my door at dawn. How horrified she would be!

'Lass,' he said as he tried to run his fingers through my hair, then grabbed my shoulder as he nearly fell. I grunted, but kept my feet and put my hands on his chest to steady him.

'What's thee done to me, lass? Been at Gate all night, couldn't stop thinking 'bout thee. Bewitched me, thee has, bewitched me with Alice's eyes.' He kissed me. Roughly this time, his whiskers – the feel of which I had so enjoyed earlier – scratched my face. He stank and tasted of Robert Grange's strong beer. Smelled like Pa after he had celebrated the sale of the wethers or a good lambing.

'Shouldn't be here, lass, shouldn't be here. Can't be anywhere else, can't help mesen.' He kissed me again, and I felt warmth flood through my body at the insistent pressure of his mouth. His arms circled me – holding me tight. I never wanted him to let me go. I stumbled back with the weight of him and he came with me.

'Oh aye, lass, aye.' I could feel a hardness against my belly, which were fluttering like dragonflies darting over the marshes, and my breath grew harder and sharper. I moved my hands over his chest, copying the way he stroked my back, my waist, my backside.

I stepped back from him again to catch my breath, overwhelmed. Nowt like this had happened to me before. Oh, Arthur Weaver had stolen a kiss last Mayday, and it had been nice, but he were only a boy – he had not made my heart pound like this, my chest heave with the effort of drawing breath. He were not a man, not like Richard Ramsgill.

'What's up, lass? Thee knows I love thee, don't thee? Thee knows thee's bewitched me with her eyes, got me thinking 'bout nowt else? Bewitched me with her eyes,' he said again. 'But thee's not her, is thee lass? Thee's even more beautiful. Thy hair . . .' He paused, this time managing to run his hand through it, carrying on, stroking my back through my thin shift, my body shuddering at his touch. 'Thee wouldn't forsake me for a stranger, would thee, lass? Would thee?' he asked again, more forcefully.

'No,' I whispered, then said it again, louder. 'No, I won't forsake thee, Mr Ramsgill.'

He laughed. 'Mr Ramsgill, is it? I think we're beyond misters, lass. Call me Richard.' He pulled back. 'Only when we're alone, though. Only when we're alone. Ahh!' He spotted his hip flask on the table. 'Thought I might have left that here.' He lurched over, grabbed it, uncorked it, and took a deep draught. 'Here, thee too, lass. It's cold, thee's shivering, this'll warm thee up.'

I took the flask from him and sipped it, managing not to cough. I had drunk some earlier, trying to feel closer to him after he had left, and the fire of it did not shock me any more.

'Aye, that's right lass, getting a taste for it, ain't thee? Just like thy mam. Have some more, go on, there's plenty.' I took a longer drink, and this time did cough. He laughed and I joined in, passing the flask back to him. He drank deeply and looked around him.

He moved to the staircase, then up, and I hurried after him, my heart thumping and my mouth dry. What on earth were he doing? I followed him to my bedroom door which I had left open, my mattress visible in the dim light. He went in and stood by it, then turned to me. 'Come here, lass.'

My heart beat faster again, but I did not move. I suddenly felt scared. *What does he want me to do? I don't know what to do!*

'Come on, lass, there's nowt to be afeared of.' He held out his hand to me and my body moved towards him, almost of its own will. *Were I really going to do this? With Richard Ramsgill? Were Richard Ramsgill really going to do this with me?*

He grabbed my arm when I got close enough and fell backwards on to the mattress, pulling me with him. I cried out in surprise and we both laughed. 'Aye, that's right, lass. Nowt to be afeared of. Nowt at all.'

He kissed me again, not quite so roughly as before, and I hardly noticed the taste of the beer now – I could only taste whiskybae. One hand were behind my head holding my face to his, and the other were on my backside again. I felt a cold draught as my shift were pulled up, his hand gathering fold after fold as he exposed my skin to the cold air. I shivered.

'Thee cold, lass?'

'No. No, I'm not,' I whispered and he smiled, then rolled us over so I were lying on my back underneath him, my shift around my hips. He propped himself up on his arms and stared at me, his eyes drifting from my face, lingering on my chest, then further down to the tops of my legs now visible below the shift.

'Take it off,' he whispered, his voice hoarse. 'Take it off, I want to see thee.'

I did not move for a moment. *Do I dare? Do I really dare to do as he asks?* His eyes rose to my face and, as we stared into each other, I slipped two shaking hands between us and grabbed hold of my shift. I took a deep breath and slowly started to pull the old, thin linen up my body. I lifted my hips to free the material and it were bunched around my waist. Then I stopped. I could not lift it further without sitting up, and I could not sit up when he were leaning so closely over me.

He realised my problem and reared up, kneeling astride my thighs, and I pulled the shift further, raising my upper body as I did so. His eyes had left mine and I pulled my belly in tight as it came into his view, my breath coming in little gasps as I watched his eyes caress my exposed body. *Is he smiling? It's hard to tell in the gloom.*

I took a deep breath and pulled my shift higher, amazed at my daring, my . . . my . . . *wantonness*. Aye, that were the word, my wantonness, and I realised I wanted this, I wanted to be with this man. I wanted never to be alone again. I drew a deep breath and pulled the shift over my breasts – I were almost sitting up now, then further until it were over my head and gone.

'Ahh, that's good, lass, oh aye, that's good.' I lay back down, naked, beneath him and he reached out to touch my breast – my left one first, his hand stroking it, circling the nipple, then cupping it and squeezing. Now both his hands kneaded my flesh and I gasped as he gripped too hard and pain shot through me.

'Aye, thee likes that don't thee, lass?'

'Mm,' I groaned and arched my back into his grip.

He stood suddenly and I looked at him in bewilderment. *What have I done wrong?* Then I realised he were fumbling with his clothes and they piled up around his feet. Jacket, shirt, breeches.

I stared at him. I had seen naked men before – it were impossible not to when families lived so closely together – but I had never seen a naked man like *this* before. He laughed and his hand closed around himself, moving rhythmically as I watched, then he moved and were once again astride me.

I reached out to touch his chest and he grabbed my hand to move it lower until I had hold of him. His hand closed around mine and he made the same movements. I tightened my grip and soon I were doing it on my own, his breathing hoarse and his hands on my breasts again. Then they were moving lower, over my belly and lower still.

I froze, my legs tight together and my hand still. He reached between his legs and started my hand moving again, then reached back to me.

'It's all right lass, there's nowt to worry about. Relax.' He leaned down and kissed me, and I took a deep breath and calmed. He pushed his hand between us.

'Oh.' I gasped as I felt his finger, slippery with a wetness I had not realised were there.

'Aye that's it, lass, move thy legs a bit.'

I did as he asked and his finger delved deeper and started moving.

'Oh!' I said again, surprised at the sensations this simple movement were causing. I parted my legs a little more. He moved his finger lower and probed, then smiled. 'Ahh, I'm the first. That's good, lass, that's good. Just lie back.'

He leaned over me and took hold of himself. I pulled my hand away and rested it on his thigh. He moved closer, till he were almost lying on top of me. I could not see his face; he were looking down there, and I raised my head, trying to see what he were doing. Then I cried out in pain as he stabbed into me.

'Don't worry, lass, just relax, it's right. Won't hurt no more now.'

I stared at the roof. I had not expected pain. Mam had not sounded in pain at night with Pa.

He pulled away, then back in. It did not hurt as much this time and I started to calm. Again, again and again. Then he groaned and fell on top of me. I held him, not knowing what to do.

'Ahh, that were good, lass.'

I had no idea what to say, so stayed quiet. He were heavy and I struggled to breathe. Finally, he rolled off me and we lay side by side in silence.

Once his breathing slowed, he heaved himself off the bed and scrabbled for his clothes. My hand found my shift and I shrugged it on, feeling exposed. Fully dressed now, he leaned over and kissed me. 'Good, really good, but got to get back, work to be done.' He stroked my face. 'Beautiful,' he said. 'Beautiful, I'll see thee soon.'

When he had gone, I hugged myself. I were truly a woman now. And not just any woman – Richard Ramsgill's woman. I smiled.

Chapter 12 - Emma
31st August 2012

I woke once again sitting up in bed, heart pounding.

'What is it, not another one?'

'No, not a nightmare – a memory. Sorry to wake you, Dave.' I couldn't say any more and got out of bed. Dave followed me to the bathroom.

'What? What is it?'

'Nothing.' I stroked his face to reassure him and did my best to smile. 'Honestly, it's ok, just a scare from the haunted house I'd forgotten about.'

'The haunted house?'

'Yes, Mark and Kathy's place before they did it up. Just kids' fanciful stuff. It's nothing really.'

He said nothing for a while then, 'Tell me again, why did you want to build here? I thought this was a happy place for you.'

'Yes, so did I. It was. It is. I don't know what's going on – you're probably right, it's just my imagination working overtime – maybe it'll all make a good book!'

'Let's hope. Are you sure you're all right?' he asked again.

'Yes, nothing a hot shower won't fix,' I replied firmly. 'Now go downstairs and put the coffee on.'

Brushing my teeth, I looked out of the window and up the hill to the haunted house. For a moment I saw it as it had been when I was a child: decrepit, burnt and filthy with a fallen down animal shed and a low dry stone wall running up the side. There had been no high garden walls or security cameras then. Hell, there'd been no glass in the windows or a staircase, and it had only been inhabited by sheep and cows.

We'd played there often, although never alone. We'd pretended we weren't scared of it, that the only ghosts were in actuality the occasional tramp sheltering from the ravages of the Yorkshire weather. But still – there'd always been *something* about the place. I shuddered, finished in the bathroom, and went downstairs, following the scent of brewing coffee and burning toast to the large kitchen-diner below the guest bedrooms on the other side of the house.

Breakfast over, Dave left to go to his office in Harrogate, and I took the dogs for a walk. This was where my day usually started – apart from waking me up, walking alongside Thruscross somehow kick-started my creative centre and I came out here making soggy notes as the beasts ran and swam and played, rain or shine, two or three times a day – sometimes more, despite the fact we had enough land that I could just let the dogs out to amuse themselves.

Today, the walk did nothing for me. Tired and unfortunately uninspired, we walked slowly (yes, even the beasts now) back to the house. I looked up at Mark and Kathy's as we passed, remembering that Dave and I were invited for dinner tonight. Was that why I'd dreamed of the place?

Half an hour later, we were all in the office. Clean-ish dogs collapsed in a heap; notebooks; pot of coffee and a plate of biscuits – all the essentials – were close at hand, and I settled down to get the next chapter of my latest book down on paper.

I cursed. Hadn't there been something in my dream the other night? An idea for their next battle? I couldn't remember, but knew the harder I tried, the further away the idea would slip. I sighed in frustration and just started writing to see what came out of my pen.

I checked my watch and massaged my neck with a groan. It was only lunchtime, yet I felt mentally exhausted. I read over what I'd scribbled and frowned. This was usually the bit I enjoyed most, where I got completely lost in the story and was just as eager to find out what happened next as I hoped my readers would be. Unfortunately what I'd written today was crap that did nothing to move the story on.

I left the notebooks on the coffee table by the sofa and crossed to the desk. I had a series of large noticeboards on the only section of bookshelf-free wall, where I had laid out the overall plot for the book. Instead of studying my plans, I spotted the old inkpot hidden away on the shelf alongside. *How had I forgotten about that?* I took it down and put it on a sheaf of papers on the desk where I could see it, then went down to sort out some lunch. I'd try again later.

Chapter 13 - Jennet
16th September 1776

I put the posset on to warm through and sat down with a sigh; I were knackered. September were a busy month with the sheep and I had spent the entire week with Richard's man, Peter Stockdale, spaining the flock. We had to separate lamb from ewes until the gimmers – the young females – were weaned and could return to breed. The wethers – males – would be moved to the best pastures down by the river to fatten them up for meat for Pateley Bridge Market, but it were exhausting to chase lamb and ewe around the moors and drag the lamb away, bleating for its dam.

I giggled to myself, remembering Peter face down in the muck after a particularly stubborn gimmer had got away from him. I had laughed so hard I fell as well, and the pair of us had rolled in mud and sheepshit with the bemused ewes looking on for a good ten minutes until the last chuckles had died away. The job had taken twice as long as it should have.

Maybe the new enclosures that Thomas Ramsgill were forcing on the valley for the king were not such a bad idea. He had a team of men – including Peter Stockdale – building the dry stone walls. They might look ugly cutting their way across moor and pasture, but his sheep had been unable to escape. His massive flock had been spained in not much more time than it had taken me and Peter Stockdale to do my twenty five beasts. I dreaded to think how long it would have taken me on my own. A couple of the ewes were past wool production as well, and I had a lot of meat to butcher and hang in the chimney.

I got up from the table to stir the posset, adding a healthy glug of whiskybae from the flask Richard had left a couple of nights ago. It were Friday night, Richard would surely be going to the Gate and then he would come here. I smiled and got out the sheep's stomach and liver I had saved, then started chopping. I had energy again.

Meat done, I prepared vegetables, then went to the well to fetch water. I wanted my body and clothes as clean and fresh as possible, and I realised I were singing as I washed; the clear, icy water making my body shudder in anticipation of what were to come. I felt like a real woman, preparing for my man.

Richard had become a regular visitor over the past month. Although daylight visits were rare, he spent two or three nights a week in my bed.

And it were more of a bed now – I did not make do with straw and heather any more, Peter Stockdale had arrived a week ago carrying a proper feather-filled mattress and bolster on his first day, then parcels containing brocades and blankets and even a cotton nightgown the next! The softest gown I had ever touched. I wondered if he knew what were in the packages. What had Richard told him he were delivering?

I had been ready a couple of hours when the door opened – he did not knock any more – and my impatience flew from me as I returned his greeting kiss. Richard had brought joy back into my life; I were not alone.

I dished up the meal, and he tucked in with relish. I picked at my own platter, enjoying the sight of him eating at my table.

'What's up, lass? Why's thee staring?'

I reddened and looked at my plate. 'Nowt.'

He put down his knife. 'No, come on, lass, what is it?'

'Well, it's just . . .' I paused, but he were still watching me. 'It's been so hard,' I continued in a rush. 'I don't know what I'd have done without thee – or without Peter.'

'Don't worry about it, Jennet, it's nowt. The least I could do.' He stretched out his hand and grasped mine briefly, then picked up his knife again and continued eating. 'We have to be more careful though, lass. Billy Gill made a crack in The Gate tonight about how well I'm looking after thee. He saw me t'other night, but Stockdale jumped in saying there were a problem with sheep. I think he took it – didn't say owt else, anyroad.'

I paled. *Does that mean he won't visit as often?*

'Don't look so worried, lass!' He laughed. 'It'll take more than Billy Gill to stop me coming here – he knows better than to put about rumour concerning me, or any Ramsgill for that matter!'

I smiled and looked up at him from below my lashes. *He's so important and powerful!*

He pushed the plate away. 'Enough of that, lass. Nice as it were, I've a hunger for summat else.' He took a swig of the whiskybae, ignoring my posset, stood, took my hand, and walked me upstairs to our richly covered bed.

Chapter 14 - Emma
1st September 2012

'Have you got the wine?'

'Yes! Both red and white,' Dave shouted back. 'Where's the torch?'

'In the mudroom, on top of the cupboard,' I called.

'Come on, Emma! We'll be late!' Dave *hated* being late.

'Hold your horses, I'm coming!'

Eyeliner, mascara, lipstick. I was ready and went downstairs to spoil the effect of my expensive linen wraparound top and black trousers with a heavy coat and wellies. Dave was still scratting about looking for the torch.

'Come on then, I'm waiting for you!' I called to Dave, laughing at his scowl.

Trudging up the lane, I was strangely nervous. I'd not been to the haunted house since it had been derelict, and Mark and Kathy Ramsgill had not been particularly keen on our build. Their invitation to dinner had been a surprise, and I hoped it was a genuine display of neighbourliness and perhaps friendship. We were very isolated out here, and I couldn't bear the thought of problem neighbours – especially since I worked from home. I hoped tonight would go well.

Wolf Farm was less than a hundred yards away over field and wall, but a couple of hundred by road – well, lane. We reached their gates only ten minutes late and pressed the intercom to gain entry. I remembered the place as open and perched on the hillside overlooking the reservoir, but now it resembled a prison with a high wall surrounding the house and garden, topped with cameras. The only way in was through heavy locked gates, and it struck me as a shame; the complete antithesis of the way of life that had built the sandstone farmhouse back in the 1600s.

'David and Emma Moorcroft,' Dave barked into the intercom and the gate slowly swung open. The front door shed a welcome rectangle of warm yellow light, beckoning us over the gravelled drive and yard.

'Welcome!' Mark Ramsgill greeted us. 'Come in, come in, just leave your boots by the door, let me take your coats. We're through here. Oh, thank you very much. Pinot Grigio and Merlot, Kathy will be pleased. Come through, come through.'

I had an impression of a friendly, cluttered, colourful hall littered with the detritus of family and dales living – lots of muddy boots, coats, umbrellas and hats – and then we were ushered into the front room, the one which no doubt looked over our house and the water. If either could be seen over that high garden wall, that is. I'd have to hope we were invited back in daylight to find out.

'Hello, hello, come in, ooh lovely.' Mark had passed the wine bottles to Kathy. 'It's nice to meet you properly at last, I'm so pleased you came. Would you like a drink? Wine or maybe gin and tonic?' she asked.

'Dry white for me, please,' I said.

'And G and T for me,' Dave added.

'I'll get them.' Mark bustled at the sideboard. 'Better not keep Kathy out of the kitchen too long. Please, sit down, make yourselves comfortable.'

'Can I give you a hand in the kitchen?' I asked.

'Oh no, no, ignore Mark, everything's under control. Roast dales beef – oh, I hope that's all right? You're not vegetarian are you?'

'No, that sounds lovely, thank you. It smells delicious,' I replied.

'Emma's what you'd call a selective vegetarian,' Dave joked. 'No red meat allowed at home, but she can't get enough of it when we eat out! I think she just doesn't like cooking it.'

'Trying to eat a balanced diet, Dave. Anyway, I wouldn't complain if you wanted to cook.'

'Yes, you would.' He laughed. 'It'd be inedible! How about you, Mark, can you find your way about in the kitchen?'

'Oh no, that's Kathy's domain.' He handed me a glass of wine and gave another to Kathy.

'Yes, the kitchen's mine. Mark can barely put beans on toast together!' Kathy sat next to me on the sofa, checking her watch.

'You have a lovely home,' I said to her with an embarrassed smile. The room was very much like the hall; colourful and full of an assortment of knick-knacks from around the world. It was a good size, painted cream to show off the paintings and textiles adorning the walls, with exposed beams and a lovely stone arched fireplace with blazing fire that took up most of one wall. They had a comfortable leather suite, an incongruous flatscreen at one end, and a rustic looking dining table and chairs standing in front of the fire. 'Do you do a lot of travelling?'

'No, not at all.' She laughed. 'I'm terrified of flying so I bring the world to me – mainly courtesy of car boot sales and TK Maxx. I love all the different cultures and types of art, I find them fascinating.'

I nodded and studied the knick-knacks. Buddhas nestled against Hindi deities and Egyptian and Chinese figurines. I spotted a boomerang, a couple of carved elephants, crystals and a collection of brass and copper plateware, including a beautiful Russian samovar.

'Are there any countries not represented?' I asked.

'Not many,' grumbled Mark.

'Oh, don't listen to him,' Kathy said. 'He picked half of this stuff out, he just doesn't like to admit it.'

Which half? I wondered. Looking at Kathy, I guessed her choices were the representations of the East. She was shorter than me, with long, dark hair pulled back in a couple of combs, bright blue eyes and flushed cheeks, although that was probably the effects of cooking, and she wore a long, floaty red and gold skirt with a gold-coloured tunic. I'd put down money that the crystals were hers, too.

Mark was taller, also dark haired, although greying now, a little plump, and dressed simply in jeans and checked shirt.

'Would you excuse me?' Kathy heaved herself off the sofa, checking her watch again. 'The stove calls for a moment.' She walked quickly into the kitchen, taking her wine with her.

'So how long have you been in now?' Mark asked with a broad Yorkshire dialect. 'Does it feel like home yet?'

'Oh yes, it's been about a month. We haven't finished unpacking yet, mind you. We love it here don't we, Dave? It was definitely worth all the hassle.'

'You were brave, doing a build from scratch. I remember all the problems converting this place,' Mark replied. 'Constant arguments with the architect and builders; I were glad to see the back of them. Never listened to a ruddy word I said!'

'Yes, they're like that.' I laughed, glancing at Dave. 'It's even worse when you're married to your architect! But we survived, didn't we, Dave?'

'Just about,' he muttered.

'You're an architect?' Mark asked, embarrassed. Dave nodded.

'So what do you do, Mark?' I asked to fill the awkward silence.

'I'm a teacher, over at Pateley Bridge. History and PE. It's where I met Kathy, actually.'

'Really?'

'Yeah, I were straight out of school myself and she were my star pupil! Oh, don't worry, we didn't get together until after she'd left, but twenty years and two kids later, we're still as happy.'

'How old are your kids?' I asked, not sure how to respond to that.

'Seventeen-year-old twins – Alex and Hannah. We're starting to think about university at the moment, which Kathy is finding difficult. But we hardly see them anyway, to tell you the truth. They're always out or staying at friends' houses.'

'So you're getting the house back to yourselves?'

'Yes. Do you have children?'

'No, no, just dogs, three of them.' Dave laughed. I sipped my drink to avoid reacting. 'And they're more than enough trouble!'

'Dinner is served!' Kathy came back in carrying bowls of soup. 'Hope you're hungry!'

'Oh, that smells delicious, Kathy.'

'Spiced pumpkin – home-grown.'

'Mark was just telling us how you met, Kathy.'

'Oh, ignore him. It wasn't anything like as sordid as he makes it sound; he likes to shock people and play devil's advocate. I'm hoping to go back to school myself once I've finished my training. I dread to think what he'll say to everyone.'

'Oh? What subjects do you teach?'

'No, not as a teacher, as school counsellor. I'm in my fourth year of training and should get my diploma in June.'

'Oh right. That sounds rewarding.'

'I ruddy well hope so,' Mark cut in. 'You wouldn't believe what it involves. I thought it would just be college once a week, but she has to volunteer as a counsellor. Volunteer! She don't get paid! Then she has to have counselling herself *and* a supervisor. It's costing us a ruddy fortune!'

'It'll be worth it, Mark, and in time I'll earn quite a bit in private practice. It'll take a while, that's all.'

'Where do you volunteer?' I asked.

'A local service that offers counselling in rural areas. It's a real lifeline to some of the more isolated, and you're right, very rewarding, even if I'm not getting paid for it yet.' She glared at Mark; it was obviously a sore spot.

'How's your beef, Dave?' Mark asked and I realised Dave hadn't said very much since the architect gaffe.

'Perfect,' he said. 'Tender and absolutely delicious. You should ask Kathy about those dreams you've been having, Emma. You never know, they might mean something.'

'Dreams?' Kathy asked.

'Yes.' I glared at Dave. They were mine to talk about, not for him to use as small talk at the dinner table. 'Nightmares really, but very real, very accurate somehow.'

Kathy and Mark glanced at each other. 'About the village?' she asked. Thruscross village dated back to the Vikings and had been flooded when the dam was built in the 1960s.

'No, just the reservoir. Why, do you dream of the village?' I asked.

Kathy nodded. 'I keep getting stuck in the mud, only it's not a foot deep like it is when the tide goes out. I sink further and further down and I know there's no end to it.'

Mark rolled his eyes. 'When the tide goes out,' he said in an exaggerated falsetto. 'It's not the seaside, eh Dave?'

'You know what I mean,' she said. 'They're always letting the water out to make sure the lower reservoirs stay full.'

'Maybe there's a book in the dreams somewhere,' I said, keen to change the subject.

'A book,' Kathy repeated. 'Are you a writer?'

I nodded. 'Yes, historical fiction, mainly.'

'Have you had any success?'

'Yes, some,' I said, modestly.

'I'm sorry, I've never heard of you,' Mark said.

'I write under my maiden name, Carter.'

'Oh! You're Emma Carter!' Kathy exclaimed. 'You write those pirate books. My daughter, Hannah, is a big fan. She loves all the description aboard the ships, says you must be a sailor.'

'Yes, I virtually grew up at the old sailing club here, actually.'

'You built your house where the old clubhouse were.'

'Yes. I loved it round here. I was very lucky to spend my childhood playing on and by the water, and couldn't imagine anywhere better to live.'

'You know, she calls this place the haunted house, don't you? Tell them about the inkpot,' Dave prompted.

'The haunted house? I'm not surprised,' Kathy said. 'There's something here. Not quite dormant; not quite finished. Waking. The dreams are only the start. Have you heard the bells yet? They say that means she walks again.'

'The dreams are only the start. She walks again.' Mark repeated his falsetto thing and I noticed Kathy grimace. My heart thumped. 'The start of what?' he asked. Do you think Jennet's coming back? Or is she still here after two hundred year?'

'Who's Jennet?' Dave asked.

'Jennet Scot,' Mark replied. 'This were her farm, or so my nan used to tell me.'

'Mark's family comes from the village, owned most of the land at one point,' Kathy added. 'His dad moved away as soon as he was old enough, but his nan only moved when the Leeds Corporation bought everything up and forced everyone to go so they could flood the valley.'

'Yeah, she were not impressed – tried to stop everyone drinking tap water! That didn't last long, though.'

'She sounds like quite a character,' Dave remarked.

'She were certainly that! Full of tales as well, and her favourite were Jennet. She were supposed to be a powerful witch, powerful enough to call up the Wild Hunt.'

'The Wild Hunt? What's that?'

'Oh, an old superstition – it goes back to when the Vikings settled here, when this were Thores-Cross, but Nan always said it were the devil riding the moors with his Gabriel hounds, collecting souls to take back to hell.'

'Charming,' said Dave.

'You're telling me. Apparently she foretold the flooding of the valley.'

'And supposedly put a curse on your ancestors – don't forget that!' Kathy added.

'Aye, my great-great-great-great-great-great-great-granddad or summat like that.'

'And now you live in her house. That's brave.'

'Oh, it's all a load of nonsense,' said Dave. 'Witches and devil hunts.'

'Wild hunts,' Mark corrected. 'And careful what you call nonsense round here, there's plenty of folk who still believe in fairies, hobgoblins and barguests and the like.'

'Barguests?' I asked. I had visions of ghosts perched on bar stools at the Stone House.

'Phantom animals – black dogs mainly. That's where the farm gets its name, Jennet were supposed to be able to turn herself into a wolf.'

'I thought it was big cats round here,' Dave joined in again. 'Wasn't one supposed to have been prowling around Harrogate a few years ago?'

'Aye, there's all sorts, especially on't moors, but it were a wolf that were supposed to have roamed in Jennet's day.'

'Did you say something about an inkpot?' Kathy asked.

'Oh yes tell them, Emma – maybe it belonged to Mark's witch!'

I glared at him. I wasn't sure if he was getting in the spirit of things or taking the piss, as he often did when the conversation turned to the supernatural. I carried on anyway.

'Yeah, I found it as a kid. I told you I more or less grew up at the sailing club. Well, we used to play up here a lot when the house was derelict. Did you know there's a natural spring in the next field? We used to collect frog spawn every year. Anyway,' I caught Dave's eye, 'I was climbing through the old dry stone wall out front – it was falling down already, honest! And I spotted a funny shaped stone, pulled it out and it was an inkpot! It wasn't just hidden, it was actually built into the structure of the wall.'

'Oh wow! Do you still have it? I'd love to see it.'

'Yes, I'll show you when you come to us for dinner. Not that it's anything special to look at, just rough stoneware. I searched online and apparently the walls were built around 1780, and the way it was built in, I reckon its original, which makes it about two hundred and thirty years old.'

'Maybe it *was* Jennet's! Perhaps she put it there so her story could be written one day.'

I didn't react. I wasn't going to tell them about the voice I'd heard, not when Dave and Mark were so scornful of the idea of ghosts. 'Who knows?' I said. 'But I'd love to set a book up here, probably in the old village.'

'Oh, yes! Mark knows all the history and has loads of books about Thruscross. Did you see the map in the hall?'

'No, I didn't notice it, I'm afraid.'

'We'll have to get you a copy as a house-warming present. It's of the village and moors in 1851.'

'Oh, I'd love to study that, and perhaps pick your brains sometime, Mark?'

'No problem, especially if they're well-oiled! Any more wine anyone?'

'Well that wasn't too bad was it, Dave? Awkward at first, but they seem all right.'

'Hmmph. She's ok, but I dinnae know about him, did you hear the way he spoke to her?'

'Oh, you're just annoyed because he doesn't like architects!'

'And what about all that witch stuff?'

'I know – fascinating. Who'd have thought it, a witch used to live in the haunted house!'

'Did you not hear about her before?'

'No, nothing. I always thought the haunting had to do with the village drowning, but maybe it's older. Maybe they're right, maybe she *will* be the plot of my Thruscross story.'

Chapter 15 - Jennet
30th September 1776

Where were he? I stared at the pottage on the fire, aware that it were already overcooked, and sighed. I stood up and moved the pot off the heat. I were not hungry any more. Another meal gone to waste to add to the others I had prepared for him over the last two weeks. Two weeks. I bit back a sob. I missed Richard so much – why had he not visited? I wiped the tears from my face. Anything could have happened. Maybe he were ill? Or somebody had seen him and he were being discreet. Maybe Elizabeth suspected something, or were he just too busy?

I walked to the door, then out into the garden, shivering in the white cotton nightgown he had given me, and tightened the thick, woollen shawl around my shoulders.

I had been out every night, staring down the lane, hoping for a glimpse of him striding towards the house as he used to. I had seen him once or twice, but he had not seen me, and he had not come. I had watched him turn right – going home after an evening at the Gate Inn.

I shivered again and stared over the moors, then lower down the valley towards the village. It were a full moon and the moors looked forbidding in the cold light.

Then – a movement. My eyes darted back to the path – he were there!

I rushed forward and he glanced up, startled. He stopped and stared at me a moment before putting his head down and turning right, his pace hurried. Going home. Again.

My heart sank and I sobbed, then turned and dashed back into the house, my hands clasped over my mouth to stifle the sound of my despair. He were not too busy. He did not want to see me.

I sat down heavily at the table, rested my head in my arms folded on the tabletop and let the sobs come – not caring if anyone heard me now. Not that they would – the nearest houses were too far away. I so wanted to see him, talk to him, touch him . . .

Why did he not want to talk to me any more? We used to spend hours talking and laughing until the dawn broke and he had to leave. Did I not touch him the way he wanted? Did he not like it? Were I no good? What were wrong with me?

Once my tears had run dry, I rose and went up to bed. He did not love me. He loved Mam. He had used me to ease his grief for her – his lost love. Tears flowed again as I thought of all the empty days, weeks, months ahead with no Richard. Years. How could he have made me love him, the selfish bastard!

My anger were refreshing – a relief from all the worry, disappointment and longing that had consumed me since I had last seen him a fortnight ago. He had got what he wanted. He had never cared. He had seen a vulnerable woman-child he could have his way with, and he had done just that. He had taken what he wanted, then thrown me aside when he were done.

God, I were so stupid! How could I have fallen for it? Mary Farmer had tried to warn me and we had laughed at her. *I* had laughed at her! In a fit of rage I pulled all the beautiful, expensive brocades off our bed. No, not our bed, not any more – only mine. I dragged my old, smelly fleece out, threw it on the mattress and crawled underneath it, sobbing once more.

I heard a noise outside and sat up, drying my face. Richard? But there were nowt. Nobody. It were probably a fox. I lay back down feeling foolish and angry at the hope that had soaked my heart. It were no good. No matter how much I yearned for him, he were not coming. Would probably never come. I were alone again.

I could not even talk to Mary Farmer – I were so embarrassed at the way I had laughed at her warnings, how could I admit what I had done? I wished he had never spoken to me at the clipping, never visited – even if that would have meant losing the farm. Would Peter Stockdale stop coming too? Would I have to deal with the sheep by myself? I should have done that from the beginning – at least I would have known where I were.

Tears rolled down my face again. My cheeks were still wet when I woke the next morning.

Chapter 16 - Jennet
15th November 1776

It had been almost two months, and I still had not heard from him. I cried myself to sleep every night, but things had changed. If only I could find a way to tell him my news, then he would come back. He would leave Elizabeth and be with me. Me and our child.

I were sure of it. My courses had only been flowing a year, and were not yet reliable. When I had missed the first I had not worried, but now I had missed a second. As a cunning woman's daughter, I knew about these things – even if I had not thought to take any precautions against it. There were no doubt at all; I had been sick every morning for weeks and my breasts hurt summat terrible. I were carrying Richard's child. He had to talk to me now. He had to see me, and help me. Oh, I knew he had a wife and a family already, but Elizabeth had only given him one son and the rest were daughters. It were common knowledge that he were desperate for more boys – and I would give him one, followed by many more. Despite his abandonment of me, he were a good man. He had been grieving Mam too – he would stand by me, help me; this were not only our child, but Mam's grandchild. He would not turn his back on us.

He had only left me because of his wife, I knew that now. The hateful stares she threw my way at church or if we passed in the village proved it. She must have found out and threatened him with scandal if he did not stop seeing me. He had not stayed away out of choice. He still loved me, I knew it, he had told me he did often enough.

That night I dressed carefully and crept outside to the fork in the lane. Ahead were the Gate Inn, to my left the lane to East Gate House – Richard's house. I kept to the shadows, hiding in the trees – I did not want anyone but him to see me.

I imagined his face – the delight and love I would see there, banishing my fears and nightmares. How would he react? Would he shout? Cry? Laugh? Pick me up and spin me round? Declare everlasting love? I hugged myself in delighted anticipation. I hoped he would not be too long, the November night were cold, despite my woollens.

I caught my breath – someone were coming! I peered out from behind the tree. John Farmer and George Weaver. Damn! I stayed as still as possible, praying they would not see me. I need not have worried; they were drunk and could barely see their way home. I listened to their raucous singing until their voices faded, and breathed a sigh of relief. If John Farmer had seen me, he would tell Mary, and I did not want to have to explain to her what I were doing out here at midnight.

I peered out from my hiding place again – were those footsteps I heard? They were, and Richard strode into view a few seconds later. I took a moment to admire him, smiling to myself. How I had missed him! Tall, with a slight stoop, greying hair and magnificent whiskers – the best in the valley. He had nearly reached me, and I checked that nobody else were in the lane, then took a deep breath and stepped out.

'By heck, lass, thee scared living daylights outta me! What's thee up to skulking in't trees?'

I hesitated. He were not smiling. I had a whole speech worked out, but it started with him taking me in his arms, or at least pleased to see me. But he were not even smiling.

'I'm carrying thy child,' I blurted out.

Silence for a moment, then, 'Thee stupid little slut!' he shouted, and before I could react, his fist connected with my face and I were lying in the dirt.

'But Richard,' I gasped, unable to understand what had happened.

'Don't thee call me Richard, thee stupid little girl!' He kicked me in the belly. I curled into a ball to protect myself and the babby, bewildered and terrified by his reaction. 'I thought thee were a cunning woman, didn't thee think to take herbs for this kind of thing? Chant a damned spell or something?'

'I-I-I'd only just started my courses, I didn't think of it!'

'Whore!' He kicked me again. I felt a stabbing pain in my back and screamed in pain and fear. 'Well, take something now and get rid of it!'

He kicked out once more, but my senses were returning and I rolled out of his way.

'Damn whore!' he said again and spat, then strode off in the direction of East Gate House.

I stayed where I were, in the dirt, stunned, tears running down my face and unable to move. I could not believe he had hurt me – I were carrying his child. Damn him! He had called me a dirty whore and left me in the dirt! He had told me to get rid of our babby!

I sobbed and struggled to my feet, my whole body hurting, then staggered home. I knew the truth now – he did not love me. Elizabeth had not prevented him from seeing me – he had chosen not to come. He had abandoned me at the worst time of my life and now he had rejected me again. My hands clasped my belly. He did not want this child.

What would happen to me? He had called me 'whore', and everyone I knew would do the same when they found out.

I could not be alone, unmarried, with a child – the whole village would hate me. I had to do as he said. I sobbed again, my heart breaking, but I had no choice. I could not bear and bring up a child alone, not a bastard child unwanted by its pa and shunned by the whole village.

I reached the house and put on a pot of water, then fumbled in Mam's remedy chest, pulling out bottles and bunches of dried herbs by the light of my single candle. I found what I wanted, then shredded leaves and pounded roots before I put the mixture into a bowl and poured on the boiling water.

I drank it all down as soon as it were cool enough, but still burned my mouth. I did not care. I did not care about anything any more.

I crumpled on to the floor, held my belly, and sobbed for the life I were killing.

Chapter 17 - Jennet
1st December 1776

'Thee ain't been to church in a while, lass.'

I glanced up. Mary Farmer stood at the open door. 'Thee can't hide away, thee knows. Folk understand thee's had terrible time losing thy mam and pa, but enough's enough. Thee ain't been to church since thy pa's sending off, there's talk of fining thee if thee don't go soon. Get changed and come along – it won't be so bad.'

I stared at her in silence a moment, then slowly got to my feet and moved away from the table. She were right. I could not put it off any longer. Mary Farmer came in and shut the door. I went upstairs, pulled off my old dirty homespun dress and reached for my Sunday best. I heard a gasp behind me. Mary Farmer had followed me.

'Jennet! Lass, what . . . what . . .' I heard a thump as Mary Farmer fell against the wall and I pulled my dress over my head. It were a bit tight round my belly.

'Lass, whatever . . . lass, thee looks . . .'

I stared at her and she took a deep breath. 'Who?' she asked.

'Richard Ramsgill.' I could not meet her eyes but stared at the floor. I had not wanted to tell her, but I knew she would not give up until she got the name out of me. 'I took red clover, raspberry, feverfew and horsetail, but it didn't work.'

'Ramsgill? But . . . but . . . that Damned bastard!'

I still could not look at her.

'Has thee told him?'

I nodded, aware that tears were rolling down my face.

'Nay need to ask how he took news.'

I shook my head, unable to tell her he had knocked me to the ground and kicked me.

'Well . . .' I looked up. I did not think I had ever known Mary Farmer lost for words before.

She stood up. 'Life goes on, lass. Thee needs church more than ever now. And it'd be better to be seen there an'all. Folk are already talking about thee not going, and thee hasn't been seen in't village neither. Best to face these things and get them over with 'fore thee gets any bigger. Come on, lass, thee's not on thy own, let's get this done.' She offered me her arm and I took it, grateful for her kindness.

* * *

It were awful. Even though I were barely showing, they all knew. I were aware of clusters of women glancing at me and gossiping. I got through the service and stood to leave the church in relief. I walked out of the cool dark of the stone building into a bright winter's day, and paused. The village were beautiful in the sunshine, the heavy frost now all but gone.

I grew aware of a silence around me, and Mary Farmer gripped my arm. Richard and Elizabeth Ramsgill stood on the path ahead of us, chatting to the curate and a couple more Ramsgills – Thomas's wife Hannah and Betsy Ward, a distant cousin. Richard saw me first. He glanced at my belly, then back at my face. I took a step back at the hate etched on his features as he glowered at me. I glanced away and saw the same expression on Elizabeth's face. So she knew. The others glanced at Richard and Elizabeth in surprise, then at me and back again. I saw realisation dawn in their faces.

'Well that's it, lass, that Betsy Ward has a tongue in her head as no one can control, least of all hersen. The whole valley'll ken afore sundown. Keep thy head up and say nowt.'

I raised my chin, aware my shame were visible in my cheeks, and we walked towards them. I kept my eyes on Richard, but his expression never wavered. I were aware that everyone watched us and my embarrassment grew sharper.

We reached them and they stepped aside at the last moment. They did not give us enough room, and I had to walk on the grass to get past.

'Whore.'

I heard the quiet whisper, and was sure everyone else had heard Elizabeth Ramsgill's insult. I glared at her, then at Richard. His face now showed disdain, and my shame turned to anger.

'Lass!' Mary Farmer said, tugging on my arm. 'Thee'll only make it worse.'

I kept my mouth shut and carried on walking. Behind us, the silence broke into whispers and titters. I realised I would have to get used to that.

Chapter 18 - Emma
3rd September 2012

I studied the sky; maybe I shouldn't have come for such a long walk after all. I wasn't going to make it back before the storm broke, but I hadn't written a word worth keeping in days, and I needed to clear my head. I turned to call the dogs, but they were chasing rabbits – they must have run a marathon this afternoon.

'Damn it.' A rumble of thunder reverberated round the valley and echoed off the dam wall ahead. I headed towards the trees as the first heavy drops of rain fell and lightning flashed.

The bridge across the Washburn and to the path up the valley side was metal – there was no way I would cross it now. I was stuck here with what little shelter I could find until the storm passed.

It was only two o'clock in the afternoon, but it seemed like dusk already: dark, heavy clouds had moved in quickly over the moors and another flash of lightning lit up the valley, the thunder that came with it so loud I thought the dam had blown up. But no, it still stood.

I huddled in the tree line, trying to remember if this was safer than being out in the open. I decided I was less likely to be hit by lightning if there were other, taller, targets nearby. I screamed as another bolt of lightning exploded overhead, suddenly not so sure of my reasoning.

The dogs, although used to thunderstorms, went mad: circling and barking, then running up the hill before returning to circle around me again, and I realised they were ignoring the rabbits that streamed about us. Something more than lightning was wrong.

I eyed the dam again. Had it been hit? Surely not, there'd be all sorts of precautions against lightning strike. It must have withstood hundreds of storms in the past fifty years. I watched it a moment longer. The amount of water coming down the overflow seemed to have increased. It couldn't all be rain, not so soon.

I glanced again at the rabbits and the odd behaviour of the dogs, and jumped to my feet. Suddenly the decision whether to shelter in the trees or not seemed irrelevant. I wanted to be on higher ground – quickly, but realised I had a problem.

I was at the bottom edge of Hanging Wood, which covered the valley side, and it was *steep*. Almost sheer. I could only climb by using the trees as a ladder; hauling myself round to brace against a trunk then reach for another, but everything was soaked and slippery already; the trunks mossy, the ground a mush of wet pine needles.

I glanced at the dam again; there was definitely more water flowing over it. Too much. I realised that lightning must have struck the water behind it and maybe cracked the overflow.

'Shit!' I screamed in terror as I slid backwards, losing the precious few feet in height I'd gained, colliding with trees, striking my elbow and scraping my legs. I looked up at the impossible slope – almost a wooded cliff – and nearly cried. There was no way I could get up there.

I spotted Cassie, the Irish Setter, barking at me and shouted at her to get on. She did, and I cursed her for leaving me until I realised how she managed the slope. That was it – thank you, Cassie!

I got to my feet again and followed, this time along a diagonal line, and soon got a rhythm going. I could dig my feet sideways into the mush and brace them against the trees at the same time. That was better: six feet, twelve feet, fifteen, time for a rest. *Surely this is high enough?* I steadied myself astride a strong pine to catch my breath and study the dam.

The sky was lightening and I had made no mistake, there was far too much water pouring into the valley. Another horrific crack, but this time not from the sky; masonry fell from the top of the dam and crashed a hundred and twenty feet on to more concrete. As I watched, the new V-shaped split in the centre became a U as cascading water forced the restraining wall out of the way. Water thundered into the valley. I needed to get higher, and started to scramble upwards again.

Another rest. I must be twenty five feet up now and my legs were shaking. I wasn't sure I *could* climb any higher. Cassie nosed up to me, whining, and I put my arms round her. She was terrified, poor thing, and I didn't blame her – I felt the same way, and completely helpless.

Suddenly, another explosion rent the air and I screamed again as a concrete boulder the size of a house fell to the valley floor. Cassie yelped and jumped, and I couldn't keep hold of her wet fur. I screeched her name as she slid down the wet slope, careening off tree trunks. Despite her efforts to stop, her claws were ineffective in the pine mush. She splashed into water and was gone.

I screamed her name again, but to thin air. I looked around for the two boys, but couldn't see them in the gloom beneath the trees. I didn't want to call them in case they tried to come to me and ended up swept away as well. I was on my own, clinging to the wet hillside above a torrent of certain death. I clung on to my tree and watched the destruction unfold in front of me.

Poor Cassie. Where would she end up? She was a good swimmer, but there was so much debris in the water, the valley would be scarred for generations. What would those trees do to Cassie? Would she manage to climb on to one of them or would they drown her? I sobbed at the image in my mind of her fighting for her life.

I gaped downstream after her, and imagined what was happening out of sight. Not just to Cassie, but to everyone in the path of this torrent. The road at Blubberhouses was impassable at every snowfall; this would definitely close it – and for how long? Three million gallons would surely wash it away completely. Then what? There were three more reservoirs downstream, would they hold this water? No way, surely their dams would crumble in its path. I had a brief vision of the *Dambusters* film, dam after dam falling away.

Then what? Otley and the Wharfe. How much would survive? What about Ilkley, Wetherby? What about York? How many homes, towns, cities would be destroyed before this brown peaty dales water reached the sea? How many people would be swept out of their lives?

My initial panic dulled and a horrified dread took its place. How close had I come to being swept away myself?

I don't know how long I perched on that hillside, watching Thruscross empty into the Washburn Valley – thrusting what was left of the dam out of the way. I'd heard of being speechless, and been afflicted that way many times, but this was the first time I'd been struck thoughtless. I couldn't grasp the enormity of what I was seeing. This was an inland tidal wave. Except this was much more than a tsunami, because there'd be no trough, no ebbing of the waters, not until the reservoir was empty. And Otley would soon be facing four times what I'd seen.

I checked my phone. I had to ring someone, anyone, to warn the people living in ignorance downstream. Nothing.

I got back to my feet to climb to the top – I couldn't afford to rest any longer, I had to get to the road at the edge of the dam where I'd have a better chance of getting a signal.

I came out on to the rocks above the road, grateful to leave the claustrophobia of Hanging Wood, and was greeted enthusiastically by two big balls of wet fur with even wetter tongues. Delly and Roddy. I hugged the two German Shepherds in tears, thinking of Cassie swept away. Then pushed them off to fumble for my phone. Emergency only – enough. I dialled 999 with shaking fingers, but had no idea which service I wanted. What could the fire brigade or police do?

'Everyone!' I shouted at the operator, 'Thruscross Dam's burst! You have to warn everyone downstream before it's too late!'

'Which service do you require?'

'Didn't you hear me? The dam's burst, water's flooding downstream, get whoever you can to move people out of the way!'

'Where exactly are you?'

'I'm at the dam.'

'Where is the dam?'

'Thruscross!' I shouted. 'Blubberhouses! Oh my God, there's a car! Get people up here quickly!' I dropped my phone and scrambled down the rocks to stop the car before it drove off the end of the road. Luckily the sight of a mud-covered, raving woman half falling towards them was enough to make the driver hit his brakes.

'Stop, stop, stop – the dam! Stop!'

'Are you all right? What's happened to you?'

'The dam!' I waved wildly. 'The dam's gone!'

'Oh my God.' The driver had got out of the car and was staring, horror-stricken. 'I wouldn't have been able to stop in time. There's nothing there! We'd have gone over the edge!'

'Steve, look! Bloody hell!' The woman passenger had jumped out and pointed at a car coming from the opposite direction. But there was nothing we could do to warn them.

There was a sharp bend just before the dam, they wouldn't have seen the gap until they were on the dam itself. We watched helplessly as the car slewed across the road, aquaplaning on the wet tarmac, then it hit the wall and scraped along the concrete towards the drop.

There was a moment at the very edge when I thought the car had caught, but its momentum was too much. I blinked as the headlights blinded me for an instant, then it plunged into the abyss.

The driver, Steve, rang 112 again. There was nothing else we could do. We couldn't get over there to warn traffic. Neither of us had enough signal to ring anybody to get down to the road before another car drove over the edge, even if I had known any numbers to ring. I hoped no one else would appear around that corner. At least it was afternoon mid-week and the road should be fairly quiet.

I walked out a little way on to the remains of the dam and peered over the wall at what was left of the reservoir. There was plenty of water at this end, but further up where the floor of the valley rose, mud-shrouded lumps had emerged. The village was rising again.

It was an eerie sight – tumbledown houses and bridges resurfacing after fifty years underwater. I realised with a jolt that Jennet would be there somewhere. The bodies from the cemetery had been moved, but she wouldn't have been buried in consecrated ground. Nobody in the 1960s would have known the site of her grave. Her waterlogged bones would be drying out, somewhere in all that mud.

I knew I had to write her story.

I sat up with a jolt. It was pitch black and I was completely disorientated. I remembered needing to see the village, wanting a closer look at the water-worn stone, but why was it so dark? Then I realised, and got out of bed fighting a panic attack. Gasping for breath, I stumbled to the window and pulled the curtains. The reservoir appeared peaceful and beautiful in the moonlight. I grasped the windowsill and stepped back, then bent over with a sob. *What's happening to me? It was so real.*

'Another one?'

I went back to the bed and Dave, and he rubbed my arms. I turned and sank against him, sobbing hard.

'It was so real, Dave! It was her – Jennet! I feel like I'm losing my mind, I don't know which reality is the true one, I don't know if Jennet is real.' I sobbed.

He held me and stroked my hair. 'You know, I don't know which is more frightening: the thought of you having a breakdown or being befriended by an eighteenth century witch,' he said in a misguided effort to cheer me up.

'Nor me,' I whispered. I wasn't cheered. There was nothing remotely amusing about this.

Dave kissed the top of my head. 'They're only dreams, Emma, she's not real, she can't be.'

'Hmm.' Logically, I accepted he was right, but it didn't help. My heart still beat madly in my chest, and I was convinced something was very wrong. 'Go back to sleep,' I told Dave. 'No point in us both being awake.'

'You sure?'

'Yes.'

'Well, lie back down then, snuggle up.' He patted my pillow.

'Maybe later.' I got out of bed. I knew I wouldn't be able to get back to sleep and was afraid it would worry Dave even more if he could feel me shaking next to him in bed. I stroked his arm to reassure him and went to the office to put the kettle on. I left the lights off and sat on the sofa, staring out at the moonlight reflected on the water. I knew exactly what was underneath that mirror-like surface. I could picture all the muddy humps and bumps, and had a clear picture of the village as it had been in my mind.

I didn't hear the kettle boil. I was already writing.

Chapter 19 - Jennet
1st December 1776

The sheep scattered before me in the moonlight as I trod through the heather, and I watched them go. The new stone walls snaked over the fields and lower moors, and it would not be long before these sheep would have nowhere to run. I knew it would make the farming easier in some respects, but they would be restricted to the same patch of field or moor, unable to roam to find better grass, and I doubted I would be allotted prime grazing land.

The barriers would also make my nightly wanderings harder. A number of the plants I used were best picked under a full moon, and the work were tiring enough without having to clamber over piles of stones or detour to go through gates. I bent to pick a clump of mushrooms and straightened, my gaze on the village below and the church.

I paused for a moment, watching the site of my humiliation that morning. *How could he have treated me that way? How could he?* And why were all the sneers and gossip directed at me alone? I might be carrying the child, but he had planted it there; how could he and his wife get away with calling *me* whore? Why were people not sniggering, pointing and whispering at *him*?

I sighed, determined not to cry any more – I had been doing that all day and did not think there was a drop of water left inside me – and carried on my search for useful plants. They were hard to find at this time of year, but I had been doing this all my life and knew where to find the most sheltered spots and the treasures they hid. Some of Mam's old customers – Marjorie Wainwright, Susan Gill and Martha Grange amongst them – had on occasion knocked on my door over the last few months asking for cures for their ailments, and in return they had helped with the sheep or paid me in winter fodder. I had hoped that word would spread that my remedies were as effective as Mam's had been, but that seemed unlikely now. Would I lose even the few customers I had? Would they turn their backs on me and make the long walk to Peggy Lofthouse at Padside? She were the next closest cunning woman to Thores-Cross, but Mam had always said she were no good. How would I manage if Mam were wrong and Old Peg took all my custom?

I pulled my shawl tighter against the cold night and tried to concentrate on the ground in my search for the ingredients I needed. If I did not, what else would I do?

I walked off the moors and trudged through the more fecund fields just above the village, stopping and bending every so often. Hazelnuts, mushrooms, rosehips and more – my basket were nearly full by the time I reached the graveyard. I closed my mind to the memories of the day and crossed to Mam and Pa's graves, the bare earth stark in the moonlight – it would be spring before nature covered them with a carpet of green.

I knelt down and pulled away the few weeds that had taken root ahead of the grass.

'Oh Mam, what am I going to do? They all hate me – Richard hates me. He never loved me – did he ever love thee, I wonder? Or did he just want what thee wouldn't give him? Oh Mam, I'm so sorry, I've been such a fool. Mary Farmer is the only friendly face left – thee can imagine!' I smiled through my tears – I did have water in me, after all.

'What am I going to do? I'm struggling with the beasts already – what am I going to do with a babby as well? Mary Farmer's getting on, she won't be much help.'

I had visions of tramping around the moors, chasing down sheep, with a child strapped to my back. I cried harder, then sat up as the wind caressed my cheek. It felt like fingers – Mam's fingers. I put my palm to my face. 'Mam,' I whispered. I sat in silence for a while longer, knowing Mam were near. I felt at peace for the first time since Richard had failed to visit.

Chapter 20 - Jennet
24th December 1776

I leaned on the garden wall and peered down at the village. A constellation of candle and lantern flames moved from house to house as the wasaillers endowed songs and blessings on their neighbours.

Every house but mine. They would not come here. They would not bless my home. The only one in the dale to be left out, and all because of an innocent child who had not yet been born. I caressed my belly. I shed no tears. The time for tears were past. I had no more upset, no more frustration, no more shame or pity in my soul.

All I had now were hate. Hate for Richard Ramsgill, hate for his wife and hate for every single villager who had pledged their condolences when Mam and Pa died, who had told me I could come to them if I needed anything. But when I needed a little compassion, a little human kindness, they all turned their backs and called me names.

Well, I did not need them. I did not need anyone. I had my wits, my home, my beasts, and I would soon have my child – only four months to go now. My first and last Christmas alone. Soon I would have everything I needed, and the whole village could go to Hell for all I cared.

The wasaillers walked up the lane. I watched their candle flames grow larger as they reached the Gate Inn. They were there a while, no doubt enjoying mince pies and spiced ale. Then the smithy. They did not spend so long there, despite the warmth of the forge. Closer now. I cursed my heart as it leaped in hope of them continuing straight up the hill to my own door, but no. They turned off, to East Gate House, home of Richard and Elizabeth Ramsgill.

Well bugger the lot of them! I did not need any of them, least of all Richard Bloody Ramsgill. I would soon have everyone I needed, once my babby were born. I already had every*thing* I needed – the moors always provided for one such as me, and the beasts had proved to be good at looking after themselves. I had meat, crops and the knowledge of a cunning woman.

They still came to me – oh aye they did. Not by day any more, no, but at night the villagers would creep up the hill, avoiding notice, coming for my cures, my restoratives and my preventatives. And they paid, by God they paid. They did not have money, nobody had actual coin to spare, except the bloody Ramsgills, but they gave me what I asked or left empty handed no matter how they pleaded. Grain, hay, meat, cheese, even whiskybae. Only what *I* needed. Only what *I* wanted. The same women who called me whore, harlot, slut when my back were turned. But I knew, oh aye, I knew. So when they came to me, they paid dearly.

I even had Hannah Ramsgill up here, can thee imagine? *She* did not go home with the remedy to cure Thomas' inattention, oh no! She got something else entirely. But she cannot tell anyone! Not without admitting she cannot attract her husband any more – and she only thirty two! She runs away from me now if she sees me in the village. Hah! A Ramsgill running from me in shame – that were more like it! I laughed out loud at the memory.

The wasaillers emerged back on to the lane. They marched straight past my house. Not a single one even paused. I watched them reach Mary Farmer's house further up the hill and gather around her door. The sound of their singing and cheers drifted down to me, and I grabbed Pa's old sheepskin coat and walked away into the blessed silence of the moor.

It were not proper silent of course, but I could enjoy the whistling of the wind and the mournful cries of owl and curlew. This were where I belonged, on the moor with bird and rodent, not with the rats of that village. Here the air were pure, there were no whispers of scorn or delight in another's fall; no sneering laughter or vicious insult. Here, everything were as it should be. Heather, bracken, sheep, grouse, and of course the ever-present owl. Sometimes audible by its hoot, often surprising as it glided past on silent wings; then a thump and squeal of its prey and it were gone. Aye, I could learn a lot from the owls.

I headed south towards the fairy spring near the rocking stone. The wind were getting up and I were frozen, but did not care. I thought I would be cold for the rest of my life. I pulled the coat tighter around myself, bent my head to the wind and trudged on. At least I could not hear the wasaillers any longer.

I reached the spring and knelt. Mam had died not far from here, and I felt close to her now. I did not like going to the graveyard any more – the village were too close. Anyroad, her spirit were out here on the moors, and this spring were where I felt close to her. She used to come here regularly, dragging me along with her, even as a toddler. She would sit for hours with me on her knee, telling me stories of the fairy folk, the giants, all the beings who were here long before us and who we ignored at our peril. I used to love the sunlight dancing in the little splashes of water as it fell a few inches off a stone and she told me those glints of light were the fairies. That if I ever needed help or a friend I should come here and make my wishes known. They would always help me, no matter what. I hoped she were right.

* * *

I shivered again as the December wind cut through my thick woollens. I looked up in alarm at a familiar but dreaded sound. The rocking stone were moving. The grinding resonated in my heart and suddenly I could not bear to be out here any longer. I turned for home and ran as best I could through the heather.

Chapter 21 - Emma
4th September 2012

'Emma!'

I woke with a start, not sure where I was, then registered that Dave was bending over me with a mug of coffee. I'd fallen asleep on the sofa. I sat up with a groan and paper and pen slid to the floor.

'How are you feeling?' Dave sat down and passed me the mug.

'What time is it?' I groaned.

'Ten o'clock.'

'What?' I looked out of the window and realised he was right.

'Where are the dogs?' I couldn't believe they'd not woken me, they must be desperate for a walk.

'They're downstairs. I let them out earlier to do their business, but I thought you should sleep. Any more dreams?'

I shook my head. I'd take the beasts out later. I could do with a long walk myself to try and clear my head and make sense of the last few days, well, nights.

I bent down to pick up my notebook and flicked through it. 'I must have been writing for hours,' I said.

'Don't you remember?'

'Not really. I was in a bit of a daze to tell you the truth. I must have still been half asleep.'

'Well you *were* writing through the early hours.' Dave tried to reassure me.

'I suppose so.' I put the notebook on the table. 'I'll read it through later. It's probably crap.'

Dave laughed. 'That's what I like to hear – optimism. You never know, it could be your next bestseller.'

I pulled a face at him. 'What time do you have to leave?' Dave had yet another business trip to Edinburgh. I knew it was important, but still, I did miss him when he was away, despite my assurances that I was fine.

'This afternoon,' he replied. 'My first meeting is over dinner. If I leave at two, I should get there with an hour to spare. Time to settle in the hotel and have a shower.' He stopped and regarded me thoughtfully. 'I could cancel if you want me to stay with you.'

'Don't be silly.' I laughed. 'It's only a few bad dreams, I don't need a nursemaid, I'm not ill. I'll be fine.'

'I know, but . . . we're so isolated here, you're on your own when I go away, I worry about you.'

'I like being alone sometimes, you know that, and I love the peace and quiet here, you know that too.'

'Those dreams are far from peaceful.'

'It's just my writer's imagination,' I said. Part of me wanted to ask him to stay and I realised I felt vulnerable since the nightmares had started. I got a mental grip of myself. I was a grown woman, and had moved here out of choice. Dave's trips to Scotland were important, I could not ask him to stay because of a few dreams, nor would I give him cause to worry. 'If I do have a problem, Mark and Kathy are up the lane. What could you do if you were here, anyway? You can't control my dreams.'

He nodded. 'Fair enough, but if you do get another one and want to hear a friendly voice, ring me – it doesn't matter what time.'

'Of course I'll ring you – you know I don't mind waking you up!' We laughed.

'All right then, I'll go and pack. Do you want to go out for lunch?'

'Oh, that's a nice idea, let's go for chips and peas!'

I waved Dave off, then pulled my scarf tighter round my neck and whistled to the dogs. They came running, and I made a fuss of all three of them. Especially Cassie.

'How do!'

I glanced up at the shout and returned Mark's greeting, then made a fuss of his border collie, who had cannoned into the mêlée at my feet.

'Delly, no!' I shouted as he went for Shep.

'Stand back,' Mark advised over the snarling. 'They're just sorting out who's boss, they'll settle down in a minute. Are you going out or coming back?'

'Setting off,' I replied, wincing at the snapping dogs, but none of them seemed to be bleeding. 'Are you sure they're ok?'

'Aye, they'll be right in a bit, can you cope with some company?'

I watched the dogs dubiously.

'They'll settle when we're off Delly's territory. Shep! Come!'

The collie ran to Mark, tongue lolling and chased by Delly; Rodney following behind.

'Delly, no!' I shouted, but he ignored me again.

Mark laughed. 'Come on, let's walk.'

I nodded and followed. All four dogs raced off down the lane towards the reservoir, Delly still snarling, but they seemed more playful now.

'I don't understand it,' I said, embarrassed at Delly's bad behaviour. 'He's the softest of dogs normally.'

'He's top dog,' Mark said. 'Mine came on to his territory, he showed him who were boss. He were protecting his pack, including you.'

'Really?' I said, pleased.

'It's what they do. See, Shep's got the message. See him licking Delly's snout? And now look, Shep's rolled on to his back, he's submitting. They'll be right enough.'

We walked down the hill after them, and they did seem best of friends now. Although Shep was a little overfriendly towards Cassie, but she was more than capable of sending him packing, especially when Delly added his own encouragement. Then Roddy spotted a rabbit and all four of them were off. I laughed, relieved, and we followed much more slowly along the shore.

'There are some good walks around here,' Mark said.

'Yes, I took them up on to the moorland the other day. They were absolutely shattered running through the heather.'

Mark laughed. 'Yes they would be! Have you walked below the dam yet? It's beautiful.'

'*No!*'

Mark seemed taken aback at the force of my denial.

'Sorry. Another dream,' I explained.

'Sounds like a bad one.'

'Yes.' I shivered. 'I was walking down there in a thunderstorm, and the dam burst. Cassie was swept away, a car drove off the edge, and I woke up crying at all the people who must have been killed downstream.'

'Nasty,' Mark said.

'Yes. But the most profound part was watching the village resurface.'

'Hang on, I thought you were below the dam?'

'I climbed up the side of the valley.'

'Dreams.' Mark nodded. 'Anything's possible.'

'Anyway.' I was annoyed. I *had* climbed up the hill; it hadn't been the dream allowing the impossible. 'As the village reappeared, I kept thinking about that witch you and Kathy talked about.'

'Jennet.'

'Yes, and how her bones are still there, somewhere in all that mud.'

'It's unlikely she were buried in the village, Emma. She'll be under the moors somewhere, probably at some sort of crossroads to try to keep her spirit contained or confused or something.'

'No, she's closer than you think,' I said, suddenly sure of myself. 'I've started writing her story,' I explained, feeling shy. I was extremely self-conscious at the start of any writing project and could hardly believe I'd told this relative stranger what I was writing about when I'd only started last night. But then I realised why. 'Maybe you could tell me more about the legends?'

'I'd love to,' Mark said. 'What have you got so far?'

I frowned. 'I'm not sure really, I haven't read it through yet.'

'Don't you know?' Mark asked, incredulous.

I shrugged. 'I started in the early hours after my dream. I must still have been half asleep. I'll read it through when I get back.'

'Maybe that inkpot you found *were* hers, and *she's* writing the story through you. Oh God, listen to me, I sound like Kathy!' He stooped suddenly, picked up a large feather and presented it to me. 'Here, a goose wing feather to go with the inkpot – it's what Jennet would have used.'

'Would she have been able to write?' I asked, surprised.

'Aye, more than likely. She were a cunning woman, her mam would have taught her to write enchantments and recipes and the like.'

I pursed my lips and raised my eyebrows as I nodded, then took the feather and laughed. 'I know I'm old-fashioned using ink and paper, but I'm not quite that old-fashioned!'

'Research,' Mark said, laughing with me. 'Use it to get into your character's skin. Isn't that what you writers do?'

I shuddered, remembering my nightmare. It felt like Jennet was getting into *my* skin rather than the other way round, but I held on to the feather nonetheless. It was from one of the Canada Geese who visited the reservoir every year. I doubted they came in Jennet's time, although they would have kept geese. Surely it wouldn't hurt to have a play with the quill, and I suddenly quite fancied putting my old inkpot to its proper use again after all this time.

'Thank you,' I said, 'perhaps I will.' Our fingers touched and I glanced up at him, then took the feather and looked away, aware that my cheeks had flushed. *What was that all about? Have we just had a moment? I don't even find him attractive!*

I called to the dogs and threw a stick towards the water. They piled into the shallows – as far as my stick had made it – and sent water splashing everywhere. The moment, whatever it had been, was broken.

'So, has Dave gone anywhere nice?' Mark asked, breaking the awkward silence. I glanced up at him in question. 'I spotted the suit carrier as he drove past,' Mark continued.

'Edinburgh on business,' I said, not sure I wanted Mark to know I was home alone. 'He'll be back in a couple of days.'

'He's brave, leaving a woman like you on your own. Sorry, I don't know why I said that,' he added, colouring. 'I guess I'm a bit star-struck having a famous author on my doorstep.'

'You flatter me,' I said, uncomfortable with the way this conversation was going. I looked at him sideways. He wasn't bad-looking, really, although he walked with a bit of a stoop, but still, I loved my husband. I didn't understand why there was this atmosphere between us. I walked down to the water's edge and searched for a flat stone to skim.

'So how long has your family lived round here?' I asked Mark after he'd skimmed a stone of his own.

'Seven! Beat that!' he said. I sighed. Save me from competitive men.

'Six, ha!' he exclaimed.

I tried again, irritated. 'There, eight, your turn,' I said, the awkwardness gone now. He laughed and threw again, poorly this time.

'I've no idea how long the Ramsgills have been here – forever, as far as I know. Long before Jennet's time, anyway.'

'So your ancestors knew her?'

'Knew her? They probably hanged her!'

'Hanged her?'

'I don't know, it's all legend. Who knows what's true? Who knows if Jennet were real at all?'

'Oh she was real all right, I have no doubt about that!'

'Why not? How the hell do you know?'

I glanced up in surprise at the intensity of his words and shrugged, not wanting to tell him how deeply I felt a connection with her after my dream. 'Women's intuition?'

I cried out as Roddy barged past me into the water after the stones and nearly knocked me flying.

Mark laughed, his bad humour forgotten. 'No, seriously, the Ramsgills were prominent sheep farmers and wool merchants. They brought a lot of work and money to the area, they owned a great deal of land and one of them were even Forest Constable, so they had plenty of power. They still had to answer to the Duchy of Lancaster though, as did the rest of those who lived within the Forest of Knaresborough.'

'Forest of Knaresborough? We're a long way from Knaresborough here.'

'Only about twenty miles as the crow flies, we're right on the edge of what were the Forest. It's funny isn't it; thinking most of these fields were once woodland, full of deer and wolves and all sorts of other wildlife.'

'Wolves? Really? Are you sure about that?' I didn't think wolves were native to Yorkshire.

'So the tales go. Our house is called Wolf Farm, although that might be something to do with Jennet and barguests again.'

'It must have been pretty isolated,' I said, getting back to reality.

'Very. They'll have had a long trek to any markets, so the village were forced to be more or less self-sufficient. My ancestors were probably the only wool merchants for miles around; all the farmers, spinners and weavers would have had to stay on the right side of them.'

I looked around. I could see for miles, but only a couple of old stone properties were visible. 'I can't imagine living up here without a car,' I said. 'I like solitude, need it even, to write. But I like to be able to leave and find other people when I want to.'

'I know what you mean. But two hundred year ago, most of the villagers would never have left the moors. Only the few more successful farmers would have made the trek to the sheep fairs – probably the Ramsgills or their men – it would have taken days.' He paused and stared at me. 'You know, I have a couple of books on the history here at home, do you want to borrow them?'

'I'd love to, yes please.' We called to the dogs and started walking back up the hill.

'I'll bring them down with me tomorrow – same time?'

'Yes.' Then a thought struck me. 'Aren't you working?'

'Term starts next week.'

'Of course.'

'Happen you'll know what you've written so far by then.'

'I'm intrigued myself.' I laughed.

I was glad to get home again and relieved to get away from Mark, although I had agreed to meet him the following day. I towelled the dogs off and fed them, then headed upstairs to my office and settled on the sofa with the dogs flat out at my feet to read last night's folios.

25th June 1776

'Here, Jennet, put them pies out on't table, lass,' Mam said, thrusting a basket of cold mutton pastries at me. 'Get a move on, will thee, that pen's nearly empty, they'll be ready for a break in a minute.'

I sighed and were about to point out that we were only late because she had not been able to find the crab apple pickle, but spotted Mary Farmer walking purposefully towards us, and did as I were told. If I were already busy, she would not be able to give me more work to do. I took the basket from Mam and carried it to the tables, the coarse heather grabbing at my skirts.

The whole village had turned out for the sheepwashing. The flocks had been driven the mile to Thores-Ford early this morning, and everyone had been hard at work since daybreak. It would have been noted that we were late, but Mam were respected as the local cunning woman and she had helped at least one member of every family here at one time or another – she would be forgiven.

This were the start of our year – even though it were midsummer – when the sheep were washed ready for shearing in a fortnight. Their wool were our livelihood and, looking round, I saw shepherds, carders, fullers, spinners and weavers. And Richard Ramsgill, the wool merchant and most powerful man on the moor. I smiled at him, shy, and looked past him to my pa who were in the ford itself, along with William Gill, ducking the sheep in the now foul-smelling water, one at a time.

The ewe thrashed as she were held underwater then thrown out whilst the next one were dumped in. It were hard, dirty, noisy, smelly work, but essential if we were to get the best out of the fleeces, and the whole valley had gathered to get it done. Another half dozen to go, then they would be ready for a break before starting on the next flock.

The washing ford were a natural widening in the stream high up on the moors, by the rocking stone. I glanced over at it now; an enormous oval rock balanced on a plinth – put there by giants to amuse their young, the old tales said. There were not enough wind now to set it in motion, but in the most powerful gales, it would move, sending a noise throughout the valley that sounded like giants' grinding their teeth. But not this day.

'Jennet! Stop dallying, lass, they're nearly ready!'

I snapped back to myself and grinned at Mam, then got back to work.

'Whoa! Watch out there!'

I glanced up at the shout. The new flock being herded to the washing ford had broken loose and were stampeding towards us.

'The food! The tables!' Mary Farmer wailed. 'Stop them!'

Mam did as she were told – everyone did what they were told by Mary Farmer, it were easier that way – and ran at the approaching flock, trying to turn them back towards the ford, but to no avail. The first ewes ploughed into the trestles sending pies, pickles and ale flying. I put my hands to my mouth in merriment – I had never seen anything so funny and I would have given anything to have seen that look on Mary Farmer's face.

'Alice!'

I stopped laughing at the panic in Pa's voice and turned. One of the ewes had knocked Mam into the water. She could not swim.

I watched Pa jump in after her and wanted to help, but could not move. Everywhere were chaos. Sheep bumped my legs, but my feet were as rooted to the moor as the heather. I could only watch.

Pa surfaced, coughing, then disappeared. I could not see Mam – not even her skirts. I could feel the blood drain out of my face as I realised what were happening and finally moved my feet. I ran to the water's edge, screaming for me mam, and got there as Pa finally pulled her up. She did not move.

'Mam? Mam? Mam!'

Pa did not look at me and Mam had not shifted. He waded to the edge and handed her up to the men gathered there, and they hauled her on to dry land. No one would look at me.

I pushed my way through the men and fell to my knees. Her usually rosy face were white and streaked with mud and sheepshite. Her eyes were shut and her lips slightly parted. She had a dark red mark on her forehead and were not breathing.

'Jennet.' Pa's hands were on me shoulders and he tried to pull me back. 'She's gone, Jennet, she's gone. Come away.'

I did as I were bid. I did not seem to be able to decide for myself, I just did as Pa bid, and the ring of people closed around Mam.

I picked up my pen to write on and find out what happened next, how Jennet carried on; but no words came and I realised I was crying. After an hour, I threw the pen down in disgust and put the kettle on. I stood at the window with my steaming cup of coffee, but found no inspiration. Thruscross was shrouded in fog, just like my brain.

With a sigh, I turned to put my mug on the desk and picked up the inkpot. Then I saw the goose feather. *Why not?* I fetched a knife from the kitchen, sharpened the shaft and poured ink into the inkpot. Feeling a bit of an idiot, I dipped in the quill, held it over the page, dropped a few blotches of ink, and started writing.

Chapter 22 - Jennet
27th February 1777

I sat back and watched the tiny lamb struggle to its feet and bleat at its dam. I rested on my heels in relief. I loved this time of year, and had not needed to give this ewe any help. At six years old she were strong and healthy and had already done this a few times.

I waited until the lamb started suckling, then got to my feet, picked up my lantern and looked around the dark moors.

I had driven my girls closer to the farm last month, where it were more sheltered with better grass – I would have to mark the new arrivals before they wandered again, to make sure everyone knew they were mine. I would give them a couple of months at least though, before I got the branding iron out and burned the initials of my great-great-great-great-grandpa on to the sides of their noses.

I stretched and glanced up at the tiny sliver of moon. I sighed, I could have done with a full one tonight. I held up my lantern and went in search of the last ewe I had marked as being likely to birth tonight.

She were the eldest of the flock, and in any year past she would have been mutton by now. But I only had one mouth to feed these days, and had decided to keep her for one more wool crop and, hopefully, another lamb.

I found her lying down, her birthing already started. I set the lantern down near her back-end and gave her face a rub before settling down to help her.

'Ey up lass, is thee all right?'

I jumped and peered at the shadowy figure behind the lantern. He held it higher, and I recognised Peter Stockdale.

'How do, Peter,' I said. 'What's thee doing here?'

'I've just finished up with Ramsgill's lambs for the night, saw thy lantern and wondered if thee needed an hand.'

'Oh,' I said, surprised. I could not remember the last time anybody but Mary Farmer had offered me aid. 'Um, she's the last one tonight, I reckon, but she's old and I think she's twinning.'

He crouched down next to the ewe and felt her belly. 'Aye, there's two in there all right.' He tugged on the ewe's ears. 'Thee's not on thy own, though, old girl.'

I glanced at him sharply. I wished he would say that to me and mean it.

Peter Stockdale caught my eye and smiled. I looked away embarrassed, back to the ewe's back-end.

'First one's coming,' I said.

'Let's have a look,' said Peter, pushing me out of the way. 'Hmm, it's taking too long, think we'd better give her an hand – give other twin a chance.'

I nodded and clasped my hands around my belly in fear. What if I had problems birthing my babby and there were no one to help?

He reached between the ewe's back legs, then pulled, emerging with the back legs of a tiny, limp lamb in his grasp.

'Dead,' he said, laid it on the ground and examined the ewe again. 'Next one's coming.'

I picked up the dead lamb, wiped the crud from its nose and mouth, then stood while holding its back legs and spun round. I had seen Pa do this successfully, but it did not work tonight.

I fell to the ground, dizzy, and sobbed.

'Never mind, lass, thee can't save them all. Here, look after this live 'un while I see to its dam.'

I took the newborn and wiped it down. It bleated at me and I grinned.

Peter Stockdale sat back on his haunches. 'Damn it,' he said.

'Oh no!'

'She's gone.'

I reached out and stroked the dead ewe's face.

'Don't fret, she were old. I'll help thee get her to farmhouse so's thee can butcher her.'

I nodded my thanks and hugged the poddy lamb.

'What'll thee do with that 'un?'

I shrugged. 'Hand-rear her, I suppose.'

'Does thee not have another ewe with a stillborn?'

I said nowt.

'Come on, lass, I knows thee's had hard time, and house must be terrible quiet, but let's give this little 'un a proper mam.'

I nodded, ashamed of my weakness, and led the way to another ewe who had lost her lamb. I rubbed the lamb on the ground around her, trying to pick up the smell of her afterbirth, then put it to the teat.

Now all we could do were wait for the milk to come through and the lamb to take it. We sat a little way back to watch.

'Thee'll not tell no one I were here, will thee, lass?'

I glanced up at him in surprise and disappointment.

'Sorry, lass.' He looked ashamed. 'But Mr Ramsgill wouldn't take kindly to this, and I can't afford to lose work.'

'Thy secret's safe with me, Peter,' I said. 'And I'm grateful for thy company.'

We sat in silence for a while and watched the lamb finish feeding and lie in the coarse grass.

'Did thee lose many?'

'Three lambs, but that one were only ewe.'

He nodded. 'That's not too bad, and at least thee'll have plenty of meat.'

'Mm.'

'How's thee faring?'

I shrugged and he nodded again. We sat in silence for a while, until the lamb had done its business.

The ewe sniffed the lamb's turds, then licked the tiny body.

'That's it, she's accepted it! I'll help thee get dead 'uns to house.'

'Thank thee,' I said as I stood. I realised I could see him properly now. He was my height, but twice as broad; with floppy, sandy hair and hazel eyes; and his crooked smile revealed crooked teeth.

'Right then,' he said. 'Let's be off.'

Chapter 23 - Jennet
26th May 1777

'Come on, lass, keep pushing! Thee can do it!'

I swore; loudly and crudely. I had been pushing for hours already; if the little bugger did not come out soon, he could bloody well stay where he were.

'I can see head!' Mary Farmer exclaimed. She were the only one here, the only one who cared. But at least I were not on my own any more. I had been for the first six hours – I had had no way of summoning Mary, but she had got into the habit of checking on me twice a day. *Thank God*.

I had made myself up a bed downstairs where it were warmest, and had forced myself up to unbar the door for her when she had finally come knocking.

'Push, lass, push!' Mary sounded more urgent.

'What is it?'

'Just push, lass.'

'Tell me!'

'The cord's wrapped round neck, I can't get me fingers in. Thee needs to push hard. Now!'

I screamed in agony at the ripping sensation as I forced the silent babby out into the world.

'Come on, Mary!' I screamed.

Nowt.

She held the babby up by its legs and I realised from the colour of him that he were dead. Mary smacked his arse.

Nowt.

She did it again with the same result and looked at me. My babby were dead. I sank back on to the filthy bedding, then screamed as another spasm of pain ripped through my body.

'Ruddy hell! There's another one! Come on, lass, don't give up now, he's been in there too long as it is, thee needs to get him out!'

I screamed obscenities at her and did my best, but I had been doing this for hours, my body felt mutilated beyond repair, and the makeshift bed were soaked in blood.

'Come on! Don't let him die too! Push, Jennet!'

I took a deep breath, gritted my teeth and heaved one last, desperate time.

'Aye!'

There were no noise. No cries. I lifted my head from the cushion of fleeces to see. 'Does he live?'

Mary were bent over the tiny body and I could not see. 'Aye, she does lass, but she's weak. See if she'll take milk.'

She handed me the tiny body she had wrapped in muslin, and I held my daughter to my breast. She moved her head slightly towards me, but did not take my nipple.

'Thee'll have to help her, lass.'

I looked at Mary. I did not like how sombre she sounded and my ravaged body flushed with panic. I took my breast, pulled the girl to me and forced my nipple into her mouth. I felt her lips close around it, but she were too weak to suckle. I looked at Mary in despair.

'I'll go to Gate for some goat's milk,' she said. 'Just keep trying.'

I nodded, and moved my breast against the tiny mouth, encouraging her to suck, but it were useless. I held the tiny body close, trying to keep her warm; trying to let her know she were wanted and loved. I realised I were muttering to her.

'Come on, Alice, come on, don't give up on me.' I had not known I had decided to call her for Mam until I heard the name pass my lips. I realised I could not feel her breath on my skin any more. I kept her in my arms, held against my heart. I did not look up when Mary Farmer returned.

'Oh lass,' she sighed. 'I'm so sorry.'

The sun were going down before I let Mary take the small bundle from me and place her on the table next to her brother. I had not cried. I did not want to cry. I stared at my only friend and all I felt were rage. It were so unfair. I had been used, berated and abandoned for these babbies, but I had wanted them and loved them, and neither had lived an hour.

'Suffer the little children,' I muttered.

'What?'

'That's what they'll say, ain't it? In that Damned church. "Suffer the little children." They'll say it's my fault, God's punishment for my actions and he . . . he gets off scot free!' My voice had risen to a shout. 'Well he won't, none of them will!'

I forced myself off the bed, staggered to the table and picked up my children. I stumbled towards the fire, hunched like an old crone, but with blood running down the inside of my thighs.

'I curse the Ramsgills! All of them! I curse them to die before adulthood!' I threw the boy on to the fire. Mary screamed and tried to grab me. I shook her off and she fell to the floor. 'Only one may live to carry the curse to the next generation, then they will suffer their losses!' My daughter joined my son.

'More peat, Mary, it needs to be hotter!' Mary backed away from me. She looked terrified. I managed to bend and knock more peat on to the pyre, then straightened as best I were able and watched my children burn. The room filled with the smell of roasting meat and the sound of the cracking of skin as it charred.

'I curse Thores-Cross! Let the Devil and his hounds be welcomed to hunt for souls here!'

I threw a handful of herbs on the flames to add potency to my words.

'They'll pay for this! The Ramsgills and Thores-Cross will pay for eternity!' I were screaming now. I turned to face Mary. She had reached the far wall, her face distorted with horror.

'Bear witness, Mary Farmer. They're all Damned now!'

Mary rushed to the door and ran. I watched her go.

Chapter 24 - Emma
5th September 2012

I sat back on the sofa, horrified at what I had written. *Where did that come from?* I put my notebook and quill on the table and massaged my right wrist. I realised tears poured down my face. Poor Jennet. Those poor babies. I propped my head in my hands and let the sobs out. I cried for Jennet, and I cried for my own lost child.

I jumped at the eruption of barking from the kitchen. Someone was at the door. I wiped my face and took a deep breath, then made my way downstairs to see who it was.

'Mark!'

I was surprised to see him, but stood aside to let him in.

'How do. I brought you those local history books I promised. Found something else you might like an'all, lass.'

I jumped at the 'lass' but managed a smile. 'That's great. I was about to make coffee, would you like a cup?'

'Aye, that'd be grand.'

I shut the door behind him and led the way to the kitchen as he greeted all three dogs jumping around us.

'Are you all right? You look upset.'

'I'm fine,' I said. 'I just got caught up in my story.'

'It must be a rum 'un if it's brought you to tears.'

'Umm, you could say that,' I replied, my voice shaking as I poured water into mugs. 'Milk? Sugar?'

'Yes to both.'

I nodded and finished the drinks, then passed a mug to Mark.

'So is it Jennet?'

'What?'

'Your story, is it Jennet's?'

I nodded, not trusting myself to speak.

'And does the quill work?'

I glanced at him in surprise.

'Your fingers.'

I looked down and managed a smile. My right hand was black with ink. 'Not the tidiest way to write! I wanted to try the inkpot and quill, I guess I got carried away.'

'Oh yes, the inkpot – you were going to show it to me.'

'Of course, it's in the office – would you bring the books up?' I led the way upstairs.

'Wow!' Mark stopped on the top tread and stared at the view. 'How can you possibly work in here? I'd be staring out the window all day!'

I nodded. 'It has been known, but these days I usually find it inspiring rather than distracting.'

I led the way to the sofa and coffee table where my notebook, quill and inkpot lay.

'Bloody hell, what a mess, Dave's going to kill me!'

Ink splotches covered the top of the wooden coffee table.

'An occupational hazard of being a writer,' Mark said and laughed.

'Hmm,' I said, horrified about the stains and concerned that I hadn't noticed them earlier. I sat down and put my coffee mug on the table. Mark joined me. He picked up the inkpot and examined it.

'You could be right, you know – about its date. If it were more ornate, I'd say it were later, but in 1700s Yorkshire, they didn't have time or inclination to make things pretty. Plain, useful and durable, that's the old Yorkshire way. This really could have belonged to Jennet.'

I glanced at my notebook. I had no doubt that it had.

'What have you brought me?' I asked.

He put the inkpot down, grimaced, showed me the fresh stains on his fingers, then wiped them on his jeans.

I smiled to myself, thinking of Dave. He'd have never done that – a quick dash to a sink with soap and scrubbing brush was more his style. I missed him when he was away, but another couple of days and he'd be home.

Mark thumped three books on to the coffee table.

'These are the best local histories I have. *Life and Tradition in the Yorkshire Dales*, *A History of Nidderdale* & Richard Muir's *The Yorkshire Countryside*, but this is the real prize.' He pulled an old, leather-bound book out of the bag. 'Old Ma Ramsgill's journal – my great-grandmother.'

'Ooh, can I have a look? I love old journals!'

'Aye. All the family history's in here, and anything interesting about the neighbours too – a right gossip, she were.'

I smiled as he passed me the book. It was filled with tiny, cramped writing. My enthusiasm faltered a little – it would take me ages to go through it all, but who knew what gems were hidden in here?

I was aware of our knees pressed together and moved my leg away as I opened the back pages of the journal.

'Oh look, a family tree!'

'Oh aye, I'd forgotten about that. The Moores – my great-nan's side are on the right, but this one . . .' he leaned over and unfolded the large sheet of paper, '. . . is the Ramsgills.'

I pored over it, excited.

'Here, these'll be them that were around in Jennet's time,' he said, pointing.

'No. Here,' I corrected, indicating the name Richard, with Thomas, Richard, Robert and Alexander below it.

'How can you possibly know that, lass?'

I shrugged, a little uncomfortable. I stared at the names, realising how strange it was that the very names I had used for the Ramsgill brothers were here, together, on the Ramsgill family tree. I shivered, then noticed something else that made my blood run cold.

'Mark – do you have any cousins?'

'Cousins? Nay. It's just me – I don't even have a brother or sister, they died when I were a nipper – meningitis.'

'I'm sorry. They?'

'Aye, twins. They run in the family, though you wouldn't know it, not many seem to survive.' He gave a small, strangled laugh.

'I thought twins only ran down the female line?'

'Aye, well, don't know about that, but there've been a lot in the Ramsgill family.'

I stared at the family tree, checking and subtracting dates. He was right – there were a lot of twins, and they had all died young.

'At first, I thought the tree was only tracing your line,' *straight back to Richard Ramsgill*, I thought but didn't say. 'But it isn't. Look. Only one Ramsgill survives to bear children. And always a man – carrying on the name.'

'Aye, we've never been lucky, us Ramsgills, but I never realised it were that bad. Let me have a look at that.'

I watched him, feeling numb. The ruddy colour drained from his cheeks as he studied the dates. I realised our legs were touching again.

'Mark, there's something I need to show you.' I felt nervous. I wasn't sure if this was the right thing to do, but he needed to know.

I picked up my notebook and found the passage, pointing to it with my finger.

I curse the Ramsgills! All of them! I curse them to die before adulthood!' I threw the boy on to the fire. Mary screamed and tried to grab me. I shook her off and she fell to the floor. 'Only one may live to carry the curse to the next generation, then they will suffer their losses!'

He glanced at me. 'That's just a bit of nonsense. You're a fiction writer – a storyteller, you've made that up, it means nowt.'

I thumbed through the notebook again and pointed out another passage.

The Ramsgills were the most important family in the valley – Thomas the Forest Constable, Richard the wool merchant, Big Robert the miller and Alexander just getting his own farm established. There were three more brothers still working their father's farm.

'Mark, how old are your twins?'

He glanced at me, jumped to his feet, and backed away.

'I don't know what you think you're doing, lass, but it ain't funny.' He turned and rushed downstairs. The dogs didn't follow, but watched him go. Cassie crossed to me and pressed herself against my legs. I stroked her absentmindedly, wondering what it all meant and thinking about the expression on Mark's face. I imagined it was very similar to the way people used to look at Jennet. But I was not Jennet.

'Why did you write that?'

'Mark, it's late . . .' And it was. I was in my dressing gown, ready to go to bed, but had somehow known who was banging on the door and had opened it.

He pushed past me and stood in the lounge.

'Why did you write that?' he asked again.

'I don't know,' I said. 'I'm not sure I did, I think . . . I think it might have been Jennet.'

'Bah!' he said, crossed to the sideboard with the whisky decanter and glasses displayed on its top, poured himself a drink, downed it and refilled his glass. I narrowed my eyes at the liberty he was taking, but nodded when he waved the decanter at me. He poured a couple of fingers into another glass.

'I don't believe in all that nonsense, Emma.'

'Neither do I, not really.' That wasn't strictly true, but I thought it the best response in the circumstances. 'Or I didn't anyway, but how else do you explain it?' I took the glass from him, my fingers brushing his. 'How did I know the names? Your family history?'

He didn't reply, but crossed to the window and stared out into the night. I followed and touched his shoulder.

'I'm sorry, Mark, I didn't mean to upset you.'

His shoulder relaxed under my touch and he turned. He caught hold of my waist and pulled me closer. We stared at each other a moment, then he kissed me. I stiffened, but didn't pull away. After a moment I returned his kiss.

I shrugged my dressing gown back on and held it tightly closed across my chest. I could not look at Mark. *Why on earth had I done that?*

'I-I-I need to get back to Kathy.' Mark looked at his watch and fastened his jeans. 'She thinks I'm at the Stone House, and it closed half an hour ago.'

I nodded, but said nothing.

'Look . . . Emma . . . I-I don't know what came over me.'

'Nor me,' I whispered, still struggling to find my voice.

'Let's just forget it happened.'

I nodded, though how on earth could I forget cheating on Dave? I hated myself. And I hated Mark.

Chapter 25 - Jennet
28th May 1777

I lay in bed, sleep impossible to find, and flinched as lightning flashed.

'*One* drunk shepherd, *two* drunk shepherd, *three* drunk shepherd,' I counted, and thunder rolled. Three miles away.

My babbies had died – both of them. I remembered throwing them on the fire and Mary running from the house. Lightning flashed again – I counted – still three miles.

I rolled on to my side and swung my legs to the floor, then pushed myself up to stand. I stood for a moment, my legs trembling and, feeling dizzy, walked unsteadily to my clothing chest. Thunder crashed again.

Downstairs and feeling a little stronger, I stared at the fireplace. The fire had gone out long before.

I hunted around in the kitchen for some food and found a pot of cold pottage that Mary had left. I wolfed it down and paused to count. Two miles.

A gust of wind shrieked in the chimney and a puff of ash scattered in the room.

No!

I found a lidded basket and cleared the grate, shovelling the ash and small bits of bone into it. My babbies could not stay in this house and become nowt but dirt.

I pulled Pa's boots on to my feet and shrugged into his coat, picked up the basket and opened the door. The force of the wind and rain near took my breath away, and I watched the dark valley flash into being for a second. Only one drunk shepherd now.

I forced the door shut behind me and headed out on to the moors.

It took me an hour to reach the fairy spring – three times as long as usual – and I sank to my knees beside it.

'They're dead, Mam, my babbies are dead!' I sobbed. 'I cursed them, Mam, I cursed the Ramsgills, and I called up the Wild Hunt!'

I lifted my head to the sky and screamed my grief and pain at the raging heavens. 'And I don't care! I don't care if the Devil comes and claims every soul in this valley!'

Lightning flashed again and thunder roared with it. The storm were overhead. I struggled to my feet.

'Do you hear me?' I screamed at the storm. 'Do thy worst! Send thy hounds! Take this whole valley to Hell!'

I picked up the basket and removed the lid, then threw the contents to fly with the wind. 'Rest easy, my loves, rest easy on these moors – I'll avenge thee, don't thee fret!'

A new noise caught my attention – a rumbling, grating. The rocking stone. The spirits of the moors had acknowledged me; they would care for my babbies.

I turned to face the full force of the wind and raised my arms. I lifted my face and felt the power of this place. 'I'll avenge thee,' I said again, my words whipped away into the dark night.

I collapsed on to the heather, my rage spent. What had I done?

'I'm sorry, Mam,' I whispered. 'Take good care of my babbies for me.'

I got to my feet and started the walk home. My woollen clothes were saturated and heavy – it would take weeks to get them properly dry again – and my legs felt like lead. My whole body hurt and I thought I could feel blood dripping inside my skirts.

I finally made it, lit a new fire, stripped, wrapped a blanket around myself, and collapsed before it. I did not sleep, but lay for hours on the stone flags, staring into the flames, my mind and heart numb and still.

Chapter 26 - Emma
19th September 2012

I stared at the house on the hill above me and swapped the bag of books to my other hand. I didn't understand why I had started this stupid affair with Mark. I loved my husband. I loved Dave. I didn't want anyone else. So why had I responded to Mark? I didn't even find him attractive! But I was drawn to him for some reason.

And why was I going up there now? I didn't need to return the books today; they could wait for another time, and Dave was coming home tomorrow, so why was I trekking up the hill to see Mark?

I reached his gate and buzzed, then jumped as Kathy's voice said, 'Yes?' What was *she* doing here? It was her evening for counselling.

'It's Emma, returning Mark's books.'

The gate buzzed and I entered.

'Hi, Emma, how lovely to see you, would you like coffee? Or something stronger?'

'Uh, coffee would be great, thank you.' I wanted to dump the books and get out of there, but knew that would have seemed strange to Kathy. The last thing I wanted to do was socialise with Mark's wife. 'I can't stay long though, I need to get back to work.'

'Nonsense, you need a break – Mark says you're always working, even when you're walking the dogs you're planning your next chapters! And with Dave being away again, it'll do you good to have company for half an hour. When does he get home?'

'Tomorrow,' I said, uncomfortable. I would just have to make the best of it, and to be honest, company *would* be nice – for a little while. Apart from Mark's visits and Dave's phone calls, I hadn't seen or spoken to anyone for a week.

'Come on through, pop the books down in here and I'll put the kettle on.'

I put the bag of books on the coffee table and followed her into the pine-laden kitchen, feeling guilty at accepting her hospitality when I was being far too . . . hospitable to her husband.

'How's the book coming on? Mark says you're writing Jennet's story.'

'Um, yes. It's flowing well actually. Um, where is Mark? I have a couple of questions for him about his great-grandmother's journal.'

'Emergency at the school. Pipe's burst or something. It's all hands on deck to clear up the mess. A nuisance, though, I'm having to miss my course so that I'm home for the twins. And they're not even here! Milk, sugar?'

'Just milk please.'

Kathy put mugs, cafetière, jug of milk and plate of biscuits on a tray and led the way to the lounge.

'Oh, you *can* see the water!' I exclaimed without thinking. 'I was wondering, what with the wall—' I stopped, realising I was being rude, but Kathy smiled.

'Yes, we needed the place to be secure, especially with two kids, but I couldn't bear for the view to be completely hidden. Mark tells me the view from your office is spectacular – I'd love to see it sometime.'

'Of course, you must pop down whenever you're free,' I said, acutely aware of the number of times she was saying "Mark said".

'How are the twins?' I asked, my eyes darting to the journal I had put on the coffee table.

'They're fine. They're both leaning towards the University of Leeds, which is a relief – couldn't be much closer!'

'That's good. Will they stay at home?'

'We're not sure yet. It'd be quite a trek for them, but certainly cheaper; we haven't worked the details out. They're both searching for jobs at the moment, anything to get some cash saved up.'

'Well if one of them has a green thumb, Dave and I could use a gardener—'

'Really? That's wonderful! Alex would love that – he's a real outdoorsman, I can't think why he's chosen business studies!'

'Oh, that's great. How about ten pounds an hour? It's quite a job to be honest, we haven't started yet, but it would be nice to have some home-grown veg and flowers – maybe some chickens too. And I'd love a herb garden: rosemary, sage, verbena and the like. Are you sure he'd be up for it?'

'Absolutely! I'm impressed, you really know your herbs. Did you have a garden at your old place?'

'No, not really, just a few pots.' I was mystified. 'I didn't know I knew all those herbs, actually. I must have paid more attention to my research than I thought.' I laughed, then realised I hadn't actually done any research – I'd little more than glanced at Mark's books, even the old journal, and had only brought them back in the hope of seeing him.

'Is that for Jennet?'

I nodded.

'Yes, she would have had a herb garden – quite an extensive one. How's the book coming on?' she asked again.

'Really well,' I replied. 'It's strange, normally I plan a book out – plot, characters, motivations, everything. But this one, this one's just flowing.'

'Mark said you're using her inkpot.'

'Mm. Though we don't know it was actually hers.'

Kathy looked at me. 'And how are you sleeping? You look tired, are you still having nightmares?'

I started to feel uncomfortable with all her questions. 'No, actually, not since I started writing her story.' I stopped. I hadn't made that connection before.

'Maybe she just wants her story known,' Kathy said.

It didn't sound like a question, and I had no idea what to say in return. I decided to change the subject. 'Have you seen the family trees in the old journal? They're fascinating!'

'Not for a long time.' She was looking at me strangely.

'In fact it's really odd, the names I used for the Ramsgill brothers in my story are all there – as brothers! And at about the right time too.'

Kathy put her mug on the table and stared at me. 'Let me see,' she said.

A little unnerved, I opened the journal and unfolded the large sheet of paper with the Ramsgill family tree. Wordlessly, I pointed out Thomas, Richard, Robert and Alexander.

Kathy traced the line from Richard all the way down to Mark.

'An unlucky family,' she said.

I glanced at her, but said nothing.

'Have you told her the rest? The curse?'

We both looked up, startled. Mark had arrived home and stood in the doorway, watching us.

'The curse?' Kathy asked.

'That's not in the journal – it's in my story,' I said.

'The story that's mirroring history,' Kathy said, pointing at the brothers' names. 'What's the curse?'

'That only one Ramsgill child survives to sire the next generation,' I said, my voice soft.

Kathy nodded and Mark threw his coat and bag on to a chair. I glanced at him; he seemed angry. 'It's nothing, Kathy – fiction. The brothers' names are coincidence, they're all traditional ones – they're pretty obvious choices! And as for the curse, *you* told her about the Ramsgill curse when her and David came for dinner!'

Kathy raised her eyebrows at me, then turned back to her husband. 'We didn't know there was a *real* curse. I'd always thought it was just a family story. How could Emma make up a curse that fits near a dozen generations of Ramsgill family history?'

'She had Old Ma Ramsgill's journal.'

'You didn't show that to me until *after* I'd written about the curse, Mark. Don't you remember? I showed it to you when you brought me the journal.'

He looked away, no doubt remembering what that had led to, and I felt ashamed. *What am I doing?*

'We don't actually know if this family tree is correct, there's nothing to worry about.' I backtracked, trying to reassure Kathy and wishing I hadn't said anything about the Ramsgill brothers and Jennet's curse.

'Aye, nowt to worry about.' Mark had poured himself a whisky and downed it in one.

'So why don't you check it?' Kathy asked him. 'You're the historian – even I know the Internet is full of these genealogy sites. Find out if these people really lived and . . . died as it's written here. Do some research.'

Mark glanced away and I realised he already had.

'Speaking of research, I must get back to mine,' I said, suddenly desperate to get out of there. 'Thanks for the coffee, Kathy, and send Alex down at the weekend when Dave's back, if you're sure he'll be interested?'

'Ten pounds an hour and no commute? Believe me, he'll be interested,' Kathy said. 'You don't need a cleaner as well do you – for Hannah?'

I laughed, pleased the mood had broken, although a glance at Mark showed he was still brooding.

'I'm not sure about that – I get distracted if anyone but Dave is in the house, but I'll think about it,' I promised.

The door shut behind me and I breathed a sigh of relief. Then raised voices from inside reached me. I hesitated a moment before turning my back and walking home.

Chapter 27 - Jennet
20th July 1777

It had been nearly two months since my babbies had died, and past time I showed my face in the village. I smiled the odd greeting, but none were returned. Hopefully it were just because of the rain. Lizzie Thistlethwaite, Martha Grange and Susan Gill, huddled on Street Bridge passing the time of day, stopped talking when they saw me, glanced at each other and scuttled off up past the mill. They were aware that I knew not one of them lived up that way, but they did not care. They had turned away from me as if I were poison. It had nowt to do with weather. I did not know if Mary Farmer had gossiped or if it were just one more thing to add to my run of bad luck.

I pursed my lips and shifted the sack of grain to my other shoulder, wondering if I would have to get used to this treatment. Let them go; stupid, silly women, what did I care? I had my house, my beasts and the moors. I went to the fairy spring regularly, and Mam and my babbies were always there. I still had Mary Farmer, too, though she were a little more reserved since the babbies, and I still had my customers.

In they crept, usually at night, anxious that nobody saw them. And they paid what I asked: a dozen eggs for a nerve tonic; a sheaf of oats for a fever remedy; a round of cheese for a love potion.

They hated me and they feared me; but they needed me and they kept me. Aye, Mary Farmer must have gossiped. I would soon sort *her* out.

I reached the mill and thumped the sack down in relief – my back ached from carrying it the mile from my farm.

I glanced up at a cough. Big Robert Ramsgill, the Royal Miller, walked out from one of the mill's dark corners. He spoke, but I could not hear him over the rumbling and splashing of the waterwheel and the grinding of the great stones. I cupped my hand over my ear, and he came closer.

'What's thee doing here?' he repeated.

I stared at him in surprise and gestured at my sack of grain.

'I'd like it grinding into flour. I've brought thy wife's herbs – three months' worth – Mam taught me the recipe.'

Big Robert Ramsgill eyed the packet in my hand and the sack of oats, then shook his head.

'She wants nowt made by thy wanton hands.' He coughed again.

'What? But I've been making them for years! And it's thy brother thee should be insulting – not me!'

'Get out of here! I won't hear abuses against my family!'

I watched him bend double with the force of his cough. I took a deep breath; I could not afford to lose my temper.

'I could help thee with that cough an'all.'

'He said leave.'

I turned. His son – Little Rob – stood at the door and glared at me. As we stared at each other, his twin sister Jayne joined him – one either side of the doorway. They were a year older than I and we had never got on. As the son and daughter of the Royal Miller, and Ramsgills to boot, they looked down on me. Even now with my own farm, I did not engage their interest – my farm were not large enough.

I glanced back at Big Robert Ramsgill. He had recovered from his coughing fit and stood firm again, though was dwarfed by his son. I sighed and bent to heft my sack on to my shoulder.

I staggered through the door and felt hands on my back. They shoved and I fell. The sack split open when it landed, and my precious oats scattered in the muck of the street.

'No!' I cried and turned to remonstrate with the Ramsgill twins.

They stood and laughed. 'That's it, slut, thee lay down in dirt where thee belongs!'

'What's going on here?' I turned to see Thomas Ramsgill, and my heart sank.

'How do, *Constable*,' his nephew stressed the word. 'This one's disturbing smooth running of King's mill. She's been asked to leave but refused – we were helping her on her way.'

His father joined him at the door, and the brothers glanced at each other.

'Why thee!' It were all I could think of to say in my rage and surprise.

Little Rob smirked and his sister giggled behind her hand.

'Be off with thee now, Jennet, there's a good lass.' Thomas Ramsgill said. 'We don't want no trouble now, do we?'

I got to my feet and gathered the remnants of the sack around the grain I could save. I glared at Little Rob.

'I know what thee did, and I'll remember. Thee ain't heard the last of this, I promise thee that.'

He laughed. 'What kind of curse is that? Thee has to do better than that, witch!'

'What did you call me?' I stepped towards him and Thomas caught my shoulders.

'Home, Jennet. Now, or I'll have to put thee in stocks.'

I looked at him. '*Me*? He's the one pushed me in dirt!'

He stared back and I gave up. I could not win here; I would have to find another way to deal with Little Rob.

I bent to pick up my grain best I could, and turned away. I paused when I saw Margaret Ramsgill at the door of Mill House. She would not meet my gaze and dropped her eyes.

I started the long trudge home – with only half a sack of grain left. I would have to grind it by hand.

I dumped the sack in the garden and went in to find the quern-stones. I poured myself a jug of ale, downed it in one, then carried the heavy, round stones outside. I were angry – I might as well use that anger in the grinding.

Ten minutes later, I paused and stretched. My back, shoulders and arms were agony, and I would have to grind for near an hour to get enough flour for a day's-worth of oatcakes.

I bent back to the grind, but knew I could not do this every day. I would have to find another way to get my daily bread.

Chapter 28 - Emma
22nd September 2012

'Emma!'

I jumped and stared at Dave.

'My God, Emma, I've been calling you for ages, didn't you hear me?'

I glanced at my notebook, then back at my husband, disorientated.

'Sorry, I was engrossed.'

'You're telling me! But you need to take a break. You've been writing since the early hours and it's nearly lunchtime. You've not eaten or washed, I'm getting worried about you.'

'I'm fine.'

'Are you? Have the dogs been out?'

I stared at him, he knew what my reaction would be if *he* hadn't taken them out. Then I sighed, feeling guilty. I was neglecting the dogs, neglecting my husband, maybe even myself, but I just – had – to – write.

I pulled my eyes away from Dave. His look of concern should have filled me with guilt, but I only felt irritation.

'Emma ...'

'What?'

He hesitated.

'Dave, what is it?'

'Don't take this the wrong way, I know you've tried counselling before, but what do you think about talking to Kathy?'

'Talking to Kathy?' I froze, *does he know about Mark?*

'Yes. Well, she's a counsellor, isn't she? She knows how to listen. Not only that, she's a friend, she might be able to help.'

'I don't need help, I just need to write this book!'

'Emma, you're not sleeping, you're always irritable, and now you've forgotten to take the dogs out. I'm getting worried – this is beyond obsession!'

I threw the quill on to the coffee table and stood. 'Fine. I'll take the dogs for a walk.'

Dave said nothing, just stared at the mess of ink splotching the coffee table. He glanced up and nodded. 'Just think about it, please.'

My irritation dimmed; he must be worried not to complain about the ruination of a perfectly good (and fairly expensive) table.

* * *

'What the hell were you thinking the other day? Kathy's in a right state!'

I didn't turn. Shep had run past me to greet my three – I had known Mark wouldn't be far behind.

'You said *you* would be there – I was taken by surprise to be welcomed by your wife!'

'You're a writer – you make up stories for a living, couldn't you have found something better to talk about?'

'I'm consumed by *this* story, Mark!' Now I turned to face him. 'It's taking me over – every waking moment I'm either writing her or thinking about writing her – it's driving me mad!'

He grabbed my arms and shook me. 'Get a grip, woman! It's a story – a tale! She's been dead two hundred year! You sound like Kathy now, going on about how Jennet walks again. It's just a bloody tale, get it in perspective!'

'Let go of me!' If anything, his grip tightened. 'Let go!' I shouted, shaking my arms free. I stared at him, then nodded past him. 'Dave might see.'

He sighed and glanced to his right, then walked to the trees. I hesitated a moment and followed.

The gloomy day was positively dark under the pines and I paused, unable to see Mark. Suddenly, he thrust my body against a tree and kissed me roughly. I pushed against him, then gave in and returned his kiss.

His hands scrabbled at my waist and he shoved my jeans down past my hips. His own soon followed. He grabbed my hips and spun me round and I grabbed hold of the tree trunk, then took a couple of steps back, the air cold on my backside.

I caught my breath in anticipation, then cried out with the force of his entry and quickly bit my lip to stop any more noise escaping me. It was fast, furious and very, very good, yet I was relieved when it was over.

I straightened up and buttoned my jeans, still with my back to Mark.

'I love my wife,' he said. 'In nearly twenty year, I've never cheated on Kathy, never! And now this. I can't help meself. I don't know what the hell this is, but it has to stop. Whatever you're doing to me, it has to stop!' He turned and walked away.

Tears rolled down my face and I stared after him open-mouthed. I wasn't doing anything to him. *He* was the one doing this to me. He was the one who had started it, who kept starting it. I loved Dave. I did. I did not love Mark – I didn't even fancy him! Yet this kept happening. And I didn't know how to stop it.

I emerged from the trees and threw stones into the reservoir for the beasts to jump after. I sat on the shore to watch the dogs swim, and tried to make sense of the mess my life had become.

Once my tears had dried and I thought I could argue the flush in my cheeks and red-rimmed eyes were due to the fresh air, I went home to Dave, none the wiser about anything.

Chapter 29 - Jennet
4th August 1777

The rain had stopped. After two solid weeks of water, the sun at last showed itself. I threw my shawl around my shoulders, picked up my basket and set off. I needed feverfew, foxglove and a number of other plants that grew in the lush meadows down the hill.

I did not want to ruin my day, so I turned left at the Gate Inn to avoid the village and followed Street Lane towards the mill. I would turn off at the bridge and follow the river downstream towards Hanging Wood. With any luck I would meet no one.

I turned the last bend in the lane and stopped in surprise at the sight of a lake. The River Washburn were in flood. I waded through on to the hump of Street Bridge to get a better view, and gaped at the sight in front of me.

I could not make out the millpond, it were part of the river now. The mill and Mill House were awash, and I smirked when I saw both Robert Ramsgills bailing water.

The grain started the grind by being hoisted up to the top of the mill, then made its way through the grinding stones until it reached the ground floor as flour. I could only imagine the mess in there.

Little Rob paused in his work and stretched his back. He spotted me watching from the bridge and shook his fist in my direction. My smile grew broader and I waved at him. He said something to his father and pointed at me. The more diminutive Big Robert stopped what he were doing to glare, then turned away and waded back into the mill.

I laughed out loud and turned to see downstream, then leaned on the parapet to get a better look. A flock of sheep were trapped by water, and the small hillock of land they had gathered on were shrinking by the minute. The whole village seemed to be on the river bank, Richard Ramsgill at their head, trying to get them on to dry land.

I peered closer and realised they were his wethers and tups – the most prized of his flock – put to graze on the lushest, most nutritious grass by the river before market.

I waded back through the water pooled over the edge of the bridge, skirts held high, and made my way down to join my neighbours.

As I got closer, I realised the sheep were all clean and closely shorn. My suspicions were right – they had deliberately excluded me from the washing and clipping this year. I gritted my teeth against a sob and took a deep breath. I would not let them get to me.

I had clipped my girls myself – not the neatest job, but I knew I would not be able to sell their wool anyroad, not when Richard Ramsgill were the only wool merchant for miles around. I would need to card and spin it for my own use – I had to be self-sufficient now.

But they were my neighbours and customers, and to live out here on the moors, we had to help each other. Maybe if I lent a hand now, some of these folk would also see themselves right to helping me some time?

'What's happening?'

Susan Gill turned to me. 'They got trapped by flood, the men are trying to get them to swim over.'

I watched the fast flowing water a moment. I knew sheep could swim, but I did not think they could swim well enough to get over that without being swept away, and said so.

Martha Grange turned to me. 'We don't need thee ill wishing us! Thee's done enough! This is thy fault – thine! Thee cursed this village and thee cursed Richard Ramsgill – and now look, his best tups and wethers are drowning!

I backed away in alarm, both at her outburst and Mary's betrayal. She were the only one who knew. She *must* have gossiped. I had thought she were my friend, how could she tell the village about that day? How could she turn the worst day of my life into tittle-tattle?

'Thee did this!' Martha Grange had not finished. 'Thee cursed Ramsgill and thee cursed this village, I heard thee!' she said again, her voice rising, and everybody stopped what they were doing to stare.

What? I stopped moving and gaped at her in confusion.

'Thee were screaming blue bloody murder that day. I were coming up to see if I could help and I heard thee curse.' She dropped her voice a little. 'Aye, saw what thee did an'all. Them poor babbies.'

She spat at me. I realised everyone else were silent and staring. It had not been Mary Farmer who had spread gossip about me after all. It had never occurred to me that Martha Grange had seen me. I turned and ran home in shame.

Chapter 30 - Emma
29th September 2012

'Emma! Emma!'

'Wha . . . ?' I blinked in the bright light and glanced up at Dave. 'What's wrong? What is it?'

He sat on the sofa next to me and held his head in his hands.

'You really scared me, Em. This isn't normal, this is . . . I don't know what this is, but I'm scared.'

'Scared? Why?'

He stared at me. 'You have no idea, have you?'

I stared back, not wanting to admit I didn't have a clue what he was talking about.

He sighed. 'I woke up and you weren't there – again. You were sitting in here – the office – in the dark, writing.'

'In the dark?' I looked at him, did he mean it or was he teasing me?

'Yes, Emma, in the dark.' His face was haggard – he was serious.

'But that's not the worst of it.' He paused, took a breath. 'When I put the light on, you didn't notice. Em, your eyes . . .'

'What? What about my eyes?' I was starting to panic now.

'They were rolled right back – only the whites were showing. Emma, you were writing in the dark – blind!'

We stared at each other, then our eyes dropped to the notebook in my lap. The writing was not only legible, but neat and straight, although it didn't quite look like my handwriting. There were fewer ink blots on the page now as well, although I noticed my fingers were still covered in ink from the quill.

We stared at each other again and tears rolled down my cheeks. Dave opened his arms and I fell into his embrace. He held on to me, hard, as I sobbed, then led me back to the bedroom.

A few hours later, I woke to my husband depositing a steaming cup of coffee on the bedside table. I smiled at him and wrapped my arms around his neck when he leaned over to kiss me.

'That's better,' he said. 'I think you got more than three hours sleep for once!'

'I actually feel like I've slept,' I said. 'I'd forgotten what that was like.'

'You needed the rest – you're working far too hard. Just take it easy this morning, hey?'

I nodded. 'What about you, are you coming back to bed?' I asked, peering up at him from under my lashes.

'Ah, I'd love to,' he replied, then glanced towards the front of the house, 'but young Alex is outside, digging a garden for us – it wouldn't be right. Anyway, I need to go to Harrogate – I've some important papers that need to go to the post, and we need a supermarket shop too – there's barely any food in the house.'

I nodded, dropping my arms from around his neck and accepting the reprimand. I realised Dave had a point, I *had* neglected things lately.

'We need to be more careful – it's isolated here, the nearest shop's miles away; we need to make sure we have plenty in. Gas is getting low too, I've rung and ordered more cylinders.'

'Sorry, I've just been—'

'Busy,' he finished for me. I dropped my eyes, guilty. He had been driving to Edinburgh almost weekly for meetings and site visits. He'd driven nearly two hundred miles home the day before, and now he was getting into the car again to drive the fifteen miles to Harrogate to stock up the fridge.

I'd spent my time writing. Oh, and fucking the neighbour – can't forget that.

I reached over and burnt my lips sipping the hot coffee. I could not look at him.

'I'll leave the front door open so Alex can come in and get himself a drink.'

'Ok.'

He gave me a peck on my forehead and left.

I waited ten minutes and went to the window to make sure his car had gone. Alex was outside the front door digging the first flowerbed, and I watched him a moment, his young muscles bulging under his tight T-shirt. I sighed, just what I needed – another bloody Ramsgill.

I turned away from the window and got into the shower, trying to drench the past month and all its implications away.

It didn't work. I felt terrible: tired, stressed and guilty. I went into the office to escape my world and write.

'Have you got a minute?'

I jumped and dropped the quill on the carpet, splattering ink everywhere.

'Mark, you scared me!'

'Sorry, the door was open.'

'What do you want?' I hadn't forgotten the last time I'd seen him, the way he'd treated me and what he'd said.

'To apologise. I made out it was all your fault and it's not, I just . . . I just don't understand what's happening.'

'No, me neither.' I shook my head, tears flooding my eyes once again.

He hesitated, then crossed to the sofa and put his arm around me. I stiffened, then leaned into his familiar body.

'This can't go on, it can't happen again, it can't. Dave and Kathy – they don't deserve this.'

'I know, I know.'

We sat for a moment in silence, then I pulled back from him, my tears calmed. His hand gripped my shoulder, and I stared at him. It felt like a tug-of-war – we were trying to pull away from each other, but instead were being hauled together.

Then a door slammed and I heard Dave's shout from downstairs, 'Emma!'

I jumped back from Mark. 'Shit!'

'It's all right, we weren't doing anything,' Mark said.

I knew he was right – this time – but it felt a lie.

'There you are, I might have known.'

'Hi, Dave.'

'Hi, oh hello, Mark, what are you doing up here?'

'Just bringing Emma some books I promised her – local history, that kind of thing.' He lifted a carrier bag from the floor. I hadn't noticed it before and I wondered if they were the ones I'd already seen or new ones.

'Hmm.' Dave frowned. 'That's very kind, but she's working too hard, look how pale she is.'

'Dave!'

'It's true, Emma. If you won't look after yourself, I'll have to do it for you.'

'He's right, Em,' Mark said. 'I was saying the same thing the other day,' he continued, glancing at Dave.

He nodded. 'You see? It's not just me.' He turned to Mark. 'She needs to slow down, she's making herself ill – this damn book's become an obsession.'

Chapter 31 - Jennet
13th August 1777

I knocked on the door of Gill Farm and glanced at the horseshoe nailed to it. I had seen a few of them as I had passed through the village – some old-style witchposts, too. I hadn't noticed the carved wooden posts before and shivered, the appearance of the charms scared me. Marjory Wainwright opened the door and gasped. 'What's thee doing here? I were going to come up to thee, later!'

'I felt like a walk,' I said cheerfully, though I were hurt by her 'welcome'. I had once counted this woman a friend. 'Is thee going to invite me in or leave me on the stoop for whole valley to see?'

She jumped back and ushered me in. She slammed the door behind me.

'Has thee got it?' she asked.

I dug in the pockets of my apron and produced a packet of herbs. Marjory's face lit up.

'Thee can't tell anyone about it, thee won't, will thee?'

I smiled at her, 'Marj, thee pays for me discretion as well as me cunning ways. No bugger will hear about it from me.'

Marjory and her husband, Bert, had been trying for a family for two years without success. They needed sons to carry on the farm, and it were said that Bert were beginning to look elsewhere.

Marj were desperate enough to have come to me, and let me inside her front door in full view of the village.

I held out the packet. 'That'll be an iron pot for the first packet. Each thereafter will cost a half-sack of flour, and thee'll be pregnant by end of year.'

'An iron pot, but, but that's too much! And Bert will notice!'

I shrugged. My own cooking pot were disintegrating, it were so old. I needed a new one, and this were the only way I would get one. 'When does he ever take note of what's happening in't kitchen? When thy courses have stopped, tell him thee needs a new, larger one for a larger family. He'll be so pleased, he'll give thee anything thee asks.'

She thought a moment, then walked through a door in the far wall. She returned carrying a large iron cooking pot with three squat legs and a handle to suspend it over the fire. She thrust it at me and I gave her the herbs.

'Thee'll need a fresh packet every four weeks,' I told her. 'Come to farm on't first day of month. And don't forget to bring flour as payment.'

'They'd better work, Jennet,' she grumbled, and I clenched my teeth.

If Robert Ramsgill would not trade with me for flour, I would get it another way – preferably without an hour's daily grind. And Marjory Wainwright would never know if some months the packets were a little light of the most potent ingredients, or that the appropriate words had not been spoken over them at the right time. No spinning work had come my way since my affair with Richard Ramsgill had become known. I had no other way of buying what I needed to survive.

She ushered me out of the door, and I started my walk home, clutching the cooking pot, staring at the people I passed in the street. They all averted their eyes rather than meet my gaze. Except one. She were a distance away, but I knew who she were at once. Elizabeth Ramsgill. I had no choice but to pass her. She never took her eyes off me, even for a second, in all the time it took me to reach her. I stared back.

Betsy Ward pulled her to one side out of my path, and I smirked. They were scared of me. The whole village were scared of me.

For the first time since Mam's death, I felt like I had a place in the world. I had power – strength. They had accused me, judged me and abandoned me. Richard Ramsgill were the one who had seduced and ruined me; yet he were still a respected man in the bosom of his family. I vowed to myself that the whole Damn village would tremble at the sight of me before I were done. I hated them. I hated them all

Betsy Ward glanced at me and hurried off, dragging Richard's wife with her, and I realised my thoughts had been plain to see on my face. I laughed to see them run, then turned up Scot Lane for home. I paused when I saw Mary Farmer up the lane, a frown on her face. She had watched it all. Not much escaped *her* notice.

Chapter 32 - Emma
6th October 2012

I jumped out of bed and ran to the bathroom, hand clasped over my mouth.

'Emma! What's wrong?' Dave called. I ignored him, focusing my attention on the toilet. I only just made it.

A hand stroked my hair. Dave had followed me, and now held my hair away from my face as I continued to throw up. I was both grateful to him and embarrassed that he was seeing me like this.

'Are you ok?' What a stupid question. 'Is it something you ate?' I managed to shrug my shoulders. 'I don't see how,' he continued. 'You've hardly been eating. I'm willing to bet you've not eaten anything except what I've made you – and what I've given you, I've had too.' He stopped. 'Emma?'

'Mm?' I managed, face down in the toilet bowl, but at least I had stopped heaving. I flushed and sat against the wall, not yet ready to move away from the toilet, even to wash my mouth. I grabbed some toilet paper and wiped my face instead.

Dave's eyes dropped from my face to linger on my chest.

Seriously? How can he possibly be feeling horny now?

He glanced up again. 'You know you've been writing at all hours?'

I groaned. *Not another lecture about working too hard and making myself ill, not now, please.*

'Well, have you been taking your pill properly?'

My breath caught in my throat. *My pill?* I thought back, but the last few weeks were a bit of a daze; I could remember little but Jennet. I stared at him in horror.

'I don't . . . I don't know,' I stammered.

He stood, opened the cabinet and took down the pink foil strip. He glanced at it, then passed it to me. Numb, I took it and looked. The next pill was Wednesday's. It was Saturday. I doubted I was only a half week amiss. I couldn't remember the last time I had taken one.

I glanced up at Dave. I could see that he wanted to smile, but was too wary to risk it.

I got up, cleaned my teeth, splashed water on my face, and put on my robe. I couldn't bear to see the rush of emotion playing over his features.

'Emma?'

I shook my head at him and went downstairs. I was terrified and needed space to think.

I stopped mid-step on the stairs and grabbed the banister to stop my fall. *Oh God, what if I* am *pregnant, but it's not Dave's? What if it's Mark's?*

In the kitchen, my hand hovered over the phone. I needed to see a doctor, to find out if it was really true and then to get rid of it – just like Jennet had tried to do.

I couldn't pick the handset up, it seemed stuck to the cradle. I couldn't. I couldn't get rid of it, what if it was Dave's? I'd already lost so much, I couldn't throw this baby away.

I grabbed my hair with both hands and pulled my head back, growling at the ceiling. I needed space, I needed time to think – a clear head, without bloody Jennet.

Chapter 33 - Jennet
6th September 1777

I stared at the ceiling, then sighed and heaved myself out of bed. I would rather stay there, nice and cosy under the brocades Richard had given me a year past. I had dug them back out of the chest where I had thrown them in disgust. Why should I not use them? Why should I not have nice things?

I dressed slowly and made my way downstairs. I had things to do – I were falling badly behind with my chores. The oats should already be in and I had not started the harvest yet. If I did not get it in soon, I would have no grain of my own for the coming year, and would be dependent on the villagers for my bread. I could not bear that thought.

I put new peat on the fire and poked at the sod that had been buried under the ash all night, until I had enough heat to cook.

I stared at the flames as I ate my porridge, thinking of the village and the hurts done to me: Robert Ramsgill – both of them; Thomas Ramsgill; Richard, of course; Martha Grange; even Susan Gill running off rather than passing the time of day. So much for the village helping me after Mam and Pa died.

I thought back to Richard's words when he first came to me; that I were quite a catch for a second son now that I had my own farm. I snorted with laughter. The only people who did not turn from me or point their crossed fingers against a witch when they saw me were the Farmers. Oh, and Peter Stockdale; he would give me a small smile if we passed – but only if no bugger else could see him.

I had not seen him properly since he had helped with the lambing in February, even though I could do with his help most days. A smile were not much use to me. It did not cut peat, clip beasts or harvest oats.

Speaking of which . . . I got up, rinsed my bowl and ale jug in a little water, then collected my weeding hooks from the toolshed out back. Inside again, I packed some oatcakes and cheese for my lunch, picked up the baskets and set off into the dawning day.

The oat fields were downhill, near the church, and I had put off tending it. I had not wanted to see anyone, and I sighed in relief when I got there – my strip were the only crop still standing – I would be working alone.

I put my baskets down near the stones that marked the strip as mine, hefted my weeding hooks and bent to my task.

The wild flowers that grew amongst the stalks were thick – I should have done this many times over the summer – and I would need to pull them all before I could cut the oats themselves. They were all useful to a cunning woman: poppy for pain; mullein for cramps and convulsions; mallow for sore throats and bruises; dandelion for upset bellies.

I would pull them, collect them, take them home, sort and dry them. Tomorrow I would be back to harvest the oats, although – I fingered a few stalks – it looked like somebody had already been helping themselves. A lot of seed heads were missing.

Fighting tears, I gritted my teeth. I would cut what they had left me, and take the stooks home to dry in the garden. I could not leave them here. All it meant were that I would have to ask for larger amounts of flour in payment for my preparations.

I looked up the hill and sighed. Pa had always borrowed Robert Grange's dray horse to haul the crops up to the farm. After Martha's outburst when Richard Ramsgill's sheep drowned, that were not possible for me. I would have to drag it up the hill myself.

I sighed again. I also had a hay crop to harvest; what state would that be in? It had been a wet summer, and hay did not do well with a lot of rain.

I pulled another clump of poppy out of the ground and frowned. My hook had caught something else and thrown it in the air. I bent to pick it up.

A corn dolly. Crudely made, but unmistakable. Arms and legs wide open in invitation, large breasts and a grotesque hole between its legs.

I stared at it, fury boiling my insides. Then I tucked it into my apron – I would deal with it when I got home.

I finished weeding after lunch and stood to stretch my back. I winced when I heard a crack, then made my way back to the start of the strip to swap weeding hooks for baskets.

By the time I had collected every precious flower, leaf and root it were growing dark and I trudged home, exhausted. I remembered the corn dolly tucked into my apron and picked up my pace – my anger feeding me energy.

Baskets on the table, I pulled a stool closer to the fire and poked it back into life.

I threw a handful of dried herbs on to it – rosemary, bay and sage – and held the corn dolly tightly in my hands.

'Let the one who made this lose her man to another.

'Let the one who made this never know the feel of a babe moving in her barren womb.

'Let the one who spited me know the loneliness I suffer.'

I threw the corn dolly on the fire and watched the flames flare up as they consumed it.

I pulled out a few ears of oats.

'Let the ones who stole from me know hunger this winter.'

I threw the oats on the fire, then more herbs, and smiled.

Chapter 34 - Emma
20th October 2012

I hung up the phone. My doctor had confirmed it – I was six weeks pregnant.

I stared out of the window of my office at the reservoir – water sparkled in the autumnal sun, but today it could not cheer me. What was I going to do?

What if this baby was Mark's? I couldn't have Mark's child, I couldn't. But then again, it might be Dave's. I'd lost so much already, I couldn't imagine getting rid of *any* child, even if it were Mark's. I had to do everything I could to give life to this baby. Whatever it took - it *had* to live.

What was I going to do? *Please let this baby live. Please let this baby be Dave's*, I prayed.

I put my hands on my belly. Instead of thinking about loss; now I thought about laughter, about cuddles, about watching my son or daughter explore the world. I thought about teaching him or her to talk, to walk, to read. I thought about taking delight in their milestones and achievements; wondering what a child of Dave and mine could achieve; what difference he or she would make in the world. I dared to hope, and finally, I dared to smile.

I turned to the sofa and coffee table, then back to the view. Jennet could wait – just for a little while.

'There you are, I should have known you'd be in here.'

I turned again at Dave's voice. 'Just admiring the view and thinking about the future.'

He smiled and walked towards me. 'That's great, Em. You need to slow down, look after yourself – and the baby.' He gazed carefully at me and I nodded, smiling. He looked relieved and I turned back to the window as he wrapped his arms around me. I leaned into him and we watched the water together. We were going to be a family after all.

The sound of barking from downstairs disturbed us, and I sighed. 'They need a walk, are you coming?'

'I'd love to,' Dave replied, and we left the office hand in hand. I glanced back once at Jennet's book on the coffee table, but forced myself to keep going. I needed a break. I needed to think about myself for a while.

* * *

At the shore, the one person I least wanted to see was walking towards us on his way home.

'Mark,' Dave greeted him and moved to shake his hand.

'David,' Mark returned the greeting, then glanced at me. 'Emma. How are you, you're looking well?'

'Thank you,' I replied, uncomfortable.

'Yes, she is isn't she? She's finally taking things easier – if I'd known a baby would have had this effect, I'd have insisted on trying again a long time ago!' Dave laughed, proud. I cringed.

'Baby?' Mark's face blanched.

'Yes, we're having a baby,' said Dave, delighted. 'It's early days yet, but we couldn't be happier.'

'Dave, we shouldn't tell people yet, it's bad luck.'

'Nonsense, with me away so much, I need to know somebody is keeping an eye on you.'

I glanced up quickly at Mark. His colour had returned.

'Congratulations,' he said, holding his hand out to shake Dave's again. I felt Dave stiffen, *does he suspect?* I wrapped both arms around his waist and leaned into him, squeezing. After a moment, he reciprocated.

'Fantastic news,' Mark had recovered himself now. 'Kathy's going to be so excited – she adores babies! You won't be short of help once it arrives.' He paused. 'Speaking of Kathy, I promised I wouldn't be long. It were good to see you, and again – congratulations!'

He hurried off and Dave dropped his arm. We walked on in silence.

Chapter 35 - Jennet
18th October 1777

Marjory Wainwright were pregnant! Already! I had counted on at least another six months' supply of flour, but that had gone now. I were happy for her, really – there were sure to be someone else who needed a remedy, a potion, or a curse – I were being asked for more and more of them now. *They* could pay me in flour – and hay; the beasts would need extra food soon. It seemed Mam had been right, and Peg Lofthouse's preparations weren't worth the walk to Padside. Despite everything, I still had customers. They may be desperate to risk knocking on my door, but that boded well for me. They would pay whatever I asked.

Shouting outside had me rushing to the door.

'What's going on here?' There were a dozen people in my yard. 'Watch my plants!' They were standing on the herbs.

'There she is, the witch! Get her!'

I gasped in fear. Had someone called me a witch? I tried to shut the door so I could bar it against them, but I were too slow.

Thomas Ramsgill were the first man through, and he grabbed my arm.

'It's the stocks for thee, lass, come on. There's no point resisting. Put on thy coat.'

I calmed a little. When I had heard the word witch, I had pictured a gallows.

'The stocks, why? What for?'

'Marjory Wainwright's cooking pot.'

'What about it?'

'Thee stole it.'

'No! It were given in fair payment, she wanted children, I helped her, she's pregnant. The pot were payment for my remedy!'

'Well, she says thee stole it, and as she's respectable married lady, and thee . . .' he tailed off, a look of disgust on his face. I gritted my teeth and stared back at him.

'Not pregnant for long, though, were she?' somebody shouted. I thought it were Digger Blackstock.

'What?'

'Aye, lost babby – thy herbs weren't up to much were they?'

'What? She's lost babby?' I asked, horrified. Poor Marjory.

'Did thee curse her, too?'

'Has thee cursed whole village? Thy babby didn't live so no bugger else's will?'

Thomas Ramsgill pulled me through the door, and I could see them all now. People who used to be friends. Martha Grange, Susan Gill. Now they cheered and spat and hated.

Tears filled my eyes. *How can they do this to me?*

We had reached the lane, and I were still shouting, 'I didn't, I ain't, I didn't!' Nobody listened. Nobody cared. Then I remembered the corn dolly – did Marjory Wainwright make it?

Past the junction – the lane Richard Ramsgill took to go home. And there he were, standing to one side, watching with Peter Stockdale. At least he weren't one of the mob.

'Richard! Richard, help me, please, I ain't done nowt!'

He stared at his boots and said nowt. I fell silent and looked at Peter. He turned away, a pained expression on his face. What more were there to say? Who to say it to?

We reached Low Green and I glanced up the lane to the church. No help there, neither.

Digger lifted the top bar of the stocks, and Thomas Ramsgill held my wrists in the half circle gaps carved into the lower plank of wood. The top came down and were secured.

I stared up at William Smith as he worked the metal links, but he would not meet my eyes. I had known him since I were a child, sneaking down to the smithy to watch him work his forge, sparks and fire flying. Now he were locking me up.

He stepped away, and I looked up at them; my wrists shackled by a plank of wood. I were bent nearly double and my back were aching already.

How long will they leave me here? Even with Pa's coat, I were chilled. To be stood here all night, unmoving, would be unbearable.

'Please, I ain't done owt, please!' I begged them, then dropped my head, it hurt to crane my neck to see them.

The crowd laughed and cheered. Nobody believed me.

Then they silenced, and I glanced up again, hopeful.

'Marjory! Please – I helped thee, I helped thee get with child, thee knows I did. I did nowt to harm thy babby, nowt! Please help me.'

She stared at me for a moment, then spat. It landed below my eye, but with my hands in the stocks, I could not wipe it away.

Then Elizabeth Ramsgill stepped forward and added her own spittle to Marjory's.

More women followed their example, and the rest of them laughed and clapped as if a band of mummers had trekked across the moors to entertain us.

Tears rolled down my face, *how had things come to this?*

* * *

They got bored after an hour or two. I mean, who would not? I only stood there, bent over, hands imprisoned.

After Marjory spat, I did not speak another word. There were no point. I heard their cheers, their laughter, their fun, but I did not listen. I did not react. Instead, I pictured myself on the moors, running free.

It were dark now and had been for some time. The crowd were long gone. The odd person scurried past; some stared, some looked away, but none stopped.

I were thirsty, hungry and cold. My wrists stung from the restriction and the wood – I were sure I had splinters – and my back had gone from ache to agony.

Thomas Ramsgill and William Smith were long gone, and I had realised some time ago that they really were going to leave me here all night.

'There she is! There's the witch, I told thee!'

I lifted my head, *now what?*

Three figures approached out of the gloom: Little Rob Ramsgill, Billy Gill and Johnny Ward.

'Go home, boys, there's nowt for thee here.'

They laughed and spat whilst crossing their fingers. I realised they were drunk. I jumped and squealed when a hand smacked my backside.

'Get out of here, boys! Thee don't want to do this!' I were scared now, and knew my fear were clear in my voice, but I had to keep trying. With my hands tied, my voice were my only defence.

'Go home, go home now!'

They laughed. 'Or what, thee'll curse us?'

'Damn right I will, if any of thee touches me, he'll lose his hand within a year!'

They laughed again, nervously now – they believed the stories. I could use that.

'Thee's calling me witch – watch out I don't grow fangs and howl at the moon! If thee don't leave now, thee'll be getting a visit from wolves first night I'm free! Who'll be first? Thee, Johnny Ward? Or thee, Billy Gill. What about thee, Little Rob?'

I realised I could not see Little Rob Ramsgill, only the other two, and grimaced as once again they spat.

'Thee don't scare me. Thee's no witch, only a trollop who opened her legs for me uncle.'

The words came from behind me and I looked round, moving away from the voice as much as possible. Bent over, in skirts, I knew how vulnerable I were.

I could not get away though, I could only move my feet half a yard or so, and I gasped when cold air hit my thighs and buttocks.

'Little Rob, stop that at once!'

I glanced up again at the new voice. A voice I knew well. Richard.

'Get away from here, all of thee!'

The two other boys ran, but I knew from Little Rob's groping hand that he were not going anywhere.

'What's wrong, Uncle Richard? Thee don't want to share?'

'Why thee little runt!'

I heard the sound of flesh striking flesh, then a body tumbled to the ground. The hand had gone from between my legs and my skirt were pulled back down to cover me. Footsteps ran off.

Chapter 36 - Emma
21st October 2012

I woke, sweating and gasping, my heart pounding. The nightmares were back. Now that I was awake, I calmed and thought about my dream; I'd dreamed of Jennet throwing her dead babies on to the fire – except that I was Jennet. It had been my own lost baby I had cremated.

I shuddered and wiped tears from my face, then listened to Dave pottering about downstairs. I was worried. He'd been very quiet since we'd bumped into Mark earlier, and he hadn't wanted to come up to bed when I came up, which wasn't like him at all. *Does he suspect?*

My life was a mess. We had been here less than three months. Where had all the laughter and excitement gone? How could everything fall apart so quickly? Now look – my new book had taken over to the point it was worrying *me* now; I'd been having an affair I didn't want; and now I was pregnant, with no idea who the father was.

Then a thought hit me – what if I wasn't the mother? If this was Mark's baby, then it wasn't me who had slept with him – it was Jennet.

Yes! That explained so much. Jennet had got inside me – that was obvious from the way I was writing. The words weren't coming from me, they were coming *through* me. Jennet's words – not mine. I had no idea of what was coming next until it was written. It was all Jennet – she'd taken me over. It was she who was drawn to Mark – a direct descendant of Richard Ramsgill. *She* was this baby's mother, not me. It was *her* book and *her* baby!

I realised I had sat up in bed. It seemed preposterous, but somehow I knew it was true. I cupped my belly with my hands. This baby wasn't mine and Dave's. It was Jennet and Mark's – Richard's.

Now I was scared. What the hell was I going to do? And how on earth would I make Dave understand?

I jumped as thunder crashed overhead. I got out of bed and went to the office. I had to finish her story – it was the only way to get her out of my head and life. I had to write her out – to exorcise her.

Dave walked into the office. I glanced up at him and he stared at me for a moment. I realised he'd been drinking.

'Is there anything I need to know?'

'What?' *Shit.*

'About the baby. Is there anything I need to know?'

I stared at him.

'Why aren't you saying anything?' he shouted.

'Dave . . .'

'What? What? It's *his*, isn't it? I saw the way he paled when I mentioned the baby. Are you fucking Mark?'

I flinched. 'It's Jennet's.'

'What?'

'The baby, it's Jennet's. I think she's possessing me and the baby's hers, not mine.'

There was silence for a moment while he processed that.

'And who else's?'

I didn't say anything, just watched him, stricken.

'I knew it,' he muttered and sat on the edge of the desk, his head in his hands.

He lifted his head and looked at me. I flinched at the pain I saw there – pain that I had caused. And the tears started.

'Dave, I'm so sorry, I really am. It's not what you think, it wasn't me, it was Jennet.'

He stared at me in disbelief. I had no option but to keep trying. No matter how ludicrous it sounded, it was the truth.

'I don't love him, I never did – I don't even fancy him! I love you, and he loves Kathy. It was like we had no choice, it was a compulsion. It was Jennet! She's inside me, and he's a direct descendant of the man she loved. It wasn't me, Dave, honestly, it was *Jennet*!'

My river of words stopped.

His face was like thunder – he looked like he'd been physically struck. 'You bitch. You *fucking* bitch! For a year you've refused to even try and I've waited. I would wait as long as I had to until you were ready, and now you're knocked up by the fucking neighbour! What is it, you think you only lose *my* babies? You want to try it with someone else's sperm?'

I flinched away from his words.

'Is it still going on?'

I shook my head. 'She's got what she wanted, she's leaving us alone now.'

'You're sick, you really are.' His voice rose, along with his temper, and red flushed his cheeks. 'Your actions are your own, not those of a woman who's been dead over two hundred years! What kind of idiot do you think I am? I don't believe in all that ghost crap! You need a doctor, Emma, a psychiatrist!'

'No, Dave, listen. What about when you found me writing in the dark, with my eyes like that? How do you explain that? And the handwriting wasn't mine – it was Jennet's! That's why I've been writing so much – it's her, using me, *forcing* me to tell her story!'

'Emma—'

'No, listen! When I found that inkpot as a kid I think it must have connected me to her, then I came to live here, so close to Mark.' Dave's face flushed darker at the mention of his name. *'Listen*! He's descended from Richard Ramsgill! She's strong, Dave, so strong, she's taking over.'

He stared at me, fists clenched, and I thought for a moment he would hit me. He took a few deep breaths and got control over himself. The emotion left him and he stared at me coldly. That was worse than his anger; he'd switched himself off from me.

'I'm away to Edinburgh again on Wednesday, for two weeks. Until then I'll be sleeping in the spare room. Please, Emma, while I'm away, see the doctor. Please.'

'And when you get back?'

'I don't know, Jennet, I don't know.'

I stared at him in horror.

'Emma. I meant Emma.' He left the room.

Chapter 37 - Jennet
19th October 1777

'Thee's safe now, Jennet, he's gone.'

'Let me out, please,' I sobbed, tears pouring down my face. 'Please get me out of here, I want to go home. I don't deserve this, I don't.'

'I can't let thee out. Our Thom'll do that at dawn. But I'll stay with thee, make sure them lads don't come back. Why don't thee kneel down? Thee'll be more comfortable.'

I cried harder. *Why wouldn't he release me?*

'I can't, me knees . . .' I managed through my sobs. I had knelt earlier to ease my back, and my knees were red raw.

Richard Ramsgill took off his coat and folded it, then placed it on the ground in front of me.

I glanced at him in surprise at his kindness, then sank down on to my knees. I sighed as my back straightened, and arched – stretching my muscles. There were a loud crack and Richard Ramsgill jumped.

'What were that?'

'My back. It's easier now, thanks to thee.' I knew it were only a matter of time before my new position became too painful, but I would take the relief while I had it.

Kneeling in front of the stocks, my hands trapped and bloody from splinters, I leaned my head against the wood and closed my eyes.

'It's a rum do, lass.'

I glanced up at him. 'Eh?' What were he talking about?

'This past year has been Hell.'

'Past year and a half,' I said.

'Eh? Oh, aye,' Richard Ramsgill said. 'I suppose things ain't been easy for thee, neither.'

I lifted my head and stared at him. *Were he serious?*

'Elizabeth has made life hell,' he carried on. 'Aye, got Pa onside an'all, she has, whole ruddy family's been punishing me.'

Did he really expect *me* to feel sorry for *him*?

'Alice's death really knocked me, thee knows lass,' he carried on.

'Mm, were a bit upset, mesen,' I said.

'Aye, that thee were,' he replied, having missed the bitterness in my voice. 'Thee knows that time with thee were happiest in a long time, Jennet. I miss thee sometimes.'

Tears dripped down my face, but he did not notice. 'Then why—?'

He glanced up at me then back at the ground. He shrugged. 'It were madness. Thee were just a lass.'

That didn't seem to bother thee at start.'

He jumped, surprised at the venom in my voice.

'Aye, well . . .' He paused, looked down again, then rose, walked over to the stocks and squatted in front of them so I could see him easily. He reached out and stroked my face, then wiped the tears from my cheeks.

'Thee were beautiful, lass, and so sad, me heart just . . . melted. I should've been stronger, I knows that, but I couldn't help mesen.'

'I loved you, Richard,' I whispered.

'Aye, lass. I loved thee too, but it were impossible.'

'Why?'

He stood and threw his arms out, indicating the village. 'Thee knows what Thores-Cross is like – folk talk. Eventually, too much talk fell into Elizabeth's hearing and she's canny – too canny.'

'What does thee mean?'

'She never said owt to me, went to me Pa and me brothers first. They beat crap out of me, and threatened to take farm off me, wool business an'all.'

'I thought they were thine?'

He shook his head. 'It all belongs to Pa. Won't be mine till he's passed.'

Now I began to understand.

'So thee abandoned me. I were grieving and alone, and thee abandoned me!'

'I had no choice, lass.'

'Then you knocked me to the ground, kicked me and called me whore – told me to kill our child!'

Finally, he looked ashamed. 'I had no choice,' he repeated. 'I'd a lost everything.'

'I *did* lose everything – look at me!'

He looked – his eyes locked on mine.

'This is what's become of me! Due to thy cowardice and weakness! Mam died and Pa followed her. Then thee abandoned me and . . .' I could not finish. Sobs wracked my body.

'I told thee to get rid of child!' he said. 'It would'a been all right had thee got rid of child! No bugger would'a known. Instead . . .'

'I tried!' I screamed. 'I tried – it didn't work!'

He sat down again. 'Oh, lass . . . I'm sorry. I thought thee'd carried on with pregnancy to spite me.'

I shook my head, then rested it on the stocks. I could barely look at him. I had destroyed my life for this man, and he thought I had set out to destroy his.

He nodded in understanding, but said nowt more. He stared at the road in thought and did not raise his head till dawn.

'Richard! What the bloody hell is thee doing here?'

'None of thy business, our Thom. Now let her out, thee's made thy point, she's had an Hellish night.'

'Where does Elizabeth think thee is?'

'I neither know nor care. Get a move on, the poor lass is crippled.'

Thomas Ramsgill glared at his brother, then motioned to Will Smith to free the locks.

He lifted the wooden bar up and gently took my numb hands out of their grooves. I glanced up at him and he smiled. I did not return it.

I straightened slowly and winced. It hurt, but I were not going to give these men the satisfaction of crying out.

'Come on, lass, let's get thee home.' I looked at Mary Farmer, grateful to see her. A friendly face.

She put her arm around my waist and I rubbed at my wrists; then stopped and studied them in surprise at the sharp pain. Dozens of needle-prick splinters were embedded in my skin.

'We'll sort that out at home, lass, come on.'

Mary urged me on with her arm, and we struggled up the hill. I could not straighten up and my legs were weak, but eventually we reached my front door and I fell into the house. Mary half carried me up the stairs to my bed, then fetched up warm ale, a bucket of warm water, cloths and some of my comfrey salve. She sat on the floor next to my mattress and started pulling splinters out of my wrists.

She barely said a word to me; an occurrence I found more frightening than a night in the stocks.

Chapter 38 - Emma
20th December 2012

'Emma Moorcroft?'

I stood and followed a nurse from the waiting area into an examination room.

'Hop up there and loosen your clothes, love, the midwife'll be here in a minute.'

I unfastened my jeans and shirt and got on to the small bed. The nurse bustled about me, pulling at my shirt. 'She needs to get to your belly, love.'

I laughed, nervous.

'Is your husband not with you?'

'No, he's away on business.' I didn't tell her we had barely spoken for the past two months and I had no idea whether our marriage would survive.

'Morning.' Another woman came in and walked to the machine next to the bed.

'Any problems?' She picked up a plastic bottle.

I laughed. Yes, I had problems.

'With the pregnancy, I mean,' she added, squinting at me, and the nurse gave my hand a squeeze.

Yes, the baby isn't mine and it's parents are over two hundred years old. I didn't say it, just shook my head.

She nodded. 'This will feel a bit cold.' She squirted my belly with gel, and I flinched despite the warning.

She picked up the ultrasound wand and placed the head on my belly, squishing the gel around.

She paused, moved it, paused, moved, paused again.

'Is everything all right?' I asked, suddenly concerned. If there was something wrong, what would Jennet do next?

'Don't worry, I'm just trying to get a clear picture,' she said. I glanced up at the nurse who gave me a reassuring smile.

The midwife pressed a button and a rhythmic sound filled the room.

'The heartbeat?' I asked.

'Yes – good and strong,' the midwife said, then moved the wand. The sound faded and grew loud again. She met my eyes for a moment. 'And that's the second.'

'The second?' I felt cold.

'Congratulations, you're having twins.'

'Twins,' I repeated.

'Do they run in the family?' the nurse asked.

Numb, I shook my head. There were no twins in my family or Dave's. Only Mark Ramsgill's.

'A bit of a shock, isn't it? Don't worry, you're not alone, identical twins are completely random and can be born to anyone – it's only fraternal twins that tend to run in families, and even that isn't set in stone – and they are more common in women your age.'

'Which are these?' I asked the midwife.

'Fraternal – there are two amniotic sacs.'

I nodded.

'Are you all right?' the midwife asked. 'It can be a bit frightening. We do have people here if you want to talk to someone?'

I shook my head. I wanted to go home. *What will I say to Dave?* No matter what these women said, he would see it as proof that these were Mark's babies. I knew it proved they were Jennet's. My blood turned cold at the thought. I was sure now that I carried Jennet's babies. I still would not have a child of my own.

Then another thought struck me, *what will Jennet do? Will she try to claim them?* I held my belly as tightly as I could, terrified. She couldn't have them. I would not lose these babies too.

I poured hot water on to the camomile teabag and stared at the phone. Maybe I just wouldn't call him.

The phone rang and I jumped.

'How did it go?'

'Hello, Dave, how are you?'

Silence, then, 'Fine. How did it go?'

'Ok. No problems. It's a boy.' I stared at the wall; I hadn't realised I had decided to lie. *Will this save my marriage, or imperil it further?*

'I see,' said Dave. 'And is everything all right with it?'

'Yes.' A pause. 'When are you coming home?'

'I'm not sure.'

'Will you be back for Christmas?'

'No. I'll stay with Ben.' His brother. I gripped the phone hard, trying not to panic. 'The roads'll be heaving, and I need to be back in Edinburgh early in the New Year. I might as well stay here,' he continued.

'I see.' Alice and the girls were supposed to be coming for our first Christmas in our new home. *What will I tell them?* My breath hitched in my throat.

'Oh, don't cry, Emma!'

I held my breath, trying to get my sobs under control, at least until we finished the phone call.

'I'll pass Ben and Julie your regards, shall I?'
'Yes.' My voice sounded strangled.
'Ok then, I'll call again soon.'
'Love you, Dave.' The phone went dead. I stared at it, put it back on its cradle, picked up my mug and hurled it at the wall.

Chapter 39 - Jennet
16th November 1777

I opened my eyes and shivered. Despite sleeping in woollens under sheepskin, I were frozen. I did not need to see the snow piled up at the window to know it had been a heavy fall. The wind whistling round the house and through the chimney had kept me wakeful most of the night.

I sighed. I were torn. I did not want to leave the bed – I knew however cold I were now, it would be nowt compared to the temperature downstairs.

Yet I enjoyed the crispness of a new snowfall, and then there were the Farmers to think about. They were getting old and John were running low on his remedy for his aches and pains. The cold made it so much worse for him, until he could barely walk. And Mary were getting frail an'all. I had made up a tonic for her, too, to help her through the winter chills – I just had not expected it to snow this heavily, this soon.

I threw the covers off and dressed, then went downstairs to stoke up the fire. The Farmers were the closest thing I had to family, and the only people in the world I could call friends. I remembered the kindness they had shown me when Mam and Pa had died – I had to go to them.

I grunted as I pulled my leg out of another thigh-high drift and planted it down, then paused to get my breath.

The moors were beautiful. Rolling hills of sparkling, unblemished white. Well, nearly unblemished. Those new dry stone walls were creeping closer and closer; black lines snaking through the snow like poisoned blood running through veins.

I pulled the coat away from my neck for a moment, sighing in the blast of cold air. Trudging uphill through this snow were hard work, and I were sweating. Well, the top half of me were anyroad. My legs – despite being wrapped tightly with sheepskin under my skirts – were numb.

I started at a sudden movement to my right and gasped. An owl! It flew past me on silent wings and soared over the moor. It were rare to see them in daylight, but snow this deep made finding food difficult – for everyone.

I scanned the hillsides again, thinking of the beasts, but couldn't spot any sheep against the white backdrop.

I had fodder for them at the house, but even if I knew where they were, I could not get it to them; they were on their own unless they made their way home. I knew they were hardy and bred to survive the winters up here, but I worried about how many would be left come spring – especially of the youngest.

That reminded me of another problem, and I stared at the walls again. When the tups were released in November to service the ewes they would roam free and I could expect a new generation to replace those lost. But what about next year when the lower moors were crisscrossed with these walls?

The tups' owners would keep them close, penned in with their own flock of ewes – and no doubt get a higher birth rate, but what about the rest of us? What about me? Where were I going to get a tup from? The best I could hope for were a shepherd with a very ill wife or child who would have my ewes tupped in return for my remedies.

I sighed again. That were next year's problem – a long way off.

I pulled my coat tight again and glanced up at the Farmers' house. I enjoyed the crisp, clean coldness of the winter air, but the smoke from their chimney looked heaven-sent.

'Ey up, lass! What were thee thinking, coming out in this?' Mary Farmer greeted me. I smiled at her as she stood aside to let me in, then bustled about getting a third stool up close to the fire.

I sat down, grateful.

'I brought John's remedy, and a little something to strengthen thee up, an'all.'

'Ah lass, thee's a good 'un at heart thee is,' Mary said. 'We could have managed till snow's gone, thee knows.'

'Could thee? This won't go overnight, Mary. I couldn't rest easy, knowing John would be in pain. I worry about thee both.'

Mary looked away and John Farmer held his hand out for the herbs. He rarely said much. He left the talking to Mary.

'Here, have some posset to warm theesen up,' Mary said, ladling some into a jug from the large pot hanging above the fire.

'Thank thee,' I said, taking it then wrapping my hands around it. 'And thee knows how I love moors, Mary, in all seasons. It were worth it, just to see them like this.'

'Thee's a rum 'un, lass,' John said, and I shrugged. He nodded and lapsed back into silence.

'Aye, he's right. It ain't normal, Jennet. Most folks are worried sick at this time of year – over food, how sheep are faring and plenty more besides. Thee be careful who thee says owt like that to – thee knows what folk round here are like!'

I laughed. 'Mary, who does thee think I talk to? Who does thee think in this village wants to pass time of day with me? Apart from two of thee, that is.'

'Aye, well, just goes to show. They're already against thee over that Ramsgill business, if anyone hears thee going on about how wonderful it is out there like this, they'll likely blame thee for snow an'all. Take care, lass, is all I'm saying.'

I nodded and sipped my posset. She were right. I were bewildered by how people I had known my whole life had turned against me. I had been fifteen, newly orphaned and barely a woman – I had known nowt of such things beyond a ram tupping a ewe. He were a middle aged man – a family man – who knew it all. Yet he were respected, and I were shunned.

'There's already rumours,' Mary continued.
'Rumours?'
'Barguests and the like.'
'Bah,' John said, staring into the flames.
'Barguests?'
'Aye, a great wolf's been seen on't moor above Gate Inn.'
'The moor above Gate Inn?' I repeated.
'Aye lass.'
'Thee means, near my farm.'
'Aye lass.'
I stared into the fire mesen. That were all I ruddy needed.

Chapter 40 - Jennet
23rd November 1777

I paused with my foot on the familiar worn step. I thought about my quiet farmhouse and the last time I had spoken to anyone but the Farmers – it had been months ago.

I needed people. I needed to give them a chance as much as they needed to give me a chance.

I took a deep breath then pushed open the church door and slipped inside. It were dark after the sunshine outside and I took a moment for my eyes to get used to the gloom. Rows of villagers turned their heads to stare at me. I glared at them then looked to the front of the church and the curate. He cleared his throat and continued with the service. I sat down on one of the pews at the back.

I stared around me at the disdain and disapproval etched on my neighbours' faces, and wondered what I had been thinking. They did not want me here. Well, bugger the lot of them. This were my church too, and I would not slink off. I stared back at the faces turned towards me, and one by one they looked away. I caught Mary Farmer's eye and she nodded at me.

Everyone stood for the first hymn, and I joined them. I had forgotten how much I enjoyed singing. One voice stood out above all the others; a voice I had always enjoyed hearing; a lovely deep tone that carried the words and tune like no other, and uplifted everyone in the building.

I watched him sing and gasped when he looked up and met my eyes. Peter Stockdale winked then turned back to the front, and I were glad of the gloomy church. No one could see my blush.

Service and sermon over, the good folk of Thores-Cross filed out into the crisp November snow. I smiled as eye after eye were averted from me. I would not let them see how much they hurt me.

I got to my feet and followed them out – I could not stay here all day. No one spoke to me or acknowledged me, not even the curate. As I passed him in the doorway, he stared straight ahead and ignored my greeting.

I moved directly in front of him – he did not shift his gaze, but stared straight through me and I grunted with laughter. 'Love thy neighbour, Curate,' I said. 'Love thy neighbour.'

I jumped as my arm were taken and relaxed when I realised it were Mary Farmer. She led me out into the sunshine, and John stood at my other shoulder.

'It's good to see thee here, lass,' Mary said. 'It's good for village to see thee at church an'all.'

'Aye,' agreed John.

I shrugged. 'Had nowt else to do today.'

Mary narrowed her eyes, but I needed my bravado – I could not show weakness in front of all these people. She said nowt and we walked down the yew-lined path.

We slowed before we reached the group blocking the way. Billy Gill, Johnny Ward and my old friend Little Rob Ramsgill were deep in conversation, and it seemed half the village were listening in.

'Aye, that's the third this week!' Billy Gill said. 'Pa went out with his gun, saw a great black dog, he said, but I were watching out window and I reckon it were a wolf!'

'Never!' Johnny Ward said.

'And it's killed three of thy sheep so far?' Little Rob Ramsgill asked.

'Aye. And Old Man Lister from Padside reckons it's had half a dozen of his an'all!'

'Grandpa and me uncles have lost a few too,' Little Rob said.

'A wolf!' Johnny exclaimed. He sounded excited.

Little Rob glanced up and saw me. 'No, not a wolf,' he said. 'A barguest. It's her.' He pointed at me. 'It's that witch! She told us she'd do it, don't thee remember? She said she'd turn into a wolf and come after us!'

Billy Gill and Johnny Ward looked embarrassed. I were stunned. I could not find any words and were aware of everyone staring at me.

'Everyone knows witches can turn themselves into animals!' Little Rob continued. 'She's the one killing the sheep! Have any of hers had their throats ripped out? No! *Her* sheep ain't been touched!'

Billy Gill glanced at me and paled. I opened my mouth to say something, but no words would come. Mary were equally silent and I stared at her in surprise. She were never backward in speaking her mind, but now she stared at the boys, her mouth hanging open.

'Oh, stuff thy nonsense!'

I glanced at Peter Stockdale, my eyes wide in surprise. I had not expected him of all people to speak up for me.

'There's no such thing as barguests, thee's letting thy fancies run away with thee!'

'Aye,' John Farmer agreed.

'There's been wolves on this moor since time began, and only reason Jennet's flock ain't been affected is because it's so small – she hardly has any sheep! Now come on, out the way, thee's blocking path.'

The boys moved to the side, and the Farmers and I followed Peter out of the churchyard.

I wondered if he saw the spitting and crossed fingers pointed at me. Whatever were going on, and despite Peter's words, folk believed Little Rob Ramsgill.

Chapter 41 - Emma
10th January 2013

'Are you ready?'

I glanced at Dave in surprise. It was the first full sentence or unsolicited comment he'd offered me since he'd arrived back from Scotland three days ago.

'You want to come with me?' I had an appointment at the doctors with a mental health assessor.

He stared out of the window at the light covering of snow. 'Whatever else is going on, Emma, you're four months pregnant and the roads are bad.'

'It's nothing the Discovery can't handle.'

'Even so, they're narrow country roads. I'll drive you.'

I narrowed my eyes, wondering if he wanted to make sure I actually went to the appointment.

'Emma Moorcroft?'

I looked up at the sound of my name, glanced at Dave, then hauled myself to my feet and followed the woman to a door. Dave stayed where he was and didn't say a word.

Inside, she introduced herself as Vicky Baxter and gave me a questionnaire to fill out. I looked at the questions that tried to gauge my mood and behaviour, and answered them as best I could. How could I explain what was happening to me with multiple choice answers?

Then the real questions started. 'How are you sleeping?'

I shrugged. 'I'm not, really. I can't stop writing, and I can't get to sleep.'

'You're a writer?'

I nodded.

'What's stopping you getting to sleep? Planning your book or worrying about it?'

'I'm not aware of the time, and can't tear myself away from writing. It's almost as if my character is taking me over.' It was the closest I would come to admitting to her that Jennet had possessed me.

Vicky nodded and made some notes.

'So, you're working hard?'

'Every waking minute,' I replied.

'It sounds obsessive.'

'I can't stop thinking about the book, or bear to be away from it.'

'And is it affecting your marriage?

I laughed, though without mirth. 'You could say that.'

There was a pause, while she made some notes. 'You've recently moved up to Thruscross?'

'Yes.'

'How do you like it there?'

'Very much. I used to go the old sailing club when I was a child. I love it there, it's my favourite place in the world.'

'It's very isolated.'

'I prefer to think of it as quiet.'

Vicky smiled. 'Do you have any children?'

My face fell and I shook my head. Tears pricked my eyes and I blinked furiously. Vicky said nothing, but pushed over a box of tissues and waited for me to continue.

'We started trying a couple of years after we got married, but . . .' My breath caught in my throat in a loud sob and I lost my battle with tears. I reached forward without looking at Vicky and took a handful of tissues. I pressed them to my eyes, then blew my nose. 'I . . . we . . .' I broke off again with another sob.

'It's ok, take your time,' Vicky said.

I nodded and fought to regain control of myself. I took a deep breath, then tried again. 'I had a miscarriage, at twenty three weeks.'

'I'm sorry,' Vicky said. 'That's terrible, and very difficult to get over.'

I nodded, tears falling freely again. 'It was just over a year ago, but it still feels like yesterday. Dave's been wanting to try again for ages, but I wasn't ready, I can't bear to lose another baby.'

Vicky nodded. 'And you're . . . at seventeen weeks now?'

'Yes.'

'With twins?'

'This is confidential isn't it?'

'Yes, as I said before, this is completely confidential unless I thought you were at risk of harming yourself or somebody else.'

I sighed. 'Yes, I'm expecting twins.'

'It sounds as if you're struggling with the idea of that.'

I stared at her, tears still falling. 'My husband may not be the father.'

She nodded, but made no comment.

'I had an affair. With our neighbour.'

She nodded again. 'Do you blame your husband for the miscarriage?'

I shook my head violently. 'No, no, of course not, it was just one of those things. If it's anyone's fault, it's mine. My body failed my baby.' I broke down again.

Vicky waited for me to calm. 'What did the doctor say?'

I sniffed and blew my nose. 'That it happens more often than people realise. He reckoned that there was nothing wrong with me, that it was food poisoning, but how can it not be my fault? I ate whatever it was killed my baby! And now with all the writing and not sleeping, I messed up my pills,' I said and stared at her, defiant. I did not want to talk about the miscarriage. She nodded and I carried on. 'Mark is a descendant of one of the characters in the book. It was like a compulsion. I didn't want to, but couldn't stop it.'

'He forced you?'

'No! No, he didn't want to either. *Jennet* forced us.'

'Jennet?'

'My character.' I stared at the floor. I had said more than I had meant to. 'I know it sounds crazy, but that's what it was like.'

She nodded again, and scribbled some notes.

'So, am I mad?' I attempted a laugh. 'Do I have that multiple personality disorder or something?'

She smiled. 'We don't use the word mad any more, and dissociative identity disorder, as it's called these days, is extremely rare. It's difficult to diagnose and to treat, and many psychiatrists don't believe it even exists. To be honest, you're describing obsession rather than dissociation, and it sounds like you've had a very stressful year, what with the move so soon after the miscarriage. You're grieving, and it's lonely up there as well. I don't think we need to worry about obscure disorders, but focus on you and your needs. Is the man you came with your husband?'

I nodded.

'Has your doctor prescribed any anti-depressants?'

'No, she didn't want to while I'm pregnant.'

Vicky Baxter nodded again. 'I think we should organise some counselling for you. CBT – Cognitive Behavioural Therapy – could help you recognise your altered feelings and behaviours and help you find ways of coping with your work/life balance. I also think some joint counselling with your husband would help as well. You can work through your grief together, as well as find a way to deal with this pregnancy. Do you think he would be amenable to that?'

I shrugged. 'I can ask him.'

She nodded. 'We would do the CBT here, over the course of three months, but for the couples and grief counselling there is a local service which would be more suitable—'

'No!'

She stared at me in surprise.

'I . . . I'm sorry, it's just that, well, the neighbour's wife . . . works for them.'

'I see, that's out then. I'll have a chat with my supervisor and see if we can offer the joint counselling here as well.'

'Thank you.'

* * *

'How was it?' Dave asked as we turned out of the car park.

'She thinks it's the stress of the move and the isolation.'

He said nothing.

'I'll start a course of counselling – they'll write with my first appointment.'

'Hmph. What good will talking do now? It's gone too far for that.'

'She says there'll be tools to help me find a better "work/life balance".' I mimed speech marks in the air. 'She also wants us to do some joint counselling.'

'No.'

'Dave . . .'

'What's the point? Either that,' he jabbed his finger at my belly, 'is mine, or it isn't. Talking won't sort it.'

'Dave it's either *ours* or it's Jennet's. Please, don't let her destroy us!'

I screamed as he hit the brakes and I was thrown forward against the seatbelt.

'Stop it!' he shouted and slammed his fists on the steering wheel. 'Just stop it! Stop saying it's Jennet's! Jennet doesn't exist! She's a figment of your imagination!'

I stayed quiet. Dave rarely lost his temper, and I'd learned to wait the storm out when he did. After a few moments, he took a deep breath and let out the clutch. We drove home in silence.

Chapter 42 - Jennet
25th November 1777

I had spent the day on the moors, gathering rosehips and nuts. It were where I felt safest; my only company the sheep, plus shrews and mice, and the buzzards, owls and hawks that hunted them. No people and plenty of warning of any approach.

I loved it up here. The biting wind fresh and clean in my face; blowing all my worries – and the hate of the village – away.

But it were time to go home. I had more than I could carry with ease and I were cold, thirsty and hungry.

I set off towards my house and saw the Farmers' place – I would stop off there; say hello. It had been over a week since I had spoken to somebody; Mary Farmer would help put off the loneliness of my empty house. Just for a little while.

'Ey up, lass, how's thee?' Mary greeted.

'I'm well, Mary, how's thee?'

'Ah well, can't complain. Come on in, lass, have a sit by the fire, thee looks nithered. I'll get thee some warm ale.'

I pulled a stool closer to the fire and hunched over, holding my hands out to the heat.

'There thee is, lass,' Mary said, holding out a jug of steaming, spiced liquid. I took it and held it between both hands, letting the warm jug finish what the fire had started and bring feeling back into my fingers.

'It'll be a hard winter, lass, will thee be able to fend well enough? I fret about thee, sometimes, alone in that house.'

'I'll be right enough, Mary. The moors give me most of what I need, thee knows that.'

'Aye, well. Much of grain's rotted in field this year, we've had that much rain over summer. Folks won't part with it, not for herbs, not this winter.'

'Oh they will, Mary, the bastards will.'

She flinched at my words.

'If they don't, I'll threaten another bad harvest next year – I'm sure they already think I'm to blame for this one – bastards!'

Mary frowned and sipped her ale.

'Thee'll never guess who came to see me last week, Mary.'

She glanced up at me – I could not read her eyes. 'Who?'

'Marjory Wainwright!'

'Marjory Wainwright? She never did! Don't tell me she were after thy help making another babby – not after last time!'

'No.' I laughed bitterly. 'Not that, she were after a curse to hex that Lizzie Thistlethwaite. Apparently Bert's been carrying on with her behind Marjory's back.'

'Oh lass, I hope thee sent her packing.'

I studied my ale and drank.

'Lass, are thy wits that addled? Thee's been in't stocks once, and thee's believed to have had curses come true – don't forget them sheep of Ramsgill's that drowned, and mill flooded not long after Big Robert Ramsgill refused to grind your grain!'

I fidgeted on my chair, but Mary had not finished and wagged her finger at me.

'They all blame thee for that – and for Marjory losing her babby. Then there's that wolf they're all convinced is thee. Thee must take better care, lass!'

I met her eye, scared. I had only been thinking about what I could do to them; not what they could do to me.

'Richard Ramsgill had a right do with Thomas over stocks – he won't lock me in them again, Mary!'

'Oh lass, how can thee be so trusting, after all that's happened? Believe me, they can – and would – do a Damn sight worse!'

I flinched, then stared at her. I finished my ale as John walked in, stamping mud from his boots, and Mary jumped up.

'John, look at mess thee's made! Get them boots off!'

He glared at her, made to answer, then spotted me. 'Oh, how do, Jennet.'

'Evening, John. I'm just on my way.'

'Thee don't need to leave yet, lass, stay.'

'No. Thank thee, but I need to get back. I'll be salving sheep starting tomorrow and I want to get some herbs sorted for a tonic for them.'

'Salving? That should'a been done last month, lass!'

'I know, I'm a bit behind, but it still needs doing.'

'Aye, well, all right then, but mind how thee goes.'

I would have to examine each ewe carefully to make sure she were healthy enough to survive the winter, while I rubbed the Stockholm tar and tallow mixture (along with my own medicinal additives) into their fleeces to proof them against water and protect them from scab and lice. The new walls were getting closer, and it might be the last time my beasts would be found by a wandering tup. I had to make the most of it – the lambs that resulted may be the last ones I would see from my girls.

I gave Mary a hug, then picked up my baskets and set off down the hill.

* * *

I breathed the fragrant air deeply. I had a great bowl of herbs steeping and the steam filled my home. They had to stay a good two hours, then I would drain them ready to mix in with the salve in the morning.

I sighed and poked the fire, then sat at the table, head in my hands. It had been a hard year, in all sorts of ways. Mary's warning ran round my head; things would only get tougher. It were not fair. Why did they treat me so?

I got up with new resolve, and fetched Mam's inkpot – there were still some ink left. And a few sheets of Pa's precious paper. I needed to tell my story. I needed folks to know my side of things.

I sharpened a goose wing feather and dipped the nib into the inkpot, then paused to think. I would likely not be able to get more ink or paper; I would have to make my words count.

I bent over the page and started to write.

Chapter 43 - Emma
14th January 2013

I put the quill down and flexed my fingers. I'd been writing for hours and had cramp. I needed a break.

I put the kettle on and stared out of the window. The reservoir was a dark grey dotted with white horses and surrounded by thick white snow. I shivered; it looked cold, forbidding and unwelcoming, and I was starting to hate it here. My dream home, built in my favourite place in the world – everything I had once loved, I now hated.

Dave was still giving me the silent treatment. But at least he was home, and the snow would keep him here for the time being.

I hadn't seen much of Mark, although I had been spending time with Kathy – she wouldn't leave me alone now she knew I was pregnant. She had no idea I was carrying twins or that they were Ramsgills.

I shivered; the unwelcome hold Mark had on me seemed to have dulled. It was as if Jennet had what she wanted – babies – and had no further need of Mark.

Dave was walking up the hill to the house, dogs jumping in the snow around him. When he was home – which seemed to be as little as possible – he walked for hours. I wiped away a stray tear; he avoided me as much as possible – not hard in a house this large.

I held a hand up in a wave, knowing the dim table light behind me meant he would be able to see me. He bent and threw a snowball for the beasts. I knew he had deliberately ignored me. I couldn't find a laugh for the dogs as, bewildered, they snapped at snow in their search for the snowball.

I gritted my teeth; enough was enough. Yes, I'd cocked up – literally – but it wasn't my fault. This was all down to Jennet. I turned and walked downstairs to the kitchen. He *would* stop avoiding me.

'Good walk?'
'Aye.' He didn't look at me.
'Where did you go?'
'Moors.'
'Dave, please . . .'
He briefly met my eye. *'Please?* Please what? Please – there's no doubt over the father of your baby? Please – my wife didn't fuck the neighbour while I was away working? Please – my wife isn't mad and doesn't think the mother of the child she's carrying is a ghost?' He threw his coat on to a chair and finally faced me, fists clenched at his side.

I took a deep breath. 'I know things have been difficult—'

'Bah!'

'—but you can't deny something weird is going on. You've seen how I've been writing – have you ever known me work like this before? You know about the nightmares, and you were the one who saw me writing in the dark – I had no idea. I've not been myself. Can you not open your mind just a little bit and accept something we can't explain is going on? Or are you arrogant enough to believe that the human race knows absolutely everything, and can explain it all with the science we know? Is there not even a tiny bit of doubt in your mind?'

I took another deep breath. 'I've told you how sorry I am. I've told you I never even fancied him, and can't understand why this happened. You've seen how Jennet's story has taken me over – why can't you see that it's even more than that – that *she's* taken me over? It's like . . . like I'm her pen or something. *I'm* not writing her story or living my life – *she* is!'

His lips remained pressed closed.

'I've done what you asked, been to the doctor and had the assessment. I'll go to counselling when the appointments come through. I know I've hurt you and I wish with every fibre of my being that I hadn't. But what's happened has hurt me too – I didn't make these choices, they were made for me by something evil and vindictive. My body was taken from me!'

I sat down at the table and put my head in my hands. 'God, I need to get away from here – from her.'

'That's not a bad idea.'

I glanced up at Dave, hardly daring to hope.

'I can't deny you've been different since we moved in. I'm not sure I can believe it's Jennet, but I want to . . .' he tailed off. 'I really do, it would mean you're still the Emma I married. It's just so . . . preposterous.'

I stared down at the table again. 'I don't want this to break us, Dave. I love you, I want to fix this, but I don't know how.'

I looked up at him, and finally he met my eyes.

'Please, let's go away somewhere – a last minute booking. A week away and leave the book here, have a complete break. Please, can we try and save our marriage?'

He watched me for a couple of minutes; I didn't look away. Then he nodded, and I felt my body crumple as the tension left my muscles.

'All right, I can't deny this place is getting to me. We'll find a last minute deal somewhere warm, and talk. It doesn't matter where we go, but I do want to see who you are away from Thruscross.'

He wasn't smiling, but I was. I got up, crossed the kitchen and hugged him. His body was tense, and his arms stayed by his sides, but he didn't push me away. We had a chance.

Chapter 44 - Emma
29th January 2013

'Cheers.'

'Cheers.' We clinked glasses and I grinned at my husband. After a tense couple of days wondering if our flight would be cancelled due to the weather, we had made it to the relatively balmy Algarve. We'd had a lovely week here, and it was our last night.

We hadn't talked – not properly – but we were speaking. We were even sharing a room. Ok, so it was a twin rather than a double, but it was an improvement on separate rooms.

We'd played golf every day. Well, Dave had played golf; I had walked and hit lots of little balls in directions I hadn't meant to.

'I believe you.'

'What?' I glanced up at him, scarcely daring to accept what I thought I'd heard.

'I believe you, about Jennet.'

'Oh, Dave.' Tears welled up in my eyes.

'You've been different here – the old Emma. You're sleeping again. I thought you'd be itching to fill the hotel stationery with Jennet, but I've not seen you glance at it once. You're a different person, you're the Emma I used to know.'

He leaned towards me and took my hand.

'I feel different, I really do, she can't—'

'Let me speak, Emma,' he said, and I shut my mouth.

'If it was psychological, the problem would have come with us and it hasn't. Therefore, the logical explanation is some kind of haunting.' He smiled wryly at the paradox.

I thanked the waiter when he put a plate piled high with fresh clams in front of me, and returned Dave's smile with relief. Finally, he got it. I took a sip of wine from the one glass I allowed myself with dinner.

'It's been awful, Dave. She's so strong, she took me over completely! I can't tell you what it means to me that you finally understand.'

He stared at my belly and frowned. 'I can't say I do understand. How can a ghost make you sleep with another man? Why is her love for Ramsgill stronger than your love for me?'

I sat back, stunned, then said, 'She doesn't love Ramsgill. It's a different motivation altogether, and I don't fully understand it yet. But please don't doubt my love for you, Dave.'

He nodded, then ate. I tucked into my own food. The clams were delicious. I had chosen them every night and would miss them once we were back home.

'So what do we do?'

I was disappointed that Dave hadn't said anything about loving me back, but maybe that was expecting too much.

'I don't know, Dave. All our money is tied up in your project, and that house and land – it won't be easy to move.'

'No, and in this housing market, we'll be hard pressed to find a buyer.'

'Even if we did move, the problem would still be there, and another family would suffer.'

'What are you suggesting?'

I took a deep breath. 'I finish her story – write her out. Maybe once what happened to her is known, she can rest in peace.'

'And what about Mark?'

'She's got what she wanted from Mark, he's not a problem any more – he didn't want to be with me any more than I wanted to be with him.'

He stared down at his plate. 'What if the baby's his?'

'I don't know. What if it isn't?'

He raised his eyes and looked at me. I needed all my willpower to meet his gaze. I was trapped in my lie about twins. We were still in trouble.

We flew home the following day. The easy atmosphere between us grew more and more strained as we approached Thruscross, and as soon as we entered the house I went to the office and started writing.

Chapter 45 - Jennet
7th December 1777

I threw a handful of scraps to the chickens and glanced up at a noise. I stared at the new wall that were slowly creeping up the lane toward my house, but heard nowt else. I threw more scraps, but kept looking at that wall. It would soon be right round the house; enclosing me; cutting me off from the moorland I loved. Soon, there would be no such thing as open space.

I bent to pick up a rare winter egg, then went back to the house.

I opened the door, stepped across the threshold and fell forward from a violent push. I heard the door slam and the locking bar fall into place and I pushed myself up; only to feel a boot in my back, kicking me down.

'Stay there, witch, on the floor where thee belongs!' It were Robert Ramsgill's voice – the young one. I heard laughter – at least two more.

I tried to speak, but Little Rob Ramsgill's boot were still on my back, and my face were pressed into the flags. Only a garbled sound came out of my mouth.

'She can't get air!' Billy Gill.

'Aye, turn her over, Rob, we're not here to kill her.' That were Johnny Ward speaking, it were the same three who had threatened me in the stocks.

I took a deep breath as I were rolled over.

'Billy Gill, what does thee think thee's doing? What'll thy mam and pa have to say about this?'

He stared at the floor, then at Rob Ramsgill, who kicked me.

'Nowt to do with thee, witch! Does thee think anyone in't village cares what happens to thee?' He kicked me again, spat, then bent and ripped my dress down the front, exposing me to the three boys. All three laughed and the other two crept closer to get a better look. Little Rob planted his boot on my belly to stop me scrabbling away.

'Don't do this, boys, thee don't want to do this,' I begged, but Little Rob only laughed.

'Who's first?' he asked.

'Don't thee dare!' I screamed at them. 'I curse any part of thee that touches me to rot and fall away!'

'Come on boys, don't be shy!' Little Rob laughed again. 'They're just words; no potions or owt like that, she's just trying to scare us. Who's up for it?'

The other two stared at the floor as I continued to scream curses at them. I tried to get away, but Little Rob put more pressure on my belly –

he stood with enough force to keep me pinned in position.

'No? Blithering cowards! Hold her down, then.'

The two boys grabbed a shoulder each. Under other circumstances, I might have laughed to see them both spit on the floor as a charm against witchcraft, before they pulled their sleeves down so their skin did not touch mine.

'Billy, Johnny, please . . .' I tried again; but neither boy would meet my eyes. Their stares were fixed on my exposed breasts.

I looked back up at Little Rob; he were untying his breeches.

'Thee won't get away with this, Rob Ramsgill—' The rest of my threat were knocked away by his kick to my mouth. My head snapped to the side; blood pooled on the stone.

My legs were pulled roughly apart and a new weight settled on me.

I struggled hard, but fingers dug into my shoulders and Little Rob's weight kept my lower body still. I screamed at a sharp pain between my legs, then again and again. It were hard to believe this were the same act I had enjoyed with Richard.

I shut my eyes and kept my head turned to the side. I gritted my teeth against more screams. I were not a party to this, so I would play no part. I tried to blank out what were happening, and welcomed the darkness that spread through my mind.

'Is she dead? Has thee killed her?'

I opened my eyes, saw the boys and sat up. They pulled away from me, startled. I covered myself as best I could with the remnants of my dress, and pushed my way backwards across the floor, away from them.

'I curse thee, Little Rob Ramsgill! And thee Billy Gill and Johnny Ward! None of thee will forget this day, all thy lives will be lost because of it!'

I lifted a shaking finger at Little Rob. 'Thee! Thee'll be first to die. Thee won't see year end, I promise thee that!'

'Remember that wolf, Little Rob!' Billy Gill squealed.

'It means nowt, they're just words,' Little Rob shouted at them, but his two friends had backed away. They were at the door, freeing the locking bar.

Little Rob glanced at me, then his friends. If he did not move quickly, he would be alone with me. I saw fear flare in his eyes, and he stepped away, spat once more, then turned and ran after the other two boys.

Chapter 46 - Jennet
8th December 1777

There were a banging at the door. I flinched and huddled under Pa's coat in fear. *Are they back?*

'Jennet! Jennet! Is thee well? Jennet!'

My body shook with sobs. It were Mary Farmer.

'Jennet! Why's door barred? What's up? Let me in!'

I pulled the coat around me and pushed myself up from the floor where I had spent the night huddled in front of the fire, though it had now burned out. I had not been able to face going outside for more peat. I kept my eyes firmly on the door and did not look at the room. I pulled up the locking bar and unlatched the door. Mary Farmer burst in.

'What is it, lass? What's wrong?'

I checked there were no one else outside, then shut and barred the door again.

'What the heck's happened, Jennet?' Mary Farmer stared at me and my swollen mouth.

I glanced around the room, but kept my face still. After the boys had gone, I had burned the remnants of my dress, then washed and washed and washed, before wrapping myself in the coat – the familiar smells soothing me. But I could not tell Mary Farmer any of that.

'John saw there were no smoke at thy chimney, we thought something had happened. What's gone on?' She reached her hand out to my face, and I flinched away from her. The coat fell open and her face paled.

'Them marks! Thy wrists, shoulders! What's happened Jennet? Tell me!'

I covered myself again and shook my head. Mary sighed and shook her head. She hunted around my cooking area.

'Why's thee got no peat in, lass? There's no watter, neither! Unbar the door, and I'll be off to well. Get theesen dressed, and get that fire going – I'll put on some posset and we'll talk.'

I did not move, but that did not stop Mary Farmer. She picked up a couple of buckets and let herself out. I barred the door behind her, then went upstairs to find some clothes.

Mary took one look at me when she returned. I wore the thickest, most shapeless woollens I had over Pa's hobnailed boots. She said nowt.

She stared at the fire. It were still dark and cold.

'I couldn't go out there,' I said, my voice sounding small and childlike even to my own ears.

She sighed and went back out, returning with a scuttle full of peat from my precious supplies in the turf-house. The fire soon blazed, then glowed with heat. She added water to a pot, along with some mutton bones I had left over and a handful of herbs. I had no cream or eggs for posset. She hung the pot over the heat, then sat at the table. She stared at me, and I sat opposite.

'Is thee gonna tell me what happened, or do I have to guess?'

I hung my head and hugged myself.

'Did they hurt thee?'

I nodded.

'Did they . . . did they . . .' She did not know how to ask. I nodded again.

She blew out another sigh and sat back. 'Who were it, lass?'

I stared at the table. I could not tell her. If those names passed my lips it would bring it all back. I could not bear to form the sounds of their names in my mouth.

Mary Farmer sighed once more and got up. She stirred the soup, then poured liquid into two jugs.

'Here, drink this, then we're off up to Thomas Ramsgill's. If thee won't tell me, thee'll tell him.'

I stared at her in horror and shook my head.

'No use arguing with me, lass. Thomas Ramsgill's Constable. It's his job to keep peace. He did thee a disservice in October, locking thee in stocks like that. He can make up for it now.'

'No! Not Ramsgills! No!'

She looked at me a moment, then shrugged. 'Can't be helped, lass. Now drink down that soup, and we'll be off.'

As usual, there were no denying Mary Farmer when her mind were set, and we walked up the hill to Thores-Green; a collection of three or four farms set in the middle of the moor itself. Thomas Ramsgill's property were stone built, as they all were round here, with a long, sloping, slate roof. Mary walked straight up to the door and banged on it. I cringed behind her.

His eldest son, Neville, opened the door. His eyes widened when he saw me. I knew he knew. 'What's thee want?'

'Thy father, is he here?' Mary pushed past him and I followed. We stood in a small enclosed hall. Tapestries hung on the walls, and lanterns lit its entire length.

'Wait here,' Neville Ramsgill muttered, and disappeared through a doorway. A few moments later, Thomas Ramsgill appeared. He were shorter than his brother Richard, and fatter, but his features were similar and it were hard to look at him.

'We's here to report a rape, Constable,' Mary said, coming straight to the point. 'Jennet here were attacked in her own home last night. Look at her face!'

Thomas stared at me; his face betrayed no expression.

'It can't be allowed, Constable, rape's a serious matter, it needs dealing with.'

I winced every time she used the word.

'Tell him what happened, Jennet, go on.'

I glared at them both in horror, *would they really make me say it?*

'Go on, Jennet, tell him!' Mary squeezed my arm and I told a very short version of my story. Mary paled.

Thomas turned back to the doorway and spoke to whoever were inside. At the same time, Mary whispered to me, 'Thee should've told me it were Little Rob, afore we come.'

I glared at her. I had not wanted to come in the first place, nor had I wanted to tell anyone at all.

Thomas came back into the hall, followed by his wife Hannah, who hid behind her husband and refused to look at me. Richard and Elizabeth followed, then Big Robert Ramsgill and his wife Margaret. Neville smirked behind them.

I watched Richard, wondering if he would help me. He had heard his nephew threaten to rape me when I were in stocks after all. He did not look at me, and dread crept through my insides with icy fingers.

'So, had to have another Ramsgill did thee, Jennet?' Elizabeth sneered. 'What is it about men in this family thee finds so fascinating?'

'Elizabeth!' Richard tried to shush her, but she ignored him and spoke louder.

'There are no secrets here, not any more, we all know about Jennet. I wouldn't be surprised if she'd cursed them into it. We all know thee's a witch, Jennet. What did thee do, call on thy Devil lover? Have him trick the boys into lying with thee? Is thee that desperate for a man?'

'Elizabeth! Enough!' Richard grabbed her arm and pulled her back into the room. The door slammed shut, but did not shut out the sound of raised voices.

Mary Farmer put her arm around my shoulders, and I realised I were trembling. Not with fear as Mary seemed to think, but with rage.

'I'll talk to them,' Thomas Ramsgill said, backing away towards the front door.

'What good'll that do?' Mary asked, but took Thomas' hint and, with a last glance at the door where Richard and Elizabeth were still shouting, led me out of the house.

She pulled me down the lane as if scared they were coming after us, then, with a glance back to make sure we were far enough away, said, 'Did thee see Hannah's face? She believes tales, and she has influence over Thomas. If Ramsgills add their weight to witch talk, thee's in big trouble, Jennet. What happened last night's just start.' She sighed, looked me in the eye, and I realised with a jolt she were crying.

'Whole village is already wary of thee – living alone in that house of thine. Then there's business with babbies and cursing. If Ramsgills are calling thee witch – and they'll do owt to protect one of their own – thee's not safe here. Is there anywhere thee can go? What about thy pa's family?'

I shook my head. There were nowhere – no one.

'I don't know anyone outside of this valley,' I said. 'And Pa never spoke about his family. All I know is that he's from Scotland.'

'Well, thee needs to think of summat, lass. Thee can't stay here.'

I shook my head. 'This is my home,' I hissed. 'They've taken everything else from me, they won't take that as well!' I were shouting now. 'I won't let them! I won't! I'll see them all dead first – and I'll start with Little Rob Ramsgill!'

I glanced up, saw Thomas watching us, and ran down the hill, cheeks streaming with water, back to the safety of my house. I hated the Ramsgills, hated the village, hated them all, but I would not run away. I would not.

Chapter 47 - Jennet
27th December 1777

I stared at the moors, then shifted my attention back to the village and the lane – something had moved.

There! A bonnet bobbing up from behind the new wall that hid the lane from view.

She walked nearer the entrance to my farm, but I still couldn't make out who it were. I gritted my teeth in frustration, then relaxed when she paused at the new gate, glanced at the house, then back to the village, Mary Farmer. I had last seen her that time at Thomas Ramsgill's. I caught my breath in anticipation. She carried on walking.

No! No! Before I knew it, my fists were in my hair and pulling my scalp backwards and forwards. 'No!' Now the word had voice.

Mary Farmer turned back, opened the gate and walked to the house. There were about fifty yards between window and lane. I were sure she could not have heard me.

I flung the door open before she reached it. 'Mary!' I cried, and sank to the ground.

She reached the threshold and I clung to her, sobbing.

'Hush, lass, people will see, get inside.'

I let go and sat back, allowing Mary to enter, then stood to shut and bar the door behind her.

'By heck, lass, thee's let theesen go! When were last time thee washed?'

I looked down at myself. I wore the same shapeless clothes Mary had made me put on three weeks ago. I could not remember venturing out to go to the well. I shook my head.

'And what's this?' She held up a dish with some meat scraps.

'For cat,' I said, embarrassed.

'What?' She stared at me in amazement. 'Is thee telling me thee's *feeding* cat?'

I nodded. It let me stroke it now.

'Thee can't be feeding cat, lass. It's supposed to keep mice from oats!' She pointed at the grain stored at the opposite end of the room to the chimney. 'If it's fed, why would it bother to hunt?'

I nodded, I knew she were right.

'Has thee been like this all Christmas?' Her voice softened. 'We were worried when we heard nowt from thee, thought thee'd be up to see us.'

Mary sighed when I did not respond, went to the fire and peered into the pot that hung there. She tutted and went to the baskets she had put on the table and which I had barely noticed. Cream, spice, and honey went into my posset.

'Keep an eye on that, lass, while I go to well. Thee needs cleaning up, then we can set about house.' She looked around her in distaste. Blood and broken egg still stained the floor, and I had no holly, ivy or any other kind of greenery as decoration, never mind a yule log.

She stared at me, sighed, rested her gnarled hand on my shoulder a moment, then picked up a couple of my buckets, unbarred the door and left. I barricaded myself in again as soon as the door had closed behind her.

I stayed at the window until I could see her hunched form struggling with the weight of two buckets of water. Guilt pierced me and I opened the door.

I took two steps outside, and panic overwhelmed me. I looked round – trying to see in every direction at once – searching for the source of my fear. I could see nowt and ran back inside. Only two steps, but I were gasping for breath. Mary followed and looked at me in confusion, but said nowt about my brief appearance and sudden dash back through the door. She thumped the buckets down and water sloshed on to the dirty stone floor.

'We'll get thee priddied up, then we'll see about getting more watter for floor.' She stared at my look of panic, but did not shift her eyes until I dropped my gaze and nodded.

'Right then, get them rags off.'

Fingers trembling, I untied and discarded. The Mary Farmer of my youth were back – the one that were impossible to deny.

She rummaged until she found a couple of clean cloths, dipped them in one of the buckets, gave one to me and started to scrub my back with the other.

Slowly, I washed my face, chest, belly and legs, and Mary moved on to my arms.

I screamed at the sound of laughter from the open window, and scrabbled round to see young Robert Ramsgill leaning on the sill, pointing. 'Look at her, being washed like a babby! Where's thy curses now, witch?'

Mary shot through the door – faster than I thought her old legs could carry her.

'Little Rob Ramsgill, thee little shite! It's high time someone gave thee a beating – knock some sense into thee! Get back here thee little runt!'

'Get away with thee, thee awd carlin! Get back to thy babby!'

Mary came back in, barred the door, closed the window shutters and lit a candle.

'It's all right, lass, he's gone.' She picked up her cloth again, ignoring my trembling, but were much gentler as she wiped off the dirt that had stuck to my wet skin as I had lain curled up on the floor.

'Right, thee's done, now get theesen dressed. We'll go for some more watter, then clean rest of house.'

'I can't! Mary, I can't go out there!'

'Nonsense, lass. Thee loves moors, we're only going to well, we'll stay out of way of village and folk – that little bugger is long gone. Thee'll feel better when thee gets back out into fresh air.'

I sighed and pulled on bodice, petticoats, and collar over my shift, then replaced my forehead cloth and coif, and finally pulled on Pa's hobnailed boots. I knew from experience there were no arguing with her in this mood. And she were right, I had missed the moors. There were no way in Hell I were going anywhere near folk though, whatever she said.

'Thee can't go out with thy hair like that, and a comb'll be no use. Where's thy carders?

I fetched the wooden paddles studded with nails normally used to untangle wool ready for spinning, and she dragged one through my hair. It hurt, but I did not scream; I remembered Mam doing this when I were a nipper, and enjoyed the memory despite the scrapes to my scalp.

'Thee needs to be seen, folk are talking about thee and way thee is now. They're afeared of thee and they have enough to fear already.'

I shrugged into Pa's coat.

'Winter, starvation, plague,' Mary carried on, oblivious to my silence. 'They'll get rid of owt else that scares them. They'll get rid of thee, lass, if thee don't take better care.'

I glanced at her and shook my head. She were just an old woman worrying too much.

'Mark me words, lass, thee needs to take better care!'

I nodded in the hope she would stop all her doom and gloom.

'Right then, where's rest of thy buckets?' she asked.

I looked at the corner of the room and she bustled over, found two more and tossed them at me, then picked up her two and led the way outside.

I hesitated on the stoop and looked around. There were nobody about. I took a deep breath and a small step, paused, then took another. Mary stood just ahead, waiting for me. I turned and shut the door, then faced her again and took another step. They were getting easier.

A breath of wind rustled my hair and I lifted my face to it, enjoying the peaty, heather smell of the moors.

'All right, lass?'

'Aye.' I walked slowly to join her. The wall had not yet surrounded the house and we could walk unimpeded up the hill.

* * *

Half an hour later we had four overflowing buckets of water and struggled back to the house. Mary had been right – this were what I had needed, and I felt like my old self again.

I were relieved to be home, though, and hurried to my door, then fell against it when something hard hit the back of my head. More stones rained around me and the water I had dropped. I cowered into a ball, screaming, and tried to protect my head with my arms. I were aware of Mary's shouts and male laughter, then Mary's arms around me.

'It's all right, lass, they're gone.'

'Who?' I mumbled, though I knew.

'Little Rob Ramsgill and his little gang of reprobates. Come on, let's get thee inside.' She opened the door and I crawled in. Mary barred the door behind us.

'Right, let's have a look at thee.' She tutted and got to work cleaning the blood from my hair and applying poultices.

An hour later, clean, tended and defeated, I crawled into bed, unable to face more of the day. Mary took her leave, promising to come back in the morning. I forced myself back downstairs to the door to bar it, checked the window shutters were secure, then back over the newly scrubbed floor to the stairs. I lay for some time shuddering and sobbing, and had never been more grateful for sleep.

Chapter 48 - Emma
8th February 2013

I dropped the quill and notebook, and buried my face in my hands. That poor girl. Tears flooded down my face as I thought of her attacked in her home, then terrified to go out – at a time when there was no running water or electricity. If Mary Farmer hadn't found her when she did, she would have died.

I wondered what had taken Mary so long to visit her, knowing what had happened. Why had she stayed away? Were the gossips of the village getting to her? Or was she scared of Jennet and her curses as well?

'Emma, what is it?' Dave had heard my sobs.

'Jennet,' I managed to say through a spasming throat. He said nothing, but sat beside me and held me until my sobs subsided.

Once I had calmed, he pulled away.

'This is getting beyond a joke, Emma. I know we agreed for you to write her out, but look at the state of you. You haven't slept since we got back from Portugal, and you look ill.

'I know the counselling starts in a couple of weeks, but what about going back to the doctor for some sleeping tablets?' he continued.

'I can't take sleeping tablets when I'm pregnant.'

'How do you know? There may be some herbal ones that are safe. Go and ask her.'

I said nothing.

'Emma, please! I'm really worried about you – you know I'm away back to Edinburgh next week – I need to know you're sleeping, at least.'

I nodded. I'd give him anything at the moment – not many men would have stayed in this situation.

'Do you have to go?'

'Aye. I've to see some potential buyers at the site to show them what's what – I've already put it off twice, I can't do it again. I'll make it as short as I can, but I have to go.'

'Ok, I'll ring the surgery now.'

'Then we'll eat.'

I smiled, kissed him and picked up the phone.

'Do you fancy going out for supper?' Dave asked. 'We haven't been up to the Stone House for a while.'

'Oh yes, that's a good idea. It'll be nice to get out of the house for the evening.'

'Great – jump in the shower, we'll go as soon as you're ready.'

I grimaced, realising I hadn't washed for a few days. My routine was all over the place; I started writing as soon as I got up – some days I even forgot to get dressed until it was time to go to bed.

Half an hour later, I was back downstairs: clean, refreshed and looking forward to an evening out with my husband.

Dave held the front door open for me and I led the way to the car. Five minutes later, we pulled into the pub car park, then made our way inside.

'Kathy! Mark.'

They were sitting near the door, full plates in front of them.

'Evening,' Mark said.

'Oh, hello!' Kathy was much warmer. I smiled at them both, but Dave ignored Mark and only greeted Kathy.

'How are you? We haven't seen you for ages!' Kathy said. She glanced at Mark and Dave in confusion.

I carried on regardless. 'We're well thanks, Kathy, how are you? How are Alex and Hannah? Have they made their minds up yet?'

'Yes, thank goodness – they've both put Leeds as their first choice.'

'That's great!' I stopped, not knowing what else to say.

'Well, better get to the bar, good to see you,' Dave said into the silence, and we escaped. I glanced back while Dave was ordering our drinks, and saw Kathy hunched over the table, questioning Mark.

'Here you go, Emma.' Dave passed me a glass of red wine, and sipped his pint of bitter. 'Do you know what you want?'

I studied the menu chalked above the bar and smiled, remembering our dinner here with Alice and the girls and how we had laughed. It seemed a long time ago now.

'Shepherd's pie,' I replied. Dave ordered, beef and ale for him. He paid, then we sat down – at a table as far away from the Ramsgills as we could find.

'Dessert?' Dave asked. 'Treacle sponge or bread and butter pudding.'

I pulled a face. 'No, they're too heavy, I'm already stuffed. I'll just have coffee, please – decaf.'

'You'll be lucky.' Dave laughed, and went to the bar.

I waited until he was back, then got up to go to the ladies.

On the way back out, I bumped into Mark. He must have been waiting for me in the narrow corridor.

'How are you?' he asked.

'Fine.'

'And the baby? He reached out to touch my belly, and I knocked his hand away, stepped back and crossed my arms over my chest.

'The baby's fine,' I said, looking over his shoulder. Had Dave seen him follow me?

'Is it . . . is it mine?' he asked. I glared at him.

'No, Mark, it's not yours. It's not mine either, come to that. It's Jennet's. It's Jennet's baby.' For some reason I did not want to tell him I was expecting twins.

'What? Oh, don't start all that again!'

'Start what? Think about it, you know it's true – neither of us wanted to do what we did – it was her! She's connected to me somehow, and you're a Ramsgill. This is Jennet and Richard's baby – not mine, and certainly not yours!'

'Mark?'

I glanced up and gasped. Kathy stood behind Mark – shock written over her face. Dave stood further back, hands in pockets, frowning.

Mark whipped round. 'Kathy, it's not what you think.' He stepped towards her – she backed away.

'How could you? Twenty years and you do this, you bastard!' she shouted, and I was aware of silence in the rest of the pub. 'And you! I thought you were my friend!'

Mark stepped towards her again, and she slapped his face. 'Get away from me, get away!' She turned and ran, barging past Dave, who stared at Mark. Mark didn't meet his eye.

'I'm sorry,' he muttered. 'So sorry.' He followed Kathy.

'Time to go?' Dave asked.

I nodded at his cold tone, and followed him through the pub and out to the car. Nobody spoke. Everybody stared. I wanted to go home and lose myself in writing. I couldn't deal with this. Couldn't think about poor Kathy. Couldn't look at Dave. I had to get rid of Jennet.

Chapter 49 - Jennet
4th January 1778

'Ey up, lass, summat's wrong.' John Farmer walked in, looking worried, and both myself and Mary glanced up at him.

'What is it, John?' Mary asked.

'Looks like fire. Lass, I think it's thy place.'

I jumped up and ran to the Farmers' door. Smoke rose from below. John Farmer were right – my house were on fire. I ran down the hill, heedless of anything but my home. Everything I had bar the sheep were under that roof. Everything I had left of Mam and Pa were in that house. I had to save it.

I ran over the last rise and stopped. The thatched turf-house, sheltering a couple of months' supply of peat, was well ablaze, and smoke poured out from the gaps in the window shutters of the house itself. A dozen people stood around, watching and doing nowt.

I hurried to the house, shouting at people to get buckets. I saw Richard Ramsgill and gave him a push to get him moving towards the smithy – William Smith always had buckets of water by his forge.

I shoved open the door and coughed. Burning peat had been strewn over the floor, and I watched the flames reach the wooden staircase, then the grain store, and take hold.

I grabbed the besom and started to push the burning peat outside. I screamed as a torrent of water hit me, then I were pushed out of the house mesen.

I fought against my attacker, trying to get back inside. All Mam's things were in there, her journal, my herbs, Pa's paper, Richard Ramsgill's gifts. I had to put the fire out.

'Thy skirts lass, thy skirts!' John Farmer shouted in my ear, and I realised he were my captor. I glanced down – the hem of my gown were charred and smoking. The water he had thrown had saved me from being horribly burned.

I let him drag me away to Mary, who held on to me while he went to refill his buckets.

Richard and Thomas Ramsgill, Robert Grange and William Smith arrived carrying full buckets, which were thrown through my front door.

'It'll be well, lass, it'll be well,' Mary soothed. 'See, it's started to rain, it'll soon be out.'

'Somebody did this, somebody set fire to my house!'

I saw Little Rob watching, not making any attempt to help or join the line of people between well and burning house, and pointed at him.

'Thee! This were thee!'

He turned to me and laughed. 'Serves thee right, witch! Thee should burn with it!'

I screeched and jumped at him. 'Thee'll regret this, Little Rob! Thee and thine, thee'll rue this day!'

'Aye, thee's said that afore! Weren't going to see year end, were I? But here I is. Thy curses mean nowt, witch!'

'Lass, hush now, come away!' Mary Farmer dragged me off. She may be old, but a lifetime of tending sheep on the moors, wrapping fleeces, carding and spinning wool had kept her strong. I collapsed in a heap and raised my face to the sky, feeling utterly hopeless.

The rain fell harder and washed my tears away.

'See, it's nearly out! Thee were lucky, lass, thy house'll be saved!'

I looked back at my home. The turf-house were still smoking, but there were only water pouring out of the front door now, not smoke.

'See, I told thee! A witch! She called the rain down, did thee see that?'

'Shut up, Little Rob!' Richard Ramsgill clouted him. 'Thee had better not have had anything to do with this!'

'Or what, Richard?' Big Robert Ramsgill, asked. 'Is thee accusing my son of summat?'

'Care, Richard,' Thomas warned.

Richard shook his head and fetched more water. He did not look at me.

The buckets were being emptied on to the remains of the turf-house now, and I shook Mary off to go back inside. I stared at the ruins of my home.

Everywhere were black with soot and running with water. There were no staircase and the boards above me were charred. I had nowhere to sleep, nowhere to sit, nowhere to eat. It were all gone.

'Walls are sound, lass, don't despair. Thee'll stay with us till we can get this cleaned up.'

I leaned my head on Mary's shoulder and sobbed. I had lost everything.

Chapter 50 - Emma
12th February 2013

'Emma!'

I jumped, splattering ink over my notebook and clothes.

'Alice! What are you doing here?'

'I haven't seen you for ages – we've hardly spoken since you cancelled Christmas, I was worried.'

'Oh.' I realised she was right. We normally spoke two or three times a week and met up for lunch regularly. I'd been neglecting *her*, too.

'I've been banging on the front door for ten minutes, didn't you hear me?'

I shook my head. 'How did you get in?'

'The kitchen door was open. You need to be more careful, Em, especially when Dave's in Scotland. Anybody could have walked in.'

'Yes, you're right. Hang on, how do you know where Dave is?'

'I rang him, I was frantic. I've been trying to talk to you for weeks – you've not taken any of my calls.'

'I'm sorry, Al, I've been writing non-stop. I don't have a phone in here.' I waved my arm around the office to demonstrate.

'I've left loads of messages, Em. On your landline *and* your mobile, you've not returned a single one.'

'I'm sorry, Alice, I guess I *have* been a bit lax lately.' I felt terrible. How could I have been so swept up in my life that I'd forgotten my family? It was Jennet's fault. I ground my teeth together. I hated her.

'Em? You ok?'

I nodded, tears pricking my eyes. 'I'm glad you came, Al. It's good to see you.'

'Mm, it's been a while. Come on, leave that, put the kettle on and we can catch up.'

'Great idea.' I threw the notebook and quill on to the table – by now it was more ink than bare wood – and stood.

'*Em!*'

I looked down at my belly, and cupped my hands around it. I grimaced. 'I've got a lot to tell you.'

'You're not kidding.' Her voice was cold. She looked furious.

We walked downstairs to the kitchen in silence. I could feel Alice's eyes burning a hole in my back. So that was everybody. Jennet had hurt everybody in my life: my husband, my sister, Kathy. No doubt my nieces would be upset too. The sooner she was gone, the better.

'Why didn't you tell me? It was hell trying to explain to the girls that you'd lost the baby and they wouldn't have a baby cousin after all! We've all been walking on eggshells around you, but don't you think we've been grieving too? It would have been wonderful to share this with you and support you! And what about Dave? He's been doing his best to look after you, who's been looking after him? I'll tell you who, nobody!'

I stared at my coffee in silence and led the way to the sofas in the lounge.

Alice sighed. 'So when did you decide to start trying again?'

'We didn't.'

'Oh! It was an accident?'

'You could say that.' I made a strange laughing noise – more like a cackle, really. 'Al, the baby . . . it's not Dave's.'

She stared at me, her mouth hanging open.

'It's not mine, either.' I made that strange cackle again, then lost my battle with tears.

'What do you mean? Of course it's yours! And what about Dave? If it's not his, whose is it?'

I held my hands over my face and fought to regain control of myself. Eventually I faced Alice and took a deep breath.

'Since the miscarriage, I've hardly been able to write.'

'What about the baby, Emma? Who's the father?'

'I'm coming to that, please listen, Al.'

She closed her mouth and sat back, arms folded, and raised her eyebrows at me.

'I hoped that would change when we moved in here, but you know what they say, careful what you wish for.' Alice's expression did not alter. I carried on.

'It started with dreams – nightmares – and I kept hearing church bells.'

'Em!' Alice knew as well as I did that the church had been flattened before the reservoir had been filled.

'No, listen Alice, please.' I filled my lungs again. 'Then we went for dinner to Mark and Kathy's – they live in the haunted house.' Alice didn't react. 'They told us about Jennet, apparently she used to live there in the 1770's.'

'And?'

'She was supposed to be a witch, and hearing the bells means she's back.' I held my hand up to forestall Alice's tut. 'She's been making me write her story – I've been in a frenzy writing it. It turns out she was in love with Mark's ancestor, and she made us have an affair.'

'Oh Em, as excuses go, that's pathetic!'

'No, it's true! It's like she's possessed me, Alice. *I* didn't sleep with

Mark, *Jennet* did. She's got into me somehow, my body isn't my own – it hasn't been since we moved here.'

'That's ridiculous, Emma.'

'I know how it sounds, but it's true. Just ask Dave – he walked in on me writing back in September. I was writing in the dark and he said my eyes were rolled up to the whites. I had no idea, Alice, none at all!'

'What were you writing or was it just scribbles?'

'It was Jennet. I was writing Jennet. It wasn't scribbles, it was legible, but it wasn't my handwriting.'

'Has anything else happened?'

I laughed, but with no humour. 'Isn't that enough?'

'Have you talked to the doctor?'

I cackled again. 'That's what Dave said. Yes, I've been to the doctor's, I've seen a counsellor, but they can't help. I need to get rid of Jennet.'

Alice leaned forward and put her mug on the coffee table. 'But . . . things like this just don't happen!'

'Yes, Alice, they do.'

'But why? How?'

'You remember that day at the haunted house when I found the inkpot?'

'So it's my fault for daring you?'

'No, of course not. It's Jennet's fault. It's her inkpot.'

Alice thought a moment. 'Do you still have it?'

I nodded.

'Then get rid of it.'

'It's not that simple, Alice. I'm using it. I need to write Jennet out.'

'But assuming what you're telling me is true, if she's getting to you through the inkpot, get rid of it.'

'No!'

We stared at each other, both of us startled by the vehemence of my refusal.

Chapter 51 - Jennet
8th January 1778

I looked down the valley at the reds, pinks and oranges splashed across the sky ahead of the sun as it woke. If I just kept my eyes on that beauty, maybe I could forget everything that had happened.

I sighed, even that beautiful sky were a harbinger of more storms to come. I turned to look at my ruined house and walked towards it.

The turf-house and its contents were destroyed. The wooden shutters were damaged and my front door were nowt but a few hanging pieces of wood. Those could be repaired. Mary and John Farmer would help feed my sheep over the coming winter, but at least the sheep themselves had been well away from the danger.

I walked inside. This were what I could not replace. Everything of Mam and Pa's had gone up in flames. All the furniture were destroyed. I would need a ladder to get upstairs, and my home stank of charred wood and burnt fleece. Everything were filthy black – covered in soot and ash.

The Christmas celebrations, such as they had been, were finally over, and there were nowt for it but to start. I grabbed a piece of wood from by my feet – a table leg – and dragged it outside. Then another and another. The fourth and the tabletop itself had disintegrated.

I used a rake to scrape the smaller debris out of the door into a pile in what had been my garden – now trampled into mud by my neighbours.

Three hours later, the ruins of my possessions were cleared – I had not had much to start with. Now I had nowt but stone walls and a few sheep. I had managed to salvage the iron- and stoneware, though it would all need a good scrub, but my wooden implements and fabric were beyond salvage – at least downstairs; I would have no idea what the situation were above my head until I could find some ladders.

'How do, lass.'

I turned quickly. Peter Stockdale had arrived with Matthew Hornwright and a cart loaded with stone to extend the enclosure wall. Nobody from the village were here to help me after my house had burnt down, but men were here to wall me in. I nodded to Peter.

'Sorry for thy troubles, lass.'

I stared at him and he stared at the ground, embarrassed. Matthew jumped off the cart beside him, stared at me, then turned to Peter.

'Got no time for thee to be courting, Stockdale! Give us an hand with this stone!'

Peter Stockdale winked at me and turned to heft stone from the cart to the ground. I took Mary's besom (mine had burned) to sweep the floor clear. Then all I had to do were scrub the soot from the walls, rinse off the floor, pull some new heather to thatch the turf-house – at least it were the right season for it – then cut peat to fill it. Oh, and find some new furniture and a ladder from somewhere – and some grain, of course, to feed me till the next harvest in August.

One thing at a time. I picked up my buckets and went back outside to fill them from the well.

I turned to the front wall – with two windows and the front door, it were the most awkward and I wanted to get it out of the way. Every stone had to be scrubbed. Soot had got into every crack and join, and the stone were rough-cut to begin with. At this rate, it would take weeks if not months to get every wall clean.

I started with the window – now little more than an empty hole in the stone. I worked my way round from the top, down each side, then the ledge. I jumped when something fell and bent to pick it up. My thumb rubbed at the soot and ash caking it – it were Mam's inkpot. I dumped it in the bucket and scrubbed the rest of the soot off, then put it in my pocket.

At least I had salvaged something that were special to me, although it were not of much use. I had nowt to write on or with. I picked up Mary's scrubbing brush and attacked the window ledge again.

Arm, shoulders and back aching, I finally allowed myself a rest. I watched Peter Stockdale and Matthew Hornwright pick up stones, examine them and discard them for others. They were making a right palaver of building that ruddy wall.

I sat on the filthy floor, back against the filthy wall and stared at the remains of my home. I took out the inkpot again, turned it round and round in my hands. My story needed to be told. Just because *I* could no longer write it, did not mean that somebody *else* could not.

I looked around for something sharp, but could not see anything. I went outside to my pile of ruined belongings, and found a knife. I went back in and cleaned it as best I could, then drew it hard and fast across the pad of my thumb. Blood dripped into the inkpot. I sucked my thumb, then went back outside and examined the ruins of my herb garden.

'Can thee salvage anything, lass?'

I glanced up with a start, then shook my head. 'No idea. I'll have to wait for spring, see what sprouts.'

'Shame,' Peter Stockdale said. 'Crying shame it is, lass.'

I nodded, then spotted what I were searching for, bent and snapped a sprig of rosemary off the bush lying in the mud. Back inside, out of sight,

I pushed the rosemary into the inkpot and held it tightly in both hands next to my heart. I whispered the most powerful words I knew; begging, no, *demanding* that somebody tell my story, wishing and praying with my deepest soul that what were happening to me would someday be known.

I put it back in my pocket, rinsed off the wall and window alcove I had scrubbed, then went back outside carrying the empty buckets.

When I got close to the new wall, I stumbled and dropped them.

'By heck, lass, is thee well? Thee should be resting after all this, not working theesen hard like thee's doing!'

I smiled up at Peter Stockdale. He had always been decent to me, although I had not seen much of him after Richard.

'Here, rest theesen. I'll fill them for thee.'

I thanked him, then stepped over to Matthew Hornwright, who barely glanced up at me.

'It looks so strong! How does it stay up without mortar or anything?'

Matthew straightened up, stretched his back and looked admiringly at the length of wall.

'It's all in't stones, lass. See? Pick right shape and fit it in snug like.'

I peered closer. 'Oh, it looks like *two* walls!'

'Aye.' He seemed friendlier now that he were talking about walling. 'See, thee's building a double wall, fitting stones together close and angled in towards each other. Then thee fills in space in't middle with smaller pieces, top it with a nice solid capstone and wall'll still be standing one, two hundred year from now.'

'No! Two hundred year?' I could not wait that long, but I did not believe him. I were sure it would fall down long before then with the winter storms up here. And no matter how well he chose his stones, there were nowt holding them together!

'Does thee want me to take them inside for thee, lass?'

'Aye, that'd be grand,' I answered Peter and, as he bent to pick up the brimming buckets again, I added, 'But what am I going to do once thee's finished wall? It'll cut me off from well!'

Peter glanced behind him at the well and frowned. 'By heck, thee's right, lass.' He looked at Matthew, then back at me. 'Don't fret, we'll build thee a stile so thee can climb over, ain't that right, Horny?'

Matthew Hornwright frowned at him and Peter waved his hand in Matthew's general direction. 'Oh, stop thy mithering, this here lass has had enough trouble to be going on with. We can't cut her off from her watter an'all. We'll stick some flat stones in, so they jut out.'

Matthew's brows drew together as he thought over the idea, then he turned and walked to the cart, presumably to choose some appropriate stones. Peter winked at me and bent again to pick up my buckets and take them to the house. I turned, took the inkpot out of my pocket and shoved it hard into the gap in the middle of the wall. Just another piece of rubble, unremarkable, hidden – until the right person came along: my storyteller.

I hurried after Peter Stockdale and thanked him, even putting my hand on his arm in the wave of relief and hope I felt knowing that my story would be told.

He ducked his head, but not before I saw the blush that stained his cheeks. I stared after him in wonder. After everything that had happened, Peter Stockdale had blushed at my touch. I put my hands to my face and were surprised to feel tears – but, for the first time in a long time, they were not tears of despair.

Chapter 52 - Emma
18th February 2013

I ran; my four legs just long enough to lift me free of the heather with each bound. As a cub it had been hard work, running through this stuff; more like a series of jumps than a run.

I reached the stream and drank deeply, then lifted my head. I'd heard something. I sniffed the air. Yes, I had not been mistaken. An animal – a young one, and alone. I took off in its direction; I were hungry.

The lamb had been easy prey. I lay beside the carcass and licked blood from my muzzle. It had been a while since I had eaten so well – the villagers had started to protect their flocks by setting traps outside the new walls; some of them even patrolled with guns.

I glanced up at the tree I lay under, and a shiver rippled my body. It weren't natural: a single big oak alone in the barren moor. It were a freak of nature, and I normally avoided the place. It stank of death and were just – wrong.

I got to my feet and trotted off. I would not have approached the death tree if it hadn't been for the promise of a meal and now I'd eaten my fill, I did not wish to linger. I headed in the direction of the village – not to cause trouble, or even to enter it, but to keep an eye on it and what they were up to. They were my enemy; I needed to know what they were doing.

The wind changed and brought a strange scent. I lifted my snout to it and sniffed deeply. I did not understand. The village normally brought smells of peat-smoke, rotten meat and human waste, but this breeze smelled clean, even fresh. A bit peaty, yes, but there were none of the disgusting elements that usually signalled the humans.

Perplexed, I carried on, speeding up a little. By the smell of things I did not need to take as much caution.

I crested the brow of the hill and stopped in surprise. The village were gone – a vast lake of water were in its place; the humans were drowned. I bared my teeth, then lifted my muzzle to the moon and howled my delight. The moors were mine.

I woke in a sweat. It had been ages since the last nightmare – they'd disappeared once I'd started writing Jennet's story. Although this hadn't been a nightmare as such, not like those early ones. Still, it had disturbed me. I reached over to Dave, but my hand met empty bedding. He may have admitted what was happening, but he couldn't bring himself to return to our bed yet.

I sighed and put my hands to my belly as tears tickled my ears. I prayed with all my heart that these babies were mine and Dave's and not Jennet's, but somehow I knew the babies were the reason for the dream. I groaned when I realised that meant I'd have another four months of them.

I swung my legs out of bed and stood, then walked to the window. Why was the wolf so happy to see the reservoir? Why was it so happy that the village had drowned? I shivered, moved to put on my robe, and went to the office. I would not sleep any more tonight. I may as well get on with Jennet's story. I wanted it finished and this waking nightmare to end.

Chapter 53 - Jennet
16th January 1778

Someone banged on the door and I dropped my scrubbing brush with a little cry. I got up from the floor I were scouring and peered through the window. I could only see the tail end of what appeared to be a ladder.

Puzzled, I walked to the door as whoever it was banged again, and jumped when my name was called, 'Jennet? Is thee there, lass?'

Peter Stockdale! I hurried to unbar the door, then flung it open.

'How do,' I said. 'What's thee doing here?'

'Well, that's a fine welcome, that is, seeing as I've missed church to bring thee this,' he said, lifting the ladder slightly.

'But, but, where'd thee get it?'

'Made it,' he said. 'Now, is thee gonna invite me in so we can see if it'll reach?'

'Oh, aye, sorry,' I stammered, standing aside.

'By heck, lass, thee's done a grand job here!' He looked around at the clean walls and the clean patch on the floor.

'Haven't started in there, yet,' I said, indicating the grain store. I were trying to make this room right again first.

'Well, I can give thee an hand with that – and turf-house an'all,' Peter said, 'but first, does thee want to take a gander upstairs – see what damage there is up there?'

'Aye,' I said. 'That'd be grand.'

He stretched and pulled a few bits of wood away that I had not been able to reach, and propped the ladder where the staircase had been. He climbed up.

'Stand back, lass,' he called, and more bits of stair joined the wood on the floor.

'Right, reckon it's safe for thee to come up,' he called down, and I made my way up the ladder. It were slow progress – I had to pull my skirts away before stepping on each rung – but before long I were stood upstairs again – the first time since the fire.

'Reckon floorboards are sound, lass,' Peter said. 'Thee were lucky.'

I glared at him – *lucky*? He did not notice. I walked into my room and Peter followed. I threw open the shutters for light and looked around.

Peter seemed embarrassed to see the bed and stayed in the doorway, refusing to meet my eyes.

'I thought thee were here to help?' I asked, all innocence.

'Aye, but . . .' he gestured at the room, 'it ain't seemly to be in here alone with thee!'

'Nonsense,' I said cheerfully. 'Everything's saturated with smoke – it needs to go outside and air. How am I gonna get it down ladder on me own?'

He nodded, but his face were still beetroot red. I stepped towards him.

'Peter, thee's only one bar Farmers who's offered me any aid, and I knows thee's an honourable man.' He glanced up at me and finally met my eye. 'Let's be honest, me own reputation can't get much worse – or is it thine thee's fretting about?'

He laughed and shook his head.

'Right then, will thee help me get mattress downstairs? I can wash cover, but it'll need repacking with heather and straw.' That were it for the soft feathers. 'Clothes ain't too bad – at least lid were down on't chest – but they'll all need washing, then room'll need scrubbing.'

'It's easy enough to get mattress down.' He had found his voice again. He picked it up, crossed to the window, and heaved it out into the garden below, followed by the brocades that had covered it. I laughed.

'See, I wouldn't have been able to do that!'

'Aye, reckon thee could do with a man around place!'

I glanced at him – his cheeks were flaming red again.

'Will thee help me haul buckets of water up? If I can get this room ready, I can move back in – give Mary and John their storeroom back.' I had been living with the Farmers since the fire, sleeping on a pile of old fleeces in a room full of them waiting to be carded and spun.

'Aye. If thee wants, I can go pull some heather for thee an'all – both for mattress, and for turf-house roof – I'll help thee rebuild that if thee wants.'

'That'd be grand, Peter, I don't know how to thank thee.'

He turned beetroot again, and I smiled.

'There's no rush though – I've no peat to put in it. No grain, neither, come to that.' I sat on my clothing chest and put my head in my hands.

'What am I going to do? It's seven months before harvest – Mary and John don't have enough spare to feed me till then. Most of my herbs are ruined too – if they're not burnt, they're mucky with smoke and useless, I can't even *earn* me bread!'

'Hush.' He crossed to the chest and put a clumsy arm around my shoulders. He squatted in front of me and lifted my chin up with his fingers.

'Will Smith has been going round village, telling everyone how badly they've treated thee, and it's time to make amends. Whole village'll each donate a couple sheaves of oats – there'll be enough to get thee through winter.'

'What? Why would they do that? They all hate me!'

'No – well, aye, some do.' My eyes dropped, and he lifted my head back up before he continued. 'But most see things've gone too far. Anyroad, they'll all need smithy at some time or other; they won't risk angering Will.'

'Oh, Peter!' I threw my arms around him. He laughed and pulled back.

'Richard Ramsgill's promised to feed thy sheep through winter an'all.'

'What? Richard?'

'Aye. Must feel guilty for summat.'

'Aye, well, his nephew tried to burn me house down – never mind all that other stuff.'

'He's treated thee bad, lass, right bad.'

I grimaced, then froze as his lips touched mine. I relaxed and held him closer as his tongue pushed against my top lip.

'Jennet!'

We broke apart and giggled at the interruption.

'Up here, Mary, I'll be right down!' I called.

Peter grinned at me, gathered an armful of clothing out of the chest, and we walked to the ladder.

Chapter 54 - Jennet
29th January 1778

The fire blazed and posset bubbled, lending a sweet spiced smell to the house, and I sat at the new table Peter Stockdale had made for me. It almost felt like home again.

Admittedly, the shelves were a little bare, but I had managed to salvage a few items – stoneware and the like. Mary Farmer had done wonders to fill the gaps; raiding her own kitchen for spare items and bullying others into doing the same.

There were still a lot missing; a lot to replace, but I had made a good start.

I had been living here again for a week and whilst I still did not like leaving the house, Peter Stockdale and Matthew Hornwright, true to their word, had incorporated steps into the wall that now stretched far beyond my farm and I could easily get over it to the well and the moors beyond.

I went to the window and stared at the wall. Mam's inkpot were there – I knew the exact spot – safe and sound. My gaze lifted and I watched the valley: sun shining on moors and glinting on the river below; hawk swooping to the catch; rabbits chasing each other in front of the house. I smiled; I had my home, and now a new friend in Peter – I had a future. And if that rabbit would run a little to the left and find my snare on its way back to its burrow, I would have a rabbit for the pot tonight.

My smile grew broader as I spied Peter hurrying up the lane. I knew he were coming here – he had visited me near every day since that first time; had made all my new furniture with his own hands and actually seemed to enjoy my company. I certainly enjoyed his.

He turned through the gate in the wall and hurried up the path to my front door. I opened the door in welcome before he reached it.

'Has thee heard news?' he gasped, and I realised he were out of breath. I frowned and shook my head.

'Little Rob Ramsgill – he's dead!'

I raised my eyebrows in surprise.

'Fool were showing off to them mates of his at Beckfoot Bridge, walking parapet, and he fell.'

'Drowned?' I asked.

'Broke his neck.'

I clapped my hands together and laughed. 'Serves little bugger right!'

Peter stared at me in horror. 'Jennet, did thee hear me? He's barely more than a child and he's broke his neck. I ken he did wrong by thee, but thee can't be rejoicing in his death!'

'I ruddy well can, Peter! That little bugger taunted me, raped me, and I'm sure it were him who nearly burned me house down. Thee's Damn right I'm rejoicing in his death! I feel like celebrating; I've some elderberry wine of Mary's here somewhere, would thee like a taste?'

'Nay I ruddy well wouldn't! I'll not celebrate the death of a lad, no matter what he's done!' Then he stopped and stared at me. 'They say thee cursed him, is it true?'

I met his eyes and stared back. 'He cursed hissen.'

'This is thy doing!' He stepped back a pace. 'He were just a lad! A bit wild, aye, but a lad – he could've made a good man!'

'He would never have made a good man!' I snapped. 'He were cruel, ruthless and had no conscience – just like rest of Ramsgills. And he'd have grown to be worst of them! I didn't kill him, but aye, I cursed him, and aye, I'm glad he's dead. There'll be nay sympathy for a dead Ramsgill in this house!'

He backed away again. 'It's right, what they're saying about thee – thee's evil! A witch! I's been consorting with Devil – I'm as Damned as thee is!'

He turned, ran through the door and dashed back down the hill. I watched him go, then something caught my eye. I smirked – rabbit for dinner.

Chapter 55 - Emma
20th February 2013

The hammering on the door eventually got through, and I glanced up from my notebook. *Who could that be? Where's Dave?* I looked at the door to the spare room, then remembered: Scotland.

I sighed, pulled my robe tighter around me, and went to answer the door. Whoever it was, they were pretty insistent; it sounded like they were kicking it down. 'Oh God, please don't let it be Mark,' I said to the ceiling, took a deep breath and opened it. 'Kathy!' I said in surprise.

She looked me up and down. 'It's eleven o'clock,' she said, then laughed, full of scorn. 'Nearly lunchtime. Or were you expecting my husband?'

'Er no, no, of course not.' I was bewildered. 'I've been writing since the early hours – lost track of time. What are you doing here?'

'I think it's time we talked, don't you?'

I nodded and moved to one side. She strode into my home, looked around, then led the way to the kitchen. I shut the door, full of trepidation. This would not be pleasant. I took another deep breath – I seemed to be doing that a lot these days – and followed her to the kitchen.

I didn't look at her, but went straight to the kettle, filled it and switched it on. 'Coffee?'

'Yes.' No please. I got out mugs, coffee and milk. I knew I was avoiding the start of the conversation, and was aware that she knew it too. I could almost hear her smirk.

Coffee made, I turned. I couldn't put it off any longer. I put hers in front of her, then sat.

'You don't have to sit so far away, I'm not going to bite.'

'Why not?' I asked, finally meeting her eyes. 'I would.'

Kathy sighed. 'I'm furious, yes, and part of me wants to throw this coffee in your face.' I flinched. 'But I won't,' she continued. 'I've known there was something wrong with this place since we did up Wolf Farm and moved in.'

I sipped my coffee and nodded. 'There's something very wrong – it's driving me insane. *She's* driving me insane.'

'Jennet,' Kathy stated.

I nodded again. 'Please believe me, Kathy. I love Dave, and Mark loves you – dearly. What happened . . . well, it was madness. It was Jennet. She made us do it somehow. She's taking over.'

'I know.'

I stared at her. 'How can you be so accepting? Dave's seen . . . well he's seen some pretty weird shit happen to me, and he's struggling to believe it. You've seen none of it.'

'I've seen plenty. I've seen the changes in Mark – strange changes. It's like in a certain light he has muttonchops – you know, those thick whiskers all down the side of his face, and there's a smell sometimes – sheep and whisky.' She shivered.

I stared at her, open mouthed. I knew Jennet had possessed *me*: it hadn't occurred to me that Richard Ramsgill was here, too.

Kathy glanced up and smiled, 'Anyway, I'll only believe my husband has cheated on me after twenty years of marriage if it's the only possibility left.'

I gave a small nod and stared at my coffee. I drank. It was getting cold. 'So, you know about these things – what do we do?'

She raised her eyebrows. 'I don't think *anybody* knows about these things – not really.'

I nodded, she was probably right.

'I've been doing some research,' Kathy continued, 'ever since I realised something – someone – was here who should be resting, and basically, all the books – the more credible ones, anyway – all say you need to give the spirits what they want. Then they'll leave.'

'I know, I need to finish her story,' I said. 'I've been saying that to Dave for weeks.'

'Yes. Finish her story,' Kathy repeated. 'And pray it's enough.'

'Why wouldn't it be enough?'

'She's been taking her revenge on Ramsgills for over two hundred years, she's got a taste for it now. She might want more than just her story known.'

I finished my coffee in silence. I hadn't thought of that. I didn't want to think about it.

Kathy stood and delved into her bag. 'I've brought you Old Ma Ramsgill's journal back, it might help.'

I took it, 'Thanks.'

Kathy gripped my wrists, hard. 'You'd better get this story told right. This is one hell of a vengeful and powerful being we're dealing with. I've read that – all of it.' She nodded at the book. 'And I'm terrified for my family.'

I stared at her, shocked by her intensity, but just as frightened.

'The Ramsgills are cursed – the evidence is all in there. You need to lift the curse – do what she wants and maybe she'll spare my children. Yours too.' She glanced at my belly. 'If it is a Ramsgill.'

'The story is what she wants, Kathy,' I tried to reassure her. 'She's in my head when I'm writing – so much so, it's like she's writing it herself. It's nearly finished. She'll be gone soon.'

'I hope so, Emma, I really hope so.' She let go of my wrists and picked up her coat. 'Don't let me take any more of your time. I'll let myself out. You get back to work. But eat something first, you've lost weight. She won't thank you if you lose that baby – she might just make another one.'

I stared after her, staggered by that idea, then obediently opened the fridge.

Chapter 56 - Jennet
30th January 1778

'Ey up, Jennet, how's thee faring?' Mary greeted me when I opened the door to her and the foggy moors afternoon.

'Mary! Has thee heard? That little bastard Robert Ramsgill's dead!'

'Aye, lass, I've heard.' Mary sat at my new table with a sigh.

'Ain't it grand? Happen there is a god after all!'

'Jennet, thee can't go round saying things like that! How many times have I told thee to take care of thy mouth?'

'Oh, who am I going to say it to? Thee's only one that speaks to me!'

'Peter Stockdale.'

'What? Oh him, he won't say nowt.'

'Aye, lass, he will. He were at church this morn, telling all who'd listen that thee rejoiced when thee heard.'

I were stunned into silence. I had thought he liked me, now he were spreading gossip?

'Well, that means nowt. No bugger could blame me, not after he raped me and burned this house.'

Mary sighed. 'Folk'll believe what they want to believe. Little Rob Ramsgill were a *Ramsgill* – no one can afford to speak ill of the Ramsgills round here, no matter what they might think. And thee, well ... a fallen woman, turned mad, who turns herself into a wolf at night and curses innocent village folk.'

'But ...'

'But nowt! I've told thee over and over to take better care! Folk are easily afeared and now they're afeared of thee!'

'But . . .' I tried to interrupt the sermon again, but she had not finished.

'I don't like the way they're talking, lass, I really don't. I'm afeared myself.'

'Thee's frit of me too?'

'Not *of* thee! *For* thee! By heck, lass, thee can be dense sometimes!'

I said nowt. I had no idea what words to use.

'That young man of thine went straight from here to Richard Ramsgill yestern – thee knew he'd been defying Ramsgill to aid thee, don't thee?'

I nodded, smiling to myself. I had loved that he had gone against Richard's wishes.

'Well, Ramsgill didn't want to know at first, sent him on his way.'

I smiled again.

'Will thee stop grinning, lass! This is serious! Stockdale had whole church up in arms this morning – including Ramsgills, all of 'em. Nobody can talk about owt else.'

I stopped smiling and stared at her.

'Aye, and they're there still, talking and crying. No one's left the place, only me, and I don't like it, lass, I really don't like it.'

Something caught my eye and I got up and walked to the window.

'They've left now,' I said.

'Eh?'

In answer I nodded at the window and Mary joined me.

'By heck,' she said.

It looked like the whole village had come; Ramsgills leading the way, looking grim – even Richard.

The villagers behind carried lit torches in the fog, and the sound of their voices singing about Christ chilled me. I spotted the curate up in the front, leading the hymn. I gritted my teeth.

I glanced round. There were no way out by the front door – if I ran that way, they'd soon be on me. I barred the door instead, then the window, and looked for something to use as a weapon.

I threw a handful of dried rosemary on to the fire for protection and uttered a quick prayer, then picked up the poker and turned to face the room.

Chapter 57 - Jennet

The door rattled. 'Open up!'

'Thomas Ramsgill,' Mary said to me. I nodded; I knew his voice well enough to recognise it.

'Jennet Scot, open this door, or we'll break it down!'

I did not move.

'Lass, the window!' Mary pointed. Smoke curled around the wooden shutter.

'No!' I screamed, dropped the poker and grabbed a bucket half full of water and threw it at the wood of both front windows. I picked up the full bucket and soaked the door, then poured water at the base in case they tried to shove a burning stick through the gap at the bottom.

'What's thee saying, lass?'

I glanced up and gritted my teeth. I had been praying to Mam to protect me and turn the villagers away, but had not realised I had been speaking aloud. Even Mary might mistake my words for a curse. 'The Lord's Prayer,' I said. I could tell she did not believe me.

The door shuddered. Mary grabbed my arm, and I almost screamed. They were trying to break it down. Another hymn started up outside as whoever it were threw himself against the door again.

I shook Mary off, and hurried over to the few herbs I had been able to salvage from the garden, and which hung from the chimney breast – it were the best place for them to dry out, which increased their potency. I made my selection and threw them in the pestle and mortar as the door shuddered again.

Muttering an incantation as I ground – bugger what Mary thought now – I walked over to the door, then scattered the mixture at the wood.

'What's thee doing, lass?' Mary had backed away from the door – and me.

'It's a protection spell – 'twill help door stand firm,' I replied, too scared to lie now, then screamed as the shutters of both windows crashed open. Two men hoisted themselves through the gaps before I could react further – Peter Stockdale and Matthew Hornwright.

Peter grabbed my arm and I stared at him in astonishment.

'What's thee doing?'

'Stopping thee before thee hurts any bugger else.'

'Peter, I ain't hurt nobody!'

Matthew unbarred the door then threw it wide open and Peter said, 'Tell it to them!'

I tried to pull away from him, but he did not loosen his grip. I threw the rest of the herbs into his face and he swore, then slapped me.

'Thee'll regret this day, Peter Stockdale! Thee'll rue the day thee betrayed me, thee mark me words!'

He slapped me again and shook me, and I realised he were afraid. I laughed.

'Jennet, no! Thee's only making things worse!'

I stared at Mary. 'There is no worse than this!' I told her, then turned my attention back to Peter, but other arms grabbed me and my hands were pulled roughly together and bound.

I screeched and tried to pull myself free, but could not break the bonds.

'Calm down, Jennet. This'll go easier for thee if thee's calm,' Richard Ramsgill said.

I turned to face him and his brothers.

'How is this going to go easier for me?' I asked, nodding at the door. Dusk were falling and all I could see were flame from the torches; all I could hear were voices raised in the praise of Jesus as my neighbours surrounded my house and watched my humiliation and fear.

Richard Ramsgill did not answer, but looked away.

Thomas grabbed my arm and pulled me through the door.

'Thomas Ramsgill! What's thee doing? Where's thee taking her? She's done nowt!' Mary shouted.

'The moors,' Thomas replied, not looking at either Mary or myself. 'She cursed young Rob to his death. We've had enough. She loves the moors so much, we're taking her to them.'

I felt cold inside and planted my feet on the ground. I would not help them by walking. Thomas pulled me and I fell. I cursed, unable to break my fall.

'She's going to turn into a wolf!' someone cried.

'Stop her! Stop her curses and witchcraft! Don't let her go now!'

I recognised the voices and shouted the names out, grinning at the terrified screams.

I were pulled to my feet, still spitting names of people I had once counted as friends – Susan Gill, Marjory Wainwright, the Granges, the Smiths, Fullers, Weavers – until a slap stunned me into silence. I stared into Richard's face and shook my head, trying to tell him that I had done nowt, but his expression were cold. He did not care.

Chapter 58 - Jennet

Richard and Thomas dragged me to the lane and heaved me on to a waiting cart.

'Walk on,' the driver said to the horse, and I froze in panic. That were Digger's voice. They had me on the back of the gravedigger's cart.

I scrabbled to sit up as the cart jerked forward. 'Stop! I ain't done nowt! I didn't do it!'

Nobody answered; just carried on singing:
'Praise God, from Whom all blessings flow;
Praise Him, all creatures here below;
Praise Him above, ye heav'nly host;
Praise Father, Son, and Holy Ghost.'

'Richard, Thomas, please! He had an accident, that's all! I didn't hurt him!'

'Liar!' Margaret Ramsgill shouted and pushed her way to the cart. 'You killed him, Witch, with your curses and ill wishing!' She spat at me. 'You killed my baby!'

'Come on, Margaret, don't fret theesen. She'll pay for what she did to our Rob.' Big Robert Ramsgill took his wife by the shoulders, glanced up and threw his own spittle in my direction.

They walked beside the cart in grim silence, Rob's sister Jayne between them, and would not look at me further. I glanced at Big Robert as he tried to keep up; he stared straight ahead. There were no point trying to convince him of my innocence. My eyes drifted to Jayne. She stared at me, her gaze unwavering and full of hate. If anyone were a witch here, it were her.

'Curate! Curate! Thee's a Christian man – thee can't let them do this!'

He glared at me and raised his finger to point. 'Thee let Devil in, lass, only the Lord can help thee now.'

'I didn't!' I screeched. *Why would they not listen? How can I make them see?* I grabbed the side of the cart as best I could as we turned on to the path over the moors to try and stop myself being thrown around with its jolting. I spotted Peter in the gloom, carrying a torch and singing at the top of his beautiful voice. I had used to love hearing him sing at church; now he were singing for my destruction.

Then I glimpsed another figure trying to push through the crowd.

'Mary! Mary help me! Please, Mary!'

The look she gave me were so worried, so despairing, that my voice dried up. I watched her catch up to Big Robert Ramsgill and plead with him. He shook her off so violently she nearly fell. I bowed my head and let the tears fall. 'Mam, help me,' I whispered.

The cart jerked to a halt, and I glanced up. It were full dark now, but I knew these moors so well, I could see exactly where we were by the flickering light of a hundred torches. There were only one place on't moors with a single oak tree amongst heather. Hanging Moor.

Thomas and Richard climbed on to the cart and pulled me to my feet.

'Stop this, please stop! She's nowt but a young lass! Don't do this!'

I tried to smile at Mary, my sole defender in this mob.

'Aye, young she may be, but she's dangerous, and we're all in danger if she lives.'

I glared at Peter Stockdale.

'Aye,' a chorus of voices rang out.

'She's not dangerous, thee daft beggars!' Mary were angry now. 'She's had an hard life, losing her pa and mam the way she did. If anyone's dangerous, it's him!' She pointed at Richard Ramsgill. 'Taking advantage of a young lass in trouble, it's shameful.'

'She bewitched me, caused me to come to her,' Richard protested with an anxious look at Elizabeth.

'Oh ballocks! She did nowt of sort! She came to thy notice, thee fancied a bit of what she had, then thee threw her down when she fell into trouble for it. Thee's only Devil here!'

'Enough!' Thomas roared.

'Not nearly enough!' Mary shouted back. 'And what about rest of thee? Standing by like good Christian neighbours? Watching it all, gossiping and shunning poor lass! That's Devil's work an'all, not Lord's!'

'How dare thee! She barely came to church, holed hersen up in that house and roamed moors alone every night! She cursed hersen by letting in Devil and brought a curse down on whole valley!'

'Aye! She cursed Ramsgill and his flock drowned!'

'Of course she cursed Ramsgill!' Mary shouted back. 'Who amongst thee wouldn't have? He'd got her with child, threw her over and her babbies died! We all curse in grief – she weren't to blame for them sheep drowning!'

'Babbies?' Richard asked.

'Aye, babbies – twins – born dead, no thanks to thee!'

'So that's why she gave hersen to Devil – revenge!'

'No!' Mary screamed in frustration.

'Shut thy mouth, thee awd carlin! She killed my brother! Why's thee defending her?' The mob cheered Jayne.

'Come on, Missus, there's nowt to be done here.' John Farmer put his arm around her shoulders and tried to pull her away. He did not look at me. I understood he had to protect his wife. In this mood, the villagers would likely turn on Mary too.

'Enough of this! We all know facts,' Thomas shouted and everyone else silenced.

'Her curses have been heard and come to pass. We know she turns hersen into a wolf to worry our sheep – it only appeared after she'd lost child.'

'Children,' I said, quietly. He ignored me.

'And I myself heard her curse Little Rob, God rest his soul. There's no doubt in my mind she's a witch.'

'Witch! Witch! Witch!' the crowd of my neighbours and one-time friends chanted. I had no hope.

'Aye! That's right! Witch!' I screamed. Nowt could save me now, but I could hurt them as much as I could before they killed me. 'And how many of thee's drunk my potions? Whispered my spells? How can thee be sure they were to heal, or for love? Which of thee men can be sure thy woman ain't snuck a "love potion" in thy ale?' I glanced round at them, in triumph. 'Everyone here's cursed by my hands!'

Richard and Thomas dragged me further back on the bed of the cart so that I were closer to the tree. I looked up at the branch above me, then at Richard as he let me go. I pulled against Thomas, but he had me in a firm grip. Richard bent and picked up a coil of rope.

'And the Ramsgills carry the heaviest curse of all.' I spat the words out. 'All of thee bar one will be dead within a year.'

Richard threw one end of the rope over the branch.

'Only one son of Richard's will live.'

'Shut up, shut her up!' someone, Elizabeth I think, screamed from the crowd.

'Every generation, only one son will live, to carry on Ramsgill loss.'

Big Robert grabbed the other end of the rope and Peter Stockdale helped him secure it around the tree trunk.

'The Ramsgill name will bring nowt but death and grief!'

'Shut up!' Richard slapped me.

I glared at him, then at the rest of the villagers. They stood in horrified silence.

'This whole valley will suffer!' I could hear my voice, shrill and panic-stricken, but I did not care – it were my only weapon, once again. 'I call down a plague on thee – on to thy flocks and on to thy families! I call floods to sweep away thy homes, I call—' I gagged when a noose were shoved over my head and pulled tight against my neck.

'Thee'll regret this.' I did not know if anyone could hear me. Richard tested the knot, then spat in my face.

'Thee were not worth all this trouble, Devil's whore! Burn in Hell!'

The Ramsgills jumped down from the cart and left me standing alone. Hands bound before me; neck bound to the tree.

'Curse thee all . . .'

The cart jolted beneath my feet and were gone. The rope jerked tight against my neck and I could no longer breathe. I kicked out, searching for somewhere to prop my feet, but found nowt but air.

I could feel the rope biting into my flesh, the tiny bit of air I could get into my throat rasping against it. My head swelled like moss put to soak. Surely my skull would burst through my skin. My eyes met Jayne's and she looked away from my gaze. No matter now, she would be joining me soon – one way or another.

Something grabbed my leg and pulled, increasing the pressure on my throat. Mary. She could only do one thing for me now, and hurry this up.

I gasped, but could not take in any air. I tried to scream, but could make no sound. Darkness closed in – a total darkness now, no torches to light my way. I succumbed to it, my last thought a promise to bring my curses to pass. I would destroy this valley. I would destroy the Ramsgills.

Chapter 59 - Emma
24th February 2013

I threw the notebook and quill on to the table in horror. No wonder Jennet was filled with enough hate to sustain her for two hundred and thirty years. I stared out of the window at the reservoir that covered the homes of the people who had hanged her, and shivered. Then had another thought, could I verify if her other curses had come to pass?

Old Ma Ramsgill's journal was on the desk and I fetched it, then sat down again. I had been writing so much that I hadn't read it when Mark first showed it to me; only glanced at the family tree, then taken it back as an excuse to see him – finding Kathy instead.

Half an hour later, I had my answer and I sat back and stared at Jennet's notebook. In 1780, after their sheep had been devastated by sheep scab, half the village, and all the Ramsgill's bar Richard's son, had died of typhus. It had taken her two years, but Jennet had killed them with her curse.

I put my hand on my belly. *What if these babies are Ramsgills? Will they die young? Or live to know nothing but loss?* An image of Alex and Hannah Ramsgill flashed into my mind. *What of them?* I picked up the notebook and crossed to the desk and computer. I needed to type up the manuscript as quickly as possible. *What if writing her story isn't enough?* I needed to get the book out there so people could read it.

Exhausted, I picked up the phone.
'Kathy? It's done.'
'Jennet's book?'
'Yes.'
'Thank God.' She blew out a big sigh into the phone and I winced. 'Can I read it?'
'Yes of course, I'll print a copy off. Would you mind popping down, though? I'm so exhausted I'm not sure I can make it to your house, even in the car.'
Kathy was full of concern. 'You all right? You sound, well . . .' she tailed off.
'Just tired. I've been up all night typing the manuscript up.'
'Well, now that it's done, life should get back to normal.'
'God, I hope so.' I tried and failed to stifle a yawn.
'I'll have to send Mark down. I'm up to my elbows in bread dough. If I leave it now, it'll be ruined.'

'Oh, ok,' I said, feeling awkward. I didn't want to see Mark, especially not with Dave away. But if Kathy trusted us ...

'Are you sure?' Kathy asked.

'Yes, yes, it's fine,' I said. 'Thank you.'

'What for?'

'Well, you know.' Silence again.

'Yes. Let's hope this is it now and she can rest in peace.'

'Amen to that!' I said, put the phone down then pushed myself up to go upstairs and start the printer going again.

The doorbell rang as I was on my way back down, and I opened it to Mark.

'Hi.'

'Hi.'

'Come through, there's a copy on the kitchen table.'

'Have you printed it off already?'

'Yes, this is the first copy. Take it, I'm printing another off for myself.'

I staggered and grabbed the table.

'Emma! Are you all right? Let me help you.' Mark grabbed my arm then put an arm around my waist and led me to a chair. 'Sit down. What's wrong?'

'I'm ok, just tired. I've been up all night typing, and, come to think of it, I don't think I've eaten anything since yesterday lunch.'

'Bloody hell, Emma, you're pregnant for God's sake!'

'I bloody well know that!' I screamed, and he took a step back. 'Sorry, Mark. I'm not myself at the moment.' I managed a small laugh.

'No, neither of us have been that for some time.'

'Kathy told me, about seeing Richard Ramsgill in you.'

I waited until he made the coffees and sat down. 'Do you think it's over now?'

He sighed. 'I don't know, Emma, I really don't.' He glanced at my belly.

'They could be Dave's.'

'They?'

I nodded.

He took a deep breath, then said, 'Hope so, for all our sakes.'

I sipped my coffee.

'So what happens now?' Mark asked.

'What do you mean?'

'With that.' He nodded at the pile of A4 pages. 'It's not a book yet is it?'

'No, not quite. Normally I'd send it to my agent, but that way it would take nearly a year before it's published.'

'That's too long!'

'I know. I'll go over it tomorrow when I've had a rest, make any corrections—'

'Corrections? Careful Emma, don't provoke Jennet by changing her story!'

I put my hand to my head and rubbed my forehead. 'No, you're right, I won't change anything, just format it.'

'Aye, ok. Then what?'

'I'll upload it to Amazon and Smashwords. It'll be published within the week.'

He sighed, 'That sounds grand. Can you not do it any quicker?'

'Not really, they have to review it and then it takes a day or two to go live, but it'll be out there as soon as possible, I give you my word.'

He nodded and looked relieved.

'My agent and publisher aren't going to be happy, but to be honest, I'm more scared of Jennet.'

'You'll sort them – tell them you had a nervous breakdown, or somebody stole the manuscript or something. Do you have to publish it under your own name?'

I stared at him, 'No, of course I don't!' I laughed. 'It's not my book, anyway, it didn't come from me, it came *through* me – from Jennet. I'll publish it under her name.' I grabbed a pen, crossed out my name and scribbled *Jennet Scot* on the title page.

'There you are then.' He gulped his coffee. 'What'll you do with the money?'

'Spoken like a true Yorkshireman!' I was starting to cheer up. 'I'll put the book on for free or as cheaply as I can, at least at first – try and get as many copies out there as possible. Then, I don't know, we can always find a charity to donate any proceeds to. Maybe that counselling service Kathy's part of? Something that would help people today who are in a similar situation to Jennet then.'

'I suppose so.'

'I can't make money from this, Mark. None of us can. We can't exploit her – it might be enough to bring her back!'

He opened his mouth, presumably to argue, but was stopped by a deep rumbling noise.

'What the hell was that?' I screamed, panicking.

Mark's face turned white and he jumped up and ran to the door shouting, 'Kathy!'

Chapter 60 - Emma

'What is it? What was that noise?' I hurried after Mark and stopped in the open front doorway. Thick black smoke poured out of the Ramsgills' house. Mark was running towards the house, then he climbed the wall into the field.

I dashed back inside to the phone and called 999.

'Fire engine and ambulance! Wolf Farm has exploded! They're inside! Hurry!'

By the time I had answered all the operator's questions and made it back outside, Mark had reached the high wall surrounding his house and was trying to climb it. I shook my head. It was too high – it had been built to keep people out.

I grabbed the keys to the Discovery, jumped in and roared up the lane. I turned in a big arc at the road so I was facing the entrance to Wolf Farm, then floored the accelerator. I screamed at the impact with the gate, but made it through, slammed on the brakes and pulled the car to one side so the fire engine would be able to get in.

I got out of the car and screamed, 'Mark!' He had managed to get over the wall and was at the front door, fumbling with his keys.

'Stop, Mark! You can't! Wait for the fire brigade!'

'Kathy!' he screamed again. 'Alex, Hannah!'

I had been moving towards him to try and prevent him running inside, but stopped. His wife and kids were in there; he would not stay out here. At last, he got the door open. Thick smoke poured out into the fresh air and he ran in. I stared at the house in disbelief, not knowing what to do.

'Emma! Are you all right? What's happening?'

I turned and fell into Dave's arms. I spotted his car abandoned down the road, and realised he'd just arrived home.

'Oh Dave,' I sobbed. 'The house exploded! Mark ran up here and has gone in – they're all in there!'

'What you mean, Mark ran up here? Where was he?'

'At our place – picking up the manuscript.'

'Is that all he was doing?'

'Yes! Kathy was baking or something and couldn't come herself, she sent Mark to get the book.'

'It's finished?'

'Yes.'

'And then the house exploded?'

I nodded, mute, and we stared at the house for a moment. There was no sign of life.

'Oh, thank God.' Sirens and flashing blue lights heralded a fire engine, which pulled to a stop in front of the house. Firefighters swarmed from it pulling hoses and ladders from the machine, and one crossed to us. He held his arm out in a shepherding gesture. 'Please move back from the house.'

We took a couple of steps and stopped when he added. 'Can you tell me what happened?'

'It just exploded!' I said, still in shock.

'How long ago?'

'Uh, I don't know, fifteen minutes? I rang 999 straight away.'

'Is anyone inside?'

'Yes – all of them.'

'Two adults, two teenagers,' Dave added.

I screamed as another explosion tore through the house, and was thrown to the ground. Dave landed on top of me and the firefighter alongside. Debris rained around us and the air was filled with noise and heat.

After a moment, Dave's weight lifted from me and I saw his mouth moving. I couldn't hear him. His mouth moved again, and I squinted, trying to lipread then nodded. Yes, I was ok.

We got to our feet and stared at the house. There was no roof, only flame – and jets of water from the fire engine. I screamed. They were still in there.

'You have to get them!' I shouted at the firefighter. I could just about hear my words now.

'We have to make sure it's safe first, I can't risk my crew in another explosion. And you need to move back.'

'But Kathy! The kids! Mark!'

'We'll get them as soon as we can.'

I struggled to hear, it felt as if I were listening underwater or had been standing by a speaker in a nightclub for hours, but realised what he was saying.

'No! No, you have to get them out!' I screamed, and stepped towards him.

'Emma,' Dave's arms were around me. 'Hush, he knows what he's doing. Are you all right? The baby?'

I sagged against him, then doubled up in a scream as a pain ripped through me. *Please no, not again!*

The ambulance is here, they'll get her to hospital,' the firefighter said. 'I need to go and talk to my crew.'

Dave half pushed, half carried me towards the ambulance, but the paramedics met us halfway with a gurney and I was bundled on to it. I screamed at them to help Kathy and the others.

'She's had a hell of a shock, she was knocked down by the explosion and she's five months pregnant.' I heard Dave tell the paramedics. 'She's had a miscarriage before, please, save her baby.'

I tried to correct him – they were Jennet's babies, *Jennet's*, but I felt a prick in my arm and everything went black.

Chapter 61 - Emma
3rd March 2013

I blinked my eyes open and looked around in bewilderment. I was in a white room, with horrible green and blue checked curtains round the bed. No, not a proper bed, one of those hospital trolley things.

'Emma! Oh thank God!' Dave leaned over and hugged me. I gripped hold of him – hard.

'What . . . what happened?'

'Do you remember anything?'

'I remember an explosion and Mark ran out to get Kathy.'

Dave nodded. 'There were two explosions at Wolf Farm – they think there was a leak from the gas cylinders. Apparently they kept them in a small alcove off the kitchen instead of outside like they're supposed to. You know what a stubborn bugger Mark— Anyway, all it would have taken was a spark . . . Mark ran in to try and get the family out—' He stopped speaking.

'Are they ok, Dave?'

He shook his head. 'They think Kathy and the kids were in the kitchen when the first tank blew, they didn't stand a chance.'

'And Mark?'

'They found him cradling Kathy's body. The second explosion . . . well . . .'

'Tell me.'

Dave looked at me, his expression concerned, and held my hand. 'They're saying at the Stone House that he was blown apart, Emma. I'm sorry.'

'No!' I gasped. 'But, but you said he was cradling Kathy?'

'Yes, his arms . . . were around her.'

I stared at him in confusion, then realised what he meant, 'Oh! Oh! Oh!' I covered my face with my hands in horror and Dave hugged me again, then pulled me close to his chest as I sobbed.

When I quietened, he eased me back on to the bed and said, 'Emma, there's something else.'

I raised my eyebrows at him.

'The baby . . .'

'The baby? Oh no! No, not again!' My arm dropped to my belly.

'We think the fall from the second explosion . . . I'm so sorry, Emma, the babies are gone.'

'Babies?' So he knew, then.

'Yes.' He took my hand. 'Twins.'

We stared at each other for a moment, then I nodded, feeling numb. I didn't know how to react. They hadn't been my babies, they were Jennet's, but my body had let them down – killed them. At twenty three weeks. Again. *Would I ever be able to give birth to a living child?*

'So she's taken them all. Writing her story wasn't enough. She killed all the Ramsgills.' I started to cry again. 'Those poor, doomed babies. None of this was their fault, and they didn't even get a chance to live. How bitter and twisted must she be that she'd kill her own babies too? When we thought we could break Jennet's curse, I never imagined that this would happen. The babies. Poor Kathy, Alex, Hannah, Mark . . .' I broke off in sobs.

'I know, I know,' Dave said, his voice soft. 'None of us guessed that this might happen. She's been hellbent on revenge for 250 years. I guess that's enough to turn anyone to such evil.' He held me and stroked my back and head until I calmed.

'I know there's not much point now, but . . .' He pulled away, reached down and handed me a plastic bag. I looked inside and pulled out a book, wiping moisture off my face. It had a picture of Thruscross on the cover. '*Thores-Cross* by Jennet Scot,' I read aloud, then looked at him. 'You published it?'

He nodded. 'To be honest, after everything that's happened, I was terrified she'd come back for you. I'm not taking any chances.'

Tears pricked my eyes again and I hugged him. Then I pulled back. 'Is it over?'

'I don't know, Emma. I hope so, I really hope so.'

I nodded. That was all we could do. Hope and pray it was over. There was nothing left for her to take. The Ramsgills were gone. Wolf Farm was gone. Her story was published.

I picked up the book again. 'Hang on a minute, it takes days to get a proper book, how long have I been here?'

'Just over a week.' I glanced at Dave in surprise. 'You had to have an operation because of the babies, and then you wouldn't wake up.' He nodded at the book. 'It was all I could think of to do. It's a bit rough, you might want to redo it properly later, but I did my best.'

I nodded. 'You did well – it worked, thank you.' I leaned forward to wrap my arms around him and held him tightly, fighting tears. He had saved my life.

After a couple of minutes, I sat back and ran my hands over my belly once more. The babies had been Jennet's and Richard Ramsgill's. They had never been mine, yet I still felt their loss. Damn Jennet for making me go through this again.

'Emma?'

I looked up at Dave. 'I was starting to believe I could finally be a mother, that it would actually happen.'

He smiled. 'You still can be. The doctors still say there's no reason you can't give birth. We can try for a baby if you want to.' His voice sounded tentative, as if he hardly dared to make the suggestion.

I regarded him a moment, then nodded. 'Yes,' I said. 'Jennet lived in fear and isolation, and look what it led to. It's time to live in hope.'

'Oh, Emma.' Tears ran down Dave's face and I hugged him as a nurse bustled into the room.

'Well now, look who's awake!'

Epilogue - Emma
9th June 2014

'Here we are – home!' Dave said as he pulled the Discovery on to the drive. He twisted in his seat. 'Her first car ride. How is she?'

'Took it like a pro.' I grinned, then tickled our daughter's chin. 'Didn't you, Louise?' She was beautiful. Only three days old, she had Dave's blue eyes and my smile. I could hardly believe it, we were a family at last. I gazed into my husband's eyes and we grinned at each other.

He got out of the driver's seat and opened the back door. I loosened the seatbelt holding Louise's carrier, and Dave picked it up to lift her out of the car. I glanced past him at Mark and Kathy's house.

'It looks like a haunted house again,' I said.

Dave turned to stare at it. Derelict once more; no roof, no glass in the windows or doors in their frames, only the garden wall was still sound. 'But it isn't,' he said. 'No ghosts here, they're all at rest.'

'I hope so.'

Louise burped and I lifted her down from my shoulder.

'Was that good?'

She gave another small burp and I giggled at her, then stood and carried her over to the cot.

'Your first night at home, I hope it's a good one, darling,' I whispered, laid her down, then pulled her blanket up to her chin and froze.

I heard it again and ran, screaming for Dave. Louise matched my screams with her own and I picked her back up, holding her close as I ran from the room.

'She's still here! Jennet! I heard the bells! Dave, she's still here, I heard them again! The church bells!'

Dave charged up the stairs and I ran into him in the office. 'She's not having Louise, Dave, she's not! I don't care what I have to do, Jennet is not taking Louise!'

He grabbed hold of me and held us tightly. 'Shh, Ems, shh. She's not here, she can't be.'

I stiffened in his arms. 'Did you hear that? Church bells! I'm telling you she's back!'

Dave said nothing.

'Dave! Did you hear them?'

He nodded slowly, and my blood ran cold. Part of me had hoped I'd imagined the sound. I pulled away from him and looked into his eyes. He looked as scared as I felt.

'You didn't hear them before. If you can hear them now, then she's definitely coming for us!'

'Ems.'

'Dave, what are we going to do?'

'Ems!'

I stared at him, then realised. 'You *could* hear them before, couldn't you?'

He nodded.

'But you made out I was mad!'

'I'm sorry, Ems, I couldn't believe what I was hearing.'

I had already pulled out of his embrace; now I stood before the windows, watching the darkness. I turned to speak, then spotted something on the coffee table.

'The inkpot!'

'What?'

'Jennet's inkpot!' I rushed over and grabbed it, still holding Louise close. 'It's this thing! This is why she's still here!'

'Then we need to get rid of it.'

'No, we have to give it back to her. Bury it in the ruins of Wolf Farm.'

'No, somebody else might find it. We'll take it to the dam, throw it into the reservoir.'

I paused, then nodded. 'Yes, that's a better idea.'

The next morning, after breakfast, we put Louise into her baby carrier and strapped her into the backseat of the Discovery. I had the inkpot in my pocket. We drove across the dam to the car park and took Louise out, still strapped in her carrier, and walked down to the dam.

Halfway across we stopped, and Dave put Louise down on to the pavement. We leaned over the parapet of the dam and stared at the reservoir. It looked calm and beautiful, the wind rippled the surface, and a flock of Canada Geese came in to land. I gave the inkpot to Dave – he had a stronger throwing arm.

'No, you have to do it, Em.'

I looked at him for a moment, then nodded. He was right. Jennet had come into our lives because of me, because I had found this inkpot twenty six years ago. I was the only one who could break the connection.

I took the inkpot back from him and looked at it one last time. Then I stepped back, leaned back and flung it as far as I could.

There was a small splash, and a few ripples spread across the water, then disappeared.

'Is that it? Do you think she's gone?' I asked Dave.

'Hope so.'

'It seems such an anti-climax.'

Dave smiled. 'What did you expect? Thunderbolts from the sky?'

'No, of course not, just . . . something. Something to tell us she's gone.'

Dave put his arm around me and stood in silence, watching the still waters of Thruscross. 'I think in this case, nothing is much better than something.'

I nodded and we turned to go home.

That evening, Dave came upstairs with me to put Louise to bed. I leaned down to put her in her cot, then paused.

'What is it?' Dave asked.

'Shh, I thought I heard something.' I stayed still and listened.

'What?'

'Nothing. It's nothing.' I smiled and glanced up at my husband. 'I can't hear anything.'

The End

Cursed

A Ghosts of Thores-Cross Short Story

From the Back Cover

"Wow, that was a great creepy story!"

Jennet's here. No one is safe.

A skeleton is dug up at the crossing of the ways on Hanging Moor, striking dread into the heart of Old Ma Ramsgill - the elderly matriarch of the village of Thruscross. And with good reason. The eighteenth-century witch, Jennet, has been woken.

A spate of killings by a vicious black dog gives credence to her warnings and the community - in particular her family - realise they are in terrible danger.

Drastic measures are needed to contain her, but with the imminent flooding of the valley to create a new reservoir, do they have the ability to stop her and break her curse?

Prologue

Thruscross, North Yorkshire

7th August 1966 – 11:30 a.m.

'Right, tea break over, lads, back to work. Rog, Steve, you're up on Hanging Moor in the bulldozers. As soon as they've gone through, Paul and Simon, you get the chippings down. And take care – don't go past the markers, that drop's lethal.'

The road crew groaned, threw their dregs of tea to the ground and refastened their flasks before clambering into their machines to dig out the access road to the new dam spanning the Washburn Valley. The valley would be flooded in a month's time, creating the new reservoir for the Leeds Corporation Waterworks to supply half of Leeds with drinking water, and the road should have been completed last month.

Rog led the way, the large bucket scraping heather and peat, then dumping it into the waiting tipper truck.

Steve followed, making a deeper cut. Together they gouged an ugly scar over the pristine Yorkshire moorland.

'Bugger,' Steve cried out and jolted in his seat, knocking the control levers. The big digger wobbled, teetered, then slowly toppled over towards the edge and a sheer wooded drop of a hundred and fifty feet to the valley bottom below.

'Steve!' Rog cried. 'Lads, help!'

The rest of the crew downed tools and diggers and rushed to the stricken bulldozer. By the time they reached it, Rog was already clambering on to the cab, desperately trying not to look at the vista that opened up before him only a few feet away.

'Steve?' he called again. No answer. His mate lay unconscious, twisted in his seat. 'No!' The digger slid a foot or two in the wrong direction.

'Rog, get down; she's going over!' Andy, the foreman, shouted.

'No – Steve's out cold.'

'You're no help to him if your weight pushes it over the edge – get down! We'll get help, but we need to secure the digger somehow, keep her steady.'

Rog took a last look at his mate then nodded. He realised he couldn't get into the cab without destabilising the digger further and he had no idea how serious Steve's injuries were. He climbed down carefully, just as Simon drew up in the tipper truck. Half full of soil and rock, it was the heaviest vehicle there.

Andy got on the radio to inform his boss at the dam where there was a telephone to call for help, while Paul ran over with a chain. He secured it round one of the digging arms, and Simon backed up – slowly – until the chain was taut.

The digger shifted, turning around the pivot point they'd created. The back end now hung off the edge of the cliff.

'Keep it there, Simon,' Andy called. 'And keep it in reverse – if the edge fails, you'll need to pull him backwards.'

'Can't he just do that anyway?' Rog asked.

'We don't know how badly he's hurt. If he's broken his back or neck, moving him could make it worse. We don't want to move him unless we have to – not until the Fire Brigade and ambulance get here. What happened anyway?'

'Uh.' Rog pulled his attention away from the downed machine. 'I don't know – he shouted out, then rolled it.'

'He shouted *before* he rolled?'

'Yes.'

'Andy, Rog. Come and have a look at this,' Paul called and beckoned them over to join him where Steve had made his last cut.

'What is it?' Andy came hurrying over.

'Uh, looks like a skull.'

'What? Oh Christ, it's a bloody skeleton! Well, that's us finished, lads, no more work here for at least a month while they sort this one out,' Rog said.

'Forget that, we'll just go round it,' Andy said.

The three men looked over at Steve, then back into the grave. Only the skull and shoulder girdle were visible. As one, they shuddered as a worm pushed its way out of the compacted earth behind the jaw bones, for a moment looking as if the skull had stuck an emaciated tongue out at them.

Rebirth

7ᵗʰ August 1966 – 7:00 p.m.

John Ramsgill rushed through the door to the Stonehouse Inn and over to the corner table by the log fire where his mother – Old Ma Ramsgill – was usually to be found at this time in the evening with a pint of stout before her.

'Ma, have you heard the news?'

'Aye, it's all these fools can talk about,' she said gruffly. No one took offence; Old Ma Ramsgill had been a regular in this pub since before most of them had been born. She called everyone 'fool', and everyone called her 'Old Ma Ramsgill', although never to her face. To her face she was 'Ma' to the whole moor, although the moor was vastly depleted now. The families who'd lived down the hill for generations had moved away over the last few years to make way for the reservoir.

'Who do you think it is?'

'Who?'

'The skeleton, Ma!' John bit back his frustration at his mother's obdurate nature. At thirty two he should be used to it, but she could still flare his impatience with a single word.

He took a deep breath and used a calmer tone. 'The skeleton they found up on Hanging Moor – where the old drovers' roads cross.'

She looked up at her son, for the first time showing interest. 'Where the ways cross? Bugger.' She said no more and again John fought to restrain his frustration.

'What do you mean, Ma? Why "Bugger"?'

'It's Jennet, she'll have been woken.'

'Jennet? What, you mean the witch? But she's just a story, she's not real.'

'Oh, she's real all right, lad.'

John turned to greet Wilf Moore as he sat to join Ma. He was almost as old – and as stubborn – as his mother, not to anyone's surprise: they were distant cousins.

'She's the reason thee's the only Ramsgill in these parts – by birth, anyroad.'

'Apart from the bairns,' Old Ma Ramsgill put in.

'Aye, apart from the bairns.' Wilf paused. 'Keep an eye on them, lad. If Jennet's awake, they ain't safe.'

'What? What are you talking about? Why would my children be in danger because an old skeleton's been dug up?'

Ma and Wilf looked at each other. 'Not here, lad, not in t' pub. We'll talk tomorrow, early. Sue too, she needs to hear it.'

John opened his mouth to say more, but Ma held up her hand, drained half her stout and said, 'Best get me another of these, John. One for Wilf too. We'll need as much fortification as we can muster.'

John sighed in exasperation and went to the bar. He knew from long experience that he would get no more from his mother – not until she was ready to talk.

8th August 1966 – 3:00 a.m.

Old Ma Ramsgill dragged herself out of sleep, sweating and gasping for breath. She fumbled at her bedside table to switch the light on, found her glasses, and peered at the carriage clock she'd inherited from Grandma Moore. Three o'clock. The time restless spirits were at their strongest.

She reached a trembling hand for a glass of water and knocked it over. 'Buggeration!' she exclaimed. Then she said it again and again, louder each time. She held her head in her hands and wept. Something she hadn't done for many a long year. Only one thing could make her weep after all she'd seen in life: family. And her family was in grave danger. She just had to make them realise it, then she had a chance of keeping them safe.

She threw the blankets back and eased herself out of bed. Her slippers were wet, but that was still better than barefoot on three-o'clock-chilled flagstones. Shuffling to the kitchen, she cursed again.

She filled the kettle and set it on the AGA – not one of those fancy new ones, but one that had been in this house almost as long as she had.

'Uh.' She bent double, hanging on to the edge of the range as images from her nightmare flashed through her mind. Dark grey clouds morphing into the face of a woman, hair flowing round an expression of sheer hatred and rage.

A wolf bounding across the moorland. Instead of taking a lamb, it snatched an infant from its pushchair.

Fire consuming not the house she stood in, Gate House, which had been in the Ramsgill family for centuries, but Wolf Farm. The farm her son, John, was talking about renovating as soon as he could save up enough cash. *Or as soon as I snuff it and he gets his hands on the Ramsgill land.* Screams of terror echoed through her head. The screams of her family.

Still no let up. Villagers drowning in the river. Babies thrown on to fires. The rocking stone grinding a sinister soundtrack to it all.

The screech of the kettle broke the spell and Old Ma Ramsgill shook her head, wincing at a sudden pain in her temple, and poured the water into her mother's old earthenware teapot.

'Dreams, just dreams,' she muttered to herself. 'That stone ain't moved for years – not like when I was a girl and a storm could set it going.'

She poured out the tea, threw in four sugar cubes, and sipped, wincing again as she burnt her lip.

'Stupid old woman,' she mocked herself. 'Get a grip, thee'll need all thy faculties to take on that witch.'

8th August 1966 – 10:00 a.m.

'About time,' Old Ma Ramsgill scolded her son and daughter-in-law when they arrived.

'We came as soon as we could,' John said. 'I had the milking to do and Sue had to feed the little ones and get Richie off to school.'

'What? Thee's never sent the boy to school? Thee fool. Thee can't let him out of thy sight!'

Sue scowled at her mother-in-law. 'It's the law, Ma, he's six, he has to go to school.'

'Tell them he's sick. This is more important.'

'What? An old skeleton. Dead. How can that be a threat?'

Ma sighed. 'Thee don't understand. Go through, I'll make another pot then tell thee the tale.'

Sue glanced at John, who shrugged. She thanked her lucky stars once again that she'd persuaded John to move away from Gate House to one of the new cottages built near the Stonehouse to provide accommodation for those forced out of their soon-to-be-flooded homes, even though he still worked the Ramsgill farm. She was still trying to persuade him out of buying that old ruined farmhouse. A couple of hundred yards up the lane from Old Ma Ramsgill was far too close for comfort; or peace.

John reached into the pram to lift the twins out, but Sue stopped him. 'Let them sleep, John, they've been up half the night.'

'And so have you.' He embraced his wife and kissed her forehead. 'They'll sleep through before long.'

'Can't come soon enough,' Sue said and led the way to the front room.

John followed, carrying the tea tray.

'Just move them journals out the way, lass.'

Sue did as Ma bid, piling the old, leather-bound books to one side of the coffee table so John could put the tray down. Her interest was piqued by them, but after seven years of being a Ramsgill, she knew better than to push Ma into an explanation.

'Thee pour, lass,' Ma said as she sank into her armchair. Sue looked at her in surprise. Old Ma Ramsgill never let anyone else pour the tea in her house. She always had to be mother.

'You all right, Ma?' John asked.

'Just a bit tired, Son. Bad night.'

'Your hip playing up again?'

'No, nowt like that.' She took a deep breath. 'It were Jennet.'

'What do you mean?' John asked at the same time as Sue's, 'Who's Jennet?'

'Thee's not told her, John?'

He shrugged. 'Why? It's just an old story, scared me silly as a lad when you talked about her. I'll not inflict that on my kids.'

Ma ignored the jibe. 'It ain't a story, Son, and I'm surprised thy mother didn't tell thee either, lass. Jennet's real. She lived in this valley 'bout two hundred years ago – in Wolf Farm as a matter of fact.'

John looked sceptical and Sue sipped her tea, unsure what was going on.

'She was treated bad by Ramsgills. Turned her rotten, our ancestors did.'

'You said she was a witch.'

'Aye, cunning woman they were called then. Healers.'

'What, like a herbalist?' Sue asked.

'Aye, summat like that. Anyroad, she became a pariah—'

'Why?'

'Had an affair with a married man.'

'A Ramsgill?'

'John, stop interrupting. Let me tell the story.'

'Sorry, Ma.'

'But yes, with a Ramsgill. Owned most of the valley then, Ramsgills did. An important family in these parts. Anyroad, back to Jennet. Folk didn't take kindly to that sort of behaviour – not like nowadays where everyone seems to be at it. They shunned her.'

'What, everyone?'

Ma glared at Sue, then her expression softened. 'Most everyone. One kept her company, an ancestor of thine, lass, Mary Farmer, that's why I'm surprised thee ain't heard of her. But it weren't enough.' She tapped the pile of journals.

'It's all in here. Couldn't cope, couldn't Jennet. Bitter she was, it twisted her. She stopped healing, started cursing. Cursed this whole valley. Look, let me show thee.'

She shuffled the pile of books until she found the one she wanted, turned the pages, then handed it to John. 'Read that.'

John glanced at Sue, then his mother, and decided to humour her. ' "Aye, that's right. Witch!" she screamed at us all. "And how many of thee's drunk my potions? Whispered my spells? How can thee be sure they were to heal, or for love? Which of thee men can be sure thy woman ain't snuck a 'love potion' in thy ale? Everyone here's cursed by my hands!" '

'Her last words, them was. She also cursed the valley, the village, and the Ramsgills in particular. Look at that bloody great dam they're building. The whole village will be drowned by end of year. Gone. Just like she said.'

'But that's just coincidence, surely,' Sue interrupted. 'Given long enough, predictions are bound to come true. It's been two hundred years, I hardly think you can blame a new reservoir in 1966 on a girl who lived in the 1700s.'

'I thought thee might say that, lass, so I drew this up while I were waiting.' Old Ma Ramsgill passed over a sheet of paper. 'It's the Ramsgill family tree going back to Jennet's time.'

'What are we looking for?' Sue asked.

'Look at the children,' Ma told her. 'See how many die? "Only one may live to carry the curse to the next generation, then they will suffer their losses." She said *that* about the Ramsgills an'all.'

The silence that followed was broken by a cry from the kitchen.

'That's Jayne,' Sue said. 'Robert will wake any second now.' Her words were accompanied by a second wailing and both parents stood to retrieve their children.

'Do you believe any of this, John?' Sue asked in a whisper.

'No, but . . .' John held Robert high and planted a kiss on the crown of his head, breathing in his milky baby smell.

'But what? It's nonsense. Witches don't exist – not in the way Ma means. And neither do curses.'

'But the family tree?'

'It goes back centuries, how do we know it's accurate? Ma's going daft, John. She's nearly eighty, living alone in this creepy old house, the whole valley about to change with this reservoir. No wonder she's seeing witches and curses. Thruscross is not haunted by a two-hundred-year-old ghost.'

'It'll do no harm to listen to her, Sue. There are things out there we don't understand.'

'You *believe* her?'

John shrugged. 'Not really but she's never steered me wrong yet, even pushing me to pop the question to you. Deep down . . . I don't know. Deep down I can't just dismiss it.'

Sue didn't reply, just raised her eyebrows and pulled in a sharp breath. She turned and went back to the living room.

'I might be nearly eighty, lass, but there's nowt wrong with me hearing.'

Sue flushed and stared at the floor.

'Aye, might be daft an'all – there's plenty round here who'd attest to that. But senile I'm not. This is real, and the sooner thee accepts that, the safer them bairns will be. Mark me words – when Jennet wakes, Ramsgills die. She was disturbed yesterday by them damn fool diggers. Taken blood too. None of us are safe.'

Relive

9th August 1966 – 7:00 am

'John, wake up, you're having a nightmare.' Sue shook her husband awake.

'Wha—? Huh? Oh, thank God.'

'You were thrashing around like anything – what were you dreaming about?'

John sat up and ran his hands over his face and through his hair. 'God, it was awful. I dreamed of that witch, Jennet. She burned the twins. God.' He shuddered. 'I'm never going to get that image out of my mind. And the smell. Christ!'

'Smell? In a dream?'

John shrugged. 'It was a vivid one. Too vivid. What time is it, anyway?'

'Bloody hell, seven o'clock, the twins have slept through!'

'Hallelujah. Well, that's something.'

'I'll go check on them,' Sue said, getting out of bed and shrugging on her robe. 'God, a full night's sleep, I feel like a new woman.'

John didn't reply, his head was in his hands again.

'John! John! Oh God, no!'

He jumped out of bed and ran into the twins' room. Sue held Jayne in her arms, tears pouring down her face. 'They're – they're cold, John, they're cold. Ring 999.'

Disbelieving, John ran to the crib and picked Robert up. His little body was stiff. Sobbing, John looked at his wife and struggled to get his words out. 'Ma was right. It's Jennet. She's back.'

14th August 1966 – 4:00 p.m.

'We have to protect Richie,' Old Ma Ramsgill insisted. 'Send him away, far enough away that he's out of reach.'

'Not now, Ma, please. It's the twins' wake. Let us say goodbye to them properly.'

'There's no time, thee fool,' Ma shouted, bringing a silence down on the Stonehouse. She took a deep breath. 'Jennet won't respect our grief. She'll come for thee or Richie next, John. Thee's the only ones with Ramsgill blood.'

'Oh not your bloody ghost again, Ma,' Tom Grange said, then laughed.

'Still thy tongue, boy.' Wilf jumped to Ma's defence. 'You know better than to speak to thy elders like that. And thee'd do well to heed Ma's words. All of thee would,' he added, his voice rising.

Ma took over. 'The whole valley's in trouble, not just Ramsgills – she cursed us all, don't forget. All of thy ancestors played a part in her story. I know it sounds like a fairy story to thee young 'uns, but this is real. This is Yorkshire, it's full of bloody ghosts and this one's a devil.'

Someone sniggered.

'Sarah Wainwright, I might have guessed. Thy ma were just as flighty as thee is.'

'Don't you talk about my ma, she ain't well.'

'Aye, soft in the head, and thee knows why? She saw Jennet the last time she woke, when she took my Jack. Ask her, go on, ask her. Helped me put Jennet back to rest she did and it broke her.'

Sarah was in tears. 'You evil old . . . *cow*,' she spat at Ma. 'You know nothing about my ma, nothing!'

'I've known her all her life, stupid girl. Know her better than thee does, I'll bet.'

Sarah screamed and dropped her glass, then pointed at the door.

'What? What is it, lass?'

'A-a-a woman . . .'

'Where?'

'The doorway. Can't you see her? Can't *anyone* see her? She's laughing at us!' Sarah's voice rose in hysteria.

'Buggeration,' Old Ma Ramsgill said and put herself between the door and the frightened girl. 'Get gone, Jennet Scot. Thee's done enough, leave us be.'

Everyone heard the laugh, then silence reigned once again. Sue nudged John and showed him her arm – raised in goosebumps. 'It's freezing in here.'

'I know.'

'Anyone else think I'm an evil old cow? No? Just as well. Get thyselves home, hang rosemary at thy doors and windows and sprinkle salt at every entrance. Oh, and pray to whatever god thee believes in – we're going to need them all.'

15th August 1966 – 6:00 a.m.

John opened his front door only to be pushed aside by Old Ma Ramsgill.

'Sarah Wainwright's dead. They're saying she was mauled by a dog. It weren't a dog, it were Jennet.'

'Wha—? Ma, no, tell me you're joking.'

'Why the bloody hell would I joke about summat like that? Damn fool boy.'

'But-but how do you know it's Jennet?'

'She used to appear as a barguest – an evil spirit disguised as an animal. Jennet's a black dog. She's up to her old tricks, and it don't look like she's happy to restrict herself just to our family. Get dressed, get Sue and Richie, and get thyselves to Gate House. We need to stop her.'

'How? How the bloody hell can we stop a two-hundred-year-old witch?' Sue asked from the doorway. 'From what you said last night at the wake, you've already tried once, yet she's back.'

'Aye. But we kept her spirit bound to her bones for near on thirty year. She'd still be sleeping if not for that bloody dam.'

'So we can do it again?'

Old Ma Ramsgill said nothing.

'Ma?' John prompted. 'Can we do it again?'

Ma took a deep breath, then heaved a great sigh. 'No. They'll be taking the bloody bones, if they haven't done already. They're no good to us now.'

'So what are we going to do?'

For the first time in many years, Old Ma Ramsgill looked her age. 'I don't know, Son. But we'd better damn well come up with something quick or this is only the start.'

7:00 a.m.

'This is my journal. The one I started last time,' Ma said. 'Thee read it out, John, my eyes ain't what they were. Then we'll go through the others, see what else our ancestors did.' She passed the journal to her son and a piece of paper slipped out. The family tree.

Sue picked it up and opened it out. 'All the twins,' she said. 'They all died together.' She passed the diagram to John and they studied it, their tears mingling amidst the names of John's ancestors, smudging the ink.

'Take care of that,' Old Ma Ramsgill snapped. 'Richie may need it one day – or his kids.'

'Not if we stop her,' John said, the emotion making his words crack, but the purpose and intent in his voice was still clear.

'Ramsgills have been trying to do that for two centuries, John. Yet still she's here. We'll do everything we can, but it may not be enough. When I'm gone, thee'll have to prepare Richie. Make sure he believes it.'

They sat with their own thoughts for a while as the implications of failure sank in, only the radio breaking the silence.

'Today's headlines. Two people died last night after being mauled by dogs. Adam Carter from Harrogate and Sarah Wainwright from Thruscross.'

All three Ramsgills listened in growing horror.

'Who's Adam Carter?' John asked.

'Shh,' Ma said. 'Listen.'

'Witnesses to both attacks describe the same vicious dog, despite the attacks being fifteen miles apart.

'A spokesperson for the North Yorkshire Police has urged local residents to be vigilant and report any sightings of a large unaccompanied black dog to them. Under no circumstances should the animal be approached.

'In other news . . .'

'Who's Adam Carter?' John asked again. 'What does he have to do with this?'

'Give me that family tree,' Ma snapped. 'Yes, look – at Jennet's time, Richard Ramsgill was married to Elizabeth Cartwright. It's my bet he's a descendant of that family.'

'Harrogate,' Sue said. 'He was killed in *Harrogate*, not Thruscross. I thought you said she only killed here.'

Ma stared at the journals. 'She's only killed here before. But then her bones were undisturbed. Either she's so angry at her grave being dug up that it's given her the energy to travel further, or her bones are in Harrogate.'

'No, they've got archaeologists and all sorts up there, *brushing* the bloody peat off the bones.'

'Then who knows how far she can go?' said Sue. 'Where can we send Richie if Jennet can find him wherever he is? Mary Hornwright from down the hill moved to Harrogate, we were going to send him to stay with her, but it isn't safe is it? It isn't safe anywhere.'

'Shh, listen.' Old Ma Ramsgill pointed at the radio.

'In preparation for the opening of the new reservoir in the Washburn Valley, Thruscross Dam has already been closed to perform a test flood. The water should be at the expected level of the final reservoir in the next few days.'

The Ramsgills stared at the radio, all thinking the same thing. *How will Jennet react to that?*

'Oh! What's that?' Sue jumped to her feet at the sound of a horn, but John beat her to the window.

'Fire engine and ambulance. They're heading to the dam. Must have been another accident.'

Silence.

It was broken by Sue, who almost whispered, 'John, do you see her?'

'Who?'

'That woman. On the edge of the wood. Staring at the house.'

'Where?'

'What does she look like?' Old Ma Ramsgill asked, joining them at the window.

'Young, long dark hair, a bit wild. Dressed in, I don't know, a wool skirt? It's plain anyway, dowdy. And she's clutching a shawl around herself.'

'That's her.'

Sue and John stared at Ma.

'We have no time to waste. She's coming after thee next. Either that or Richie.'

'She's smiling,' Sue said. 'Waving. Now she's gone. What does that mean? Why did she wave? She looked almost – friendly.'

'Let's hope she recognised thee.'

'Recognised her – what do you mean, Ma?' John asked.

'Remember I told thee last week – the only one in the village that didn't shun her were Mary Farmer. Thy great-great-great . . . Bugger it. Thy ancestor, Sue.'

'So am I safe?'

Old Ma Ramsgill shrugged. 'Who knows? She might have been mocking thee, but thee've a better chance than the rest of us, lass.'

'Does that mean Richie's safe too?'

Ma stared out the window. 'Doubt it, lass. He may have Farmer blood, but he's also a Ramsgill, and he bears the name of the one she hates most.'

A banging on the door made them all jump. John went to answer it. He came back into the room with Wilf.

'I've seen her, Ma, I've seen her. So's the Stockdale girl.'

'So have I,' said Sue.

'She's going to kill the whole damn lot of us,' Wilf said, sinking down on to the sofa.

'Not if I can help it,' Ma said and shuffled back to her armchair. 'But we're going to have to move quick.'

'What can we do? Her bones will soon be gone, and anyway, we can't get near them. We can't bind her to them as you did before,' Sue said, her fear evident in her strident voice.

'The reservoir,' John said from the window. 'It's already filling, if we bind her to one of those buildings, she'll be under the water and can do no harm.'

'Aye, that might work, Son.'

'But which building? What has the strongest connection to her?'

'The church,' Ma said. 'She hated it, as it did her. And it'll be the strongest protection.'

'Can you do it, though? Can you stop her, Ma?' Wilf asked.

'I bloody well hope so, but I don't know, Wilf. I don't know. She's stronger this time and I'm old. Old and tired. But I can tell thee one thing – I'll have a damned good go at it, thee see if I don't.'

Return

15th August 1966 – 7:00 p.m.

Sue opened the door to the cottage to let Ma in. 'God, what an awful night,' she said as her mother-in-law entered.

'God has nowt to do with it, lass. This is Jennet. Good to see thee's nailed horseshoes on the door, at least thee's listening now. Has thee a fire lit?'

'Yes, come through.'

Ma sat in the chair nearest the fire and held her hands and feet to the heat. 'A glass of stout wouldn't go amiss.'

'Here you are, Ma, all ready for you,' John said, offering a pint of Samuel Smith's Oatmeal Stout to his mother. 'Got special supplies in from the Stonehouse.'

'Good, I'm going to need it.'

'Are you sure you wouldn't be more comfortable at Gate House?'

'Don't be a fool, boy, she knows it too well, it's the first place Jennet will look for me when she realises what we're up to. Did thee get the stone from Wolf Farm?'

'Here.' John picked up the stone he'd prised loose from the hearth of Jennet's old home. 'Ma . . .'

'What, Son?' Ma waited. 'Spit it out, what's up?'

'Have you seen the water level?'

'Aye.'

'Well, what do we do?'

'What does thee think thee bloody does? Swim.'

All three jumped at a flash of lightning and immediate thunderclap.

Ma relaxed into her chair and sipped her stout.

'Ma?'

'Give me a minute, Son.' She closed her eyes. 'Aye, she's strong all right. This storm? It's her. She's watching the valley flood and she loves it. Her curse is coming to pass.' Ma opened her eyes. 'We have to do this now, while she's distracted. Any news from Wilf or Stockdales?'

'Haven't heard anything.'

'Good. We'd know if either had been harmed. She's forgotten about them – at least for the moment. We can't waste any time. Pass me my bag, Son. And get ready with that hearthstone.'

John passed her the rucksack and she pulled out a canvas drawstring bag, then the journals.

'Do you really need all of those?'

'Hope not, Son. But better to have 'em. Just in case.'

John nodded.

'Right, thee two, both ready?'

John and Sue nodded.

'Where's nipper?'

'With my sister in York,' Sue replied.

Ma nodded. 'Let's hope that's far enough. At least we know she's here.'

'Stand by with that stone. I'll tell thee when I'm ready.' Ma heaved herself to her feet and stood directly in front of the fire, bracing herself against the stone wall before she stood straight and opened her canvas bag.

She pulled out a cloth figure.

'What the hell's that, Ma?'

'A poppet. It's filled with moors' peat and heather.'

'Is that supposed to be Jennet?' Sue asked.

'It's supposed to represent her.'

'How? It's just a doll, and a bloody rough one at that,' John said.

'Did thee not hear me? It *represents* her. It has the earth of her home and a slip of paper with her name and family history inside. Now, is thee going to ask me for a lesson or let me get on with this and save thy son?'

No answer.

'Right then, glad we've got that sorted, now hush while I do this.'

She glared at her son and daughter-in-law then, satisfied, took a deep breath and held the poppet out before her.

'Woman of cloth thee is now.

'Woman of flesh and blood thee once were.

'I name thee Jennet Scot.

'No more shall thee do me and mine wrong.

'Never again shall thee take the life of a Ramsgill.

'By the power of the gods, my will and that of the Ramsgills I command this.'

She threw the poppet on to the fire and John and Sue jumped back at the flare of flame and spark.

'I bind thee, Jennet Scot, to this valley.' Ma threw a handful of salt into the fire, which burned green and blue.

'I bind thee, Jennet Scot, to this valley.' A handful of rosemary followed.

'I bind thee, Jennet Scot, to this valley.' Heather this time.

'Is that it?' Sue asked.

'Not nearly,' Ma replied. 'If we're lucky she won't have noticed yet.' She turned back to the fire. 'Throw in that stone.'

'What?'

'Thee heard me. Get it in the fire, quick.'

John did as he was told.

'I bind thee, Jennet Scot, to this hearthstone of Wolf Farm.' Salt.

'I bind thee, Jennet Scot, to this hearthstone of Wolf Farm.' Rosemary.

'I bind thee, Jennet Scot, to this hearthstone of Wolf Farm.' Heather.

Ma turned to John and Sue. 'Get it out of the fire. Use them tongs. And get it to the church, quick as thee likes. She won't notice, yet. This cottage means nowt to her, it's new. But she ain't daft, she'll work it out soon enough.'

John fished the stone out of the fire with the poker and tongs and it clanged on the hearth.

'Care, boy! Don't break it, this is our only chance.'

'Sorry, Ma.'

Sue passed him a folded towel and John lifted the stone and headed out the door.

'Go quickly, Son. Thee too, Sue. I'll distract her best I can.'

'I bloody well hope so,' John muttered.

'John, look how deep it is already.'

'I know.'

'How can we get this bloody great big stone out to the church by swimming? It'll drown us both.'

'Wait here.' John dashed off and returned ten minutes later dragging a small rowing boat along the edge of what was now most decidedly looking like a reservoir.

'Wilf's old fishing boat,' he said with a grin. 'The old bugger had me rescue it from the river and drag it up the bloody hill last month. Can't bear to see anything go to waste or be chucked out until there's nothing left of it to chuck. It should get us and the stone out there, at least.'

They heaved the stone into the bottom of the boat, then John held it steady while Sue climbed in. He pushed off and launched himself inside – a sprawl of legs and arms that she could not help laughing at despite the severity of the situation. Her laughter cut off at a vicious blast of lightning and thunder. 'That struck the bank – she only just missed us.'

'Bloody hell! She knows what we're doing – quick, get rowing, we haven't got much time. I hope to God Ma knows what *she's* doing.'

The boat bumped against the stone wall of the church and Sue only just managed to grab hold of a gargoyle on the roof edge to hold them in place.

'John, the door's underwater already – how are we going to get the stone inside?'

'I'll break a bloody hole in the roof if I have to,' he said. 'Richie's life depends on it. I won't lose another child to this bitch – however old or powerful she is.'

Sue said nothing, just held on tighter with gritted teeth.

John clambered on to the roof of the church. 'Pass me the stone.'

'How? I need both hands to hang on!'

'I'll hold on to the boat. Just put the stone on the roof.'

Sue let go, noticing John's knuckles turn white as he took the strain from his awkward position. She needed both hands and a knee to heave the hearthstone up, and as soon as she let go it started to slide.

'No!' they both cried, and John let go of the boat's gunwale to stop it slithering into the water.

'John!' Sue shouted and grabbed for the edge of the church roof. Her momentum forced the boat from under her and she splashed into the water, kicking hard to help herself gain purchase on the wet, slippery slate tiles. Lightning and thunder cracked overhead.

'Sue!'

'Get the stone inside, I'm okay.'

'No, grab my hand.'

'John, please, this could mean Richie's life.'

John said nothing, but turned himself around, his leg securing the stone. He began the laborious task of pushing it up the steep roof, but every inch he gained was immediately lost again. The roof was too wet, too mossy, and too steep. He had no choice but to begin prising away slate tiles where he was.

'They won't budge – they're fixed tight,' he called.

'Then smash them!' Sue had managed to get a leg on to the roof and hauled herself to safety.

'Grab hold of the stone and brace yourself, don't let it slip.'

She shuffled over and used her body as a brace between the stone and the gargoyle she'd anchored herself to earlier.

John sat back and used the heel of his boot to smash the roof tiles. When he had a hole large enough, he started to push the hearthstone towards the gap.

'John, no!'

'What?'

'Is the inside flooded?'

He peered through the hole. 'I don't think so, not yet – the water level's still low.'

'The stone can't break, it's our only chance. We need to wait until it's deep. Then it can sink and stay in one piece.'

John looked at her. 'You're right, but can we wait that long?' He glanced up as another flash of lightning lit them from above and cringed at the force of the thunder.

'We have to.'

* * *

Old Ma Ramsgill continued her chanting of, 'I bind thee, Jennet Scot, to this valley. Thee'll do no more harm here. I bind thee Jennet Scot—' She screamed as something knocked her down. Screamed again as her body broke. Then resumed her chant.

The storm above the valley intensified.

'Got thee now, bitch,' Ma whispered. 'Got thee on t' run – too busy celebrating thy freedom, forgot what was—' She screamed again as lightning struck nearby.

'Missed, bitch!' She cackled into the sudden dark as the lights went out. 'That's all thee's got? Terrorise my family, would thee? Ha!'

Another scream as her leg was twisted and she felt – and heard – another bone break. 'Do what thee likes to me – I've lived a long life, more than thee ever did. Too late to stop me now!'

The fire flared and sparks leapt out into the room.

'No!' Old Ma Ramsgill screamed, louder than she had for sixty years. Sparks landed on the pile of journals and bred flames. As they took hold, Ma forced her broken body along the floor and reached out. She found her own journal, dragged it out of the inferno, beat it against the floor, then rolled on top of it to smother the flames. She passed out.

'John!' Sue screamed as lightning struck the steeple. 'Do it now – she's too strong.'

John glanced up at the sky then turned to Sue. 'I don't know if it's deep enough.'

'It has to be, just do it before she stops us.'

He nodded, once, then pushed the heavy stone towards the hole in the church roof.

Right at the edge he paused and looked at his wife. 'Are you sure?'

'Yes. Just do it.'

Lightning struck again, blinding them both.

As Sue's sight slowly came back, she searched for her husband. 'John? John? *John!*' The last word was a shriek. He had gone.

Sobbing, she pulled herself to the hole in the roof and peered down. All was black. She could see nothing.

Lightning flashed again and she had a split-second image of John's twisted body, floating face down in the water below.

'Nooo! John, no!' She turned her face to the sky as distant thunder rumbled and the church bell pealed.

Another flash. John still didn't move. There was nothing she could do. She couldn't get to him and Richie needed a mother.

The bell continued to ring and she realised: it was Jennet. She'd claimed another victim, but the bell was the only way she could now express her fury.

The ringing faded. It was over. At least for now.

Soundlessly, Sue slid off the roof and into the water. She swam ashore, silent tears adding to the new Thruscross Reservoir. She was a widow but her son was safe. The only person left on this earth who carried Ramsgill blood.

16th August 1966 – 2:00 p.m.

'Here thee goes, Ma,' Wilf said, passing her a heavy carrier bag. 'Don't let the nurses see.'

Ma peered into the bag and grinned before pulling out one of many bottles of Oatmeal Stout. 'That's good of thee, this'll do a damn sight more good than them pills they keep making me take.'

'Don't be daft, Ma. Everyone knows what thee did – thee'll never have to pay for another drink in the Stonehouse, that's for damn certain.'

'Right, well give Sue one then and thee can bring some more tomorrow.'

Wilf chuckled as Sue walked back into the room and took the bottle Ma held out to her.

'Is it really over, Ma?'

'I bloody well hope so, lass. At least for now.'

'What do you mean? Will she be back?'

'She's always managed it in the past. Just promise me one thing.'

'What?'

'Don't drink the bloody tap water and don't let Richie have even a drop.'

'What?'

'That reservoir. It's to supply drinking water. Don't use the tap water and *never* let Richie – or his kids – drink it.'

Sue stared at her.

'Jennet's in there – in that water. She's bound to it. If even a drop of Thruscross water makes it into the glass of a Ramsgill, Jennet will gain strength. Maybe enough to come back.'

21st August 1966 – 2:00 p.m.

'Ey lass, thee's a good 'un to visit me every day as thee does.'

'Ma, Ma, Ma!'

Sue lifted Richie up on to Old Ma Ramsgill's hospital bed and he snuggled up to his grandmother.

'Did thee rescue any of the journals?' Ma asked once she'd hugged her grandson.

Sue shook her head. 'Only the one you saved. But rain stopped the house burning.'

Ma nodded. 'Keep that journal safe, and make sure thee passes it on to Richie and he knows to pass it on to his kids. There's a lot of stuff from the others in there. I hope I've copied all the important bits. Should have left the others at Gate House.'

'Ma, about Gate House . . .'

Old Ma Ramsgill looked up sharply at her daughter-in-law.

'It-it was struck by lightning. I'm sorry, it's gone. But you'll be all right, you'll stay with us.'

Ma said nothing, but her sorrow was clear on her face.

'There's something else. They're going to demolish the church,' Sue added quietly.

'What's that thee's saying?'

'Someone must have seen us that night on the church roof. They're concerned about people swimming out to it if they leave it. Part of the steeple was still above the water when the reservoir was full. Anyway, they've decided it's too much of a risk. When they let the water out, they'll take it apart and take all the internal fittings to that new monstrosity they've built on the other hill.'

'Buggeration!'

'Does that mean she'll be free again?'

'Don't know, lass. It'll still be holy ground, it depends on whether they move her stone. Did it go right to the bottom?'

'I don't know.'

'Then we can only hope, lass, nowt more we can do now. Pass me another of them stouts.'

The End

Jennet is stirring once more and will return to the moors at Thruscross in the full-length novel, **Jennet: A Novel (Ghosts of Thores-Cross #3),** *due to be released in 2018.*

Please sign up to Karen's newsletter on her website: www.karenperkinsauthor.com and/or join her on Facebook for regular updates.

Knight of Betrayal:

A Medieval Haunting

Ghosts of Knaresborough (Book 1)

From the Back Cover:

"A pacy, page-turning ghost story with a twisted difference! A must read."

The repercussions of an horrific crime reverberate through the centuries as the 12th century ghosts seek redemption and revenge, with no thought for anyone unlucky enough to get in their way.

1170, Canterbury Cathedral:
Four knights break sanctuary to brutally murder Archbishop Thomas Becket for their king, Henry II.

Running from their crime, the four knights - Hugh de Morville, William de Tracy, Reginald FitzUrse and Richard le Brett - flee north to Knaresborough Castle where Morville is overlord. Initially celebrating ridding their king of the pest that Becket had become, they find themselves increasingly isolated as the Church and public opinion turn against them.

2015, Knaresborough, North Yorkshire:
August is feva time - a celebration and festival of the arts. The Castle Players are to perform a play of their own creation: Knight of Betrayal, based on the events leading up to Becket's murder.

Taking the honour seriously, they work hard to get into character - but after they experiment with a spirit board, are they channelling more than just the characters of the knights they are portraying?

Cast List

Main Historical Figures and Titles

Henry II – King of England, Duke of Normandy, Duke of Aquitaine, Lord of Ireland
Thomas Becket – Archbishop of Canterbury

Sir Hugh de Morville – Baron of Burgh-on-the-Sands, Lord of the Manor of Cnaresburg
Sir William de Tracy – Baron of Bradninch
Sir Reginald FitzUrse – Lord of the Manor of Williton
Sir Richard le Brett (also known as Richard le Breton/de Brito)

Cnaresburg and Yorkshire:
Sir William de Percy – Baron of Topcliffe, Lord of Spofford and Wetherby
Sir William de Courcy – Lord of Harewood
Sir William de Stoteville
Lady Helwise de Morville

Other:
Sir Hamelin Plantagenet – Earl of Surrey
Sir William de Mandeville – Earl of Essex
Sir Richard de Humez – Constable of Normandy
Sir Ranulf de Broc – Overlord of Saltwood Castle
Hugh Mauclerk

Modern Characters
Helen Forrester – director and scriptwriter
Paul Fuller – plays Henry II
Charlie Thorogood – plays Thomas Becket
Ed Thomas – plays Hugh de Morville
Mike Bates– plays William de Tracy
Dan Stoddard – plays Reginald FitzUrse
Sarah Stoddard – plays Richard le Brett
Alec Greene – sound and lighting technician
Donna – owner of Spellbound
John Stoddard – son of Dan and Sarah
Kate Stoddard – daughter of Dan and Sarah
Richard Armitage – feva committee member

Place Names
I have used the historical spellings of place names in the knights' timeline and modern ones in the Castle Players' timeline:

Cnaresburg – Knaresborough
Goldesburgh – Goldsborough
Plumton – Plompton
Riche Mont – Richmond
River Nydde – River Nidd
Screven – Scriven
Spofford – Spofforth

Chapter 1

Saltwood Castle

29th December 1170

'This is our chance. You heard the King's words,' Sir Reginald FitzUrse said. 'Becket has shamed him.'

'He called us all drones and traitors for allowing Becket to get away with it,' Sir William de Tracy said.

'Yes!' shouted FitzUrse, and slammed his fist against the table to emphasise the word. The four men sitting with him flinched at his exuberance. Sir Reginald FitzUrse, or The Bear as he liked to be called, resembled the ursine creatures he was named for in more ways than one. Large, hairy, loud and strong with a temper to beware of, his friends and vassals were afraid of him, although were eager to please him – even the mature yet impressionable Sir William de Tracy. Sir Hugh de Morville exchanged an exasperated glance with Sir Ranulf de Broc – the overlord of Saltwood Castle and the knights' host.

'No one has avenged me,' FitzUrse quoted their king, Henry Plantagenet of England, leaning forward now and staring at each man in turn. 'No one has avenged me,' he repeated.

'A clear plea,' Broc, FitzUrse's master in the King's household, agreed. 'King Henry raised Thomas Becket from a low-born clerk to Archbishop of Canterbury, for God's sake, and look how he has repaid him.'

Tracy nodded with enthusiasm. 'Yes! He excommunicated l'Évêque, Foliot and Salisbury, and for no good reason.'

Broc glanced at him in annoyance. 'As I was saying, two bishops and the Archbishop of York excommunicated and damned for eternity for crowning the Young King.'

'Well, his father, King Henry, still lives.' Morville tried to calm the rising tempers as Broc signalled to his steward to refill the jugs of fine Rhenish wine. 'It may be customary for a king to crown his successor before his own death in Normandy, but it is rare in England. Only King Stephen did it, and that was just to spite the Empress Matilda.'

'It is King Henry's prerogative!' FitzUrse slammed the table again, and Sir Richard le Brett – still a boy – steadied the now full flagon of Rhenish, then proceeded to empty it into goblets. Morville sighed as he watched Tracy down half in a single gulp.

'Yes,' Tracy slurred. 'It's nothing to do with Becket. It would not surprise me if Becket meant to depose the Young King and try for the crown himself.'

'Always was an ambitious bastard,' Brett agreed, then picked up a bone and noisily sucked the marrow from it.

'Are you sure we arrived on England's shores before Mandeville and Humez?'

'Yes, I have had my men patrolling the coasts to slow them down. They failed me when they allowed Becket to beach from France. They will not fail me again.'

'How can you be so sure?' FitzUrse asked, pointing a half-eaten pheasant leg at his host.

Broc laughed. 'Oh, I can be sure. One captain lost his head – the rest all want to keep theirs.'

Morville drained his wine, once again regretting FitzUrse's choice of ally. The other men laughed, and Morville realised they were well into their cups. He poured more wine and drank again – in their cups may well be the only way they'd survive this day.

'So we shall beat them to Becket?' Tracy asked.

'We have to,' Broc said. 'If they arrest Becket, they shall receive all the accolades – the two of them already hold more castles and titles than the five of us put together. If we can take Becket to the King, he will surely be indebted to us and who knows what his favour may bring?'

'Then what are we waiting for?' FitzUrse roared, pushing himself to his feet. His fellow knights followed suit, throwing down the remains of the meat they'd been gnawing on and draining their goblets.

The men-at-arms seated in the hall below shoved as much meat in their mouths as possible before following their masters to the stables. Half an hour later the company of over a hundred armed men cantered through the imposing towers of the castle's gate and took the road to Canterbury.

While Broc garrisoned his men in the town, FitzUrse, Morville, Tracy and Brett – along with a small retinue of their most trusted vassals – clattered through the gatehouse to the Archbishop's Palace and dismounted in the courtyard.

Morville glanced at his companions, still concerned at the glazed eyes which the three-hour ride had done nothing to clear.

FitzUrse produced another wineskin which he passed to Tracy after taking a large slug himself. 'Are you ready for this?'

'We need to disarm,' Morville said before the other knights – still focused on the wine – could reply.

'Disarm? God's blood, Hugh, we are here on the King's business.'

'This is a house of God – the Archbishop will have mere monks, priests and clerks about him. No men-at-arms and no weapons. We shall not need arms to arrest him.'

'He is correct,' said Brett, 'we can kill him with our bare hands if necessary.'

'Richard!' Morville was horrified. 'We are not here to kill him, merely to arrest him and take him to King Henry to deal with as *he* sees fit.'

'If necessary, the boy said. If necessary,' FitzUrse jumped to his sycophant's defence.

'Why should it be necessary?' Morville asked.

'Thomas Becket stands against not only the Young King, but King Henry himself. He has just returned from exile. Look what he has done already, who knows what he would do when called to account? We must be ready for anything.'

'But we leave swords and mail here,' Morville insisted. Despite FitzUrse's bluster, as Baron of Burgh-on-the-Sands, Sir Hugh de Morville held the highest status amongst the four men.

FitzUrse hesitated, then succumbed to him. 'Very well, if it shall make you happy. Arms and mail stay here.'

Mauclerk, Morville's clerk, helped the knights out of their heavy hauberks and mail hoods and piled the armour, along with their long blades, under a nearby mulberry tree. 'They will be safe here with me,' he said.

FitzUrse glanced round the knights. William de Tracy in particular looked nervous and vulnerable without his arms or armour. Despite his thirty seven years and own barony, he appeared younger with a boyish clean-shaven face, copper curls and slim build. At this moment, if one ignored the lines of worry around his eyes, he appeared a child.

FitzUrse passed him the wine. 'Who are we?' he called.

'The King's men,' the other three chorused.

'Who are we?' FitzUrse shouted louder.

'The King's men!'

'Who are we?' Louder still.

'The King's men!'

'Á Henry Plantagenet!' FitzUrse roared, and the others joined in, the wineskin forgotten and trampled on the cobblestones.

FitzUrse crossed to the door of the great hall and banged his clenched paw upon it. 'In the name of the King, open up!' Then again, and again, the other knights joining in the cry and the thumps on the door – even Morville was carried away now with the purpose of their mission.

'Thomas Becket, in the name of King Henry, permit entry or we shall break down this door!' Tracy yelled, then stumbled back at the sound of bolts being drawn.

Chapter 2

'This is an insult,' FitzUrse fumed. 'He affronts the King by keeping us waiting.'

'I suspect it is the four of us he intends to disrespect,' Morville countered.

FitzUrse glared at him. 'We are the King's men. He affronts us, he affronts King Henry.'

The entrance of a monk interrupted the resultant awkward silence. 'The Archbishop shall see you now.' He backed against the open door as the knights passed through.

Thomas Becket was still seated at table in the company of near half a dozen men, and Morville recognised John de Salisbury, Benedict de Peterborough and William de Canterbury. A monk seated at Becket's right hand glared at them, but the knights dismissed him. He was of no consequence.

'Ahh, Hugh, Reginald, William, how good of you to welcome me back to England's fine shores. It has been long that I have been away, and there is no sweeter pleasure than returning home and reuniting with old friends.'

The knights faltered, unsure of how to proceed in the face of this effusive and seemingly sincere welcome. Then FitzUrse stepped forward.

'We are not here to welcome you, Becket.' The Archbishop's brows rose at this calculated insult; the proper form of address was Your Grace. 'We are here to return you to Normandy. You have grievously wronged the King.'

'Wronged the King? My Lord, what do you mean? What evil and disgusting lies have been told of me?'

'No lies, Becket.' FitzUrse's face reddened further under the mass of hair that covered it. 'Do you deny that you have excommunicated three loyal subjects of King Henry? Roger de Pont l'Évêque, Gilbert Foliot and Jocelin de Salisbury – the King's most loyal Archbishop of York and two of his most loyal bishops. What say you to the charge?'

'Those facts are correct. Pray, what is your complaint?'

'What is my complaint?' FitzUrse's voice rose and he stepped forward, then glanced back at his fellow knights who stayed where they were and showed no sign of speaking. He grunted in exasperation.

'Those three honourable, devout and loyal subjects met the King's wishes in crowning his son, Henry the Young King, as his successor. As you know this is normal practice in France and a custom that our king desired to be enacted on England's shores. Yet you bring down the worst punishment on these good, God-fearing men – a punishment worse even than torture and death, for it will condemn their souls to reside in Hell for eternity.' FitzUrse paused for breath, and Archbishop Becket waved him to continue with a smile. He looked as relaxed as if he were enjoying a much anticipated reunion with the friends he had claimed them to be.

FitzUrse continued with another aggravated glance at his silent companions, 'By excommunicating them for the crowning of the Young King, you have declared yourself against not only the Young King, but King Henry himself.' FitzUrse pushed himself to his tallest and thrust out his chest. 'As such, by the command of King Henry, I arrest you for the good of England, and charge you with sedition and treason.'

'Sedition *and* treason? Surely it must be one or the other, Reginald. Committing treason or inciting others to commit treason. King Henry would know that you cannot charge me with both. Which tells me that you and your friends are here on your own recognisance, perhaps to find favour with Henry, hmm?' Becket stood as he spoke and planted his fists on the table before him, pulling the full force of his position as Archbishop of Canterbury about him. FitzUrse stood his ground, but the others shrank back.

'Henry also knows that it is the duty of the Archbishop of Canterbury to crown a king, an obligation not given to the Archbishop of York nor any other man. King Henry accuses you as traitor. You shall come with us.'

'Do I need to remind you that you are my sworn vassal, Reginald? Your good self, Hugh de Morville, and you, William de Tracy, all swore fealty to me. You,' he peered at Brett, 'you have not, although I know you, do I not?'

Brett ground his teeth, but said naught.

'No matter. As my sworn vassals, I demand you leave my presence. I shall hear no more of this nonsense.'

FitzUrse strode forward to Becket's table and planted his own fists upon it. 'Yes, we swore fealty to you, but as Chancellor of England, not as Archbishop of Canterbury. Yet even so, the fealty sworn was second to King Henry. I – we—' he glanced behind him, disgusted that his fellow knights still hung back, '—serve the King above all others. Including you.'

'Then tell Henry I have no issue with either himself or the Young King. Coronations in England are performed by the Archbishop of Canterbury and no other. Now leave my presence and explain to *our* king that I am his loyal servant still. The excommunications stand and are an issue between myself, the bishops concerned, Pope Alexander III, and no other. King Henry has my love and fealty, as he has yours. Please try your best to understand that and depart. This has grown tiresome. I bid you goodnight, My Lords.'

Becket turned, his green robes swirling, and left by a door the knights had not noticed, followed by his clerics. At a loss and alone in the great hall, the four knights turned to depart.

Chapter 3

'Where is he?' Broc – standing at the head of a column of men-at-arms – demanded. The knights looked at each other and said naught. 'Are you telling me that four knights of the realm, four of the King's own warriors, were no match for one paltry churchman?'

FitzUrse stepped forward. 'We offered Becket a chance to come gracefully. He refused. Now we shall take him.'

Broc glanced at the pile of swords and mail with contempt. 'You had better dress yourselves then.'

The knights hurried to the mulberry tree and Brett hauled up the first heavy hauberk: FitzUrse's. He held the coat of mail wide, heaved it up, and dropped it over FitzUrse's outstretched arms and shoulders. The Bear grunted as the weight landed on him, then straightened up and shrugged it over his torso. Mauclerk did the same for Morville, then Tracy and Brett helped each other into theirs.

'Ready boys?' Broc taunted.

'Always, My Lord,' FitzUrse replied, hefting his sword, then strode back to the door of the great hall of the Archbishop's Palace. It remained barred to them.

Tracy glanced behind at the smirking Broc, and called, 'Round the back! There must be another way in.'

Without a word – or a glance at his master – FitzUrse led the way round the great building to the administration buildings attached to the north side of the cathedral.

'There.' Tracy pointed at a window under repair. 'The masons have left it incomplete!'

'Up you go then, William,' FitzUrse said. 'Climb in and unlock the door.'

Tracy glanced at him, then back at the window. His fear of FitzUrse was greater than his fear of heights, however, and he searched the stonework for a path up to the open invitation.

Just as he was about to start his climb, Brett called, 'One moment, William.'

Tracy turned and smiled when he saw the young knight dragging a ladder.

'The masons must have thrown it into the shrubbery and fled when they saw the men.' Brett nodded at the score of men-at-arms behind Broc.

'Your lucky day,' Broc said. 'What are you waiting for?'

Tracy glanced at him, then led the way up to the window, followed by

Brett. Morville was the only man to think to hold the ladder steady for them.

When both had disappeared through the narrow aperture into the archive building, then made their way downstairs to let the others in, FitzUrse led the way to the chancel door to gain entrance to the cathedral itself, sword drawn.

'It's locked,' Tracy said.

'Then we'll break it down,' FitzUrse said. He raised his hand to bang for entry but the door swung away before his fist connected, causing him to stumble.

He glared up at the monk, expecting to see mirth, which he would have sliced off his face in an instant. Instead, he saw fear.

'The cathedral is open to all,' the monk at the door said in a shaky whisper, blanching at the sight of steel. FitzUrse ignored him and brushed past, searching the gloom of the great cathedral for his quarry. His eyes lit on a huddle of men. 'North transept. By the high altar. Onward.'

He strode forward, heartened by the sound of purposeful boots on flagstones behind him.

'Becket! Traitor! You will come with us by the order of the King.'

'I am no traitor, Reginald. The traitors here are you and your friends. You are my sworn vassals yet you dare enter the sanctuary of Our Lord with swords drawn?'

'We are the sworn vassals of the King, above all other men!'

'And what about God? You insult Him by entering His house so armed?'

'Traitor!' FitzUrse accused again, unable to conjure a more ribald riposte.

'And what are you?' Becket taunted, pushing past two of his monks who were doing their best to shield him. 'A procurer! And I see the Lord Broc, the King's most senior whoremaster is here too. Good afternoon, Sir Ranulf. Has the King really sent his pimps to procure an archbishop rather than whores? He must think highly of you after all!'

FitzUrse roared with rage and rushed forward, his impetus enough to carry Morville, Tracy and Brett in his wake.

'Reginald, are you mad?' Becket's voice at last portrayed fear, but it only drove the knights on and broke the paralysed terror of Becket's men as half of them fled. Now it was four against four, although the knights had an army at their backs; the clerics had naught but an altar.

FitzUrse and Brett grabbed the priest. 'Tracy, bend over,' FitzUrse ordered. At Tracy's bewildered look, he explained further. 'We shall get him on your back, then carry him outside.'

'No!' Becket lunged at the nearby pillar, clutching it to his bosom as if his life depended on it.

FitzUrse burst into bellows of laughter as Brett tried to pull the Archbishop's grip from the pillar and Tracy attempted to heave the man away. Morville stood, sword raised to keep those clerics who had stayed under guard, whilst Broc and his men stood back, seemingly viewing the proceedings as a mummers' show.

FitzUrse flicked out his sword and caught the Archbishop's fur cap which he flung towards the altar, then smacked the holy man's rump with the flat of his blade. Becket roared in outrage and Tracy gave up the tug of war, dumping the Archbishop in an ungainly heap on the floor.

'Sire!' one of the monks, Grim, cried out, and escaped Morville to rush to his master's side.

Becket jumped to his feet, his face red, and confronted FitzUrse. 'You *have* gone mad, Reginald. You have lost what few wits you were born with! This is no way to treat any man, especially in God's house, never mind *me*. You swore fealty to me! Yet you make a mockery, not only of yourselves, but of My, *Our* Lord, and His sanctuary! Leave this place and do not return!'

In reply, FitzUrse took hold of the Archbishop's cloak and pulled the man closer. Before he could speak, however, Becket spat in his face.

'Unhand me, *pander*. You are not worthy to touch this cloth.'

'By God, men, if you do not shut him up, I shall rip the very head from his body,' FitzUrse roared. He let go his hold of the holy cloth and stood back to give himself room to swing his sword. Becket bent forwards, clasping his hands before his face in prayer, beseeching God to be ready to welcome him through the gates of Heaven.

Tracy lunged before FitzUrse finished his backswing. The monk – Grim – raised his arm to protect his master, but Tracy did not flinch. His blade glanced off the top of the Archbishop's head, sliced a deep gouge through Grim's upper arm, and parted the flesh of Becket's shoulder until he struck bone.

Grim screamed in agony, yet Becket barely paused in his prayers. 'Into Thy care, Lord, I commend my spirit.' He sank to his knees as the blood flowing from his wounds weakened him.

Tracy struck at his head once more, screaming as he swung his blade and the priest fell.

Tracy rested on his sword, the effort of such a heavy swing winding him, and Brett stepped forward.

Shrieking in rage, he thrust his blade at Becket, slicing the crown of his head clean away. Sparks flew, momentarily gracing Becket with a halo as the steel blade shattered. 'That's for William, my friend, the King's brother! He died of a broken heart when you refused his marriage. Now you have paid the price for his suffering,' Brett shouted.

Grim fell over his master, weeping, and Hugh Mauclerk – Morville's clerk – stepped forward. With the tip of his sword, he scraped the pinkish-white brain matter from the holy skull and smeared it over the bloody flags. 'That's one pesky priest who shall give no further trouble.'

Morville grabbed him, horrified at the callousness of his man – a man who had played no part in the actual deed. 'Hurry, we must depart.'

The knights turned to leave but paused at the glare of Broc and the horrified faces of the men who stood with him. 'What have you done?' Broc said.

'We have cured the King of his priestly troubles,' FitzUrse said, 'and you stood by and watched.'

Broc gritted his teeth in thought then said, 'Go. Back to Saltwood Castle. Take your belongings and ride north. Scotland may be safe for you.'

'And you?' Morville enquired.

'Me? I shall go to the King and plead your case.'

A man burst into the cathedral and hurried to his master. He hesitated at the sight before the high altar, then whispered into Broc's ear.

'Mandeville and Humez have beached. Hurry, you must leave.'

Chapter 4

12th June 2015

Friday night rehearsal over, the cast and crew of Knaresborough's amateur drama group – The Castle Players – headed out of the Castle Theatre to the Borough Bailiff for a pint or few and the debriefing. The rehearsal had not gone well and everyone had more anticipation for the alcohol than the discussion.

Helen Forrester's phone rang. She checked the display, then called to the others to order her a large gin and tonic and she'd catch them up.

'Hello?' she said into the phone, a mass of nerves as she prepared to hear the verdict on her proposal.

Half an hour later she joined the rest of the group in the pub. 'That was Richard Armitage from feva. They want us to perform *Knight of Betrayal*.'

'Bloody hell, that's fantastic news,' Paul Fuller said, 'well done, Helen!'

Feva was Knaresborough's annual festival of entertainment and visual arts, attracting authors, poets, musicians and artists of all persuasion from all over the country, as well as hosting a number of local attractions. It was quite a coup to have been chosen to put on a play as part of the event – and would be a definite boost to the Castle Players' status.

'They liked the idea of a play about Thomas Becket's death, given that the knights responsible hid out here afterwards. Apparently the BBC set a play here about fifty years ago, but since then nothing. Most events have been centred on John of Gaunt or Isabella – Edward II's queen.'

'But Morville and the others are barely acknowledged here – did you know there's not one book about them in the bookshop?'

Helen shrugged. 'I guess the feva committee aren't so eager to brush history under the carpet.'

'Well, thank God for that,' Charlie Thorogood said. 'Otherwise we'd have been wasting our time with the play.'

'Charlie! We've only just started rehearsals,' Sarah Stoddard said.

'True, it's Helen who's put the time in writing the script,' agreed Sarah's husband, Dan.

'The main thing is we've got the green light,' Helen said. As writer and director, the hardest part of her role was to keep the egos of her actors in check, and she was well used to intervening before squabbles erupted into full-blown fights.

'We have until August to rehearse – that's two months and, judging by tonight's performance, we'll need every day of that.'

'Plus the sets to paint, props to source and costumes to make,' Ed Thomas said.

'And the sound and lighting programme, and equipment – don't forget that,' Alec Greene added.

Helen held her hands up. 'Yes, we have a lot to do, but it's nothing we can't handle. We've been given a grant of £500 to help with expenses so we can buy some props in.'

'What? They said yes? That's fantastic!'

Helen grinned. 'I know. We'll all pitch in with the sets and costumes. This is our big chance to play to a full house. If it goes well, we may get into Harrogate Theatre for a run too – maybe even York or Leeds.'

'Let's just focus on Knaresborough first,' Alec cautioned. 'Bad luck to count our chickens.'

'True enough, Alec. First things first,' Helen said. 'Speaking of the first things, what on earth went wrong tonight?'

Silence.

'Well?' Helen prompted. 'I can't be the only one who noticed. You know the lines, but it just didn't flow.'

Everyone looked at Charlie – who was cast as Thomas Becket – and Paul – cast as Henry II.

Finally Charlie spoke. 'It's difficult to get into the characters. They lived nearly eight hundred and fifty years ago, spoke a variation of French, and not only is there little source material, but what does exist is contradictory. I'm struggling to get a sense of who Becket was as a man as opposed to an archbishop.'

'I second that – there is more information out there about Henry, but it focuses on his temper, dress sense, and marriage. Everything is just . . . one dimensional.'

'And there's even less known about the knights,' Ed, cast as Morville, said. 'They only feature in the history books on the night they assassinated Becket.'

Helen nodded. 'I had the same problems when writing the script, but I had hoped the dialogue would be enough to convey their characters.'

'We're not criticising your writing, Helen,' Charlie was quick to say. 'It's just that the twelfth century was so long ago and life and culture so different, we're struggling to get a handle on it.' He looked around the table for support, aware he'd inadvertently spoken for everyone.

'I'm finding the same,' Paul said. 'Royalty then was different to royalty now.'

'Well at least that's an easy one,' Helen said. 'Henry II was your quintessential dictator and warlord. Think Mugabe, al-Assad, Gaddafi, Hitler, Stalin et cetera.'

'But that's a simplification,' Paul persisted. 'Yes he was a dictator, but he didn't have total control of power over his subjects – he shared it with the Church and was second to God and, by association, the Pope. There is no situation or role today that compares.'

Helen nodded and finished her gin. Mike got up, took a couple of notes from the pile they had pooled together in the centre of the table and went to the bar to get the next round in.

'I have an idea,' Helen said. 'Sarah, are you free tomorrow?'

'Yes, I think so. Why?'

'Meet me at nine, we have some shopping to do before tomorrow's rehearsal.'

'What for?' Dan asked.

'You'll see.'

Chapter 5

'So what's this mysterious shopping trip about?' Sarah asked as Helen approached.

'Ah, wait and see,' Helen said, looping her arm through her friend's and leading her through the market square. 'To be honest I'm not sure if it's genius or madness but we're about to find out.'

'Now you really have me intrigued,' said Sarah with a nervous laugh. 'What are you up to?'

'Well, you know the new shop that's opened up on Kirkgate?'

'Which one? Oh, you don't mean the witchy one, what's it called, Spellbound?'

Helen laughed. 'Oh yes. Desperate times and all that.'

'Not that desperate, surely?'

'Did you not see them last night? They were so wooden they may well have been planted in Knaresborough Forest. We need to do something drastic to loosen them up and help them embrace Becket and Henry.'

'But spells, seriously?'

'No, not spells,' Helen said. 'We're here, come on.'

The smell hit them first, a mix of herbs and incense, and both women relaxed. A large display of crystals adorned the table in the middle of the shop which drew them closer, both of them compelled to touch the beautiful diodes, points and tumble stones.

They wandered around the rest of the filled interior; books, tarot cards, bags of herbs with appropriate spells, wands, dreamcatchers, all inspiration to their imaginations.

'Okay, I give up,' Sarah said, hands full of crystals, angel cards and incense that she felt she just had to have. 'What are we here for?'

Helen said nothing, but pointed up to the objects displayed on top of the bookcases.

'No, oh no, Helen, you can't be serious.'

'I'm very serious,' Helen said. 'No one is connecting with their characters, we've tried the conventional exercises – picturisation, sense memory, circle of concentration – but nothing is working. We have eight weeks to put on a play to wow feva, Knaresborough, and every visitor who pays good money to see us. How better than to ask the men themselves?'

'But a *spirit* board? They scare me, Helen.'

'We'll be fine as long as we're careful and responsible.'

'Good morning, ladies, I'm Donna.' A petite blonde woman dressed in purple, and with a genuine smile on her face approached them. 'I couldn't help but overhear, and you're right to be wary of the Ouija. The boards need to be used properly and with care, but if they are, they can be a powerful tool.'

'But isn't it like opening the doors to your home and inviting any passing stranger inside? Dead strangers I mean,' Sarah said.

'It is if you don't take precautions, but I don't let anybody buy one of these from me without full instructions to ensure that does not happen.'

'Which is the best one?' Helen said, studying the half dozen designs, all featuring the letters of the alphabet, digits 0 to 9, yes, no and – very prominently – the word goodbye.

'Whichever you feel drawn towards,' Donna said.

'That one,' Helen said, pointing at one with the Spellbound branding. 'I want yours.'

'Thank you.' Donna pulled a footstool out from behind the counter and plucked a board and planchette from the shelf. She went back behind the counter and rummaged through some paperwork to find a three-page sheaf of A4. 'Please read this carefully before you use it.' She put the paper, board and planchette into a black paper bag. 'It tells you everything you need to know to make sure you use the board safely.'

'That's a lot of advice,' Sarah said, still nervous.

'Not really, it basically says the same three things in a number of different ways. Be positive, protect yourselves, and close the board at the end of your séance.'

'Close the board?' Helen asked.

'Yes. Say goodbye. Make it clear that the session has ended and the spirit is no longer welcome.'

Helen nodded but said nothing.

'That's £30 please.'

Helen handed over her credit card, then Sarah emptied her hands of her own prospective purchases and paid for them.

'Are you sure this is a good idea, Helen?' Sarah asked as they walked to the High Street and the Castle Theatre.

'Nothing else has worked,' Helen said. 'It's different, we can have fun with it, and hopefully it can connect the cast with their characters.'

'By bringing forth their spirits?' Sarah asked.

Helen laughed. 'You don't believe that crap do you? There's no way Thomas Becket, Henry II and those knights will visit us. I just want the guys to open their minds and embrace their characters. It's all psychological. If they believe their spirits are with them, they'll become them – I just need them to break through whatever is blocking them at the moment. We don't have long and they need to be perfect or the Castle Players may as well disband. I'll do everything I can to make sure we pull this off.'

Chapter 6

'Henry has decided on Becket for Archbishop of Canterbury,' Helen said, her voice projecting throughout the empty theatre.

Paul and Charlie stood on stage, scripts in hand. 'So are they still friendly at this point?'

'At the beginning, yes, but Becket doesn't want the archbishopric – he realises that it will cause problems and it will be impossible to marry his loyalty to Henry with duty and service to the Church.'

'But if they're such good friends, why doesn't Henry listen to Becket?' Paul asked.

'Henry is a twelfth-century king – he listens to no man but himself,' Helen said. 'Basically, he's a dictator who believes he has a divine right to rule and is always right.'

'So, a typical man then,' Sarah said with a laugh, but accepted with good grace the playful thump on the arm from her husband, Dan.

'As I was saying,' Helen's voice projected once more, bringing the Castle Players to order. 'Henry makes Becket archbishop, despite him not being ordained as a priest. Becket has no choice but to make the best of it, and chooses his role as the Church's highest representative in England over friendship and Chancellor to King Henry II. He resigned as Chancellor . . .'

'But is this important?' Charlie asked. 'What does it have to do with his murder? I thought that's what the play's about.'

Helen sighed. 'It is, but it's also about the motivation and why a man who had been such a good and trusted friend of Henry's ended up assassinated in his name. This is where it starts. Making him archbishop was Henry's first mistake as far as Thomas Becket was concerned.'

'Oh,' Charlie said, nodding. 'I see.'

'From the top,' Helen said.

HENRY II (PAUL FULLER)
Thomas, 'tis my will and pleasure that thee succeed Theobald in the archbishopric of Canterbury.

THOMAS BECKET (CHARLIE THOROGOOD)
'Tis an honour too great, Sire. Why, look at me (indicates fine clothing). *I am hardly a man suited to the purity, poverty and abstinence of this holy office.*

'Okay, stop there,' Helen said. 'Paul, Charlie, this is a monumental request, you sound as if Henry is asking directions to Canterbury not appointing a new archbishop. Give me more – emotion, import, passion. Try again.'

HENRY II (PAUL FULLER)
No better man can I depend upon to act as mediator 'twixt King and Church. Together we shall bring England to glory.

THOMAS BECKET (CHARLIE THOROGOOD)
Sire, I would not gainsay thee, but consider it further, please. I would not the Church came betwixt us.

'Enough,' Helen shouted. 'Paul, Charlie, I'm still seeing and hearing you up there – I need to see Henry and Becket.'

'Well you're not going to see them two, are you? Not when we're dressed in jeans. It's not exactly medieval costume.'

'Costumes aside, you sound like Paul and Charlie, not Henry and Becket. We don't have long to get this right, and it could be our big chance.'

'Well, what do you suggest?' Charlie said, sounding irritated.

'Something a bit different,' Helen said. 'For all of us. We need to embrace the twelfth century – the culture, politics and the characters – and we need to do it quickly. Everyone on the stage, please, now. Paul, Charlie, will you bring that table into the centre? And we need chairs too.'

The octet of Castle Players sat around the circular table, most looking resigned to yet another game to release their inhibitions and take on the mantles of their characters. All but Helen and Sarah – they both seemed nervous, and Dan narrowed his eyes at his wife.

'What the hell is this?' Charlie exclaimed when Helen produced the black and purple spirit board and placed it in the centre of the table.

'You have got to be joking,' Dan said.

Helen looked at each of them in turn. 'No, I am not joking. We need to do something to channel these characters. We've tried most of the usual exercises and nothing's worked.'

'Well it's hard to play a man who's nearly eight hundred and fifty years dead,' Paul said.

'I agree, so why not ask for help from the men themselves?' Helen said.

'Assuming I believe in ghosts, which I don't,' Charlie said, 'why would their spirits come and talk to us?'

'As you pointed out yesterday, there are so few surviving accounts of their lives – and all contradictory – why wouldn't they want the truth of their lives told?' Helen said.

'I'm not sure about this,' Mike said. 'I don't like messing in things I don't understand.'

'It's okay, Mike,' Sarah said. 'The woman in the shop gave us loads of advice about how to use it properly and be safe.'

'Us?' Dan said. 'So this is what your secret shopping trip was about?'

'Helen asked me not to say anything,' Sarah said, refusing to look at him, 'not until she brought it up.'

'Since when do you put your friends before your husband?' Dan said, colour rising in his face.

'When that friend is her and her husband's director,' Mike said, staring at Dan.

'It's my fault, Dan,' Helen said. 'If you're angry at anybody, be angry at me, I'm the one who put Sarah in a difficult position.'

Dan looked at her, opened his mouth, then shut it again. He played Reginald FitzUrse and was still hopeful of a promotion to Henry II or Becket should Paul or Charlie prove unequal to their roles. He did not want to antagonise the script writer and director; he would continue the discussion with Sarah, later, in the privacy of their home.

Chapter 7

'Are we seriously going to do this?' Paul asked.
'Yes,' Helen said, 'and please try to be positive, or at least have an open mind.'
'Come on, Paul,' Sarah said. 'It might be fun and help us connect with the guys we're playing.'
'But we just— It's not something to be messed with,' Mike said.
'Have you used it before?' Sarah asked.
Mike hesitated.
'You have, haven't you?'
'Yes,' he admitted. 'At a party, years ago, these girls made one out of paper.'
'What happened?'
'Not a lot really, the glass they used instead of that thing,' he pointed at the triangular planchette, 'flew across the room and smashed.'
'Then what happened?' Helen asked.
'Nothing, we were all freaked out, so we burned it.'
'Somebody just flicked the glass,' Dan said with a smirk, 'to freak you all out.'
'Maybe.' Mike shrugged. 'But I don't see how.'
'You said it was at a party,' Sarah said. 'Were you all pissed?'
Mike grinned. 'Well . . .'
'There you are then,' Helen said. 'Stop worrying. I know what I'm doing. Are we all ready?'
'I suppose so,' Mike said. 'But we stop if things get too weird, okay?'
'Fair enough,' Helen said. 'What about the rest of you?'
The others shrugged or nodded with varying degrees of assuredness, which Helen took as assent. She placed her fingers on the planchette.
'Paul and Charlie, you have the two main roles, I'd like you to touch the planchette as well, then everyone else put your hands on top.' Helen said and waited until they'd complied.
'Okay, I'm going to protect us first – we don't want anything flung against walls,' she said with a smile at Mike. 'I call on our angel guardians and spirit guides to protect us here tonight.'
'Are you serious?' Dan asked, pulling his hand away.
'Yes, I am. Please, Dan, stay positive.'
'But angels and spirit guides?'
'Would you rather I called on the devil?'
'No, of course not!'
'Then let me carry on.'

'I'd rather we at least put the intention out there for angels, Dan,' Sarah said.

Her husband stared at her, then returned his hand to the tower of fingers on the planchette.

'Thank you, Dan,' Helen said. 'I call on our angel guardians and spirit guides to be with us tonight as we try to contact Henry II, Thomas Becket, and Sirs Morville, FitzUrse, Tracy and Brett. We ask that you surround us in a protective white light and facilitate contact with the spirits we are asking to communicate with.' She bowed her head and fell silent.

'Did they answer you?' Dan said. Helen ignored him.

'Henry Plantagenet, Thomas Becket, Hugh de Morville, Reginald FitzUrse, William de Tracy, Richard le Brett, I humbly beg you to join us this evening, your presence is welcome and we would be honoured if you felt able to help us tell your story.'

'Overdoing it a bit, isn't she?' Dan whispered to Sarah.

'Shush. She's speaking to medieval nobles, including a king. They would expect nothing less,' Sarah hissed back. Dan shrugged.

'Henry Plantagenet, Thomas Becket, Sir Hugh, Sir Reginald, Sir William, Sir Richard, will you speak to us? You are most welcome here.'

Everybody stared at the planchette. It didn't move.

'Now what, oh high priestess?' Dan said.

Helen glared at him.

'Maybe we're asking for too much at once,' Sarah said.

'That sounds plausible,' Paul said. 'Why not focus on Henry and Becket first?'

Helen nodded. 'Good idea. Okay, just Paul, Charlie and myself touch the planchette.'

'Why you, Helen?'

'I'm acting as medium, Dan. The notes from the lady in the shop said one person should be in control of the board.'

'And of course that's you,' Dan said under his breath.

'Pardon?'

'Nothing. By all means carry on.' Dan made an expansive gesture with his hands, leaned back in his chair and folded his arms.

Helen ignored him and looked at Paul and Charlie. 'Ready?'

They both nodded and Helen took a deep breath. 'I humbly invite Henry Plantagenet, King of England, and Thomas Becket, Archbishop of Canterbury, to join us,' she said. 'Are you there?'

The planchette moved to point at the word *yes* on the board. Everybody – including Helen – gasped in surprise and lifted their hands away.

'Who did that?' Dan said. 'Who moved it?'

Helen, Paul and Charlie looked at each other – all innocent.

'It must have been one of you,' Dan insisted.

'It wasn't,' Helen snapped. 'Shall we continue before whoever it is leaves in disgust?'

'I'd have thought both Henry and Becket would feel quite at home with this squabbling,' Ed said, breaking the tension.

Helen smiled, placed her fingers back on the planchette, and looked up at Paul and Charlie. 'Well boys?'

They glanced at each other, then followed Helen's lead and assumed the Ouija position.

'Who are you?'

The planchette moved almost immediately and pointed at the letter *H*, then to the *2*.

'Are you Henry Plantagenet, the king of England we know as Henry II?' Helen asked.

The planchette moved to indicate *yes*, then moved back to the empty space in the middle of the board.

'One of you is moving it,' Dan said. 'This isn't real, it can't be.'

'Shh,' said Paul.

'Thank you, Sire, for joining us, you are most welcome and we are honoured you have chosen to be with us this evening.'

No movement.

'You need to ask a question,' Sarah hissed.

Helen swallowed. Deep down, she hadn't thought this would work and hadn't prepared any questions.

Paul came to her rescue. 'Greetings, King Henry. I am Paul Fuller and have the very great honour of representing you in our play.'

Dan guffawed with laughter, and Sarah elbowed him to quiet him. Paul ignored him, and Sarah was the only one to see Dan's look of anger.

'I humbly beseech thee—'

'He's getting into the lingo now, at least,' Dan mocked.

'—to help me give a true and flattering portrayal of Your Majesty,' Paul continued. 'Would you be willing to help me tell your story?'

The planchette stayed still, then shot back to *yes*.

'My humble thanks, Sire.'

'If anyone says humble one more time, I'll sucker-punch them,' Dan said, then screamed as his chair shot backwards, tipping him over and dumping him on the boards.

'Nice try, Dan, grow up,' Mike said.

'That wasn't me.'

'So what, you *do* believe in ghosts now?'

'It wasn't me, the chair moved by itself!'

'In that case, I suggest you show more respect, Dan,' Mike said. 'You are disrespecting the first Plantagenet king of England, the head of one of our greatest dynasties.'

Dan said nothing, just glared at his fellow actors, then picked up his chair and gingerly sat down.

'Come on, Paul,' Sarah said, earning a more intense glare from her husband, which she ignored.

Helen glanced between the two of them, concerned at the marital discord on display, but pushed her worries to one side for now, and turned her attention back to the spirit board, Paul and Charlie. 'We all thank you for joining us, Sire,' she said, 'and apologise for our colleague's cynicism. He means no disrespect.'

Nothing. Helen looked at Paul, whose colour had drained to white.

'Forgive me, Your Majesty,' Charlie said into the silence. 'May I respectfully ask if your great friend, Thomas Becket is with you?'

The planchette vibrated, but did not move.

'Ask Becket,' Mike hissed and Charlie nodded.

'Thomas Becket, are you here with us?'

Again the planchette vibrated, then inched its way to *yes*.

'Welcome, sir,' Charlie said, swallowing. 'I am humbled that you have chosen to join us and ask you the same question, would you be willing to help me tell the true story of your later life?'

The planchette moved again to *yes*, then back to the empty place, then *yes*, back, *yes* over and over, gaining speed and ferocity.

Charlie, Paul and Helen snatched their fingers away all at the same moment. 'Hot,' Helen said, protecting her fingers under her armpits. 'It's just got hot.'

'But the room's freezing cold,' Sarah said.

Helen looked around and shivered. Sarah was right. 'When did that happen?'

'The first time the planchette moved,' Sarah said.

Nobody spoke. All wondered what the hell they'd been thinking.

'Our turn,' Mike said and everyone looked at him in surprise. He shrugged. 'Well, in for a penny, in for a pound, right? We've set this in motion, might as well follow it through. This is gonna be one kickass play,' he said, shuddered and placed his right forefinger on the planchette.

'Come on Sarah, Ed. Dan, are you up for this?'

With all attention on him, Dan coloured then added his finger to the planchette. 'If this goes tits-up, it's your fault, not mine.'

'Way to be positive, Dan,' Mike said. Everyone laughed and the atmosphere lightened.

'Come on, Helen, you're the medium, remember,' Sarah said. 'Give us your finger.'

More laughter, and Helen complied. She took a deep breath, glanced at Sarah, Dan, Mike and Ed, who all looked apprehensive with their fingers on the planchette, despite the laughter and bravado.

'Come on then, Helen, the surprise is killing me.'

'Not the best choice of words, Ed,' Alec pointed out.

Helen broke the ensuing silence. 'We are most grateful for the presence of King Henry and Archbishop Becket, and now respectfully ask that the barons and knights Morville, FitzUrse, Tracy and Brett also join us.'

The planchette quivered.

'Sir Hugh de Morville, are you here?'

Yes

'Sir Reginald FitzUrse . . .'

The planchette moved away then back to *yes* before Helen could complete her sentence and Dan smirked at her.

'Sir William de Tracy, are you here?'

Yes

'Richard le Brett, are you here?'

No

'No?' Sarah exclaimed. 'Why is my character the only one who says no?'

'If he's not here, how did he say no?' Mike asked. 'Ask again, Sarah.'

'Sir Richard le Brett, are you here?'

Yes

'Ask again, best out of three,' Alec suggested.

'Sir Richard le Brett are you with us?'

Yes

'Our thanks and gratitude to you all,' Helen said. 'History is vague and we know not the true circumstances leading up to and after that fateful day of 29th December 1170 . . .'

'Less speeches, more questions,' Dan interrupted.

Helen made to retort, then thought better of it. He was right. She looked at Charlie and Paul, then back at the planchette. They both understood and added their fingers to the others.

Helen took a deep breath, then said, 'Did you, King Henry, mean to order the assassination of Archbishop Thomas Becket?'

Board, planchette and table were thrown against the back wall of the stage, only missing the heads of the assembled company because all eight of them were thrust backwards from the epicentre of their séance, their chairs splintering as they fell against the wooden boards of the stage.

'I told you this was a bloody stupid thing to do,' Dan shouted, the first to get to his feet. 'We've messed with things that shouldn't be messed with. God knows what we've unleashed. Bloody stupid woman!' He looked around, then added, calmer, 'Where's Helen?'

The rest of the cast got to their feet, shocked, but only bruised, and looked around.

'There! She's down there,' Sarah called, pointing to the front row of seats.

'Shit,' Paul said, and jumped off the stage. 'Someone call an ambulance!'

Chapter 8

January 1170

'There she is, Cnaresburg Castle,' Hugh de Morville declared with evident pride as the knights emerged from the forest.

'God's blood, Hugh,' FitzUrse said. 'Even if Broc does turn the King against us, no bugger's going to get to us up there.'

The castle's keep, newly built from stone, perched atop the cliff, the deep gorge more of an obstacle than any man, or siege engine, would be able to conquer. The sight of it stunned the men; despite being of Norman descent and used to sights of the strongest castles in Europe, none were familiar with the rugged landscape of Yorkshire.

A deep, clear river sparkled in the late afternoon sunlight before them, above which the red-orange sandstone cliff towered. Trees and lush vegetation grew to the very banks of the River Nydde.

As the horsemen approached the river, a group of young goatherds looked up from their charges and spotted them.

'Á Morville,' they cried and a couple ran up the steep bank towards the town.

'Á Morville?' Tracy asked with a smile. 'You have them well trained.'

Morville shrugged, pleased at the welcoming war cry, but trying not to show it to his companions.

He led the way, his palfrey splashing through the shallow waters of the ford. 'Take care not to stray too far to either side, the waters can be treacherous,' he called to the following men. The knights glanced at each other and smirked, knowing full well that Morville was enjoying his role as overlord and the chance to assert the authority this status gave him, over Reginald FitzUrse in particular. All the men, not just the knights, but the accompanying men-at-arms of each house, had had more than enough of The Bear's overbearing bluster on their exhausting ride north.

'What are the defences on the far side?' FitzUrse called to Morville. 'I doubt you are as well-protected from the town as you are from the river.'

'The curtain wall is twenty feet high and four feet thick. The ditch is being deepened, but will be completed shortly, especially now that I'm here to oversee the work.'

'Towers?'

'At all four compass points, including those of the gates, although the southern tower is still under construction, as you can see.'

'It sounds like there is much still under construction.' Tracy laughed.

Morville turned in his saddle. 'When I was entrusted with the castle, it was little more than motte and bailey. That was seven years ago. In that time, the curtain wall has been raised, towers constructed, and the keep is now of stone. If you disapprove, you are more than welcome to continue to Scotland as Broc suggested and try your welcome there.'

Tracy held up his hands in mock surrender. 'No offence meant, My Lord. It is a wondrous castle.'

The others laughed and Morville screwed up his face in disgust, faced forward once more and spurred his palfrey up the steep bank of Brig-Gate.

'My apologies, My Lord,' Tracy whispered once they'd reached flatter ground. 'I did not mean to insult. It just struck me that we may be under siege here before long should the King take up arms against us.'

Morville glanced at him and sighed. He knew that Tracy was suffering larger and longer pangs of conscience than any of the others. He was not a killer by nature, merely a follower of killers.

'The King needed Becket stopped before he did any more harm. He was a traitor. Had we not taken care of the problem he would have revolted against not only the Young King, but King Henry himself. You know this to be true, we have talked of little else since we left Canterbury.'

'Bad things happen, William,' FitzUrse bellowed from behind them. 'We served our king well, he shall reward us.'

'And Broc?' Morville asked.

'Yes, he shall reward Broc as well,' FitzUrse replied with a grin. 'Handsomely, no doubt.'

'Broc won't . . . betray us?' Richard le Brett asked. As the youngest, of lowest status, and the man who had dealt the fatal blow, he had become the quietest, most timid of the quartet.

'He would no doubt attempt it should it be to his benefit,' FitzUrse laughed, 'but he hosted us at Saltwood Castle. He accompanied us and he supplied men-at-arms. We had more than enough between us, but he wanted a share of the glory.'

'And the loot,' Morville muttered. The four of them had helped themselves to gold plate and coin as they left. Broc and his men had taken everything else of value in the Archbishop's Palace, although had left the cathedral treasures. That would have been a sacrilege too far.

'He cannot betray us without betraying himself,' FitzUrse continued.

'But what of his suggestion for us to flee to Scotland?' Tracy asked.

FitzUrse bellowed laughter. 'His idea of a jest, is all.'

'A jest? To send us to a man who would gladly hang us as Englanders?'

'He has an evil sense of humour.'

'Á Morville! Á Morville!'

The knights' conversation was halted by the cheers as the townsfolk swarmed out of the alleyways to greet their returning overlord.

Morville raised his gauntleted hand in acknowledgement of the praise.

'They love you here,' FitzUrse said in wonder.

'No, they love the coin we will have to spend in the market. Look behind you.'

The knights twisted in their saddles to view the trailing men-at-arms. A force drawn from four houses.

'The population of Cnaresburg has just doubled.'

Chapter 9

Morville led the way over the drawbridge and through the north gate, and the knights clattered into the courtyard of the outer ward. Grooms rushed from the stables at the noise and the men jumped down from their mounts.

'Welcome to Cnaresburg Castle, My Lords,' Morville said. 'Make yourselves at home, we may be residing here for some time.'

The knights grimaced, all of them wondering the same thing: how had King Henry received the news of their deeds?

Morville led them through the inner gate to the bailey of the inner ward and pointed out the chapel and administration buildings. Nobody paid much attention. Once past the grandeur of the situation of the castle, the innards were nothing remarkable. The curtain walls and keep were the only stone edifices; all else was timber. Whilst it was apparent much building work had been undertaken, it was just as apparent there was a great deal still to be done.

'Helwise, welcome our guests,' Morville said to his wife, who stood at the door to the stone tower of the keep.

'Husband,' she acknowledged and nodded.

Brett, the last to be admitted, wondered at the faint trace of a smile on Lady de Morville's face at such an abrupt greeting.

Hugh de Morville flung open the doors to his great hall and stopped in shock. The force of FitzUrse blundering into his back pushed him onward and he took a couple of paces forward before once again coming to an abrupt halt. Cursing, FitzUrse, Tracy and Brett stepped around him before halting themselves and Brett understood the reason for the young Helwise de Morville's pleasure in spite of her husband's rude homecoming.

Morville remembered his manners and bowed to the men seated at the lord's table, instigating equivalent gestures from his companions. 'My Lords, I-I-I welcome you to my castle.'

'Not your castle, Morville, my brother's, King Henry. You are merely custodian here. For the present, at least,' said Sir Hamelin Plantagenet, Earl of Surrey. Seated at the overlord's place – Sir Hugh de Morville's seat – at the lord's table at the head of the hall, it was very clear to all present who held authority at Cnaresburg Castle this day. It was not Sir Hugh de Morville, Lord of the Manor of Cnaresburg, Baron of Burgh-on-the-Sands, Lord of Westmoreland.

Morville gathered his composure and greeted the other great men seated at his table.

Sir William de Courcy Lord of Harewood, and Morville's close neighbour Sir William de Percy Baron of Topcliffe, Lord of Spofford and Wetherby, sat at either side of Hamelin Plantagenet. None of the three appeared pleased to see the four travel-worn knights.

Morville looked around the bustling hall, nearly full he now realised, his awareness of his surroundings having been paralysed by his shock of seeing three great lords; three of King Henry's innermost and most loyal circle. He noted who else was present: Nigel de Plumton; Sir John Goldesburgh; Gamellor, Lord of the Manor of Beckwith; Morville's brother-in-law, William de Stoteville; and even his forester, Thomas de Screven. Everyone of any import in the vicinity was here, dining at Morville's pleasure, and cost, without his knowledge.

'H-H-How . . . ?' he stammered and FitzUrse poked him in the back. Morville drew himself to his full height and tried again. 'Forgive me, My Lords, it is of great surprise to find you here. We rode like the wind . . .'

'Yes,' Plantagenet drawled. 'From Canterbury. We heard. Then we sailed with the wind to ask you what the hell you were thinking.'

'Becket,' Morville began.

'Yes, Becket. Pray, enlighten us.'

'He was a traitor.' FitzUrse stepped forward, unwilling to allow Morville to plead his case on his behalf. 'He was planning to depose the Young King and, more than likely, King Henry himself. He was a man of great ambition, it is of no surprise to anyone that he had his sights on the crown of England. King Henry wanted him stopped. We stopped him.'

'You certainly did that,' Plantagenet said.

'How did King Henry take the news?' Morville found the courage to ask.

'Ahh, the pertinent enquiry.' Plantagenet pushed his trencher aside, crossed his arms and leaned forward on the table, glaring at the nervous knights.

He pulled back and addressed the men sitting either side of him. 'How would you say my brother took the news of the horrific murder of his closest friend of, what, twenty years?'

Courcy and Percy solemnly shook their heads.

'Panic-stricken,' Courcy said.

'I have never heard such lengthy lamentations,' Percy said.

Plantagenet nodded, then braced his elbows on the table once more and regarded the knights. The hall, filled with near two hundred men, was silent, every ear turned to hear the Earl's words.

'Panic. Lamentation. Yes. He then fell into a stupor, gentlemen.'

The knights winced. Whether at the news or the insult of 'gentlemen' was not clear.

'He fell into a stupor,' Plantagenet repeated. 'Took to his bedchamber and naught was heard nor seen of him bar his groans of grief and constant prayers for the safekeeping of Becket's soul.'

As one, the knights paled and stepped back at this most dreadful news.

'He would admit no one, nor any succour; no flesh of any kind. And you know how my brother enjoys flesh.'

The lords at the table laughed, banging their fists on the wood. Henry had an appetite befitting a king; he loved his food and his women, and could never have his fill of either. This was serious.

The knights stayed silent.

FitzUrse glanced behind, but the door to the great hall was closed, with pikemen stationed to either side. There would be no escape that way. Just as there had been none for Thomas Becket.

'What say you to that, gentlemen?'

Morville fell to one knee, followed by Tracy, Brett and, after a pause, FitzUrse.

'My Lord, I am grievously wounded to hear such news. The King demanded vengeance on the Archbishop, our only aim was to obtain that for His Majesty.'

'He demanded action from Mandeville and Humez!' Plantagenet roared, leaping to his feet. 'He gave you no such instruction!'

'But My Lord . . .' Morville faltered as Plantagenet raised his eyebrows and scowled.

'The eve of the Great Council,' FitzUrse broke in. 'At supper, the King demanded vengeance from anyone who had the courage to obtain it. We had that courage. My Lord,' he added, casting his eyes down once more.

'Courage? Courage, is that what you call it? Stupidity to the utmost degree, say I! You broke the sanctity of Canterbury Cathedral! You killed an archbishop on his altar steps. An archbishop armed only with a hair shirt! How is *that* courage?'

A hair shirt? All four of the knights blanched. *He was pious after all?*

'My Lord, we attempted to take him peacefully,' Morville ventured, swallowing the lump in his throat at the unwelcome news. 'We did so without arms and without mail. He laughed at us and laughed at the King.'

'He *laughed* at the King?' Plantagenet asked.

'He did, My Lord,' FitzUrse said. 'So we regained our arms and returned for him. He refused to leave the cathedral, made it impossible for us to remove him, and taunted us. By taunting us, the King's men, he taunted the King. We could not permit that.'

'I see.' Plantagenet retook his seat. 'I see, well, that does shine a different light on things.'

'It does?' Tracy asked, speaking his first words since entering the hall.

'Well, it would had Ranulf de Broc not already made that clear.'

'My Lord?' Morville asked, confused.

Plantagenet laughed. 'It has been said that had my brother not been high-born, he would have made an excellent mummer, is that not so?'

Courcy and Percy looked at their trenchers and made no reply.

'Oh come now, My Lords, I hear the talk, we are amongst friends here. I ask you again, is that not so?'

Courcy relaxed and nodded. 'Yes, it has been said, My Lord.'

'Excellent. And what say you, do I have some of his skill?'

'Worthy of a prince,' Courcy said.

The knights glanced at each other in confusion, unable to understand what was happening.

'Oh stand, My Lords, stand.'

The knights regained their feet.

'My brother has to put on a show. He must appease the Pope, do you understand?'

The knights nodded, yet still appeared uncertain.

'*Before* he secluded himself, he sent messengers to Rome, and included details of his seclusion within his missives.'

The knights glanced at each other, now starting to understand. Or at least, they hoped they did.

'As long as Henry's messengers reach Pope Alexander first, this unfortunate incident shall be brought to an amenable close.'

'And if they are not first?' Morville asked.

'Well, then all Hell and the fury of Christendom shall descend on your souls.'

Chapter 10

Jack, the head steward of Cnaresburg Castle, placed dishes of thrice-cooked pork, onion and beans on to the lord's table and the hungry knights speared large pieces with their eating knives. For a while, all was silent as they sated their hunger and thirst.

FitzUrse was the first to sit back, signalling for more wine. 'That was quite a welcome,' he said. 'I thought it would end with our heads on pikes on the towers of the gatehouse.'

'I fear it was a near thing,' Morville said. 'Let us hope that the King's messengers are the first to give Pope Alexander the news.'

'They had me in fear and no mistake,' Tracy said, emptying his goblet which was immediately refilled.

'Am I to understand that you . . . killed the Archbishop, husband?' Helwise de Morville said.

'Hush, child.' Morville swept his hand to the side, catching Helwise on the side of her face and rocking her back in her chair. Her face reddened and her eyes filled, but she gave no other outward reaction.

'Hugh!' her brother, William de Stoteville, exclaimed in her stead from her other side and placed a comforting arm around his sister's shoulders.

Morville leaned forward and pointed his eating knife at him. 'Do not *you* disrespect me at my table, William, as does your sister.'

Stoteville gritted his teeth together to prevent his retort, knowing his sister would likely pay for it later.

Helwise shrugged his arm away and patted his knee with a small smile. Twenty years Morville's junior she had been his wife seven years, since she was nine, and although Morville had only taken his marital dues in the last couple of years, she already knew to recognise his moods and behave accordingly.

Despite the coldness in their marriage, she was glad of it; it had enabled her to not only remain in Cnaresburg, but run the castle and care for her town during her husband's absences, which were frequent and lengthy.

'Why do you think the lords did not remain to sup with us?' Brett asked, gallantly coming to his hostess's rescue. He gave her a small yet kind smile as soon as Morville's attention was turned.

'I fear they would withhold any outward show of favour until they hear of Pope Alexander's reaction,' Morville said and took a large gulp of wine.

'What shall we do should Alexander condemn us?' Tracy said, panic lacing his words.

'He shall not,' FitzUrse said with confidence. 'He would be condemning King Henry should he do so and would not risk making such a powerful enemy.'

'He may already view King Henry as an enemy,' Morville said. 'Remember I witnessed the Charter of Clarendon? It took away the freedom of the clergy and made them accountable in law to King not Church. Henry crowed about how he had beaten Alexander. I doubt the Pope took it lightly. He may see this as an opportunity for revenge.'

'God's wounds,' Tracy muttered, emptying another goblet; an action repeated by his fellow knights as they considered the possible implications of their deeds. 'No wonder the lords departed so hastily for Spofford.'

'Calm yourselves, Percy is past his prime, eighty years and more has he not, Helwise?' Morville turned to his wife who gave a curt nod. 'An old man enjoys the comforts of his own home.'

'And they'd supped their fill at your table, Hugh.' FitzUrse roared with laughter.

'Indeed,' Morville said, spearing another slice of pork.

'At least we need not explain ourselves further to them,' Brett said. 'And can rest and dine well after our ordeal.'

'Indeed,' Morville repeated and raised his goblet in a toast. 'Comfort, safety and sanctuary.'

The knights drank, as did Helwise and William, albeit reluctantly. They shared a quick glance acknowledging the hypocrisy of the toast to sanctuary.

A serving girl leaned between Morville and Helwise to place a pie of apple, damson and dates before them. Helwise ignored her husband as he – heading into his cups – fondled the girl's leg and rump at length.

'That will be all, Mable,' Helwise said, and the girl scurried away. Morville glared at his wife.

'Now I see why you insisted on coming to Cnaresburg, Hugh,' Tracy said, his words becoming slurred. 'Such a beautiful and young wife.'

Helwise glanced at him, grateful he had commanded her husband's attention.

'My wife is beautiful too,' Tracy confided very loudly. 'Although no longer young.' He laughed and drank again, then leaned forward to look past FitzUrse and Morville and addressed Helwise.

'She is with child,' he said, his face a picture of pride. 'Borne me two fine sons already.' He paused. 'Olion and Oliver, both knights themselves now. Fine men, the pair of them.'

'They are indeed,' Brett said. 'I last saw Oliver in Normandy before we departed for England. He has grown so strong, he bested me at a wrestle in no time at all.'

'Verily. A fine warrior,' Tracy said, holding his goblet up to toast but spilling most of its contents on to the sleeve of his tunic.

'Pomperi,' he said, oblivious, 'my beloved wife. I hope to see her again.'

His face fell, then he looked up. 'I *will* see her again, will I not, Reginald?'

'Without a doubt, William. Without a doubt.' FitzUrse pulled a passing serving girl on to his lap. 'Until you do, there are plenty here who would enjoy your attention, is that not so?' He nuzzled the young girl's neck.

'Of course, My Lord,' she squeaked before extricating herself and scampering back to the kitchens.

The table of knights roared with laughter. Even Tracy smiled, drained what was left in his goblet then stared at the table in morose silence.

Chapter 11

Helwise was awoken by fingers fumbling beneath her shift. Her heart sank as she realised her husband was already awake and had recovered from the excesses of the previous evening.

He had fallen asleep as soon as he'd lain down, but Helwise's relief had turned to irritation as the volume of his snores did not diminish throughout the night hours. She felt as if she had only just fallen into slumber and was not yet prepared for the new day.

She did not move or indicate she was awake, and kept her legs still and heavy, resisting her husband in the one way open to her. On occasion it had worked, but not this morn. Hugh de Morville would not be denied his wife.

With a groan of frustration, he flung aside the bed covers, rose and knelt over Helwise, pushed up her shift and forced her legs apart.

Helwise remained still and silent, taking no part in the act, then cursed herself as her body responded, despite her wishes and his sour breath.

She clasped her legs around her husband with a moan, who reacted in both strength and vigour until they cried out together.

Morville rolled away and levered himself off the bed. He poured a little water into a bowl, splashed his face, then pissed into the fireplace before donning hose, smock and cote.

'Hurry yourself, Helwise. I wish to hear the progress made on the tower and ditch and view the work done in my absence. You would be my guide.'

'Very well, husband,' Helwise said, reluctantly climbing out of bed. She wished for another hour or two of slumber, but knew this would hold no sway with Hugh.

She dressed in a long chainse with tight-fitting sleeves, then chose a dark-blue bliaut. It fitted snugly under her breasts, the voluminous skirts draping to the floor. She adjusted the sleeves until they were comfortable; closely tailored from shoulder to elbow then draping to the same length of the skirts.

After donning a coif to cover her hair, then adding the face-encircling barbette that Queen Eleanor had made so popular, she added a fillet around the top of her head to secure everything in place. She fastened her emerald-green cloak at her neck and hurried down the spiral stairs to join her husband at the south tower.

* * *

Helwise found Morville in the inner bailey, surrounded by smiths, ropewalkers, carpenters and wood-turners. He turned to study the complete towers of the east, north and west gates, then stared to the south. No gate here at the top of the cliff, but the new defensive watch tower was less than half the height of the completed structures.

'I had thought it to be raised higher by this time,' he said.

'The weather has been inclement,' Helwise said, 'making the quarrying difficult, affecting the mix of the mortar and turning the scaffolding treacherous. The masons have done well in the circumstances.'

Morville harrumphed and led the way through the doorway to climb the spiral staircase, then scrambled out on to the scaffolded platform at the top.

'My Lord,' the mason said in surprise, finished tamping down the stone he had placed, then laid down his tools. 'I bid you welcome.'

Morville nodded. 'How goes progress?'

'We are making the most of the break in the weather, My Lord.' He nodded towards the treadmill. 'That was damaged in the last storm, but as you can see is working once more.'

Morville said nothing, but watched the two men inside the contraption walking the wheels around. Presently, a plank carrying a load of sandstone rose over the edge of the platform and was manhandled on to the platform to be sorted by colour. The strongest dark-grey stone would be used for the facing and structure of the wall, which would be infilled with the reddish and softer yellow stones, giving great strength to the thick defences.

Morville ran his hand over the faced stone of a completed section and nodded in satisfaction at its smoothness.

He peered over the edge to examine the ditch below. More quarry than dry moat at this time, it was abustle with activity; men quarried stone, the rhythmic clanging of the masons' chisels facing the blocks for the inner and outer skins as well as the steps for the spiral stair was as effective as a drummer marking time for rowers or marching soldiers.

'It is quite a distance down, is it not, Hugh?' Helwise said at his side.

'It is indeed,' Morville said, happier now despite the lack of height of the tower. Any attacking force would be more than daunted by the height of the cliff and depth of the ditch, and even at this low elevation, he had a view of the valley for miles in all directions. Although there was plenty of ammunition for siege engines about the quarry, there was no flat ground for them to be situated and used against him. Cnaresburg Castle was in no danger from the south.

He glanced up at the sun, then turned to his wife. 'It is near time for dinner, Helwise, let us re-join our guests, see how they fare this day.'

'I am concerned for Sir William, Hugh. He seemed ill at ease last evening.'

Morville made a sound of disgust. 'He is weak of heart, blaming all but himself for his present circumstances.'

'He misses Pomperi,' Helwise said.

'Bah. He has two fine sons yet continues to bleat about his wife and the child she carries. It is unnecessary.'

'He is concerned, Hugh. It is good to witness.'

Morville glared at her, and she spoke no more but followed him away from the construction of the tower and back to the keep and great hall.

Chapter 12

19th June 2015

'Thank you, everyone, for coming,' Helen said. 'I know our last rehearsal was a little – strange – and am relieved none of you have given up on our production.'

'To be honest, Helen, we're all a bit freaked out,' Paul said. 'We can't explain what happened, and the possibility it was real scares the shit out of me, and I think everyone else, right guys?'

He got a few nods, but not from everyone, yet pushed on regardless. 'Was it worth dabbling in things we don't know, and to be honest, shouldn't know or have contact with in this life?'

'I appreciate your concern, Paul, and apologise to everyone – I had thought the spirit board was a way to allow you to tap into your psyches and your creative cores, to channel your characters, and become them when you're on stage. I honestly did not expect what happened.'

'How's your arm?' Alec asked.

'Broken wrist. It could have been a lot worse. Was anyone else hurt?'

'No,' Sarah said, 'just you.'

'Okay then, shall we start?'

Helen sat in the middle of the front row of seats; no gods, no boxes, no circles, just rows of seats on one level, more like an assembly hall than a theatre, yet it hosted a wide variety of acts and plays.

'We need to plan the sets – they'll take the most time to create – as you know it's mainly a two-hander between Henry and Becket, and they're rarely together geographically so we have to get creative.'

'Huh? How will that work?' Dan said.

'We need a set to represent a castle in Normandy for Henry's scenes, and Canterbury Cathedral for Becket's – and of course, most of their arguments and fallings out happened when they were separated by the English channel, and done by messenger, but that won't work in a play.'

'So what do you suggest?' Ed asked.

'One set split into two. The left-hand side as the audience looks on will be a Norman castle's great hall, the right-hand side Canterbury Cathedral. Most of the play will focus on these two locations – often at the same time.'

'But how will that work?' Sarah asked. 'We can't have two locations on stage at the same time.'

'I think we can – one stage, two locations. Henry in his, Becket in his, and use lighting to distinguish between the two. So when Henry makes

Becket archbishop, the Norman castle and Henry are spotlighted, whilst Becket and Canterbury is dark. Then when Becket denounces his chancellorship, Canterbury is lit and Normandy dark. The lighting will switch between the two, following their dialogue. Is that possible, Alec?'

'Yes, absolutely. It will take quite a bit of setting up to programme, but there shouldn't be any problems.'

'Great,' Helen said. 'What about sets? Do we have enough time?'

'Just about,' Ed said. 'But they'll be rough – I can't go too detailed in the time we have. I think we can manage with one backdrop in a masonry design, so we can use it for the final scene too, then use different furniture and props to show the difference between castle and cathedral.'

'Okay.' Helen paused, knowing she had to ask the next question. 'So, does anybody feel any ill effects after what we did last week?'

'Aside from your broken wrist, you mean?' Alec said.

'Well, yes,' Helen said.

Silence.

'We didn't close the board,' Sarah said. 'The woman in the shop, Donna, said we had to close the board.'

'I think the board closed itself, babes,' Dan said, and Sarah glanced at him in annoyance at the annoying pet name.

Chapter 13

THOMAS BECKET (CHARLIE THOROGOOD)
Great Hall, Archbishop's Palace, Canterbury Cathedral.
So here I be, yesterday a layman, today the Church's highest authority in the land. What is my friend Henry thinking? And why does he not take my advice in this of all things?
(Sits at desk with quill, ink pot and parchment)
I may have no say in the archbishopric, but I shall resign as Chancellor, if only I could find the words to express my ire at Henry.

'Okay, stop there, Charlie,' Helen called. 'This is where we need to get to know Becket as a man. Who is he? What's his character?'

'Why don't you hold another séance and ask him?' Dan said, sarcastic as ever. Helen glared at him, then softened.

'Not one of my better ideas, I admit,' she said. 'Where is the board, anyway, has anyone found it? I think we should burn it.'

Dan look surprised. 'I thought you'd taken it.'

Helen shook her head. 'Not me, anyone else?'

Sarah, Mike, Ed, Alec, Paul and Charlie all shook their heads.

'Well, never mind, I'm sure it will turn up,' Helen said and brought her attention back to Charlie on stage.

'Becket's an important man. Up until now he's been the closest man to the King, Charlie.'

Charlie nodded. 'And now he's a priest, with no choice about the matter, I get it,' he said.

'Do you? He likes the finer things in life – clothing, food, hunting, women,' Helen said.

'Should fit right in then,' Paul said with a laugh. 'The bishops can go hunting together!'

'Ah, that they may have done, My Lord. But that shall not follow now I am the Primate of All England.'

'That's it, Charlie! You're getting it – you sound just like Becket,' Helen said, striking her knee with her good hand in place of clapping.

'My thanks, fair maiden,' Charlie said, bowing to his director.

'Thomas, my friend, thee must leave the ladies of the kingdom alone now,' Paul said, mounting the steps to the stage.

'Ah, so that is why thee foisted this most unwelcome honour on me. Thee is scared of the competition!'

Paul laughed and clapped his friend on the back. 'Not at all, Thomas. With thy help I shall bow the Church to my will and the will of England.

No more of this petty squabbling that has become so arduous.'

'But Henry, thee has given me a great duty. As Archbishop of Canterbury, I must serve God above all else.'

'Thee serves me, Thomas,' Paul said. 'Me, thy King.'

'Of course, Sire,' Charlie said. 'I serve thee after God.'

'Thomas, I warn thee now, consider thy actions with care,' Paul said, balling his fists. 'I have not risen thee so high to stand against me. That does not follow. Does thee hear me, Bishop?' The last word was a sneer.

'Verily, Sire, and I shall bring all my powers to the task of tallying my spiritual duties with those demanded by thee.'

Paul opened his mouth to retort but was interrupted by clapping from the auditorium.

'This is going to work, isn't it?' Dan said. 'This is really going to work.'

Helen grinned. 'Oh yes, and a great bit of improv, guys. Can we try again with the scripts now? Scene three, from the top.'

Paul moved back to his position, and Charlie readied himself to restart his monologue.

THOMAS BECKET/CHARLIE THOROGOOD
I cannot fathom why my king has forced this upon me. Archbishop of Canterbury and Chancellor of England? Nay, 'tis too much, how do I reconcile such conflicting differences in my duties? I cannot.

'Hold it there, Charlie,' Helen said. 'You're wooden again.'

'Maybe it's the monologue,' Sarah said. 'It just isn't natural. Why don't you combine this scene with Paul's monologue in scene four? Have them both on stage and interacting – we can use that trick with the lights and sets you talked about.'

Helen pursed her lips in thought, then nodded. 'Okay, let's try it. Just improv for the moment and I'll rewrite.'

'Sire, 'tis with great reluctance, with not fear nor favour, that I must tender my resignation as your Chancellor,' Charlie said, pretending to write as he spoke. 'I find my pastoral duties too great to be able to fully apply myself to both positions.'

Paul crossed to the table and grabbed a piece of paper. 'Need a prop,' he said by way of explanation, then retook his position, cleared his throat and pretended to read.

'By God's eyes,' he exclaimed. 'I am betrayed and by my greatest friend in the nation! Is he now to be my most formidable enemy?' Paul appealed to the audience, arms spread wide.

'I fear I have angered my king,' Charlie said, head in his hands, then he sat up straight. 'But *he* has brought us to this pass.' He stood and approached the audience, putting Becket's case forward.

'Did I advise him to follow this road? Nay, I did not. Did I not warn him against taking this step? Indeed I did. Did he listen?' he said, voice rising, then softened once more. 'Of course, he did not.' Charlie gave a small laugh and shook his head.

Paul stepped forward. 'Betrayed!' he shouted. 'Betrayed by my most faithless friend! Whom now shall I trust? Who now is deserving of their king's favour?'

Silence.

'Indeed,' Paul said softly. 'No man in England is worthy of my faith, no man but myself.'

'I don't think they need that rewrite, Helen,' Dan said. 'They seem to be doing pretty well on their own.'

Helen nodded. 'Well done, guys, time for the pub, first round's on me.'

Chapter 14

The Borough Bailiff was one of the oldest pubs on the High Street. Named for the stewards who collected the rents for their lords, it was friendly, down-to-earth and a favourite of the Castle Players.

'Same again?' Dan asked and grabbed a twenty from the pooled money in the centre of their long table.

'Keep 'em coming, mate,' Mike said and laughed.

'Are you okay, Mike?' Sarah asked.

'Fine, Sarah, just peachy,' Mike said, leaning back on the bench seat and dropping his arm along the back of it. 'They did well today didn't they?' he added, leaning into Sarah's shoulder.

'They did. Though I don't think Helen is too pleased that her script went out of the window.'

'Too bad. The improv came across natr . . . nature . . . smoothly,' Mike said.

'Hmm.'

'What's wrong?'

'Well, you don't think it had anything to do with that spirit board, do you?' Sarah asked quietly.

'No, that was just a bit of silliness.'

'But the way we all fell! Helen broke her wrist – that's more than silliness.'

'Power of suggestion,' Mike said, finding it easier to get his words out with a little concentration. 'That's all, don't worry about it.' He stroked Sarah's hair and left his arm about her shoulder.

'Get your hands off my wife.' Dan slammed pints of bitter and lager on the table.

'Sorry mate, nothing meant,' Mike said, lifting both hands in supplication.

'Like hell there wasn't!'

'Hey, settle down guys,' Paul said. 'We're all friends here.'

'This bastard's getting far too friendly with my wife,' Dan said, leaning over the table towards Mike.

'Well, maybe you should treat her better,' Mike said.

Silence.

'What the hell do you mean by that?' Dan's voice was low and measured, and Sarah panicked.

'Nothing, Dan, he doesn't mean anything, he's just had too much to drink.'

'And why are *you* defending him?' Dan switched his ire towards his wife. 'Are you sleeping with him?'

'Dan!' Sarah said, shocked. 'Of course not.'

Dan stood upright. 'Yeah, now I see it, the pair of you have been too pally for far too long. And you enjoyed the kiss in the last play far too much. I see it now, you've been banging each other since then, haven't you?'

'Dan, how many times?' Sarah said, exasperated by not only having this fight again, but in company. 'It was a stage kiss, we're actors just as you are. There was nothing more to it.'

'Yeah, I bet,' Dan sneered.

'Dan, calm down, mate,' Mike said. 'You're embarrassing yourself.'

'Embarrassing? You're pawing my wife and call *me* embarrassing?' Dan lunged across the table and grabbed the front of Mike's T-shirt. The table collapsed, beer foaming over the carpet as Sarah screamed.

'That's enough!' the landlady shouted. 'Get him out of here!'

Alec and Ed had already jumped up to grab Dan. He shook them off and slapped Sarah. 'Whore!' he shouted. Alec and Ed caught hold of his arms and wrestled him out of the pub.

Helen pulled Sarah into a hug.

'I'm so sorry, I'm so sorry,' Sarah said. 'I don't know what's got into him lately. This isn't him, it really isn't. Yes he can be a prick sometimes, but not like this.'

'I'm sorry, Sarah,' Mike said. 'I was just winding him up, I didn't mean . . .'

'I think you've said enough, Mike,' Helen said.

'No,' Sarah said. 'Mike's right, they take the piss out of each other all the time.' She reached out a hand and clasped Mike's forearm. 'It's not your fault, it's Dan. I don't know if something's happened at work or what, but he's been in a right mood for ages.'

'What's happening out there?' Helen said, trying to peer through the window in response to a crashing sound.

'I don't know, but I don't think I'm the best person to go and find out,' Mike said.

Helen nodded. 'I'll go. Mike, you and Charlie look after Sarah, okay?'

Both men nodded and Mike and Sarah sat down, Mike's arms around Sarah as she sobbed into his chest.

'I'll help clean this mess up,' Charlie said. 'And pay for the damage.'

'Charlie, no, I should do that, it's my fault,' Sarah said through gasping breaths.

'No it isn't,' Charlie said. 'Quite the opposite. Anyway, it'll come out of the Castle Players' fund, not my own pocket.' He winked at Sarah and went to attempt to placate the landlady.

Chapter 15

February 1171

'You are joining us?' Morville asked his wife as she entered the great hall, dressed in a forest-green bliaut over a sky-blue chainse.

'I am,' Helwise replied. 'I have been training a new merlin, she has done well on her own. I should like to try her in a full hunt.'

Morville nodded and the men shifted on the benches to make room for the lady of the castle to sit. The four knights had been joined by Helwise's brother, William de Stoteville; Gamellor, Lord of the Manor of Beckwith; Sir John Goldesburgh and Sir Nigel de Plumton.

No lord's table this morning; the knights had gathered around one of the low tables where they had more room to huddle together to plan the hunt. Warmed by a roaring fire, in front of which half a dozen greyhounds stretched, spirits were high and all were looking forward to the day's activity.

FitzUrse helped himself to another hunk of bread and lump of cheese as Thomas de Screven, the forester and head huntsman, strode into the hall, accompanied by two very happy looking lymers. The dogs rushed over to the fire to greet the greyhounds and Screven joined the knights and Helwise.

'Well?' Morville asked.

'A white hart, My Lord, in Haya Park. Twelve points. I have been keeping an eye on him for some time, he is a fine beast.'

'And you have his trail?' FitzUrse asked.

'Yes,' Screven replied and unrolled a scroll depicting the hunting grounds. 'He is in this area here,' he indicated the eastern quadrant, 'near Ferrensby.'

'Not far from Spofford,' Morville said.

'Yes. I met with Sir William's man, the Baron is on his way here to join you.'

'Excellent,' Morville said. 'I had feared he would not accompany us, I have received no reply to my message.'

'Another of his jests,' FitzUrse said with a scowl. 'He has been spending too much time in the company of Hamelin Plantagenet.'

'God's blood, they had me going,' Tracy said.

'Yes, you looked as if you had soiled yourself,' FitzUrse said.

'I think you all did,' Goldesburgh said, and the company of nobles roared with laughter. FitzUrse took a moment, then his colour calmed and he joined in the merriment.

'By God, he had us going,' Morville said, repeating Tracy's earlier words. 'I surely thought King Henry wanted our heads.'

'No, we served him well by cutting out the canker of England.'

'Henry's heroes,' Helwise said.

'Henry's heroes! Hear that, My Lords? We're Henry's heroes! All is well, we shall soon return to Normandy and to our king's side.'

'To our king's right hand,' FitzUrse corrected. 'We are the best of his knights now. To Henry's heroes,' he toasted, raising his goblet high.

The men and Helwise drank, with varying degrees of enthusiasm, then Morville brought their attention back to the business of the day.

'What better way to celebrate our great feat than to bring down a white hart? That rarest of beasts, his head can go right there.' He pointed at the far wall behind the lord's table. 'He will grace Cnaresburg Castle and boast of our success for generations to come.'

'I shall drink to that,' Tracy said, upending his goblet once more.

'Which way is the beast headed?'

The men turned as one, then stood to greet the aged William de Percy, Baron of Topcliffe. Helwise curtsied.

'I bid you welcome, My Lord,' Morville said, and Percy crossed the room to place a gallant kiss on Lady Morville's hand.

'Lady Sybil sends her regards, Helwise, alas her hunting days are behind her, but she bids you be successful and teach these men a thing or two of the chase,' he said with a twinkle in his eye.

'I shall do my utmost, Sir William,' Helwise said and Percy patted her hand. Their families had known each other for many years, and Percy was as fiercely protective of her as he was of his own daughters.

Trying not to show his irritation, Morville called for more bread and cheese as well as more flagons of Rhenish for his esteemed guest, then ushered Percy to the central position on the bench facing the fire.

The others shifted once more to realign the pecking order, and Percy sat down, raising his eyebrows at Screven.

'I spotted him here, My Lord, heading north,' the huntsman said, pointing at the chart. 'I suggest relays of hounds at these points.'

'Hmm,' Percy said. 'Put one of the relays there.' He indicated the place he meant. 'That terrain is rough, he may bear west for flatter, faster ground.'

'As you wish, My Lord.'

Screven bowed to Percy, then again to Morville, before calling the dogs to heel and exiting.

'Your marshal has your mounts ready?' Percy asked Morville.

'Yes, My Lord.'

'Then let us depart. Tally-ho!' He raised his goblet and the men and Helwise toasted to the success of their hunt.

Horns announced the nobles' departure from Cnaresburg Castle, warning the townsfolk that a horde of horsemen would soon be tramping through the marketplace and up the High Street towards Haya Park.

Traders and tradesmen scurried to shift carts and stalls to expose a thoroughfare through the centre of the marketplace, which was soon turned to chaos. The nobles were a clash of colour in their finery, each trying to outdo the other in their garishness: Morville in blue and white, Tracy red and white, and Brett and FitzUrse in red and yellow. Percy even had his courser, smaller than the destriers ridden in war, but a powerful beast nonetheless, decked out in blue and yellow to match his cloak.

The local butcher had a battle to keep the hounds from his wares; although well-trained, the dogs were hungry and excited at the prospect of the hunt, and the smell of fresh, even less-than-fresh meat, proved to be too much. Screven's shouts and blows of his horn to keep his charges in order merely added to the confusion, and the townsfolk, bar the butcher, revelled in the spectacle; cheering and applauding their lords as they passed. They knew that a hunt meant a feast later that day, with a surplus of leftovers to be distributed amongst the commoners of Cnaresburg.

Hugh de Morville, as overlord of Cnaresburg, basked in the glory and love shown, waving and showering the spectators with quarter-pennies. Thanks to his wife and her family, the de Stotevilles, who had lived here since the days of King William, he was well respected in this town and surrounds, and his wedding day had been one of the best of his life; principally because he had been awarded the custodianship of Cnaresburg Castle by a generous King Henry.

As the nobles walked their mounts away from the merriment, their minds turned to the fynding, wondering how long Morville's lymers, the best breed of dog for tracking, would take to find trace of the white hart.

Their mirth was cut short by the tolling of the church bell and the men glanced at each other in consternation as the peals added up. Ten. Twenty. Thirty. Announcing the death of a man. A local resident? Or had news of Thomas Becket reached Cnaresburg?

Chapter 16

'How is Pipsqueak now we are away from the hounds?' Helwise called over to Richard le Falconer.

He raised the wicker cage perched before him on his saddle so his mistress could see the small brown-grey merlin inside. 'She is well, My Lady. Has been since we hooded her and she could no longer see the lymers.'

'Poor thing, those dogs scared the feathers off her.'

'She's not used to seeing so many at once excited for the hunt, My Lady.'

'True. Well, let us hope she gets used to them soon.'

'Aye, My Lady. 'Tis a pity we could not go with the main hunting party, that white hart would be a sight to see and no mistake.'

'But a shame to see such a fine beast brought down for the table,' Helwise said. 'I am gladdened we had need of taking a different path, Pipsqueak needs open ground to hunt.'

Richard le Falconer made no comment and they rode in silence until they reached their usual larking grounds to the west of Haya Park.

Falconer reached into the cage, pulled the falcon out and unhooded her. The small bird of prey squeaked as soon as she laid eyes on Helwise – and continued squeaking. Even her small brain knew the appearance of the lady of the castle meant food, and she flew to Helwise's gloved fist to receive her first treat of a one-day-old-chick's foot.

Helwise raised her arm, the falcon's cue to start hunting. Pipsqueak launched, then swooped, flying low to the ground to flush out her first prey: a meadow pipit. Chasing and gaining height on the bird, Pipsqueak then dived at a seemingly impossible speed, and her talons plucked the unfortunate bird out of mid-air and brought it back to Helwise to be rewarded with another chick's foot.

Having been hand-reared and trained from the egg, Pipsqueak viewed Falconer as her father and Helwise her mother. She had not worked out that she would get more to eat for less effort if she simply feasted on the birds she caught.

'She's doing well, My Lady – a dozen larks and a couple of pipits in the last hour alone.'

Helwise smiled with pride, then gasped and stared at the treeline. A white hart bounded out from the trees, gracefully making ground at high speed, and dashed across the open moorland before making a sudden direction change and racing for the nearest trees to the north.

'He's magnificent,' she said. 'So handsome.'

'My Lady!'

Helwise glanced at Falconer in irritation.

'They're on the chase, that means—'

'The hounds!' Helwise scoured the sky, searching for her bird and knowing that if she did not secure her and hood her before the merlin falcon saw the dogs, they may well lose her.

Too late. The lymers and greyhounds, hot on the scent of the hart, disrupted the peace as they chased hard, followed by the hunting party of nobles.

'My Lady!' Falconer called, and Helwise returned her gaze upwards, to see a confused and panicking Pipsqueak launch a new dive.

She held out her fist, tapping it, while Falconer threw her a chick's head to tempt the falcon, but Pipsqueak picked up none of the visual cues, focusing instead on the object of her dive. The feather in the cap of Sir Hugh de Morville.

Talons outstretched, Pipsqueak arrowed in on her prey, grabbed what she thought to be a songbird, then struggled to lift the heavy woollen headwear.

She grounded amidst flying hooves and the shouts of an infuriated baron, and hopped in a desperate attempt to release the woollen encumbrance and take off to safety.

'God's wounds!' Morville shrieked. 'That bloody rat of a bird took my cap!' He rubbed his head, refusing to acknowledge the pain and shock of the strike from a six-ounce bird diving faster than the speed of a shot crossbow bolt; at least before his fellow knights. Helwise would hear more of it later, in private.

'Pipsqueak!' Helwise screamed, and ran over to the mêlée to rescue her youngest and favourite falcon.

'Get back, woman, do you want to be trampled?' Morville accented his warning with a flick of his crop. Helwise flinched to save her face from its sting.

Morville moved away from Pipsqueak. 'Retrieve my cap, Helwise, and train your bird better.'

Helwise rushed to Pipsqueak and untangled her sharp talons from the cap. The falcon hopped on to her fist and she passed the hat back to her husband.

'She is but a young bird, Hugh. She has not flown with the hounds before, they scare her.'

'Bah! A hunting bird scared of hounds? You'd do well to wring its neck.'

'No!' Helwise stepped back, away from her husband, her free arm held out in defence of Pipsqueak. At Morville's glower, she added, 'Begging your pardon, My Lord. I shall continue with her training. She is a good hunter – near two dozen larks for the table already.'

'Hugh,' FitzUrse called, 'we are losing the hart!'

'Hmpf.' Morville glared at his wife a moment longer, then pulled his courser's head around, kicked, and re-joined the chase.

Once the hunting party was out of sight and hearing, Helwise launched Pipsqueak once more.

'She missed! That's the first one she hasn't taken,' Helwise said as the falcon recovered from her unproductive dive, hugged the ground for a few wingbeats, then soared once more.

'And again. What's wrong? Do you think she's hurt?' Helwise asked Falconer.

'No, she would not be hunting if she were hurt. She's just unsettled.'

'We'll call it a day, then. Give her a rest.'

'Best to let her catch one first, else she'll learn she does not need to hunt to be fed.'

'Just this once?' Helwise implored.

Richard le Falconer shook his head. 'Sorry, My Lady, these birds are lazy and will not hunt if there is no imperative to eat. Best to wait and give her time, else your husband *will* wring her neck.'

Helwise nodded, knowing he was right, and examined the sky for a glimpse of Pipsqueak. 'She's diving,' Helwise said, excitement and apprehension inflecting her words; if Pipsqueak did not catch a lark soon, her future looked short.

Both Helwise and Falconer held their breath as Pipsqueak stretched her talons and snatched the skylark out of the air.

'Yes!' Helwise shouted, jumped and clapped her hands in exuberance, then turned and hugged Richard le Falconer.

'My Lady,' he reproached, stepping back.

'Oh, I beg your pardon, Richard. But she's done it, my little Pipsqueak has done it!'

She turned sideways on to the bird to make herself appear smaller and stretched out her right arm. Pipsqueak dropped the skylark into her waiting hand then circled round to fly on the wind and landed on Helwise's gloved left fist.

Helwise dropped the dead lark into her hunting bag and rewarded Pipsqueak with a full chick, squeezing the yolk from the head before offering the meal.

Richard le Falconer took the hunting bag from Helwise and stowed it on his horse, then returned with Pipsqueak's cage. The falcon hopped inside to finish tearing the chick apart and swallowing.

Chapter 17

Morville caught up his fellow nobles just as the chase ended. He saw the hart turn to face them – at bay and ready to defend himself against his pursuers.

He was a magnificent creature, standing taller than a man; his proud head with the dozen points lifted high, nostrils flaring, eyes staring and ears flicking at every bark of the restrained hounds.

The nobles spread out, surrounding the creature, and Morville glanced at Percy. Despite being the host, he indicated with a hand that the elderly Percy should take the kill.

William de Percy acknowledged the honour of the mort with a small nod, then drew his sword and walked his courser forward.

The hart took a couple of steps back, but stopped at a halloo from Tracy behind him.

Percy came on, drew his sword high, then slashed at the animal's throat, immediately backing up his courser to avoid the fountain of blood.

In silence, the hart fell to its fore-knees, his frightened eyes already dulling, then collapsed to the ground to the cheers of the gathered noblemen.

Morville was the first to congratulate Percy on the kill. 'It will make a fine course tonight, Hugh,' Percy said. 'I hope your cook can do it justice.'

Morville swallowed at the insult – etiquette dictated that the man who made the kill should host the resultant feast; they should be dining at Spofford Castle tonight not Cnaresburg – but he refused to let any sign of it show on his face or in his voice. 'Adam shall make a fine job of it, My Lord. Will you be gracing us with your company?'

Percy nodded. 'I shall.' He wheeled his courser around and cantered in the direction of Spofford Castle, leaving Morville to preside over the unmaking.

Screven stepped forward, unsheathing his knife, and began the job of dissecting the beast, starting with its guts before skinning it.

Once the hart had been unmade and the haunches of bloody meat and the proud head piled on to the small cart that had followed the nobles, Screven began the curée to reward the hounds.

He soaked stale bread in the blood of the hart, then mixed it with the intestines and pushed the resultant porridge into the gaping hole of the hide.

The dogs ran in excited circles, but their base instincts had long ago been beaten out of them and they held back until the sound of Screven's horn gave them permission to eat.

Morville watched the mêlée with interest – the deer carcass under the roiling mass of hungry dogs having a strange fascination – before he pulled the head of his courser around and led the way back to Cnaresburg Castle. He caught and rode past Helwise with no acknowledgement, and she fell in beside her brother, William de Stoteville.

Stoteville reached over and placed a hand on his sister's arm. He held no regard for Morville as a man, yet had a great deal of respect for his titles, in particular the barony of Burgh-on-the-Sands.

'Do not fret, Helwise. He will not be here long. There have been no repercussions to his deed and he will surely re-join King Henry in Normandy before too much time passes.'

Helwise smiled at him. 'It cannot come soon enough, Brother.'

He gave her arm another squeeze, then withdrew it. They both knew well the realities of marriage. Helwise would have to bear her husband's presence – whatever his demands – for as long as he chose to remain in Cnaresburg. Then she would be free to enjoy her position as Lady of the Castle until Morville deigned to return once more.

'William, what's happening?' Helwise asked, sitting straighter in her saddle and looking about her at the near empty High Street. 'Where is everyone? It's market day.'

William said nothing, but nodded his head towards the marketplace ahead. The townsfolk stood in silence, watching Morville and the others parade towards the imposing towers of the northern gate to Cnaresburg Castle.

One or two people smiled at the Stotevilles as they rode past, but there was none of the usual welcome. Whilst Morville was accepted as overlord, the Stotevilles were loved here, having lived amongst and advocated for these people for generations. Helwise was used to greetings, cheers and even the occasional posy of riverside flowers when she was about Cnaresburg. She looked to William in consternation.

'It appears that the news has reached Cnaresburg,' he said, his face grim as rotten fruit was thrown at the mounted noblemen ahead. Morville pulled his horse up and shouted at the assembled crowd.

'Murderer!' a young boy shouted. 'You murdered the Archbishop! May you rot in Hell!'

Morville jumped off his courser and forced his way into the crowd, reappearing with his fingers clasped around the ear of a young boy.

'Robert Flower!' Helwise gasped. 'Oh no.' Robert was a strange young boy – wiser than his years – whose outspoken ways often got him into trouble, yet Helwise – and most of the town it had to be said – had a soft spot for the young tearaway. Whatever trouble he got into or caused, there had always been good reason – at least in the boy's mind – whether it was stealing bread to give to a starving family or stealing cloth from Tentergate to present to his mother for a new gown. The people of Cnaresburg held him in a kind of exasperated regard.

Morville struck the lad, hard, and he fell to the dirty cobbles. As Morville made to kick him, the townsfolk rushed forward as one; the crowd becoming a mob.

FitzUrse grabbed his friend, pushed him to his horse and the four galloped to the castle, ignoring the pedestrians who fled from their path.

'Come on, Helwise,' William urged, spurring his own courser into a gallop.

Helwise screamed as a stone glanced off her skull, and William wheeled around, putting himself between his sister and the people gathered about the prone body of Robert Flower.

Screven placed himself on his mistress's other side as they galloped to safety.

Helwise took a last look around before the portcullis clanged down and the drawbridge over the ditch rose, relieved to see a dazed Robert Flower sit up just before he was lost to sight.

William reached up to help his sister dismount. 'Are you hurt?'

Helwise shook her head, then grimaced at the pain. She put her hands to her skull, then looked at her reddened fingers.

'Come, I'll help you to your bedchamber,' William said. 'Where is your husband?' he added, his face colouring with fury. 'He has not even paused to see if you are safe.'

'What do you expect?' Helwise asked. 'He has concerns only for himself.'

After a short silence, William said, 'I am sorry, Sister, you must prepare yourself. If Cnaresburg has reacted with this fury, the rest of Christendom must feel the same. I fear your husband will be present here for some time.'

Helwise said nothing.

'I shall stay here with you as much as I am able,' William added. 'I will not leave you alone with these men.'

Helwise nodded, then grimaced again. 'My thanks, Brother, your company will be most welcome.'

William glanced at the door to the hall at the bottom of the keep, then helped his sister up the narrow stone stairs to the bedchambers. The sound of the night's anger carried clearly up the steep round stairwell and his heart sank. Difficult times lay ahead.

Chapter 18

At first glance around the great hall, nothing seemed amiss. Fires blazed in the three large fireplaces. The candles of the chandeliers and candelabra flickered with flame, adding to the uplifting spirit of celebration.

Morville and Helwise sat at the centre of the lord's table with the knights and lords, from Sir Reginald FitzUrse to Nigel de Plumton, arranged to either side in order of status – other than William de Stoteville, who had ensured that he sat beside his sister in defiance of the higher titles of FitzUrse and Tracy. Lesser nobles, such as Pulleine of Fewston and Bilton from Hampsthwaite, sat at the centre of the low tables along with Thomas de Screven and other important local men, the richest merchants, and the parish priest. The rest of the available seats were occupied by the various vassals and men-at-arms of the gathered nobles.

Music was provided by a flautist, and tuneless but well-wetted voices grew louder and merrier with each jug of wine or ale.

Morville glanced around the gathered throng once more. There was no sign of William de Percy or any of his men. Morville grimaced in annoyance. Not only had Percy insulted him earlier by taking the mort, then issuing no invitation to feast at Spofford Manor – whilst Percy insisted on calling it a castle it was in reality no more than a large manor house, but Percy – one of King Henry's favourites – had not deigned to join the knights for the feast of venison; an unforgivable insult.

Meat was a rarity – banned by the Church on Wednesdays, Fridays and Saturdays – and with Lent imminent a feast such as this night's was something to savour. Yet it was all ruined. Not only by the events of the afternoon and Percy's absence, but each course was slow in being brought to the table, and the larks, one of which he had just demolished, had been cold long before they had been placed before him and his guests. He threw the small bones on to the table in disgust and shouted for his steward, Jack.

Helwise stared at the half-eaten bird – one of the many caught by herself and the merlin – a feat of which she was proud with such a young bird accompanying a full hunt for the first time. A pity about the incident with her husband . . . She glanced at him as she remembered his near panic when he'd felt those talons at his head. True, the bird could have had his eye out, but it was the highlight of Helwise's day.

Morville caught her glance and smile, and scowled. She looked away and fell into conversation with her brother, sitting to her left.

'Is there any news of young Robert?'

He shrugged. 'The boy is fine, although a little dazed still. And recounting his narrow escape from Becket's murderers with some zeal.'

'Enough!' Morville roared, slamming his fist on the table. 'Do not mention that boy's name in this castle! And never, ever, refer to myself or my fellow lords as murderers, or you shall drive me to commit that very crime. Do you understand me?'

Stoteville lowered his head in acquiescence while a terrified Helwise grabbed his hand under the table.

Morville stared at his brother-in-law a moment longer then took hold of his wife's chin, tilting her head and pushing her hair and fillet away from her forehead to expose the now ugly bruise and gash on her pale skin. 'That is what those rogues did – to their lady! The lady who cares for their troubles, feeds the poorest and most wretched, and advocates for their needs. This is what they did!' He thrust Helwise's face away, ignoring her cry of pain and the tears that had escaped her lashes.

'You are hurting her, My Lord,' William de Stoteville said, his tone low and calm.

Morville stared at him a moment and let go of his wife's face. 'Steward!' he roared. 'Where in Christ's name is the venison?'

Jack leaned forward to speak in his lord's ear. 'Begging your pardon, My Lord. Many of the cooks and servers were at the market today. Not many have returned to the castle.'

Morville stared at him. 'Ensure that they are replaced forthwith,' he eventually said. 'And bring out that bloody venison.'

'Yes, My Lord,' the servant said, bowing and taking the half-full platters of leftover pork and skylark down to the lower tables to be gnawed over.

The venison arrived half a dozen goblets of wine later. Morville was morose, FitzUrse and Tracy loud and belligerent – mainly with each other, to the relief of everyone else present – whilst Brett gazed around him with unfocused eyes and a vague smile.

Nobody spoke to Morville, FitzUrse, Tracy and Brett except Morville, FitzUrse, Tracy and Brett, and the only ones who noticed were Helwise and William de Stoteville. Stoteville caught the eye of his vassal, Nigel de Plumton, Lord of the Manor of Plumton, who looked worried. Stoteville would have given anything to hear the opinions and words of his peers, but was reluctant to leave his sister's side when her husband was in such foul spirits.

She leaned into him, knowing her brother well enough to guess where his mind had turned. 'Go and join them,' she whispered. 'With my husband so hated, we must strain to retain good relations with our friends.'

William nodded and moved to stand but was stilled by Morville's roar.

'Hated? How dare you speak of your husband as such?'

The chatter and music silenced and the entire room of near two hundred souls stared at their lord and lady. Helwise wisely said nothing, knowing any attempt at appeasement would result in more ire.

'Am I not your friend, wife?' Morville asked.

Helwise nodded.

'Then do not betray me.' The words were uttered calmly, so calmly that Helwise only understood them when her husband's fist connected with her cheekbone and she fell, screaming from both the pain at the blow, plus fear at the crack she heard on its impact.

William stayed silent, but pulled his dagger as he climbed on to the bench and threw his entire weight at his brother-in-law.

Helwise crawled to safety as the other knights jumped to their feet. FitzUrse, Tracy and Brett attempted to heave Stoteville away from Morville, and the local nobles tried to heave FitzUrse, Tracy and Brett away from Stoteville.

Soon the entire hall was at odds with each knight's men fighting their master's rival's men. Staring at the carnage, Helwise was reminded of hunting hounds fighting over a kill. She alone witnessed William de Percy, favourite of King Henry, enter the hall, stare around him in contempt, then abruptly turn, his scarlet cloak swirling, to leave the troublesome knights to their brawl.

Chapter 19

11th July 2015

'Dan, no, I have a headache.' Sarah wasn't quite sure if she'd spoken the words aloud, she was still more in sleep than out of it, and Dan didn't stop. He rolled her unresponsive body on to her back and her entire focus was on keeping her legs together.

He persisted. There was no sensuous touching, no loving caresses, just fingers between her legs, trying to force them apart and gain access.

Sarah forced herself awake to again grunt, 'No,' then rolled back on to her front. She despaired when she felt those same fingers still seeking the depths of her body. She held her legs together, determined not to be used like this.

She tumbled back into dreams, thinking she was safe, then jerked awake as she was intimately touched.

'No, Dan, stop, let me sleep,' she mumbled, curling up into a ball.

'Oh come on, Sarah, it's been ages,' Dan said and smacked her backside.

Sarah started awake – properly now – sat up, and pulled both covers and legs up.

'What the hell's wrong with you, Sarah? I thought we were doing better lately.'

'I'm not against a little morning glory, Dan, but I was asleep and woke to you mauling me. I feel like a piece of meat.'

'Is it so wrong for a husband to desire his wife?'

'Of course not, if the husband takes the time to turn his wife on, so that she wants it too, rather than just taking what he fancies.'

'You make it sound like rape!'

'Well, to be honest, waking up like that kind of feels like rape.'

'But you're my wife!'

'Yes, and I love making love with you. But not when I'm asleep!'

'You bitch. You *are* shagging Mike, aren't you?'

'Oh my God.' Sarah rested her head in her hands. 'For the last time, I am not having an affair with Mike. I wouldn't do that to you.'

'How can I believe that? You don't even want to have sex with me any more.'

'Of course I do, I'd just like to be an active participant, that's all!'

'There you go again with the rape accusation.'

'I didn't say that, you did.'

'But how can a man trying to have sex with his wife be rape?'

'Are you kidding me? What, are you living in the Middle Ages now? You do not have an automatic right to my body. It's *my* body. And if I want to say no, then you respect that.'

'You *are* sleeping with Mike, aren't you?'

Sarah stared dumbfounded at her husband. How many times could she deny an accusation without foundation? 'No, Dan, I'm not,' she said, weary.

'Then who?'

'No one. And unless you can trust me, not you.'

'Fucking bitch!' He bent over her as she lay whimpering in their bed. 'Going off sex is the first sign of cheating,' he hissed in her ear. 'I know you're being untrue. I know it.'

He jerked back and stormed naked out of the room, fists clenched. Sarah stared after him, knowing she'd had enough and wondering how she could separate their lives in a divorce. And where the hell could she go?

'Hi Helen,' Sarah said as Helen stood to embrace her friend.

'How are you?' Helen asked. 'I've been worried about you.'

The women both sat and Sarah shook her head. 'I don't know what's got into Dan lately. He was jealous after that love scene with Mike in the last play, but nothing like this, it's exploding out of him now.'

'Exploding? What do you mean? Has he hit you?'

'Oh no, no,' Sarah shook her head, then paused. 'Not yet. No more than the slap he gave me in the pub the other week, anyway.'

'Not yet?'

'No. No, sorry, I'm being silly. I didn't sleep well. There is no yet. Dan isn't like that.'

'He did a damned good impression in the Bailiff,' Helen pointed out.

Sarah stayed silent for a moment, then said, 'I'm going to the bar, what would you like?'

'No, I'll get them, you need a bit of TLC.' Helen reached across the table and squeezed her friend's hand, aware that Sarah's eyes were glistening.

'Large dry white wine, please. Thanks Helen.'

'Anytime.' Helen stood then sat back down. 'You know if it gets too much and you need some space, you're very welcome to stay with me.'

'Thanks, but things aren't that bad. He's my husband and he's clearly going through something. You know what men are like, he'll tell me what's going on eventually.'

'Yes, when it's all sorted.' Helen laughed, then went to the bar.

'I got a bottle,' Helen said, and stepped aside for the barman to put it and two glasses on the table. There were some advantages at least to having a broken wrist. 'I have a feeling this is going to be a long lunch.'

Sarah laughed. 'You know me so well.' She picked up the bottle and poured two large glasses, while Helen sat down.

'He does like you, you know.'

'Who, Dan?'

'No, Sarah. Mike.'

'Well, we're friends.'

'He likes you more than that and you know it.'

'Oh don't be silly.'

'I'm not, it's obvious to everyone – except you it seems.'

Sarah said nothing but looked thoughtful.

'Oh, you like him too, don't you?'

'Helen, no, I'm married with two kids.'

'So? I'm not asking if you're sleeping with him, just if you fancy him.'

'Helen!'

'You still haven't answered the question. You do, don't you?'

'Well okay, he's sweet.'

'Sweet? Could you find a more insulting compliment?'

'It's a married women's compliment,' Sarah said with a grin, 'and all I'm giving.'

'Giving me, anyway,' Helen said, laughing.

'Giving anyone,' Sarah insisted. 'Mind you, I'm paying the price as if I were giving Mike more – might as well do the crime if I'm already doing the time. Cheers.' She raised her glass and took a large gulp while Helen spluttered over her own wine.

'I'm joking! Only joking!' Sarah said as they both descended into helpless giggles.

'Well, be careful who you tell that joke to, Sarah.'

'Only you.'

'That's good.' Helen was serious again. 'You know, I *am* worried. Not only about you but the rest of the players too. If Dan's cracking, it could fracture the whole group.'

'Thanks.'

'Oh don't be like that, Sarah, you know I'm here for you.'

'Yes, of course, sorry Helen. I'm just tired. Sick and tired of my husband and my marriage.'

Helen leaned over again to squeeze her hand. 'Is it really that bad?'

Sarah looked at, eyes steady. 'Pretty much, yes. We've fought before, but this time I just don't have the energy to fix things.'

'You don't love him any more.'

'I didn't say that.'

'Yes, Sarah, you kind of did.'

Chapter 20

'Are you sure we can afford this, Charlie?' Helen said as Charlie got up to get another round in.

'Absolutely. We still have a large chunk of the grant money left. We deserve a celebration, and as treasurer I officially declare that we can afford to do it in style.'

'Okay, if you're sure.' Helen relaxed and beamed. 'I still can't quite believe that we got funding.'

'It's about time,' Charlie said. 'We've been operating on a budget for years. It feels good to earn before the doors even open.'

'Well, hurry up and get the drinks in then,' Helen said with a laugh.

'Yeah, get a move on, mate, we're dying of thirst here,' Paul said.

Charlie flicked two fingers at him, then went to the bar.

'Oh, bloody hell, that Catherine lass is here – no wonder he was so keen to get up for the next round,' Paul said. 'He's not beating me with this one, too.'

'Oh don't tell me you two have bet on a woman again,' Sarah said.

'It's just a bit of fun.'

'No it isn't, it's degrading. Why don't you try to be nice and – I don't know – talk to her?'

'Where's the fun in that?' Paul asked.

'Yes, you might win the bet that way, mate,' Mike said at the same time.

The others laughed at the comical impression of a light bulb illuminating that Paul was barely aware he'd done, before he hurried to the bar asking Charlie if he could give him a hand.

Sarah smiled at Mike, pleased he'd taken her part, then glanced at Dan as he slammed his empty glass on the table. 'Off for a piss,' he said and got to his feet, knocking the table, and staggered off in the direction of the gents.

'Is he okay?' Ed asked.

Sarah sighed. 'He's fine, just drunk. He's been drinking all day,' she said, her exasperation with her husband clear to her friends.

'How long has that been going on?' Alec asked.

Sarah shrugged.

'We should try and talk some sense into him,' Alec added.

'Won't do any good, even if you can get him when he's sober,' Sarah said.

'We have to do something,' Helen said and laid a gentle hand on her friend's arm. 'It's affecting his performance on stage – I won't let him ruin this for us.'

Sarah shrugged again. 'I don't know what to tell you. I don't know what to do,' she said, tears threatening.

'Shush, it's okay, love,' Mike said, putting his arm around her shoulders and pulling her close. 'We're all friends here, and we're here for you.'

Helen widened her eyes at Sarah in warning, but she either didn't see or she refused to see. She patted Mike's knee. 'Thanks, Mike.' She straightened before Dan came back. Mike reluctantly dropped his arm and gave her a small smile.

Helen froze. *Shit, he's in love with her,* she thought. *Oh shit, shit, shit. I didn't realise it was that bad.* Her thoughts were interrupted by Dan thumping back down in his seat.

'Have they got the drinks yet?' he said, peering at the bar in search of Paul and Charlie.

'Could be a while yet,' Ed said, turning and spotting them both talking to Catherine. 'Doesn't look like they've even ordered them.'

'Bloody amateurs,' Dan sneered and levered himself back to his feet to hurry up his mates. Ed, Alec, Helen, Sarah and Mike looked at each other in silence.

'He'll be okay,' Mike said, patting Sarah's back. 'He'll sort himself out and soon.'

'What if he doesn't?' Sarah said. 'What then?'

'Then we find someone else to play FitzUrse,' Helen said.

Sarah looked at her. 'That's not what I meant, Helen.'

'Sorry.' Helen flushed and looked at the table.

'I'll have a word with him,' Mike said.

'I don't think that's a good idea,' Alec said. 'Ed and I will do it.'

'Why?'

Alec didn't reply, but turned to Ed. 'You're up for that, aren't you?'

'Yeah sure, whatever I can do to help,' Ed said.

'Here you go, sorry about the delay,' Charlie said as he put two pints and a couple of gin and tonics on the table, followed by another four pints from Paul. Everyone held the table steady as Dan retook his seat – just in case – then the other two sat down.

'Took you bloody long enough,' Mike said.

'Ah, but it was worth it,' Paul said, holding up a scrap of paper with numbers scribbled on it. 'Pay up, Charlie.'

Charlie grumbled, but got his wallet out. 'Enjoy it while it lasts – I'll get the next bird, then you'll be giving me that tenner back.'

'When did you two get so callous?' Sarah asked, disgusted with her friends, then erupted into giggles as Catherine poured her drink over Paul's head and plucked the tenner out of Charlie's fingers.

'That'll pay for the drink I've just wasted,' she said. 'Grow up, boys.' She sashayed to the door, turned and gave Sarah a wink before she left.

'I bloody paid for that drink,' Paul shouted after her, to even more amusement from his friends.

'I'm off to clean up,' he said. He punched Charlie on the arm. 'We both had a lucky escape with that one.'

Charlie tried to retort, but could not form any recognisable words through his laughter. Eventually, holding his stomach, he managed to say, 'Priceless, bloody priceless, well worth a tenner. I think I'm in love.' He collapsed into helpless laughter again, infecting the whole table – including Dan.

When Paul returned to the table, still wet, but at least not quite as sticky, Helen couldn't resist. 'Now careful, guys, we're already barred from the Borough Bailiff, we don't want to get barred from here too. We'll be running out of pubs at this rate.' Even Paul managed to see the funny side.

'I'm off to the loo, will you let me out, Dan?' Sarah said once the giggles had subsided enough.

Exiting the ladies, she was surprised by Mike, who grabbed her arm and pulled her into a hug.

'Mike, what are you doing?'

'Shush,' he said. 'Don't worry, I just want to say, well, I know things aren't great with Dan at the moment . . .'

'Mike, this isn't the time, we're both pissed and if Dan sees us, he'll kick off big time.'

'No, it's okay, the boys are having a word with him, he didn't even see me leave the table.'

Sarah nodded. 'Okay.'

'Sarah, I just want to say . . .'

'Well hurry up and say it then.' She laughed to take away the sting of her words.

'I just want to say, if you're not happy, you know, with Dan, you don't have to stay.'

'Mike, he's my husband and the father of my children.'

'I know, I know, but if he's making you unhappy . . . oh, sod it,' he said, grabbed Sarah's head and kissed her, hard.

Sarah squeaked and tried to push Mike away, but as he persisted, she found her resistance wavering, replaced by tingles in her belly and a quickening of her pulse. As she melted into Mike's kiss, the tingling spread until she was kissing him back with the same intensity.

Mike pulled back to look into her eyes as she pushed away, horrified at the realisation of what she'd done.

'I can't, Mike. I can't, I'm married, that shouldn't have happened.'

She broke the contact between them and rushed back to the bar, her thoughts and feelings in such a whirl she didn't see Helen standing against the wall, watching.

Chapter 21

'I don't get this scene,' Dan said.

Helen sighed, paused a moment, then explained again. 'We're covering the major incidents between Henry II and Becket to understand how such a close friendship ended so brutally.'

'Yes, I know that, but you keep talking about Clarendon – what the hell is Clarendon?'

'A palace near Salisbury,' Helen said, her teeth gritted. She took another breath to calm her irritation – she had explained this three times already, and her fears over Dan's mood and attitude were becoming reality. He was rude and surly to everyone – not just Sarah and Mike.

Helen just stopped herself from glancing at the pair of them – they were giggling like teenagers. She kept her attention on Dan. *Thank God I cast him as FitzUrse*, she thought – not for the first time – *at least this attitude suits The Bear perfectly.*

'Henry has called a council to meet at Clarendon Palace. He wants Becket and the bishops to make an oath that Henry has final authority in all things – including the sentencing of crimonious clerics.'

'Crimonious clerics?'

'Priests and monks who have broken the law.'

'But what's all the fuss about, surely the Church can sort them out?'

'No – they can only fine and defrock. Not a fitting punishment for robbery, rape or murder.'

'Huh. Fair enough. So what's Becket's problem?'

'Becket isn't popular with the English clergy – he wasn't even an ordained priest when Henry made him archbishop, remember – they don't trust him and he's trying to prove he's on their side. Henry is simply asking for too much.'

'Doesn't sound like it to me,' Dan said.

'Oh for God's sake, Dan,' Paul said, his patience running out. 'Can we just get on with the scene?'

'I don't understand why I'm in it,' Dan replied. 'How do we know it was our knights who were there?'

'We don't,' Helen said, all attempts at relaxed conversation now abandoned. 'We know Morville was there, the rest is dramatic licence.'

Dan opened his mouth but Paul interrupted before he could speak. 'Enough of this nonsense.' He paused in the shock of silence – Paul was usually mild mannered. 'Sorry guys, but seriously, we're here to rehearse. Let's just run through the scene, then we can talk it through later in the pub.'

'Okay everybody, positions please,' Helen called.

'Charlie, you as Becket centre stage. Ed and Sarah join him, you're bishops for this scene – Ed you're the Archbishop of York Roger de Pont l'Évêque, Sarah you're taking the role of Bishop Gilbert Foliot. Dan and Mike, I need you in the wings, with Paul as Henry behind you,' Helen instructed. 'From the top,' she said when everybody was in place.

Henry's voice reverberated from offstage. 'Get in there and force those damnable priests to submit. I'll castrate or execute any damned cleric who defies me!'

The bishops glanced at each other, clearly terrified.

'Calm thyselves,' Becket said. 'The King can be . . . dramatic at times. 'Tis an idle threat, purely for show.'

The bishops relaxed, though only a little – they had been locked in this room for the past two days. But their archbishop knew their king better than any other man in Christendom. They had to trust him. To be fair, they had no other choice. The oath that King Henry demanded of them was too great; they were more than happy to leave the awkward and potentially life-threatening negotiations to the unwanted primary legate the King had forced upon them.

As one, they shrieked and retreated as Morville and FitzUrse burst through the door, flung away their cloaks to reveal their coats of mail, and unsheathed their broadswords.

'Definitely dramatic,' squeaked Roger de Pont l'Évêque, cowering away from the armed knights and clutching the arm of Gilbert Foliot.

'Submit in the name of the King,' Morville shouted.

'He has had enough of vacillating!' FitzUrse yelled into the face of Becket. The Archbishop stood his ground, but words failed him, for the moment at least.

'This is unacceptable.' L'Évêque stepped forward, only to retreat as Morville and FitzUrse turned their attention to him.

'Put down thy swords,' Becket quietly commanded. 'We are men of God and unarmed. Should the King wish to talk, we shall converse, but there is no need for this.'

'The King,' FitzUrse shouted, 'wishes agreement to his demands. Refusal of such is treason. And we do not countenance traitors.'

'My Lord, please, we are no traitors here – merely servants of God and the Church.'

'And the King!' FitzUrse shouted, brandishing his sword at Becket.

Becket studied the faces of the two men threatening him and realised he had no choice. 'Very well, I consent to the demand of my king. Please, sheathe your arms and allow the King and myself to discuss my oath.'

* * *

'Fabulous,' Helen cried. 'Even without costumes, it felt like the characters speaking. Well done!'
'Pub?' Mike said.

Chapter 22

29th March 1171

'It is good to be outside the curtain walls again,' said Richard le Brett, turning his face up to the sun.

'And out of the chapel,' FitzUrse growled.

The four knights had spent a particularly pious Lent, hearing Mass twice daily. On Easter Sunday – yesterday – they had donated the best cuts of meat in Morville's kitchen for the townsfolk to enjoy. Today was their first opportunity to hunt since Lent had begun, and the knights of Cnaresburg Castle intended to make the most of it.

Nigel de Plumton had joined them at the behest of Sir William de Stoteville, but William de Percy was once again absent, as were Sir John de Goldesburgh and Gamellor. Helwise had also elected to abstain from the day's activities.

Despite their reduced numbers, the men were determined to enjoy themselves and had elected boar as their quarry. The kill would not be as prestigious as the white hart they had brought down on their last outing, but it promised to be better sport. Boar could be dangerous and would test all of their wits, and hopefully lift their spirits. Relations between the men were tense after their confinement and the constant fights.

'I had the pleasure of dining with William de Percy at Spofford yesterday, William,' Nigel de Plumton said at length, while they waited for Morville and the others.

'Easter Sunday?' William de Stoteville asked.

Plumton nodded. 'It was a prestigious affair. Hamlin Plantagenet was in attendance, as well as William de Courcy, Lord of Harewood.'

'King Henry?'

Plumton shook his head. 'No, he dare not leave Normandy until he has heard from Pope Alexander.'

'He *dare* not? That does not sound like the King.'

'There is a great fear of excommunication.'

'I see. Is that why Percy did not invite us to Spofford for Easter?'

'Yes, I fear it is true. If Henry's messenger did not meet the Pope first, your brother-in-law and his cronies may be facing great trials ahead.'

'And my sister,' William muttered, watching an argument develop between Morville and FitzUrse over the courser The Bear had been given to ride. 'What was the tone of your dinner?'

'Sombre,' Plumton said. 'I owe you much, William, and must warn you. If the Church condemns them,' he nodded towards Morville and the other knights, 'they will find no support amongst the barons.'

Excommunication was the harshest punishment the Church could inflict on a man, and William nodded at the implications of Plumton's statement.

'That puts you in a delicate position, William.'

'Yes, it does indeed. I have no love for Morville, but I cannot abandon my sister to whatever fate befalls *him*.'

The men paused to watch Tracy and Brett physically restrain FitzUrse, whilst Morville, with his newly bruised jaw, was attended to by Mauclerk and Thomas de Screven.

'There may yet be no problem,' William said, his disdain evident on his face. 'They are likely to kill each other before Pope Alexander's judgement reaches their ears.'

Morville shook off his man and rushed FitzUrse. Tracy stepped forward, receiving a violent shove for his trouble and Morville and The Bear rolled in the mud like street urchins, whilst Brett backed up out of their way. Neither Plumton nor Stoteville made any move to intervene, and Henry Goodricke, Cnaresburg's bailiff, walked up to join them.

'I like the idea of this hunt less and less,' he said. The other two nodded.

'We need to make our allegiance plain,' Plumton said. 'William de Courcy is holding a tournament at Harewood Castle next week. We should attend, and fight under the red and gold of King Henry, make sure they know whose side we are on.'

William and Henry nodded their agreement, but before either could say more, Richard le Brett spoke.

'A tournament at Harewood? God's blood, that's just what we need – we've been cooped up in this damned place for too long.'

The three lesser nobles looked at each other in dismay as Brett strode over to the squabbling knights.

'Stop that, save it for the tournament next week – at Harewood Castle!'

'What's that?' FitzUrse got to his feet and gave Morville a withering glare that stopped his next attack before it began. 'A tournament? Hugh, William, did you hear young Richard? A tournament, by God, there couldn't be better news. I for one am sick of the rain, the sights and the smells of this damnable town. A knights' tourney at Harewood? A hundred marks to the best placed of us. Who shall take the bet?'

All three took him up on it, their dispute forgotten.

Plumton, Goodricke and Stoteville stared at each other.

'They were not supposed to know about it,' Plumton whispered.

'Don't fret, Nigel, they were likely to hear a loose word from a groom or serving girl. But we shall make our own way there, we shall not travel with Morville and the other assassins.'

'Agreed,' Plumton and Goodricke said. 'Agreed.'

Morville led the hunting party into the marketplace, glancing warily around him as he did so. A complement of men-at-arms accompanied the nobles – a larger quota than Morville had ever needed before in Cnaresburg, but the townsfolk offered no threat. They simply and silently turned their backs as the knights rode past.

'Hugh,' Stoteville said, pointing down a narrow alley as they emerged on to the muddy high street.

Morville peered into the gloom, then quickly drew back his head as the smell of the rotting heap of meat struck him. It was the Easter meat the knights had foregone and given to the peasants and villeins.

'Even the bloody dogs don't want our food,' Morville growled, both angry and hurt at the dishonour shown him. The other knights were close behind and grumbled at the waste.

'Á Morville,' FitzUrse shouted, the battle cry a warning to all present. Then he laughed. Loudly.

'Shut up, you fool,' Stoteville said, pulling his courser up and turning to face the man.

FitzUrse's colour rose until his face was nearly as red as the cloak he wore.

'You do not speak to me like that, boy.'

'Then do no more to antagonise this town,' Stoteville replied, equally angry. 'These are *my* people. My family has lived amongst them since they arrived on these shores with King William.'

FitzUrse made to reply, but Morville intervened. 'Stop it, both of you.' He glanced behind FitzUrse at Tracy and Brett, then beyond them. The knights turned in their saddles to see the way behind blocked. Judging by the tools the men carried, peasants, villeins, butchers and more had gathered together to stand against the man they called lord.

The knights and men-at-arms positioned themselves to meet an attack, riding abreast boot-to-boot, and brought their boar spears to bear.

As one the townsfolk dropped the tools of their trades and turned their backs.

'They're pretending to be Becket,' Stoteville said with a glance at Morville. 'Non-threatening and unarmed.'

Morville ignored him, stared at the wall of backs before him, then yanked his courser's head around, kicked, and galloped towards Haya Park.

The other nobles glanced at each other, then followed. William de

Stoteville brought up the rear with Plumton and Goodricke, at a walk, noticing how worried both Tracy and Brett looked as they continually glanced behind.

The three local men said nothing as they walked their mounts on, each of them lost in their own thoughts.

Chapter 23

April 1171

'Harewood Castle is at the top of this hill,' Morville said for the benefit of FitzUrse, Tracy and Brett, 'the other side of that wood.'

Nobody acknowledged him. They were all exhausted by the early start and seven-league trek, although it was the palfreys they rode that had done all the work.

Morville glanced behind him and grimaced at the state of his fellow knights; too much indulgence the night before a tournament never boded well, but there was no stopping Tracy and FitzUrse when they had the taste of wine in their gullets. And Brett was just as bad, as was Morville himself. Morville laughed out loud at the truth of it, to the consternation of his mount, which shied at the sudden noise. But it was no surprise that they took to the table and their cups quicker and more enthusiastically these days.

There had been no further word from King Henry since Hamelin Plantagenet's 'welcome' at Cnaresburg in January, and it was becoming apparent that his favourites – not only Plantagenet, but Courcy and Percy in particular – were keeping their distance. Even Goldesburgh, Plumton and Goodricke were more often staying away, and he was well aware of Stoteville's view. Though the two of them had never been friends, they had tolerated each other since Morville's marriage to Helwise; the marriage which had brought Morville a castle, the Stoteville's titles, and was an excellent match.

Morville glanced back again, this time at the destriers, the warhorses the knights would ride at the tournament. A risk to bring such fine beasts, but Morville at least recognised they were sorely in need of friends, and if the sacrifice of a destrier in ransom bought them a friend or two, it would be well worth the loss of horseflesh. That was relatively easy to replace.

The cart with their armour and weapons lagged behind, the two packhorses barely able to drag it up the steep hill, but Thomas de Screven and Hugh Mauclerk were in attendance and would ensure that their belongings did not fall too far behind.

'Ah, it feels like civilisation again,' Tracy said with a broad grin at the sight of knightly entourages approaching the gates of Harewood Castle from three separate directions. 'It is good to be in the company of knights rather than peasants.'

'And what in God's name do you think we are?' FitzUrse demanded.

'Calm yourself, Reginald, I was including you in my observation. Is it not good to gaze on colour and riches rather than dirt and poverty?'

FitzUrse grunted, his temper calming, and a rare smile was just discernible behind the hair of his full beard. 'Is that not Stoteville and Plumton?'

'Yes, it is indeed,' Morville said. 'Goldesburgh too, even Gamellor.'

'Why did they not ride with us?' Tracy asked, his voice petulant.

'There's far more prestige in accompanying William de Percy, it appears,' Morville said nodding at the blue and yellow livery of the men-at-arms.

'More prestige?' FitzUrse growled. 'Shame on them. We're the only men with enough courage to have cut out the canker of England!'

Morville said nothing, and noticed that Tracy looked worried. Very worried. Maybe the drunken sot had some sense in his head after all, not that it would do him much good if he persisted in toadying to Reginald FitzUrse.

It escaped none of the knights' attention that not a single greeting was passed their way, but as one they all chose to ignore the fact.

'William,' Morville greeted his brother-in-law. 'I did not know you would be attending.'

'Hugh! What are you doing here?'

'That's a fine way to greet your sister's husband, why would I not be here?' Morville said, knowing full well that Stoteville had been aware of his intentions to attend.

'Well, with the Church's attitude to tournaments, I assumed you would not risk antagonising them further.'

'I do not answer to the Church, William, only the King.'

William de Stoteville nodded. 'Begging your pardon, My Lord.'

Morville changed the subject. 'It seems Courcy has attracted a good turnout.'

'Yes, Henry is more confident in the Church's favour after events just past – it has been a very quiet few months, more than time enough to tourney.'

'Most of the barons and knights of England have made the journey,' Morville remarked, glancing around at the garish colours declaring the wealth and status of their wearers; or their wearers' masters.

'There has been scant opportunity to win coin or settle old scores this year,' Stoteville said then added sotto voce, 'Mandeville is here. Beware him, Hugh, he was furious that you reached Becket before him and has been disclaiming your name to anyone with an ear.'

'What? Because he was tardy and we accomplished the task in his stead?'

Stoteville grimaced but stilled the retort ready on his tongue.

'He will have to beware me should I spot him in the mêlée,' Morville continued, oblivious to Stoteville's reaction.

'There will be no mêlée, Hugh, it is a joust of peace – the quintain and ring.'

'What? By the name of all that is holy, why?'

'Henry does not wish to antagonise Pope Alexander further. No swordplay and no mêlée. Courcy did well to obtain permission for this only.'

'God's blood, what is a tourney without swords or mêlée? Where's the opportunity for ransom?'

'There is none, the knights entering the joust are required to pay a fee. The best man will take the purse.'

'But where's the fun in that?' Morville asked.

Stoteville glanced at him in frustration. If the oaf could not recognise the enmity in the glares of the gallant knights, and realise they all suffered the consequences of his and his cronies' actions that fateful night, Stoteville would not be the one to enlighten him.

Chapter 24

The heralds' trumpets silenced the crowd of nobles and men-at-arms, and every man turned their attention to the lists.

'Earls, Barons, Knights, Gentlemen. Sir William de Courcy, Lord of Harewood, bids thee welcome at Harewood Castle,' Courcy's pursuivant-of-arms announced as the trumpet notes faded, 'for a celebration of the joust.'

The knights roared approval and FitzUrse turned to Tracy and said, 'Though we are not per se jousting.'

'No, indeed, a mere practice,' Tracy said.

'Although it is good to be away from Cnaresburg, even if only for a day or two,' Brett said. Morville glanced sharply at him, but his words were drowned out by another blast of trumpeted notes.

'Bid thee welcome to Sir Hamelin Plantagenet, Earl of Surrey. Most esteemed guest of honour, and our first contender!'

The gathered noblemen and their entourages burst into tremendous applause and cheers, each plying further admiration for the King's brother, despite the fact that his entire head was enclosed by the steel of his modern helm and he was essentially deafened.

Although Plantagenet's opponent was a mere quintain, he rode into the lists in full armour: padded gambeson; mail coat, hood and even legs; spurs attached to his boots, and heavy lance held erect.

He circled the field, then guided his destrier to the head of the lists. A wooden rail ran down the centre of the field, and a blue shield adorned with the golden fleur-de-lis of Louis VII was mounted on a crossbar attached to a ten-foot pole.

He flicked his visor closed: an act of affectation as he faced no opponent, but the gathered nobles got the message nonetheless. Plantagenet would do this virtually blind, no man could beat him.

Plantagenet kicked his horse, who strode straight into a canter, then a gallop. He levelled his lance, balancing it on his thigh, and aimed it at the quintain dead ahead. He leaned back to adjust his aim and struck it squarely. The shield sprung back, allowing the Earl safe passage.

He pulled his mare up, wheeled around and circled the field, delighting in the applause as the quintain was reset.

'Will he not attempt the ring next?' Brett asked, confused.

'No,' Morville replied. 'Each man will have three tries at the quintain today, three attempts at the ring tomorrow, then the best of them will strike at both the day after.'

They looked up as Plantagenet took a second turn at the quintain, a glancing blow not as true, but the quintain swung away nonetheless. The applause was just as raucous. The King's brother could fall and still be heralded, at least in public, as champion.

His third attempt was as clean as his first and he lifted his visor, stood in his stirrups, and thumped his chest in triumph as he completed his final lap of honour.

'We're losing the light,' FitzUrse said. 'We have not been called yet, it will soon be dark.'

'Maybe that's the idea,' Morville said, then looked up as his name was called. 'Damn them, they give me no warning? Mauclerk! Bring my horse, now!'

Brett helped him into his mail, he grabbed his helmet – of the older and most common design: conical with only a nose guard to protect his face – and hurried to the entrance to the lists, accompanied by the impatient slow handclap of the waiting nobles.

Flustered, Morville grabbed the reins from Mauclerk and lifted his foot, ready for his clerk to clamp his hands together and heave him into the saddle.

Morville took a deep breath to steady himself. He scanned the silent crowd, then tapped his helmet to ensure it was secure on his head. He was unnerved. He knew he had kept everyone waiting, through no fault of his own, but he had never known a cavalcade of knights be so quiet.

He took another breath, brought his lance to bear, and kicked his spurs into his horse's flanks. Shutting out the disapproval of his peers, he focused on the quintain, aimed, and hit it square. The wooden shield sprang back and he heaved on the reins to slow.

Morville glared at his silent audience, determined not to show his unease. One gaze in particular caught his attention. A priest, no doubt Harewood's parish priest, stood with arms crossed, his eyes full of a hate so malevolent, Morville had only seen the like on a battlefield.

Shaken, he turned his destrier's head and trotted back to the head of the lists for his next attempt.

Once again he pushed his helmet down hard on his head, took a calming breath and kicked. He leaned to his right in a last-minute adjustment of his lance, but was too late, his mind not on the task at hand. The ten-foot lance connected with the edge of the quintain, and the force of the blow was thrown back into his shoulder, knocking him off balance. The quintain stayed in place and his body connected with it at full gallop.

Winded, he allowed Mauclerk to help him to his feet, pulled off his helmet, then wished he hadn't as the crowd's cheers and catcalls penetrated through the ringing in his ears.

He limped away from the lists, head hanging as Brett chased down his horse and the pursuivant announced FitzUrse.

Sir Reginald FitzUrse, mounted, sat at the head of the lists and surveyed the crowd of silent barons, knights and assorted lords surrounding the jousting field.

He reached up to secure his helmet, then changed his mind and snatched it from his head and threw it to the turf. If they would force him to the lists at dusk, he would not hamper himself any further – no matter what Hamlin Plantagenet had done in full daylight.

Shutting out the mutterings of the gathered nobles, he brought his lance up, couched it against his shoulder and focused on the quintain. He could only just see it. No wonder Morville had missed.

He kicked his horse into action, adjusted his direction, and aimed. Dead centre.

He turned his horse into a lap of honour, but heard not a single cheer. His peers were silent.

He realised the futility of what he was doing, realised he could not win, and finally realised they held his recent deeds in abhorrence, no matter that the act had been instigated by their king.

He cast his eyes around the crowd in contempt, lingering on those of Hamlin Plantagenet as the man closest to Henry, then turned and cantered out of the lists.

Morville, Tracy and Brett were at the gates. With one gesture they followed him, back to Cnaresburg.

Chapter 25

'But how could they treat us so?' Tracy whined before emptying his goblet.

'Does this mean that the King has forsaken us?' Brett asked before any answer was given.

'How the damnation do I know?' FitzUrse said. 'We're cut off here, far from Normandy. Has Percy not said anything to you, Hugh?'

'Of course not, I would have told you should he have spoken to me. This turn of events is as much of a surprise to me as you.'

'But what shall we do?' Tracy said. 'We are naught without the favour of our king.'

'The Church must be holding sway over him,' Morville said.

'And you know Henry, he'll put himself above all others,' FitzUrse added.

'Indeed,' Morville said. 'If he is in such straits with the Pope, he would not hesitate to cast us aside.'

'So, we are on our own,' FitzUrse said.

'Yes, we are on our own – at least for the time being,' Morville said. 'If only you had stayed your hands and merely arrested Becket.'

'Hugh! You saw how hard I tried to talk sense into the man,' FitzUrse said. 'I was the only one who tried, if I recall. The rest of you scurried away like rats.'

'Yes, but what else could we have done?' Tracy said. 'We did all we could to persuade him.'

'You call slicing off the top of his head persuasion?' Morville said.

'I was only trying to help!' Brett said. 'Put him out of his misery.'

'Yes, but murder, Richard. Murder,' Tracy said, emptying another goblet and reaching for the flagon of Rhenish.

'He was a traitor,' Brett said. 'It was not murder but execution sanctioned by the King.'

'He did not order Becket's death, Richard,' Morville said.

'No, but he demanded vengeance,' Tracy said. 'He wanted the Archbishop silenced.'

'Well, we've done that all right,' FitzUrse said. 'We've resolved his problem, and now he abandons us. What reward is that for his most loyal knights?'

'No reward,' said Brett, 'but vilification and shunning.'

'Have a care, Richard, your talk is nearing sedition,' Morville said.

'I was just saying.'

'The point is,' FitzUrse said, 'what do we do about it?'

'What can we do?' Tracy asked. 'Without the King's favour, we are doomed.'

'William, that's putting it a bit strongly,' Brett said. 'Why don't we just stay here until Becket is forgotten?'

'That could take a lifetime,' Tracy said.

'I'm only trying to help,' Brett said. 'Would you pass that flagon or have you drunk it all?'

Tracy slammed his goblet on the scarred wood of the table. 'And what if I have? Hugh has plenty more in his cellar.'

'Speaking of more,' Morville said, 'where the blazes is my steward? We've been sitting here a half-hour and have no repast.' He stood and strode to the door, then roared for Jack. When no server was forthcoming, he roared instead for his wife.

'Helwise, what the devil is going on?' he said when she arrived.

Flustered, the long sleeves of her bliaut whipped around her knees. 'There's illness in the town, My Lord,' she said. 'They believe it punishment from God.'

'Punishment? What the devil for? What have they done?'

'Harboured you,' Helwise said, staring at her husband, her face expressionless. Morville said nothing, although his mouth worked frantically.

'They have heard word of your reception at Harewood Castle, My Lord. They believe you against the Church *and* against the King,' Helwise continued.

'The ungrateful buggers,' FitzUrse said, and Morville spun round. All the knights had congregated behind him. 'We ridded the King and his kingdom of a serious threat. The Young King is now safe, thanks to us. And this is how we are repaid?'

Morville recovered his composure. 'And what of the garrison?' His blood ran cold at the thought that his men-at-arms may have also absconded.

'Still present, My Lord,' Mauclerk said, stepping out of the shadows. 'The castle is still strong.'

'Blacksmith? Marshal?'

'The marshal is yet here, although minus a couple of grooms. The smith . . . the smith was persuaded to stay.'

'Persuaded? By you?'

Mauclerk nodded.

'Good man. Keep a close eye on him, and ensure the blades and crossbow quarrels he crafts are of strength and high standard.'

'Of course, My Lord.'

'And go to the sergeant-at-arms, have him put his best cooks in my kitchen. You can bring us wine. My Lords, please, return to the table. We are in need of a plan of action.'

Chapter 26

Tracy lunged forward, swinging his sword. FitzUrse blocked his thrust, continued the arc of his parry, then reversed direction, aiming for Tracy's head. Tracy ducked, then caught FitzUrse's mailed wrist with his blade.

FitzUrse stepped to the left to keep his balance, prepared to strike, and this time connected with Tracy's helmet.

Both men stepped back to regain their breath, then Tracy again swung low. Blocked by FitzUrse. Right to left, this time high. He grinned at the solid thunk of his sword striking FitzUrse's helmet, swung his sword back – knowing he was exposed and taking the gamble that FitzUrse would not yet have regained his wits from the ringing in his ears – and swung on a diagonal to catch FitzUrse's arm.

'That's five, my turn,' Morville said. FitzUrse had already initiated his answering blow and did not pull it, but caught Tracy's thigh.

Tracy fell, howling in pain and outrage. Not only had FitzUrse's turn in the practice circle ended, but Tracy was not wearing leg mail. Padded leather did little to soften the blow of a heavy sword strike, even that of a dulled practice blade.

'Reginald, enough!' Morville shouted.

FitzUrse took off his helmet and cupped his ear, feigning deafness, then reached out a gauntleted hand and hauled Tracy to his feet. Tracy glared at him but said naught, instead turning to face Morville.

Five strokes later, he turned to do the same with Brett then took his place in the circle as FitzUrse entered the centre and faced Morville.

Too soon, FitzUrse turned to Tracy, who had not yet recovered from his gruelling turn in the centre of the practice circle. FitzUrse seemed unaffected by his rounds with Morville and Brett, despite his heavy mail and padded gambeson on a warm spring day.

Tracy scowled at him, still smarting from the blow to his thigh, and stepped forward, lunging at his opponent, despite the convention that the man in the centre be the aggressor. FitzUrse grinned and countered, then launched a heavy and rapid sequence of thrusts, slices and strikes; once more sending Tracy to the ground.

'My turn,' Morville announced, stepping forward. FitzUrse spun round, adding momentum to his sword, which Morville only just managed to block. He struck back, but FitzUrse had anticipated his move, fended him off, then spun again to block Tracy's sword.

Both knights swung at The Bear, one sword glancing off FitzUrse's shoulder, barely registering with him. His face a mask of concentration and effort, his total awareness was captured by his sword.

As the three men turned, Brett stepped in alongside FitzUrse, then all four knights engaged in battle, the only sound the clash of sword against sword, mail and helmets, accompanied by grunts of exertion. Not one of them had strength enough for words.

Minutes later, all four backed away, resting their sword tips on the ground and leaning on the pommels, panting heavily.

Morville was the first to regain his composure. 'Enough for today.' The others nodded in relieved agreement and, as one, sat, dropping the swords and pulling off helmets. Morville gestured to Mauclerk, who hurried over with a large flagon and four goblets.

FitzUrse topped up Tracy's goblet then glanced at the southern curtain wall and tower. 'It's coming on well.'

'Yes,' Morville said. 'They should have it finished soon, then we'll be able to withstand any attack.'

'Do you really think it will come to that?' Brett asked.

'You witnessed our reception at Harewood,' FitzUrse said. 'If Henry has turned against us, there will be no shortage of volunteers to rid the kingdom of us.'

'Surely Henry hasn't turned against us in truth,' Morville said. 'We carried out his bidding.'

'Yes, but all it takes is one intemperate proclamation falling on the wrong ears,' FitzUrse said.

All four remained quiet, none of them daring to voice the concern that they themselves had acted on an 'intemperate proclamation' rather than a carefully considered order.

'Ah, the crossbows,' Morville said, breaking the uncomfortable silence. The others turned to see thirty men-at-arms approaching. 'Good, I want to see how true their aim is.'

'We should move,' said Brett, nodding in the other direction at the bales of straw being set up as targets. 'We are in the line of fire.'

Morville and FitzUrse glanced at each other, both wondering how true Brett's ill-considered words would prove to be.

Chapter 27

22nd July 2015

Helen saved her work and got up to answer the door with an audible curse. 'Why does someone always have to knock on the door when I'm in the zone and the words are flowing?'

'Oh thank goodness you're in, Helen,' Sarah said. 'It's so great you work from home.'

Helen opened her mouth to say, 'Yes, work being the point,' but changed her mind as she realised that Sarah was barely holding back tears. 'Come in, Sarah, what's wrong?'

Sarah didn't answer, but took off her hat and coat, then looked up at Helen and pushed her hair away from her face to reveal a purple bruise on her temple.

'He hit you?'

Sarah nodded and lost the control she'd been holding on to. Helen hugged her and led her to the sofa in the living room, her heart sinking.

'I'm sorry, Helen, I didn't mean to break down on you.'

'Don't be silly, Sarah, I'm your friend, you can always come to me if you're in trouble.'

'Th-th-thank you.'

Helen reached to the coffee table for a box of tissues and handed it to Sarah, who took a handful, mopped her face, and blew her nose.

'Feel better?'

Sarah nodded, but tears started to fall again. 'I'll be okay in a minute,' she said, taking a deep breath.

'I'll go put the kettle on, you could do with a cup of tea.'

'I could do with a bottle of wine,' Sarah said, with a shaky laugh.

'I can do that too,' Helen said. 'I'll just be a moment.'

'What happened?' Helen asked, back on the sofa, both women clutching glasses of Sauvignon.

'He laid into me about Mike, said I was getting too friendly and leading him on. Asked me *again* if we were sleeping together.'

'Are you?' Helen asked.

'No! Not you too – Helen, you know me better than that.'

'I saw you, Sarah, kissing him outside the ladies at the pub.'

Sarah buried her face in tissues again, then when Helen said nothing more, she took another gulp of wine.

'It was nothing, really. We've just been getting on so well lately and Dan and I have been going through a rough patch for what seems forever.'

'So you got a bit carried away.'

'Yes! That's it exactly.'

'Is that the only time it happened?'

Sarah looked down at her wine and emptied her glass.

'I guess that answers that question,' Helen said and refilled it.

'Anyway, back to Dan,' Sarah said. 'We were having a full-blown row – another one – when Mike called.'

'You answered it, didn't you?'

Sarah nodded. 'Dan said that it showed that Mike meant more to me than he does, and proved that we were sleeping together.'

'Then what happened?'

'I—'

'Sarah?'

'I denied it, but by this time I was so furious with him, I mean talk about double standards – I've lost count of the number of times I've caught him watching porn on his phone.'

'What did you say?'

'I said I wasn't but I wished I was. That I've had it with Dan's moods and aggression and told him that he couldn't control me any more and it would be his fault if I did get with Mike.'

'Oh Sarah.'

'And he hit me. So it's my own fault.'

'No. No Sarah, it's not your fault. Yes, you could have handled it better, but that's no excuse for him to punch you in the face!'

'I was shocked more than anything,' Sarah said, taking another sip. 'Dan's never been violent before.'

'But he has been getting more and more belligerent.'

'You've seen it too! Yes – ever since we started this play. It's like I don't know him any more. He's not the man I married.'

'And Mike? I know you've always been friendly, but not like this.'

'Yes, he's different too. He's there for me, and makes me laugh. He even listens.' Sarah gave a hollow laugh. 'Just like Dan used to.'

'So what now?'

'I can't go back there, I just can't.'

'No, of course you can't, and you're welcome to stay here, but what about the kids?'

Sarah rested her head on her hand and Helen rescued the glass of wine before the remainder slopped on to her sofa.

'What am I going to do?' Sarah wailed through sobs.

'John and Kate shouldn't be in the middle of this, Sarah.'

'I know.'

'Where's Dan now?'

'At work.'

'Right. Then we'll go and get your stuff, the sooner the better.'

'Thank you, Helen, but I don't want to impose – you don't want me underfoot all day when you're working. I'll stay with Mike, he won't mind.'

Helen shut her eyes for a moment and took a deep breath, then said, 'Sarah, that's not a good idea. Running off to Mike will not help things – you can't throw away a ten-year marriage like that.'

'I'm not! Dan did that when he hit me!'

Helen nodded. 'But think of the kids – how would they handle it? And if Dan gets help, some counselling and anger management, maybe he can work out where this aggression is coming from and deal with it.'

'The way he is now, he won't even hear of it,' Sarah said.

'Okay, but still give it some time before shacking up with Mike.'

'Maybe you're right,' Sarah said and leaned forward to refill her glass. 'Thanks, Helen, you're a good friend.'

Helen clinked her own glass against Sarah's. 'Always.'

'I just don't know what's got into everyone.' Sarah said. 'It's not just Dan and Mike who have changed. Paul and Charlie are competing over everything. I know they always had a rivalry, the two of them always being up for the main parts, but it's gotten ridiculous. Do you know Charlie even took Catherine out to dinner?'

'The girl who threw her drink over Paul?'

'The very same. Paul's furious. He's getting so bossy as well – in the rehearsals it sounds as if he's the director these days. What's got into everybody?'

Helen hesitated. 'Nothing. I hope.'

The two women looked at each other and paled.

Chapter 28

'Thanks for coming, everyone – I appreciate the hours you're putting in,' Helen said.

Mike laughed. 'Not too hard to come to the pub for the evening.'

'Cheers to that!' Paul said, raising his glass in a toast.

'When did you start drinking wine?' Charlie asked.

'Just got sick of the beer, mate, fancied a glass of Rhenish.'

'A glass of what?'

Paul shrugged. 'Just fancied a change.'

'Anyway,' Helen said, a little uneasy, 'let's get down to business. I need an update on costumes, props and sets. Sarah, are John and Kate still on board to help?'

'Yes, I want to keep them busy, take their minds off things.'

'What things?' Alec asked.

Sarah took a deep breath. 'Dan and I have split.'

Silence.

'What did you say?' Paul asked, his voice measured and low.

'You heard her,' Mike said.

'Is this anything to do with you?'

'No. It's to do with me and Dan,' Sarah said quickly.

'Well, nice timing, Sarah. What the hell have you done that he won't join us?'

Sarah stared at him and pushed her hand through her hair to display the bruise faintly visible under her make-up. 'I've done nothing, the fault is his. And he's not here because he's in the Borough Bailiff, getting pissed and chatting up the landlady.'

'I thought he was barred from there,' Alec said.

'It seems the landlady has a soft spot for him,' Sarah said, her voice pitched high.

'Shush, it's okay, Sarah.' Mike stroked her back to calm her.

'Yeah, I'm not surprised, looking at the two of you,' Paul said.

Sarah opened her mouth to retort but Helen spoke first. 'This isn't helping. Dan will come around, he just needs a bit of time. Alec, I know you're sound and lighting, but will you understudy Dan as well, just in case? At least he's only in the one major scene.'

'But if Alec plays FitzUrse, who will do the lighting in the final scene? It's the most complicated,' Ed said.

'I will,' Helen said. 'Alec will do all the programming ahead of time anyway and I can follow instructions. And it's only plan B. Dan's never let us down before. It will all come together on the night.'

'I bloody well hope so,' Paul grumbled. 'It's looking a bloody shambles at the minute.'

'All right, mate, calm down,' Charlie said. 'It sounds like Helen has everything under control.'

'Thanks, Charlie. Enough of Dan, where are we with the costumes, Sarah?'

'Costumes we're all right with. It's mainly tunics and hose, which are pretty simple to put together. I've bought *The Medieval Tailor* so have patterns for everything I need to make, and Kate's helping me.'

'That's great, Sarah, do you need any more help?' Helen asked.

'No, I'm fine for the moment – to be honest, it's good for me to keep busy.'

Helen nodded. 'Alec, Ed, where are we on the sets?'

'We have the main backdrop in a masonry design, and I think it will work if we then use different furniture to show the difference between castle, great hall and church,' Ed said.

'Good,' Helen said.

'We already have the basics, I'll use one of the tables as an altar, so just need an altar cloth and a cross.'

'We,' Alec said.

'What?'

'You said "I". It's "we" who are doing the props.'

'Yes, of course, that's what I meant.'

'Didn't say it though.'

'My sincere apologies, Alec. *We* will use one of the tables for an altar. Then *we* will keep an eye on the local auction house for a suitable chair that *we* can upholster to create a throne.'

'Good,' Helen said, trying to quell the unexpected animosity between the two men. 'What else do we need?'

'A crown for Paul,' Mike said. 'A crook, or whatever they're called, for Charlie, and parchment, quills and inkpots.'

'Did archbishops have crooks back then?' Ed asked.

'We need to check,' Helen said. 'Then there's mail coats and hoods, and those conical helmets with a nose guard for the knights.'

'And swords,' Mike put in.

'Okay, that all sounds a bit pricey,' Helen said.

'eBay is a good place to start,' Sarah suggested. 'Plenty of theatrical outfitters and LARP companies. I can have a look if you like.'

'Great, thanks Sarah,' Helen said. 'How much do we have to spend, Charlie?'

'What? Erm, not sure to be honest.'

'What do you mean you're not sure? You're the bloody treasurer,' Paul shouted, slamming his wine glass on to the table then cursing as the stem broke. 'Oh, for God's sake! Someone get me another wine.'

Mike jumped to his feet to go to the bar. 'Anyone else?'

Helen looked around the table and realised everyone was on wine. *When did we all start drinking wine?* she thought, the sinking feeling in her belly gathering depth. 'Here Mike,' she said, brandishing a £20 note. 'Get a couple of bottles.'

'That won't be enough.'

'Then add to it,' she snapped. 'Sorry, Mike, that's all I have. Anyone else?'

'It's okay, Helen, I've got it covered,' Mike said and rushed to the bar.

Helen took a deep breath, but Paul beat her to it.

'Charlie? You haven't answered my question. How much money is left?'

'I don't know, about fifty quid I think.'

'Fifty quid? How the hell is that all we have left from a £500 grant? We haven't bought the bloody props yet!'

'Well, we had that night out, I had to pay for the damage Dan did in the Bailiff, and there's the fees for hiring the theatre for the rehearsals . . .'

'So you've spent it,' Paul said.

'No, *we've* spent it,' Charlie said.

'Have you got the accounts?'

'Well, no, not really. The cash is in a jar in my kitchen and I reckon there's about fifty quid left, but I'll add it up and let you know.'

'Are you telling me you've not kept accounts?' Paul demanded.

'Well, yeah, I guess I am. No one's needed them before, so I've not bothered. Come on, mate, you can trust me.'

'Can we? You've spent over four hundred quid and don't have much to show for it. Are you sure the money's gone on this drama group?'

'Just what the hell are you accusing me of, *mate*?' Charlie spat the question and stood.

Paul rose to match him, braced his hands on the table, and leaned over to push his face into his friend's. 'I think it's quite clear what I'm accusing you of, *mate*.'

'Guys, guys, stop it, what the hell are you doing?' Helen said, standing herself and putting her good arm between the men in an attempt to keep them apart. 'Charlie, can you put some figures together – some accounts?'

'Yes, sure, I'd have done it already if I knew you didn't trust me.'

'We do trust you, Charlie,' Helen, Sarah and Alec chorused.

'But I see the rest of you don't,' Charlie said.

'Shit, shit, shit, shit,' Helen said, slowly retaking her seat.

'What the hell's wrong with you, woman?' Paul demanded.

'It's not what's wrong with her, but what's wrong with the rest of us, isn't it, Helen?' Sarah said.

Helen nodded. 'We've got a big problem.'

'What? God's wounds, tell us!' Paul said.

Helen looked up at him sharply. 'Remember the spirit board?'

'Oh don't be bloody ridiculous.'

'She's not,' Sarah said. 'Look at us, we're all . . . different.'

'And what's just happened also happened between Henry and Becket – they fell out over Becket omitting to make accounts and Henry accused him of embezzlement,' Helen said. 'Don't you see? The spirit board worked – we brought them through.'

'Oh don't get hysterical,' Paul sneered. 'What the hell are you doing here anyway? This is the business of kings, begone, Saxon.' He looked around at everybody. 'What? It was a *joke*.'

Chapter 29

June 1171

'My Lord, horsemen approach,' Mauclerk said as he burst into the great hall.

'Who is it?' Morville demanded.

'They fly no banner, but one of the riders is Sir William de Percy.'

'Percy? I wonder what's brought him so low, that he graces us with his presence,' FitzUrse said.

'Should we unbar the gates?' Mauclerk asked, ignoring FitzUrse's scowl.

Morville hesitated. 'How many men does he have with him?'

'A company, near enough, perhaps fifty men or more.'

'So many?' Tracy asked, then turned to Morville. 'He's here to attack.'

Morville glanced at him then rose. 'I need to see them.' He hurried up the stairs to the top of the keep and peered out at the approaching men.

'Permit them entry,' he told Mauclerk.

'Hugh, do you think that's wise?'

'If he were here to attack, he would have more men and brought siege engines.'

'Yes, but it may be a trick,' Tracy said.

'Only one way to find out,' Morville said and led the way out to the courtyard to greet his guests. 'My Lord Percy, what brings you to Cnaresburg?'

Percy dismounted but said naught, instead gesturing to the other riders. Morville recognised Hamelin Plantagenet and William de Courcy then focused on the fourth man briefly before dropping to one knee. 'My Liege, welcome to Cnaresburg,' he said.

FitzUrse, Tracy and Brett knelt a fraction after Morville, with an audible gasp from Tracy.

Henry Plantagenet pulled his hood from his face. 'It is a dark day indeed when a king must ride through his own kingdom in secret lest he be recognised.'

'Welcome,' Morville said again. 'May I offer you some refreshment after your journey?'

'You may indeed,' Henry said, striding towards the keep and great hall within, without making any indication the knights could rise.

The four glanced at each other, then regained their feet the moment King Henry turned his back to them. Percy smirked at them, but Hamelin Plantagenet and Courcy's expressions remained unreadable.

'Hugh, where is Helwise?'

'William, I did not see you there, why did you not send word you were coming?'

Stoteville glared at him. 'The King did not wish it. Where is my sister?'

Morville shrugged. 'About somewhere – the mews perhaps, she seems to spend most of her time with the hawks these days.'

Glancing around the table filled with dishes of venison in wine sauce, stewed swan, beef pottage and a spicy Leche Lombard, amongst many other delicacies, Morville was satisfied he had provided a meal fit for his king, even if it was being served by men-at-arms rather than young, pretty and buxom girls. He noticed Henry glare at the men as they brought more rich fare to the table, then the King glanced at Morville, eyebrows raised.

Morville filled his king's goblet, unwilling to explain that his servants had deserted him. 'What brings you to Yorkshire, My Liege?'

'I am on my way to inspect my new mighty castle at Riche Mont, which perchance provides the perfect opportunity to speak to you.' He raised his goblet to include FitzUrse, Tracy and Brett.

'It is our very great pleasure and privilege to receive you, My Liege,' Morville said. 'To Henry Plantagenet, King of England, Duke of Normandy, Duke of Aquitaine, and Lord of Ireland.' He raised his goblet in toast as he spoke and king, earl, barons, knights and men-at-arms drank as one. Silence fell over the gathering.

Henry glanced around, seeming to enjoy the discomfort of the assembled men, and prolonged it further by taking a large gulp of Morville's finest Rhenish and helping himself to a large portion of venison. The others took this as their cue to help themselves, although Tracy and Brett in particular found their appetites diminished by the atmosphere in the hall.

It was a great honour to host the King, but they could not help but reflect that Henry had arrived incognito. He wanted no one but his most trusted men to know of his presence in Cnaresburg. That did not bode well.

Henry looked around the almost silent hall, then said, 'It may be advisable to dismiss your men-at-arms before I continue.' He stared at Morville and FitzUrse, and all four knights gestured to their sergeants. A noisy five minutes later, the only men present were the nobles and their king, although Mauclerk hovered behind his lord.

Chapter 30

'What news have you of Canterbury?' Henry began.

'None, My Liege,' Morville said. 'We receive little word of events here in Cnaresburg. What has occurred?'

'Miracles. At the Archbishop's tomb. Healings. There is talk of canonisation.'

'A saint? They talk about making a traitor a saint?' FitzUrse exclaimed.

'So it seems,' said Hamelin Plantagenet. 'It appears that however high Becket was raised in life, you have raised him further in death.'

Morville opened his mouth to speak, then closed it when no words came forth.

'But he was a low-born clerk,' FitzUrse said. 'He stood against the Young King!'

'And was murdered before his altar!' Henry roared. 'Within the sanctuary of his cathedral!' He slammed his fist on the table then stood, heaved up the platter of venison, and hurled it to the floor. 'You have made a holy martyr of him!' He swept his arm across the tabletop, scattering trenchers, meat, goblets and full flagons of wine. Tracy squeaked in protest, then fell silent at his king's glance.

Henry leaned both fists on the table and bowed his head, then pulled himself up to his full height, and turned to glare at his knights.

'I gave Mandeville and Humez a simple task. Arrest Becket and bring him to me. I would have dealt with him. Instead you interfered. I have lost my battle with the Church over the Constitution of Clarendon and will not now be able to hold the English clergy accountable. I was even under threat of excommunication and eternal damnation! Four more troublesome knights I have never had!' He slammed his fist on the tabletop once more. 'I would have you all executed did I not think that would ensure my excommunication!'

'Excommunication? My Liege, that would be unconscionable,' Morville ventured.

'Apparently not. The four of you were excommunicated on Holy Thursday.'

Silence.

'But that was three months ago. We have been damned for three months?' Tracy whined.

Henry laughed. 'Three months is nothing, William. Your soul is damned for all time!'

Tracy refilled his goblet and downed the wine in one. Morville, FitzUrse and Brett followed suit.

'What did you expect?' Henry shouted. 'You had all pledged fealty to Becket, then you murdered him. In his cathedral! Did you not expect the Pope to react?'

'Just as he pledged fealty to King Louis of France, then took his wife Eleanor and half of his lands,' FitzUrse whispered to Morville.

'What was that, Reginald?' Henry asked.

'Naught, My Liege,' FitzUrse simpered. 'I am gladdened our excommunication did not extend to you.'

'Well it might have.' Henry frowned. 'Well it might have.'

The men paused, each taking another drink and contemplating: *What to say next?*

The King broke the silence. 'I suggest you each commit yourselves to earn back Rome's favour.'

'How do we do that?' Tracy asked. Henry frowned. 'My Liege,' he added.

'I would not know, although I suggest building and improving churches would make a noble beginning. Rome responds to the chink of coin,' Henry said, sitting down. 'The louder the better.'

Tracy nodded and emptied his goblet once more. He appeared close to tears.

'There is also talk of the four of you serving the Poor Fellow-Soldiers of Christ and of the Temple of Solomon in the Holy Land for a period exceeding ten years.'

'The Knights Templar, My Liege?' FitzUrse and Morville protested together.

'Fear not. It is unlikely to come to that. But the whole of Christendom wishes to see you punished. They need to believe you are contrite. Although if you do not build enough churches—' Percy and Courcy grunted and suppressed laughter '—you may have to serve if you wish to save your souls,' Henry warned.

'You need to tell Pope Alexander what he wants to hear and keep the Saxons quiet,' Hamlin Plantagenet added. 'Do not embarrass our king any further.'

The knights nodded, chastened.

'You must present yourself to Pope Alexander at your earliest convenience. Do what you can to repair your reputation – and mine – before then,' Henry ordered.

'Yes, Sire,' the knights said.

'We shall take our leave,' Henry said, rising once more, and the knights escorted him and his party to the bailey and their horses.

'There will be a joust of peace at Riche Mont Castle in a sennight,' Henry said, mounting. 'Do not attend. Do your penance before you show your faces again.' He dug his spurs into his mount's flanks.

Morville held his breath, but his men were paying attention and the gates to Cnaresburg Castle opened as King Henry reached them.

Chapter 31

25th July 2015

Helen took a deep breath and opened the door to Spellbound.

'Oh hello,' Donna said from behind the counter. 'How are you?'

'Hi, I'm fine, thanks,' Helen said, then hesitated. 'Well, not really, to be honest.'

'What's wrong?'

'You remember that spirit board I bought from you?'

'You'd better come through,' Donna said, and pulled back the curtain from the alcove behind the counter where she did her tarot readings. 'Take a seat,' she said, and took the far chair for herself. 'Tell me.'

'You know feva is coming up?'

Donna nodded.

'I'm with the Castle Players and we're putting on a play about Morville and the other knights who murdered Thomas Becket then hid out at the castle here.'

'I see,' Donna said, drawing the words out.

'The guys were having trouble connecting with their characters and I thought the spirit board would be a fun and different way to embrace them.'

'I told you when you came in, the Ouija is not "fun" – it's serious and you need to treat it with respect.'

'I know, I know, and I did – I followed all your instructions.'

'And the others, did they take it as seriously?'

Helen said nothing.

'Let me get this straight – are you telling me you used the spirit board to contact a medieval king, four of his knights and the priest they murdered, as – what – a theatre game?'

'Exercise rather than game,' Helen said. 'And it worked, the improvement is amazing! I thought at first that they'd let go, relaxed and embraced the characters, but now . . . now I think it's something more.'

'Why?'

Helen took a deep breath. 'Everyone's . . . changed.'

'Changed – how?'

'Well, Dan and Sarah have split after ten years and two kids – and it's nasty. He's become aggressive and belligerent, which he never was before, and Sarah . . . Well, Sarah's lost her mind. She's taken up with one of the other guys – someone she's always been friendly with. I reckon he's fancied her for years, but she never felt the same.'

'Are you sure?'

'Yes. I can't count the number of times we've talked about him and she's always thought he was sweet, but boring. He never did anything for her, and now she's besotted.'

'Is there any correlation between that and their characters?' Donna asked.

Helen thought for a minute. 'I guess so. It's hard to know for sure, the historical record's sketchy at best, but Sarah plays Richard le Brett, who served William de Tracy, who Mike plays. They were the meekest of the four knights, so it stands to reason they were close.'

'And the husband?'

'Dan plays Reginald FitzUrse – a brash, vulgar bully. Which is what he's turned into.'

Donna nodded but remained silent awhile before asking, 'And what of the others?'

'Well, Paul and Charlie – they play King Henry and Becket – they're acting oddly too. They were always good friends with plenty of banter, but lately it's more – they're so competitive it's unreal, and Paul's getting to be a right pain, throwing his weight around and taking everything over.'

'Just like a medieval king,' Donna said.

'Exactly. Alec and Ed – to be honest, I'm not sure, with the drama of the others, I've not really noticed.'

'So what in particular prompted you to come and see me?' Donna asked.

'Last night there was an argument over money – Charlie's the treasurer – and Paul practically accused him of stealing. It echoed an argument between Henry and Becket and it was just one coincidence too many. I think they're possessed.'

'Possessed is a strong word and unlikely, but it *is* possible that spirits have attached themselves to your friends.'

'What does that mean?'

'They're here, feeding off the energy of their "hosts" and influencing their behaviour.'

'But how can that be? Henry was a Norman king, he didn't speak English, and the English language that Becket knew bears little resemblance to the one we speak today. How can they be influencing the speech and actions of men they can't communicate with?'

'But Charlie and Paul speak English. Language is a function of our brains not our spirits. The guys are just tools for the spirits to use. One more question, did you close the spirit board?'

Helen looked down at her hands.

'You didn't, did you?'

'We couldn't. Something happened—' she paused and Donna waited for her to continue. 'It was weird, it was like an explosion of – nothing. But we were sent flying. I fell off the stage and broke my wrist,' Helen pushed back her sleeve to show her tatty pot, 'everybody else landed on their arses, and the spirit board just vanished.'

Donna drew in a sharp breath. 'And you haven't found it?'

'No. To be honest, we didn't look very hard – we were all freaked out. I was hurt, and I don't think any of us actually wanted to see it again.'

'You have to find it. That's what is connecting the spirits to your friends.'

'So if we find it, then what, destroy it?'

'Yes, burn it and cleanse the place where you held the séance – was it at the theatre?'

Helen nodded.

'We'll also cleanse each individual and hopefully it's not too late.'

'What do you mean, too late?'

'It sounds like the connection is strong. It's unusual for spirits to exert so much control unless the person is in trance. Judging by their history, the spirits have unfinished, extremely emotional, business to put right. When was the murder?'

'1170.'

Donna released a breath and seemed to shrink into herself. 'So that's what, eight hundred years?'

'Nearly eight hundred and fifty.'

'That's a long time for unresolved issues to brew, even in the spirit world.'

Helen didn't know how to reply to that, so said nothing. Then, 'How much will it cost?'

Donna glared at her, then her expression softened. 'Don't worry about that at the moment – the main thing is to stop the spirits replaying their past or exacting vengeance, and make sure everybody is safe.'

'Safe? You think we're in danger?' Helen asked, horrified.

'They've already hurt you and broken relationships,' Donna said. 'God knows what else they're capable of – it sounds like they're gathering strength every day.'

Chapter 32

'Hi Donna, thank you so much for doing this,' Helen said as she let the Wiccan into the theatre.

'No problem. How long have we got before the others get here?'

'About an hour.'

'That should be fine, but let's get started. Where did you hold the séance?'

'On the stage.'

'Of course you did.'

'What do you mean?' Helen asked.

'Oh I'm sorry, there's no need to be defensive.' Donna laid a hand on Helen's arm. 'It's just that the spirits were given centre stage – it will have given them extra energy. You know how you feel during a show – that high?'

'Yes.'

'All that energy over countless shows – by everyone who's ever performed there – leaves an energetic signature behind. Over the years that would have built up, and when the spirits were invited to join you, it would have given them a sizeable boost. That's probably why they were able to get rid of the spirit board and attach themselves so firmly. Did you look for the board?'

'Yes. Yes I did, but I couldn't find it.'

'Maybe one of your friends took it and put it "somewhere safe".'

'But why would they do that?'

'They didn't – the spirit they're hosting did.'

'Oh.'

'Not being able to deal with the board makes this much harder. Keep an eye out – especially when visiting your friends. See if you can find it.'

'Okay. Will this work without it?'

'That depends on how strong they are and how badly they want to see this through.' Donna frowned, then brightened and smiled to reassure Helen. 'Only way to find out is to try. Let's get started. The stage first.'

Helen took a deep breath, then followed Donna through the auditorium and up to the stage where she deposited the large bag she was carrying.

'What's all that for?' Helen asked as Donna pulled out bundles of herbs, a lighter, dish, coloured candles, a box, and a cup ornate enough to be labelled a chalice.

'I'll cast a circle first,' Donna said, picking up the ornate box. She opened the lid and showed Helen the contents. 'Salt,' she said. 'It will start to purify the place.' She walked around the stage area in as large a circle as she could fit, sprinkling the salt as she went.

'That covers the main area of the stage,' she said. 'Whatever you do, don't step out of the circle. I'll cleanse this area first, then go around each part of the theatre, then outside.'

'Okay,' Helen said, feeling like an extra from *Supernatural*.

Donna bent, picked up a compass, and checked that she was in the exact centre. 'Will you put the green candle there, it represents earth,' she said, pointing. 'Left a bit, perfect,' she added as Helen did as she was told. 'Now the yellow candle in the east for air. Then a red candle for fire to the south and blue for water in the west. Then come to the middle and stay still.'

Donna picked up one of the bundles of herbs and the lighter. 'Sage,' she said by way of explanation. She walked to the green candle and lit it, muttering under her breath, then round to light the others, ending up back at the green candle. She held the bundle of sage to the flame until it caught, then blew on it until it smoked copiously with no flame.

'With earth I cleanse this place of fear, pain and anger. Henry Plantagenet, Thomas Becket, Hugh de Morville, Reginald FitzUrse, William de Tracy, Richard le Brett, thank you for your time here, please leave now. We send you home and invite light, love and peace to dwell in this place,' she intoned, walking around the circle anticlockwise, then she came back to the centre, placed the herbs in the dish, and picked up another bundle.

'Cedar,' Helen said, recognising the smell when Donna lit it.

Donna said nothing but repeated her chant as she walked around the circle waving the smudge stick.

'Sweetgrass,' Donna said as she lit the next bundle, this time walking clockwise.

Helen looked nervously at the amount of smoke and made a mental note to check the smoke alarms. *Surely at least one of them should have gone off by now.*

Donna blew out the candles, and Helen strained to hear what she was muttering – it appeared to be a number of thank yous.

'Now for the rest of the theatre,' Donna said with a smile, picked up the still-smoking bundle of sage and wafted the smoke into every corner and along every boundary of the stage, auditorium and the areas backstage.

'Are we done?' Helen asked, checking her watch – the others would be here soon expecting a rehearsal not a Wiccan ritual.

'Not quite, I'll go outside and do the same all around the building – everything I can get to, anyway,' she said, referencing its semi-detached nature. 'Then I'll need to do each member of the cast.'

'What? They'll never agree to that, not the way they are now,' Helen said.

'Then find a way to persuade them – and do it on the stage – that has received the most intense cleanse and the spirits' hold on them should be weakened.' Donna recognised the distress in Helen's face and hugged her, careful to keep the burning herbs well away from their bodies. 'Don't worry, I'll help you fix this.'

Helen nodded and sniffed, surprised to find herself emotional. 'Thank you,' she whispered.

'Have a drink of water and just sit quietly and gather your thoughts,' Donna said. 'I'll be back soon.'

Helen jerked in surprise. The smoke alarms were finally doing their job and an ear-splitting howl transformed what had been a tranquil moment into a nightmare – at least until she realised what the noise was.

'What the bloody hell's going on here?' Paul demanded. 'Dan, shut that thing off will you?'

Dan waved his script under the sensor to clear the smoke, and the alarm silenced. Until another emitted a high shriek. One by one they were silenced. One by one they screamed.

Finally, a quiet that lasted. Until Paul broke it.

'Well, Helen? Are you going to tell us what in the name of God you've been doing?'

'Actually, that was me,' Donna said from behind him.

He spun around and stared at her – eyes insolently examining her from her short blonde hair, down her long pink dress, to her pointed black patent boots, then back up. 'And who the hell are you?'

'Hi, I'm Donna,' she said brightly, holding out her hand for a shake. 'From the Wiccan shop.'

Paul kept his hands by his sides, then slowly turned back to Helen and arched an eyebrow in question.

'Come and sit down, everyone. We need to talk,' Helen said, indicating the circle of chairs she'd arranged at the centre of the stage.

'Come on, mate,' Charlie said, tugging at Paul's arm. 'Let's see what she's got on her mind.'

'I don't have time for this,' Paul said.

'Of course you do. Stop moaning and sit – whoa.' Charlie dropped Paul's arm and stepped back as Paul's hand bundled into a fist.

'Sorry, mate,' Paul said after a moment and relaxing his hand. 'Don't know what's got into me lately.'

'That's kind of what I need to talk to you about,' Helen said and led the way to the circle of chairs.

Chapter 33

'This is Donna,' Helen said loudly enough that everyone could hear her, 'from Spellbound.'

'A witch?' Charlie said, his voice full of disgust.

'Wiccan,' Donna corrected. 'Very different to what the Church portrays as a witch.'

Charlie muttered something under his breath that sounded remarkably like, 'Heathen'. Donna glanced at Helen but did nothing else to acknowledge the comment.

'A few weeks ago, you experimented with the spirit world,' Donna said.

'Load of nonsense,' Dan scoffed.

'I don't think so,' Helen said. 'Since then, you've all been . . . different.'

'Different how?' Ed asked.

'Well, for one thing you've become your characters on stage—'

'That's what we're supposed to do,' Paul said. 'We're actors!'

'—and offstage,' Helen continued as if he hadn't spoken.

'How do you mean?' Sarah asked, and Helen narrowed her eyes. *Surely Sarah out of everyone realises what's going on?*

'Well, as you said yourself, Sarah, the friendship between Paul and Charlie has changed – you're far more competitive with each other than before.'

Paul and Charlie looked at each other and shrugged.

'And you yourself, Sarah – it's no secret that Mike has fancied you for months . . .'

'Hey,' Mike said, but Helen ignored him as well as Dan's cursing.

'But you've never entertained him as anything but a friend before – now you've moved out and are seeing him. It's just not you!'

'I bloody knew it, you cheating bitch!'

'Is there any point to this?' Paul interrupted, holding a hand up at Dan to quieten him.

'Yes Paul, there is a point, you're not in control.'

'So you're saying this . . . this *mess* is down to, what, ghosts?' Dan asked.

Helen's heart sank at the tone of hope in his voice. Whatever the reason, what had been done had been done and there was no going back from it. 'Yes, that's exactly what I'm saying.'

'So all this, the breakup of my marriage, my kids' heartache, mine, it's all because you brought that, that, *thing* here and made us use it?'

Helen had no answer.

'No,' Donna said. 'Many people use spirit boards every day with no problem. Unfortunately, the spirits you contacted are angry, powerful and have no doubt waited centuries for a chance to come back and put right what was done in their lifetimes.'

'So just bad luck, huh?'

'I'm afraid so.'

'What can we do about it?' Charlie asked, his voice hesitant as if he had to force the words out.

'We've cleansed the theatre, and now, with your permission, I'll cleanse you. But to be honest, it may not be enough. We need to find the spirit board too – do any of you know what happened to it?'

'It just . . . disappeared,' Ed said and Donna stared at him.

'Do you know where it disappeared to?'

'No, of course I don't. I'd have said.'

'Okay, shall we start with you for the cleansing?'

'What? I-I don't know about that, what does it involve?'

'It's nothing to be worried about – I'll just cleanse your aura with sage and ask any spirits to leave.'

'Sounds like pagan devilry to me,' Charlie said.

'Pagan yes. Devilry no. Everything I do comes from a place of light and love,' Donna said.

Charlie's thoughts were clear enough on his face that he didn't need to voice them. Donna glanced at him nervously then turned her attention back to Ed.

'Okay, I want you to uncross your legs and arms, close your eyes and relax. Just concentrate on your breathing and let any thoughts drift away.'

Ed looked relaxed enough and Donna took a smudge stick from her bag, then lit it. She wafted it around Ed, surrounding him in smoke, then placed the sage in a dish and stood behind him, hands on his shoulders and face upturned. 'I call on my angel guardians and spirit guides to join with Ed and cleanse him of the spirit of . . .' Donna opened her eyes and looked at Helen in question.

'Hugh de Morville.'

Donna repeated the name, then repeated the mantra twice more as she waved her hands rapidly upwards from Ed's feet to the crown of his head, finally clapping her hands together above his head.

She placed her palms back on Ed's shoulders and asked him how he felt.

'Okay, I guess,' he said slowly, blinking as he refocused on the group. 'Yeah, okay.' He smiled up at Donna, who moved to Sarah, carried out the same ritual then went on to Mike.

'You're not touching me, witch,' Dan said as Donna finished Mike, stood in front of him and picked up the sage.

'I won't harm you,' Donna reassured.

'I don't care, you're not casting your spells over me!' He hit out, catching Donna's hands and she dropped the smoking bundle of herbs.

'Dan!' Sarah shouted. 'Stop it, she's only trying to help.'

'You don't get to tell me what to do any more, whore,' Dan sneered. 'What you think and want is nothing to me, do you understand?' He jumped to his feet and Sarah recoiled in her chair.

'Fucking heathen bullshit,' Dan said and kicked the bundle of herbs off the stage.

'Dan!' Helen cried and ran offstage to retrieve the bundle. 'You'll set the place on fire.'

'Oh stop bleating, woman! It's always melodrama with you. I'm going to the pub, anyone want to join me or would you rather chant spells and set fire to yourselves?'

'Reginald's right,' Paul said. 'Hold on, I'm coming too.'

'And me,' Charlie said and they both followed Dan out of the theatre.

'Did Paul just call Dan Reginald?' Sarah asked.

Helen nodded, her face ashen.

'Things have gone too far,' Donna said. 'This is more than I can deal with.'

'So what do we do?' Helen asked.

'I'll make some calls,' Donna said. 'But to be honest, I think the only people who can stop this are Dan, Paul and Charlie.'

The others stared at her, then at the exit door.

'Fat chance of that happening any time soon,' Mike said, then pulled his chair closer to Sarah's and put his arm around her. 'You okay, love?'

'You have to find that spirit board, Helen,' Donna said. 'It's probably your only chance.'

Chapter 34

'Dan! Dan, wait up! Where are you going?' Paul shouted.

Dan turned. 'Harrogate. Had enough of Knaresborough for one night. I can't stand seeing those two huddled together. I want some real pubs – and some real women – preferably ones I don't know.'

'Amen to that,' Charlie cried. 'Wait up, we're coming with you. Next bus in what, five or ten minutes?'

'There it is,' Paul shouted. 'Come on!'

They ran in front of the bus, preventing it from leaving the stop outside Sainsbury's, and giving the driver no choice but to wait and let them board – though he clearly wished to avoid it.

'Onward, Coachman, á Harrogate,' Paul cried and the three of them creased up in laughter. The young woman sitting near them got up and made her way to the front of the bus where she felt safer, which only amused the three actors further.

Half an hour later, a relieved bus driver pulled into Harrogate bus station and opened the doors. He'd expected more trouble than raised voices and raucous laughter, but was glad to wash his hands of the three unruly men nonetheless.

'Where to?' Charlie asked.

'I fancy somewhere grand but cheap,' Paul said.

'Wetherspoons then,' Dan said. Situated in the historic Royal Baths, once a place visitors flocked to in their thousands to sample the Harrogate spa waters, the pub had kept the soaring decorated ceilings yet boasted the same prices as any other Wetherspoons in the country.

'Lead on, my good man,' Paul said, sweeping his arm expansively.

'So what the hell was all that crap about?' Dan said once they all had full glasses in front of them.

'Devil worship,' Charlie said.

'Women's troubles,' Paul said and raised his glass. The other two spluttered, clinked, then drank.

'Another round, boys?' Paul said, eyebrows raised. They had all drained their glasses.

'Keep 'em coming, Sire,' Charlie said, and they burst into laughter once again.

* * *

'So what's going on with you and Sarah, Dan?' Paul asked.

Dan scowled and thumped his glass on the table, sloshing red wine on to the polished wood.

'What's there to say? She's shacking up with that bastard, Mike.'

'What? She's moved in with him?'

'Well, she reckons she's staying with Helen until I move out, but she'll be with him.'

'And she's making you move out?' Charlie asked.

'Yeah. Then no doubt she'll move lover boy in.'

'And you've agreed to this?' Paul asked, incredulous.

'No choice.'

'Why?'

Dan shrugged. 'If I don't she'll go to the police, tell them I hit her or something.'

'And did you?' Charlie asked.

Dan looked uncomfortable then, 'Fuck, yeah I did.' He drained his glass. 'We were arguing about Mike, then she ignored me to answer his call.'

'Sounds like she deserved it,' Paul said.

'Damn right she did, embarrassing me like that, and with a mate. I should do it again!'

'She's making a fool of you, Dan.'

Charlie noticed the looks of disdain from the women on the next table and felt uncomfortable for a moment, although he wasn't quite sure why. He ignored the feeling. 'All right, darling?' he said and the women pointedly turned their backs. He laughed and went to the bar.

'Bloody hell, he's pulled,' Charlie told Paul, half a dozen glasses of wine later. Paul turned in his seat to see Dan at the bar talking to a group of women, two bottles of red wine on the bar beside him.

'It doesn't look like he's bringing them over,' Paul said.

'What? The wine or the girls?'

'Neither!' Paul stood up too quickly and knocked his chair over. He left it where it was and lurched to the bar, Charlie in his wake, bowing and making apologies for his friend, though not caring if he received glares or smiles in response.

Paul approached behind two of the women and cupped their hips as he pushed his head between them to greet Dan. 'Aren't you going to introduce us?' he said, oblivious of the women recoiling from him – one of them straight into Charlie's arms.

'Forgive my manners,' Dan said. 'These are my good friends Henry and Thomas.' He raised his glass to Paul with a wink and a smirk. 'And I'm Reginald.'

'You mean you've been hogging these lovely ladies and haven't even introduced yourself, uh, Reg?' Paul asked, laughing. 'Hey, where do you think you're going?' he added as the woman lucky enough to avoid Charlie's clutches almost succeeded in freeing herself from Paul – who just gripped tighter. Hard enough for her to cry out and push him away.

'All right, that's enough, leave the ladies alone.' A short but burly man dressed in a black suit grabbed hold of Paul's shoulder.

'And who might you be?' Paul said, his voice full of disdain.

'I'm the bloke who's kicking you out. You can go quietly, but if not my friends and I will help you on your way.' He jerked his head towards the door but did not take his eyes off the drunken men.

Paul pushed closer to him. 'You do not lay a hand on me or my friends, do you have any idea who I am?'

'I don't give a shit who you are, you're not welcome here.'

'You insolent . . .'

The doorman caught Paul's swinging fist easily and used his momentum to spin Paul around, twist his arm behind his back, and propel him towards the doors.

'Hey, you can't do that,' Charlie shouted, moving to come to his friend's aid. 'He's King Henry!'

'Yeah, he's King Henry and I'm William the Conqueror,' the doorman muttered, all patience evaporated – if he'd had any in the first place.

'He is.' Dan descended into giggles as two more security staff grabbed him and Charlie and marched them all out of the pub, the crowd of patrons parting before them.

'You're not welcome back,' the first doorman said. 'So don't even try it.'

'Why, you cretin,' Paul said, lunging for the man and catching him on the jaw with his fist. The doorman quickly wrestled the 'king' to the ground, kneeling on him to keep him subdued while his two colleagues dealt with Charlie and Dan's drunken and ineffectual attempts to free their friend. Soon all three were on the ground amidst a growing circle of concerned onlookers.

Within minutes a police van arrived and the doormen let the three friends up. They immediately spun again, but the men were expecting a clumsy attack and stepped back to avoid it. Each actor was grabbed from behind by police officers, then thrown against the side of the van, where more officers fastened handcuffs on their wrists.

'I am arresting you for being drunk and disorderly,' one of the officers – a sergeant – said. 'And if you don't calm down, I'll add assault to that. What are your names?'

He received only verbal abuse in return and indicated that the officers should put them into the back of the van.

When the cage door was shut and locked behind them, the sergeant tried again. 'What are your names? It'll be worse for you if you don't answer.'

'Reginald FitzUrse,' Dan said and cackled with laughter. 'And this is Thomas Becket and Henry Plantagenet.'

'I see,' the sergeant said with a sigh. 'At least that's more original than Mickey Mouse.' He shut the van door and thumped on it to indicate that the driver could go, then turned to ensure the pub security staff were okay and ask what the hell was going on.

Chapter 35

July 1171

The knights and their men-at-arms gathered in the outer bailey; the marshal and grooms in a flurry of activity to ensure the horses were tacked and ready to ride. One of Tracy's men lost his battle with the frayed nerves of his mount and it bolted; scattering men, weapons and horses until it was brought up short by the curtain wall.

Morville and FitzUrse glanced at each other in despair at the chaos.

'Just as well no one attacked or laid siege,' said FitzUrse. 'All that training and it's a shambles.'

Morville shrugged. 'No one knows what to expect, and you all have a long journey ahead – especially Tracy. Plus the men don't know what to think – I'd be surprised if you didn't lose a few on the road.'

'When I find out who told them of the Pope's sanction, I'll strangle him with my bare hands,' FitzUrse said.

'You would never keep that news quiet,' Morville said. 'The whole kingdom is aware.'

'Yes, well, this shall not be a comfortable ride.'

'Think of poor Tracy. When you and Brett arrive in Somerset he still has almost a sennight's ride to his estates in Cornwall.'

'It seems an awful lot of trouble to go to – all to build a few damnable churches.'

'The King wishes it. We need his favour and that of the nobles. I just hope it shall be enough to pacify Pope Alexander.'

'You know Tracy is talking about building three,' FitzUrse said.

Morville shook his head. 'Damned fool, can't do anything in moderation.'

FitzUrse shrugged. 'He's keen, too keen at times, but you know he'll always do his best for you.'

Morville stayed silent as Tracy and Brett approached.

'Are you ready, Reginald?' Tracy asked. FitzUrse gave a curt nod. 'Then we bid you farewell, Hugh.'

'Godspeed and safe journey,' Morville said. 'I shall see you in a month or two.'

'Yes, and all of us considerably poorer,' FitzUrse said.

'It is a small price to pay to regain the favour of all of Christendom,' Tracy said. No one could gainsay Tracy's piety, although FitzUrse scowled. Morville rested his hand on his fellow knight's arm to forestall any rebuke.

'Godspeed,' he said again. 'Build your steeples tall and your naves wide. Let these churches be a beacon to sinners and saints alike.'

'Amen,' Tracy said, crossing himself. The three knights turned to go, FitzUrse at the rear shaking his head. Morville suppressed a smile. Despite The Bear's outward show of scorn, he had not overly protested at riding to Barham Court to raise a church dedicated to Thomas Becket as his declaration of repentance. He was as shaken by the news that Becket was to be canonised as he was by his own censure.

Once his guests and their retainers had cleared Cnaresburg, Morville set out on his own mission of penance.

'What made you settle on Hampsthwaite?' William de Stoteville asked.

'It is a new parish and growing, yet has not a stone church,' Morville replied, 'and is close enough to also serve the new hamlet of Clint.'

'Would not a church serve you better in Cnaresburg itself?'

'Cnaresburg has the church of St Mary Magdalene and Nostell Priory. It needs not another place of worship and would likely be seen as a bribe by the populace.'

'You may be right,' Stoteville said, surprised that Morville had thought this through.

'The population of Hampsthwaite has grown in recent years and a stone church would fulfil a true need. A much better penance do you not think?'

'Yes, I do indeed.'

'Although I have charged Robertson of Cnaresburg as master stone mason and given him full authority over his team of masons.'

'And he is happy to carry out the work?'

'There are few commissions of this size to be had. He is very happy indeed.'

'And so shall many families in Cnaresburg be happy,' Stoteville said with a wry smile at Morville's cunning. 'Which will go a great way to restoring your good name.'

'Let us pray it is so,' Morville said. 'If I can turn the hearts of Yorkshiremen, turning the heart of an Italian pope shall be a simple task in comparison.'

Stoteville laughed as Morville kicked his horse on into the ford through the River Nydde at Hampsthwaite, and followed him into the shallow water.

A few yards further and Morville pulled up his mount to the right, where the current chapel was situated. 'We shall replace this shack. Those woods shall supply the timber for the fitments, it is near the heart of the village and by the crossroads, so also easy for the folk of Clint to attend,' he said, glancing around at the abundant green fields and woodland, and the small wooden structure already standing.

'But it is not on a rise,' Stoteville objected.

'No,' Morville said. 'I do not want to put my church above the village.'

'Becket's Church,' Stoteville could not help but correct.

'Indeed,' Morville said.

'The ideal spot. Ah, here is Robertson now.'

'That went exceedingly well,' Stoteville said on their return journey to Cnaresburg at dusk.

'Yes, Robertson is very pleased with the opportunity – especially as I did not object to the number of masons he wishes to employ,' Morville said.

'If it brings harmony back to Cnaresburg Castle, it is a low price to pay,' Stoteville said.

'Yes, my thoughts exactly. Although I am concerned about how many carpenters Foster will foist on me when he hears of it.'

'Your pockets will be much lightened,' Stoteville observed with a smile.

Morville sighed. 'What price Heaven, William? For let us face it, that is what I am buying.'

Stoteville could find no answer and they rode in silence.

'What's that?' Morville exclaimed as he topped the rise of the hill leading to Bond End.

Stoteville joined him. 'God's bones – fire!'

Both knights kicked their spurs into their horses' flanks and galloped into Cnaresburg.

The marketplace, surrounded by flimsy thatched timber buildings, was well ablaze and both men stared in shock.

'Go to the castle!' Morville shouted. 'Raise the garrison, maybe we can save the rest of the town.'

'But what if it's a trap?'

'It's no trap, William, hurry!'

'But Percy or even Courcy could have instigated this to weaken your defence of the castle.'

'They would be more direct, William. Tarry no longer, to the castle with you!'

Morville jumped off his horse, giving the rump of Stoteville's a hearty smack as he did so.

'Hurry, before I have to rebuild the whole town,' Morville shouted, then joined the line of men and women passing buckets.

Stoteville galloped down Butter Lane and Castle Gate to the

gatehouse, his horse spooking at flares of ashes and airborne embers.

As he led the garrison back out, he remembered Morville joining the line of peasants and shook his head. He had underestimated his brother-in-law.

Approaching the marketplace at the head of a column of men-at-arms, Stoteville spotted Morville, black with soot and dirt, grasping the arm of an equally encrusted man, and he grinned. Morville had done much to repair his reputation and standing this day.

A thought flitted across his mind. He dismissed it but it would not leave him be. *Had that been Morville's plan?*

Chapter 36

26th July 2015

Helen looked at her watch. 'Well, we can't wait any longer, let's get started.'

'How can we rehearse Becket's exile scene without Becket or Henry?' Ed asked.

'Not very well, clearly,' Helen snapped, then she sighed and ran a hand through her hair. 'Sorry, Ed. Everything just seems to be falling apart.'

'It's the ghosts.' Mike chuckled.

'Don't laugh, love, it probably is,' Sarah said, her hand on Mike's knee.

Helen sighed again. Nothing had changed much since Donna's cleansing – not enough, anyway. 'We'll talk through all the practical stuff, use this time to get everything sorted.'

'I don't see why they can't be here,' Alec grumbled. 'We're all giving up our time and Paul and Charlie have the leads.'

'I'll ring again, see if I can find out what's going on,' Ed said and left the theatre to find a signal.

'I think we need to expand plan B,' Helen said. 'Just in case things don't get any better.'

'They can hardly get worse,' Alec said.

'What do you have in mind?' Sarah asked.

'Understudies,' Helen said.

'You have got to be joking, Paul and Charlie have the leads!' Mike echoed Alec's earlier words. 'Most of the play is the two of them! It's not the same as understudying Dan.'

'What do you suggest?' Helen retorted. 'Cancel the show?'

'No way, being part of feva is massive for us, I'm not walking away from it,' Alec said.

'Are you willing to understudy then?' Helen asked.

Alec sighed and looked around at the others. 'I guess so,' he said. 'I know Henry's part best, I'll learn Paul's lines. But that means somebody else will have to understudy Dan.'

Helen breathed a sigh of relief. 'Thanks, Alec. Mike, how about you? It's you or Ed for Becket.'

'What about me or you?' Sarah asked.

'I'll take one of the knights' roles if need be,' Helen said.

'John or Kate might take one on,' Sarah said.

'Yes, fantastic.'

'Why can't I play Becket?' Sarah asked again.

Helen stared at her. 'I think we can get away with women playing the minor roles, but having a woman playing a medieval archbishop won't go down well.'

Sarah pouted and sat back in her chair, arms crossed, but didn't argue.

'I'll do it if Ed refuses,' Mike said grudgingly. 'But with work and all I'm not going to have much time.'

'Thanks Mike, I appreciate that. We'll ask Ed when he comes back in, but to be honest we've got some serious work to do to pull this together for opening night.'

'Plan A or plan B?' Sarah asked, still petulant.

Helen was saved from having to answer by Ed running back into the auditorium. 'They were all arrested last night!'

'What?' the others shouted, all but Sarah who frowned and shook her head.

'Tell us, Ed,' Helen said, fighting the urge to weep as she saw everything she'd worked so hard for fall into ruin.

He gave them the story, then added, 'They've been charged with drunk and disorderly, but wouldn't accept a caution, the stubborn idiots. So it will go to court. They've been knocked around quite a bit apparently – Paul's spitting feathers, talking about suing Wetherspoons and the police.'

'Bloody typical,' Alec muttered.

'How badly hurt are they?' Helen asked.

'Not sure to be honest, Paul was too busy ranting about the police.'

'They'll be fine then,' Sarah said. 'And Dan?'

Ed shrugged. 'They'll be here soon. You can ask him yourself.'

'I need a coffee,' Sarah said and stood. 'Anyone else?'

'I need a bloody bottle of wine,' said Helen and everyone laughed. 'I guess coffee will do for now though.'

Sarah led the way back into the theatre. 'The convicts are coming,' she said amid peals of laughter. Her husband, Paul and Charlie followed, carrying the coffees and scowling.

'Give it a rest, Sarah,' Helen said, noting the expression on Dan's face in particular. 'How are you doing, guys?'

'Battered, bruised, knackered,' Paul said. 'How do you think?'

An awkward silence fell on the group.

'At least you're here,' Sarah said. 'Why don't you sit down and have your coffee?'

Dan glared at her, but the others took seats at the front by the stage.

'So what happens now?' Helen asked.

Charlie shrugged. 'We have a court hearing in a couple of weeks.'

'What, like a trial?' Sarah asked.

'No, just a hearing. I think we just say not guilty, then it will go to trial a few months later.'

'A few months? So after feva?' Helen said.

'Yes, after feva, Helen,' Paul said, sarcastically. 'The show won't be affected.'

'Sorry, Paul. If there's anything we can do to help, you only have to ask. And honestly, the show's already been affected,' Helen said.

'We were just talking about plan Bs,' Alec said. 'I'm to be your understudy, Paul, you know, just in case anything else goes wrong.'

Paul said nothing, his face unreadable.

'And who's to be my understudy?' Charlie asked.

'I'm not sure, it's between Ed and Mike,' Helen said. 'And I'm sorry guys – it is only plan B. So much has already gone wrong, I'm just trying to be prepared.'

Nobody said anything until Ed broke the silence. 'I'm happy to do it – not that I expect I'll be needed,' he said, looking at Charlie, who nodded.

'So who's my understudy?' Dan asked.

'Helen,' Sarah said, not quite hiding the glee in her voice at the dismay on Dan's face. There was a reason Helen stayed offstage.

Silence again.

'Shall we get on then?' Paul asked. 'Can't sit around here gossiping all day.'

The resultant laughter broke the tension and Helen gave him a grateful smile before briefing them.

'Becket's exile,' she began, but Paul interrupted.

'The year's 1164 at Northampton Castle. Becket's gone too far and thinks Henry is a tyrant. Henry is determined to bring him to heel. Becket's conduct has crossed into treason with a lot of insults and bickering. Nothing is achieved. Becket's been embezzling – which reminds me, Charlie, have you done those accounts yet?'

'Sod off, Paul, I've been a bit preoccupied of late, I'll bring them next time.'

Paul nodded then turned back to Helen. 'Where was I? Oh yes, embezzlement. Attack and counter-attack. Vicious war of words, Becket grovelling.'

'Hardly grovelling,' Charlie said. 'Making sound legal argument and proposing excellent compromises.'

Paul waved his friend's words away. 'Then Becket – guilty coward that he is – flees to France.'

'It's a little more complicated than that—'

'Okay, okay,' Helen interrupted. 'You know the scene, do you want to take the stage and run through it?'

'See – you're worrying about nothing,' Sarah said, leaning toward Helen.

'I hope you're right.'

Chapter 37

'No, guys, that's not high enough,' Helen said. 'I want Henry overlooking the murder, saying the words that drove the knights to Canterbury. He needs to be higher, overlooking the entire scene, almost godlike. I want to draw the parallels between the two great influences over everybody in England – the Church and the Crown – and the conflict between them.'

'But you said the platform just needed to be raised a bit,' Alec protested.

'It doesn't sound like that was what she said. Just admit it, you cocked up!' Ed said. 'All that work for nothing.'

'Don't go putting all the blame on me,' Alec said. 'You were there too.'

'No I wasn't, I was off getting the swords and other stuff.'

Helen held up a hand to forestall further protests. 'I don't care whose fault it is, we don't have time for blame. Opening night is in one week – we need a higher platform. Henry needs to be above the heads of everyone else – the position he believed he held.'

'But that's a massive job,' Alec protested. 'Can't we just make do?'

'Make do? Are you kidding me?' Ed shouted. 'All the work we've put in and you want to make do on the final scene – the scene it's all been building up to?'

Alec shrank back from the venom in Ed's voice. 'Sorry, it's just . . . I don't know how we're going to do it in time, along with everything else.'

Before Ed could tell Alec exactly what he wanted him to do, all three were distracted by more acrimonious voices backstage.

'Stay here and work it out,' Helen said and dashed off towards the sounds of the screams and shouts, leaving Ed and Alec bickering despite the commotion.

'What the hell is going on?' Helen demanded, rushing to Sarah who sat on the floor in a huddle together with John and Kate. She looked to Dan for an explanation, but he stood silent, fists clenched and face red.

'Mum asked Dad for a divorce,' Kate said solemnly. 'Dad didn't take it very well.'

Speechless, Helen looked from Sarah to Dan and back again. *They've done this now? And in front of their kids? What the hell is wrong with everyone?*

Helen's blood ran cold as the thought registered, then took control of herself. 'Dan, go and help Ed and Alec, they have a problem with the set for the final scene and need an extra pair of hands.'

Dan didn't move.

'Go, now Dan. I'll sort everything out, just go and help the guys.'

Dan finally looked at her, nodded, and left, all without saying a word.

'What's going on?' Mike rushed over to Sarah. 'Love, what happened?'

In answer, Sarah's sobbing increased. Mike took her face in her hands and drew in a breath through clenched teeth. 'He hit you again, didn't he? The bastard! I'll sort him out!'

'You'll do nothing of the sort, Mike,' Helen said. 'Stay here and look after Sarah. John, Kate, can I have a word with you?'

The teenagers looked to their mother – a silent question if she was okay – then followed Helen. Kate was shaking, John trembled with rage.

'Come and sit down,' Helen said, and led them out to the auditorium, choosing seats out of earshot of everybody else. The argument between Ed and Alec was still going strong on stage – she wouldn't be overheard.

'I know everything's a mess, but don't blame your parents,' Helen began.

'Are you *serious*?' John asked. 'Dad *hit* Mum – in front of us, we *saw* him.'

'And it's not the first time,' Kate said. 'Mum keeps getting bruises and lies about them.'

Helen took a deep breath, shocked that things were far worse than she'd realised. 'Your dad isn't well,' she said, then stopped at the looks of scorn from John and Kate.

'It's difficult to explain,' she tried again. 'But this is my fault and I'll fix it.'

'How is it *your* fault?' John asked.

'When we started rehearsing, I tried something a bit different to help everyone get into character.'

'Oh, the spirit board,' Kate said. 'Yeah, Mum told me about that.'

'You're not serious? Why are you messing about with that stuff?' John asked.

Helen sighed. 'I know, it was stupid, but – as with most bad ideas – it seemed like a good one at the time.'

'Are you trying to tell us that Mum and Dad are what – possessed?' John asked incredulously.

'Not possessed exactly,' Helen tried to explain. 'But I think the spirits of their characters have . . . attached themselves to everybody.'

'Attached? What does that mean?' Kate asked.

'I'm not sure I understand it properly myself, but somebody is trying to help me sort it out.'

'So you're saying that Dad is really FitzUrse, and Mum is Richard le Brett?' John asked.

'Well, in a way, yes. For the moment.'

'Does that mean Mike's gay?'

Despite herself, Helen choked a laugh and the teenagers joined in.

'I doubt it, everything is just . . . mixed up at the moment.'

'What do you want us to do?' Kate asked.

'I want you to get out of here – can you go and stay with your grandparents for a while? Your nan's in Harrogate isn't she?'

'Um, yeah, we've been staying there anyway but I'm sure she'll let us stay longer. What are we supposed to tell her? Hi Nan, Mum and Dad think they're medieval knights and we're scared to be around them?'

Helen laughed again, then realised it was inappropriate and stopped. 'Maybe not that – just say your parents need some alone time.'

John nodded. 'Okay.'

'But what about the costumes? I'm helping Mum with them and we haven't finished,' Kate said.

'Don't worry about it – I'll help your mum finish them. I just want you both out of the way and safe.' Helen reached over and gripped their arms. 'Trust me. I *will* fix this. Then your mum and dad will be back to normal.'

'Promise?' Kate said in a small voice.

Helen took a deep breath then nodded. 'Yes,' she said. *Shit, what have I just said?* she thought.

Chapter 38

August 1171

'Horsemen!' The lookout on the tower of the east gate shouted, and the cry was echoed to the inner bailey where Morville was going through his paces with sword and Mauclerk. He stepped back and removed his mail hood.

Mauclerk panted with exhaustion for a few seconds and followed suit, but his lord was already running to the tower, despite his mail tunic and recent exertions, to see for himself.

Up in the battlements he peered into the morning sun. 'Can you make out who it is?' he asked his sergeant-at-arms.

'Not yet, My Lord. Maybe when they approach Brig-Gate.'

Morville pointed; children were running towards the castle, their faces and voices excited and hearty. 'They are friends not foes. Open the gates.' This last a shout, and minutes later the heavy gates were unbarred and swung open, the portcullis was raised, and the drawbridge dropped.

FitzUrse was the first through, followed by Brett and an assortment of their men-at-arms and retainers, all looking weary but relieved to have arrived. Tracy followed, escorting a cart, in which Morville was surprised to see a woman holding two newborns. He guessed this must be the wife Tracy had been bleating on about when in his cups. Finally some good news – Tracy had healthy twins.

'Reginald, William, Richard, welcome! It is good to see you again, my friends. How was your journey?'

'Long,' FitzUrse said. 'The less said the better.' He looked behind him at the gates, still open. 'I was surprised by Cnaresburg's welcome. It appears things have changed.'

'They have. I am in favour again, at least in my own town.'

'Although not to the extent of leaving the gates open,' FitzUrse interrupted.

'No harm in a little caution. How went it with you?'

'Difficult,' FitzUrse said. 'The bastard masons tried to charge me at least triple, the carpenters more still. I refused. Tracy fared the worst, insisted on funding three churches, the fool. They've left him near penniless, but at least the weeping and wailing when he's in his cups is reduced to bearable proportions, although he cares about naught but his wife and the babes now.'

Morville laughed, put an arm round each of FitzUrse and Brett's shoulders, and addressed Tracy as he guided them to the keep. 'Come, your old bedchambers are ready for you. I'll have baths prepared, then rest awhile and I'll have Jack organise a feast for dinner. Plumton and I took a venison a sennight since. It's well hung and will serve.'

'Jack is back?'

'Yes, as are they all, down to the serving girls. Sheepish and eager to please, just how I like them.'

The men guffawed and climbed the narrow stone stairs to their respective bedchambers, Tracy solicitously aiding his wife.

'Ah, I am ready for this,' FitzUrse said, striding to the lord's table. 'Those bastards at Teston virtually besieged me in the manor house, it has been some time since I sat at table like this.'

'You should have paid them what they wanted, Reginald,' Tracy said. 'Ease tempers rather than inflame them.'

'Ah, but then I would not have been able to make a loan to you, William.'

Tracy coloured and glanced at Pomperi, who diplomatically turned to Helwise with a compliment about the stones-and-roses decoration on the walls of the great hall.

'It is but small and temporary,' Tracy said.

Morville interrupted before tensions rose higher between the two knights. 'And what of you, Richard, how did you fare?'

The young man shook his head and grabbed his goblet to drink.

'Sir Simon barred the gate to him,' FitzUrse answered in Brett's stead. 'Refused to acknowledge him. The boy lived as an outlaw in Sampford Brett, despite the place carrying his name. Sir Simon only admitted him once the first stones of the new church had been laid.'

Lost for words, Morville drained his own goblet and called for more of the fine Rhenish wine.

FitzUrse grabbed the serving girl as soon as she deposited full flagons on the table, and pulled her on to his lap. 'This is better, Hugh, too much hard muscle on a man-at-arms to be serving table.'

Morville's men, seated below the knights in the body of the great hall, roared with laughter, every one of them relieved to be sitting to dine rather than cooking and serving.

'Beyond Teston,' Morville said with a glance of frustration at FitzUrse, 'our favour appears to be growing once more.'

Tracy and Brett nodded. FitzUrse ignored the jibe and wrenched a huge mouthful of venison from the joint before him.

'Yes, England is becoming friendly again,' Tracy said with a fond look at his wife. A smile flitted across Pomperi's face and Morville wondered at the strain apparent on her countenance. He glanced at his own wife and for the first time recognised the marks of a similar strain on her features.

'And not before time,' FitzUrse said, the words fighting their way out around the half-chewed meat in his mouth.

Morville forgot his inspection of the women and reconnected with his train of thought. 'I think it's time to call on that favour and grow it further,' he said.

'What do you have in mind, Hugh?' Tracy asked.

A slow smile spread on Morville's face and he paused before answering, judging his timing well. 'A tournament,' he said. 'Tourney for the nobles and a fair for everyone else.'

'God's wounds, Hugh, a tourney! Just what I need. But a real one, a proper joust of war and a mêlée. If we do this we do it well.'

Morville grinned. 'Just as I was thinking, Reginald. A real spectacle, something for all to enjoy.'

Brett clapped his hands together with a grin.

'Is that wise?' Tracy asked. 'We have risen in favour due to repentance, would not holding a tournament risk losing it again, especially from the Church?'

'Nonsense, William. Why, even the parish priest attended at Harewood. The Church's position on tournaments is posturing, naught else.'

'Maybe so, but remember what else happened at Harewood,' Tracy persisted.

'How could I forget?' FitzUrse said, and pointed a half-gnawed bone at Tracy. 'One tourney unmade us, another will remake us. Nothing gladdens a noble's heart more surely than a tournament done correctly, with proper ransoms and every opportunity to shine. Now, to business. Where would be the best place to host the mêlée, Hugh?'

As the men plotted, Helwise and Pomperi held each other's eyes for a moment, the despair in each clear enough to require no accompanying words.

Chapter 39

September 1171

'Fortune has smiled on us,' Brett said. 'It is a good sign the sun has joined us.'

'Yes, and soon so will the nobility of England,' Tracy said.

'You have decided this tournament is a good thing then, have you, William?'

'Yes.' Tracy couldn't quite meet FitzUrse's eyes. 'It looks as if the townsfolk are enjoying the fair already.'

The others squinted into the morning sun. The field ahead was filled with striped tents of every colour. Blue and yellow, red and green, orange and white. Morville counted the peaks of the apexed canvas 'roofs'. 'Over a score. Good, and plenty of people too.'

'Any knights?' Tracy asked.

'Not that I can see, but they will still be on the road, I don't expect the nobles to arrive until afternoon.'

The knights entered the fair grounds and dismounted, leaving Mauclerk to see to the securing and well-being of their palfreys.

The noise and activity of the fair gave them a moment's pause; each recalling the occasions they had been shunned, by commoner and noble alike. The sight of so many people gathered together at their behest was welcome indeed.

The local tradesmen had erected tents – butcher, baker, candlestick maker amongst them – and minstrels and stilt walkers added to the chaotic atmosphere, each desperate to bring custom to their benefactor's tent of wares or goods. The more their benefactors sold this day, the more they would themselves earn.

The knights walked past a small enclosure where a group of children were pitting their cocks against each other – the youngsters almost as raucous as the birds.

'A quarter-penny on that one.' Morville indicated a bedraggled-looking bird missing a sizeable quantity of feathers.

'Hugh, are you crazed? It's barely standing,' FitzUrse exclaimed.

'Are you taking my wager?' Morville asked.

'Assuredly. Let me see.' FitzUrse scanned the birds, ignoring the expectant faces of their young owners. 'That's the one.' He pointed to the largest, preening its feathers.

Morville accepted the wager and both men gave quarter-pennies to Tracy to hold.

As the children chased down their cocks to place them in the fighting circle, Morville remarked, 'It looks like this is the first fight for yours, Reginald.'

'Yours looks like it's lost every fight it's engaged in.'

'To me, he looks like he's come out of a good scrap still standing.'

'We shall see,' FitzUrse stated. 'I stand by my choice.'

'And I mine,' Morville said.

Both cocks were released and FitzUrse's brute charged Morville's scraggy favourite. It uttered a loud squawk, jumped in the air, clipped wings flapping, and met Brute's challenge with extended talons. Another squawk and beating of feathers made it clear Scraggled's tactics were effective. FitzUrse said nothing but looked a little worried. Scraggled did not back off but continued his offensive, jutting his sharp beak into the side of his opponent, yanking out feathers with every peck.

'Come on, Brute, fight back damn you!' FitzUrse roared above the noise of the children's insulting encouragements to both birds.

Scraggled was remorseless. A veteran of many cockfights, as Morville had rightly assessed, he knew well the only way to avoid pain and injury was to inflict pain and injury. And he did so, remorselessly and unflinchingly. Within minutes, Brute lay near dead and bleeding in the fighting circle, the victor strutting and preening even fewer feathers.

'Well done, Hugh.' FitzUrse made an exaggerated bow to the victor, and Tracy passed the two quarter-pennies to Morville, who in turn flicked them both to the boy who had gathered his prize cock in his arms.

'Well done, boy, you breed them well.'

'Thank you, My Lord,' the boy said, his embarrassment at being addressed by the controversial Lord of the Manor of Cnaresburg evident in his red cheeks.

Morville glanced at the boy staring at his unmoving prize cock. 'Here, lad,' he said, and flicked another quarter-penny in his direction. 'Let this be a lesson to you, the quality of the warrior is not evident in his armour, but in his strength of heart and his will to win. Look for those qualities in the next cock you bring to fight.'

'Thank you, My Lord,' the boy squeaked, scrabbling in the dirt for his piece of coin. 'I surely will.'

'Percy,' Brett said, interrupting them. The other three knights looked up to see William de Percy striding towards them.

'He doesn't look happy,' Tracy said. 'And why is he on his own?'

Morville and FitzUrse glanced at each other, both aware that this did not augur good tidings.

'Greetings, My Lord Percy,' Morville said. The formality of his welcome was not lost on anybody present and even the cocks seem to hush their squawking.

'Greetings,' Percy replied, but gave no smile. 'What were you thinking, Hugh?'

'In what regard, William?' Morville replied, incensed at being called into question within the hearing of the children and citizens of Cnaresburg.

'A joust of war? Really? You are in need of King Henry's favour, so why flout his ban?'

'Ban?' Morville asked, his heart sinking.

'Yes, ban. Jousts of war are banned in England, and have been for some time.'

'But . . . Harewood? And Riche Mont?'

'Special dispensation from the King and jousts of peace for the practice at the quintain and ring,' Percy said.

'I, uh, we were not aware,' Morville said.

'I told you it was a bad idea,' Tracy said, and FitzUrse elbowed him so hard he staggered to keep his feet.

'You know you are out of favour, why did you not ascertain the current state of affairs before sending your invitations?'

'Why did you not advise us when you received yours?' FitzUrse said. 'It was a fortnight since, yet you only advise us now.'

Percy turned and stared at The Bear. 'I have only last night returned from Normandy. Enjoy your fair, My Lords, but there shall be no tournament. When Henry hears of this, and no doubt he has by now, you will be even further in disgrace. Good day to you, and good fortune, you are all in dire need of it.' Percy turned and strode away. The four knights stood, rooted to the spot in shock, unable to voice a sound.

'I told you it was a bad idea,' Tracy said again. 'I told you. We were making good progress, and now look, we've defied the King. Ruined, we are all ruined.'

'Hush, William!' FitzUrse shouted, his face red and fists clenched. 'Stop your whining, or by God I will stop it for you!'

Tracy stepped back, partly in surprise at FitzUrse's reaction, partly in fear.

'Calm yourself, Reginald,' Morville said. 'This is a time for clear heads.'

'Everything we've done, everything we've endured, and now we've gone against the express wishes of the King,' FitzUrse shouted. 'He shall not forgive this easily.'

'He will understand,' Brett said. 'We were ignorant of his ban, he will understand that.'

'Understand? What the devil makes you think King Henry is understanding? Do you know nothing? He is a man who does not need to understand, he is *King!* Events are as he decrees, no matter the truth of them. He sent us to silence Becket, which we did, and look how we've been treated since. Has he taken responsibility for his part? No. It has fallen on us, his loyal servants.'

'If his character is as you say, then why has he left us here to live? Surely it would serve him better to have us dead!' Tracy said.

'Care what you say, William. He may well yet decide on that course of action.'

'But, but, we were acting at his behest!' Tracy protested.

'What does that matter? A year ago Becket was a troublemaker, an impious archbishop intent on sedition. Now he is a martyr and will no doubt be canonised. We killed him in his cathedral, before his altar. When his body was prepared they found his hair shirt, so he is no longer impious. Now he is a devout man whom we killed in God's sanctuary. When we dealt with him he was hated. Now he is loved. Where we were loved, now we are hated.' FitzUrse stopped, overcome by his passion and words.

Tracy gaped at him. Morville and Brett looked on, both silenced by FitzUrse's analysis of their situation.

'What are we going to do?' Brett whispered, his querulous tone betraying his youth. Morville felt sorry for him: he had not yet seen his twenties, but had dealt the killing blow and Morville could see no future worth the pain of living ahead of him.

Silence, then: 'We go to the Pope. We throw ourselves on his mercy and take what punishment he decrees,' Tracy said.

'By God, no,' FitzUrse shouted. 'It is Henry we need to appease, not the Church.'

'We are excommunicated. Our souls are damned for eternity,' Tracy said. 'By your very admission, King Henry does not need to understand, he will do what is most propitious for himself. If we are pardoned by Pope Alexander, we will be pardoned by King Henry.'

'Don't be so sure,' Morville said. 'From what I have learned of our king these past months, I feel he would consider himself injured if we put the approval of the Pope over his own.'

'Yes, you speak well, Hugh,' FitzUrse said. 'I am in agreement.'

'I am not.' Tracy drew himself up to his full height. 'And I will no longer follow your lead, Reginald. You led us here. I will leave for Rome to prostrate myself before His Holiness Pope Alexander. I will prepare Pomperi and the babes, escort them to Bovey Tracy, then take my leave of England. Will any of you accompany me?'

Morville said nothing, Brett would not meet Tracy's eyes. FitzUrse was the only one to speak, once again holding the fate of his companions in his hairy fist. 'You are on your own, William. We shall take all necessary steps to regain King Henry's favour before we attend to Pope Alexander.'

Tracy drew in a sharp breath. 'Very well. I bid you good fortune and hope our paths shall once again cross.' He walked away, slowly but deliberately, having finally chosen his own path, at the age of thirty seven.

Chapter 40

30th July 2015

Paul stood stage left, spotlighted and dressed in purple tunic, hose and crown, a short cloak slung about his shoulders. Helen smiled – that faux fur had been a wonderful find in the charity shop, and Paul looked every inch the medieval king, strutting in his leather boots.

She looked up as Donna sat in the seat next to her. 'Sorry I'm late.'

'Not at all. Thanks for coming. We're just building up to the final scene.'

'Ah, England's fine shores,' King Henry proclaimed. ' 'Tis good to be treading her fertile soil once more. Come, Henry,' he called offstage to his son. 'This will all be yours one day, 'tis time to claim your rights as my heir.'

The light on Paul doused, and a new spotlight shone on Charlie, sitting stage right, dressed in a brown monk's habit and with a table of papers before him.

'Ah, Henry, my old friend, you test me so,' Becket said, reading a scroll. 'You insist on insulting my Church and my Pope – not to mention my good self. What to do with you? How to bring you to heel?'

The lights switched once more, illuminating Henry standing, legs apart and arms akimbo. 'This is *my* kingdom. *I* rule here and no other. My son shall be crowned as my heir and I shall brook no argument. Close the ports!' He swept his arms wide. 'Becket can stay in France, cowering from my wrath. He shall not oppose me in this too.'

He turned and began to pace the distance of the lighted area. 'With the ports closed, neither he nor any messenger can defy me. Not even communiqués from the Pope can be brought. I shall have no interference from the Church in this matter.'

Back to Becket, now joined by an uncomfortable-looking Sarah dressed in a nun's habit.

'Mary de Blois, my dear Princess, you are my only hope.'

'Archbishop, I am pleased to serve you, Your Grace.'

'I have a task for you. A task only you can succeed in, and you shall have your retribution against Henry for the unholy marriage he forced upon you.'

'I need no retribution, Your Grace. I only wish to serve our Lord in the company of my sisters.'

'Indeed,' Becket said. 'Both myself and Pope Alexander are most grateful that you have chosen to leave the convent to assist us.'

The lights switched once more. Paul had now been joined by Ed playing the role of young Henry – the King's eldest son.

'Prepare yourself, boy, this is a great honour.'

'Yes, My Liege,' Ed said, playing a bewildered boy terrified of a tyrannical father.

Henry adjusted the ermine cloak his son wore, then looked up in fury as Sarah walked into the light.

'What is the meaning of this?' he roared.

'I am a royal princess, Sire, daughter of King Stephen and your cousin. Your closure of the ports could not stop me attending the coronation of young Henry.'

'I see,' Henry said, his eyes narrowed in suspicion. 'Have you brought Rome's blessing?'

'Indeed I have not, Sire. I hold papal decrees for Archbishop l'Évêque, Bishop Foliot and Bishop Salisbury,' Sarah said, producing three scrolls bearing the intersecting circles of the seal of Rome. 'They are forbidden to continue with this coronation in the absence of the Archbishop of Canterbury.'

'Ah, so Thomas still thinks he has power over me, does he?' Henry said.

'Indeed not, Sire, only over the bishops who are subordinate to him,' Sarah – as Mary de Blois – said.

'Hah,' Henry shouted. 'Becket holds no power in a land in which he is too cowardly to set foot. The bishops are subordinate to *me!*' He grabbed the scrolls and ripped them, throwing the pieces back into the nun's face. 'The coronation shall proceed. My son shall be proclaimed the Young King this day.'

The stage plunged into darkness and Helen stood, applauded carefully as the lights came back on – grateful her pot had finally come off – and shouted, 'Well done, guys. Sarah and Ed, you could both be a little more relaxed on the night, but well done!'

Helen sat back down and turned to Donna. 'What do you think?'

Donna sighed. 'It's not good news, I'm afraid. Both the main guys had spirit with them – I've never seen spirits so close to a living man before. They didn't just stand behind or to the side, they walked in.'

'Walked in?'

'Yes. Almost blended with the men. Have you ever seen a trance medium work?'

Helen shook her head.

'It's quite remarkable to witness. The spirit of the medium withdraws and gives permission for another spirit to enter – at least temporarily.'

'That sounds . . . frightening,' Helen said.

'No – it's done with permission and great respect, and the trust is never betrayed. The disembodied spirit needs the full approval of the medium. But here . . .' she paused. 'This is something else. I've never seen anything like it. The auras of both the main men—'

'Paul and Charlie,' Helen said.

Donna nodded. 'Their auras changed as soon as they started speaking. Even their appearance changed, did you notice?'

Helen stared at her hands and did not speak.

'When they finished . . .' Helen looked up at Donna, waiting for her to gather her thoughts. 'The spirits withdrew,' Donna continued, 'but not completely, they're still attached by their auras.'

'Is that bad?' Helen asked.

'It isn't good,' Donna said. 'Especially as I don't think the guys are even aware of it. I think this is without their permission and they're being violated.'

'So what do we do?'

'We hold another séance and ask the spirits to leave.'

'And will they?'

'That depends on how strongly and faithfully Paul and Charlie tell them to go.'

'Faithfully?'

'If it's a deep and genuine wish to be left alone.'

'And we need their cooperation and belief?'

'Yes.'

'They don't believe.'

'That they want the spirits to withdraw?'

'That the spirits exist in the first place.'

'Then we really do have a problem,' Donna said.

Chapter 41

'Okay, let's pick up from where we left off yesterday,' Helen said. 'We have a few days left, let's make them count. Places everyone.'

Paul and Charlie walked on to stage, Charlie taking Becket's place to the right, Paul to the left. The rest of the cast settled into their seats to watch, Dan sitting as far away as possible from his wife and Mike.

Helen turned to the sound and lighting booth to give Alec a thumbs up. 'From the top.'

Charlie's spotlight focused its glare on to Thomas Becket. He sat at a table, scroll in hand, and paused as he read, then looked up to the audience, stood, and brandished the parchment.

'By God, that man shall drive me to apoplexy! His son is crowned – *crowned* – and by a hand other than mine! The lion of justice? No – a rat of betrayal! He shall be the death of me, by God, I swear it.'

Becket approached the front of the stage and lowered his voice. 'But I shall not submit to his tyranny. Yes, *tyranny*! Once my good friend, he has become a caricature of himself – of a king. I shall bring him back to actuality – bring him back to himself, the good man he once was. I shall save him if it is the last thing I do.'

Becket returned to his chair, picked up a quill from the table and began writing on parchment. The spotlight dimmed and Henry's blazed into life.

'Damn that man!' Henry shouted, both fists clutching sheaves of parchment. 'Will he never do my bidding? Look at these, *look* at them!' He thrust the parchments towards the auditorium. 'Papal mandates, letters of interdict from Becket and Pope Alexander! They're threatening excommunication. Imagine, *me*, Henry, King of England, excommunicated! It's unthinkable!' He threw the parchment into the air as he stamped his foot, grabbed fistfuls of his hair and cried out as if in pain as he doubled over.

Straightening, he calmed and his hands dropped to his sides. 'I have no choice. I must extend peace to Becket and bid him return to England. That should take care of these.' He kicked at the scattered parchment. 'At least in England he shall once again be within my reach.' He smiled in cunning.

Becket's spotlight came on and the men met centre stage and embraced as the lights dimmed to nothing.

'That was great, guys, well done,' Helen called to the stage, standing and clapping. The other Castle Players did the same.

Helen turned to give Alec a clap too, the complicated lighting sequence having been executed perfectly, then spotted another audience member at the back of the theatre. 'Donna! What are you doing here?' Helen said as Donna stood and moved to join her.

'What's she doing here, *again*?' Dan called and made his way to join the rest of the crew. 'Come to do an exorcism?'

Donna shook her head. 'No, no exorcism, you're not possessed by demons, but are being attacked by spirits. That's very different.'

'So why are you here?' Helen asked.

Donna gave her a strange look. 'You invited me, don't you remember?'

Helen looked puzzled and glanced at Sarah, who shrugged.

'After I called Richard Armitage and told him what was going on.'

'You did *what*?' Sarah said.

'Don't worry, he didn't believe me. Sarah, what have you done to your face?'

'Ask my husband,' she snapped.

Donna looked around at everyone, eyes settling on Dan, who looked furious. 'Can I have a word in private?' she asked Helen.

'Uh, yeah, I suppose so.' Helen looked to the others and they all drifted towards the stage and Paul and Charlie.

'What's going on?' Donna asked Helen. 'Has Dan been hitting Sarah?'

'Only a couple of times, but they're staying well away from each other now. Well, at least when they're not on stage.'

'Has she been to the police?'

'The police?' Helen looked blank. 'No.'

'Why not? She's a victim of domestic abuse.'

'I didn't really think about it like that, they'll sort it out between themselves.'

Donna stared at her in a moment. 'Oh my God, you've got one too.'

'What are you talking about? I'm fine.'

Donna lowered her eyes and looked up at Helen through her lashes. 'No, you're not. You have a man standing in your aura – too close. He's in mail so is another knight. Hang on, I'm trying to get his name. Brought, rock, something like that.'

'You mean Broc? Ranulf de Broc.'

'Yes, that's it. Who was he?'

'The Lord of Saltwood. He hosted the knights and rode to Canterbury with them, then smoothed the waters with Henry.'

'So he was the man behind the scenes? The director?'

'I suppose so,' Helen said.

'As are you.'

Helen said nothing.

'We have to hold another séance, ask the spirits to leave.'

'No.'

'Why not?'

'We open on Saturday. You saw the guys, they're good. Better than good, they're great! It could be Becket and Henry up there.'

'It *is* Becket and Henry up there! Don't you understand? We have to make the spirits leave, they're too strong, and they're still increasing their hold on their hosts!'

'Not until after the show.'

'That may be too late! Look at what's happening to you all – Dan and Sarah, Mike, you're always in the pub, and I heard your two leading men were arrested a couple of weeks ago. Your lives are already being affected, and they're getting stronger. Things will only get worse. You *have* to cancel the show!'

'No. We're not cancelling.'

'But Helen, don't you see? The spirits have such a strong hold I'm afraid they'll only leave when they right the wrongs that were done to them in life.'

'We're not cancelling the show.'

'But anything could happen. It's too dangerous to go ahead!'

'You heard. We're not cancelling the show.'

Donna looked up to see that the rest of the Castle Players had rejoined them and stood as a pack in the aisle. She turned to Helen again, but realised by the set of her jaw and folded arms that the woman wasn't listening.

'Oh God,' Donna said. 'Oh my God. It's already too late.' She hurried out of the theatre.

Chapter 42

October 1171

'How do you consider Tracy fares?' Brett asked.

Morville shrugged and FitzUrse said, 'Probably hasn't reached Rome yet.'

'What will happen to him?'

'Pope Alexander will no doubt hand him over to the Dominicans,' FitzUrse said.

'No! They would torture him, even burn him!'

'We don't know what else the Pope would order, unless it be serving at the pleasure of the Knights Templar. Percy said that Henry and Rome are on better terms these days, so I doubt he shall be given to the Dominicans. The Pope will not burn Tracy, that would necessitate taking strong action against King Henry too. He will no doubt be ordered to the Holy Land as the King suggested.'

'You think so?' Brett asked, his youth evident in his shaking voice.

Morville held up a hand to forestall FitzUrse's probable brutal reply. The boy needed encouragement, not fear. 'It is sure to be so, Richard. Do not fret, William will live, and no doubt welcome his penance, his conscience was deeply troubling to him. This is the right course of action for him.'

Brett nodded. 'Then why did we not travel with him?'

'Bah! Prostrate myself before the Church, throw myself on Pope Alexander's mercy? I'm not minded for that course of action. Let us regain King Henry's favour, then he will help us with Rome,' FitzUrse said.

Brett nodded again.

'Begging your pardon, My Lord,' Mauclerk interrupted them, speaking from the door to the great hall. 'Sir William de Percy has arrived.'

'Percy? Again? Well, show him in, Hugh,' Morville said, then glanced at Brett and FitzUrse. No words were said, but all thought the same: *What now?*

Percy strode into the room, wasting little time on greetings. 'I am here on the King's business,' he said, holding up a scroll bound with ribbon and Henry's distinctive double-sided seal.

He handed the scroll to Morville then helped himself to wine. He winced at the rough Spanish vintage; he much preferred the far superior Rhenish.

'We are bid come to Ireland,' Morville said. 'We must leave at once to join King Henry's expedition.'

'Is there unrest, William?' FitzUrse asked Percy. 'With Dermot dead and Strongbow's surrender, I thought all was well.' He glanced at Morville and Brett. 'After the débâcle with the tournament, I took it upon myself to employ a number of my men-at-arms as messengers.'

'Messengers or spies?' Percy asked.

FitzUrse stared at him. 'News bearers, to ensure I keep abreast of events.'

'What has happened to occasion an expedition?' Morville asked in an attempt to defuse tempers.

'Strongbow is above himself. Yes, he surrendered but with the condition that he is granted the fiefdom of Leinster.'

'That is on the east coast is it not?' Morville asked, unwilling to admit to Percy that he had no idea what trouble Strongbow – Sir Richard de Clare – had caused to necessitate a surrender.

'Yes,' Percy replied. 'Too close to England's shores for a man with such recent aspirations as King of all Ireland. Richard de Clare is far too strong in an unruly land, Henry does not trust him, despite his promise to turn over the key ports and castles to England. Henry wishes to show Clare who is king, and to leave nothing to uncertainty.'

'And he has requested our assistance?' Morville asked, pleased at the portent of this.

'Most assuredly,' Percy said to beams of relief from the three other knights. 'He has lost much this past year. The Charter of Clarendon and the reform of clerical courts – a charter you were witness to, were you not, Hugh?'

Morville gave a small nod, saying nothing, wishing people would stop reminding him. No smiles were evident now.

'Then of course the favour of Rome, which he has had need to address with the Charter of Reconciliation. A turn of events most embarrassing and expensive to him. He wishes to keep you close so you can cause him no more harm, nor gold. The restitution he is required to make to Canterbury in particular would have paupered most nobles.'

Morville, FitzUrse and Brett glanced at each other in unease.

'We did as we were ordered . . .' FitzUrse started, but Percy held up a hand to forestall him. 'That is between you and King Henry. In this instance I am a mere messenger. We ride to Harewood to join Courcy at dawn tomorrow then on to the west coast. A ship awaits us.'

Morville rose. 'We shall be ready in good time. We are King Henry's knights, it is a great honour and we shall put our all into battle for our king.'

'Á King Henry,' FitzUrse and Brett chorused.

Percy gave a wry smile, but gave no opinion. 'Very well. I shall return at dawn with my men. Good eve to you.' He drained his goblet and strode out of the hall, leaving the three knights to stare at each other, wondering what this augured for them.

Chapter 43

It had been a hard ride, conducted mainly in silence, and every man in the party – baron, knight, man-at-arms alike – was relieved to see the gleaming blue strip of sea and smell salt on the air. Every attempt at conversation on the week-long trek had failed, and all were eager to see a change in circumstance.

The men, led by Courcy and Percy, rode on to the beach and loaded themselves, their armour, weaponry and what was left of their supplies into the small boats waiting for them.

'Do you think this means we are back in favour?' Brett asked, the three knights having managed to board the same boat without Courcy, Percy or any of their men.

'Sure to be,' FitzUrse said, full of confidence as ever. 'Henry would not have asked us to join his endeavour should he not value us.'

'Unless he means to rid himself of us under the guise of war,' Morville said.

'Damn and blast, Hugh, why do you always look at things so darkly? King Henry cannot denounce us without denouncing himself, I tell you.'

Morville shrugged. 'Very well, I hope you speak true.'

'Sure to be,' FitzUrse said. Brett said naught, but did not appear encouraged.

The Spirit of Aquitaine grew closer as the sailors pulled on their oars, and with some trepidation the knights regarded the vessel to which they would be entrusting their lives over the next stage of their journey.

She was of a good size, more than fifty feet in length, and near a quarter of that in breadth. With a single mast and large sail, she had fighting platforms fore, aft and aloft. There were no cabins. This was a warship, built for everything but comfort.

Once the goods, men and horses were loaded, there was barely space for the sailors to work. Brett, never a good sailor, ensured that he had a place against the side, knowing he was likely to spend the voyage across the Irish Sea hanging over the rail, and hoping he had picked the right board. The last thing he, or any of his fellows, wanted was a youngster vomiting into the wind.

At last the anchor was hauled up, the sail loosed, immediately catching the wind, and *The Spirit of Aquitaine* started her voyage west. To glory or humiliation, no man knew, but every man aboard determined to believe in glory.

* * *

'I don't understand why King Henry is invading Ireland,' Brett said, clinging on to the side of the ship. 'What are we facing?'

FitzUrse heaved a large, dramatic sigh, as if in exasperation, but said nothing.

Morville suppressed a smile. He realised The Bear didn't fully understand either but was loath to admit it. 'All I know is what Percy told us,' he said, then started as Mauclerk joined them.

'It appears Strongbow was sent to represent King Henry's interests,' Mauclerk said. 'But then allied himself with King Dermot, insisting, or forcing, that he be made his heir. Dermot died, and sure enough, Strongbow was named. The high king, Rory O'Connor, did not accept that, but Strongbow routed him on the battlefield.'

'How do you know all this?' FitzUrse demanded, his distaste of Morville's clerk clear.

'I ask questions, My Lord. And I listen to the answers,' Mauclerk replied, staring at FitzUrse.

'Continue, Mauclerk,' Morville said, disinterested in FitzUrse's dislike of his most loyal man.

'King Henry ordered Strongbow home to England, but he did not obey, so the King placed an embargo on supplies to Ireland – including men.'

'What did Strongbow do?' Brett asked.

'Nothing,' Mauclerk said.

'And Henry will not have a baron call himself king, of any land,' Morville said. Mauclerk gave a small nod. 'And so he mobilises his knights into an army and we take Ireland.'

Mauclerk nodded again.

'Some army,' FitzUrse said, watching Percy and Courcy, 'when two of Henry's most trusted lords avoid all unnecessary time in our company.'

The four men stared at the two nobles, chilled by the fact – hitherto unremarked – that they had made a place for themselves as far away as possible in the confines of the deck of *The Spirit of Aquitaine*.

'Ugh, the wind's getting up,' Brett said, hauling himself to his feet then being violently sick over the rail. Thank goodness he'd chosen the right board, the wind blew at his back and the contents of his stomach were swept away from the ship, deck and gathered knights.

'Umm,' Morville said, the tang exacerbating his own distress as his stomach disagreed with the more urgent lurch and wallow of the ship's motion.

'Oh calm yourselves, it is a gentle breeze, is all,' FitzUrse scoffed.

Morville jumped to his feet and joined Brett over the rail to empty his stomach. He sat back down and could not resist a glance at Percy and

Courcy. They appeared to have found a subject of much merriment; Morville feared he knew the cause.

The wind continued to increase as *The Spirit of Aquitaine* fought her way west. As she did so the waves deepened and the warship may well have been a cork navigating rapids. Within minutes, knights and men-at-arms alike were spewing. The horses, gathered and tethered amidships, squealed their terror, their hooves threatening to stave in the boards of the stinking deck.

One – Hugh de Morville's finest destrier – reared, snapping the rope securing him, and the men closest to those flailing hooves screamed in alarm, having no weapons to hand and no room to run.

The stallion's distress increased the fear in the rest of the herd, and soon the waist of the ship was a mass of panicking men, horseflesh and blood, as the frightened animals kicked out.

Morville, FitzUrse and Brett stared in astonishment, with no idea how to calm the beasts in such confined quarters.

'Clear the way,' a voice roared, and men-at-arms and sailors parted to let Sir William de Percy through.

He stepped forward, drew the edge of his sword against the throat of one destrier, then plunged the tip into the chest of another.

He kept going, and in seconds, every horse lay dead or dying on the deck.

'Heave them overboard,' Percy said. 'Our king needs us. Not horse nor man would delay us.'

Chapter 44

'The Emerald Isle,' FitzUrse said as they waited to disembark. 'Ha, the greenest things in sight are the pair of you!'

Morville and Brett ignored him and looked forward to setting foot on terra firma once again; whatever their reception by Henry may be.

Staring ashore, the town of Waterford was visible in the distance, but before that all traces of green had been commandeered by Henry's camp.

Hundreds of gaily coloured tents stretched for near a league in each direction, knights and men-at-arms milling between them; the one almost indistinguishable from the other in the basic living conditions. Each lord's entourage was marked by colour. Blue and yellow for Leicester, red and white for de Lacy, blue and white for Tyrell; every combination of colour was represented.

The sea of canvas was broken up by a mesmerising array of siege engines: mighty trebuchets towered over smaller catapults and ballistas, each of them capable of hurling enough rock and iron to batter down any curtain wall, not to mention more creative payloads such as beehives or hornets' nests; the bloody carcasses of soldiers felled in battle; or the worst of the lot, Greek fire. A substance brought from Hell, it would stick to any unfortunate until it burned out; not water nor sand would dowse it, the only chance a man had was for his friends to piss on him as copiously as possible. Of course, it would only help if they had also pissed on him, at least twice, before he'd been hit by the sticky flames. Morville shuddered. He had seen its effects more than once. The very sight of a siege engine had given him chills ever since.

The highest point of the camp was taken by the most magnificent marquee. Adorned in the red and gold of Plantagenet, it was a palace of canvas. King Henry's quarters, along with his household.

The three knights stole a brief glance at each other, the only betrayal of their anxieties, then followed Courcy and Percy down the gangplank and set foot on Irish soil.

The party of five, followed by a gaggle of men-at-arms and retinues, marched through the narrow alleyways formed by rows of tents towards Henry's abode.

Morville, FitzUrse and Brett kept their heads high and their feet moving, refusing to react to the stares of every man they passed.

'Assassins!' someone hissed. 'The traitorous assassins.'

Morville caught hold of FitzUrse's arm and heaved him forward. 'It is King Henry's opinion that is important, once we know how he holds us, then all else will too. Brawling on our first audience with him in four months would not endear us to him.'

FitzUrse controlled himself with clear difficulty, his face flushed and fists clenched white, then gave a curt nod and continued to move forward. He faltered for one pace on seeing Courcy smirk, then continued onward, staring at the Lord of Harewood until he turned his back and marched forward.

Morville and Brett glanced at each other in consternation. Morville had used the word audience, but in truth it felt more like they were about to attend their own trial and execution.

At long last, they reached the brow of the hill and were admitted to King Henry's presence. All five knights dropped to one knee and bowed their heads in deference to their king.

'Ah, I have been wondering when you would arrive, I bid you welcome,' Henry said. Dressed in his habitual hunting clothes of hose and short tunic he strode over to the group of kneeling knights. The knights rose, the relief of Morville, FitzUrse and Brett almost palpable.

Henry grasped the hand of Courcy then Percy, wrapped an arm around each of their shoulders and led them to the high table, laden with meats and delicacies. 'How went the voyage? I hear the Irish Sea was rough today.'

'We fared well, Sire,' Courcy said.

'Some better than others,' Percy smirked.

Morville glanced at FitzUrse and Brett to see a look of consternation on their faces, no doubt mirrored on his own. Their king had ignored them.

'What think you of my siege engines? An impressive sight, no?'

'Indeed, Sire,' Courcy said. 'Strongbow and O'Connor will be in no doubt of your intentions.'

'Ha! Strongbow has already capitulated, he is due soon to pledge fealty. That upstart shall never call himself King of Ireland.'

'Indeed not, Sire. He has shamed himself and his house by his actions here.'

'Verily,' Henry said. 'Far too many do the same.' He glanced at Morville and the others. 'Now, be seated and feast while I deal with these three reprobates.'

He turned back to the three knights, each of whom now dreaded his attention.

'So, you saw fit to ignore my instructions. Only Tracy had the good sense to depart for Rome?'

'We fully intend to join him, Sire,' FitzUrse interjected.

'Once you learn of his punishment and not before, I suspect?'

'No, Sire. We had heard of the difficulties Strongbow has been causing you . . .'

'Strongbow? Show some respect. He is Sir Richard de Clare, ensure you address him as such in future.'

'I humbly beg your pardon, Sire,' FitzUrse said, falling back to one knee.

Henry stared at him and made no indication that he should rise. He glared at Morville and Brett, who both hastily joined FitzUrse in his gesture of humility.

'What a pity you did not ignore my words spoken in anger in the way you ignored my clear direction to present yourselves to Rome.'

'Sire?'

Henry stamped his foot. 'Damn and blast it, you snivelling buggers, you know well to what I refer!'

The three knights bowed their heads, knowing from long experience not to respond when Henry was in the grip of one of his furies.

'Do you understand what you have done? *Do you?*' He screamed and hurled his goblet to the floor. Fine Rhenish vintage soaked into the fresh rushes.

'All is lost! My court reforms, the Constitution of Clarendon – all gone! The clergy will never be accountable to me now. Instead I am accountable to Rome! Me! King Henry of England, Duke of Normandy, Duke of Aquitaine accountable to a feeble old man in Rome.'

Henry paused for breath, his face puce. A steward handed him another goblet of Rhenish and he drank half of it in one swallow. Not one of the gathered knights, men-at-arms or servants made a sound nor dared to move for fear of attracting their king's ire.

He thrust his face into Morville's, who resisted the urge to flinch back from the hatred in his king's eyes and the stink of sour wine on his king's breath.

'Alexander banned me from entering a church. Me – banned from the heart of God! He threatened to excommunicate me – me! And Thomas . . .' He paused to catch his breath. 'Thomas, that brilliant, frustrating, true and treacherous friend, whom I raised up from naught. Thomas will be canonised. *Canonised!*' The last word was screamed as the King lost all semblance of control; all memory of having already told the knights this news lost. He fell to the ground and hammered his fists and feet upon it. As he rolled in his fit and spilled Rhenish, only occasional words were audible: 'Saint', 'Devil', 'Friend', 'Martyr'.

The knights dared not so much as glance at each other, all shocked that their actions had reduced their king to such paroxysms of fury. They had observed such behaviour before – all the men in King Henry's service had witnessed such displays – but had never before brought their master this low themselves.

The sound of heralds' trumpets outside the canvas palace finally penetrated Henry's awareness and he stilled, rose, adjusted his clothing, held out a hand for more Rhenish, emptied the goblet in one, then took his seat, waved the knights aside and awaited his visitors, all composure restored.

'Sir Richard de Clare, Lord of Strigoil and Pembroke. Sir Maurice de Prendergast, Sir Richard Tuite, Sir John Baret.'

Four nobles entered as their names and titles were announced, removed helmets and mail hoods, unbuckled sword belts and handed them to waiting servants, then approached Henry and fell to one knee in obeisance.

Henry nodded, then the first man, Sir Richard de Clare – Strongbow – stepped forward, once again fell to one knee, then clasped his hands together as if in prayer and extended them. Henry placed his own hands either side of Clare's and grasped them for a moment.

A Bible was brought close as the men loosed hands, Clare placed his right hand upon it, and met his king's eyes.

'Sire, My Lord King Henry, I beg you to hear my oath. I pledge on my faith that I would for all days be faithful to you, never cause you injury, and would give my life to your service. I would observe my homage, reverence and submission to you completely, against all men in good faith and without deceit.'

'I, your Lord King, Henry of England, Duke of Normandy and Aquitaine, accept your fealty, Sir Richard de Clare, and grant upon you the fief of Leinster. May you serve me equally in peace and war, and with loyalty and honour.'

'I thank you, My Liege.'

Clare rose and backed away, allowing Prendergast then Tuite and Baret to take his place and make the same oath.

Once the rebellious barons had been accepted back into Henry's fold, FitzUrse stepped forward but was checked by Morville's hand on his arm. These proceedings had been negotiated and agreed in advance. Henry had no use for a spur-of-the-moment pledge of fealty from them, no matter how deeply meant. He would need to forgive them first. And that did not look likely.

Chapter 45

Morville, FitzUrse and Brett set up their tents on the outskirts of the main camp, ensuring their temporary homes were surrounded, and well-protected, by those of their men-at-arms.

They sat around the campfire with a plentiful supply of wineskins and Brett poked at the brace of coneys roasting above the fire; the only meat they had been able to find. The mood in the camp was so hostile they had forgone the supply tents and caught their own dinner in the surrounding woods; woods that had been hunted daily for weeks. There was no bigger beast left in them than the bobtail coneys, and their entire party had caught not nearly enough to feed the knights and men-at-arms. Thank goodness they had thought to bring a plentiful supply of wine in their haste to depart Cnaresburg.

'That was not the reception I had expected,' FitzUrse said at last. 'We did as Henry instructed, we carried out his orders and carried them out well. And look how we are vilified.'

'Hush, Reginald,' Morville said. 'You do not know who may be listening, this is no time to speak ill of the King.'

'Indeed it is not,' a new voice said, surprising the knights. Its owner stepped into the firelight.

'Mandeville!' Morville exclaimed.

Sir William de Mandeville, Earl of Essex, grinned, although there was nothing friendly in the rictus. A second and third man stepped up, all three dressed in full mail and helmets, swords at their sides. Richard de Humez and Ranulf de Broc. The two men who had originally been sent to arrest Becket and whom Morville, FitzUrse, Tracy and Brett had beaten to the prize. And Broc, the man who had encouraged and led them to Canterbury, then turned his back on them and left them to suffer the consequences. They had not heard a single word from him since they had left Saltwood Castle nearly a year ago.

FitzUrse glared at his old master, who stared back with equanimity; no emotion or expression evident on his face.

'What is this, Ranulf?' FitzUrse asked.

'What does it look like, Reginald?' Broc replied, his tone mild. 'You have shamed our king, and by doing so you have shamed all of us.'

FitzUrse worked his mouth for a few moments before he could find coherent words. 'We shamed you?' he said quietly. 'We shamed you? We *shamed* you?' His voice and temper rose with each utterance of the phrase.

'You did.'

'But, but, it was you . . .' FitzUrse stopped, speechless once more.

'I gave you every assistance and opportunity to arrest Becket. Yet you slaughtered him in his cathedral and made him saint and martyr. You betrayed your king, your earls and your fellow barons and knights when you did so.'

'But, but . . .' FitzUrse spluttered.

Broc smiled. 'You have much to learn about politics, my friend.'

'Friend? *Friend*? You have been no friend to me!'

Broc shrugged and unsheathed his sword. Morville and Brett stepped forward, having taken the opportunity of FitzUrse's 'conversation' to don mail and helmets. Brett slapped FitzUrse's helmet with slim nose guard on his brother-in-arm's head. There was no time for FitzUrse to don mail, but all three had kept their weapons close, unnerved by Henry's reception of them.

FitzUrse glanced around and realised Broc, Mandeville and Humez' men had surrounded their outlying camp. He was gratified to see their own men-at-arms had remained, and stood between the gaggle of knights and the small encircling army. Then he realised these same men had let the visitors through and his pleasure soured.

'So you intend murder?' FitzUrse asked Broc.

'No. Murder is despicable and unchivalrous,' Mandeville said in his stead.

FitzUrse's temper rose once more and both Morville and Brett stiffened, recognising they were being taunted into stupidity. 'Reginald, care,' Morville warned.

FitzUrse didn't hear him. Or, more likely, chose not to.

'This is your fault,' he said, advancing on Broc. 'This is all your fault.' In one quick movement he unsheathed his sword and struck. But Broc was fast and parried with apparent ease. Morville recognised a smile on his face and realised he had intended to taunt FitzUrse into striking the first blow, yet he also felt a respect for the man; he knew well from their many practices with swords at Cnaresburg Castle how strong FitzUrse's blows were. Even in his fury, The Bear's strength made little visible impact on his old master.

'To arms!' Morville shouted, drawing his own sword and stepping up to William de Mandeville. He held his blade defensively, determined not to fall into the same trap as FitzUrse. Unfortunately Brett did not have the same sense or experience, and he flailed his blade at Humez, who defended with ease, with plenty of breath to taunt the young knight further.

FitzUrse, meanwhile, had lost all sense, striking at Broc quickly and ferociously, delivering a devastating sequence of strikes. Broc's mail held up to the blows that he was unable to deflect. He would be badly bruised on the morrow, but as yet his skin was unbroken.

The surrounding parties of men-at-arms were in much the same mind as FitzUrse; months of uncertainty at the actions and manoeuvrings of their masters releasing in the familiar arena of battle. At last, all was simple. The masters of the opposing men meant to harm their own masters. They would fight to the death to defend their lord. They had all spent their lives in training for these moments. This was what they knew. This was what they did. They fought. Some with swords, others with axes, still more with maces. Whatever their weapon, they struck, parried, ducked and danced around their opponent, then struck again.

Morville and Mandeville, the eldest and most cognisant men on the battleground, were the only two who had not yet landed a blow. They circled, feinted and taunted, each determined to place the other in the wrong. Each determined he was in the right.

'Cease! Cease! In the name of King Henry, cease this madness!' Hamelin Plantagenet, mounted on a large destrier in full barding, cantered into the throng of warriors. Percy and Courcy, similarly mounted, accompanied him. 'How dare you disrespect my brother, the King? Cease, damn you!'

The men separated, lowering their weapons.

'What is the meaning of this?' Plantagenet addressed Mandeville.

'Settling an old score, My Lord,' he replied.

'Consider it settled,' Plantagenet said. 'Return to your quarters.'

Mandeville, Humez and their men-at-arms retreated, faces impassive.

'The King demands an audience with you, FitzUrse and Brett at dawn,' Plantagenet said to Morville. He glanced around. 'Where is Reginald?'

Morville searched the diminishing circle of men and could not see him. 'I am unsure, My Lord.'

'Find him before dawn.' Plantagenet wheeled his destrier around and moved off. 'There is to be no further discord,' he proclaimed. 'We are here to challenge the Irish rebels, not each other. In the name of the King!'

'In the name of the King!' shouted the gathered knights and men-at-arms, both those so recently fighting and those who, Morville now recognised, had gathered to witness it.

Morville met Percy's eyes for a brief moment. Neither spoke, then both Percy and Courcy turned their horses on the spot and followed the King's half-brother.

Brett stood, having been felled by Humez. 'Where *is* Reginald, Hugh?'

'I know not, Richard. Nor where Broc has disappeared to. We must find them before we face the King. I fear there will be no rest for us this night.'

* * *

'Here! My Lord, here!' The shout was taken up by more men-at-arms and both Morville and Brett turned as one in the direction of the cry, and hurried through the trees as best they could to see what had been found.

'No! Reginald!' Brett sank to his knees, shaking. 'Why? My God, why? He did not deserve this!'

Morville said nothing, but approached his comrade-in-arms, his own men retreating to give him room. He looked up.

Reginald FitzUrse swung and twisted at the end of a rope; his face purple in the predawn light. Very clearly dead.

'Cut him down,' Morville said.

As the body of his late friend thumped on to the mulch beside him, Morville bent over him. 'Pass me a torch.'

He held the flaming pitch-soaked branch over FitzUrse and the men around him gasped. Brett erupted into further moans.

FitzUrse had not only been hung, but disembowelled, snakes of his guts writhing around his body, still slithering from the impact of his fall.

Morville held the torch close to the face to make sure of the man's identity, and gasped. Clear in the light of the fire, the letters T R A I T O R had been written on Sir Reginald FitzUrse's forehead in his own blood.

Morville stared for a moment, then handed the torch back. 'Bury him,' he said, walked over to Brett, and hauled the young knight back to his feet.

'But who . . .' Brett said.

Morville did not answer. 'We must prepare for our audience with the King,' he said instead, marching the boy back in the direction of the camp.

'What do we do now?' Brett asked after Morville had sat him in front of the fire and forced a goodly amount of Rhenish down his throat.

'We have little choice, Richard. We stay and die as Reginald did. We flee and live as outlawed excommunicants in a vicious and strange land. Or we petition the King to allow us free passage to Rome and throw ourselves on the mercy of Pope Alexander.'

'But the Dominicans?'

'We pray that we are sent to serve the Knights Templar and not the Dominicans.'

They stayed silent for some minutes. Then Brett asked, 'What are our chances?'

Morville looked at him, shook his head, and emptied his wineskin.

'So,' Henry said, still in his hunting hose and tunic. 'Sir Reginald has departed us.'

'He has, Sire, in the most gruesome manner,' Morville said.

'A shame. He was abased when he fell. I would not have wished eternity in Hell for him.'

Morville and Brett said nothing.

'And Broc? What of him?' Henry asked the gathering of interested knights.

'Spent the night with his whore,' Mandeville said. 'He is not responsible for this.'

Henry laughed. 'Yes, that sounds like Broc.'

Morville gritted his teeth and clamped his fingers into Brett's arm to stay any reckless statements.

'Well, what to do with you two?' Henry mused, steepling his fingers and looking at his two most errant knights.

'Begging your pardon, Sire,' Morville ventured and took Henry's raised eyebrows as permission to continue. 'Richard and I beg leave to depart Ireland for Rome, there to throw ourselves upon Pope Alexander's mercy and subject ourselves to the penance of his choosing for our misdeeds.'

Henry nodded in thought, held out a hand into which was immediately placed a fine goblet of Rhenish. He took a long drink then relinquished the goblet and looked back at Morville and Brett and nodded. 'God have mercy on your souls.'

Chapter 46

1st August 2015

Donna glanced around as she handed in her ticket at the door, her hand trembling. She was relieved to see that no Castle Players were front of house, but was dismayed at the steady stream of cars entering the car park. There were too many. Far too many.

She ignored the door to the auditorium and hurried to the ladies, glad that she'd had the opportunity during the cleansing to explore all the theatre's nooks and crannies. She shut herself into the far cubicle, closed the toilet lid and sat down to wait.

By her watch there were ten minutes left before the curtain rose, giving Henry and Becket centre stage and a captive audience. She waited a little longer until she was sure no one else was in the ladies, then emerged from her cubicle.

In the hallway she took off one of her shoes – she'd worn stilettoes in preparation for this performance – took a tight hold of it and smashed the heel into the fire alarm.

She breathed a sigh of relief as the siren wailed – she'd half expected the spirits to put a stop to her plan and somehow take the alarm system offline. She felt a brief pang of pity for Helen and the other players, then hardened herself once again. However much work they'd put in, and however important this was to them, she *had* to put a stop to it. Nothing else had worked.

Half an hour later, huddled in the car park in the wash of blue flashing lights from two fire engines, Donna held her breath once more as Helen stood at the top of the steps with a firefighter at her side and called for everyone's attention.

Please cancel, please cancel, please cancel.

'Thank you everyone for staying, I'm relieved to announce it was a false alarm – a prank.' Helen stared at Donna as she said this and Donna glared back, her heart sinking. 'We can all go back in, the show will go on!'

Helen raised her hands to quell the surge of words her announcement had ignited and added, 'And in apology for the inconvenience, your interval drinks will be on the house.'

The crowd of theatregoers applauded and made their way back into the auditorium.

'Not you.' Helen stepped in front of Donna as she tried to re-enter. 'I know it was you, but you won't stop us. You're not welcome here.'

The firefighter stepped behind Donna, giving her a disgusted look and effectively trapping the Wiccan.

'Helen, please – you're putting the safety of all these people at risk. You can't *do* this!'

'These gentlemen would like you to go with them.' Helen indicated two police officers who stepped forward.

'Hoax fire alarms are serious, miss. If there'd been a real fire elsewhere, people could have died.'

'People will die if you don't stop this show!'

'That's a serious threat.'

'It's *not* a threat! I'm trying to stop something awful happening. These people are being controlled by spirits, they're not in their right minds!'

'I see. Have you taken anything tonight, miss?'

'What? What are you talking about?'

'Drugs, Donna. He's asking if you're high,' Helen said.

'No! Of course not. You have to believe me!'

'Come along, miss. We'll have a doctor check you out at the police station.'

Defeated, Donna allowed herself to be escorted away. She took one last look back at Helen, and saw the shape of a medieval knight standing behind her, almost melding with the director.

Helen gave Paul a thumbs up as he rushed to his new position on the balcony, then turned to Mike, Dan, Ed and Sarah. 'This is our best opening night ever, despite all that nonsense with Donna earlier. They're loving it!'

All four nodded with smiles and prepared themselves for their final scene.

Helen opened her mouth to give more encouragement, then closed it and turned to watch as the stage was lit once more.

Charlie was barely visible, kneeling before his table which had been transformed into an altar by cloth and cross.

Paul, standing on the new platform Ed and Alec had constructed, was six feet above the stage, shining in the full glare of the spotlight. He watched Becket pray for a moment then turned to the audience.

In the wings, Helen silently clapped her hands: his timing was perfect.

'A man who came to me with naught. A man I raised up from *naught* treats me with such contempt as *this!* And you, you do naught!'

'What miserable and cowardly drones and traitors have I nourished and promoted that allow their king to be so shamed?

'Who here shall take vengeance for the wrongs that I have suffered? Which man that swore fealty to me, to redress all injury done to me, and pledged their loyalty and honour to me shall make good on their vow now?

'Are you so weakened by castles, wealth and comfort that you no longer care to fight for your king?

'Damn the lot of you for weaklings – allowing a troublesome, low-born clerk to treat their king with such *scorn*!

'I am ashamed to call you my vassals. *England* is ashamed of her lords! Who shall cut this canker from England's breast?'

A recording of loud male cheers and the thumping of booted feet on wooden floors and goblets on wooden tables reverberated throughout the theatre, and the knights rushed on to stage, passing underneath Henry and confronting Becket who rose to meet them as the spotlight on him brightened.

'What insanity is this, that you would enter Canterbury Cathedral bearing arms?'

'We are the King's men, come to take you to Henry to answer for your crimes,' FitzUrse declared.

'Crimes? Crimes? Of what crimes do you speak? I have committed no act that could be so described.'

'You excommunicated your king's bishops – a traitorous act! By so doing you have declared yourself against the Young King, the Crown of England, and King Henry himself!' FitzUrse turned and pointed at Henry.

Becket laughed, shook his head, and looked up at his king, who returned his stare as he braced himself on the railings of his balcony.

'King? You are naught but a small boy, stamping your foot in anger when he has lost the game!'

'What are you doing? You should not be talking to Henry! Get back to the others!' Helen hissed, gesticulating to get Charlie's attention. He ignored her.

'You have gone too far, my old friend,' Henry said. 'All I have done for you, and you betray me so heinously.'

'*I* betray *you*? You sent your knights to silence me!' Becket protested. 'You betray not only my own person but the Church and God Himself.' He smacked the fist of one hand into the palm of the other.

'Do not presume to chastise your king, Thomas. You shall only make matters go worse for you.'

Helen gave up her protests and watched silently, as did the two hundred people in the auditorium, all captivated by the two powerful men on stage.

'Cease this nonsense, Henry.' Becket indicated the stage with a wave of his arm. 'We have chased each other through Heaven and Hell for near a millennium, and now look,' Becket gestured to the auditorium, 'we are naught but a mummers' show, displayed for the entertainment of commoners.'

'You call *this* a mummers' show?' Henry asked, incredulous. 'What do you call the farce at your so-called shrine? Saint Thomas – that is the most heinous fallacy of all! You are a *low-born clerk*!' He slammed his fist on the rail, his face turning purple with rage. 'Look how you have been raised up both in life and in death, by *me!*' The last word was a roar.

'Raised up? Hounded and murdered!' Becket roared back. 'Murdered by my closest friend. And for what? Because I carried out the duties of the Archbishop of Canterbury. The duties *you* laid on me despite my protests!'

'You were my friend, my ally, together we could have transformed both England and the Church.'

'Your demands were unjust, Henry! You wanted power over the Church, nothing more. You wanted to use me to weaken the Church. You were not a king but a tyrant, too full of his own glory!'

'A tyrant you say?' Henry's voice was quiet, menacing, yet carried to every ear in the auditorium. 'You talk to me of tyranny? You, who refused the just demands of your king? You, who raised the Church against me? A low-born clerk challenging the rule of his king and *you* talk to *me* of tyranny?' Henry's voice rose in a crescendo. 'You, who damned my bishops? You, who would deny my son his crown? You, who incited the common folk of this good country against me?'

'The common folk of this country know what is just,' Becket answered, fumbling in the folds of his green robe. 'The common folk of this country need both King *and* Church. The common folk of this country have the sense to know that one without the other breeds only terror! *Yes*, I gave voice to the common folk of this country. *Yes*, I spoke and acted for the common folk of this country. And you – you still stand above them on a pedestal of your own making! You still send your knights to murder!' Becket indicated the four men behind him, a flash of light from the blade he had retrieved from his robe blinding Henry for a moment.

'Not this time! You shall not murder me again, tonight our story *changes*.' Becket threw the dagger, and laughed as the blade sank into Henry's chest, blood spurting from the wound and splattering his upturned face. 'Tonight I finally have my revenge!'

'Sire! King Henry!' the knights shouted as the audience gasped and Paul toppled over the railing of his balcony to thud on the boards below.

'You have murdered the King!' FitzUrse shrieked. 'Murderer! Traitor!'

Charlie staggered and looked around in shock, his eyes fixed on the body of his friend. 'Paul? What, what happened?' He screamed as FitzUrse's blade sank into his shoulder at the point where it met his neck.

'Dan, no!' he gasped as he fell to his knees, blood spurting from his wound.

The four knights stood and stared at the felled men in shock.

Tracy dropped his sword with a clatter. 'The King . . . the King is dead. We shall be blamed.'

'Silence, William,' FitzUrse shouted.

'But we will be blamed! You've done it again and led us to ruin!'

'Silence!' FitzUrse roared and swung his sword.

Mike jumped backwards, avoiding the blade. 'Dan, stop! What are you doing?'

'Charlie!' Sarah sobbed as she knelt beside her friend in a growing pool of blood, then looked up at her husband. 'You've killed him!'

Dan stared at his wife, then at his bloody sword and dropped it in shock. 'N-n-n-no. No. No.' He fell to his knees, hugged himself and swayed back and forth, still uttering the denial.

Chapter 47

8th August 2015

The remnants of The Castle Players walked away from the police station, down Castlegate towards the centre of Knaresborough a week later, after being questioned by the police yet again.

'Helen!'

They turned to see Donna running towards them.

'Are you okay?'

'Not really,' Helen said. 'They keep asking us the same questions, as if they think the answers are going to change!'

'Asking if we killed our friends,' Sarah added.

'It's been a nightmare,' Ed said.

'But they've let you go,' Donna said.

'Reluctantly,' Helen said. 'They couldn't charge us with anything. Everyone could, could s-s-see . . .'

Donna held Helen as she fought against tears. She'd already shed more in the past week than she had in the past year.

'They still think we did it, though,' Mike said. 'You could see it on their faces. I'm sure they're convinced we poisoned them or slipped them some acid or something.'

'But you didn't and there's no evidence of any drugs or poison.'

'No. They've put it down to mass hysteria,' Alec said. 'Blaming it on the pressure of putting on the play.'

'You know it wasn't that,' Donna said, and the others nodded.

'I'm sorry I didn't listen to you,' Helen said. 'Did you get into much trouble?'

'No, they let me go the next morning.'

Helen nodded. 'Have you heard about Dan?'

'No,' Donna said. 'What's happened to him?'

'He still hasn't spoken,' Sarah said. 'Other than repeating "No".'

'It's a catatonic state, apparently, probably to do with post-traumatic stress or something,' Mike added.

'Oh my goodness, tell me he isn't still in police custody,' Donna said.

'No, he's at the Briary,' Sarah said. Donna looked puzzled. 'The psychiatric unit at Harrogate District Hospital,' Sarah explained. 'I've been to see him a couple of times, and he's just . . . just *not there*.'

'What do you mean?'

'It's his body, but it's like no one's home.'

'So he won't be fit to stand trial,' Donna said.

Sarah broke into sobs and Mike comforted her.

'No,' Helen said. 'He doesn't even know his own name. There won't be a trial.'

'But he killed Charlie in front of everyone,' Donna said. 'Or rather, Reginald FitzUrse did.'

'He's lost his mind,' Ed said. 'He'll never get out of hospital.'

'I'm so sorry,' Donna said.

'So you bloody well should be,' Alec said. 'Selling crap like that spirit board, destroying people's lives. It's dangerous! *You're* dangerous.'

'Alec,' Helen said.

'No, he's right, Helen,' Donna said. 'Nothing like this has ever happened before. I've burned all my spirit boards and I know most other retailers have as well, despite the way people have reacted.'

'What do you mean, despite the way people have reacted? People have condemned them on the news.'

Donna shrugged. 'Hasn't stopped everybody wanting one. I could have sold a couple of hundred these last few days. People have come from Leeds, York and even further away to buy the exact same type that you used.'

The Castle Players stared at her, mouths open.

'Nowt so queer as folk.' Mike recovered first.

'I need a drink,' Helen said.

'I think we could all use one of those,' Donna said, smiling. 'The Borough Bailiff?'

'*No*! No,' Helen said, the second word calmer. 'I don't want to be in public, I can't face people, I'm sick of phones being stuck in my face to take pictures for their blogs and whatever. We can go to mine, it's on Finkle Street.'

The others nodded and, in silence, they crossed the Market Place and walked through the narrow alleys to Helen's.

'Wine, beer or gin,' Helen said, flicking lights on.

'Gin and tonic please – a strong one,' Mike said. 'Beer just won't do it tonight, and I never want to drink wine again.'

'I'll give you a hand,' Donna said, following Helen into the kitchen while the others found seats in the lounge and sat in a shocked silence.

Helen busied herself collecting glasses and ice cube trays. 'The gin's in that cupboard to the left,' she told Donna. 'And there should be tonic in the fridge.'

Donna opened cupboard doors, looking for the right one. 'Did you ever find the spirit board?'

'No. I don't know how many times we searched, but we covered every inch of that theatre and it was nowhere to be found.'

'Then how did it get into your kitchen cupboard?'

'What?' Helen turned and dropped the glass she was filling with ice and lemon when she saw Donna holding the board. She pressed herself back against the counter, her face white with terror, arms stretched out as if to fend Donna and the board away.

'What happened, are you okay?' Alec said, rushing into the kitchen. 'I heard . . . Where the hell did you get that? How dare you bring another one of those things in here!'

'I didn't,' Donna said. 'It's the original one, I just found it.' She indicated the cupboard.

'Helen?' Alec said quietly. 'What's going on?'

Helen looked at him and her other friends gathered behind Alec in the doorway. 'I-I-I don't know. I don't know how that got there. Honestly, I don't.' Her gaze flicked between Donna and the others, eyes wide. 'You have to believe me, I didn't put it there.'

'You must have,' Sarah said. 'Who else would?'

Helen just stared at the lettered board.

'It will have been Broc,' Donna said.

'Broc? What are you talking about? We didn't call on Broc,' Ed said.

'Doesn't matter. He was connected to the others, they must have pulled him through with them.'

'Pulled him through?'

'From the spirit world,' Donna said. 'I suspect he's been with Helen from the beginning.'

'What about me? Does that mean a spirit's been with me too?' Alec asked.

'I think that's likely, otherwise you wouldn't have gone along with everything.'

'Mauclerk,' Helen said.

'How do you know?' Donna asked.

'It makes sense. Behind the scenes, though very much involved, and particularly close to Morville who was played by Ed, Alec's best friend.'

'I see,' Donna said, then paused as they all digested Helen's words. 'Well, that's not important now. We need to deal with this board, close it—'

'Destroy it,' Sarah said.

'Yes. Destroy it. Helen, Sarah, you finish off in here. The rest of you come with me to the garden, we need to make a fire. Do you have a barbecue stand or something, Helen?'

'Yes, in the shed.'

'Lighter fluid, matches?'

Helen nodded, pointing to one of the kitchen drawers.

* * *

Helen and Sarah, calmer now, joined the others in the garden, carrying six gin and tonics which they put on the table. 'Is it done?' Helen indicated the fire blazing in the barbecue.

'Not yet. I want all of you to do it,' Donna said. 'Mike, can you break it up somehow? Smaller pieces will burn better.'

Mike nodded, gingerly picking up the board, and he carried it to the back steps. Placing it down so it overhung, he stamped on it, splitting it, then again and again.

'That should do it, Mike,' Donna said, taking a gentle hold of his shoulder. 'Mike?'

He paused, took a deep breath, and nodded. They collected the splinters and handed them out round the group so each Castle Player had part of the board to throw on to the fire.

'Goodbye,' Donna said and indicated to the others they should say the same as they burned their pieces of wood.

'Goodbye, goodbye, goodbye, don't come back again. Goodbye you evil, murdering bastards,' Helen said, stopping only when Donna handed her a drink. She took a long, large gulp. 'Goodbye,' she whispered.

The others made similar sentiments as they threw the splinters of board on to the fire, 'Goodbye, good riddance, leave us alone. Piss off back to Hell.'

'Is that it, have they gone?' Ed said after they had watched the flames for a while.

'To be honest, I think they left in the theatre, once Henry and Becket had . . .' Donna couldn't finish. She took a deep breath, then, 'This is just closing the door, to make sure they stay gone. Let's go in, though, and I'll double check.' She led the way, carrying her still full glass.

Inside she knelt before each actor in turn, closed her eyes a moment, then looked up at them from under her lashes. 'There's no one here that shouldn't be,' she said after a couple of minutes. 'Your auras are clear.'

'That's that then,' Alec said.

'Not quite. You've all been exposed to the spirit world, I want you to protect yourselves spiritually every day to make sure nothing else attaches to you.'

'You mean this could happen again? What, we're targets now?' Sarah asked. 'I've lost my husband, my children have lost their father, and two of the best people I know are dead, and this can happen *again*?'

'Possibly. Don't worry,' she added quickly, recognising panic in Sarah's rising voice, 'it's very unlikely, more to be safe than sorry really.'

'Too late for that,' Alec said.

Donna broke the ensuing silence. 'I want you to imagine wrapping yourselves up in a cloak of white light, so your whole body is covered, head to foot, can you do that now?'

Helen and Sarah nodded and closed their eyes, then the men agreed. 'Okay.'

'Now call on your guardian angels to protect you and keep you safe.'

Alec's eyes snapped open, then he closed them again – protest gone before it was uttered.

Donna waited a moment, then said, 'That's it, that's all you have to do, but do it every morning and every night. Make it part of your routine, when you brush your teeth, something like that, so you don't forget.'

'So what happens now?' Helen asked.

'Now you get on with your lives,' Donna said. 'As best you can.'

'How are we supposed do that?' Alec said.

'Well, Mike and I have been talking – I want to get away from this place, start again where nobody knows us,' Sarah said. 'Give John and Kate a chance at a normal life.'

'You'd take them away from Dan?' Ed said, incredulous. 'Hasn't he been through enough?'

'He doesn't even know who they are,' Sarah said. 'It nearly broke Kate when he looked through her and didn't recognise her. I know Dan's in hell, and I feel so sorry for him, but I won't consign our kids there too.'

'Well, you two bugger off then, take Dan's kids, *I'll* stick by him,' Ed said. 'I'll make sure he has someone fighting for him.'

'Yes, me too,' Alec said. 'We'll get him the best medical help, then the best legal help. He didn't do this, he was used by a vengeful ghost. It's not fair to just leave him in there.'

They sat in silence for a while, Sarah burying her face into Mike's shoulder, then Donna asked, 'What about you, Helen, do you have any plans?'

'I've had a lot of time to think about that,' she said and managed a small smile. 'I'm going to write a book about what happened.'

'What? Do you really think that's a good idea?' Sarah said. 'Surely it's better to try to forget, put it all behind you, not immerse yourself in it by writing about it.'

'How else will the real story be told? Everyone thinks that Paul, Charlie and Dan went mad – some kind of mass hysteria. As Ed just said, they weren't mad, and I want to set the record straight. I started all this by doing that bloody séance, I owe them that much, and maybe it will help Dan too – at least the proceeds may help pay for his care.'

'It's your penance,' Donna said quietly.

'Exactly. My penance.'

The End

KAREN PERKINS

Parliament of Rooks
Haunting Brontë Country

Ghosts of Haworth (Book 1)

From the Back Cover:

"Lush and atmospheric, this novel is dark and moody with supernatural elements and accurate historical details." - The BookLife Prize by Publishers Weekly

Parliament of Rooks, the new historical paranormal novel by Karen Perkins, contrasts the beautiful, inspiring village of Haworth today with the slum – or rookery – it was during the industrial revolution: rife with disease, heartache, poverty, and child slavery in the mills.

**In 2017, life expectancy in the UK is 81.
In 1848 Haworth, it was 22.**

Nine-year-old Harry Sutcliff hates working at Rooks Mill and is forever in trouble for running away to the wide empty spaces of the moors – empty but for the song of the skylark, the antics of the rabbits, and the explorations of Emily Brontë. Bound together over the years by their love of the moors, Emily and Harry develop a lasting friendship, but not everyone is happy about it – especially Martha, Harry's wife.

As Martha's jealous rages grow in ferocity, Harry does not realise the danger he is in. A hundred and fifty years later, this danger also threatens Verity and her new beau, William. Only time will tell if Verity and William have the strength to fight off the ghosts determined to shape their lives, or whether they will succumb to an age-old betrayal.

"You are my Demon.
This is my Exorcism."

— Verity Earnshaw

One for sorrow,
Two for mirth.
Three for a funeral,
Four for birth.
Five for Heaven,
Six for Hell,
Seven for the Devil, his own self.

— Old English nursery rhyme

Prologue

Haworth, March 1838

Martha hitched up the bundle strapped to her front. Satisfied Baby John was secure, she grasped the handle and began to haul the full bucket up the well shaft.

John barely mewled in protest at the violent, rhythmic action, already used to the daily routine, and Martha pushed thoughts of the future out of her mind. Her firstborn was sickly, and she was surprised he had survived his first two months. He was unlikely to live much longer.

She stopped to rest, her body not yet fully recovered from the rigours of the birthing, then bent her back to her task once more. She had too much to do to indulge in a lengthy respite.

Once she had the water and had scrubbed their rooms clear of coal dust and soot, she'd be up to the weaver's gallery to start on the day's pieces.

She stopped again, took a couple of deep breaths, then coughed as fetid air filled her struggling lungs. Bracing herself, she continued her quest for water, cursing the dry February that had caused the well to run so low.

At last she could see the bucket, water slopping with each jerk of the rope. Reaching over, she grasped the handle and filled her ewers.

Adjusting Baby John once more, she bent, lifted, and embarked on the trudge homeward.

'Blasted slaughterman!' she cried, just catching herself as she slipped on the blood pouring down the alley past the King's Arms and on to Main Street. She'd forgotten it was market day tomorrow. The slaughterhouse was busy today.

Another deep breath, another cough, and Martha trudged on, the bottom of her skirts soaked in blood.

She heard the snort of the horses and the trundle of cart wheels on packed but sticky earth just in time, and was already jumping out of the way before the drayman's warning shout reached her.

'Damn and blast thee!' she screeched as she landed in the midden anext the King's Arms, which stank of rotten meat and offal from the slaughterhouse next door.

She clambered back to her feet, checked Baby John was unharmed, then noticed her empty ewers lying in the muck beside her.

Covered in blood and filth she ran after the dray, cursing at the top of her voice, then stopped. That wasn't the drayman sat atop his cart of barrels. It was a trap carrying a passenger.

She watched the carriage come to a halt by the church steps, and a jealous rage surged in the pit of her stomach as the passenger alighted.

Emily Brontë had returned to Haworth.

Part One

December 2016

"I wish I were a girl again,
half-savage and hardy, and free."

Wuthering Heights
Emily Brontë, 1847
Haworth, West Yorkshire

1.

'There she is, about bloody time! I have better things to do than hang about here,' the van driver said, just loudly enough for me to hear.

At the same time, he returned the rude gesture of the Range Rover driver who had just squeezed past the van on the narrow, cobbled lane.

Out of breath from my steep climb up Main Street, I smiled weakly and jangled my new keys at the man and his mate.

'At least there's not much to shift,' I heard one of them say as I unlocked the front door. I wondered if I'd been meant to hear this comment too, but decided I didn't care. No, I didn't have much to shift – just clothes, books, a laptop and a few personal things I could not bear to leave behind in the ruins of my marriage.

I had taken only the furniture and furnishings I'd had when I met Antony; none of the joint purchases. I'd left our CD and vinyl collection alone – the CDs were already in my iTunes library and I had nothing to play the vinyl on anyway – and had even left all the kitchen paraphernalia. Everything held memories; memories I knew I had to leave behind else turn mad.

The only thing I had brought out of the divorce was money – enough to buy the old restaurant, turn it into a guesthouse, and start again. That was all I wanted.

'Them bloody roads ain't fit for vehicles,' the driver's mate said. 'Some bugger's knocked the wing mirror off!'

I landed back in reality with a bump – the actuality of my dream move was car horns, angry men and chaos. Not quite what I'd hoped for from this quaint West Yorkshire village clinging on to a steep hillside in Brontë Country.

I tuned the noise out again and smiled. *Brontë Country.* Charlotte, Emily and Anne had lived a minute's walk away from where I now stood and lived. I could *see* the parsonage from the top windows of my new home. I'd been a fan of their books since discovering them at school, and had dreamt of living here one day.

'That'll be going on the bill,' the driver said, stomping through the entrance, arms full of suitcases.

'I told you to park in the museum car park,' I said.

'I'm not paying four quid to park the van and carry stuff further than I need to.'

'Seems cheap now, though, doesn't it?' I smiled at him with no sincerity. He'd done nothing but complain since he'd arrived to collect my belongings. He hated the roads, hated his satnav, hated the hills, hated the cobbles, hated his job, life and pretty much everything else. I was beyond irritated, but I would not let him spoil this for me.

'I want everything upstairs in one of the guest rooms. Through that door, up the first set of stairs, then left through the arch. I'll take it from there.'

'Are you sure you don't want us to sort it into the right rooms for you?' the driver's mate asked.

'No – I have a load of work to do first.'

'Ain't that the truth,' the driver said, looking around at the empty, damp and dingy foyer. 'Not exactly welcoming, is it?'

I stifled a retort and forced myself to smile again. 'It will be by the time I open,' I said. 'Is there much more to come in?'

'Give us a chance, love, this is only the first load.'

I nodded, my point made, and went outside, unwilling to spend any more time in the man's company. A few seconds later, I was in the heart of the village.

Whatever the removal men's faults, I had to admit they had a point. These roads had not been built for cars; their narrow blind bends and cobbles were far more suited to slower horse and cart.

I looked up, startled at the clop of a horse's hoofs, and waved at the rider – a young girl in a high-vis vest. For a moment I'd half-expected to see a nineteenth-century carrier's cart loaded with barrels or coal sacks.

Having left Leeds that morning – for good – I felt like I'd stepped back in time, such was the contrast.

Instead of a bustling, modern city centre, Howarth Main Street plunged in its full cobbled glory into the Worth Valley below. The moors rose opposite in magnificent frosted green and winter shades of brown – heather, grasses, bracken and gorse – with snow heaped against the dividing dry stone walls.

Slate roofs slanted, soot-stained and age-darkened millstone grit walls leaned, and cobbles rose to trip the unwary or infirm. Even the accoutrements of modern living – benches, telephone poles, red telephone box (yes, Haworth still had one), lamp posts and the rest – tipped, dipped and sloped, all having to accommodate at least one unexpected angle, rejecting all human effort to tame this wild land.

Yet people were still here. They carved out a living; they enjoyed a holiday; they walked, shopped, explored.

It was an uneasy balance, made even more precarious by the flocking tourists anxious to follow in the footsteps of their literary heroines and characters. But something told me Yorkshire was not yet done; the power of the earth was too strong here, too prevalent. Nature would yet prevail over this insidious human invasion.

'Hello? Where the hell has she got to?'

I sighed at the driver's distant, grating voice and turned back, unable now to summon even a ghost of a smile for him as I approached.

'All done, you just need to sign the worksheet, then we'll be on our way.'

'Right then,' I said, took his pen, and hesitated. Much as I wanted this annoying man out of my dream home as soon as possible, I could not bring myself to sign without checking everything first.

I led the way back into what would soon be my guesthouse, ignoring the heaving sigh of irritation behind me, and examined the piles of boxes, suitcases, and scraps of furniture, mentally checking everything off.

'And the van is definitely empty, is it?' I asked when I re-emerged into daylight, my head swimming.

The driver glared at me, but his mate grinned, slid open the side door and I inspected the interior. If anything had been left behind, it wasn't in there.

I signed the paperwork and the driver snatched it out of my hands, clambered behind the wheel, and slammed the door.

'Good luck in your new home,' the mate said, touched his cap with a grin, then sighed before joining his colleague. I had never been so glad to see anyone drive away in my life.

I walked back into the building and looked around me. The proud smile drained from my face as the enormity of what I had taken on hit me. I had left everything I knew behind me, and my future was blind.

2.

A shriek outside made me jump, then I relaxed and smiled at the sound of high heels and laughter accompanied by the rumble of trolley bag wheels on cobbles. Lara and Jayne.

Opening the door, I stared pointedly at Lara's feet as she tottered down the steep, icy ginnel, clutching an enormous bouquet of flowers. Jayne was pulling two cases and wincing at the ferocity of her friend's taloned grip on her arm.

'I told you to wear flats,' I said. 'You'll break your leg in those things here.'

'I don't do flats, darling,' Lara said, unconcerned. She let go of Jayne to swathe me in a floral-scented hug. 'Welcome to your new life, Verity.' She handed over the flowers. 'It's very . . . you.' She beamed, clearly pleased with her non-committal phrasing.

I turned to hug Jayne and was almost knocked off my feet by an excited Irish terrier the colour of sandstone who'd been chased from the car park by Lara's ten-year-old daughter, Hannah.

'You need to keep hold of his lead,' Jayne admonished, bending to pick up the leather leash. 'He has no car sense whatsoever.'

'Sorry, Aunt Jayne, he's just so strong and excited.' Hannah took back possession of Grasper and tried to pull him away from me and all the interesting smells around the front door. He only acquiesced when I ceased petting him and finally embraced his mistress.

Accepting a bottle bag with a very promising gold-foil-covered offering inside, I led the way. 'Welcome to The Rookery,' I said.

'So where exactly are we sleeping?' Jayne asked, perched on her case and clutching a mug of champagne. She peered around the foyer. 'Are the guest rooms at least serviceable?'

'No, not yet,' I said. 'I've a camp bed set up in the best one for myself. I thought you three would put your sleeping bags out here – you did bring sleeping bags, didn't you?' I eyed their cases.

Jayne spluttered champagne, Hannah clapped in delight at the prospect of camping, and Lara grinned.

'Nearly had me going there, Verity,' she said. 'Now put Jayne out of her misery and tell her where we're really staying.'

I smiled. 'Sorry, ladies, I couldn't resist. No, I'm not inflicting this place on you – not until it's furnished anyway. I've booked you into the Old White Lion; it's literally thirty seconds down the street. I'll take you over in a bit so you can check in, then I thought we'd have dinner there.'

'Cowbag,' Jayne said, and Hannah giggled. 'How long will it take to get this place ready for guests?'

'I have three months. I'll make the website live and sign up to all the booking sites as soon as the wiring is done and I have broadband. With any luck, I'll be taking bookings from the first of March for Easter onwards.'

Lara looked around the foyer and Jayne laughed. 'I hope you have reliable tradesmen – that doesn't leave you much time if anybody lets you down.'

'They've all been highly recommended and they start on Monday. I've been speaking to the foreman, Vikram, quite a bit on the phone and so far I'm impressed.'

'Oh yes, Vikram is it? What does he look like?' Lara said, eyebrows raised.

'They're starting the week before Christmas, are you serious?' Jayne said.

I chose to answer Jayne. 'Yes, the joiners are in first to wall off part of the back there – they'll make another guest room, then the remainder of the space will be a kitchen for the guest breakfasts, plus an office. The electricians and plumbers will do their thing too then start on the existing bedrooms upstairs, and the joiners will move up to partition off the en-suites when they've finished down here. I don't have to have every guest room ready for Easter, but I do need the downstairs area, as many guest rooms as possible, and my own living quarters to be ready on time.'

'Then what, you'll have work carrying on while guests are here?'

'If need be, although only after breakfast hours for as little disturbance as possible.'

'But it'll all come to a grinding halt before they even get started,' Jayne predicted.

'Only for a few days over Christmas,' I said.

'Do you really think it'll be ready in time?' Lara asked.

I looked around me, unwilling to admit my doubts from earlier.

'You don't, do you?' Jayne was far too good at reading people.

'Yes, it'll be ready. Okay, okay.' I raised my hands to hold off more naysaying. 'I admit when the movers left and I was here on my own for the first time, I had a moment of doubt, but I can do this, I know I can.'

'Of course you can, Verity,' Lara said, putting down her champagne mug.

I really must get some proper glasses, I thought as she tottered across the flagged floor and embraced me.

'Don't listen to old Grumpy Drawers over there, and don't be too hard on yourself. You've gone through hell with the divorce and everything. This is your new start. It sounds like you have everything organised and you'll be on site to keep an eye on things – and we'll help as much as we can. I know the village seems isolated, but it's really not that far away – it only took us half an hour to get here, we'll be here all the time!'

'Don't forget she needs the rooms for guests.' Jayne joined the huddle. 'She has a business to run, you know. Sorry, Verity, I didn't mean to come across grumpy.' I felt her lift her head to glare at Lara. 'I was just trying to make sure you're on top of everything and have a good plan.'

'Always bloody planning,' Lara said.

'And just as well, too – my planning has got you out of more than one scrape, remember?'

'Enough!' I laughed. Jayne and Lara were so different on the surface, one a building society manager: practical and stern; the other a complementary therapist and single mum, and one of the strongest women I'd ever met. But both of them had big hearts and matching values, and despite the outward bickering, all three of us had been best friends for years.

'What's wrong with Grasper?' Hannah's voice penetrated our hugfest.

Jayne swung around in concern, then smiled at her pet's antics. 'He's just bored, probably needs a walk and some attention.'

'Hmm,' Lara said, digging in her bag for her phone. She ignored Jayne's scoffing and filmed the Irish terrier as he jumped and twirled about, tongue lolling in delight.

'Have a look at this,' she said, playing the video back.

Jayne and I peered over her shoulders.

'There – did you see it? And there – another one.'

'Let me see, let me see,' Hannah begged.

'Just a moment, Hans.' She ran the video again. They were still there: two circles of light dive-bombing and circling the dog.

'Those are orbs, Verity. Spirits. You've bought a haunted house.'

3.

'Oh good thinking, Verity,' Jayne said, sitting down on the padded bench next to me and pouring a glass from the bottle of Prosecco on the table in the bar of the Old White Lion Hotel.

'Well, it's a celebration,' I said. 'It's not every day you finalise a divorce, complete on a haunted guesthouse, and move to a village where you don't know anybody.'

'Cheers to that,' Jayne said with a smile at my attempt at a joke, and we clinked glasses.

'What are we toasting?' Lara asked as she sat down.

'Verity leaving her cheating husband, upping sticks and moving to the middle of nowhere,' Jayne said.

'Don't forget the bit about the ghosts,' I added.

'Pour me a large one,' Lara said. 'I'll drink to that!'

'Pour your own, you lazy cow,' Jayne said. Lara stuck her tongue out at her and did just that.

'Can I have a glass, Mummy?' Hannah asked, and Jayne spluttered over her next sip.

'No, you can't have wine, Hans. Water, squash or apple juice.'

'Coke!'

'Not at teatime, you won't sleep. Water, squash or apple juice.'

'Aww, please, we're celebrating, Auntie Verity said so. Please?'

'Water, squash or apple juice.'

Hannah sat back, arms folded in a sulk.

'Let me know when you've decided,' Lara said, then turned back to us. 'So how does it feel, Verity?'

'What? My cheating husband or the haunted guesthouse?'

'Cheating *ex*-husband,' Jayne said.

'True.' I raised my glass in a toast once more and took a long gulp, blinking back unexpected tears. I'd thought I'd already shed all those.

'Did he ever give you an explanation?' Lara asked.

I shook my head, thinking back to the day I'd found Antony's emails and messages not to another woman, but to many, going back years. 'He didn't seem to think he'd done anything wrong – once the initial shock of being found out had worn off, anyway. Apparently virtual cheating doesn't count. Despite the intimate pictures, the webcam sessions, the fact that he proposed to at least one of them, and declared his undying love to a few more. He just can't understand why I'm so hurt or feel so betrayed.'

'Idiot,' Jayne said.

'Bastard,' Lara countered.

'Mummy!' Hannah admonished.

'Sorry, Hans, quite right.'

'Well, at least the judge understood,' Jayne said.

I said nothing, and sipped my wine. Finding out what Antony had been doing for so long had turned my world upside down. We'd been together for years, I'd thought we would always be together. It had turned out that I didn't know him at all.

'Have you decided yet?' Lara asked Hannah, and I gave her a grateful glance for changing the subject.

'Juice.'

'Juice what?'

'Juice, please.'

'Okay. I'll get us another bottle as well, ladies. Might as well make a night of it.'

'You're a bad influence, Lara,' Jayne scolded.

'Rubbish, you were both thinking it.'

I looked at Jayne and laughed. Lara's observation was spot on.

'This is supposed to be a working trip, not a girls' weekend,' Jayne complained.

'The work starts tomorrow,' Lara said. 'Tonight is the celebration. Relax and enjoy yourself, Jayne.'

'I hope Grasper's okay over there. Those light things were freaky.'

'He'll be fine,' Lara said. 'Dogs aren't allowed in here, there's no way he can sleep in the car, and the orbs were friendly, they were playing with him.'

'Let me see it again,' I said, and Lara dug out her phone.

We watched as Grasper jumped at a ball of light, then spun in a full circle as it teased him before shooting off. I could almost see the indecision on the terrier's face – torn between chasing the one and playing with the other. The second orb hovered around his head then shot to his tail, where it followed the wildly wagging appendage as best it could – not an easy task as Grasper was also circling madly, trying to catch it. I realised I could see the orbs more clearly each time I watched the video.

Then the first rejoined the fun and Grasper was truly lost. Snapping at one then the other, he settled for watching them, tongue hanging out in a sappy grin. He only joined in their whirling dance when one approached him.

A moment later, they were gone, and Grasper settled down on the floor, exhausted but happy, looking up at Jayne with his usual level of adoration.

'Whoever they are, they're friendly,' Lara said. 'Grasper would react very differently if they were dark forces.'

'*Dark forces*? What nonsense!' Jayne said in exasperation. 'They're flies or something, that's all. Not spirits or ghosts, and certainly not demons!'

'They're not flies, Jayne. Look at them, they're circular balls of light. Have you never watched *Most Haunted* or *Ghost Adventures*? They're orbs – spirits.'

'You're freaking me out,' I said before Jayne and Lara descended into a bickering spat. 'I'm going to be on my own there most of the time – at least until I open. I don't want ghosts around.'

'Ghosts? Oh, you must be the lady who bought Weavers.'

We looked up at the waitress – blonde, pretty and young; it seemed very strange hearing her talking about ghosts.

'Yes. I'm Verity Earnshaw,' I said. 'I'm turning it into a guesthouse, and should be opening in April.'

'Earnshaw? Well, you'll fit right in round here then.' The girl laughed. 'I'm Tess, welcome to Haworth.'

'You know about the ghosts?' Lara asked.

'Village is full of them, but I only know about one at Weavers, the Grey Lady. She's not seen very often, but the sightings are consistent – she's a bit of a celebrity round here. People reckon she's Emily Brontë.'

'Are you seriously trying to tell us that Verity's guesthouse is haunted by a Brontë sister?' Jayne asked.

'No one knows for sure, but she only appears around December 19th, the date of Emily's death.'

'Next week,' Lara said, glancing at me.

'Yeah, she's said to climb up a flight of stairs that are no longer there – the wall that adjoins the row of weaver's cottages. But she's always smiling and has never done any harm,' Tess added quickly, no doubt in reaction to me. I felt cold and horrified, and presumably had paled considerably.

'Don't worry,' Jayne tried to reassure me. 'It's fanciful tales, that's all.'

'Oh no, that's where you're wrong. There's plenty of ghosts round here,' Tess said. 'Nothing fanciful about them – you should go on the ghost tour, find out all sorts of tales you will.'

'Verity, relax,' Lara said. 'It's Emily Brontë – how wonderful is that? That's why she played with Grasper, she loved animals and even had a dog herself called the same, that's where Jayne got Grasper's name from.'

Jayne nodded in agreement.

'And I told you,' Lara continued, 'those orbs are friendly. You've nothing to worry about.'

'Orbs?' the girl asked. 'What orbs? What did you see?'

Lara showed her the video, which she watched in silence.

'Well, I've never seen owt like that before,' Tess said. 'Will you show me mam? She's behind the bar – if there are any stories, she'll know.'

She didn't wait for an answer but shouted across the bar, her Yorkshire accent broadening further.

'Ey up,' her mam said after viewing the clip. 'Now there's a thing.' She turned and went back to the bar, and the three of us looked at each other in confusion.

'Don't worry. She takes a while to warm up to strangers. If she knew anything, she'd have said. But she'll find out, you can be sure of that. Are you ready to order?'

Subdued, we ordered food and wine – and an apple juice for Hannah. When we were alone again, Lara reached over and grasped my forearm.

'Don't worry, Verity. You'll have Grasper with you tonight, and I'll cleanse the whole building for you in the morning. You'll be fine.'

I shuddered. Spirits were unknown and unknowable, and I hated the idea of strangers in my new home. Then I grinned at the absurdity of that thought. In a few months, I'd be running a guesthouse – constantly inviting strangers into my home. I raised my glass and took a long gulp, realising I was committed. The Rookery was my home and would soon be my livelihood. I had nothing else. I was stuck here, ghosts or no ghosts.

4.

The camp bed creaked as I turned over, and I startled awake, the image of a man clear in my mind. Dark-haired with black eyes and sun-baked skin. I shivered, rolled over again, and went back to sleep.

He beckoned to me and I joined him, walking across the car park behind my guesthouse, wincing as my bare feet found stones and the debris of tourists.

Towards the parsonage then down Church Lane to the graveyard, I followed the enigmatic figure in shirt and breeks – barefoot like myself.

I chided myself at every step, yet could not halt my feet. He pulled at me, beseeched me, drew me in, yet never touched me.

Past the early graves, the slabs of stone flat against the earth and butted up to each other so closely, Nature had no chance to exert a living presence. Some altar graves, then the newer, tall, carved monoliths standing sentinel and guarding the valley below.

I hesitated, shivering again as the man I followed disappeared into fog. What was I thinking?

I took a couple of hesitant steps backwards, but was too late; the fog was quick, falling down the hillside, enveloping me until I could see naught but grey and white swirls of cloud.

Then light, and I moved towards it, the misty tendrils releasing me, and I saw him again.

Standing with the sun behind him, shining on him, he spread his arms wide as if to show me something. I looked past him and gasped at the majesty of the moors: grim, yes, but also beautiful in their barrenness.

But no, not barren. Buzzards, hawks, even red kites circled above. I spotted a kestrel, hovering in place despite the wind, then diving down on to its prey.

I looked closely at the ground, a mixture of heather and tough, tussocky grass, and spotted rabbits playing, then scattering as a young fox cub bounded into their midst – too young and unskilled to do anything but scare them away. That would soon change.

The man pointed, and I twirled to see a herd of deer run past on the hillside below me. I grinned in utter delight, clasping my hands together, and watched the hardy beasts until the last flash of white from their hindquarters disappeared. I turned back to the man.

He beckoned again and I stepped forward, but he turned and walked away. I followed, hardly thinking about what I was doing, back into the swirling, enveloping fog, then jerked to a standstill as it cleared and I found myself perched on a rocky ledge at the edge of a precipice, the man's hand on my arm to steady me.

I opened my mouth to berate him, to tell him to be more careful, but he gestured to the valley below, and my complaints died in my throat.

The moors stretched out in all directions, a seemingly endless and full palette of browns and greens, yellows and oranges, maroons and purples, all swirled together as if by the hand of a great master in a grand passion of artistic creativity.

I pulled my gaze down and looked over the valley, only now seeing the towering, elongated chimney stacks belching black smoke to mingle with the clean moorland mist.

All that burning coal to produce the steam needed to run enough jennies, mules and looms to clothe gentlemen and ladies alike in the finest worsted wools.

I counted what now looked like vents from Hell as I pictured the children crawling about under that relentless machinery, literally risking life and limb with every crash and rattle of iron, every yard of yarn. A dozen, no, more – eighteen – factories of slavery and torture littered the valley, and I realised they must provide work for the occupants of near every house I could see.

The small slate roofs jumbled together in clusters, mimicking the outcroppings of ancient rock that interrupted the swathes of colour on the moorland above.

How many people lived and worked in those tiny cottages? Streets swimming with filth, children close to starvation, disease rampant.

I shook the dreary thoughts away; the vista was so beautiful, why did I feel sad?

I gasped as the man pulled me, and mist eddied around us once again until we were on the edge of the moors and I recognised the parsonage by the church – although something was wrong. The parsonage was missing a gable; the museum buildings at the back, as well as the car park, were not there. Neither were there any trees in the churchyard, and all the memorial stones were flat. Everything seemed very . . . bleak.

Six children walked up the lane and I smiled, charmed by their fussy Victorian clothing, the smallest girls looking the cutest of all in bonnets, clogs and aprons over full skirts.

I looked more carefully and realised they were all close in age; no more than a year or two between each, and they were not all girls – a boy walked in the middle, herding and shepherding his charges along. Well, trying to; his sisters did not appear to appreciate his efforts.

It struck me who they were, and I turned to my companion to confirm my suspicion of the identity of the family, but he was entranced by the large black rook perched on his wrist.

It took flight, was buffeted by the wind, but soon righted itself and swooped low to the gaggle of children.

One of the smaller girls – Emily, I decided; there was only one younger who would be Anne – raised her face to the bird in delight and stretched out her arm.

The rook alighted on its new perch, shuffled and flapped its wings, then settled.

The children stepped back from Emily in amazement, either scared of frightening the creature away or of its sharp, curved beak, but Emily took the visit in her stride. She lifted her arm close to her face to whisper a few words to the bird, then looked up at us and waved with her free hand.

The man waved back, and a smile – the first expression I had seen from him – broke across his harsh features, softening them, animating them, and my heart thumped hard at the sight of the crinkles around his eyes, the love and sheer delight reflected in his pupils, and the shape his mouth formed.

I gasped at the crushing pain in my chest and clawed my way to a sitting position, blinking in utter confusion at my surroundings. Then I realised I'd been dreaming.

The sense of crushing disappointment was accompanied by a strange smell – one I could not place, but knew belonged to the moors – and I felt in the bed next to me for Antony.

Reality coalesced as I touched no husband nor soft, luxurious bedding; merely a sleeping bag and the frame of a camp bed. A moment of sadness, then I remembered the man from my dream and identified the still-lingering smell as wild garlic.

Heathcliff, I thought, smiling. *I just met Heathcliff.*

I hugged myself tightly, and realised a wide smile – a smile to match his – stretched across my face, despite the absurdity. I was in Brontë Country after all; I'm sure plenty of women dreamed of meeting Heathcliff when they visited this village.

Feeling lighter and more positive than I had for many years, I disentangled myself from my sleeping bag, eager to get on with the day.

5.

'Coo-ee, Verity, are you here?'

I made my way downstairs to greet my friends. 'Goodness, you're early, couldn't you sleep?'

Jayne gave me a funny look. 'Verity, it's nine thirty, we were expecting you for breakfast an hour ago, are you okay?'

'What? Nine thirty?' I fished my phone out of my pocket to check and saw I'd missed three calls from them.

'Goodness, I'm sorry, I completely lost track of time and I didn't hear your calls.'

'Are you sure you're all right?' Lara asked. 'You look a bit flushed.'

'I'm fine.' I blushed a deeper red – I'd been fantasising about Dream-Heathcliff. 'I slept really well, got up early and took Grasper out, then started cleaning. I only meant to do half an hour, then meet you for breakfast. I guess I got carried away.'

'Well, find somewhere to sit,' Lara said. 'We brought breakfast to you – a bacon butty and coffee, hope that's okay.'

'Perfect,' I said, realising I'd built up quite an appetite. I had no furniture yet, so used the windowsill as a table.

'Verity,' Jayne said slowly, 'aren't the workmen coming in on Monday?'

I nodded, my mouth full of bacon and soft, white, fluffy bap.

'Then why are you cleaning now? There doesn't seem to be much point.'

'I was working in my quarters, trying to make them a bit more habitable – I'm not having too much work done up there and it would be good to set up a sleeping area and be able to use the kitchen and bathroom. The basic fittings are still here from the previous owners, and they'll do until I can afford to upgrade.'

'Oh, we'll give you a hand – we'll soon have it right when the three of us get going on it.'

'Thank you.' I looked around, startled, just noticing the quiet. 'Where's Grasper gone?'

'Hannah's taken him out again,' Jayne said. 'How was he last night? No more weird stuff?'

'He was fine, Jayne, no trouble at all, and nothing weird, don't worry.'

'And what about you, how did you get on?' Lara asked.

'I went straight to sleep, I was shattered,' I said. 'No ghosts, no ghouls, orbs, nothing.'

'Did you dream?'

'I did actually – very vividly,' I said, then stopped. I didn't want to share the dream man with them.

I changed the subject to forestall what looked like the makings of another question I didn't want to answer. 'Weren't you going to do a cleansing or something, Lara?'

'Yes, it's always a good idea to cleanse a new home anyway to clear it of old energies, and I brought some sage with me so I could do the guesthouse for you. We'll get started when you've finished your breakfast.'

'What does it entail, exactly?' I asked.

'Sage is cleaning and protective. I'll light the smudge stick—'

'The *what*?'

'Smudge stick, Jayne. Don't look so sceptical, it's been used for centuries.'

Jayne grimaced but stayed silent.

'Anyway,' Lara continued, 'I'll use the smoke to clear out the old energies of the people who used to live and work here, and invite in all things positive for Verity. You'll be surprised at the difference it will make to the feel of the place.'

'And will it get rid of those things, those orbs, from last night?'

'I don't know to be honest, Verity. We can only try it and see.'

'I've been thinking about that. There's all sorts of things those could have been. Insects or moths, for example,' Jayne suggested once more.

Lara pulled her phone out and played the video again. 'Do you see any wings, Jayne? And anyway, it's December, not exactly bug season.'

'Dust, then.'

'When have you ever known dust to move like that? Plus we'd have been able to see it when we were watching Grasper without the phone. And before you say it, they weren't lens flare, else Grasper wouldn't be reacting to them, they weren't torchlight or headlights, nor were they dandelion clocks or any other kind of seed in December. And we're inside, so they're not raindrops.'

'It does smell a bit damp in here though, it could be moisture.'

'When have you ever known water droplets to form and move like that? They're orbs, Jayne, accept it. What else can they be?'

Jayne said nothing.

'All right, I'm done, let's get started with this smudge-sticking or whatever it's called,' I said to break the charged silence.

Lara smiled. 'Smudging,' she said. 'Come on then, we'll start upstairs and work our way down.'

* * *

'Just what *exactly* is this supposed to achieve?' Jayne asked, disapproval distorting both her face and her words.

Lara ignored her and continued dancing around the room, waving the smoking, tightly bundled baton of sage into every nook and cranny. She finished her circuit of the window frame, then of the rest of the room before standing in front of us.

'As I said before, I'm clearing out any and all energies that no longer belong here,' she said slowly, staring into Jayne's eyes. 'I'm getting rid of any and all negativity so that Verity's positivity, hopes and plans for her new life can flourish. Your attitude is not helping the process, Jayne.'

Jayne scowled and I hurried to speak before she could pour more scepticism on to Lara. 'It can't hurt, Jayne, and it might help – I like the idea.'

'It smells like dope,' Jayne said.

'It's not cannabis, it's pure sage – grown in my own garden,' Lara said, her irritation barely concealed. 'Just keep an open mind, Jayne, that's all I'm asking. Now, you're in the way.'

We moved from the door to let Lara finish, then she stepped into the corridor and moved on to the other rooms. Jayne and I followed behind, staying out of her way.

'This will be my quarters,' I said, taking the conversation away from Lara, herbs and energies. 'Kitchen and lounge up here, bedroom and bathroom below.'

'Isn't that upside down?'

'What does that matter? This house is four nineteenth-century cottages converted into one property – you've seen the maze of rooms and staircases. I can get four double and one single guest room – all with en-suites – from it without having to knock through any stone walls, apart from doorways, and this is the space that's left.' I spread my arms, indicating the doors around us.

'I'd rather have a larger lounge than bedroom, and a bigger kitchen than bathroom, wouldn't you?'

'Fair enough.' Jayne went back into the room behind us – the lounge – and looked out of the window. Finally, she smiled. 'It's one hell of a view, Verity. You can see right up on to the moors. Oh, what's that?'

I joined her and looked down at the line of smoke. 'Steam train. It runs from Keighley to Oxenhope. They used one of the stations to film *The Railway Children*.'

'Oh wow, can we go on it?'

I laughed at her transformation from stern disapproval to almost childlike delight. 'Absolutely.' I turned to look back into the room. 'I'm going to paint everything white.'

Jayne nodded. 'A blank canvas,' she said.

'Exactly! I don't know what my future will hold – other than this place, of course – or who I'm going to, or even want to be. I like the idea of clean, fresh walls. A new start in every way.'

'What about the guest rooms?'

'I'm taking my inspiration from the Brontës,' I said.

'What? Wild moors and crumbling ruins? Mad wives in the attic, that kind of thing?'

I laughed. 'No, from their home, the parsonage. It's all very tasteful and understated. The wallpapers are floral, but two-tone and are as masculine as they are feminine – delicate patterns intertwining. Classy.'

'And the furniture?'

My face darkened. 'Well, all dark wood, nineteenth century of course, but I don't want it to overpower the space. I'll have to go to Ikea.'

'What? You can't be serious!' Jayne scolded, loudly enough to bring Lara running.

'What's going on now?'

'Verity has this wonderful plan for beautiful wallpaper in the guest rooms, then wants flat-pack furniture!'

'I can't afford solid wood,' I said. 'I can only do what I can to furnish five bedrooms.'

'Nonsense,' Lara and Jayne said together, then looked at each other and giggled, best of friends once more.

'What's your budget for each room?' Jayne asked.

I shrugged.

'Well, that's the first thing to do. We'll sit down this afternoon and go over the figures, work out what you can afford to spend.'

'Then we'll go round the second-hand shops and auction houses,' Lara said. 'I bet we'll find some nice stuff in Ilkley and Skipton, and even Harrogate isn't that far away. We can sand it down and varnish or paint, the rooms will look stunning.'

'And everything you do have to buy new: beds, mattresses and the like, well, its sale season in a couple of weeks, the perfect time to buy.'

All of a sudden, I felt like bursting into tears. I couldn't afford to do everything at once, and had made the decision to focus on the basics – plumbing, electrics, structural alterations – then gradually upgrade the furniture in the rooms as and when I could. It hadn't occurred to me to buy used pieces and renovate them. 'That could work,' I mumbled, and grinned at my friends.

'It would add character too,' Jayne said.

'Thank you, I don't know what I'd do without you two.'

'Well, you'll never have to find out,' Lara said.

'Probably starve,' Jayne said, and we both looked at her in confusion.

'You have no food, no microwave and no kettle. As soon as Lara's finished her smoking—'

'Smudging.'

'Whatever. And when Hannah's back with Grasper, we're off to Asda. We'll get these rooms liveable this weekend and move your camp bed in, but there's no way you can put us to work without regular cups of coffee!'

6.

'Fish and chips times four,' Jayne said, puffing as she came through the door and put the bag on my new kitchen table. 'Bloody hell, Verity, you'll soon get fit living here – there are hills everywhere. And then this place, I've never been somewhere where I've actually had to *look* for the next staircase! I nearly got lost on the way up.'

'It's a great place for hide and seek,' Hannah piped up. 'I could hide for *hours*! You'd never find me, I'd win easily!'

I laughed as I found the salt, vinegar and ketchup in the array of Asda bags lined up along the wall ready to be unpacked into the newly cleaned kitchen cupboards. We'd eat out of the boxes for tonight. 'Yes, you probably could, Hannah. Once all the alterations and decorating are done, it will look very different though, and should be easier to navigate.'

'I bet your guests will still get a bit lost though,' Lara said.

'You'll need lots of signs guiding people to their rooms,' Jayne said, ever practical.

I brought the condiments to my new camping table, and Lara carried wine and glasses.

'We did a good job today, thank you, ladies,' I said, looking around the upstairs of my flat. We'd scrubbed, washed and swept, and I had a living space with basic cooking facilities. 'I'd never have got this done without you, not before Monday.'

'I know it's rudimentary,' Jayne said, glancing at my 'furniture': camping table, four foldaway chairs and a camp bed doubling as a sofa in the large, open-plan kitchen and sitting room. 'At least you have somewhere to escape to while all the work is going on.'

'We can decorate next weekend,' Lara said. 'It won't take long to slap some paint on the walls and then you'll be ready for proper furniture as soon as the New Year sales start.'

'Are you both coming for Christmas? Have you decided?'

'Definitely,' Lara said. 'Jayne talked to the receptionist at the Old White Lion about Christmas lunch and rooms, and we're all booked in, so we can help out here over the holidays. It's our Christmas present to you.'

'I don't know what to say,' I said, feeling emotional as I hugged them both. 'I can't believe you're giving up your Christmases.'

'We're not,' Jayne said. 'We're spending Christmas with friends. Now come on and eat, the food's getting cold.'

Lara and I laughed, and Hannah sidled up to her mother. 'We're not giving up Christmas, are we?'

'Oh, no, Hans,' Lara said with a laugh. 'Don't worry, it's just an expression. We're going to come here for Christmas.'

'We'll still have turkey?'

'We certainly will – at the hotel where we're staying now.'

'So you won't be cooking?'

We all laughed at the hopeful expression on Hannah's face. Lara was an enthusiastic cook, but rarely followed a recipe or the recommended cooking times. She usually got away with it, somehow, but there had been one disastrous Christmas lunch two or three years ago which had come with an extra gift of food poisoning for all who'd tasted her undercooked turkey.

'No, I won't be cooking,' Lara said with good grace, 'and Grasper will be here to play with.'

'Yay!' the girl said, clapping her hands and hugging the dog.

'Right, wash those hands again, young lady, then come and eat.'

Jayne poured the wine. 'To your new home,' she toasted.

We all clinked glasses and I looked around. Yes, this could be a home – my home. I started to relax. I could be happy here, couldn't I? Okay, at the moment it reflected my life: bare, empty, and in need of decoration and filling, but that would not last.

I looked at Lara and Jayne, and raised my glass again. 'To best friends and an empty guesthouse,' I said with a wry smile.

'From small beginnings are grand dreams realised,' Lara said.

'I'll drink to that,' Jayne said.

'So what's the plan for tomorrow?' Lara asked, closing the lid of the cardboard fish-and-chip box.

'Day off, it is Sunday, after all,' I said. 'I thought we could do the touristy things, explore Main Street, visit the Brontë Museum, ride the steam train, maybe even go for a hike over the moors.'

'What, with Lara in high heels?' Jayne laughed. 'You know its stilettos or bare feet – nothing in between.'

'Too right,' Lara said, lifting one of her legs and wiggling her toes. 'A girl has to have standards.'

Jayne snorted, but said nothing.

'I don't want to go to a museum,' Hannah said from the camp bed where she was cuddling – and surreptitiously feeding – Grasper.

'Someone needs to look after Grasper anyway,' Jayne said. 'Unless we lock him in which doesn't seem fair when there's so much countryside about.'

'I can take him for a walk!' Hannah said.

'Is it safe?' I asked.

'Grasper will look after her – she's part of his pack,' Jayne said.

'Okay, as long as you don't go far and you have your phone switched on – but only while we're in the museum, all right, Hans? And you go no further than I say.'

'Okay, Mum,' Hannah sang, then she turned to Grasper. 'We're going to— oh!'

'What is it, Hans?' Lara turned to her daughter. 'Oh my God. Verity, Jayne, look!'

Grasper leaped from the camp bed, high enough to clear Hannah's seated form, although she had ducked out of his way, then circled a couple of times and jumped back on to the bed, ran over Hannah's lap, then tumbled back on to the floor.

'What the hell was that?' I cried.

'I saw it too,' Lara said, fumbling in her large handbag. 'Damn it, where's my phone? We need to video this.'

'I'm on it,' Jayne said, iPhone in position and already recording her pet's antics. 'I want to make sure it wasn't a glitch or a special app on yours, anyway.'

'An app?' Lara was insulted at the suggestion, but was distracted by Hannah's giggle as she dived away from . . . nothing. Although I did think I saw a flicker of light near her head as she ducked.

I glanced at Lara and knew she had seen it too. 'Wasn't that sage-smudging stuff supposed to get rid of those orbs, or whatever they are?'

'It would have if they were negative energies. If they're still here, they must be of the light – good.'

'Then why have you gone white?'

'It just dive-bombed my daughter and I don't know who or what it is!' She rushed to Hannah's side, although Hannah didn't need comforting; she was still giggling.

'Oh settle down, Lara,' Jayne said. 'You're over-reacting.'

'Am I? Don't you want to know what Grasper's playing with? If anybody is interacting with my daughter, I want to know who they are and what they intend.'

Jayne did not answer.

'I need to know. We have to hold a séance.'

I looked at Jayne and shrugged. I didn't expect it to help in any practical way, but if it put Lara's mind at rest then I was happy to do it.

'You can't be serious, Lara!' Jayne was not so easily persuaded.

Lara raised her eyebrows at her friend. 'Why not?'

'You can't mess with things like that, you're likely to make things worse, not better.'

'I'll be careful. Anyway, do you have any better ideas?'

Jayne shook her head, then looked at me. 'Verity?'

I glanced at Grasper, who was still dancing with things we could not see. I spread my arms and held my hands high, palms up. 'I don't think we have much choice.'

Jayne nodded, although she did not look happy about it. The three of us might bicker like siblings most of the time, but when we needed each other, we were there, no matter what that entailed.

'I'll go put Hannah to bed and see if that Tess girl will keep an ear out for her, then I'll be back.'

7.

Lara, Jayne and I sat at the camping table, which we'd covered with a new white cloth. Under Lara's direction, we spread our hands out and connected our little fingers to make a circle.

Lara took a deep breath before intoning, 'Is anybody there?'

I glanced at Jayne, then immediately looked away. Both of us felt it was ridiculous and clichéd.

Lara breathed heavily again, but didn't comment, yet I felt chastened, and knew Jayne felt the same way. I glanced up at Lara and smiled to encourage her to continue.

'We only want to talk to you, we will not harm you. Will you talk to us?'

Silence.

'Please talk to us or give us some kind of sign that you're here. Can you knock on the wall or tap on the floor?'

Silence.

'Knock once for no, twice for yes.'

Nothing.

'Please,' I said before Lara could continue. 'We'd really like to talk to you, don't you want to talk to us?'

Grasper barked when two sounds echoed through the near-empty room. He jumped off the camp bed and ran in circles around the table.

Jayne broke the circle to reassure her pet, and I snatched my hands away, shocked that we'd elicited a response.

Grasper calmed, but refused to budge from Jayne's side. 'Are you okay if we try again?' Lara asked her.

Jayne glanced at me then said, 'Maybe we should leave this.'

'No,' Lara said. 'I need to know who this is and what they want with us.'

'Are you sure?' I asked, glancing at Grasper. Although quiet now, he was still alert, his eyes wide.

Lara nodded and I pursed my lips to indicate my agreement.

We placed our hands back on the table.

I shivered and blew out. My breath condensed and the mist of it dissipated within the circle. Lara and Jayne simultaneously blew a long breath and the same happened.

'It's so cold,' Jayne said.

'It's an old house,' I said. 'The heating isn't working yet.' I wasn't sure if I was defending my new home or trying to deny the sudden drop in temperature.

We gasped when two knocks reverberated around the room.

'Lara,' Jayne warned, 'don't push it.'

I realised our hands had split again and wordlessly splayed my fingers on the tabletop. I was not in the mood for banter now.

Lara took a moment to gather her thoughts, then asked, 'Did you live here?'

One knock.

'No. Did you work here?'

Two knocks. Yes.

'Are you the Grey Lady?'

Nothing.

'Are you a woman?'

Silence.

'Are you a man?'

Two knocks.

I gasped and pulled my hands away.

'Oh calm down, Verity, that's hardly conclusive,' Jayne said.

I couldn't speak; an image of the man in my dream last night filled my head. I knew it was him; just *knew* it. The thought crossed my mind that this was the time to tell my friends about my dream, and how much it was affecting my thoughts, but I stayed silent. I wanted to keep him for myself; I was not yet ready to share him.

'Jayne's right,' Lara said. 'We need to be careful not to get carried away.'

Jayne raised her eyebrows at her and Lara smiled, then became serious once again.

'Spirits can lie, just as people can. We need to keep in mind the Law of Three. Ask the same question in three different ways and only trust the answers if they concur.'

'That makes sense,' Jayne said, albeit reluctantly. 'And those answers didn't meet that criteria.'

'No,' said Lara.

'But the temperature,' I said slowly, ready now to face the truth of it. 'I could see your breath – I know it's winter, but it isn't that cold in here, despite what I said about the heating not working. Anyway, we've had the new portable heater going.'

'I didn't say nobody was here,' Lara said. 'I just said we shouldn't blindly trust what they're saying.'

I shivered when I noticed she was picking the nail varnish off her nails, something she only did when very stressed or nervous. Grasper barked and chased his tail for a couple of circuits.

'I think we're done,' Jayne said. 'Grasper needs his night walk, we're all spooked, and to be honest, I'm ready for my bed.'

Lara looked as if she would protest, then said, 'Yes, time to call it a night.' She stood. 'Sorry, Verity, I feel I've given you more questions than answers.'

I hugged her. 'Well, I'll be here for quite a while – plenty of time to find those answers.'

'Goodnight, Verity, hope you sleep well.'

I jumped. For all the world, it had felt like somebody had blown a breath on the nape of my neck. I put my hand there but felt nothing.

'What's wrong, Verity?'

'Nothing. Goodnight, sleep tight.'

8.

I put the rubbish out before the whole Rookery took on the smell of fish and chips, then climbed back upstairs to my bathroom, below my kitchen. It didn't feel quite *right* down there, as if I hadn't moved in on that floor yet, and I was glad to get back upstairs and climb into my sleeping bag and camp bed, despite the dog hairs Grasper had so kindly left both on and somehow inside the sleeping bag.

As I thought this, he made a chuffing sound and I stroked his head; he'd stretched out alongside the camp bed, putting himself between me and the rest of the room.

I wondered briefly if Jayne would mind leaving him here when she went home. Somehow he just fitted in here at The Rookery, and I felt safer for his presence. I knew there was no way she'd go without him though.

Antony rolled away from me and I reached out to him, imploring him to stay in bed just a little while longer, even though I knew he was on the breakfast shift.

I let him go, reluctantly, and he walked naked to the bathroom to shower.

I stretched out in the bed, luxuriating in Egyptian cotton sheets, wondering if he'd have time to bring me a coffee before he had to leave for the hotel and its hungry guests.

A flashing light caught my eye and I realised Antony had left his phone on silent. I rolled over, grabbed it and dropped it in shock as my eyes focused on an intimate picture of a stranger that had just been sent to my husband via WhatsApp.

I scrolled through, and saw picture after picture, some of her, some of him.

The images sliced though my brain, preventing coherent thought, and dropping a depth charge straight into my heart.

I knew I could not hide from the truth any longer; no matter what I wanted the truth to be, it was time to face the reality of my life and my marriage.

I scrolled to the main menu, and saw a list of names I didn't know. Gina, Isa, Patsy, Sindi. I tapped on one and dropped the phone when I read the words written there amidst naked pictures of *another* woman. *I love you so much, I can't wait to marry you.*

'What?' I whispered, amazed at how calm I was as I struggled to grasp what was happening. I guessed I was in shock; my voice hadn't caught up with the emotions racing through my body. Whoever these women were, I wanted to leap through the phone, shove my arm down their throats, rip out their hearts and drive a stiletto heel through them. Then spit on them, chuck them on a fire, and feed them to the pigs. Then do something else that I wasn't yet capable of thinking of at that moment.

I dropped the phone, then belatedly realised I hadn't cleared the screen and could still see the evidence of Antony's betrayal, but I could not – would not – bend to his mistress, no, mistresses. Had he really proposed to someone? How many women was he swapping intimate pictures with? When and how had he met her – them? He was a chef in a five-star hotel and when he wasn't working, he was with me. And even when he *was* working, I was at the reception desk; most of the time, anyway.

When had he found the time and opportunity for one affair, never mind multiple betrayals? It certainly wasn't at work. Yes, okay, hotels were notoriously incestuous, but I had my ear very definitely plugged into the gossip grapevine. He was not doing the dirty at work, I was sure of that. Anyway, everybody there knew we were husband and wife.

Antony walked back into the bedroom, mostly dry and still naked after his shower. I glared at him, stared at his groin. I'd trusted him. Had he really stuck that elsewhere? Did I need to get tested? I looked away in disgust.

My practical side crumbled, the emotion overtook me, and I scowled at him, pouring my hatred through my eyes until I found my voice.

'Babes, what's wrong?' Antony rushed over, full of concern, and took me in his arms.

'Get off me!' I screamed. 'Don't touch me! You bastard, you cheating scum bastard!' Too late, I thought about playing it cool, then dismissed my own recrimination. There was no way I could handle this coolly – my heart had just broken. If I didn't take my anger out on him, I would take it out on myself.

'What? What the hell's wrong with you?'

In silence, I pointed at the phone on the floor, still displaying his proposal to another woman.

'Babes, babes, I'm so sorry. I can explain. I love you, I do, honestly. I've never even met her—' he picked up and brandished the phone at me '—not in person, just playing online.'

His words stabbed me and I lost the tenuous control I had over my temper. I grabbed his phone, opened the window and got ready to throw it on to the patio below.

I was too slow. He caught me; grabbed hold of my arm – hard

enough to make me scream in pain – but I did not care. I flicked the phone up, caught it with my left hand and launched it through the window. Not as hard as I'd have managed to do with my right arm, but it was still somewhat satisfying.

Antony ran to retrieve it.

I followed as far as the top of the stairs and thought I should have gone after him and locked him out as soon as he went into the garden, but I didn't think of it in time. Instead I stood there, numb, unable to comprehend what had happened.

We'd been married for thirteen years, and we'd never tired of each other. Our sex life was still healthy; we had no shortage of conversation or laughter. I'd thought we were happy; solid; soul mates. What a fool I was.

He came back inside and climbed the stairs. Stood in front of me.

'She's nothing, it was just a game,' he said. 'It's you I love, we can fix this.'

I stared at him. *Is he for real?*

My fists clenched at my sides and it took every ounce of willpower I possessed not to raise them. I wanted – so desperately – to lift them; to launch them at him; to push him; to thrust him back down those stairs; to kill him.

I forced them to stay by my sides. I stared at my husband and his face changed. He wasn't Antony any more, his features morphed to those of the man in my dream the previous night, and I relaxed. Heathcliff. Heathcliff was here.

He held out his hand and took mine, then led me back to the bedroom, I climbed into the bed and he sat on the mattress next to me and stroked my hair; calming me, soothing me, sending me deep into sleep.

Except I wasn't falling into sleep, I was falling out of it.

Slowly, awareness coalesced. I wasn't snuggled in Egyptian cotton on a soft mattress; once again I was in a sleeping bag, on a flimsy canvas camp bed.

I tried to roll over, but couldn't. My mind was awake, I knew where I was, what had happened, the challenges that lay ahead; but I couldn't move. I couldn't even twitch.

But I wasn't scared; I just watched myself sleeping in that bed.

His hand stroked my hair. I knew I should be terrified, but I also knew I was asleep so I was not frightened; I was just aware, observing, fascinated.

I grew more cognisant; realised my mind was awake even if my body was not. I enjoyed the feeling of relaxation and peace that I had rarely known before.

I grunted as my body tilted, but I did not have the capacity to fend off whomever was there.

My awareness grew and I understood the camp bed was sloped and skewed as if someone were sitting on one side of it. But there was no one there. I could no longer see my dream man.

The bed lifted and I felt a hand in my hair again, smoothing it.

My heart pounded, jerking me awake, and I stared wildly around the room.

No one was visible. But I *knew* somebody was there. I stretched my hand down to find solace in the fur of Grasper's head. He didn't need any more encouragement and jumped up to join me on the bed.

I realised he was just as confused as I was.

9.

'Blimey, that lad in the old Hovis ad had some legs, didn't he? He almost *ran* up this hill,' Jayne said, stopping for breath yet again.

I didn't need any persuasion to rest with her. 'It gives new meaning to the words "high street", that's for sure. I feel more like Ronnie Barker than the Hovis lad – do you remember that TV sketch?'

'Hill? More like mountain,' Lara complained from behind us before Jayne could answer. 'And these bloody cobbles will be the death of me.'

'Well, they might be the death of one of your ankles,' Jayne said. 'Why on earth wouldn't you just borrow a pair of Verity's trainers?'

'Heels, darling, heels,' Lara said. 'When they make a pair of trainers with heels, then I'll try them. Until then, not a chance.'

She caught us up, bags flung over each shoulder – she'd stopped at almost every shop on Main Street as an excuse to have a rest from the climb – and I took pity on her. 'We're nearly there, Lara. The pub at the top is just there – see?'

'Pub?' Lara said, hope in her voice. 'Pub? Why didn't you say so? Come on, Hans, help me up this last bit – it must be lunchtime and it's definitely wine time.'

Recovered, refreshed and replete, we left the Black Bull and made our way up the lane, past the church, and towards the parsonage for a gentler afternoon exploring the home of the Brontë sisters.

'Oh wow, look at that graveyard,' Lara said. 'That is seriously spooky.'

'It's definitely atmospheric,' Jayne agreed. 'Shall we have a look around?'

Lara was already halfway down the path, Hannah and Grasper in her wake, and Jayne grinned at our friend's enthusiasm for a cemetery.

'Are you all right, Verity? You're very quiet today.'

I squished my lips together in a pathetic attempt at a reassuring smile, then gave up. 'Bad dreams,' I said.

'Antony?'

I nodded. 'That morning I found his phone and found out about those women. I know it was months ago, but it still hurts.'

'Of course it does.' Jayne put her arm around me and squeezed. 'It devastated you – Lara and I have been really worried. But it's a good sign you're dreaming about it, it means you're processing it, starting to deal with it, deep down.'

'You sound like Lara.' I attempted a laugh and faltered.

'Well, I spend enough time with her.' Jayne's smile was genuine. 'But seriously, Verity, dreams are how we deal with what life throws at us. You've not stopped since it happened; the divorce has only just been finalised, and you completed on the guesthouse two days ago. The past *is* now the past, and you've embarked on a different future; it's no wonder you're dreaming about him – you're getting him out of your system.'

'I hope so.' I shuddered. I hadn't told anybody just how close I'd come to pushing Antony down the stairs. Did the fact I dreamt about that moment mean I still wanted to kill him?

'What? There's something else,' Jayne said, as astute as ever.

I decided on the lesser of two evils. 'Well, it was weird – I relived the phone call, the arguments, the emotion, everything—' I broke off before I said too much. 'But right in the middle of it, Antony changed.'

'What do you mean, changed?' Jayne sounded guarded.

'He became . . . well . . . someone else.'

'Did he *look* like Antony?'

'No – nothing like.'

'Well that's a relief! I thought for a moment you'd changed the way you think about him, but it sounds like you might be getting ready to meet someone else.'

'Don't be ridiculous, Jayne. No one's ever getting the opportunity to hurt me like that again.'

'I know, honey,' she said. 'But don't tell Lara or she'll be signing you up to all the dating sites.'

This time my laugh was genuine. 'Not a bloody chance,' I said. 'Don't you dare say anything to her!'

'Anything about what?' Lara said. 'What's up with you two? Come on and have a look at this place, it's amazing.'

We followed her into the graveyard, and I understood why she was so enthralled. Six-foot-by-three-foot stone slabs lay so close together not a blade of grass could grow between them. Just like my dream. If not for the names etched on them, it would look like a patio.

'There must be ten names on that one,' Lara said, pointing. 'How deep would the grave need to be for ten coffins?'

I shook my head, unwilling even to think about it.

'Oh God, they're so young!' Jayne said. 'Look – aged two, four, six, twenty six. I haven't seen any age above thirty yet.'

'Not a great place to live in Victorian times,' I remarked, then jumped as a flock of birds took off as one from the nearby trees.

'A parliament of rooks,' Lara said. 'How fitting.'

'What are you talking about?'

'That's what a flock of rooks is called, a parliament. They were believed to be the souls of the dead. It's quite profound to see them in a graveyard.'

We walked on in silence, all of us a little overawed by our surroundings.

'Is that the parsonage?' Jayne asked, pointing between the trees.

'Yes,' I said. After my dream it looked strange with the extension, although the addition now looked as aged as the rest of the building.

'What a place to grow up, looking at this through your windows every day,' Lara said. 'Those poor children.'

'I don't think there were trees then, either,' I said, then shrugged at Jayne's enquiring glance. 'I did a bit of reading up on the village and its famous residents before I moved in.'

'Glad to hear it. At least this bit has more character than the patio down there.'

The graves here were still flat, but some were raised – either a couple of inches or a foot – resembling altars of death. I wondered what it would have been like as a child, growing up with intimate knowledge of a working graveyard like this, surrounded by death every day.

'Apparently at the time of the Brontës, life expectancy was about twenty two,' I said, falling into the defence mechanism of tour guide to avoid the emotion of it. 'Patrick Brontë performed about three hundred baptisms a year, and then did the funerals for most of them, often only a few years later.'

Jayne shivered and hugged herself. 'Goodness, and think how many babies would have died even before baptism. It doesn't bear thinking about.'

'It wasn't a healthy time to be alive, that's for sure,' Lara said, staring at a stone filled with names. 'Where's Hannah?'

I started at the panic in her voice, then spotted her. 'Over there, look, by the upright stones.'

Lara hurried off and I glanced at Jayne, both of us fully understanding of Lara's sudden protective instincts. It was humbling to see so many children's deaths recorded in stone.

'Mummy, Mummy, stop it, I'm playing with Grasper.' Hannah squirmed out of her mother's arms and chased after the Irish terrier.

'Grasper!' Jayne called, and I glanced up at the sharpness in her voice. She was more spooked than I'd realised. 'Here boy!' The terrier ran to his mistress and she took hold of his lead then passed it to the child. 'Keep hold of him, Hans. He shouldn't be running around the graves, it's disrespectful.'

'Yes, Aunt Jayne,' she said solemnly and clenched the leather leash with both fists.

I looked up at the hillside, dotted with six-foot-high carved monoliths to celebrate and mourn the dead. 'They look like sentinels,' I said.

'Guarding the village below from the moors above.' I realised I was lapsing into my first dream and quietened.

Lara and Jayne said nothing, and we stood in silence for a while, contemplating the rows of individually engraved millstone grit.

'I don't know which is sadder,' Lara eventually said. 'The stones with a long list of names, or the ones that are only half full.'

I followed her gaze and spotted the stone that was affecting her. Two names at the top, then four feet of blank.

'Their family didn't survive,' I said. 'They died before they could have children.'

'Can we get out of here?' Lara said. 'I've had enough.' She shuddered. 'There's something about this place, something not right.'

As one we turned and left the dead to re-join the living.

10.

I climbed into my camp bed utterly exhausted. I couldn't remember the last time I'd seen Lara so spooked. She wouldn't leave Hannah alone, even for a second, and had said she could not 'cope with the museum and more death'.

Instead, we'd come back to The Rookery, Hannah had become fractious and emotional from the unaccustomed fussing from her mother, and they'd left just after an early tea.

I missed them already. I knew I had a busy week ahead, but it seemed to stretch out emptily until Friday evening when they would return.

The phone buzzed and I jumped, then scrabbled for it, a sinking feeling in the pit of my stomach as I wondered what had happened.

With relief I registered that the caller was not Lara or Jayne and swiped the answer icon. I instantly regretted it when Antony said, 'Verity? Hello?'

'Hello Antony,' I said, resigned to the conversation, but determined to keep control of my temper and emotions. 'How are you?'

'Not good, Verity, not good.'

My heart sank. It was one of *those* calls: self-pitying and maudlin drunk. 'What's happened?'

'Nothing, I'm just really low. I miss you, I've messed everything up.'

'Yes, you have.'

Antony huffed in frustration. He wasn't sorry, he just wanted absolution. And probably the divorce settlement back. 'I know, I know, things were just so hard – we hardly saw each other, always on different shifts, and we weren't getting pregnant.'

I gritted my teeth. I would not cry. I would not.

'I was lonely, Verity, so lonely.'

'We worked at the same hotel, Antony, we lived in the same house. If you had put the effort into us instead of that slapper—' I broke off and squeezed my eyes shut in frustration. The last thing I wanted was to argue with my ex-husband. Even by being on the phone he was tainting my new home; my new life.

He said nothing for a while, then changed tack.

'You can't put it all on me, you know. You could have made more effort.'

I said nothing, wondering if I should hang up or if that would make things worse.

'You were so cold, and always complaining, it's no wonder I looked for comfort elsewhere.'

'What? You can't put this on me! *You* were the one cheating!'

'We were arguing all the time.'

'Probably because you were chasing other women!'

'Verity—'

'No! No, I've had enough. Please, it's over, it's done. We're divorced, we're separated. You go marry your slapper, and I'll get on with *my* life. Goodbye, Antony.' I finally hung up.

Within seconds, the phone buzzed again. I ignored it.

And again.

I switched it off, lay back down, and stared at the ceiling somewhere above me in the dark.

Tears rolled down the sides of my face and pooled in my ears. I stifled a sob, furious with myself for allowing him to upset me again. I'd cried a river since that day. It was time to move on, to get over it, over *him*.

But how *did* you get over a broken heart? How did you put the pieces back together again? How did you ever let anybody in again?

I sobbed once more as a lonely, empty future stretched out before me. *Would* there ever be anybody to share it with me?

A face swam in front of my vision. Dark, handsome, piercing eyes, infectious smile. He held out a hand to me. I took it, and sank, swirling into a dark mist, letting go, drifting away from the bleak reality of my life.

11.

I woke with the image of those same eyes staring into mine, and lay frozen for a moment, my heart beating hard. My chest seemed to be the only part of me able to move as my breathing matched my heart in its intensity, clouding the air above me with evidence of life. For a moment I had been so disorientated I'd been unsure if I were alive or dead.

I caught my breath. What was that noise? And again! *Footsteps*? I listened until I had to release air and take in fresh – the action violent enough to shake me out of my torpor. I laughed at myself – in silence and without mirth – of course it hadn't been footsteps; just an old house on a winter's day, and the remnants of a nightmare.

I remembered Antony's call last night. That would have been enough to spark all sorts of weird and frightening mirages in my sleeping brain.

Shaking it off, I forced myself out of my warm bed into the cold morning air – the sooner the heating system was sorted properly, the better.

Shuffling to the shower – thank goodness for fluffy slippers and fleecy onesies! – I remembered the eyes I'd woken to. They hadn't been Antony's blue irises; they had been dark, brooding, intense.

'Oh for God's sake, Verity, it was a bloody dream, stop spooking yourself!'

I laughed at the sound of my own voice in the emptiness and switched the shower on. Time to be thinking about the day ahead, not the night behind. I undressed and stepped under the thankfully warm spray, then lifted my face to the waterfall.

The builders would be here before too long, ready to start work on making the place mine.

I soaped myself, thinking about my plans, my dream of how the next part of my life would be.

The Rookery would have five bedrooms, and I was determined to make it spectacular, going that extra mile to make people feel welcome and valued. After living and working in the centre of Leeds for so long, I wanted to embrace country living: fresh air, a real community, and a slower, more enjoyable pace of life.

I loved the Brontës' books, and couldn't be closer to the parsonage – one of the reasons I'd chosen this property – and I wanted to reflect the history of this place in my design and management decisions.

The house was attached to a row of weaver's cottages, so I'd use plenty of local textiles, and it stood to reason that Emily Brontë, and then Charlotte would have been regular visitors to the people who lived and worked here. In the 1840s, Emily had returned to live with her father and Branwell, and carried out the duties of curate's wife – even though she was daughter. Then Charlotte when she returned to Haworth after a small taste of fame and the city life in London to care for her father, then as Arthur Bell Nicholls' wife until her own premature death in childbirth in 1855.

I sighed at the tragedy of so many talented and driven siblings dying so young. Poor Patrick; first burying his wife, then seeing all six of his children in their graves. Maria, his firstborn, at age eleven through to Charlotte, the most famous of his brood, at thirty eight.

The pain and unfairness of it had me close to tears and I lifted my face to the spray of water and leaned back into the comforting hand around my waist. It had been a long time since Antony had joined me in the shower.

Then I remembered and spun around, my grasping hand on the tiles only just saving me from a nasty fall.

I yanked the shower curtain back and used it to cover myself in one movement, then peered into the small bathroom as I fumbled around for the shampoo bottle. Not much of a weapon, but all I had to hand.

I listened hard to silence as the steam cleared, then stared at empty tiles, mirror and closed door.

There was no one there.

12.

Chaos had never felt so safe. Noise, people, dust, destruction, rubbish. If I couldn't have Jayne and Lara, Keighley Building Services would do until the girls could get back to Haworth.

I handed out mugs of strong, sweet tea and looked at what had been accomplished so far. The build team – Omar and Woody – had ripped out a couple of internal walls in the lobby, covering everything with rubble and curses.

They had not yet managed to find a single level surface – on any plane – and had launched into a constant bicker with each other and the project manager, Vikram, about how to go about turning the drawn plans into reality.

Sarah, or Sparkly as she seemed to be quite happy to be called, was the only female electrician within twenty miles and very proud of it. She was not taking the state of The Rookery's wires very well; mainly because she was struggling to even find them, and she took every frustration out on poor Snoopy, her apprentice, real name Charlie Brown.

Thick, stone walls were introducing themselves at most inopportune moments, and two hours in, nobody understood the original construction or subsequent alterations of the building.

'Look at this,' Omar said, gesturing at the architectural plans I'd had drawn up at great expense. I hung back, not wanting to get embroiled in yet another row.

Vikram leaned in closer, a look of resignation on his face. He was a funny bloke; big features in a rugged face, and I suspected he'd get better looking as he got older and grew into his looks. But he definitely looked interesting. Tall and surprisingly strong – he'd heaved some pretty heavy loads out to the skip along with Omar and Woody – I was not quite sure where his lanky frame was hiding the muscle. I wondered what he looked like when he smiled – if he ever did. I'd seen no hint of one so far, not even in greeting.

'Architect has us moving this wall 'ere, but its bloody stone. Then there's this en-suite upstairs – I've got no idea how the plumbers are going to pipe it in.'

'And the wiring will have to be completely redone,' Sparkly put in. 'And I can't go off these plans, I'll have to go through the whole place and find out for mesen which walls are stone and which I can work with.'

This was beginning to sound expensive. I couldn't just leave them to it. 'But why are there so many issues? Surely the architects sorted all that out when they surveyed the place.'

'It doesn't look like they did survey it,' Vikram said. 'It looks like they've just gone off the plans that have been lodged with the Land Registry and not checked to see if they're correct. And with a building this old . . .' He shrugged.

'So what was the point of me paying them all that money?'

Vikram shrugged again. 'First off, you'll have needed them for planning permission for the alterations, and to be honest, having architects come out to the property to survey it really would have cost a fortune.'

'And we'd still probably have had to chuck it all out when the real work started,' Omar interrupted.

'Don't worry, love, we'll work out how to sort it, you don't have to bother yourself,' said Vikram.

'My name's Verity, and this is my home, business and livelihood. I will very definitely bother myself with it.'

'All I meant was, we'll work out how to sort it,' said Vikram. 'Verity. We've all grown up and spent our working lives in buildings like this. If we can't understand the place and make it work, no one can.'

I nodded, mollified. 'That's good to hear.' Then, keen to ease the tension, I said, 'So what do you think we should do about that wall?' I pointed at Omar's most urgent problem: the stone wall that bisected my proposed reception area.

'Give us a minute, love. Verity,' Vikram corrected, glancing up at me.

I gave him a small smile and he held my gaze a moment, then returned his attention back to the plans and room.

'Well, we can't knock it down,' he said at last. 'It's original and solid – it's been there over a hundred and fifty years, and ain't shifting without some serious resistance.'

'So we need to work around it,' Omar said.

'How about instead of having your reception area against that front wall, you move it there.' Vikram pointed to the left of the back wall. 'Then that wall can stay and we can widen the doorway into an arch,' more pointing, 'and you've still got room for seating and stuff there and there. Would that work?' He looked to Omar and Sparkly first for approval before turning back to me.

I walked to the doorway in the problem wall and looked into the space that would have to house my guests' breakfast room. 'It's a bit tight. I need five tables with chairs as well as a buffet table, and I don't want everyone on top of each other.' I looked at the far wall. 'It might work if that's moved back.'

Vikram sighed, strode to the latest offending wall, knocked on it a couple of times then opened the door to examine the other side. 'It's timber and plasterboard,' he said. 'It can be done, but it'll mean a smaller kitchen.'

'I realise that. But I'll only be cooking breakfasts, not three-course dinners as the restaurant did.'

'Don't forget we'll be putting a bedroom in over there.' Vikram pointed again.

'I haven't forgotten.' I took a deep breath and did my best to speak builder. 'If this wall was moved back two feet, and with the new room and en-suite at that end, what would the dimensions of the new kitchen be?'

'Omar?' Vikram barked, clearly not amused to be challenged.

'Well, if we put the new wall in here,' Omar laid a batten on the floor, 'and the wall for the new bedroom will come to— Hang on a minute.' He nipped back into the lobby, presumably to check the plans, then reappeared and paced, thinking hard. 'Here.' He placed another batten, then turned and spread his arms. 'This will be your kitchen.'

I looked at the large space, then up at Vikram. 'Perfect. We'll do that, then. Can I leave it with you? I have a few errands to run.'

Vikram nodded – still no smile – but Woody grinned at me as I escaped.

It would take more than two months to be ready for guests, and I was ready to pull my hair out after two hours. I couldn't do this alone.

I fished my mobile out of my bag and dialled. 'Jayne? Tell me again why this was a good idea . . .'

13.

'Oh you've got to be kidding me,' I muttered as I drove down West Lane. Builder's vans and skips had taken over and there was nowhere to park. *Not the best way to introduce myself to the neighbours.*

I drove on, crawling down the almost vertical Main Street, managing not to hit any of the winter tourists – even though a fair few of them didn't realise it was a functioning road with actual traffic – and made my way back round to the top of the village. I'd have to park in the museum car park and unload the car later.

I glanced over at the rear gable of The Rookery and walked in the other direction. I simply could not face Vikram and his army yet. Maybe later – when they knocked off for the day. His comment about not bothering myself tickled at my memory, but I shoved it away.

I continued walking. Past the parsonage and into the graveyard. It seemed quiet, peaceful. The odd tourist was wandering around, but the bustle of village life was absent. Best of all: no builders.

I sat and sighed, feeling my shoulders physically drop as I relaxed. Then I jumped as my phone beeped.

Embarrassed, I fumbled it out of my bag, pulled off my glove, and checked the text. Antony. *I'm sorry about last night. I didn't want to argue. I miss you. Call me xx*

I stared at it then switched the phone off. Why couldn't he leave me alone? Did he not realise how deeply he'd hurt me? How much I was still hurting? Every reminder of him and his betrayal just made it worse. I shoved away the memories of that night and what might have been, took a deep breath, and looked around me; searching for the calm that had descended on me when I first sat down; furious with myself that despite it all, I missed him too.

The clop of horses' hoofs broke into my reverie and I smiled – that was such a sound of the past. I realised I couldn't hear any cars or any other noise denoting the twenty-first century, just the buzz of insects, the horses, and a cock crowing. Even the distant voices could have come from the age of the Brontës.

I sniffed. No exhaust; no ozone; just damp fresh earth with a hint of something familiar. A distinctive smell I recognised. I'd smelled it the first morning I'd woken in my new home: wild garlic. *In December?* I dismissed the discrepancy as the bare trees above rattled their smaller branches in response to a gust of wind, and a rabbit shot across the path in front of me as if being chased by a ferret.

The millstone grit slabs of stone themselves stayed stoic, whether laid on the ground or standing upright in rows. Each was a different shape, a different design, and heavily carved, but all were of a similar imposing size. Indifferent custodians of the dead.

I shivered when I remembered 44,000 people were believed to have been buried in this vastly inadequate patch of earth; far too many of them children. I counted the names on the nearest upright stone. Twelve. Twelve people in one grave. I shuddered, remembering Lara's question about how deep these graves must be. Had they dug it deeper every time there was a death in the family? How often in the past had this cemetery been scattered with rotting coffins as more room was cut out of the earth below?

Was my dream man one of them? Were his bones commemorated by one of these stones? Had those forceful eyes rotted away into the earth beneath my feet?

I caught a movement between the stones – a flash of white. Him? I stared. There it was again, but too far away to make sense of it. Then again, in the other direction.

I shook my head. This was getting ridiculous; at best I was descending into a world of fantasy and ghosts, at worst I was losing my mind.

Startled, I looked up as the rooks took wing as one, lifting from the skeletal treetops in reaction to some unseen threat.

I shivered as I realised they had done so silently – with no cawing of warning or intention – before settling once more in their roosts. Somehow it felt a portent.

I shook myself, ashamed of being so melodramatic, and I glanced around at the stone sculptures surrounding me. *Well, no wonder my imagination is running away with me in here.*

I stood and belatedly realised my bench was in fact an altar grave. I silently apologised to the occupants and peered at the worn letters.

After a few moments, I picked out *cliff* and my heart leaped. *Heathcliff, really?* I sank to my knees and activated the flashlight app on my phone, then shone it from the side to pick out the rest of the letters in the winter's afternoon gloom.

Not Heathcliff, Sutcliffe.

I hung my head and snorted with laughter at my ridiculous assumption, then got back to my feet and went home.

I shouldered open my front door, cursing at the shopping bag straps digging into my arms and shoulders, then swore more violently as Woody barged into me and sent me flying.

He didn't even stop to apologise, never mind help me up or pick up the food and wallpaper samples now scattered over the dusty, rubble-strewn floor.

'What the hell?' I shouted at Vikram as he rushed in to see what all the noise was about. 'Your bloke just shoved me over! What's going on?'

'I'm sorry, love, I don't know what's got into him. One minute he was measuring up, the next he bolted.'

I rubbed my elbow, then pushed up my sleeve to try and examine it, but couldn't see.

Vikram took hold of my arm. 'That'll bruise, you should get some ice on it.'

I snatched my arm back. 'One of your staff assaults me, and that's all you have to say?'

Vikram stared at me. 'Don't worry, love, I'm sure it was an accident, but I will deal with him, don't doubt that. Are you hurt anywhere else?'

'No, no, I don't think so.' I was mortified to hear my voice shake, and stepped forward, but winced and rubbed my hip. 'Spoke too soon.' I tried to smile. It was a poor attempt.

'Get yourself upstairs and pour yourself a nip of summat. I'll bring this lot up.'

'What's happened? Is everything all right?' Sparkly appeared at the door to the stairs.

'Where's Woody buggered off to? What's going on?' Omar said, pushing past her.

'I dunno, he just bolted, knocked Verity over.'

'What? Are you okay?' Sparkly asked.

'What's he done that for?' Omar said. 'What's got into the lad?'

'I'm fine, just a bit shaken,' I answered Sparkly.

'Dunno,' Vikram repeated to Omar. 'He never said a word, just ran. But he was as white as a sheet.'

'I'll go after him, find out what's up.'

Vikram nodded and bent to gather up my shopping as Sparkly led the way upstairs, asking new questions with every step.

That nip of something Vikram had mentioned was getting more and more tempting, and I found myself praying the bottles had survived the tumble.

14.

I stared at the ceiling, alternately willing sleep to come, then doing my utmost to stay awake when I felt my eyelids falter. I desperately wanted my dream man to visit again, but at the same time he scared me. When my lids finally closed I remembered the caress in the shower this morning and snapped awake.

If I wasn't already going mad, it wouldn't take much longer at this rate.

I drifted awake, becoming aware that I must have succumbed, but with no idea how long ago. The mixture of relief and disappointment I felt at not having dreamt dissipated in a flash. Was that a footstep? And another?

I tried to move, but once again was paralysed, helpless to do anything but listen and wait.

There was no doubt now: footsteps climbed the stairs, growing louder and resonating deeper the closer they came.

They were in my apartment now, approaching the room where I slept. I cast my mind back, wondering if I'd closed my bedroom door – I didn't think I had.

A floorboard creaked – that was in my room!

I still could not even open my eyes, never mind move my limbs, and now my breath faltered too. I focused on expanding my chest then pushing the air back out, trying to dismiss the creaking footsteps as imagination.

My breath caught and I forgot to expel it. My mattress had dipped as if someone had sat on the edge of my bed. My chest strained, but I still did not breathe, then I felt fingers brush my cheek and I let out the stale air with a yell and sat up.

I scrambled to switch on the bedside light and stared around the room – eyes wide and breath now panting in and out of my abused lungs. No one. The room was empty.

I bolted out of bed, showered with no further incident, dressed and was downstairs fifteen minutes later. I'd get breakfast from the closest café.

When I got back to The Rookery, Vikram and the build team were waiting for me. The expected complaints didn't come as I let them in, instead Vikram introduced the new face amongst them.

'This is Gary, he'll be working with Omar to replace Woody.'

'Morning, Gary, pleased to meet you.' I held up my hands full of coffee and bacon butty to indicate I couldn't shake, but he wasn't bothered.

'Hiya, mush. That smells good.'

Mush?

Sparkly saw my expression and laughed. 'And you thought "love" was bad! Best just to ignore them – I've been trying to train them for years, I'd have better luck with pit bulls.'

I smiled, still too shaken by this morning's rude awakening to get upset about the pet name.

'Pit bulls are very intelligent,' I said with a smile and Sparkly gave a very loud, very throaty laugh that had the men grinning along.

'So what happened to Woody?' I asked.

'He saw the Grey Lady,' Sparkly said. 'Freaked him out – he doesn't believe in ghosts.'

'Sparkly!' Vikram admonished. 'I thought we'd agreed—'

Sparkly flapped her hand at him. 'She'll find out eventually, and it's not as if she's evil or anything. Woody's just a wimp. Verity, are you okay?' Her tone changed. 'You've gone as white as Woody did.'

'Just get to work, all of you,' Vikram barked. He dragged a sawhorse closer. 'Here, sit on this.'

I nodded at him gratefully and perched on the paint-splattered trestle.

'You've seen something too, haven't you?'

I shook my head. 'No,' I said, ignoring Grasper's antics with the orbs, then to moderate the lie, added, 'but I've felt things, and had dreams. What did Woody see?'

'The Grey Lady – he's not the only one, plenty have seen her over the years, here and in the row of cottages next door. She's said to be Emily Brontë.'

'Yes, the waitress in the White Lion said something about that.' *But if The Rookery is haunted by Emily Brontë, Who's the man with the dark eyes?* I thought but did not say.

'Oh Tess, yeah, she loves all the ghost stories, does amateur ghost hunts and puts stuff on YouTube. There's not much evidence it *is* Emily, to be honest, just that she's only seen at this time of year, and she wears the right era clothing – big bonnet with a bow, full gown, that kind of thing.'

'Why grey? That was a mourning colour wasn't it?'

'I don't know about that.' Vikram screwed his mouth up. 'People say there's a grey haze around her, which is where the name comes from.'

I sipped my coffee, my bacon butty forgotten. 'So what did Woody see? What actually happened?'

'Right over there.' Vikram pointed to the wall separating The Rookery from the cottage next door. 'She walked up the wall in a diagonal, as if there were stairs there, then disappeared through the wall.'

'That's all?'

'It was enough for him.'

Despite myself, I laughed.

'It sounds like you've had more scares than funny feelings and dreams,' Vikram said.

I smiled up at him, touched by his concern, but reluctant to tell him too much. I didn't want him to talk about me in the same dismissive way he'd spoken about Woody's reaction to the Grey Lady.

'Just intense dreams and a few touches. A man though, definitely not Emily Brontë.' I laughed. 'Probably just my imagination – new start, new home, and in a place with so much history.'

'Not heard of anything like that here,' Vikram said. 'Right, better get on.'

So much for not being dismissed.

15.

I had to admit, despite the problems, Vikram and his team had made good progress. The new floor plan downstairs was coming on – the walls that we'd finally decided would come down were down, although there was still a lot of tidying up to be done. The new dividing walls should be in place by the end of the week, then Omar and Gary would start on the bedrooms after Christmas, although finding workable room for all the en-suites was going to be a challenge.

Sparkly was happier with the wiring. She'd found most of the existing network and had enthusiastically ripped out every wire. Which meant I was reliant on candles, torches and woolly jumpers until she could get lights and sockets working in my apartment again.

My candles flickered and I switched on the torch and looked around. I really had not thought this through. Instead of a romantic adventure, this was far too spooky. I liked a good ghost story – but not when there was the possibility I was featuring in it.

I unscrewed my bottle of wine and poured my first glass. I didn't normally drink alone on a Tuesday evening, but I told myself the circumstances were exceptional. It would keep me warm and was quite possibly the only way I would sleep tonight. If I drank enough, I might not even dream.

I'd called Lara and Jayne earlier to give them the news that the place was definitely haunted, and wished I'd made Jayne my second call for her calming, logical reassurance. Instead, I'd been left with Lara's excited squealing and talk of Ouija boards and more séances. Just what I didn't need.

I took a big gulp of wine and called Jayne back.

She answered my call, laughing. 'You called Lara didn't you?'

'Yes.'

'How badly has she freaked you out?'

'Well, I'm sitting in a hundred-and-fifty-year-old haunted house. I have no electricity. I'm drinking wine by candlelight, one of the builders was so scared he ran, even though it might cost him his job, and the man in my dreams keeps touching me. I'd say I'm about nine out of ten on the freaked-out scale.'

'What? The man in your dreams, plural? And he's touched you? You didn't tell me that before.'

I winced and took another gulp of wine. 'Sorry, I didn't mean to tell you now – it's probably just imagination. It's always when I've just woken up and my subconscious is probably dealing with all the Antony stuff.'

'So is the man in your dreams Antony?'

'Well, no.'

'What does he look like?'

'Dark, handsome – very handsome!' I giggled and had another drink. 'And his eyes – the complete opposite to Antony's – they're dark too, I feel like they're looking straight through me, into the core of me. I know I'm only dreaming him, but it's like he's staring into depths of me I don't even know are there.'

Jayne was silent a moment. 'You know who you've just described, don't you?'

'Who?' Although I knew what she was going to say.

'Heathcliff.'

'Great, I'm being haunted by a fictional character!' I laughed and sipped again.

Jayne was the first to stop laughing.

'What?' I said into the silence on the line.

'I just had a thought. He'll have been inspired by *somebody*, the Brontës did draw on the people in Haworth for their characters – more than a few of their neighbours were upset when they realised who authored those novels.'

'So who inspired Heathcliff?'

'Exactly.'

I drained the bottle into my glass, a little embarrassed at how quickly I'd emptied it, and made Jayne promise not to tell Lara about the dreams. I ended the call but dropped the glass before I'd brought it halfway to my lips.

There was a figure, glowing grey, almost brighter than the candles. A woman, and slim. She wore a large bonnet, and a dress tight about the upper torso and gathered in the back to accentuate her shape. *A bustle*, I thought, *it's called a bustle.*

She carried a basket over one arm – I could see it was full, but not what the contents were – and as I watched, she calmly disappeared into the wall.

I stared open-mouthed. *Have I just seen Emily Brontë?*

Or have I just had too much to drink?

This was too much. Feeling completely sober despite the wine, I grabbed my handbag and coat and left. Hopefully the Old White Lion Hotel had an empty guest room as well as a warm, comfortable bar with real, *live* people.

16.

The boy bolted and was on the moors before the mill bell had stopped ringing to announce the end of the children's long working day. There was still a glimmer of the late spring daylight left, but the shadows were fast encroaching on the bleak landscape.

He lost his battle with the tears he'd been fighting all day and ducked down behind an outcrop of millstone grit to give in to them in privacy.

He gasped for air between sobs and fell into a violent coughing fit as fresh moors' air hit his wool-fibre-lined lungs. Only one day at the mill and his chest hurt. The fibres had prickled the back of his throat all day, and nobody had paid any attention to his complaints.

Mind you, nobody could hear him over the relentless cacophony of the spinning jennies and mules.

It had been worse than thunder, and there had been no let-up; not from the mill bell at five that morning until the children's bell at six that evening. Even the worst thunder didn't send merciless steel backwards and forwards, threatening to crush unwary hands, feet, or heads.

Fresh tears flooded down his cheeks as the seven-year-old realised he would have to do the same tomorrow, and the day after that, and the day after that, for the rest of his life; however short that may be.

'Why are you crying?'

The boy startled and rubbed his face at the thin but strident voice, then peered at the girl in confusion, unable to decipher her words through the ringing in his ears. She repeated her question and Harry studied her lips to understand what she was saying, then recognised her as water cleared from his eyes.

Emily, one of the parson's daughters. He cringed; to show such weakness in front of a girl!

'I'm not, I just have soot in my eye. I started working on mill floor today.'

'Is that why you're covered in black dust?' Emily asked. 'You'll get the moors dirty.'

He looked down at himself. She spoke true; he was covered in sooty wool fibres. He shrugged. 'Maybe Mr Baalzephon will clean mill up.'

She hooted with laughter. 'Old Man Rook? He'll do nowt of the sort!'

The children laughed, united against the owner of Rooks Mill.

'What's thee doing here?' the boy asked, remembering Emily was a couple of years younger than he. 'Where's thy brother or thy sisters?'

'Oh they're in the parlour,' Emily said, dismissive. 'I crept out, I wanted to see if the lapwings had hatched.'

'Lapwings?'

'Aye, there's a nest over yonder with eggs. Listen, the mama and papa are calling! Do you want to see?'

'All right then, happen I do.'

'But you'll have to be quiet or you'll scare them away. Why are you shouting, anyroad?'

The boy stared at Emily. 'I'm not shouting.'

'Yes you are, you're really loud.'

He thought for a moment. 'Is thee sure lapwings are calling? I can't hear them.'

'Yes!' Emily stamped her foot. 'Listen! There, did you just hear her peewit?'

The boy cocked his head but still heard nothing. 'I think mill's made me deaf already,' he said, then looked at Emily in alarm. 'Has mill taken lapwing's call away from me forever?'

Emily stared up at him. 'They're this way,' she said in lieu of answering his question, and ran up the hill.

The boy followed Emily through the bracken and grass of the lower moor, then through the heather until the little girl turned with her finger to her lips.

She pointed ahead and the boy squinted. There she was! Difficult to see unless you knew she was there, her brown plumage camouflaged her well against the heather stalks, her crest imitating the new growth above that sheltered her and her eggs from the overhead threats of owl, buzzard and kestrel.

'How does thee know there are eggs? It's late in season to be laying,' the boy whispered.

'Shh,' Emily hissed, but too late, the lapwing hen took wing.

'There, see?' Emily said. 'You'd better not have scared her away for good or the chicks won't hatch. I wish I'd never shown you. Come on, come away.'

The boy followed his diminutive young guide back down the hill.

I woke with tears flooding down my face. I could *feel* the despair of the boy and somehow understood exactly what it was like for the child to crawl underneath the working spinning mule, brushing down its moving parts, as well as the floor, as it operated; the metal frame clanging into its final position, then making its return journey; back and forth three times a minute, every minute, of every working hour. And there were an awful lot of working hours. No wonder employment of children in the mills had been termed The Yorkshire Slavery.

As I grew more aware, I shrank against the wall before remembering where I was. The Old White Lion. I clearly didn't need to be at The Rookery for Heathcliff, or whatever his real name was, to visit. He could find me anywhere.

17.

Sitting in comfort, having breakfast served to me and my coffee cup refilled regularly was exactly what I needed and went a long way to bolstering my spirits.

I didn't want to leave the comfort of the White Lion and return to my building site, but it had to be done, and eventually I settled up and walked home.

The build team had beaten me again and were sitting in their vans outside, waiting.

'Morning,' I said as they exited their vehicles and trooped into The Rookery. I received a few grunts in return and a reluctant 'how do' from Vikram.

My good feeling from breakfast disappeared and I wondered what was going on now.

'None of 'em slept well.' Vikram had recognised the look on my face. 'They all had nightmares, but none of 'em will talk about it.'

'So it's catching.'

'What?'

'Nothing. How about you, did you sleep okay?'

He shrugged. 'Well enough. What happened here?'

I followed his gaze and saw the shards of broken wine glass. I'd forgotten about that – they still lay where they'd shattered before I'd fled last night. 'Woody's Grey Lady paid another visit.'

'You saw her?'

I glanced away from him, then back. 'I-I think so. But I was spooked after the Woody thing, and had no lights but candlelight. Now it's daylight, I-I'm not so sure.'

'What did you see?'

'Well, what you said. A woman glowing grey with a big bonnet, a gown gathered at the back into a bustle, and carrying a basket.'

Vikram said nothing.

'What?'

'I don't remember telling you about the basket.'

'What?'

'I didn't tell you about the basket. Everybody sees it – sometimes that's all people see – but I realised when I got home I hadn't told you about it.'

'Oh.'

Vikram made his habitual shrug. 'It seems your imagination isn't quite so rampant after all.'

I sighed. 'Thanks for that. I feel much better.'

Vikram's answering smile was gone before it was complete as a crash echoed from upstairs and Sparkly's voice carried through the building.

'You daft bugger! I told you to hold on to them wire strippers! Where the hell are they?'

'Sorry, sorry, I don't know where they've got to. I just had them!' Snoopy said. 'Sorry, Sparkly.'

'And why the hell does everyone have to call me Sparkly? My name's Sarah, and I never wear bloody sparkles!'

'You're a female sparky, lass, so you're Sparkly. Get used to it,' Omar butted in.

'I'd better go calm things down before Gary calls her "mush", and she really loses it,' Vikram said, finally smiling and hurrying through the broken glass still on the floor, towards the stairs.

'What on earth is going on here?'

I twirled at the sound of her voice. 'Jayne! What are you doing here? I wasn't expecting you until tomorrow.'

'It sounded like you needed a friend, so I pulled a sickie. Lara can't make it today because of Hannah's school, but she sends her best and wishes she was with us.'

I embraced her and hung on tight. 'Thank you,' I whispered. 'It's so good to see you.'

She hugged me back a moment, then pulled away. 'Right, well, we'd better get that glass cleaned up and then you can fill me in properly on what's been happening.'

'Okay, but not here. Let's take Grasper for a walk – I need to get out of this place.'

By the time we had completed a very slow stroll to the bottom of Haworth Main Street, it was almost lunchtime.

'Let's try Haworth Old Hall,' I said. 'I haven't eaten there yet.'

'Lead the way, Verity. I hope that place isn't haunted!'

I slowed my step. 'In a place this old, with this much history, *everywhere* is probably haunted,' I said, aware my chest was tightening again.

Drinks and menus in situ on the table, Jayne sat and stared at me.

'What?' I asked.

'I think you're worrying too much.'

'Okay,' I drawled, hoping she was right but knowing deep down in the pit of my stomach that she wasn't.

'Antony's put you through hell in the past year, it's no wonder you're having weird and vivid dreams, especially about a man, and especially about a man who's the opposite in looks to Antony.'

'But what about the touches? The footsteps and sitting on the bed?'

'You said yourself, you were either still half-asleep or had only just woken up. You were probably still dreaming.'

I thought back to the caress in the shower. That had not been a dream, I was sure of it. I'd been fully awake for that one. Although, if I was honest, I *had* been daydreaming about Antony, hadn't I? Maybe Jayne had a good point.

'What about the Grey Lady – seeing her last night?'

'Power of suggestion. You're already on edge with the dreams and sleeping alone in a strange house – and a very old one at that. That builder bloke had already freaked out about the Grey Lady – more suggestion, judging by the legend that's passed about. And you'd been drinking by candlelight. It wasn't real, just a shadow.'

'But I knew about the basket.'

'Lucky guess.'

I pursed my lips. 'Maybe.'

I'd run out of arguments, and I really, *really* wanted her to be right.

18.

''Scuse me, love.'

I stepped aside for a strange man carrying plastic piping and watched him climb The Rookery stairs. The plumbers had arrived.

'Does that mean central heating?' Jayne asked.

'I think it might,' I replied, and knocked three times on the closest door frame.

'Wonderful.'

'I doubt it will be operational by tonight.' I laughed at the crestfallen expression on her face. 'We'll still be camping upstairs around the fan heater, I'm afraid.'

Jayne shrugged. 'Why is it so quiet?'

I stopped and listened, confused, then realised what Jayne meant. Whilst there was plenty of banging and clattering – plus the constant rumble of the generator – there were very few voices, and none of the banter I'd become used to.

'I'm not sure I want to know,' I said, glancing at the wall where I'd seen the apparition the night before. 'Come on, let's go up, out of their way.'

'Why can't you leave the generator running for us?' I asked Vikram. 'There's plenty of cable to run lights and heater.'

'Sorry, love. Health and safety. Can't run it when there's no staff on the premises – insurers won't let us.'

'But . . .'

He shrugged. 'Nowt I can do about it, love, sorry.'

'It's okay, Verity, the lamps have plenty of batteries and I'm sure we can work out how to get the camping stove running,' Jayne said.

'They'll have rooms at the White Lion or Black Bull,' Vikram said.

'No, they're booked up for Christmas,' I said. 'I was lucky to get a room last night, but it was the last one.'

Vikram nodded. 'I'll stop in later, if you want – make sure you're okay.'

'We'll be fine,' I said. 'But thank you.'

'Sparkly's not far off getting the wiring sorted,' Vikram said. 'If she doesn't finish it tomorrow, she won't be going home Friday till you have lights and heat for Christmas.'

'Thanks, Vikram.'

'No problem, goodnight.'

'Did you see the way he looked at you when he was talking about staff being on the premises?' Jayne asked once the door had closed behind him. 'He was after an invite to stay!'

'Don't be daft.'

'I'm serious – he's definitely interested.'

I shook my head. Vikram had warmed up since Monday, but he was very definitely not interested in me. 'Shall we go see if the fish and chip shop is open?' I asked to change the subject. 'Then we don't have to bother with that camping stove.'

Jayne wasn't fooled, but let it slide. We wrapped up and stepped out into the freezing December evening.

'It looks so eerie,' Jayne said. 'The way the streetlights look like old gas lamps, and the haze around them; all the stone and cobbles, it really wouldn't have looked much different a century ago.'

'Longer,' I said. 'I think the gas came in the 1860s, so that's a hundred and fifty years at least.' I shivered as we walked. 'You can almost feel the history embracing us.'

'You're not kidding,' Jayne said. 'If not for the odd parked car, I honestly wouldn't be sure *when* we are.'

'We should walk back through the graveyard,' I suggested. 'If you think this is atmospheric, try that place at night!'

'You'll not get me in there after dark! It was spooky enough in full daylight.'

I smiled. I wasn't sure 'spooky' was the right word – it was something more than that; something *heavier*.

'Thank goodness, they're frying,' Jayne interrupted my reverie. 'What are you having?'

Half an hour later, with hot food before us, glasses of wine poured, Jayne's lamps brightening my apartment, and wrapped up in sweaters and blankets, I felt at ease. I wasn't concerned about Haworth's ghosts, not in Jayne's company. I smiled at the thought that she'd shooed them away.

'What?'

'Nothing. I was just thinking how glad I am you're here.'

She grinned. 'What else are friends for but to freeze to death with you in a haunted house four days before Christmas, eating fish and chips and swilling wine?'

I laughed. 'I do appreciate it, Jayne, honestly. More than I can say.'

'I know, love.'

'Oh don't you bloody start calling me love, too!'

'That's better! I was surprised to hear you take it from Vikram.'

I ignored her raised eyebrows. 'I've given up. Anyway, one of the builders calls everyone "mush", so being called love doesn't seem so bad now. I've decided to ignore it.'

'Oh my God, it would drive me crackers!'

'How are Jenny and Michael?' I asked when the laughter had died down.

Jayne's smile relaxed and she sipped her wine. 'They're fine – great. Jenny's well on with her final year assignments, and Michael seems to be settling down at the ad firm okay.'

'Will you be seeing them over Christmas?'

'No. It's their father's turn for Christmas this year, I'll catch up with them in the New Year.'

I nodded, careful not to comment. Jayne had been divorced fifteen years and still hated her ex with a passion.

'Next year, there'll be rooms here for them too,' I said and leaned over to squeeze Jayne's hand.

She shook me off and took another bite of battered fish, making me wait until she'd finished her mouthful before replying. I refilled her glass while I waited.

'That would be lovely – I just hope they won't be too busy in their new lives. They're literally only going for the meal this year, apparently John's furious.'

She smiled and gulped her wine. I followed suit and refilled again.

'But I guess that's what happens.' Jayne visibly pulled herself together – sitting more upright and squaring her shoulders. 'They grow up, don't they, boy?' She ruffled Grasper's fur and fed him some fish.

The subject of children was still too raw for me too. 'I wonder if he'll come tonight.'

'Who, Vikram?'

'No!' I slapped her arm with the back of my hand. 'Behave. I meant the dream man.'

'Ah, Heathcliff.'

'I wish you wouldn't call him that.'

Jayne smiled. 'Well, I hope he isn't Heathcliff,' she said, standing up and clearing away the empty plates. 'You've had enough of dysfunctional men. Ow!'

I leapt to my feet at the exclamation, Grasper's frantic barking, and crash of dropped plates. 'What happened? Are you all right?'

'Someone pushed me!'

'What? Who? There's no one here!'

We looked at each other.

'Are you sure?' I asked. 'It was definitely a push?'

'Yes! Two hands on my back. I was lucky I didn't fall.'

'The floor's pretty uneven, are you sure you didn't just trip?'

Jayne stared at me, worried, then shrugged. 'Maybe. I must have done. It's just this place, it's got me spooked.'

We both jumped at a bang from the window.

'Just a bird,' she said.

I gave a shaky laugh. 'Now you know how I feel.'

We both looked at Grasper who was still very vocal and seemed to be doing a little dance; leaping and twisting, his eyes following something neither Jayne nor I could see.

'Is there more wine?' Jayne asked.

'Plenty.'

19.

'What have you found, Emily?' Branwell called from further down the hill. 'Don't go too far away, you know Papa said I'm in charge and I'm staying over here with Anne.'

Emily gave no sign of hearing her brother, and crouched motionless in the heather over the treasure she'd found.

'Can you hear them?' she asked.

'Only a little bit. How did you know I was here?' Harry asked.

Emily looked at his wooden-soled clogs, and he understood.

'I ran away from mill again,' he confided.

Emily made no reply. Harry watched her, intrigued as she studied the lapwing nest of chicks. She didn't speak to him very much, but he didn't take offence. She didn't speak to anybody very much, except her brother and sisters, and then only when she had a mind to.

He liked her silence; his world was normally filled with noise: the spinning machines at the mill, and the constant clack of the handlooms in the weaver's gallery which took up the entire top floor of the row of cottages where he and his family had their home. The clop of horses, rumble of wagon wheels and shouts of draymen on the street. And of course the little ones' cries and Ma's sobs at the house.

He lived with his eight brothers and sisters – seven now. The baby had died before even earning a name, and someone was always sickly. It was Mary and Robert at the moment, keeping everyone's nerves on edge with their constant coughing and crying. As if on cue, Harry himself coughed, feeling the tickle of the fluff from the spinning room within his throat.

'Hush.' Emily rounded on him, her little face fierce. 'You'll scare them!'

'Sorry,' Harry whispered. 'Can I see?'

Emily regarded him with large, round eyes, considering whether he was worthy of the sight, then nodded and moved aside.

Harry took her place then gasped as the dull, grey drizzle that had offered no respite for over a week turned to a sudden, drenching downpour.

The sky turned so black it almost seemed night, high on the moor above Haworth, despite it yet being early afternoon.

Harry regained his composure and bearings in the violently changed conditions, then lost them again as he saw Emily Brontë twirling in the heavy rain, arms outstretched and face turned to the sky.

'Emily, Emily, come on, we have to find shelter or we'll catch our deaths,' Branwell called, to no avail.

Branwell's small face, turned up towards them, was serious and worried, but he had Anne to take care of, and the seven-year-old took his duty very seriously. Besides, he knew just how stubborn Emily could be.

'*Emily!*' Harry saw him scream. Saw because nothing could be heard over the enormous, thunderous roar that exploded around them.

Lightning flickered, followed by a lesser thunder.

Something wasn't right.

Harry looked uphill and his mouth dropped open in shock. It was moving. The hillside was moving.

Peat, heather and rock slid towards them.

'Emily!' Harry shouted, and ran to grab her. She had seen the danger, but instead of running for safety, she was trying to gather the lapwing nest with its brood of chicks into her hands.

Harry pulled at her, but she resisted, and he had no choice but to pick up the child – thankfully small and thin for even her young age – and run, stumbling out of the path of the relentless, tumbling moorslide.

The four children, Emily still clutching the lapwing chicks, hurried along a path that would take them out of danger, and also bring them back together; Branwell dragging a screaming five-year-old Anne alongside him, and Harry still carrying Emily.

He put her down, his arms shaking, and she barely looked at him, her attention still wholly occupied by the birds. Did she not understand the danger she had been in herself?

'Emily.' Branwell sank to his knees when he reached his sister, and he and Anne clung to her. 'Is all well?'

'I think so,' Emily said, holding out the nest. 'I don't know how their parents will find them, though, they had better come home with us.'

Branwell and Harry looked at the way home. It was a river of gloopy, rocky mud.

'How will we get home?' Anne asked, her voice small and terrified.

Branwell didn't answer, but looked at Harry.

'We'll have to go round,' Harry said.

'No,' Branwell said. 'We'd have to go right round by Top Withens. That's too far, especially in the rain and with Anne. Ponden Hall is much closer. We'll go there and the Heatons can get a message to Papa. He shall come to fetch us.

'Whoever heard of an earthquake in Haworth?' the parson said when he arrived, having ascertained those of his children not yet in the custody of a school were all present and unharmed.

He stared at the lapwing nest, still protected in Emily's hands, then glared at Harry.

'Mam says it were the bog that burst,' Robert Heaton said.

'Nonsense, did you not hear it? It was an earthquake,' the parson dismissed him and his mother. 'Now, who is this?'

Harry stayed silent, scared of the stern cleric who thundered from the pulpit every Sunday. A tall figure, dressed in black with high, white collar, Harry had always been scared of him.

'Harry Sutcliffe,' Emily said. 'He works at the mill but keeps running away.'

'Does he now? You know you'll be beaten for that, boy?'

Harry nodded. 'Yes, sir.'

'He saved Emily, Papa,' Branwell said, unhappy at being left out of the conversation. 'I was with Anne, looking after her like you told me to, Papa, and Emily was up the hill with her lapwings. I told her to come, but she didn't, Papa. And then Harry came, just before the big roar, and Emily was dancing in the rain and she wouldn't come and she saved the lapwings and Harry picked her up and ran away from the bogslide.' Branwell stopped, out of breath.

His father regarded him in silence a moment, no doubt making sense of his son's rushed monologue.

'I see. Well, young Harry, it appears I and my family owe you a great debt.'

Harry looked up at him in hope. Mrs Heaton had fed them all pork and apple with hot posset when they'd arrived, soaked to the skin and shivering. Dare he ask for more food to take home for his family?

'You work at the mill, boy?'

'Yes sir.'

'Which one?'

'Rooks, sir.'

'And you do not like the work?'

'No sir.'

'But is it not good to have work so your family have food and shelter and cloth on their backs?'

'Yes sir.'

'Then why do you run away?'

'It is so loud, sir. I can't hear the lapwings call, and I cough all the time, and my brothers and sisters cough all the time, and I keep getting hurt.' He held out an arm showing thick red weals on the pale skin. 'And—'

'Enough.' Patrick Brontë held up a hand. 'I have heard enough.' He glanced at Emily.

'Do you miss the lapwings' call, Harry?'

'Yes sir.'

'Well, I cannot find you work with birds,' the parson said, and Mrs Heaton tittered. 'But the mason is looking for an apprentice. There is just too much work for him these days . . .' He lapsed into a thoughtful silence, then blinked. 'It is hard work, but skilled work and would give you a trade. Would you like that, boy?'

'Yes sir, thank you, sir.'

'Very well, report to the mason's workshop behind the parsonage first thing tomorrow morning. I shall inform your father and Mr Rook.'

'Yes sir, thank you, sir,' Harry said again, so overjoyed at not having to return to the mill, he had not yet considered that he would be carving memorials for the remainder of his life.

'What about me, Papa?' Branwell asked, a little sulkily. 'I looked after Anne and saved her. I dragged her away out of the danger, didn't I, Anne? Didn't I?'

Anne nodded. She had not spoken since reaching safety.

'I should expect nothing less from you, Branwell. It is your duty to care for your sisters.'

At Branwell's crestfallen face, his papa ruffled his hair. 'Now, let's get you all home, Tabby and Aunt Branwell are very worried about you all and are making an extra special supper for us all tonight: liver and onions. And you have earned a double helping, Branwell. What do you think of that?'

'That will do very well, Papa, thank you,' Branwell said and beamed at his father. It was his favourite.

20.

'Morning, Vikram, what's the plan for today?'

'Morning, love.'

Jayne smirked at my continued non-complaint about the generic pet name. I ignored her.

'Plumbers want to finish getting the pipe laid for the central heating so they can crack on with the pipework for the en-suites after Christmas. And Sparkly's putting the final touches to the wiring – with any luck, you'll have light and sockets by the end of the day. But it might be best to stay out of her way. Things can get a bit . . . fraught when she flicks a switch and things don't happen quite as they're supposed to.'

'I know the feeling,' Jayne muttered, and I grinned.

'I think we can all relate. Well, what do you think about visiting the museum, Jayne? I don't think Lara's too bothered about it, so it would be a good opportunity.'

'I don't mind where we go as long as we get out of here for a while.'

I glanced at her, realising she was more affected by last night than I'd appreciated.

'More ghosts?'

'Something like that.' I smiled at Vikram, took Jayne's arm and led her out of The Rookery, then stopped at Vikram's touch on my back.

'Verity?'

'Wait for me outside,' I said to Jayne, then turned to Vikram, surprised at the way my heart had speeded up at the sound of my name in his voice.

'Is everything all right?'

I shrugged. 'A bit stressful, to be honest, but that's to be expected.' I gestured at the chaos in the room.

'Are you sure that's all?'

'Yes. I'm fine, honest.'

He had no choice but to believe me, although we both knew I was lying, but I smiled, turned and left; at least for the day.

We entered the front garden of the parsonage and I almost felt Jayne's shudder.

'Jayne . . .' I started, but she shook her head, clearly not yet ready to talk about what had happened.

'I didn't realise the extent to which death surrounded the Brontë sisters,' she said after a while. 'They lived surrounded by gravestones.' She indicated the churchyard bordering two sides of the garden.

'I know, it must have been a very strange way to grow up, although of course the graveyard would have been much smaller then.'

We both looked up as the resident parliament of rooks took wing and wheeled about the memorials before settling to roost once more. Jayne shuddered again and I looped my arm through hers.

'Even though the front looks down over the older part and the church, the standing stones are newer, so it wouldn't have been so obvious they lived surrounded by graves. And there would have only been a few to the side as well. It wouldn't have been quite as grim then as it appears now.'

'Yes, but still – young kids growing up here?'

I shrugged. 'They were different times. Death was very much a part of life and childhood then, no matter where you lived. And look at the house they enjoyed – other kids their age were sleeping nine to a room, and a small room at that.' I gestured to the handsome, millstone grit building as we turned.

Framed by the moors behind, it was true that the nine windows on the front aspect regarded the church and its yard, but each was made up of smaller panes, and lined with the darker stone that picked out the corners of the building. A white portico framing the front door was in vast contrast to The Rookery – once four cottages, each housing large families.

'Come on, let's go in,' I urged. 'Enough doom and gloom. Whatever you think about its situation, wonderful books were inspired and penned here.'

'I'm starting to see why they're so bleak.'

'Come on, Jayne, this isn't like you. And I know you love *Wuthering Heights* and *Jane Eyre*.'

Jayne sighed. 'I know, you're right, sorry, I'm just a bit out of sorts this morning.'

I opened my mouth to speak as we climbed the steps to the front door, but she rushed on to stop me. 'Not yet, I don't want to talk about it yet, Verity.'

I nodded, handed our tickets in, then led the way into the Brontës' dining room and became lost in the world of Charlotte, Emily and Anne, and the tragic tale of their family and lives.

'Even the pub backs on to the graveyard,' Jayne said as we settled into our seats at the Black Bull.

'Worse than that,' I said. 'We're downhill, bordering it, and one of the village's main wells was in the backyard here.'

'You are kidding me!'

'Nope. The water from the moors filtered through the cemetery then ran into the village's drinking water.'

Jayne stared at me in horror.

'No wonder the churchyard is so full,' I said. 'Now, what would you like to drink?'

Jayne pulled a face at me. 'Something fermented, and preferably shipped in.'

'Sauvignon blanc?'

'That will do nicely.'

I fetched two glasses and a bottle, which Jayne frowned at.

'I know its lunchtime, but it's nearly Christmas.' I smiled.

Jayne paused and said, 'It's strange to think those wonderful books were all plotted and written in that dining room. I could almost see Charlotte, Emily and Anne walking around the table in a frenzy of creativity, skirts swishing.'

'They didn't have much room, did they?'

'I guess they didn't need it,' Jayne said. 'They needed each other more.'

'Yes, it was interesting to see all that stuff about Angria and Gondal, the fantasy lands they created together as children.'

'I know, and those tiny books!'

'No wonder there's so much fascination about the sisters and their lives,' I said. 'The whole family certainly did things their own way.'

'You can say that again. Can you imagine waking up to your father discharging a pistol out the window every morning?'

'Not really.' I laughed. 'That's one hell of an alarm call!'

'It must have been awful to live every day – and night – in fear, and if the father felt it, the children must have too.'

'Yes, I guess the threat posed by Luddites and campaigners against the working conditions in the mills was a lot deeper than I thought.'

We both sipped our wine, then I tried to lighten the mood. 'What did you think about the décor? I want to decorate the rooms at The Rookery in the same style, although keep each different and original.'

'That sounds like a great idea, and very appropriate given the building's age and location.'

'Yes. I also thought about naming the rooms rather than numbering them, just because everything's on different levels and numbers wouldn't flow – they could cause more confusion than assistance. What do you think about Charlotte's Room, Emily's Room etcetera?'

'A bit clichéd isn't it?' Jayne asked. 'Might be a bit over the top.'

I shrugged. 'Maybe. I'll give it some more thought.'

'Are you ready to order?'

'Oh, sorry,' I said to the waitress. 'Too busy chatting, can we have a couple of minutes?'

'Of course.'

We sat in silence to study the menu, ordered our food, then I topped up our glasses and looked at Jayne, my eyebrows raised in silent question.

21.

'It was a definite push, Verity.' Jayne took another gulp of wine. 'I felt hands, and they had force. How can that be?'

'I don't know, Jayne. Maybe Lara can shed some light on it when she gets here tomorrow.'

'Has anything like that happened to you?'

I shook my head. 'Just the dreams, which are getting more vivid, and seeing the Grey Lady.'

'But you've been touched?'

I said nothing.

'Verity?'

I took a deep breath, then a sip of my own wine, then nodded. 'A couple of days ago. In the shower.'

'In the *shower*?'

'Yes, but it wasn't trying to hurt me, it was more of a caress.'

'So, let me get this straight.' Jayne pressed together her index fingers to emphasize her first point. 'The Grey Lady, supposedly Emily Brontë, has only been seen occasionally over the years, yet has appeared twice in the last two days to two different people.'

She moved to her second finger. 'You're dreaming about the same man every night, and occasionally the Brontës as children as well.'

I nodded.

'Three. You're getting caresses while wide awake and I was pushed by invisible hands. So what does that tell us? Verity—?'

I'd stopped listening, jumped up, knocking the table, and rushed out of the pub. I stood staring down Main Street when Jayne caught up with me.

'Verity? What is it? You're white as a sheet.'

'I thought I saw . . .'

'Hey!' The waitress had dashed after us, holding two plates of food. 'You haven't paid!'

'Sorry,' Jayne said. 'My friend was taken ill. It's okay, we're not doing a runner, we'll be right there.'

The girl looked at us dubiously, then behind us at our table and realised our coats were still there. She went back inside, carrying our lunch.

'Verity?' Jayne said. 'What happened?'

'I just . . . I thought I saw . . .' I stopped, not quite sure now what I'd seen. 'Sorry, Jayne, I thought I saw the man I've been dreaming about, but he was gone by the time I got outside.'

'You saw his ghost?'

'No, I don't think so. He was wearing jeans and a parka, no Victorian costume.' I shivered. 'Come on, let's go back in.'

'Okay, but I want to know every detail about the dreams. Something is going on here and it's escalating. I have a bad feeling. Oh, and there's no way we're sleeping there tonight. If the White Lion's still booked up, we'll find rooms elsewhere.'

'*Everywhere's* bloody haunted around here. You'll not get away from Haworth's ghosts that easily.' I managed a laugh and followed Jayne back into the Black Bull, though I had lost my appetite.

I regarded the age-blackened wood panelling which had been hacked into to accommodate modern plug sockets, and the uneven stone flags that had been shined by centuries of shuffling feet and which were now breaking away to reveal more stone beneath. The building was a complex jigsaw of colour, texture, age and use, and I wondered just how many ghosts were resident here, too.

The waitress gave us a funny look as she checked on us and watched Jayne pick up her phone despite our half-full plates. 'There *was* a bog burst,' she said. 'On Crow Hill in 1824. And Patrick Brontë *did* think it was an earthquake.' She looked up at me. 'If that's true, the rest is likely to be as well, but I don't see how we can check it.'

'What about the name? Harry Sutcliffe.'

'Nothing comes up online, but it's a common enough name. We could have a look at gravestones, see if we can find him.'

I shuddered, remembering the altar grave I had sat on in error. The name on that had been Sutcliffe. 'But even if Harry is real and I am dreaming real events, that doesn't explain the caress in the shower or the push last night.'

'No,' Jayne mused. 'Oh God, I wish Lara were here, this is more up her street than mine.'

'I know, but it's good to talk about it now. You know what she's like, she'll get all excited and carried away and I could really do with getting my head round it all first.'

'I don't think there's much chance of that,' Jayne said. 'By the sounds of it, the story your dream man is telling you has only just started.'

'You think he's telling me a story?'

'Isn't he?'

I shrugged.

'Well, whether he is or isn't, maybe you should keep a dream diary. It might help us put the pieces together and understand what's happening.'

'That's a good idea,' I said. 'We'll stop off at the Tourist Information shop on the way back to The Rookery and I'll pick up a notebook.'

'Verity?'

I looked up to see Vikram. 'What is it? Is anything wrong?'

'No, not wrong, but Sparkly's panicking a bit over the security cameras. She needs you to confirm exactly where you want them.'

'Cameras?' Jayne asked.

'Yes, I'll be running the place on my own so I'll need to be able to see the public areas and front door from the kitchen and my apartment. There's the security aspect too.'

Jayne nodded, and I scrunched up my napkin.

'Oh, finish your meal first, love. Sparkly will wait – as long as she knows you'll be back after dinner.'

I nodded and smiled at him and he took his leave.

'If your dream man is jealous of *me*, that guy had better watch out,' Jayne said.

'Oh Jayne, stop it.'

'You like him, I can see it in your face.'

'It doesn't matter. I'm not ready, not after Antony, it's still all too raw.' I sipped my wine and shared out the remainder of the bottle. 'Drink up, it could be a trying afternoon.'

'Things have been trying enough already,' Jayne said, picking up her glass. 'I'm not sure I can cope with more just yet.'

22.

'Coffee, please,' Jayne said. 'Plenty of it and keep it coming.'

The waitress – Tess – smiled. 'No problem, I'll bring the pot. And for you?' she asked me.

'I'll share her coffee,' I said.

Tess glanced at Jayne. 'I'll make it a large pot.' She visibly relaxed as Jayne smiled.

'Are you always this grumpy in the morning?'

'Only until my third cup of coffee. Ah, at last.'

I glanced up at Tess with an apologetic smile. She really could not have been any quicker. I dreaded to think how Jayne had behaved earlier when she'd taken Grasper out while I was still getting ready.

Jayne poured, sipped hers – black and scalding – and sighed, her shoulders discernibly lowering to a more natural posture.

'All right now?'

'Much better. I'm so glad there was a cancellation and my room was available a day early.'

'And that it's a twin,' I added.

'Definitely. You know we can share for the rest of my visit, too.'

'What, and face a coffee-less Jayne every morning? I'd rather deal with the ghosts over the road!'

Jayne scowled at me, then laughed. 'Well, it's up to you – the offer's there.'

'Thank you. I do mean that, Jayne. But The Rookery is my home, I need to claim it.'

Jayne nodded. 'That makes sense. But wasn't it a relief not to dream? I'm also worried about that push – if whatever it is, is getting violent, you might not be safe.'

'He's not been violent to me – quite the opposite – and there's never been any hint of threat from the Grey Lady either.'

Jayne pursed her lips. I didn't want to tell her my nightly visitor could find me here.

'Anyway, this place is haunted too, you know.'

'What?'

'Yes, a balloonist who died in the '20s, Lily Cove. She fell to her death on the moors and apparently still haunts her old room at the White Lion.'

'Which room?' Jayne had gone very still.

'Seven, I think.'

She relaxed again. She was in Room Six. 'Is there anywhere *not* haunted in Haworth?'

'I doubt it. There's a lot of history here, and much death over the centuries, much of it . . . unpleasant.'

'What do you mean?'

'Well, Lily for one. Then there's a witch's house up the road connected to Pendle. And don't forget all the mills, the accidents and lung diseases there, plus horrendous living conditions: overcrowding, bad water, shared privies, TB, cholera and all sorts of other diseases.'

Jayne shuddered. 'But it's such a pretty, picturesque village.'

'Well yes, it is now. Wasn't so great living here in the 1800s.'

'So what do you think about that Sparkly woman yesterday?'

I raised my eyebrows at Jayne's abrupt change of subject, then shrugged.

'She's normally lovely, I don't know why she's been in such a bad mood the last couple of days. I guess she's just under pressure with such an old and complicated building to rewire.'

'Strange her tools keep going missing, though. You don't think your ghosts are stepping up their game?'

Ah, so it hadn't really been a change of subject after all. 'I doubt it, it'll be the lads winding her up – they seem to really like her, but are constantly on her back.'

'Or hope to be.' Jayne sniggered and I laughed with her.

'Probably, yes.'

'Come on, let's order some food.'

'It was strange Vikram turning up like that last night,' Jayne mused, as she refilled her cup.

I shrugged. 'It's a small village – no real surprise we bumped into him in one of the main pubs.'

'I suppose,' Jayne said, smiled at me, then focused on the rest of her breakfast.

'Lara's just texted,' Jayne said as we approached the door to The Rookery. 'She'll be here after lunch.'

'Great,' I said, then looked up as a flock of birds cawed above us. 'I wonder what she'll make of everything that's been happening.'

Jayne groaned. 'I don't even want to think about it. She'll be in seventh heaven and having us do all sorts of weird and wonderful stuff. We'll be like *Ghost Adventures* or *Most Haunted*!'

'We might get some answers,' I said as I pushed open the door to my guesthouse and stopped dead.

Sparkly was in full flow, ranting about missing tools and cable, the lads shuffling awkwardly, trying to defend themselves, but only succeeding in angering Sparkly further. Even Vikram looked lost for what to do.

'What's going on?' I asked, and was ignored.

Jayne slammed the door and I asked again, this time at the top of my voice, and hush descended over the rabble of squabbling tradesmen and -woman.

Sparkly took a deep breath, faced me, and opened her mouth, no doubt to begin her tirade afresh, but Vikram stepped in front of her.

'The cameras have disappeared,' he explained. 'Expensive ones.'

Sparkly shouted over him, 'And I know you guys have done it for a joke, but it's gone too far. I need to get them all up today. I've got everything else finished. There's only the cameras left to fit, then I'll be done – I want to finish today. Just tell me where they are, you buggers!'

Vikram held up a placating hand. 'I'm not denying we don't wind you up for a laugh – but none of us want to hold the job up. The sooner we get done, the sooner we get off for the Christmas break. Nobody's taken the blasted cameras. They must be here somewhere.'

'I've looked top to bottom, and in every damned cranny in the place!' Sparkly stamped her foot and Vikram's face reddened.

'I suggest you look again, start at the top.'

She opened her mouth to argue, then shut it again. Vikram had turned away from me so I couldn't see his new expression. Judging by Sparkly's about turn, followed by the rest of the gang, it was probably just as well.

He turned back to me. 'Sorry about that. Things are just a bit fraught for her around Christmas – family stuff, you know.'

I nodded, I was feeling a bit fraught myself to be facing my first Christmas as a divorcée – but at least I had good friends around me.

'How is everything else coming on?' I asked.

'Pretty good, actually,' Vikram said. 'We're a little behind, but not much. Sparkly's got all the sockets and lights working, and the plumbers are well on with the new pipes for the en-suites. I was hoping to have all that done before Christmas, but we're not quite there I'm afraid. Nothing to worry about though,' he added hastily. 'It's to be expected in an old building. We'll have you ready to open on time. It's just these blasted cameras . . .' he tailed off.

'I'll help you look,' I said. 'Sorry, not much fun for you.' I glanced at Jayne.

'Don't worry, I need to take Grasper for a long walk, get rid of most of his energy before Lara and Hannah arrive.'

I nodded. 'That sounds like a good idea – he'll likely tear the place up again if you don't. Joke,' I added, seeing the look on Vikram's face. 'He'll be fine.'

'He'd have to face that lot if he isn't,' Vikram said, jerking his thumb at the stairs, still flooded by the sound of animosity.

I grimaced.

'He'll behave,' Jayne said. 'Verity's just having you on.'

'I'd like to get some mince pies and mulled wine in as well, just as a thank you for everyone working so close to Christmas.'

'They'd like that, although would probably prefer cans of Stella and Black Sheep to mulled wine,' Vikram said. 'Have a word with them at the Black Bull, they'll sort you out. Assuming we find those damned cameras, we'll be done by two.'

'Great, I'll sort it for then. Would you split this between everyone too?' I passed him an envelope.

He laughed. 'They'll appreciate that even more! Thank you.'

'One way to make sure they'll come back in the new year,' Jayne said.

'Oh, go and walk your dog. And have another coffee.' I smiled to take the sting out of my words, realising the atmosphere of the constant arguing was getting to me. 'Sorry,' I added. 'I'm feeling a bit on edge with all this going on.'

Jayne nodded and gave me a hug, then called to Grasper who, we just noticed, was once more doing his crazy dance – presumably chasing more invisible balls of light.

23.

'Everyone seems much happier,' I remarked to Vikram, watching the build team tuck in. The Black Bull had been more than happy to cater the beer and wine, and one of the local cafés had done us proud with sandwiches and nibbles. Everything looked . . . festive, despite The Rookery being more building site than guesthouse.

'Yes the cameras turned up, and we all pitched in. Sparkly's relaxed, and that makes all the difference.' He swigged from his can and I wasn't quite sure how light-hearted his comment truly was. I decided to ignore it and mentally apologised to Sparkly for my lack of female solidarity.

'Where were they in the end?'

'Well, that's the strange thing,' Vikram said. 'They were on the top stairs – that's what all the shouting was about earlier. One camera on each tread. Cables neatly coiled, all very carefully. Sparkly went ape.'

'So had one of the guys done it to wind her up?'

'I don't see how. She'd searched the place top to bottom, there's nowhere they could have hidden them – then they were set out in plain view. No one's been on their own, and everybody swears it wasn't them. I believe them.'

'Sounds like your ghost is playing tricks.'

I swung round at the familiar voice. 'Lara! How wonderful to see you!' We hugged, then I released her to hug Hannah while Jayne embraced Lara.

'How long have you been standing there?'

'Long enough to hear you've been having fun and games without me, and apparently not long enough for anyone to offer me a drink.'

'Oh sorry! Mulled wine?' I turned to pour her a glass without waiting for her nod. 'What's up with you anyway? It's not like you to wait until you're asked – you certainly know you don't need to stand on ceremony here.'

Lara shrugged. 'You have company, I was trying to make a good impression.'

'That ship sailed with your ghost comment,' Jayne said, laughing. 'Seriously though, it's good to see you.'

Lara raised her eyebrows. 'Why do I get the feeling I don't know even half of what's been going on?'

Jayne and I shrugged in unison, and Lara narrowed her eyes but checked her curiosity for the time being and turned to her daughter who was tapping her arm, trying to get her attention.

'Can I take Grasper for a walk, Mummy? Can I? Can I?'

'You'd best ask Aunt Jayne.'

'Can I, Aunt Jayne, can I take him walkies? Pleeeaasse.'

'Well, now you've said the magic word—'

'What, walkies?' I said, laughing as I indicated Grasper's excited and downright manic circling.

Jayne smiled. 'Of course you can. Just watch out for that Main Street – I took him down there earlier and it was lovely. The only problem was getting back up it!'

The adults laughed, but Hannah looked confused. 'Why? It's just a hill.'

The laughter died and Jayne held out the Irish terrier's lead with a resigned smile. 'Now I feel old,' she said. 'From the mouths of babes . . .'

'I'm not a babe, I'm ten!' Hannah said, full of indignation. She clipped on Grasper's lead and marched out of The Rookery, head held unnaturally high.

'You've got a right one there,' Vikram said.

'Oh, Lara's more than a match for her,' Jayne said. 'She keeps us all on our toes, though – doesn't let us get away with anything!'

We all sipped our drinks, then Lara said, 'Oh, I meant to tell you, Verity – you need to get some netting or spikes on the window ledges and gutters. You know, the ones town centres use to keep the pigeons from roosting and messing up the front of the buildings.'

Vikram scowled. 'We don't really have much problem with pigeons here – the buzzards tend to scare them off.'

'Well, whatever they are, there's loads of birds perching outside. I dread to think what your window cleaning bill will be if you don't sort it out.'

Jayne and I looked at each other in confusion. 'I haven't noticed anything,' I said.

'No, nor me,' Vikram added. 'Let me go and have a look.'

'Good idea,' Jayne said, and we moved to the door.

'Mistletoe!' someone shouted from behind us – Omar or Gary, I'm not sure, and the build team filled the place with laughter as Vikram and Jayne looked up to see the offending greenery with white berries hanging over the doorway.

'Bad luck not to give her a kiss, boss,' Gary – definitely Gary this time – called.

'They won't stop,' Vikram said to Jayne and she gave a slight nod to permit his peck on her cheek, then glanced at me in a mixture of apology and embarrassment.

I smiled and we trooped outside – in single file.

'Worse than Spin the Bloody Bottle,' Lara muttered.

Outside we looked up and I gasped. Every window ledge, door lintel, the edge of the roof – every available roost – was occupied. I had a brief flashback to Daphne du Maurier's *The Birds*, then shook myself. They weren't doing anything, they weren't threatening, and they weren't attacking.

All the same, the sight of so many rooks, wing to wing, was unnerving.

'I've never seen owt like it,' Vikram said.

'What made you call this place, The Rookery, Verity?' Lara asked. 'Where did the name come from?'

I shrugged. 'I don't know really, I was playing around with more Brontë-like names, Wildfell, Thrushcross, that kind of thing, then The Rookery popped into my head and just kind of stuck.'

We stayed staring at the façade of the building for a minute or two more, then the build team emerged – in single file again to avoid the mistletoe – to say their thanks and goodbyes.

'I'll leave you to it as well, ladies. Happy Christmas,' Vikram said.

Lara, Jayne and I returned the greeting then went back inside and I topped up our glasses.

'I think you two had better tell me exactly what's been going on,' said Lara.

24.

'There's something you're not telling me,' Lara said, looking at Jayne after I'd told her about my dreams, the touch in the shower, and the sightings of the Grey Lady. 'Jayne, you're too quiet, and too accepting of everything. Why haven't you made any jokes or suggested rational explanations?'

Jayne shrugged, clearly uncomfortable, but said nothing.

'Something happened to you too, didn't it?'

'I don't know. Maybe. It was probably nothing.'

'Jayne?'

She sighed. 'Verity, you tell her.'

I wasn't sure if she was scared, in denial, or just reluctant to admit what had happened after years of poking fun at Lara for believing just this kind of thing. Whatever was going on with her, I did not want to make things harder, and told Lara about the push.

'Do you feel safe here?'

I was surprised at Lara's response, but nodded. I did feel safe. I was curious and confused, but I didn't feel threatened.

'No.' Jayne's reply was unequivocal. 'And I worry about Verity staying here. I think she should sell up.'

'What?'

'Something's going on, Verity – something strange, something powerful, and even if you feel safe, I don't. I could have been badly hurt. The builders don't like it here either – one's run off already and the others all keep falling out, and it's centred around this place and you. You've only been here a couple of weeks and it's escalating. I think you should go.'

'Verity?'

I was flabbergasted and needed Lara's prompt to gather my thoughts. 'I can't go. Look at the place, I could never resell with it like this, and I've invested everything into it. Anyway, I don't want to move.' I sat back and folded my arms.

'To be honest, it sounds like it may already be too late,' Lara said.

'What do you mean? How can it be too late?' Jayne asked.

'There are different types of hauntings,' Lara began. 'Take the Grey Lady – from the sound of it, she's a residual impression of something that happened a hundred and fifty years ago. It may be something that happened often and regularly, or maybe something else happened around the woman – whether she's Emily Brontë or not – that has kept her stuck in that action. It's almost recorded into the fabric of the building – a bit like the way sound used to be recorded on to iron oxide in the days of cassette tapes. There's no interaction, no consciousness there, just a repetitive image.'

'Okay,' Jayne said, drawing the syllables out. 'I guess that makes sense.'

To her credit, Lara didn't bat an eyelid at this apparent acceptance of her theory. 'But the man – the man's different. He's communicating – at first just with Verity and through her dreams, but he's getting stronger. The dreams are becoming more focused, he's touched not only Verity, but you too, Jayne, and I think he's connected to Verity rather than the building. He's sentient, and if Verity leaves, I think there's a good chance he'd go with her.'

'But he didn't last night,' Jayne objected. 'Verity didn't dream about him last night when we stayed at the White Lion.'

'He may have overexerted himself, weakened himself. Plus you were both relaxed, focused on each other, and I'm guessing had quite a bit to drink.'

'Well . . .'

'That's a yes then. Even if you did dream about him, Verity, your sleep could have been so deep that you just can't remember it.'

'Oh. Yeah, I guess.' I wasn't sure if the prospect of having to drink to silence him was more unsettling than the idea that if I did drink, I would miss him.

'Talking of drink, I need a refill,' Jayne said, rose and fetched a bottle of merlot. On her way back to our makeshift seats of sawhorses and trestles that Vikram and the team had left us, she stopped, visibly shook herself, then rushed over.

'You're freaking me out,' she complained.

'What happened?'

'I just came over all cold.'

Lara stood and moved around the same area that had frozen Jayne. 'A cold spot. He's here.'

'Well, tell him to go!'

Lara slowly shook her head at Jayne as she returned to her seat. 'No. He's here for a reason. We need to find out what that is, then maybe we can help him and he'll leave us alone.'

'What if what he wants is Verity?'

We looked at each other – Lara and I now sharing Jayne's fear.

'Then we protect her,' Lara said at last.

Neither Jayne nor I asked her how. We were both too scared that she may not have an answer.

'So what do we do?' I asked after more silence.

'We find out all we can about this place and the people who lived here,' Lara said. 'We do our research – books, the museum, and is there a ghost walk or anything? This is a tourist village, there must be a ghost walk.'

'Yes, there is,' I said. 'But I don't think they're running at the moment, we may have to wait until the New Year.'

'Well, I'll get stuck into the books and Google,' Jayne said. 'You two can do the ghost walk, then all of us can go to the museum again – I'll find out when it's open over Christmas and the New Year, and if we can access their library.'

'Oh ghost walk, ghost walk! Can I go on the ghost walk, pleeaasse?'

'Hans, are you sure?' Lara turned to greet her daughter as Grasper hurled himself at Jayne. 'It might be scary.'

'I'm not scared of stupid ghosts. Anyway, Grasper will look after us.'

'Well, okay, if you're sure, but tell me if you get too scared and Auntie Verity will bring you back here, okay? I need to stay to the end of it, I don't want to miss any of the stories.'

'I won't get scared, Mummy, promise. Can we go tonight, can we? Can we?'

'No, not tonight, Hans, we'll have to find out when the next one is. Anyway we're all a bit tired, we'll just have a nice evening together and an early night.'

'Okay, Mum.' Hannah looked crestfallen. 'Do you promise we will do it, though?'

'I promise.'

'Hans,' Jayne said, 'did you see the birds when you came in, are they still there?'

'What birds?'

Jayne breathed a visible sigh of relief.

'Mum, what's Grasper doing?'

We turned and looked. Hackles up, growling – something I couldn't remember hearing him do before – Grasper had placed himself between us and the cold spot Jayne and Lara had found earlier. He did not like whatever it was he could see.

25.

Harry stood back watching Uriah Barraclough – the master stonemason and the man he was now apprenticed to – and John Brown, the sexton, push the tiny coffin into its final resting place within the Brontë family vault underneath the church.

Opened just four years ago for Maria, the parson's wife, ten-year-old Elizabeth had now joined her mother and elder sister,

Her father, Patrick, remained stoic and calm, but Harry had already seen enough pain etched into too many faces not to recognise the same in his.

And no wonder. When his wife died he had been left with six children to care for. Now, consumption had taken the two eldest within little more than a month. What would become of those surviving: Charlotte, Branwell, Emily and Anne?

Harry risked a small smile at Emily, but she turned her head. He kicked himself. It was hardly the place for a smile.

He concentrated on watching Mr Barraclough and Mr Brown carefully secure Elizabeth's carved memorial in place next to those of her sisters, then they stood back and the Reverend Brontë cleared his throat to speak.

I woke with a sob. *Those poor girls. That poor family.*

I rose, went to the loo, washed my face, and took a long drink of water. Maybe Jayne had been right and I should have joined them at the White Lion after all.

No. I shook my head to emphasise the thought. This was my new home, my new business, my new life. I could not run away from a few dreams. I pushed thoughts of caresses, pushes, orbs, cold spots and Grasper's odd behaviour out of my mind and went back to bed, accidentally on purpose leaving the bathroom light on and pretending not to notice.

Harry found Emily in one of her favourite places; the little waterfall only half a mile up the moors, over the clapper bridge. She was sitting on a rock and staring at the summer trickle of water, her new puppy, Grasper, at her feet. Harry suspected she would find a wild winter torrent more to her taste today.

'How do,' he said, and she grunted.

'It's hard,' Harry tried again, 'when a sister dies. I remember when our Rebekah went last year, it were like a light had gone out of the world.'

'Two,' Emily said.

'Beg pardon?'

'Two sisters. *Two* sisters died. *Two* sisters in their coffins. *Two* sisters in the vault. Two, two, two, *two*!'

She jumped to her feet and ran through the heather – her sure feet jumping from tussock to tussock as she somehow kept her skirts away from the grasping branches of the tough, hardy plants.

The inevitable happened and she fell.

'Emily!' Harry cried. He had been following as quickly as he could, but heather was not easy to run through – poor little Grasper had to bound in a series of jumps to make any headway.

Harry reached down to help his friend up, and she kicked and scratched. 'Don't touch me, don't touch me, get away!'

He sat next to her and stared, waiting for her to calm down.

'I still miss Rebekah,' he said. 'And Charlie, and John.'

'Who's John?'

'The babby. Died before he got a name really, but I allus think of him as John. Don't know why.'

Emily sat up. 'I remember Rebekah. She cried when Black Tom caught a chaffinch.' Black Tom was Emily's cat. Even by age seven she'd collected a menagerie of stray and injured animals, not all of them four-legged. 'I liked her.'

Harry nodded. 'The consumption took her too.'

Emily pulled Grasper on to her lap and tugged on his ears in affection. 'It was that school. That school killed them. I'm not going back, neither's Charlotte. They can't make us.'

Neither spoke, knowing full well that Emily and Charlotte had no choice in the matter.

'I want to be here,' Emily said. 'Nowhere else. I just want to be here. In Haworth, on the moors. Here.'

Harry shuffled sideways and put his arm around her. 'I want thee to stay here too,' he said. Emily relaxed into his embrace and sobbed her grief for her beloved sisters.

Harry was just glad she couldn't see the tears on his own face.

26.

'Morning, ladies. Happy Christmas Eve,' I said as I opened the door to my friends. We all looked up, startled at the thrash of wings, and a dark cloud lifted to the sky.

Hannah ducked as the rooks rose overhead and all three dashed into safety as Grasper raced around in circles, barking at the birds.

'I think you're right about that pigeon netting, Lara,' I said.

'You might need spikes to deter that lot,' Jayne said.

'I'll get Vikram on to it as soon as they're back at work,' I promised.

'Ugh,' Hannah said. 'One's messed on me!'

We laughed then immediately sobered as the child neared tears.

'Don't worry, Hans, it's supposed to be good luck,' Lara said. 'Take your jacket off and we'll give it a good wash.'

'Yes, the new washing machine is working,' I said. 'Come on up and I'll put the kettle on.'

'Oh goody, I'm ready for a coffee,' Jayne said, and Lara and I laughed.

'When are you not?' I spluttered.

'You know, when we came down this morning, the breakfast staff had a pot ready brewed and waiting for her.'

'Well-trained,' Jayne said.

'Terrified of you more like – you've only been here a couple of days and you have your name on a coffee pot!'

We laughed again – even Hannah – the tension broken.

'They had a cup-to-go ready for me when I took Grasper out first thing,' Jayne admitted, 'with two extra shots.'

'Do you bleed red or coffee brown?' Lara asked sweetly.

'Definitely red,' Jayne answered, 'but the nurses swore they could smell coffee brewing last time I donated blood!'

Laughing, we reached my rooms and I filled the kettle.

'Guess which room Lara and Hannah have,' Jayne said after she'd taken a scalding sip.

'No,' I said. 'You're not in Room Seven?'

'Yep,' Lara said, hugging Hannah to her. 'Aunt Jayne told us all about the stories at breakfast.' She glared at Jayne. 'But it's a lovely room, isn't it, Hans?'

Hannah nodded but said nothing.

'Come on, give me that jacket – I'll rinse it off and get it in the wash,' I said. 'You can borrow one of mine if you want to take Grasper out later, okay, Hans?'

Lara handed me the jacket as Hannah nodded and slid to the floor to play with Grasper, looking a bit more cheerful.

'What the hell is that noise?' Jayne asked, lifting the sash window and leaning out. 'Oh, Christ!'

'What is it?' I joined her at the window, closed my eyes and sighed.

Antony's car was blocking the narrow lane, and neither he nor the man trying to drive in the opposite direction were giving way.

'That's all I bloody need,' I muttered.

'Do you want us to go and give you some privacy?' Lara asked.

'No – thanks, Lara, but no. You are invited, he is not; you are the ones I want to spend my Christmas with, not him. He is not chasing you out of my home, no way.'

She nodded, but cast Hannah a worried glance.

I looked out of the window again. The men had sorted out who owned which bit of the road, Antony had parked up, and was hammering at the door.

'I'd best go and see what he wants,' I said, 'before he upsets the rest of the neighbours.'

'Happy Christmas!' Antony beamed and held out a box.

I looked at him, stared at the box – unwrapped – for a moment, then lifted my eyes back to his. 'What are you doing here?'

'I just wanted to wish you well,' he said. 'It is the season of goodwill after all.'

I arched my eyebrows at that.

'It's a Christmas tree.'

'What?'

He waggled the box. 'Just a small one. I didn't think you'd have had time for decorations or anything and thought it might brighten the place up for you. First Christmas . . .' He faltered and reddened.

'First Christmas alone, you mean?'

He cast his eyes down briefly then gave me a small smile. 'For both of us. I just hoped, well . . .'

'Yes?'

'Well, that we could start afresh, you know, put the divorce behind us and move forward.'

I stared at him. 'You want us to move forward? What – get back together?'

'No.' He squeezed his eyes shut a moment then said softly, 'No, I don't mean that, I know we're over. But we shared a lot of years together, a lot of laughs, and yes a lot of tears, but we had some good times. I just don't want us to be strangers.'

I nodded in understanding, but wasn't ready to respond to that. 'You'd better come in.'

He looked around the lobby, horrified at the mess and all the work that still needed to be done.

'I've only been in a couple of weeks,' I said, angry with myself for feeling defensive. 'The build team have worked like Trojans to create this chaos.'

He disguised his mocking smile with a sage nod. 'When do you open?'

'Easter, all being well. There'll be a lounge and breakfast room down here, plus a bedroom through there, and a kitchen of course.' I led the way to the stairs, pointing out the rooms as I went.

'Will it be ready in time?'

'Early days yet, but I don't see why not.' I tapped the wooden bannister three times for luck, then started to climb, before stooping to pick up an iPad from the next tread. I looked at it in confusion for a moment, I was sure it hadn't been there on the way down. 'The electricians are more or less done, and the plumbing and partition walls for the en-suites started. As long as everyone comes back to work after Christmas and don't let the ghosts scare them off, I'll be fine.'

'Ghosts? You're kidding, aren't you?'

I shook my head, annoyed at myself for opening up to him, even a little.

He seemed happy to drop the spectral subject though, and opened one of the doors I'd indicated as we passed. 'Good-sized room this.' He crossed to the window and peered out. 'Oh, is that the parsonage?'

'Yes, great view, isn't it?'

'One of the best.' He walked towards me and I backed out of the doorway and continued up the next flight of stairs to my private quarters, Antony following close behind, still carrying the box.

'And these are my rooms,' I said, stopping in and turning just in time to catch his look of dismay as he spotted Lara and Jayne.

27.

'Oh, hello,' he said to the cold glares he was greeted with, then glanced at me. 'Not a Christmas alone after all then.'

'No, I'm not alone,' I replied. 'You can put the tree down over there.'

'Tree? Is it a Christmas tree, Uncle Tony?' Hannah asked, and I winced at the 'uncle'.

'It is, do you want to help me put it up?'

'We can do that later,' Lara said.

'Of course. I can't stay long anyway, I'm on a split shift, and the restaurant's full tonight.'

'Would you like a coffee?' I asked, depositing the iPad on the table.

He glanced at Lara and Jayne, then shrugged. 'Sure, why not?'

I glared at Jayne to warn her not to answer that question, and went to fill the kettle.

'You could have told me *they* were here,' Antony hissed in my ear and I jumped. I hadn't heard him follow me.

'Why? Our lives are separate now, Antony. I don't need to run things past you or check with you before I make a decision or plan, *or* invite my friends to stay.'

'I know, but you could have warned me downstairs, I wouldn't have come up.'

'Why, too ashamed to face us?' Jayne approached us.

Antony said nothing.

'Hannah and I are going to take Grasper for his walk,' Lara said, and I smiled at her in apology, recognising her desire to get Hannah away from the souring atmosphere and threatening argument.

'Check in my wardrobe for a jacket for her,' I said. 'My fleece should be in there.'

'Thanks, Auntie Verity. Bye, Uncle Tony.'

'Bye Hannah, happy Christmas.'

She ran over and gave Antony a quick hug before Lara could stop her, then turned her attention to the increasingly agitated Irish terrier. Come on, Grasper, walkies!'

Hannah and the dog pounded down the stairs as Lara collected my fleece, looked at Antony but said nothing, then followed her daughter.

Silence filled The Rookery, and we sipped coffee.

'You're right, Jayne,' Antony said at last. 'I am ashamed, I deeply regret the way I hurt Verity.'

Jayne snorted. 'Only because you were caught. How could you do it? Lie and cheat all that time?'

A red flush of anger crept up Antony's neck and jaw. 'I don't have to justify myself to you. I've already been through this with Verity. We're divorced, I've paid for my mistakes, just leave it.'

'Just leave it? Are you kidding? Lara and I were the ones who picked up the pieces while you indulged in your fantasy life.'

'I'm not doing this with you, Jayne. It's between me and Verity.'

'No, it isn't. You mess with her, you mess with me.'

'Jayne, please, it's all over and done with. Leave it,' I said.

'No, I will not leave it!' She slammed her mug down and looked at me, 'Don't you remember what it was like, Verity? You were a wreck.'

'Jayne, please,' I said, glancing at Antony in embarrassment. I did not want him to hear this.

The twitch of his mouth sent a chill down my back. Was he amused? Pleased? *Proud*? My eyes narrowed and I clenched my jaw in an effort to refuse my emotions.

'And what the hell were you thinking, turning up here, at Verity's new home, new *life*, and on Christmas Eve? Haven't you done enough? Can't you just stick to your cheap tarts and leave Verity alone to get on with her life?'

'We broke up.'

'I bloody know you broke up! She found you out and kicked you out for God's sake, that's hardly news.'

'You broke up? With *her*?' I interrupted Jayne. If anyone was going to argue with my ex-husband, it should be me, not her, however passionately, and I was letting the side down.

Antony nodded and a feeling of vindictive smug satisfaction spread through me – echoed on Jayne's face with the ugliest smile I had ever seen her pull.

'So did she check your phone too?'

Antony paled but said nothing.

'And so you've come crawling back to Verity,' Jayne sneered. 'I wouldn't expect anything better from you. Did you think she'd warm your bed for you while you trawled the Net for your next bint?'

'I thought nothing of the sort,' Antony retorted. 'I just came to wish her a happy Christmas.'

'I am here you know,' I said, my emotions finally under control.

'Well, you're too late,' Jayne said in triumph as if neither of us had spoken. 'She's already moved on.'

'What?' Antony and I said together.

'Am I interrupting?'

I whirled round to see Vikram standing in the doorway.

'I – er – I've misplaced my tablet,' he said into the sudden silence. 'I need it to work out the wages. I must have left it here somewhere.'

'Hi, Vikram, sorry,' I managed to say, quite calmly. 'This is Antony, my ex-husband. Um, yes, I found it on the stairs, I meant to ring you.' I crossed over to the table to pass it to him.

'On the stairs? What was it doing there?'

I shrugged.

'Anyway, thanks. I'll leave you to it.' He glanced at Jayne and Antony, recoiled from the animosity of Antony's stare, then glared back until Antony dropped his eyes. 'Well, thanks again.' He waved the iPad at me. 'Have a good Christmas, and I'll see you next week.' He rushed out, his footsteps beating a rapid tattoo on the stairs.

Antony rounded on me. 'Is that him? Are you seeing him?'

I shook my head.

'It's only a matter of time,' Jayne crowed. 'She's a catch is our Verity, and now with her own business too, she's causing quite a stir in the village.'

I shot her a warning glance, but she was far too interested in winding Antony up and doing her best to hurt him.

'She's not the meek little wifey you thought she was, not any more, not now she's free of you. She can do anything she wants, with whomever she wants – she doesn't need you!'

'Jayne, please, enough.'

She ignored me, her full attention on Antony. She'd been waiting a long time for a chance to tell him what she thought of him.

A slow grin spread across his face and my heart sank. I knew that look.

'Antony, I think you should go.'

He ignored me too.

'Meek little wifey, is that what you think? Maybe you don't know our Verity as well as you think you do, there's nothing meek and mild about her, not when she gets going – a right little hellcat she is.'

Jayne sneered.

'You haven't told her, have you?' He turned to me. 'And I thought you told your girls everything. Not so honest when it comes to your own shortcomings, are you, Verity?'

'Antony, please don't.'

He turned back to Jayne. 'What has she told you about the day we broke up?'

I jumped as my coffee cup fell off the table, but Antony and Jayne didn't notice.

'I know she found your catfishing harem on your phone,' Jayne shouted. 'I know the messages went back months – years – with different women. How many *were* there? You're a fantasist, you've got a serious problem!'

'Just words,' Antony said. 'A bit of fun online, none of it meant anything.'

'It did to Verity! How do you think that felt, her reading your declarations of undying love, never mind the webcam footage and phone sex?'

'I've got a fair idea,' Antony said. 'She made it pretty clear at the time.'

I jumped at another crash, this time from the kitchen area, but was more fearful of what Antony was about to say. I grabbed his arm, but he shook me off. There was no stopping this.

'I should bloody well hope she did,' Jayne shouted. 'I'd have killed you if it had been me!'

'She tried to!'

'Antony!' I shouted.

Antony opened his mouth to say more, but was startled by a loud bang from the kitchen.

'What the hell was that?' Jayne said.

This time I ignored her. I glared at Antony in silence.

'Verity?' Jayne said. 'What's going on? What did you do?'

I sighed. 'Nothing. I was just so angry and hurt and humiliated. He wouldn't get away from me; he kept trying to hug me, talk to me, *lie* to me. And I wanted, wanted to—'

Tears were running down my face now and I was dimly aware of noise but I was lost in the memory of that moment.

I screamed as Antony launched himself at me and we crashed to the floor. Winded, I struggled feebly, then with more strength.

'Stay down!' He rolled on top of me, his weight pinning me, and I screamed and struggled harder.

Jayne's screams matched mine and I grew aware of the other noises: the banging of cupboard doors; smashes and crashes as plates, glasses and mugs hit the walls above our heads, showering us with shards as sharp as knives; the whistle of the kettle, suddenly come to the boil; the gush of water as the taps spouted torrents of water.

I squirmed my head free just in time to see a bottle of wine on the worktop explode, coating the walls behind with streaks of red. Hysterically, I thought of the TV show, *Dexter*, and wondered how he would analyse the splatter. Then it stopped.

The door opened.

'What have you done to them?' Lara launched herself at Antony, kicking him off me. 'Are you all right?'

'Nothing, I didn't bloody do anything!' Antony pushed himself off me, clambered to his feet, and backed towards the door, his face white with shock. 'What the *hell* is going on here?'

He turned and ran.

Lara offered me a hand up off the floor and all three of us looked around the mess of the room.

'I guess your ghosts like Antony even less than they like me,' Jayne said.

'At least they have good taste,' Lara said, breaking the tension. All three of us gave a high-pitched giggle, then sobered at the desperate sound of it.

'Well,' Jayne said. 'I think it's time for a drink.'

'White Lion,' Lara said, and hustled Hannah down the stairs, Grasper leading the way.

Jayne and I hastily gathered up our coats and handbags, then I dashed downstairs to collect a change of clothes and my toiletries bag. Nothing would induce me to sleep in The Rookery tonight.

Part Two

28th December 2016 – January 2017

"Be with me always – take any form – drive me mad! Only do not leave me in this abyss, where I cannot find you! Oh, God! It is unutterable! I cannot live without my life! I cannot live without my soul!"

Wuthering Heights
Emily Brontë, 1847
Haworth, West Yorkshire

1.

The twelve-year-old girl trudged towards the parsonage, exhausted and chilled after a day in the fresh winter air, yet reluctant to descend from the moors.

'Emily!'

She stopped at the shout and turned towards the stonemason's workshop.

'Thee just walked past without passing the time of day,' Harry complained.

'Good afternoon, Harry.'

'That's better, see, no harm in passing a friendly greeting is there?'

Emily smiled at him and Harry beamed in response to the rare show of affection. Emily didn't make friends easily – not of the two-legged variety anyway. He glanced at the strange collection of animals that seemed to be forever in attendance on Emily Brontë, and smiled when he noticed the new additions of a goose and a pheasant amongst the usual cats and dogs.

He was proud of the fact he was likely Emily's only friend outside her family. He knew no other who was as self-sufficient and happy in her own company as Emily – even her siblings were social extroverts in comparison – and he was honoured that she viewed him as friend – even if the other lads in the village teased him over her, calling her savage. And when her temper was roused, she certainly could be; but they had never seen her charm a hurt lapwing on to her hand to be carried home and nursed back to health. They had never seen her free a coney from a snare and care for it until it could return to its warren.

Although it never had gone back to its own kind, he mused, as he watched it awkwardly hop up to join the rest of Emily's coterie. The fur never had grown back on that hind leg and, although slower than the rest of its kind, the little bobtail was never too far away from its saviour.

'Thee'd live up there if thee could, wouldn't thee, lass?' Harry said, nodding at Haworth Moor rising behind Emily.

She turned and looked at the landscape. Most would consider it grim and barren at this time of year. Not Emily; she saw naught but life up there and loved it all, even the wind, no matter how hard it bit.

'I'd love to,' she replied, her voice childlike in the simplicity of her answer. 'Away from the cesspit of human habitation.' She wrinkled her nose at the stench of the privies and midden heaps of Haworth – a smell diluted by the position of the parsonage and mason's workshop beyond the church and away from Main Street, but still powerful enough.

'It would be much better to live with the coneys and the foxes, the buzzards and the owls. They drink the purest water and eat the freshest meat.'

'Apart from the foxes that scavenge from the midden heaps,' Harry said with a grin.

Emily shrugged. 'Only in the winter, when there's less food about. Then they're back on the moor, the air fresh, and the footing sound.'

Harry grimaced, knowing what Emily was referring to. The recent rains had sent a river of waste from the privies and middens at the top end of Main Street down to the bottom. The steep hill had been lethal, even more so than normal; and people, horses and carts had slithered down it with a filthy, stinking regularity over the past few days.

He shuddered. 'The sooner they lay them cobbles they keep talking about, the better.'

Emily didn't appear to have heard him. 'I love the . . . space . . . up there. No one else to annoy you, just fauna and flora.'

Harry scowled at her fancy words mixed in with her Yorkshire dialect, itself not as strong as most in the village. That more than anything highlighted the differences between them, and at times he struggled to understand her meaning.

He glanced at the parsonage then thought of his family's cottage. Nine of them in two rooms; and that was only because four of his siblings were already in their graves.

'Been up to Top Withens today,' Emily continued, having mistaken Harry's silence for interest. 'Love it up there.'

'Aye, thee can see for miles and there's no folk to spoil the view,' Harry said.

'Yes,' Emily exclaimed. 'That's it exactly!'

'Mebbe one day we'll live up there, together.' Harry blushed fiercely, wondering if he'd gone too far, but Emily didn't seem to have understood his meaning. Either that or she had far more tact than people credited her with.

'I'd love to live up there,' she said. 'But Papa would never allow it. What time will Mr Barraclough release you?' She looked at Harry, irritated, and he knew he'd taken too long to respond to her change of subject. He popped his head inside, and received a nod from his master.

'Whenever thee wishes. What service can I do thee for?' He smiled and winked, but again Emily failed to react.

'Come to the parsonage for tea. In about an hour. Papa was complaining this morning that he doesn't see enough of you.'

* * *

'Have another sandwich.' Charlotte proffered the plate. The eldest at fourteen, Harry knew, yet she was so diminutive, even her youngest sister Anne more than matched her for height.

But whatever her stature, she was the perfect hostess, with impeccable manners, even if she did have a strange manner of peering intently at her guests.

Must be all that reading she does, Harry thought, *that makes her squint so. Bad for thy health, all them books.*

'I've just finished *Don Juan*,' Branwell announced. 'I found it to be an absolutely fascinating, if a little shocking, study of today's society. Have you ever read Lord Byron, Harry?'

Harry refused to let his true reaction to this pretentiousness show on his face. He couldn't abide Branwell, who lorded it over boys of his own age, especially those of the village. He idolised his father's sexton, John Brown, and tried to pretend he was of the same age and life experience, despite the thirteen-year gap. Little did Branwell know, instead of appearing learned and a man of the world, he was viewed as a pompous ass by everyone in Haworth under the age of sixteen – unless their surname was Brontë.

'No, I have not, Branwell,' Harry replied, mocking the other boy's upper-crust way of speech. 'My reading tends to be limited to the memorial stones Mr Barraclough carves.'

Charlotte reclaimed the conversation with a small rebuke to her brother as she defended their guest. 'Don't be silly, Branwell, Harry doesn't have time for such pursuits as poetry, he must feed his family, especially with young Mabel so poorly. How does she fare, Harry?'

'Ailing at the minute, Miss Charlotte, but still breathing so there's hope.'

'Well, you must take the rest of these sandwiches home with you. Some apples too, we have a good stock, they'll do her the power of good.'

'Thank you, Miss Charlotte.'

'Ha!' Branwell interrupted, determined to regain the upper hand from his elder sister, and waved a newspaper over the children. 'Look at this! Mr Rook will have a fit when he sees it.'

'Sees what, Branwell?' Charlotte asked. 'Which publication is that?'

'*The Leeds Mercury*.' Branwell cracked the paper open in emulation of his father.

'That scoundrel, Richard Oastler, is at it again, he's blatantly calling for millworkers to strike!'

'No scoundrel, Branwell,' Emily said. 'He speaks for many, and there is truth in what he preaches, even Papa says so.'

Branwell scowled. 'He should not talk against the mills. Without them Haworth would starve.'

Emily snatched the newsprint from her brother. 'You know as well as

I the perils of working in the mills. Even now Harry's sister is in her bed, barely able to breathe for the fluff in her lungs, and only ten years old, the same age as our Anne!'

'Emily,' Charlotte cautioned with a concerned glance at Harry. His face was white, but he showed no other sign of emotion.

Emily ignored her sister. 'Richard Oastler speaks for all the mill children who have no voice. Their parents too.' She jumped to her feet in her passion, her features pinched as she struggled to express the outrage flooding through her. She pointed at the newspaper, then her brother, and stamped her foot.

'The Yorkshire Slavery he calls it, and slavery it is. Nippers crawling under them awful machines, and girls not much older running those huge spinning frames.'

'Have a care, child. I will tolerate no Luddite tendencies under this roof.'

Emily jumped, paled, and sat down all in one motion at the sound of her father's rebuke.

'I am sorry, Papa. I am not speaking against the machines, only the lot of their operators.'

'Those operators are lucky to have the work,' a new voice said. 'Without it, their families would starve. Is that not so, Mr Sutcliffe?'

'Yes, Mr Rook,' Harry said.

Baalzephon Rook, as owner of Rook Mills the employer of the majority of Harry's extensive family, nodded and put a hand on the shoulder of his son, Zemeraim.

'What say you, Miss Brontë?' he said, glancing at Emily. 'Should I allow those families to starve?'

Emily met his gaze, lifted her chin, and opened her mouth.

'Come now, Baalzephon. You shall get no sense from a child,' Patrick Brontë said with a cautionary glance at his most wayward of daughters, who blessedly kept her silence.

'They show rather too much interest in a world they neither understand nor have no business therein,' Rook Senior pronounced.

'Nonsense, Baalzephon. 'Tis good for the new generations to learn about their world, surely?'

'They do not seem to be learning, but passing judgements beyond their capabilities.'

Patrick shot another warning glance at Emily, then replied, 'Merely a step on the road to enlightenment, my friend, 'tis all.'

'And I'm surprised at you, Harry Sutcliffe, keeping such company.'

Patrick narrowed his eyes, unsure whether Harry or his own offspring were being insulted, but before he could enquire, Baalzephon and Zemeraim had taken their leave and departed.

Emily looked at Branwell, whose face resembled a thunderous sky at the perceived slight, and giggled.

Patrick sighed in exasperation.

'I think I should also take my leave,' Harry said, flustered. *Why could folk not just say what they mean?*

'I shall see you out, Master Sutcliffe,' Patrick said, and Harry fled.

'Not so fast, boy.'

Harry froze on the stoop.

'She's not for you.'

He did not turn.

'I encouraged your friendship, I know. My Emily does not make friends with ease, not the human kind. You have been good for her. You have saved her life at least once. But she will never be your wife. My largesse shall not extend to that. Set your sights on another.'

Harry walked away. He did not look back. He would not allow Patrick Brontë to see the angry flush his words had ignited on his cheeks.

He passed through the gate from the parsonage garden to the churchyard, past the grave of his sisters, past the church, towards home on Weaver's Row.

Patrick watched him go, wondering if he had done the right thing. Harry was the only person outside the family and household who understood Emily, who accepted her as she was, who loved the birds and animals as she did.

But he was a stonemason's apprentice, and a weaver's son. Emily was a parson's daughter.

With a heavy sigh, he swung shut the front door and turned to see Emily staring at him.

One of the few things in the world that could make the Reverend Patrick Brontë flinch, was his daughter Emily's fiercest stare. He not only flinched, but stumbled backwards against the closed door.

2.

'Are you sure you should move back in there?' Lara asked.

'Yes, I can't afford to stay at the White Lion indefinitely when my own place is just across the street. It was lovely over Christmas, but I need to face whatever is going on at The Rookery. Anyway, Vikram and the gang are back today, I can't put it off forever, and nothing has happened since Antony's visit.'

'And you've had no more dreams?' Lara asked.

'No,' I lied, and Lara narrowed her eyes, but with a glance at her daughter, she stayed silent. 'And even if I had, the dreams aren't the problem.'

'No, just your friends and your ex-husband,' Lara pointed out.

'Well, I don't think Antony will pay another visit.'

Lara laughed. 'You can say that again – I've never seen anybody run so fast. Or look so pale.'

'Like he'd seen a ghost,' Hannah repeated the joke we'd been telling all over Christmas. 'Like Scrooge.'

'Just like Scrooge,' Lara agreed, and Hannah buried her nose back in her book. I was struck anew by the way Hannah seemed to cope so well with such strange and frightening events. Yes, she was terrified when these things happened, but within a day she'd accepted it as normal. I envied her.

'Anyway, I have to check out today, the room isn't free again until after New Year. Apparently there's a big do on in the village and they're booked up already.'

'I just wish Jayne had been able to stay longer,' Lara said, and I looked at her in surprise.

She shrugged. 'We may not agree on everything, but we do agree on looking out for you.'

I nodded and Hannah looked up from her book again and said, 'And Grasper could have looked after you too, Auntie Verity.'

'He certainly could, Hannah. What are you reading?'

Hannah showed me the book – a history of Haworth. 'It has all the ghosts in it,' she explained.

'Hannah woke up on the floor this morning,' Lara said. 'Seemingly, it's because of the ghost of the balloonist.'

'Yes, Lily Cove,' Hannah explained. 'She parachuted out of her hot-air balloon, but the parachute didn't open and she just fell.'

'And you're not scared?'

'No. I was at first, but she just wants to tell people what happened to her and it's difficult because she doesn't have a voice or a body any more. That's what Mum says. Maybe that's what your ghosts are doing, Auntie Verity, trying to tell you what happened to them.'

'You could be right, Hans,' Lara said. 'Have you finished your breakfast?'

Hannah nodded, put a large black feather into her book to mark her page, then closed the book.

'Where did you get that?' Lara asked with a shiver.

'Outside Auntie Verity's house. There are lots on the ground from those big black birds.'

Lara and I exchanged a glance, then I threw my napkin on to the table. 'Right, come on. I need to get my stuff and settle my bill, then once I've spoken to Vikram and the build team, the rest of the day is ours.'

'What's that lot for?' I pointed at the bag of crystals, amulets and other odds and sods Lara had bought from the new-age shop on Main Street.

'If you're moving back into that place, you'll do so with some protection,' Lara said.

'Stones, herbs and symbols?' I scoffed.

'I'm willing to try anything,' Lara said. 'And don't mock this stuff, used properly it can be very powerful.'

'But you've already cleansed The Rookery. That didn't do much good.'

'How do you know? You've no idea if things would be even worse without that cleansing.'

I stayed silent, but knew my apprehension was clear in the set of my face and shoulders.

'We'll cleanse again tonight after the builders have gone, then every evening – and you need to carry on doing it after Hannah and I go home.' She stopped in exasperation at the look on my face.

'Look at it this way, Verity, it can't hurt and you'll keep me off your back.'

I relaxed. 'You're right, Lara, sorry.' I gave her a quick hug. 'I guess I'm a bit freaked out by it all. When the stuff in the kitchen started smashing, well . . .'

Lara glanced at Hannah, who was peering into shop windows and not paying us any attention.

'It must have been terrifying,' she said. 'But no one was hurt – and they could have been had the spirits wanted to. They're clearly capable of it.'

'They?'

Lara shrugged. 'Well, yes, there were two orbs, remember?'

'My dream man and the Grey Lady,' I said.

'I don't think so – I don't think the Grey Lady has anything to do with this. But whoever they are, we need to make sure you're safe.'

'I don't think they want to hurt me,' I said. 'If anything, I think Hannah's right, he – they – want to tell me something.'

'Maybe, but to be honest, they're going to a lot of trouble and energy to merely tell you a story. No, there's something more going on here, and I'm not sure we want to find out what.'

'I doubt they'll give us the choice, they've been pretty insistent so far.'

'That's what's worrying me so much,' Lara said. 'How much further will they go to make you understand?'

I hesitated, then said, 'Okay, I'll do whatever you want: spells, potions, rituals, the works. Even dance naked in the graveyard under the full moon if that'll make you happy!'

Lara laughed with me. 'We don't need to go that far, Verity, not unless you really want to.'

'I'd rather not – even if it appeases the ghosts, which is unlikely, I can't see my new neighbours taking kindly to that spectacle!'

'Why are you laughing, Mum?' Hannah had grown bored of window shopping and re-joined us.

'Oh, just picturing Auntie Verity dancing around the gravestones with no clothes on.'

Hannah looked thoughtful for a moment. 'Why would you picture that, Mum?'

I joined in Lara's laughter. 'Yes, why would you picture that, Lara?'

'I wish I never had,' she spluttered. 'Shall we get on with the shopping instead? Didn't you want to have a look at the art gallery?'

Still laughing, I linked arms with Lara, Hannah taking her other side, and we made our clumsy way over the cobbles.

3.

'Auntie Verity!' Hannah bumped into my back and I managed to put one foot in front of the other to make slow progress into the art gallery. The man behind the counter stared at me as intently as I stared at him, but neither of us spoke.

'Hi,' Lara said with a concerned look at me. 'We're interested in local landscapes . . .' she tailed off, glancing between me and the man, then plonked her handbag on to the countertop with an audible thump and broke the spell.

The man diverted his attention to her and finally smiled. 'Over here.' He moved towards the far wall of the shop. 'They're my speciality – if there's a local landmark you're thinking of in particular and it isn't here, just let me know and I'll paint it for you.' He shot another glance at me, his colour high.

'Oh, you're the artist too?' Lara asked.

'Aye, William Sutcliffe. At your service.' He gave an awkward bow, the blush in his cheeks undiminished.

'How wonderful,' Lara said.

I still could not form words of my own and thanked my lucky stars that we'd done this today and Lara was here to speak for me.

'Do you paint people too?' Hannah asked.

'Aye, sometimes, if someone takes my fancy.'

I met his eyes again then looked away just in time to catch Lara's smirk.

'Have you ever had your portrait painted, lass?'

'No, only photographs,' Hannah said, deadly serious. 'I'd love a painted portrait, though. Mummy, can I have one?'

'I think that might be a bit too expensive for your pocket money, Hans,' Lara said, with a smile.

'Ah well, you'll just have to save up, lass. I'll do you a good deal.' He winked with a smile.

'Or I could get a job, just like Aunt Jayne.'

'Maybe in a few years. Come and have a look at these,' Lara said. 'Which do you think would look nice in Auntie Verity's hotel?'

'The spooky ones,' Hannah answered promptly. 'So the ghosts feel at home.'

I laughed – finally finding my voice. 'They already seem to feel quite at home, Hannah, don't you think?'

Hannah shrugged as the man – William – said, 'Ghosts? You've bought in Haworth then, there's barely a house without a ghost story on this hill.' He smiled at me as I gave another nervous laugh.

'Yes, we're getting that impression.' I stuck my hand out. 'Verity Earnshaw,' I said as we shook. 'I've bought The Rookery – the place on West Lane with the skip outside,' I added as I remembered that nobody but myself, Jayne, Lara and the build team knew the building by that name at the moment.

'Ah, the old weaver's cottages. Aye, I know the place. Have you seen the Grey Lady yet?'

'Auntie Verity has, and one of the builders did. He ran away scared, didn't he, Mummy? I'm not scared though, not any more, not of her or the man. Or the ghost in our room at the hotel. I'm not, am I, Mummy?'

William looked rather taken aback by this, but rallied valiantly. 'It sounds like you're a very brave girl – that's a lot of ghosts not to be scared of.'

'It is, isn't it, Mummy? A lot of ghosts. They don't scare me though.'

'Okay, Hannah, how about we look at these pictures?' Lara tried again to distract her daughter.

Hannah's babbling had at least given me time to recover my wits, and I turned my attention back to William. 'I'm looking for a couple of dozen landscapes,' I started.

'Prints or originals?'

'Prints – preferably related to the Brontës and the village.'

William nodded and I realised he'd hear this criteria from most of his customers.

'They're to go in the guest rooms as well as the public areas,' I continued, 'and be available for sale to guests, so I was hoping we could make a sale or return arrangement.'

'Sale or return,' he repeated. 'And when would you return them if they didn't sell?'

I stayed quiet, unprepared for this question, but he took pity on me and broke the silence.

'I can't do that I'm afraid,' he said. 'If I did I'd have prints hanging in every guesthouse and hotel in the dale, but I'd have no money coming in. This is how I make my living, I do need to sell my work.'

He sighed and rubbed his hand over the dark stubble on his chin. I wondered if the growth was from overnight or if he had indeed shaved that morning, then caught myself and brought my mind back to the business at hand.

'As you'd like a bulk order, I can offer you a 25 per cent discount on the lot, or you can buy half at full price, and I'll let you have the rest on sale or return – but only for six months. If you don't sell any, I'll take them back, or you'd need to buy them.'

'At 25 per cent off?'

He shook his head. 'One or the other, I'm afraid. It's up to you and how many you think you can realistically sell.'

I stayed silent, thinking.

'And if she buys them at the discount, then sells, what would you offer at that point?' Lara asked.

William smiled, but didn't take his eyes off me. 'If you're making sales, then we can definitely renegotiate.'

He stared at me a moment longer, his colour rising once more. 'When do you open?'

'Easter,' I said.

'So you wouldn't need them straight away,' he mused, then met Hannah's eyes – big, grey and round, staring back at him, full of hope – and his face softened, then hardened once more as he returned his attention to me.

'Earnshaw did you say your name was?'

'Yes, my father grew up in Keighley, but his ancestors came from this area. He always joked one of his relations inspired Emily Brontë's Cathy.'

'But you're Verity.'

'My middle name's Catherine.' I blushed; I hated admitting that.

William nodded. 'Well, you're a local then.' He smiled. 'Tell you what, if you let me hang the pictures and have my card in the frame, I'll let you have them for three months after opening, on spec. Then you decide which deal you want. Can't say fairer than that.'

Hannah clapped her hands, but was silenced by her mother's hand over her mouth.

I considered for a moment, then held my hand out. 'Deal,' I said. 'Nice doing business with you.'

He took my hand and I jolted at the sensation of our palms touching again. By the look in his eyes, he had felt it too.

We let go at Lara's cough and I wondered just how long we'd been standing in the gallery holding hands. I was surprised to hear myself say, 'When would you like to pop in to have a look around The Rookery? We'll be in tomorrow.'

'Tomorrow it is then, as soon as I've shut up shop.'

'See you then.' I hesitated, unwilling to leave, but eventually followed Lara and Hannah back out on to Main Street.

Hannah ran on ahead up the steep hill and Lara linked her arm with mine as we followed far more slowly.

'What was all that about? Why were you acting so weird in there?'

'That,' I said, 'was the man I've been dreaming about.'

4.

'I clear this space of all negative energy and call in angelic light and love to fill this place,' Lara intoned yet again, then held the smouldering bundle of sage under the tap before putting it into a bowl.

'When it's dry you can relight it and do the same again,' she said.

'Uh huh,' I replied, my arms folded and my nose wrinkled in scepticism.

Lara glanced at me, frustrated. 'I thought you were going to try this, Verity.'

'We are trying it.'

'No, you're watching me try it – again. This is your home, you need to embrace it or the intentions have no power.'

'It'll only work if I believe in it, you mean?'

Lara sighed. 'Essentially, yes.' She held up a hand to forestall my mocking harrumph. 'It's all about intention. If you believe and mean the words, that gives them the power to manifest – become true.' She paused and looked at me in exasperation.

'Have you ever lost something?'

'Of course I have.' I laughed.

'And what do you say to yourself while you're looking for it? Say for example, you can't find the TV remote, what's running through your head while you're searching?'

'Um, where's the bloody remote? I can't find it anywhere. Something like that.'

'And do you find it?'

'Eventually.'

'But not while you're telling yourself you can't find it, right?'

I thought for a moment and relaxed a bit. 'Well, usually I've given up, gone to get a cup of coffee or glass of wine, come back into the lounge and then I find it.'

'Probably somewhere you've already looked, right?'

'Well, yes, usually. That could just be age though.' I laughed.

Lara smiled. 'Or it could be that you didn't see it because you were telling yourself that you couldn't find it, and you believed that.'

I shrugged. She was starting to make sense.

'Next time you lose something, instead of telling yourself you can't find it, tell yourself it will be in the next place you look.'

'If I tell myself that often enough, it *will* eventually be in the next place I look.'

'But I bet you find it long before you give up, get a drink, then find it somewhere you've already searched.'

I said nothing. I'd have to try it first.

'It's the same thing here – the cleansing we're doing with the sage and candle is about setting your intention. In the same way as telling yourself you will find what is lost, you are telling yourself and anything listening that you want only peace here.'

'Okay, I guess that makes sense,' I admitted, 'but do I really have to wave burning herbs around? I can't imagine my guests enjoying the smell, it stinks like a doss house!'

'Yes, unfortunate that burning herbs all smell the same – including cannabis, as Jayne so kindly pointed out before Christmas.' Lara smiled. 'No, just do the sage when the place is empty and you're cleaning and airing the rooms anyway. The rest of the time use a candle.'

'How do I do that?'

'I'll show you, we'll do it now.' Lara dug into her shopping bag and pulled out a small votive candle in a glass holder. She lit it and handed it to me.

'I want you to move it in continuous clockwise circles,' she said. 'Get into every corner of every room, and spend a bit of extra time in the well-used places like I did with the sage: over your bed, the dining table, sofa, that kind of thing. And keep repeating the intention.'

I nodded and started. 'I cleanse this place of all negative energy— I feel like a right wally,' I interrupted myself, self-conscious again.

'No one's laughing at you, Verity, and being a right wally may not be the best intention to set, no matter how apt it is at the moment.'

I narrowed my eyes at her and she laughed.

'Keep going. I did it and I'm none the worse for wear.' She smiled to reassure me. 'It doesn't feel so weird after you've done it a few times. Trust me.'

I held her gaze for a moment, then nodded. I did trust her, and I had no better ideas.

I raised the candle again and started to move through the rooms, circling and chanting – with the odd prompt from Lara.

'I cleanse this place of all negative energy and call in angelic light and love to fill this space.'

We moved through the rooms, pausing in my bedroom to check on Hannah – fast asleep on my bed, exhausted from her insistence on running up Main Street ahead of us, then returning to chivvy us along up the steep slope.

'Downstairs too?'

'Every single room on every single floor,' Lara said. 'And every single day, too.'

'What?'

'You need to keep doing it until you fully believe in what you're saying, until the intention of light and love is as much a part of you as the blood that runs through your veins. Then you'll be safe.'

'How long will that take?'

No answer.

'Still feel like a wally?'

'No-no, I don't. I feel weird, peaceful somehow.'

Lara nodded, smiling.

'Probably all the candle and sage smoke gone to my head!' I joked.

Lara's smile grew wider, her eyes crinkling in honest pleasure. She said nothing, though, just poured us both a glass of wine. 'I think we've earned this,' she said. 'Cheers.'

We clinked glasses and drank.

'What?' I said, defensive again at the look in her eyes over the rim of her glass.

'What do you think about a tarot reading?'

'I don't know, Lara, that makes me uncomfortable.'

'You're spending too much time with Jayne,' she said. 'There's nothing to worry about, nothing sinister about the cards, they're just a tool to allow us to understand what our subconscious and intuition already know.'

'Oh what the hell,' I said. 'In for a penny, in for a pound. Just don't go telling me when I'll die or anything like that.'

'The cards don't predict death,' Lara said, 'only the most likely outcomes of current situations.'

'I thought there was a death card.'

'There is – but it means change, a letting go of a way of life, not the end of a life.'

I nodded. To be fair, I was intrigued by the tarot. Lara had never been wrong in the past when she'd persuaded me to sit for a reading. Something about them just unnerved me though, and I'd never embraced the cards.

'Best to do it quickly before we have more wine,' Lara said, and I laughed as she took another gulp, then I gulped myself, took the bottle and followed her to the table.

As she unwrapped her cards from the silk purple scarf in which she kept them, I topped up our glasses.

'Dutch courage.' I shrugged at her frown and took a sip.

She said nothing, but shuffled the cards, her eyes closed and face blank in concentration.

I sipped again as I waited, then took the cards when Lara proffered them, and shuffled them myself as she instructed.

Handing them back, she laid them out, face down in three columns of three cards each, then looked at me. 'Ready?'

I gulped my wine, noticing that Lara had drunk no more, then took another drink and set my empty glass down. 'Ready.'

Lara turned over the top row of cards.

'This represents your past,' she said, 'and there are no surprises here – always a good thing at this stage.' She smiled up at me and I refilled my glass.

'Seven of Cups. That's delusion, believing somebody who's been lying to you.'

'Antony,' I confirmed, sipping again.

Lara nodded. 'Then the Three of Swords. Discord – that's the divorce card – and the third one is the Tower. Your old life falling down.'

'Sounds about right,' I said, lifting the glass to my lips again. I quirked an eyebrow at my friend. 'Are you sure this is a good idea? I think we'll need more wine if it carries on like this.'

Lara reached over and laid her hand over mine. 'This is a reflection of the past, Verity. It's nothing you don't already know, and actually the Tower is a good card to end on.'

I stared at the picture on the card. A bolt of lightning striking a tall, lone stone keep, fire spewing from the upper floors, stonework tumbling.

'It means the slate's wiped clean and you can rebuild, with stronger foundations. It means a new life is beginning.'

I grinned, looking around me and opening my arms wide to indicate The Rookery. 'Very apt.'

Lara smiled and bent her head back to the spread of cards. 'The next row is your present. The Fool, the Chariot and the Eight of Wands.'

'The Fool, that sounds about right.'

Lara ignored me. 'The Fool means you're at the beginning of a new journey, and judging by the Chariot that follows it, it'll be quite a ride!' She looked up and took a sip of her wine. 'You'll need willpower and hard work, but you have both of those in you in spades. And you'll persevere.' She spread her own arms out, repeating my earlier gesture. 'I think this place will be a success.'

'I'll drink to that.' I giggled, growing tipsy now.

'Then this one.' Lara tapped the Eight of Wands. 'These are the arrows of love.'

'The arrows of love? Christ, I don't need any of that, thank you very much. Antony has very definitely rid me of any appetite for love!'

'Really? Watching you in that art gallery today, I could have sworn I saw you salivating.'

I blushed, but I wasn't ready to talk about that – I needed far more wine before I could even start to get my head round meeting that man.

'And what about the next cards, the future?'

Lara unsuccessfully tried to hide a smug smile, then grew serious again. 'The Moon, the Hanged Man, and the Lovers,' she said as she turned the cards over.

I stayed silent, my heart doing funny things at the appearance of the last two cards.

'The moon is about your dreams,' Lara said, eyebrows raised.

'You're joking!'

She shook her head. 'Pay attention to them, truths are contained within your dreams, truths you need to know and understand.'

I sipped my wine, feeling unaccountably sober again. 'And the Hanged Man?' I almost whispered the words.

'Does *not* mean death,' Lara reassured, her hand once again atop mine. 'It can mean sacrifice, or can be about perspective. Coming after the Moon card, I think it's telling you to look at things in a different way. See how the man is hanging upside down from his foot? He's telling you to be open-minded, don't jump to conclusions, and look at things from every angle before acting.'

I nodded then giggled again. 'You don't have to tell me what the Lovers means!'

Lara tilted her head to her right shoulder. 'Not quite what you're thinking – it indicates choices to be made, although probably to do with a lover. It can often mean the start of a significant relationship.'

I giggled again, my earlier protestations forgotten.

'Verity.' Lara grabbed my hand again and I winced at the strength of her grip. 'Make the right choice – be very careful.'

I wrenched my hand away. 'Lara, what the hell?'

She blinked a few times and looked confused, then gasped.

Two balls of light hovered over the spread of cards on the table, then slowly moved around each other and rose to the ceiling, where they circled around the room.

I jumped to my feet, Lara a split second behind me, when I spotted the hazy figure of the Grey Lady standing in the kitchen area, her back to us.

Lara and I grabbed each other and stood frozen, fingers intertwined, and stared as the figure turned to look at us.

She was petite, barely taller than Hannah, and very slender. Her hair – it was impossible to see the colour of it but it seemed dark – was bound up under a bonnet, but careless curls, not quite ringlets, escaped its confines and framed her bony, pinched face.

Her gown was modest; the lace trimming the neck of it brushed the base of her skull, the sleeves puffed from the shoulders, and the waist was impossibly nipped in.

Corset, I thought. *She's wearing a corset.*

The skirt bloomed large from the hips and brushed the floor – no, extended *through* the floor.

I raised my eyes again to her face, and gasped. She was staring at me with such a look of pity and – sorrow – yes, that was it, sorrow, I felt tears prickle my eyes.

She turned her face forward again and moved, very slowly, until the kitchen units, then the wall swallowed her up.

She was gone.

Lara dragged her hand out of mine and fell back into her chair – hard enough to hurt. She stretched out a shaky hand, took hold of her glass, and after a couple of attempts, drained it in one.

I retook my own seat and stared at her.

'Bloody hell, Verity,' she said. 'Tha-that was a ghost. That was a real ghost.' She took a deep breath. 'I've never actually *seen* a ghost before!'

5.

The Reverend Patrick Brontë regarded the couple standing before him, and a rare smile flitted across his face as his eyes met the groom's. *The lad's left it long enough,* Haworth's parson thought, *but it's good to see him wed at last.*

'Harry Sutcliffe, wilt thou have this woman to be thy wedded wife, to live together after God's ordinance in the holy estate of Matrimony? Wilt thou love her, comfort her, honour, and keep her, in sickness and in health; and, forsaking all other, keep thee only unto her, so long as ye both shall live?'

'I will.'

'Martha Earnshaw, wilt thou have this man to be thy wedded husband, to live together after God's ordinance in the holy estate of Matrimony? Wilt thou obey him, and serve him, love, honour, and keep him, in sickness and in health; and, forsaking all other, keep thee only unto him, so long as ye both shall live?'

'Aye, I will.'

Emily watched from the back of the church with her siblings. Charlotte and Branwell were in charge of taking the collection, and it was Emily and Anne's duty to distribute then re-collect the prayer books and hymnals before and after every service; whatever the service may be: wedding, funeral, christening or Holy Communion. It was a nice change to attend a wedding, the most common service by far was the funeral.

Emily was glad to see Harry wed before she left for her teaching post at Law Hill. She knew he'd been holding out to wed her, but had finally given up hope. *A pity,* she mused, *if I am to have a husband, Harry may have been a tolerable one. But better to have a teaching life, than be a stonemason's wife, that's what Papa says. Maybe I'll find a husband on the moors one day.*

Emily's attention was brought back to the church as the congregation stood to sing. It was her favourite hymn, *All Creatures of our God and King*, and she joined in with gusto until Charlotte elbowed her in the side, and she lowered her voice to a more melodious tone.

Martha looks lovely, Emily thought when the hymn was over. *Not like her usual slovenly self at all.* The bride wore a new cotton gown, especially made for the occasion. It would have taken the Earnshaws a couple of years to save up for the material, but was worth it. A lovely earthy pattern of dark red stripes on a gold background, it would likely be Martha's best dress for the rest of her life, worn for every special occasion.

I hope they've been able to leave plenty of spare material at the seams, Emily thought. *If Martha's anything like her mam, she'll be needing to let it out plenty afore too long.*

Emily breathed deeply as the distinctive, fresh smell of wild garlic wafted over her. *Garlic for courage and health*, she thought and squinted at Martha's bridal bouquet to see which other flowers she'd chosen; what her hopes for the future were.

Gorse: endearing affection. Emily scowled, that wasn't Martha at all. Maybe Harry had given her that. White heather for dreams to come true, honeysuckle for the bond of love, and of course pussy willow for motherhood. Hence all the garlic. Babies rarely saw their first birthday, and nearly half of those that did would not see their seventh.

Papa's certain it's the wells. If water stinks that much outside, what does it do to us inside?

Emily smiled at Harry as the couple passed, genuinely happy for her friend, then recoiled at the strength of Martha's glare.

The two had never got on, not even as girls, but Emily hadn't paid too much attention. She didn't care what the village girls thought of her.

They had never hated each other though, but that's what Emily saw in Martha's face as she walked out of the church, her new husband on her arm: a deep, malevolent hatred. And something else too. Triumph?

Verity jerked awake, her fists clenched, heart racing. But not for love, her heart was racing in anger.

Her breathing calmed as she grew aware of her surroundings and century. The dream had seemed so *real*, and that was William who'd been getting married – for all he was called Harry in her dreams.

Verity's gut twisted at the thought. *Jealousy? Am I seriously jealous from dreaming about a man I don't know getting married over a hundred years ago?*

She threw the covers aside and jumped out of bed. *This is getting ridiculous.* Even more ridiculous when she caught herself hoping that Harry would visit her in the shower again.

6.

'It's not good enough, Gary,' Vikram said into the phone. 'You and Omar swore to me you'd be fit for work this week.'

He listened a moment, then, 'Food poisoning, my arse. Alcohol poisoning more like. Just get here when you can – I don't care how much your head hurts.'

He hung up with a curse, then winced and apologised for his language when he saw Hannah.

'Problem?' I inquired.

'The labourers have hangovers,' he said. 'It'll slow us down some.' He indicated the two men standing behind him with cups of tea. 'Both Pramod and Darren are qualified plumbers, and now they'll have to work together on one en-suite rather than getting on with two.'

I shot an enquiring glance at Lara, then said, 'Can we help? If it's labourers you need, we're more than happy to help out – we can fetch and carry with the best of them.'

Lara laughed. 'Yes, we'd been planning to visit the museum but it's closed until after New Year. We have the day free if you can use us.' She stared innocently at Vikram as he blushed.

'Well . . . if you're sure . . .' He hesitated and looked to his colleagues, then shrugged. 'If you two can help Pramod, I'll help Darren. We'll be laying pipe for the bathroom suites, and connecting everything up.'

'Like the pipes game on your phone, Mum,' Hannah butted in.

'Well, something like that,' Vikram said. 'It shouldn't be all day, with any luck, those two layabouts will drag themselves here at some point. They'll need to earn some dosh for their next pub crawl! You'll need safety gear though, hard hat, high-vis vest and steel toecaps.' He paused and stroked his chin.

'Steel toecaps? Do those come with heels?'

Vikram stared at Lara, for a moment lost for words, then he seemed to decide she was joking. 'I should have enough gear in the van, but I don't think I'll have anything to fit you, lass.'

Hannah looked crestfallen.

'Not to worry, Hans. It'll be all dirty and dusty,' Lara said. 'You wouldn't like it. Why don't you go up to Auntie Verity's rooms and do some colouring?'

'I want to read,' she replied, lips pouting in a sulk.

'Okay, I'll pop over to the hotel and get a book. Which one do you want?'

'*Gangsta Granny.*'

I raised my eyebrows at the title, then followed Vikram to the van as Lara and Hannah crossed the road to the White Lion.

'I was sorry to intrude on Christmas Eve,' Vikram said.

I shook my head. 'Don't worry about it, you weren't the one intruding.'

'The ex?'

I nodded.

'Are you okay?'

I gave a smile that I knew barely touched my cheeks. 'Yeah, I'm fine. He won't be back in a hurry.'

'Is that a good thing?'

'Definitely.' This time my smile was genuine.

He nodded and clambered into the back of his van, emerging with an armful of safety gear. 'Boots'll be a bit on the big side, you'll have to stuff socks in them or summat.'

'No problem, it's not as if we'll be walking far. Oh, you've got three hats, Hannah will be chuffed!'

'Aye, three vests an'all. It'll be too long for her, but at least she won't feel left out.'

'That's very thoughtful of you.'

'Aye, well, I've three nippers of my own, I know how they get.'

'Oh, I didn't realise you had children.' I mentally kicked myself; his private life was none of my business.

'Yeah. Don't see enough of them, though.'

We were interrupted by the return of Lara and Hannah, who immediately cheered up with the presentation of a hard hat and a fluorescent yellow vest, then we turned to go back inside.

'Bloody hell,' Vikram said. 'Sorry,' he added with a glance at Lara. 'Again.'

'She's heard worse,' Lara said. 'What's wrong?'

He pointed. 'The rooks again. I've not known them roost on the buildings before – they tend to stick to the graveyard, away from folk. Well, living folk, anyroad,' he amended.

'Yes, I was meaning to mention that to you. Can you put up netting or spikes, something to keep them away? As soon as possible.'

'Aye, no problem. It'll have to be in the New Year though, when I've got a full team back.'

'That should be okay – as long as it's before guests start arriving.'

He nodded. 'You know, it's said they're lost souls.'

'Yeah, I'd heard something about that.'

'Aye, unable to find their way to peace, that's why they congregate in graveyards.'

I shivered and noticed Hannah step closer to her mother, pressing against Lara's side. Vikram must have seen too.

'Load of superstitious nonsense,' he said, his tone brighter. 'Shouldn't have brought it up. Right, are you ladies ready to go to work?'

'I am absolutely exhausted,' Lara said, collapsing on to one of the camping chairs.

'Hey, watch it, you're filthy.'

'I'll clean it later.'

I took pity on her. 'Tell you what, grab a quick shower and change, and I'll treat you and Hannah to lunch as a thank you for this morning.'

'Done,' Lara said. She held her hands out. 'Drag me off this chair and I'll do that.'

I laughed, grabbed her hands and hauled her to her feet. 'You've only done two hours' work, and most of that was sitting and holding pipes in place!'

'Harder than it looks,' Lara said. 'Right, Hans, are you coming with me or staying here with Auntie Verity?'

Hannah cast a disdainful look over her mother's dust-laden and generally grimy appearance and stuck her nose back into her book. 'I'll wait here.'

Lara and I grinned at each other, then went our separate ways in search of cleanliness.

'Meet you in the Black Bull?'

'Half an hour.'

As it transpired, Hannah and I passed the Old White Lion just as Lara emerged.

'You look like a new woman,' I said.

'Good job too. You don't scrub up too badly yourself.'

Giggling at Hannah's eye roll, we linked arms and followed Hannah to the Black Bull and lunch.

I stopped dead as soon as I stepped through the interior door.

'Is that . . . ?'

'Yes.'

'It's the painting man,' Hannah exclaimed and ran over to him. 'Hello, have you painted my picture yet?'

William Sutcliffe glanced down at her, stared a moment, then raised his eyes to mine. He lifted his hand to his flat cap and tweaked it, then regarded Hannah once more, tilting his head first one way then the other.

'Not yet, lassie, but one day. Setting has to be right, though.'

'Mummy, Mummy, he's going to paint me!'

'That's lovely, Hans.' She raised her eyebrow at William, and he shrugged.

'She's persuasive, that one.'

Lara relaxed. 'Yes, she certainly can be.'

He turned his attention to me. 'Ms Earnshaw.' He touched his cap again.

'Mr Sutcliffe.'

'I'll be seeing you later as agreed?'

I nodded, then followed Lara and Hannah to a table.

'Seeing him later?' Lara asked.

'He wants to come and see The Rookery,' I reminded her. 'To get an idea of where his pictures will hang.'

'It seems a bit early for that.' Lara pursed her lips, but amusement shone in her eyes.

I shrugged.

'Lara,' I said, 'can I ask you a serious question?'

'Of course, what is it?'

'How can he be a ghost if he's flesh and blood?'

'Why, Verity,' Lara laughed, 'he can't be. You must have seen him on one of your trips here before you moved in, he's made an impression on your subconscious and that's why he's popping up in your dreams.'

'No. No, that's not it, it's more than that. Besides, if I'd seen him, I'd have remembered.' I blushed at the lifting of Lara's eyebrows, then recovered myself.

'There are at least three ghosts, right? The Grey Lady and the two orbs.'

Lara nodded.

'Because of the dreams and what else has happened – Jayne being pushed, Christmas Eve when Antony was here, last night . . .' I tailed off then gathered my thoughts, grateful that Lara had the patience to wait for me. 'Well, how can he be a ghost if he's standing right there?'

'He can't.'

'So what is he?'

'I have absolutely no idea,' Lara said, and reached over to grasp my hand. 'I'm sorry, but I don't. We don't even know that the man you've been dreaming of is one of the orbs. At least we know the Grey Lady and the orbs don't mean you harm.'

'How do we know that?'

'They still appeared after we'd cleansed and protected The Rookery. They're not evil or demonic.'

I stared at her in shock.

'Don't look so worried, Verity. Those orbs were white light, and the sense around the Grey Lady was one of peace. They're beings of light.'

'But what do they want?'

Lara opened her mouth then shut it again. She had no answer.

I looked up in time to see William tip his cap to me again and leave the pub.

7.

William Sutcliffe eyed me from head to toe, then frowned at the birds overhead and pushed past me into The Rookery.

'I'm going to dinner with Lara and Hannah when we've finished here,' I said, then mentally berated myself. Why on earth was I explaining my outfit to this man? Although, I had to admit, I hadn't chosen my V-neck dress for Lara . . .

'Uh huh,' he said, scanning me once more, then he lifted his eyes to take in the building site that was still my foyer. 'Still got a bit of work to be getting on with.'

'Yes,' I said. 'They're getting the en-suites sorted at the moment, then the plasterers and decorators can take over.'

'It'll take time for the plaster to dry.'

'Yes, I know that,' I said through gritted teeth. 'It's all in hand, the schedule's been devised for an Easter opening.'

He nodded. 'Are you going to give me the tour then?'

I bit my lip, wondering if he was being deliberately rude or if this was his habitual manner. I decided to give him the benefit of the doubt. For now.

'These will be the public rooms,' I began. 'Lounge area there, reception desk, then breakfast room through there.'

'And will you have pictures on all the walls?'

'All but that one and the corner.' I pointed. 'Those will be covered with book shelves.'

'I see.' He looked at me expectantly.

He was older than the man in my dreams, I suddenly realised, his skin more weathered and tanned. The eyes and the shock of curly dark hair were the same, though – apart from the threads of grey at his temples.

He still hadn't shaved, and the stubble was nearly long enough to be called a beard. I wondered if my dream man had the same need to shave so often, then realised I was staring.

I tried to hide my blush by rushing towards the stairway. His smirk told me he had noticed my colour.

'There will be one bedroom through here.' I placed my hand on the wall. 'They'll knock through and partition it off from the existing kitchen, but it's a bit of a mess at the moment.'

'Double or single?'

'Double with wetroom, and accessible for a wheelchair.'

He nodded, then pushed past me to the stairs.

'What will be down here?' he asked, indicating the first corridor.

'Housekeeping cupboards, then a single room at the end. Branwell's Room.'

He cocked an eyebrow in question.

'I'm calling each room by the name of a Brontë sibling. Charlotte's will be the room downstairs, Emily's and Anne's will be doubles on the next landing, then Elizabeth and Maria's at the top.'

'I thought you said five bedrooms.'

'Yes, Elizabeth and Maria's will be a twin.'

He said nothing, but opened the door to Branwell's Room and crossed to the window.

We were at the front of the building, away from the parsonage, and looking out over the rolling, green hills of the Worth Valley.

'You'll be able to see at least six mills from here when it's light,' William said. 'An image of the mill race and waterwheel would look well there, then a study of the mill floor on that wall.'

'I was thinking more of Brontë landscapes.'

'You can't have the Brontës without the mills,' he said. 'The mills were a major part of life here when they lived. The whole village depended on them. It would add a bit more interest too, rather than the same old images you see everywhere. England's dark satanic mills,' he quoted. 'William Blake, *Jerusalem*.'

'Well, I suppose so – you're the expert.'

He nodded, pointed to the door, then brushed at his face, cursing cobwebs. He pushed up his sleeves: he meant business now, and I led the way to the next rooms, listening to his suggestions, not only on subject matter and placement, but lighting too.

My initial shock at meeting him yesterday had morphed into a combination of suspicion, trepidation and . . . fascination. Yes, that was the word; he fascinated me. Why was I dreaming about him? Or a version of him, anyway.

'You know the place is haunted, don't you?' he said.

'What? Well, yes, I do as a matter of fact.' I laughed.

He held out his arm for me to inspect before I could elaborate.

Cautiously, I stepped closer and gasped when I saw every hair on his arm was standing on end. I stretched out a finger to stroke the strands and was rooted to the spot by a rush of electricity.

More energy lifted my chin – his finger, I dimly realised – and our eyes met.

'That's not static,' he said, his voice hoarse and gruff.

'No,' I said – or tried to; my own voice was misbehaving and it came out as a whisper. 'I don't think it is.'

His head lowered and my breathing accelerated. Very slowly, his lips inched closer, until his breathing was mine and mine his.

My phone rang, startling us both, and I pulled away and fumbled it out of my pocket; partly with relief that the spell, whatever it had been, was broken, and partly with exasperation at the loss.

Crestfallen, I hung up.

'Not going to dinner then?'

'No. It was Lara, Hannah's poorly – only the sniffles and a headache, but she's running a temperature and Lara's put her to bed.'

'Guess you're on your own then.'

I frowned at him, my patience running out and my mind whirling with confusion. Then my heart lurched as a smile transformed his gruff, whiskery, taciturn features.

'Sorry, that was rude. What I mean to say is, I'm dining alone as well, will you join me? Only at the Black Bull like,' he added, 'but they do a mean curry.'

I heard myself agree before I was aware I'd decided. I didn't feel as if I had any choice; not one inch of me wanted to depart from his company.

8.

The noise was tremendous, a surreal cacophony that shut out the world and exhausted the senses. Five floors of wheels, gear levers, travellers, carriages, and row upon row upon row of spinning bobbins created a rhythm more urgent and regular than her own heartbeat.

It took over everything; every movement was made to the percussion of the spinning frames. Those working the cap frames walked to a different beat to those at the ring spinners, who were out of step with the mule spinners, their wooden clogs – no hobnails allowed in here for fear of sparks – reinforcing the beat of the iron machines they tended.

The only thing out of rhythm was the staccato coughing of the women and children in attendance on these marvellous monsters of modern ingenuity. Throats dried within seconds of walking on to the spinning floor, and lungs breathed in the fine wool fibres flying off the machines like spider silk.

Even kerchiefs tied around mouths and noses couldn't keep the stuff out, and most didn't bother. For some, it filled their bellies, driving away the hunger pains, despite providing no sustenance.

Martha doubled over with the violence of her coughing fit. She had been drifting, standing with her mouth hanging open like an old clodhopper. Sarah grabbed hold of her and yanked, then pointed to forestall Martha's swinging hand; a verbal protest had no power in this place.

Instead, Martha mouthed, 'thank you', knowing Sarah would understand. Even the five-year-olds could read lips in this place.

The carriage of the spinning mule thumped into position at the end of its traverse, gears changed, and it trundled back to reunite with the rack of bobbins. Had Sarah not acted as she had, Martha would have gone with it, screaming at the top of her lungs and unheard.

Pull yourself together, lass, she scolded herself. *No point worrying unduly. What shall be, shall be.* She took a deep breath and immediately regretted it as another coughing fit racked her body. She clutched a protective hand to her belly, just in case, and her mind wandered back to her growing concern.

With her mam so poorly, and Harry's passed, there was no one at home to look after a bairn; all her sisters and Harry's were on this mill floor. She'd have to stop working and stay at home and they'd never manage without her few shillings a week.

Harry seemed not to be bothered, but Martha couldn't believe Mr

Barraclough would up his wages by that much, even if he *was* a married man now. She'd have to see about doing some weaving, Old Dan Walker was struggling to grasp the shuttles now his fingers were so crooked. Maybe she could do the weaving and him take a cut for the use of his loom? The money wouldn't be as regular, but better than nowt.

Dan worked in the weaver's gallery over the row of cottages she lived in with Harry and his family. She could easily keep the bairn in a basket by her stool. No one would hear it cry over the noise of the looms, and the rhythmic whooshing of the shuttles soothed bairns. It would be perfect.

'What's going on?' Sarah's voice penetrated the ringing in Martha's ears, and she startled back into the present. The machines weren't moving.

She'd never known the machines to still in the middle of a shift.

Martha met Sarah's eyes, wide with fright. Martha knew her own betrayed a similar emotion.

Bartholomew Grange, the overlooker, stood by the door, silent and unmoving. More confused now than scared, the women and children gathered together to hear the news. Whatever had happened was serious to bring the mill to a halt.

Baalzephon Rook, his son Zemeraim, and even the youngest, Jehdeiah – rarely seen on the mill floor – entered amidst the sound of shuffling feet and constant coughing. Now the overpowering noise had stopped, Martha noticed the smell for the first time: lanolin and grease; a sickly combination.

Suddenly she missed the unholy racket that had been the overwhelming signature of her days for as long as she could remember.

'Silence,' Grange roared, slapping his dreaded alley-strap, the one he liked to call 'The Dasher', against the door frame. It made a completely different sound against wood than skin, Martha mused. Even she could hear that.

The mass of shuffling wooden-soled clogs against wooden floorboards stilled, but not even the threat of the overlooker's leather paddle could silence the coughing.

The Rooks, at least, understood that, despite Grange's scowl.

Baalzephon Rook stepped forward and cleared his throat against the fine wool fibres still dancing in the air. 'The king is dead,' he announced. 'His niece, Victoria, has taken the throne.' He just managed to utter the final word before a coughing fit overtook him.

'Long live the queen,' Zemeraim finished his father's speech.

Martha and the other spinners, piecers and mule rats stared at him in silence. A girl of eighteen their queen? No king? How could a young lass be their queen?

9.

'She's recovered quickly.' I indicated Hannah, who was chasing rabbits across the heather, squealing in delight as their white tails flashed.

'Resilience of youth,' Lara said.

I narrowed my eyes at her. 'Was she even ill or was it just an excuse so you could play Cupid?'

'Verity! How could you suggest such a thing? You really think I'd lie about my child being ill?'

I said nothing, but stared pointedly at Hannah, who was standing, hands on hips, searching for her next four-legged victim in her game of hoppity tag.

Lara sighed. 'It turns out I may have been a little over-cautious,' she allowed. 'But you can't be too careful – especially with kids. You just don't know what will be a temporary sniffle and what will knock them on their backs for a fortnight.'

'Well, thank goodness she's okay,' I said, and Lara grinned at me.

'So, are you going to tell me? What happened last night?'

I shot another glance at Hannah to make sure she was out of earshot, then returned Lara's grin.

'It was . . . interesting.'

'Interesting? In a Chinese curse kind of way or an, I met the man of my dreams kind of way?'

I laughed. 'I'm not sure – could be either, or both, I suppose.'

Lara grimaced, then brightened again. 'Come on, stop stalling, spill.'

'Well, after you interrupted our first kiss—'

'What? How did *I* interrupt anything?'

'When you rang to cancel dinner.'

'But that was early on! Are you telling me you were already snogging?'

'No. Well, not quite, but I think he was about to kiss me.'

'Fast mover,' Lara remarked. 'Or was something else going on?'

I quirked one corner of my mouth. 'Something else. All the hair on his arm was standing on end, and it was like we were being pulled together; caught in an energy tow or something.'

'An energy tow?'

'Yes, electricity was literally shooting through me and I couldn't step away from him. Even if I'd wanted to.'

'The arrows of love,' Lara whispered. 'So then what happened?'

'You rang and broke the spell.' I laughed. 'Then we finished the tour and talked about the pictures – he has some really good ideas, you know.'

'Yeah, yeah, get on with the juicy bits.'

I gave a snort of laughter, then pulled my expression into one of seriousness. 'And then we went out for dinner.'

'Thank God for that,' Lara said. 'Things aren't as serious as I thought. There's life in you yet!'

I gave her a playful shove, then grinned at her.

'And it looks like you lived very well,' she said.

I nodded. 'We just couldn't stop talking. Once the shock of seeing him wore off, it was like we'd known each other for years. Although I can't remember what we were talking about now!'

'Hmm. Both of you *did* look shocked when we walked into that gallery.'

'Yes, but it's weird, he's not quite the guy I've been dreaming about. He's older for a start.'

Lara shrugged. 'That doesn't mean very much, it could still be the same man.'

'No, there's something in his face – the jawline. It's subtle, but it's not the same.'

'Did you dream about him last night?'

'No, not really. He took me to the mill and left me there. It was frustrating actually – I couldn't get a proper look at him.'

'Mum, Auntie Verity, the waterfall's just up here.' Hannah grabbed the hands of both Lara and myself, and tugged us up the path to the Brontë Falls. I glanced to the side where the path fell away into a steep valley, and felt a touch of vertigo, but Hannah pulling my hand kept me steady and we allowed her to drag us along.

Sunshine had greeted us this morning and we'd come up Penistone Hill to make the most of a perfect winter's day. Blue skies contrasted with the grim brown moor, and pockets of frost lingered in the hollows. The wind was biting, but luckily not too strong, and was no match for the layers of cotton, fleece and Gore-Tex we all wore. Although Lara and Hannah – and no doubt myself – sported red noses; their eyes were bright and skin glowed with health and fresh air.

I reflected that this was the very land that the Brontës had loved so much and thought I could understand how it inspired such wild and dramatic novels in the young girls.

From where we stood, the moors stretched for miles over rolling hills, bare but for the hardy heather and the odd weather-battered tree or farm standing sentinel and providing the only shelter for the creatures that made their home here. I spotted a couple of farmhouses – in ruins now – and I wondered which one was Top Withens – the farm

Emily had supposedly used for Wuthering Heights. Probably neither – that one would be further 'oop dale', I thought, coining the Yorkshire expression as I stared at the horizon: a dark, unbroken, unwavering line of hills against the blue.

'Just how much further is it, Hans?' Lara asked.

'Not far, just up past this big stone. Look, there they are!'

I stared at the small stream tumbling over little rocks and shrugged at Lara as she mouthed, *waterfall?*

The falls we had trekked to see were little more than a stream cascading through a cleft in the moor. Pretty and quite dramatic after the recent snows, the waterfall was not as large as I'd expected.

Lara perched herself on a nearby rock.

'Your throne, madam?' I asked.

'Just keeping an eye on things,' she said, watching her daughter, and swinging her feet to tap against the stone.

'Have you forgiven me yet for making you wear walking boots?'

Lara lifted her legs to regard her feet and frowned. 'I suppose I'd better get used to clodhoppers now you've moved to the country.'

I laughed then sobered as I thought about one of my early dreams – the bog burst – and remembered it had probably happened near here. I decided not to remind Lara about it.

'You didn't tell me how the evening ended,' Lara said. 'Did you . . . ?' She left the question hanging.

I kept her in suspense a moment then shook my head. 'It was a close run thing, though.' I laughed, remembering my parting from William. We had stood, still talking, outside the Black Bull for an hour, neither of us wanting to separate, neither quite daring to take the next step so soon.

I was sure the bereft expression of regret on his face as I finally broke away from his arms, had been echoed on my own face.

'When are you seeing him again? Tonight?'

I shook my head, although the temptation had been almost unbearable. 'Tonight is for my girls.' I smiled. 'Jayne's back this evening, and I thought we could all try out the ghost tour.'

'And tomorrow?'

'Well, he did let slip he'd be in the Black Bull, but we really should make the most of New Year's Eve, don't you think? There's a torch-lit procession planned – all in Victorian fancy dress, it should be very atmospheric, and a bit different.'

Lara grinned. 'A torch-lit walk to the Black Bull it is then. I'm looking forward to it.'

'Hmm.'

'What's wrong?'

'Everything's just so . . . odd. And sudden. I don't know what to make of it all. The dreams, the orbs and birds at the house, the *ghost*. And now him. One minute I'm overjoyed, the next I'm terrified.'

'To be fair, that's normal for anybody falling for someone new.'

'Who said anything about falling for him?'

By way of reply, Lara arched her eyebrows.

'Well, okay, maybe I did give that impression, a bit,' I admitted.

'*Aren't* you falling for him?'

I looked at her, helpless, unable to deny it yet afraid to confirm it.

She jumped down from her stone throne and hugged me. 'It'll be okay, Verity. Just take your time, don't do anything before you're ready, be careful of your heart, but above all, enjoy it! The last year has been hell, you deserve a bit of fun, you deserve smiles and laughter; you deserve to love and be loved.'

'But what about all the weird stuff?'

'Well, if he's connected to the man you've been dreaming about, which he must be, somehow, then he's likely to be connected to the answers too. But I think you need to decide now – do you want to understand what it's all about?'

'Yes,' I said. 'If I don't, it'll drive me mad, and someone's likely to get hurt too.'

'Then we spend New Year's Eve, or at least part of it, at the Black Bull,' Lara said. 'And we travel this road wherever it takes us.'

'Jayne may not like that idea – what if it makes everything worse?'

Lara met my eyes, then said, 'That's a risk we have to take, Verity.'

'A risk *I* have to take, you mean.'

'No, I meant what I said. Jayne and I are in this with you, wherever it takes us.'

10.

'Aunt Jayne,' Hannah cried, waving madly before dashing to hug Jayne.

I smiled as Jayne's face lit up in an expression of pleasure I'd seen nobody but Hannah evince in her since her own son and daughter had left home. Hannah had been the one who had convinced her to join us this evening.

Escaping Hannah's clutches, Jayne greeted Lara and me, waiting patiently on the church steps.

'Auntie Verity's got a boyfriend,' Hannah announced before we'd barely had chance to say hello. 'He's going to paint my picture. And Mum wore walking boots without heels. All day!'

'Are you serious? I've been gone less than a week!'

'We've got a lot to tell you,' Lara said, then approached the gentleman dressed in top hat and tails to collect a couple of lanterns he was handing out.

Jayne squeezed my arm and looked at me. 'Verity?'

'Not now,' I said, nodding at the top-hatted man. 'The tour's about to start, we don't have time – I'll fill you in later. I could do with your advice.'

'Okay,' Jayne drawled. 'Are you all right?'

'I'm not sure, to be honest.'

'Ladies and gentlemen, boys and girls,' Top Hat said, forestalling all conversation for the moment. 'The ghosts of Haworth welcome you and invite you into their world.'

'Had enough of that already,' I hissed to Lara.

The man glared at me, then bade the small group across Main Street to Gauger's Croft.

I leaned against the stone wall of the narrow, covered passageway and relaxed as I listened to the man weave his story of inns and slums, horses and carriageways, ladies in full skirts dropping small curtseys in response to the lifted top hats of gentlemen's greetings.

I peered out at Main Street; it seemed to have grown darker, much darker, and I blinked when I realised the modern-day streetlamps – fashioned to resemble olde worlde gaslights – had disappeared. In their stead were the broad, dancing naked flames of pitch torches.

I gasped and clamped my hand over my mouth as I emerged on to Main Street to investigate further. The place stank. The underlying smell of burning pitch and coal fires added a singed accent to the overpowering stench of raw sewage and rot.

I lifted my foot to investigate what I had stood in, and realised the entire street was filth. The cobbles were gone and muck flowed down the steep hill.

I jumped backwards to avoid the two gentlemen about to walk into me, and shouted after them, but they did not acknowledge my presence.

Turning to Lara, my mouth dropped open. She was gone, as were Jayne, Hannah and the rest of the ghost tour group. They hadn't passed me, so they must have moved deeper into Gauger's Croft. I hurried after them and was again halted by the overpowering stench of sewage.

Horses were crammed together so tightly the air could barely circulate around them, and I did not want to think about the constituents of the stinking piles the dim torchlight revealed.

Midden heaps, I thought. *Those are midden heaps.*

Fear solidified into a twisted ball in my stomach and I stepped back into the passageway then whirled around at the crack of a whip and a shout behind me.

A horse loomed above me, whinnying crazedly, and I screamed as the cart it pulled bore down on me.

White faces stared at me, and Jayne and Lara both put hands on my arms.

'Verity? Are you okay?'

'What happened?'

I gaped at the strange faces watching me with a mixture of curiosity and contempt, and apologised. 'It's nothing, I just got a bit carried away.'

The tour guide moved the group on, past the Black Bull, the King's Arms and the White Lion, but I barely listened, still spooked by the experience I'd had in Gauger's Croft.

It had seemed so real; the smell, or the memory of it, still stung my nose, and I had honestly believed I was about to be trampled.

Hannah's squeal brought me back to the tour, and I saw we were outside The Rookery. I was one of the stops on the ghost tour.

Flanked by Lara and Jayne, I listened in fascination as Top Hat described numerous sightings of the Grey Lady, painting a picture of exactly what I had seen, although there was no mention of orbs of light, or people being pushed.

'Auntie Verity's seen her, twice,' Hannah informed the tour guide. 'That's her house and she keeps seeing the ghost. Mum's seen her too, but I haven't, not yet. I've only fallen on the floor in that other place, the White Lion, that's the only ghost I've seen,' she continued, oblivious of Top Hat's irritation at this interruption to his narrative.

His eyes narrowed as he shifted his gaze to me and I nodded, then shrugged in apology. His expression grew thoughtful and he moved us on, introducing the 'witch's house' at the end of West Lane.

'I don't like it here, Mummy,' Hannah said. 'I feel funny, I want to go.'

'Shush, we'll be moving on in a minute,' Lara said. 'I want to hear the story about the witch.'

'But I don't like it,' Hannah cried. 'I *really* don't like it.'

'I'll take her back to the White Lion,' Jayne said, taking Hannah's hand. 'We'll have hot chocolate by the fire and wait for you there.'

'Okay, Aunt Jayne, let's go.' Hannah almost dragged Jayne away, casting an accusing glance back at her mother, and Lara met my eyes.

I couldn't decipher the expression in them, and wondered if she was feeling the same sensation I was: my chest tightening so much I was having to make a conscious effort to deflate and inflate my lungs for air.

Top Hat raised his voice as he came to the climax of his story – either that or he was just sick of the interruptions caused by me and my friends. I heard the words 'hanging from the rafters' and reached my limit. I glanced at Lara, who nodded, and we placed our lanterns on the low wall bordering the path, walked away from the tour, and hurried after Jayne and Hannah.

'Whatever that is in there, Pendle witch or not, it does not come from the light,' Lara said. 'That's a dark energy, thank God Jayne took Hannah away so quickly. I should never have brought her on this tour.'

I said nothing. I'd had enough of ghosts; I wanted hot chocolate by the fire with my friends.

II.

Martha glanced into the churchyard as she passed, able to see the site of the Sutcliffe grave where they had lain Baby John to rest before he had seen his first year out. She sighed at the memory of him, then turned her attention back to the living and stooped to pick up Edna – her little legs not quite up to the full walk to Harry's workshop. Mr Barraclough was handing more and more of the work to Harry these days, and he was fast gaining a reputation as a master stonemason in his own right.

Not surprising, all the work he does in that churchyard, Martha thought. Memorial stones had grown more intricate in latter years, the more successful families opting for altar stones rather than the more usual flat slabs laid directly on the ground, and were happy to pay for elaborate carvings to commemorate the passing of their loved ones.

Martha stopped in her tracks at the sound of voices rather than the regular percussion of hammer and chisel. *That's a woman's voice.*

She hefted Edna in her arms, and strode to confront her husband – the pail of bread and cheese she was bringing him for his dinner swinging, despite the coughing the exertion brought on.

Her expression hardened when she recognised the interloper's voice. Emily Brontë.

'It's a travesty,' she was saying, 'throwing Richard Oastler into The Fleet.'

'Aye,' Harry replied. 'It's nowt to do with debts, neither, that's just trumped up. It's to stop him acting against the mills.'

'They just don't know what to do with him – a Tory organising strikes!'

'That Thomas Thornhill has much to answer for – it's his doing, mark my words. Oh hello, love. Has thee brought me lunch?' Harry noticed Martha in the doorway.

'What's going on?' She put Edna down, who waddled over to her papa.

'They've arrested Richard Oastler, you know, The Factory King. Him who's against young 'uns working in the mills so much,' Harry explained.

'The Yorkshire Slavery he calls it,' Emily said. 'Have you read about him?'

'She don't read much,' Harry said. 'Worked in the mill since she were not much older than our Edna here. Never got to go to school.'

Emily nodded but said nothing more.

Martha added embarrassment to the cauldron of emotions boiling within her. She glared at Emily. 'Had to work for food,' she said, her voice strident. 'All of us did, couldn't swan off to no fancy school.'

Harry shot her a look of rebuke. Emily's two eldest sisters had died as a result of their time at Cowan Bridge School, something Martha knew well.

He noticed Emily's expression darken, and hurried to forestall Emily's words; trying to protect his wife from the wrath of his friend.

'Mr Oastler is for the Ten-Hour Movement,' he said, his voice unnaturally loud. 'No more getting out of bed at four and working till nightfall. And no young 'uns to be working in mill afore their tenth year.'

'But how will families manage?' Martha protested. How will they feed little 'uns without that wage?'

'Mills will have to pay a better living to them that do work,' Emily said.

'I can't see Rooks or any of other mill owners agreeing to that,' Harry said. 'Law or no law. They've paid no mind to the Factory Act, and that's been in place seven year now.'

'Aye, but there was no way of proving a child's age,' Emily argued. 'Nearly every child in the mills is "small for his age" or undernourished. Now the queen is forcing every birth to be registered, they'll not be able to get away with it no more, they'll have to prove their age with a certificate.'

'Aye, that's true enough, lass. Though for folks like my Martha here, there's not a lot of point to a certificate they can't read.'

Martha thumped Harry's lunch pail down and glared at him.

He cast his eyes down in apology, but Emily didn't seem to notice Martha's pique.

'But the authorities can read it. People like my papa write them out, and the mill owners will be kept in check. Things will come good.'

'I hope so, lass, I really do,' Harry said, then switched his attention to a safer subject by picking up his daughter to swing her round in a circle, confident Edna's giggles would soften Martha's mood.

He risked a glance at his wife, and grinned when he saw his ploy had worked.

I woke with a smile at the delightful sound of Edna's simple joy. Then realised where I was, alone in my new bed in The Rookery. My hand drifted to my stomach, a belly that had never expanded with new life, and I felt a sense of profound loss. Surprised and feeling a little shaken, I got out of bed to start the new day.

12.

'Wow, just look at that!' Lara exclaimed as Haworth Old Hall came into sight. Morris dancers were in full swing, their shin bells marking the steps of their dance, as they wielded their sticks in minutely choreographed strikes.

Flames glanced off top hats and canes, breeks and clogs, bustles and bonnets, and I staggered as the tarry smell of the burning pitch hit my nostrils. For a moment I was back in Gauger's Croft, the horse and cart bearing down on me.

A tug on my arm brought me back to the here and now. 'What's that, Auntie Verity? Is that woman holding a dog? Why isn't it moving?'

I chuckled. 'No, it's a muff, Hans. It keeps the lady's hands warm.'

Hannah looked thoughtful. 'Why doesn't she just wear gloves?'

'Back in Victorian times, ladies didn't wear big, thick gloves, only thin, dressy ones.'

'But it's like her hands are tied in front of her.'

'Not really, she can get her hands out easily.'

'Oh.'

'Welcome.' It was the man who had led the ghost tour. 'No scares tonight, hopefully,' he said as he recognised us. 'Just a walk back in time before we see the New Year in.' He held his flaming torch aloft. 'Lanterns are over there, and there's plenty of mulled wine left. Please help yourself, and we'll be setting off soon.'

'Can't we have a torch?' Hannah asked.

'No, 'fraid not. Only the organisers have those – health and safety.'

Ten minutes later, the procession of tourists and locals, all dressed in a sometimes curious mix of nineteenth-century fashion, began the climb up Main Street, the flickering torchlight reflecting off dark windows and wet slate lending an eerie atmosphere to the walk, despite the mulled wine and music, as Top Hat weaved his tales of the history of each building we passed.

The pace was slow, and slowed further the higher the cobbled street rose. The distant sound of a brass band urged us on, our feet trying to march in step to the deep beat of the tuba, although with little success, until we neared the church.

We reached the church; rebuilt in 1879, the base of the tower and the crypt below were the only parts of this building that the Brontës would have known. The sandstone almost glowed in the light of half a dozen torches, and the Haworth Band was arranged on the steps and into the square at the top of Main Street with a full complement of tuba, trombones, and trumpets.

We paused to listen. There was something almost magical about the music in this atmosphere of biting cold, pitch torches, and centuries-old buildings. I could almost imagine the Brontës enjoying a similar spectacle, and wondered if they had even listened to the same tunes.

'Well, I've worked up a thirst now,' Jayne said, hitching up her skirts yet again after catching the heel of her ankle boots in her extravagant petticoats. I smiled, she'd been very quiet since Jenny had called to say she and her brother Michael had decided to go to Edinburgh's Hogmanay celebrations for New Year, and would call in to see her on their way back south.

'What those women went through,' Lara said, pulling at her stays. 'Corsets *hurt* – and that's without the tonne of cotton silk and lace we're hauling about. Everything digs in and pinches, and *squeezes*. Who thought it would be a good idea to climb *that* hill in this lot?' She flared her skirts in a sulk.

'We'll be at the pub soon, then you can loosen up. Your corsets, I mean,' I added quickly at Lara's glare and Jayne's laugh.

Lara gave a pretend swipe at my head with her palm, then giggled. 'I can't wait to get back into jeans. Even bras don't seem so bad anymore.'

'So,' Jayne said. 'Black Bull, King's Arms or White Lion?'

'Verity'll want the Black Bull,' Lara said.

'*William* will be there,' Hannah said, drawing the name out, then her face grew serious. 'Should I call him Uncle William?'

'No!' I said, too loudly, then, 'Sorry, Hans, I didn't mean to startle you. Just William is fine, he isn't your uncle.'

'But you're not really my aunt, and I still call you Auntie Verity.'

'That's because your mum and I have been such good friends for so long, we're sisters in all but blood. We've only just met William.'

'Oh.'

'So,' Jayne said, 'Black Bull, then?'

They moved in that direction, but I hung back.

'What's wrong?'

'Let's make tonight about us,' I said. 'No men, no ghosts, no dreams, no complications, just us. It's New Year's Eve – I want to celebrate with you, not William, or Harry, or whoever he is.'

Lara and Jayne walked back and linked arms with me.

'Verity, are you crying?'

I wiped awkwardly at my face, almost dislodging Lara's arm, surprised to find it wet.

'I-I—' My breath hitched in a sob.

'Verity, it's okay,' Lara soothed.

'I'm sorry.' I got a tenuous grip on myself. 'I don't know what just happened.'

'Don't worry about it, and there's nothing to apologise for,' Jayne said as Lara rubbed my back. 'You've had a lot going on. Getting divorced and moving house are two of the most stressful things you can do. Add to that starting your own business, the renovations, and the hauntings, I'm surprised you're not having a breakdown!'

'Oh, a breakdown sounds good,' I said, forcing a laugh. 'Can I go somewhere quiet and have a rest?'

Lara laughed. 'That's what a guesthouse is supposed to be about – quiet and rest!'

My chuckle was genuine this time. 'I suppose you have a point, but that tends to be the guests, not the proprietor.'

'You can always come and stay with us – anytime things get too much,' Lara said, and Jayne agreed.

'Vikram seems very capable, I'm sure he'd cope if you spent a few days with one of us,' she said.

'Thank you.' I gave them both a squeeze. 'Even the thought of it makes me feel better. Look, no tears!' I raised my face up and showed them first one cheek then the other. 'But I am ready for a large glass of something.'

Arm in arm, we crossed the road and made our way to the White Lion, only now realising Top Hat was standing nearby, awaiting the return of his lanterns.

13.

'Ah, that's better, loose corsets and wine,' Lara said, sinking down on to her seat, her skirts narrowly avoiding knocking drinks off three tables as she did so.

'Saucy,' I said. 'Careful, you'll give people the wrong impression.' I smiled at the family on the next table.

'Or the right one,' Jayne said, deadpan.

'I'll drink to that,' Lara said, unfazed, and lifted her glass. Giggling, Jayne and I joined in.

'Better?' Lara asked me.

I nodded. 'Things just got a bit much,' I said. 'Plus it's New Year's Eve, and that always gets me – especially this year with the divorce and everything.'

'Yes, it's definitely been a year of big changes,' Jayne said. 'But you're moving forward positively. New home, new business, new man . . .' She raised her eyebrows and smirked.

'Ghosts, spooks and nightmares.' I aped her expression.

'We'll fix all that,' Lara said. 'It's only frightening at the moment because we don't understand what's going on. But don't forget, the cleansing and protection I did doesn't work.'

'You say that as if it's a good thing,' Jayne said, eyebrows raised.

'It is,' Lara insisted. 'It means the spirits, whatever or whoever they are, mean no harm.'

'Is that why one tried to push me down the stairs?' Jayne shot back. 'Or destroyed Verity's kitchen and sent Antony running.'

'Maybe that was the point – getting rid of Antony,' Lara said. 'Protecting Verity.'

'And me? Does Verity need protecting from me, too?'

'Of course not. What was going on when it happened though?'

Jayne paused, then a strange look crept across her face. I remembered at the same time.

'We were talking about my dream man. Don't you remember, Jayne? You were wondering if he was Heathcliff, and warned me off dysfunctional men.'

'That's interesting,' Lara said.

'Enough,' I said, forestalling Jayne's reply. 'Sorry, but can we just have a break from it all tonight, please?'

Lara nodded as Hannah climbed on to her lap. She stroked her daughter's hair as Hannah's thumb found its way into its owner's mouth. 'Are you sure you don't want to go to bed, Hans?'

She shook her head.

'She's determined to stay up till midnight,' Lara said with a smile. 'First time ever.'

'Sunday tomorrow,' Jayne said. 'We can all have a lie in and a quiet day.'

'Actually, I wondered if it would be a good idea to go to church tomorrow.'

'Church?' I repeated.

Lara shrugged. 'Can't do any harm, and a bit of prayer may help.'

'I'm willing to try anything at the moment,' I said.

'Talking of willing,' Jayne said, indicating the door behind me. 'I didn't know they were friends.'

I turned to see William and Vikram standing at the door looking awkwardly around the room.

'I almost didn't recognise him,' Lara whispered, and I pulled my eyes away from William's to consider Vikram. He looked more the artist than William did, and without a trace of builder. His chunky black collared sweater hugged his body and suited him almost as much as his black flat cap and dark-rimmed glasses. I smiled; Lara and Jayne would be fighting over him before the year was out.

My eyes slid back to William. He hadn't made as much effort as Vikram, but was simply dressed in a white, open-necked shirt and jeans. The ensemble set off his dark eyes perfectly, and his freshly shaved jaw took years off him.

Thank goodness he hasn't got dressed up, I thought, shifting uncomfortably in my Victorian-style gown, *I'd have thought him to be Harry.*

Vikram led the way to our table, but before the greetings were completed, William escaped to the bar and I stared after him, my heart beating hard, then glanced at Vikram in consternation.

Vikram shrugged and looked embarrassed. 'I hope you don't mind.'

'Of course not, it's good to see a friendly face,' Jayne said. 'Why don't you sit down, join us?'

We shuffled round and Vikram squeezed in on the bench next to Jayne.

'Happy New Year,' I said to him, draining my glass. 'I'm surprised to see you here, I just expected tourists – I thought you'd be going up to town.'

'No, it gets too much – full of teenagers falling over,' he said. 'I'd rather just go down the pub with my mates.'

'I didn't realise you and William knew each other.'

He gave me a funny look. 'Known him since I were a lad. I didn't know *you* knew him.'

I opened my mouth then closed it again. Why had I said that? Vikram was right, *I* was the incomer here. *I* was the one who didn't know anybody in Haworth, who had no ties here.

William plonked a couple of pints of bitter on the table, then left again, all without saying a word.

I glanced at Jayne and Lara, who asked Vikram, 'Is he always so friendly?'

Vikram smiled and sipped his beer. 'He's Yorkshire. Tends to keep himself to himself, but he'll speak when he has summat to say. Then you won't shut him up.' He replaced his pint glass on the table and looked thoughtful. 'He has been a bit out of sorts, though, lately. He was gutted when you didn't show up at the Bull, Verity.' He winked then jumped as a bottle of Sauvignon blanc was slammed on to the table.

William glared at his mate, then turned to me and said, 'Tess behind the bar says this is the one you're all drinking.'

'Th-thanks, yes,' I stammered, and shifted on my seat to make more room.

Jayne coughed and I realised she hadn't met him yet.

'This is Jayne,' I said with a hand flourish. 'And this is William.' I flourished my other hand.

'He's the painting man,' Hannah said, proving she was still determined to stay awake. 'Auntie Verity's boyfriend.'

William spluttered into his beer and I shut my eyes for a moment then busied myself pouring wine, unsure what to do or say, and unable to look at him.

Lara came to my rescue. 'I think it's a bit soon to be saying that, Hans.'

I gulped my wine, still not daring to look at William, yet very aware of him squashed up beside me.

'Yes, the rule is three dates,' William told Hannah, his voice serious, and Jayne nudged my leg on my other side. 'You're not boyfriend and girlfriend before three dates.'

'And by then you'll know whether or not you want to be,' Vikram added, laughing, then leaned towards Jayne and muttered something I couldn't hear.

'Oh, I see,' Hannah said and paused. 'Is this a date?'

'This is just friends meeting up to celebrate a new year,' Lara said.

'So what would make it a date then?'

'I'll tell you later,' Lara said, 'in private.'

'Ah, kissing,' Hannah said, stuck her thumb back in her mouth and wriggled on Lara's lap until she was comfortable again.

'How did you enjoy the procession?' Vikram asked, covering Lara's shocked silence, Jayne's poorly stifled giggles, and the matching blush on William's face and my own. 'Looks like you went to a lot of trouble.'

'You didn't fancy the Bull then?' William spoke softly in my ear as the others discussed the merits of various items of Victorian dress.

'I'm sorry, it was rude of me to stand you up.'

'So why did you?'

I sipped my wine, then looked up at him. 'Everything's just been so full on lately, then with all the brass band stuff, the Bull was heaving, I just felt overwhelmed. I guess I needed a quiet evening with the girls. I'm sorry, it was a last minute decision.'

'You don't need to apologise,' he said. 'Are you okay with us being here? Do you want us to go?'

'No,' I said, a little louder than I'd intended. 'No, it's good to see you, I'm enjoying this.'

'Not too full on?' he teased.

I said nothing, my mind whirling.

'I know what you mean, though,' he added. 'Something's going on here – it has me a bit, well, freaked too.'

'Freaked?' I raised an eyebrow then put my hand on his knee before I realised I'd done so. I moved quickly to hold my wine with both hands. 'Sorry. Yes, freaked is a good word.'

He leaned towards me at the same time as I turned to him.

'Ow,' he said, holding his nose as I rubbed my temple.

'The fireworks are starting!' Hannah shouted, scrambling off her mother's knee, and I looked round in surprise to see the bar was almost empty.

'Blimey, is that the time?' Jayne said, echoing my own thoughts and we grabbed drinks and shawls, then hurried outside.

Fully aware of William standing next to me, I did my best to ignore him. I couldn't decide whether I wanted to engage him in intelligent conversation, or tell him to leave me alone, so instead I oohed and ahhed with everyone else at the white, green and red flowers depicted in the skies above Haworth Moor.

'Ten, nine, eight, seven . . .'

My breath froze as I realised what the chant meant. What it was leading up to. It had been so long since I'd enjoyed a New Year's Eve celebration as a single woman, I'd forgotten about the pressure.

My heart beat faster and I could feel the warmth spread over my chest and head.

'Four, three . . .'

'Verity?'

'Umm?' It was all I could manage, and I risked a glance upwards, just as an almighty barrage of rockets, Roman candles and mines put everything that had gone before to shame.

His lips were on mine before I registered he'd leant in, and the scratch of his new stubble tickled my jaw.

That's really going to irritate my skin, I thought, before sensation took over doubt, fear and sense.

I kissed him back, my tongue meeting his, teasing, playing, exploring. My lips allowed him to lead the dance and my misgivings melted away – at least for the moment.

We parted with a gasp, both of us short of breath, and my flush deepened at the stares of Jayne, Lara, Hannah and Vikram.

14.

'Let us confess our sins in penitence and faith,' the vicar of St Michael and All Angels intoned.

'Verity!' Lara nudged me and passed me a packet of tissues.

I gave her a puzzled glance.

'Your nose,' she hissed.

'Live in love and peace with all.'

I put my fingers to my face. They came away bloody. I fumbled a tissue out and held it to my nose – just in time as blood gushed from me.

'Head back,' Jayne whispered, then smiled reassuringly at the woman in the pew in front of us who'd turned to see what was going on. I kept my head bowed, not wanting to swallow the blood.

'Lord, have mercy.'

Lord have mercy, indeed, I thought, echoing the vicar's words. *Why now?* I had suffered from regular nosebleeds in the early days of my breakup with Antony, but I hadn't had one for months now. Until today.

'Keep it back,' Jayne insisted, passing me a fresh tissue.

I glared at her, but this was not the time to debate the correct head position during nosebleeds.

The congregation stood to sing a hymn, and I risked moving the tissue away. A mistake.

'I need to go,' I said as best I could.

'You take her, Lara,' Jayne said.

'You're not coming?'

'No, I'd like to stay. Unless you need me, Verity?'

'No.' It came out more like 'doe'. 'I'll be okay. You stay too, Lara.'

'I'm coming,' Lara said in a tone of voice I knew not to argue with. 'But we'd better hurry.'

Jayne slipped out of the pew to let us out and I hurried out the door, closely followed by Lara and Hannah, grateful we'd chosen a pew at the back.

'Why was that lady staring at us?' Hannah asked. 'Couldn't she see Auntie Verity had a nose bleed?'

'Probably thinks I did something to deserve it or there's something wrong with me,' I said dryly, 'and shouldn't set foot in a church.'

'Stop that right now, Verity,' Lara said. 'It's a nosebleed, nothing more, nothing less.'

I handed her the packet of tissues to extract another for me, then placed the fresh tissue to my nose.

'I think it's getting better, Auntie Verity.'

'Yes, it's definitely slowing,' Lara added. 'Come on, let's get you home and cleaned up.'

'Jayne's taking her time,' Lara said as she handed me a mug of coffee and took away the now-melted bag of peas to replace them in the freezer.

'Umm,' I said. 'She's up to something.'

Lara shrugged, sat beside me, and sipped her coffee. 'How are you feeling?'

I brushed my fingertip under my nose, and gave it a quick check. Clean. 'It's stopped.' I touched the tip of my nose and winced. 'All a bit sore, though.'

'You've got a red nose, like a clown, Auntie Verity,' Hannah informed me.

Lara laughed, which somewhat negated the impact of her, 'Don't be rude, Hans.'

She recovered herself and touched my arm. 'It's just the frozen peas, Verity.'

I smiled. I knew well what I must look like, and doubted Hannah was far wrong. I pulled a face at her, immediately regretting the nose scrunch, but the laughter was worth it.

'I think I'll just go and change,' I said, tugging my top to show off the blood drips, but was stopped by Grasper's frenzied barking.

'Aunt Jayne's back,' Hannah announced from the window. 'She's got the vicar with her, he's still wearing his dress.'

'Cassock,' Lara corrected as she joined her daughter at the window and peered below. 'Looks like you were right – she *is* up to something.'

'Well, that was a waste of time,' Lara said as we found a free table.

'Couldn't hurt to try,' Jayne said. 'Do you both want wine, shall I get a bottle?'

'Coke, please, Aunt Jayne.'

'Apple juice or water for you, miss,' Lara corrected.

'Apple juice.' Hannah pouted then added, 'Please,' at her mother's raised eyebrow.

We sorted menus while Jayne went to the bar.

'It was a good idea, Jayne,' I said when she returned. 'Thanks. Though I'm surprised you persuaded the vicar to come straight over after the service.'

'He said it's not the first time someone's had a spontaneous nosebleed in his church,' Jayne said. 'He said if you were that stressed, the least he could do was come round as soon as the congregation had left.'

'He probably wanted a look-see at what you're doing to the place,' Lara said. 'You know what these villages are like, everyone wants to know everybody else's business.'

'Probably,' I said with a laugh. 'Either that or he was looking for the Grey Lady.'

'Behave,' Jayne said. 'It was good of him to give up his time to bless the house – it's his busy day, you know.'

We all laughed then, the tension broken. Truth be told, I had found the blessing comforting – and very similar to Lara's cleansings. I couldn't quite understand why she was being so sarcastic and resistant. I shrugged; maybe she just wanted to be the one to solve the issue.

'What's up?' Jayne asked.

'Nothing, just trying to make sense of the last few days,' I said.

'Are the dreams back?' Lara asked.

'No.' I blushed. 'I couldn't sleep last night – not a wink.'

'Ah, thinking about William,' Jayne teased.

My blush deepened.

'You're one to talk, Jayne, did you dream about Vikram, or did he keep you up all night too?'

'What?' I stared at Jayne, whose blush was in competition with mine. She was the scarlet of a hunting jacket.

'Yes, Vikram and our Jayne at midnight,' Lara said. 'Giving you and William a run for your money – I had to cover Hannah's eyes.'

'No, I saw them.'

'Oh, thank goodness,' Jayne said as Tess approached with our wine. 'I need a bloody drink.'

'Roast beef and Yorkshire puddings all round, please,' Lara said to Tess. Then, to us, 'What?'

'We might have wanted something else!'

'Tough – it's a Yorkshire roast for you while you both fill me in on your men. And be aware of young ears!'

15.

Deep breath. You can do this, I thought, then reached out and pushed my way through the inner door to the Black Bull.

I paused, self-conscious, my eyes scanning the interior, trying to check each nook and cranny without appearing too obvious.

Then I saw him. Hand raised. Smiling. At the bar. Waiting for me. William Sutcliffe.

The worry that he wouldn't be here, and the fear that he would be, coalesced, but now the churning in my stomach was infused with warmth. He was here, and I was here. Everything else – caution, memories, Antony, my dreams – hadn't been powerful enough to keep me away. Whatever the evening would bring, I was here; he was here.

I realised I was still standing near the entrance, blushed, smiled, and walked towards him.

'Hi, I was worried you were going to stand me up again.'

My heart leapt into my mouth, and I realised I'd made a mistake. 'You weren't expecting me to turn up? You didn't mean it?'

'Oh,' he held the flat of his hand out to me, 'no, that's not what I meant. I was just trying to make a joke.'

'Oh,' I said, 'I see.' I was lost. Was this a date or wasn't it?

'Shall we start again?' He grinned, and my heart leapt again, this time more pleasantly, at the lopsided smile and resultant dimple in his right cheek. I nodded.

'Hello Verity, it's good to see you.' The dimple deepened. 'Would you like a drink?'

'Yes please, a large one.' I found myself wishing for dimples in my own cheeks to match his.

'That bad is it?'

'Getting better.'

Deeper still. A pause, then a quirk of his eyebrow.

'What's wrong?'

'*What* would you like to drink?'

'Oh, yes. Umm, dry white wine please.'

He ordered it, plus another pint of Black Sheep for himself. 'Haven't done this for a while.'

'No, I'm a bit out of practice.'

'I meant me.'

'Oh.'

'Shall we sit down?'

'I think we'd better.'

We found a seat in the corner by one of the lopsided leaded windows, and looked at each other in silence for a few moments.

'Shall we start again?'

'Okay.'

We laughed then, the awkwardness dissipating in the absurdity of the situation. A couple of nights ago, we'd been in each other's arms at the birth of a new year, a couple of nights before that we'd hardly been able to stem the words; now we seemed incapable of conversation.

'It's good to see you,' William said.

'You too. Cheers.' I held my glass up to clink, then we drank, our eyes locked on each other.

I realised he was younger than I'd originally thought – probably mid-thirties rather than early forties. His face was tanned, but what I'd taken for wrinkles, I now saw were pale lines – crease lines, I realised. He must spend a lot of time outdoors, squinting into the sun.

'You've shaved,' I said, out loud, then gasped and clamped my hand over my mouth.

'Well, I am on a date,' he said dryly, his eyebrows raised. 'Though it's a damn strange one so far.'

'Sorry, I'm out of practice,' I reaffirmed.

'Good.'

I took another drink, cursing myself for injecting discomfort back into the evening.

'It looks good.'

'What does?'

For answer, I stroked my chin, though in truth it wasn't a good look on him, the skin of his jaw was two shades paler than the rest of his face.

'Thanks.'

'Have you ever grown a beard?'

He shrugged. 'Once or twice, but it comes in grey and is a bugger to trim. Easier to shave it off.'

I nodded and sipped my drink again. *Why on earth am I quizzing him about his shaving habits? How would I like it if he asked me about mine?*

'Should get rid of these really, too,' he continued, running his fingers through his sideburns. I realised he was just as nervous as I was, and glad to have something – anything – to talk about. 'Rebekah won't let me though, insists they make me look distinguished.' He wobbled his head in mockery with the last word.

'Rebekah?'

'My sister.'

Relieved, I said, 'She's right, they suit you – give you a certain . . . gravitas.'

'Gravitas?'

I shrugged. 'When the word fits.'

'I'll tell Rebekah that next time she comes to cut my hair.' The dimple reappeared.

'Is she a hairdresser?'

'No, a historian.'

I laughed. 'And the sideburns now make perfect sense!'

We clinked glasses again.

'So how is The Rookery coming on?'

'On schedule so far – thanks to Vikram,' I replied and surreptitiously tapped the wooden table three times. I noticed William watch my fingers, but he didn't remark on the habit. He definitely had better manners than I did.

'Aye, he's a good man is our Vikram. He's very taken with your mate, you know.'

'Jayne? Yes, I heard they got close New Year's Eve.'

Silence fell again as our eyes met, both embarrassed as we remembered how we'd 'got close' at the same time, and I wondered if he felt the same tingle of excitement I did.

'So, Sutcliffe,' I said, 'no relation to Peter?'

He groaned. 'Why do women always ask me that? No, I'm no relation to the Yorkshire Ripper. Another wine?' He got up without waiting for a response and went to the bar.

When he returned, I thanked him for the drink and apologised.

'No, it's fine, it's a fair question. The man terrorised the area – I can remember my sister being banned from going out alone, most lasses were – thank God he's rotting in Broadmoor or wherever they moved him to. I just hate that we share a surname, does me no good on dates.'

I smiled at the sight of his dimple.

'Tell me about your family,' he said. 'Why did you choose Haworth?'

'Well, I got divorced about a year ago – the details have only just been finalised.'

'So you're starting over?'

'Exactly.'

'Why here?'

'My dad was from Keighley, we used to come here at weekends when I was a child – this place holds my happiest memories – in fact, my dad's family may have originated here, they definitely worked in the local mills.'

'Have you never looked into it, ancestry.com and all that?'

'Have you tried sticking "Earnshaw" and "Yorkshire" into any search engine? There are millions of hits thanks to *Wuthering Heights*.'

'Yes, I can see that would be a problem.' He smiled. 'Maybe Emily based Catherine on one of your ancestors.'

'God, I hope not!'

16.

'Your turn,' I said when I rejoined him, fresh drinks in hand. 'Have you always lived in Haworth?'

'Born and bred,' he said, his pride evident in the smug cast of his smile – no dimple. 'Apart from three years at art school. This is my home – I hated being away, and I can't imagine living anywhere else. We can trace the family back here over three hundred years. I love the moors, the people, the way of life here, both past and present. I just have to paint it, all of it.'

'Wow, so you're not an adventurous breed then?'

I cringed, wondering if I'd been inappropriate again, but he continued without a flinch.

'My grandda and his before him, and his before him, were stonemasons – carved most of the stones in the churchyard they did, and built most of the houses of their time.'

I felt cold and faint headed, but if I'd paled as well, he didn't notice.

'The business struggled when they stopped burying people in the churchyard.'

'Why did they stop?'

'Overcrowding, and the stones were laid flat, so the gases and rot from decomposition were trapped in the ground. Some of those graves are twelve corpses deep, and there's no spaces between them. Supposed to stop in the 1850s they were, after the Babbage Report pretty much condemned the village. But nobody took much notice – folk want to be with their folk, it takes a lot to come between family in these parts.'

I nodded. 'Who was Babbage?'

'An inspector in the 1850s from the General Board of Health – Patrick Brontë had him come out, actually, the sisters' father. Anyways, the living conditions here were atrocious: life expectancy early-twenties; at least one funeral every day; over two thousand people sharing four wells and twenty five privies. Not good.' He shuddered, and I joined him.

'One of the wells was out back here by the graveyard, and another next to the morgue, where the Tourist Information is now. Can you imagine? Even the cows wouldn't drink from it, folk had no chance. Anyroad, things started improving after he came, and eventually they stopped digging graves.'

'Not before time, by the sounds of it.'

'But it meant no one needed new headstones. I think it was a blessing really when the museum people bought the parsonage – they knocked down the old mason's workshop to make room for the car park.'

'That must have been difficult for your family,' I said. 'The stonemason's workshop must have been a big part of Haworth's history, especially with it having been so close to the parsonage.'

'Aye, just not the sort of history that brings in the tourists,' William said with a smile – dimple evident this time – and took a long drink.

'Anyway, they didn't do too badly from the sale of the land, enough to set the family up in other businesses. My father had the shop on Main Street – shoemakers it was in his day, then when he retired, I took it over and reopened as an art gallery.'

'What did he think to that?'

'Not a lot,' William admitted, 'but he's starting to come round now.'

'How long have you been open?'

'About ten years.'

I laughed. 'And he's just starting to come round to the idea?'

William shrugged. 'Yorkshire folk don't like change. Things are best done the way they've always been done.'

I raised my eyebrows and pouted. I had plenty of memories of my dad saying exactly the same thing.

'I didn't have it as bad as Rebekah, though. You should have heard my dad when she told him she was going to university to read history. Well, most of the village did hear him!' He laughed, but with no mirth, and took another drink.

'Still complains to this day, though we're both making good livings. Not sure he means it now, though, just does it to keep up his curmudgeonly reputation.'

I giggled. 'He sounds like quite a character.'

'Oh aye, that he is, right enough. Just beware when you meet him, he'll have all sorts to say about you opening yet another guesthouse.'

'When I meet him?'

'Aye, well.' He coloured. 'Bound to before long, living here.'

The bell behind the bar rang, and William jerked his head round to stare at the barman.

'Bloody hell, last orders already? Can't be.'

I checked the time on my watch. 'Eleven,' I said. 'Funny, living in Leeds, I haven't heard a last orders' bell in years. Everywhere just stays open.'

'Aye, well, you're in the country now. Things are done the way they always were,' William said. 'And we forgot to eat! Everywhere will be closed now too, dammit.'

'Not to worry, let's get a last round in, then we can go back to mine – I should be able to rustle up an omelette or something.'

'You sure?'

'Yes, but I'm only offering food, mind, it *is* only a second date.'

We smiled at each other, eyes locked together, then William pulled away at the shout of 'Last orders, please!' from the bar.

'Blimey, what's going on?' William ducked as a couple of birds swooped at us.

'Oh yes, they seem to like roosting here – it turns out calling it The Rookery is very apt!'

William looked up at the gable and windows of The Rookery. 'They never used to roost here before.'

'Really? They've been bothering me since I moved in. I'm sure there are more of them every day.' I gave a nervous laugh and found the keyhole with my still unfamiliar key.

'I've only ever known them roost in the churchyard,' William said. 'My sister used to tell me they were the souls of all the babies buried there. Scared the life out of me, she did – I couldn't go near the place for years.'

'She sounds lovely!' I laughed.

'Aye, but she's also a big sister – had to have her fun with me.'

I switched the lights on and led the way to the stairs. 'The only working kitchen at the moment is the one upstairs, I'm afraid.'

'Vikram's still got a lot to do, hasn't he?'

'Yes, but there's time. They're doing well, actually, on schedule so far, despite the holiday season.'

'That doesn't sound like him – mind you, I guess he's only just started.' William laughed, then realised what he'd said when I turned to him.

'What do you mean? Should I be worried?'

'No, no, not at all. Sorry, me and my big mouth. He's one of the good ones is Vikram, we were at school together. When he does a job, he does it proper – even if it takes him a bit longer. He'll see you right, don't worry about it.'

I nodded, mollified, and led the way up the narrow staircases.

'So why didn't you come to the Black Bull on Saturday – the real reason?'

I didn't turn. I couldn't look at him. 'I-I'm sorry. I shouldn't have stood you up like that. I've taken so much on with The Rookery, and especially after all the stuff with the divorce, it just seemed too much. And Hannah was with us, too, of course.' I paused. 'I'm glad you and Vikram came to the White Lion, though.'

'Yes, me too. I wasn't sure if you'd turn up tonight.'

I giggled. 'I couldn't do that to you again. Anyway, I enjoyed New Year's Eve.' Now I did turn, smiled, and led the way to my apartment.

* * *

I opened the fridge. 'Wine or lager?'

'No bitter?'

'None I'm afraid.'

'Guess I'll have to make do with lager then.'

I glanced at him, ready to apologise, but relaxed when I saw his dimple, and passed him a bottle of Becks. I poured myself a glass of wine, then regarded the fridge once more.

'Well, it looks like cheese omelette – that do you?'

'Cheese? At this time of night? You'll give us nightmares.'

'To be honest, it doesn't seem to take cheese to have strange dreams at the moment, I've been having them since I moved in.' I glanced at him, then away again as I put eggs and cheese on the worktop.

'Strange dreams?'

'Hmm.'

'Verity?'

I turned and looked at him properly.

'I've been having strange dreams too,' he said.

'Really? I bet mine are stranger!'

He grinned. 'I've been dreaming about you.'

'What?'

'I've been dreaming about you, for a couple of weeks now. Then you walked into my gallery and I felt pretty much how you look right now. Come and sit down.'

He took my arm and led me to the sofa. A loud crash made me scream and my glass fell, smashing and drenching the floor with Pinot Grigio. 'What the hell was that?'

William left me at the sofa and rushed to the window. 'One of the birds,' he said. 'Must have been mesmerised by the light. I'm afraid it's cracked the window. More work for Vikram.'

'Is it dead?'

'Unlikely. It landed on the tiles, probably just stunned. Best thing is to leave it to sort itself out if it can.'

'And if not?'

He shrugged. 'Nowt we can do. Why did you look so shocked when I told you I'd been dreaming about you? It sounds like a corny pick-up line, I expected you to laugh.'

'Get me a new glass of wine, and I'll tell you.'

17.

'You romantic devil!' Martha exclaimed as Harry presented her with a bouquet.

'Well, three years to the day since we were wed,' he said. 'Look, I got gorse, garlic, pussy willow.'

'And the honeysuckle too – the same as my bridal flowers!' Martha held the blooms to her nose and breathed the scent in. She could just make out the delicate scent of the honeysuckle under the more powerful wild garlic.

'Lizzie's happy to have Edna, one more don't make no difference to her now.'

'What, all day?' Harry's sole surviving sister was not normally so free with offers of help.

'Aye, well, special occasion, ain't it?'

'Thee's paid her, ain't thee, Harry?'

He shrugged. 'Special occasion,' he repeated. 'And we're doing all right. I've plenty of work on, and there'll be no let up, not with the smallpox rife. We can afford it, love. Relax and stop worrying, at least for today.'

Martha did as she was bid and leaned her head on her husband's shoulder for a moment. 'So what does thee have in mind?'

'Get out of this village, for one. I've bread and cheese,' he kicked the pail by his feet, 'and a couple of bottles of porter—'

'Thee *is* splashing out!'

Harry raised his eyebrows at her and she stilled her protest.

'I thought we could go up to Harden Woods, it'll be pretty there, the bluebells might be out, too.'

'That sounds lovely.' Martha smiled at her husband and kissed him full on the lips.

'Hang about, woman. We're in public! Plenty of time for all that later.' He grinned and smacked Martha's rump, enjoying the sound of her resultant squeal. He hadn't heard that mock-protest in a very long time.

Harry dropped the pail of food and beer, grabbed Martha – to another squeal – and spun her around in much the same way he usually did with Edna, then kissed her. Not like the way he did Edna.

He pulled Martha to him as she responded, their bodies reacting to each other in the way they used to. It had been some months since they had shared more than a discreet fumble in a room full of sleeping bodies, and both wanted to take their fill of each other.

Martha pulled back and smiled at Harry, brushing away the hair that flopped over his eyes, then stroked his whiskers.

'You're looking very distinguished these days,' she said.

'Well, I'm a master mason now. Folk expect a bit of distinguishment.'

Martha giggled. 'Is that even a word?'

'Don't know, I'll have to ask Emily.' He could have bitten his tongue. Of all the stupid things to do – mention Emily Brontë to his wife.

He didn't understand Martha's antipathy towards her, apart from the usual wary regard most of the village folk had for Emily. But with Martha it was something different, something more.

'She'll likely not know either,' he added in an attempt to undo the harm. He kissed his wife again, melting her heart towards him once more, and grabbed her rump to pull her close.

He was rewarded with another squeal and he hooked her legs, bent her body, and landed her on the ground with a thump. He got slightly more than a squeal for that, but there was no real sting in her slap.

He straddled her and gazed down at his wife of three years. *Why can she not accept that I love her and no other?*

Along with the grief of losing their firstborn, John, that was his only sorrow, knowing that she had no real faith in him. God knew, he had done nothing to deserve her distrust; had always been true to her, unlike many of his peers. But nothing would persuade her of his fidelity and loyalty.

He pushed the thoughts away and smiled down at Martha. Today may well help in that regard.

'You're as pretty as a picture,' he said, and meant it. Her flaxen curls framed her face, and she was surrounded by the greenest grass which brought out the little flecks of green in her otherwise blue eyes, a similar hue to the bluebells which nodded their trumpet heads in the April breeze.

The smile he was granted warmed his heart and he bent his lips to worship it.

I woke, blinked and groaned. I tried to move my arm to grasp my aching head, but it was trapped. I shifted and tried to roll, then realised my body was not the restraint.

Wide awake now, I scrambled to a sitting position, throwing away William's embrace and startling him to wakefulness.

'What the hell?'

I stared at him, stricken, then relaxed in the warmth of his smile and

the slow realisation that he was still dressed. I glanced down. So was I.
Thank God.

William wiped his face with his hands, then seemed to be brushing something away. He looked at his hands, bemused, then turned his gaze back to me and shrugged. 'Felt like cobwebs, but there's nothing there, must be the remnants of a dream.'

'Cobwebs?'

He smiled and showed his hands. 'No. Nothing there. Good morning.'

I relaxed a little more. 'Morning.' I smiled, shy. I had not woken up with a man since Antony. It had been a long time since I had been so intimate, even if we were still fully clothed.

Slowly, the events of the evening before materialised in my memory. The rook striking the window and cracking it, the draught, the cold. Me freaking out, knowing those birds were just outside that broken pane of glass.

We'd made omelettes so quickly we could qualify for the Saturday morning omelette challenge, scarfed them down, then brought the rest of the alcohol into the bedroom, closing the door on the cracked window.

Then we'd talked.

And talked, and talked.

I'd fallen asleep in William's arms and, thinking back now, hadn't felt so safe for a very long time.

Then I'd panicked when I'd woken in those same arms.

Ashamed, I cuddled up to him. 'I had the strangest dream.' I blushed, remembering the bluebell wood.

He gave a humourless laugh. 'I'm not surprised, with everything that's been going on, I had a weird one too. Very interesting it was.' Our eyes met, and I saw he was as embarrassed as I was.

As one, we reached for each other and kissed. Lips soft against mine, tongue gently exploring, his breath feathering my cheek. My heart thumped then settled into a faster rhythm and I could feel his matching mine.

My hands moved down his arms as his crept down my back and cupped my waist as I reached his hips.

Then we broke apart – together – and rested our heads on each other's shoulders, panting hard.

Again as one, we sat up straight and found each other's eyes.

'I can't quite believe I'm saying this—'

'But I need to wait,' I interrupted.

William nodded. 'This is something – I mean *really* something. I don't want to rush it or get it wrong. I want to do things right.'

'Me too,' I whispered. 'These old-fashioned values are quite romantic, really,' I said with a smile, brushing my thumb over his lips.

'Hmm. Not quite sure when I adopted them, though.' He laughed.

'Nor me.' I lowered my face with a smile and glanced up at him through my lashes. 'Coffee?'

18.

I opened my front door the following Friday evening, and flung it wide to usher in Lara and Jayne. I cast a suspicious glance upwards, but the rooks were no threat.

Today, at least.

We hugged, then I stood back and saw a glance pass between Lara and Jayne.

'What?'

'It's just good to see you,' Lara said.

'We haven't heard much from you the past week,' Jayne said with a sidelong glance at Lara. 'We've been worried.'

'Worried?' I scoffed. 'I'm fine, better than fine, I'm in love!'

'Already?' Jayne asked.

I glared at her.

'A week ago you were avoiding William,' Lara pointed out. 'Now he seems to have taken you over. We're concerned, that's all.'

'Yes, you've been through a lot lately, we just want to be sure that life is being kind to you now – for as long as possible.' Jayne smiled.

I hesitated before answering, then relaxed. 'It is, it *is* being kind. William is amazing. I'm so sorry I've been quiet all week, truly I am.' I smiled and held my arms out to embrace my friends once more. The hug was slightly awkward, but none of us remarked on it.

'It's like we've been in our own fantasy land,' I continued, leading the way upstairs.

Lara and Jayne didn't answer.

'Our own little Gondal, that's what we say.' I giggled as I turned to them. 'After the world Emily Brontë created with Anne.'

Jayne gave a small smile, and I faced forwards again and began the climb up the next staircase in silence, wondering what they were both thinking. I couldn't remember the last time I'd felt so awkward around my friends.

I opened the door to my apartment and ushered them in, then stared at the empty staircase behind them. 'Where's Grasper?'

Jayne's jaw tightened and I was embarrassed that I had only just noticed his absence.

'I left him at home with a neighbour. Didn't want him distracting us tonight.'

'And Hannah's with her dad,' Lara said, clearly hurt that I'd missed Jayne's dog before her daughter. 'After virtually ignoring her over

Christmas and New Year, he thinks a weekend at Center Parcs will make up for it.'

'Selfish bastard,' I said. 'Glass of wine, ladies?'

I watched as Jayne and Lara shared another glance, then they acquiesced.

'What the hell is that?' Lara exclaimed, staring at the window.

'Oh, CDs,' I said. 'William strung them up for me to scare away the birds until Vikram can put something more permanent in place. They're actually not too bad now, can be a bit unnerving in the morning when they first catch the sun, though.'

'What happened?' Jayne asked, noticing the three small panes covered by cardboard and brown tape. 'Why are so many windows breaking?'

'It's the birds, isn't it?' Lara said, her voice soft. 'They're attacking.'

'They're not *attacking*,' I said. 'They're just . . . congregating. And the lights are confusing them, that's all.'

'Is that what William says?' Lara asked.

I shot her a sharp look, hearing the scorn in her voice.

'What does Vikram say?' Jayne interceded, breaking the tension.

'The same,' I said. 'Here.' I passed glasses of wine round, then sipped my own, staring at my friends over the rim of my glass.

Lara and Jayne

'The bar's still open,' Jayne said as she and Lara entered the White Lion.

'Thank God for that. You collect the keys, I'll order us a bottle.'

A couple of minutes later, Jayne joined Lara at the table in front of the fire, which was still blazing, and handed her the key to Room Seven.

'I'd have thought you'd had enough of that room,' Jayne said. 'Isn't that the haunted one?'

'It's not the ghosts in this place that worry me,' Lara said as Tess deposited a bottle of Sauvignon blanc and two large glasses on the table. She looked up to thank the girl, and smiled. 'Don't worry, no strange happenings here.'

'Yet,' Tess said, turned and walked away.

Lara looked stunned, then burst out laughing at Jayne's equally shocked expression. She shrugged. 'Must be a true Yorkshire lass – they're not given to hysterics in these parts.'

Jayne relaxed and joined in her laughter. 'That's probably just as well.' She picked up the wine and poured two generous glasses.

Lara said nothing, but took her first sip before Jayne had even replaced the bottle on the table.

Jayne followed suit, the mood now sombre. She shivered despite the heat of the fire. 'You noticed it too.'

Lara nodded. 'When *did* you last hear from her?'

'I spoke to her yesterday, but only because I rang her – she didn't even text back from my calls earlier in the week.'

'Same here. It's not like her.'

'I thought meeting a man would be good for her,' Jayne said, 'but it's like she's forgotten us. She's just not *Verity* anymore.'

'I know. It's natural to be wrapped up in each other in the beginning, but Verity . . . Normally, the slightest thing happens and she's straight on the phone to tell us about it.'

'Every detail.' Jayne smiled. 'But this time, nothing. It's almost like when Antony was at his most controlling, and she withdrew into herself, do you remember?'

Lara nodded and took another sip of wine.

'What do you think he's doing to her?' Jayne almost whispered the words.

'I don't know. Have you spoken to Vikram much?'

Jayne coloured and glanced down at her hands. 'Just a few texts.'

'Has he said anything about William?'

'We haven't been texting about William.' Her blush deepened.

'I hear you.' Lara smiled. 'I'm glad it's going well.'

'Early days,' Jayne said. 'Hopefully I'll see him tomorrow, but back to Verity. What do you think William's doing?'

Lara didn't speak at first, but sipped her wine again. 'I'm not sure it's him.'

'What do you mean?'

'Whatever's going on, I don't think it's a destructive relationship.'

It was Jayne's turn to silently sip her wine.

'But whatever *is* happening, I think he's as much a part of it as she is.'

'What do you mean? I thought it was the building that's haunted, not Verity.'

'Oh it is – the Grey Lady is definitely connected to the building. But the other, whatever *the other* is, I think that has to do with Verity. And William.'

'But how? I don't understand.'

'There's the million-dollar question. I don't know either, but whatever it is, I don't like it.'

'If we don't know what the problem actually is, how do we solve it?'

Lara smiled at the typical Jayne question.

'Well, to quote someone I know,' she smiled at her friend, 'our first task is to quantify the problem.'

Jayne grinned. 'You're never going to let me forget that, are you?'

'Nope.' Lara swigged her wine, her eyes dancing at the memory. Jayne had been on a problem-solving course at work the previous year and had taken it very much to heart.

'So how do we quantify this?'

'Well . . . I do have an idea,' Lara said.

'Yes?'

'You're not going to like it.'

19.

'Blimey, I didn't realise it was fancy dress,' Vikram said when William and I opened the door of The Rookery.

'It isn't,' William said.

'Really? Never seen you in that getup before, mate,' Vikram replied, unperturbed and indicating William's black slacks, white shirt and embroidered waistcoat. 'Apart from the Victorian dress-up days the village makes us do every year, that is,' he added.

'It's a dinner party.' William shrugged. 'This is the smartest gear I have.'

'Fair enough. Good to see you, mate.'

Finally Vikram and William shook hands, and Vikram led the way into The Rookery.

Glancing skyward and looking relieved to get under cover, Lara and Jayne followed.

'You look nice, Verity,' Jayne said with a glance at Lara.

'Thought I'd get into the spirit of things.' I'd also adopted the Victorian theme with a high-necked, lace-trimmed white blouse and long black skirt. 'Come on through, it's good to see you both.'

I took my friends' coats, draped them over a dustsheet-covered sawhorse and gestured them through to the first of the staircases and upward.

'Wow,' Lara said. 'This looks great, Verity.'

'Thanks, William and I have spent all day getting it ready.'

Jayne and Lara shared another glance, and I remembered the way they'd looked at me when I'd told them to relax and go to the museum or something, and that I'd see them tonight.

'Don't forget my team,' Vikram said, sounding wounded. 'We've worked ruddy hard to get your new kitchen installed and ready for tonight.'

'Aye, you have that, mate,' William said. 'It's appreciated, and why you've been invited to the inaugural dinner party.'

Vikram took the beer his childhood friend proffered, but didn't say anything.

Lara and Jayne exchanged yet another look, and I sighed inwardly. *What's their problem?*

I relieved them of the bottles of wine they'd brought, checked the labels and deposited them in the fridge, before removing one already chilled. I opened it and poured three glasses.

William opened his can of bitter and raised it in a toast.

'To Verity and The Rookery.'

I smiled at William as the others repeated the toast and drank.

'How's that meat coming on, love?'

'Oh.' I'd forgotten about it. I set down my glass and rushed to my new oven – this was its first use and I really had no idea how efficient it was.

I basted beef and turned potatoes and veg in the roasting pan, then replaced it in the oven, along with an empty Yorkshire pudding tin.

Then back to the fridge and out with a plate of smoked salmon on Ritz crackers with lemon wedges.

I realised the room was silent and caught yet another look between Jayne and Lara.

'What?'

'Nothing.'

'There's definitely something.'

'Well, I was just reminded of when you were with Antony,' Lara said. 'You hated the focus on the food rather than the people in the room.'

'And tonight you seem to be embracing it,' Jayne added, with a glance at William, who was focused on me, helping me with the meal.

Don't they realise how much work we've put into this for them? I swallowed my ire, and said, 'Sorry, the whole day's been a mad panic.'

'You've definitely been busy this week, Vikram,' Jayne said, lightening the mood. 'You've done a great job in here.'

'Thanks,' he said, visibly relaxing. 'The guts of the job are mostly done, now it's everything else.' He laughed. 'We're going from the top down now, getting Verity's accommodation sorted, then each guest room, then the ground floor. Should be a decent place when it's all finished.'

'Oh!' Jayne exclaimed, spinning around on one foot as Lara grabbed her arm – to steady herself as well as her friend.

'It's the CDs we strung up to deter those damned birds,' Vikram said, having rushed to the window to determine the source of the clatter that had startled everyone, then swiping at his face. 'The string's failed.'

'Failed or pecked through?' Lara whispered to Jayne.

Vikram recoiled as a bird landed on the windowsill, opened its beak, and – it seemed – tried to bite the glass with a clack audible in the room.

'Like *that's* not going to get annoying,' Jayne said as the feathered beast did it again, her nervous laugh betraying the confidence of her words.

'The pigeon spikes are due Tuesday,' Vikram said.

'Will pigeon spikes be enough?' Lara asked. 'Those rooks are twice the size.'

Vikram laughed. 'Not quite that big, but the principle's the same. They'll stop roosting here once we've got them all in place.'

He jumped as another beak clawed one of the nine small glass panes that made up each window. 'Can't come soon enough.' His following laugh did nothing to ease the nerves of the others.

'Maybe curtains should go to the top of your shopping list, Verity,' Jayne suggested.

I pouted. 'We're on the third floor, and uphill of the other houses on the other side of the street. I have no intention of blocking any of my view – not considering what I've gone through to get it.'

Jayne's mouth opened, then shut without making a sound.

'These look lovely, Verity,' Lara said to break the tension. She helped herself to one of the smoked-salmon canapés. 'You're really treating us.'

'Then it's sirloin of beef from the local butcher,' William said with pride. 'I could even tell you the colouring of the cow it came from.'

Vikram grinned. 'Old Ed Stockdale,' he said, wiping his face. 'He loves telling people that – picks his beasts out personally he does.'

Lara and Jayne stayed silent, seeming almost grateful for the thump from the window from yet another bird. It meant they didn't have to reply.

'Time to get the Yorkshires in,' I said. 'William, would you help me?'

Vikram squeezed on to the sofa next to Jayne, forcing her and Lara to shift up, then he rubbed his face again.

'Why do you keep doing that?' Lara asked.

'What?'

'Wiping your face. I've seen you do it a few times tonight, but can't remember seeing you do it before when we've met.'

'Oh.' Vikram looked surprised, then regarded his hand before lifting it to his cheek once more. 'It's weird, I keep feeling like I've walked into a cobweb.'

'Really?' Lara glanced at Jayne, who looked confused.

Another rook trying to bite its way through the glass distracted them and conversation stopped for a while.

I gave Lara a quick smile as I caught her eye and poured batter into the piping hot Yorkshire pudding tin, whilst William basted the meat again, then glanced at Jayne who was smiling shyly at Vikram.

Lara sighed, rose, walked to the fridge, extracted a bottle and took it back to the sofa.

'Thanks, Lara,' Jayne said as she topped up the glasses.

Lara's answering smile was small. She looked like she'd made her mind up about something. Something unpleasant.

'I hope you're all hungry,' I said as William and I rejoined our friends in the lounge area. 'Dinner will be ready in twenty minutes.'

20.

'That was absolutely delicious, Verity,' Lara said, pushing her cleared cheesecake plate away. 'You must have been flat out all day.'

'Pretty much,' I said, pleased that the atmosphere seemed to have lightened from earlier. I rested my hand on William's arm, 'But I had a lot of help and I really wanted to treat you after the way you've both helped and supported me through the move and everything.'

'Any time, Verity,' Jayne said.

'We're always here for you, you know that,' Lara added.

Vikram thrust his chair away from the table, startling the others, and swiped his hand over his face.

'Seriously, mate, what's wrong with you?' William demanded.

'It's this place, Will. Something keeps touching my face. It's freaking me out.'

Jayne and Lara exchanged one of their silent glances that expressed so much.

'You okay, Vikram?' Jayne asked.

'Yeah, yeah, it's gone,' he said and pulled his chair back to the table.

'Has anything else been happening, Verity?' Lara asked.

I shrugged, but could not stay my glance towards the window and the bird that was still snapping at the glass. I leaned into William as he grasped my hand. I didn't need to say anything for my friends to understand.

'We need to find out what's going on here,' Lara said.

'You've been saying that since I moved in. So far, nothing's worked.'

'Cleansing and blessing the house hasn't worked,' Lara qualified. 'I think it's time we tried something else and found out exactly what or who we're dealing with and what they want.'

'And how do you propose to do that?' Vikram asked, his scepticism clear in his voice, yet belied as he wiped at his face once again.

'We ask them,' Lara said. 'We hold another séance. Properly this time, and we don't stop until we get answers.'

'What, table tipping and ectoplasm out of your nostrils, all that nonsense?' William asked.

Lara laughed. 'Not quite, but whatever is here does seem to be trying to interact with us – or Verity at least.'

'And William,' I said. 'He's been dreaming too, like me.'

'Of the same man?'

'No, of a woman who looks like me.'

'Okay.' Lara drew the word out as she absorbed this. 'So it does seem there are two of them and they're trying to get through to the two of you.'

'Let's see if we can help them,' Jayne said.

'You're on board with this?' I asked her in surprise.

'Yep. She's quantified the problem and accepts this as the most effective solution,' Lara answered for our friend.

We laughed while both men scowled, not understanding the joke.

'Let's give it a go,' William said, to Vikram's obvious surprise. 'What, mate? Something's going on—' He broke off at another interruption from the window and an opaque crack snaked across another small pane of glass.

He looked back at his friend. 'This ain't normal, and I can't think of anything else to do.'

Vikram didn't remove his stare from the destructive avian, which seemed to gaze back at him – the light from the streetlamps reflecting in its one visible eye. He nodded.

Jayne and William helped me clear the table, and Lara flung her scarf over the standard lamp.

'What?' she asked in response to Vikram's raised eyebrow. 'It adds to the atmosphere.'

He didn't reply.

Lara pulled three pillar candles from her large handbag and set them on the table.

'You came prepared,' Vikram said.

'Always,' Jayne answered for Lara, and gave Vikram's arm a friendly squeeze. 'You haven't done anything like this before, have you?'

He shook his head. 'Shouldn't mess with things you don't understand.'

'Don't worry, Lara knows what she's doing.'

'I hope so,' he said, then flicked off the overhead light at Lara's instruction.

The room seemed to glow; the pink of Lara's floral scarf complementing the candlelight, and all five of us jumped as a rook pecked again at the cracked pane.

Vikram twisted suddenly.

'What's wrong?'

'I thought I saw something.'

Silence for a moment – even from the birds.

'I think we should get started,' Lara said.

We took our seats and joined hands.

Lara took a deep breath.

'Is anybody there?'

Nothing happened.

'Please come forward, we would like to help you.'

I gasped as the candle flames flickered.

'If you would like to talk to us, please knock or rap the table.'

The candles flickered again.

'It's just the draught from the window,' Vikram said as a second bird cracked another of the small panes.

'One tap for no, two for yes.'

'You'll have no sound windows left at this rate,' Vikram said as a third pane split. 'Mind you, you could probably claim on the insurance if the birds are doing it.'

'Shh,' Jayne said and squeezed his hand.

'One tap for yes, two for no,' Lara repeated. 'Please talk to us.'

Another pane broke.

'It's the birds,' Jayne blurted out. 'They're tapping —answering.'

I screamed as glass showered to the floor, and hung on to William's hand as the others jumped to their feet. The table juddered and thumped against my new rug, and all three candles extinguished as one.

More smashing from the windows and the room was suddenly full of beating wings and outstretched talons.

I heard Jayne shriek as she dived under the table and Lara jumped out of the way as Vikram swung his chair at the invading birds.

'Out, out, out!' he shouted, and I screamed as a bird pecked at my hand.

William threw himself at me, and I fell from the chair to the floor, William's bulk landing on top of me. I welcomed the dark as it rushed to embrace me. I did not want to be inside The Rookery a moment longer.

KAREN PERKINS

Part Three

1830-1848

"Terror made me cruel"

Wuthering Heights
Emily Brontë, 1847
Haworth, West Yorkshire

1.

Martha used the foot-treadle to shift the warps then sent the shuttle flying through the resultant gap between the two rows of woollen yarn. Weft picked, she beat the new pick up against the fell of the woven piece, ensuring the new weft was snug against the one before, then worked the treadle and flicked the shuttle back with the next pick. Then repeated. Endlessly.

She had been at this near a year now, and could match most of the men for speed, now that she'd built up the strength needed for beating-up. Though she was still waiting for the day when Old Man Barraclough dropped his chisels for good and Harry could take over the mason's shop.

She wouldn't need to work at all then. She could stay at home, or swan about on the moors like that Brontë lass. She avoided even thinking her name these days, and was furious that Harry still gave her the time of day.

'Her father's the parson,' he'd say. 'They're important in the village. And if I'm to take over from Mr Barraclough one day, I need to keep in with 'em. Most of our trade's memorials. Thee kens that, Martha. Where would we be without the church?'

Martha had no answer.

A cough interrupted her thoughts and she brought her attention back to the piece she was weaving, checked the let off and take up to ensure everything was regular, then glanced down at Edna who was in her basket, playing with her poppet and a couple of bobbins. Happy enough.

She was finding her feet quickly now and Martha did her best to tire the child out throughout the morning, so that when she took over the loom from Old Dan after dinner, Edna would stay in the basket where she put her. The rhythm of the looms seemed to calm the child, but then she'd heard it all her life.

Martha smiled at her daughter, then checked her piece and picked the shuttle. This was the only machine Edna would know, Martha was determined to it. No mill for Edna Sutcliffe, not if she could help it. As a daughter of the master stonemason, she'd be in line for a decent husband who'd keep her in a fine house.

She coughed, adjusted the take up a little on the loom and worked the treadle. *That's better.*

Aye, mebbe it is worth putting up with the Brontë girl if it means Edna and whoever comes next have a decent chance at life.

She caressed her belly, certain more life was growing there, then returned her hand to the loom.

She thought back to that wonderful day in the bluebell woods, certain that was when the child had started. Aye, she was a lucky one to have snared Harry Sutcliffe, though it had taken long enough to get him to the altar. Sarah was green with envy when she told her.

Martha smiled again then glanced down to check on Edna. The basket was empty.

Sighing, Martha scanned the floor of the weaving gallery for her independence-seeking offspring, then a shout alerted her. 'Ower 'ere!'

'Thanks, Alf,' she called and halted the loom to retrieve Edna. Crawling around the way she did, she could easily get trapped under a working foot treadle.

Standing, Martha stretched, then put her hand to her mouth as a more violent cough shook her. She looked around in alarm at the gallery of weavers mesmerised by the rhythm of their looms, recognising a smell that every textile worker dreaded.

Smoke.

'Edna! Edna! Where is she?'

A couple of weavers looked up at her, recognising the note of alarm in her voice.

'Smoke!' she cried. 'There's a fire! Where's my baby?'

2.

'Fire!'

Harry heard the shout, dropped his chisel and mallet – mindless of the memorial stone for Richard Smith's second wife – and dashed outside.

'That's Weaver's Row,' he shouted. 'Martha! Edna!' He ran downhill to his family.

Men flocked to West Lane: slaughtermen, innkeepers, cloggers, druggist; every trader on Main Street. No one from the mills though, they were too far away. It would be up to the village tradesmen to save the cottages; home to near a dozen families, including the Sutcliffes.

'The gallery, is the gallery afire?' Harry cried as he pushed his way through the throng of men.

'Nay, 'tis woolcombing shed. Gallery's safe for now.'

'Where are the weavers?'

No one answered him, and Harry could do naught about Martha as a full bucket was pressed into his hands. A line of men already stretched from the well to the wooden woolcombing shed attached to Weaver's Row, and Harry was one of the closest.

He threw the water at the flames that were singeing the whiskers on his jaw. He didn't notice.

Despite his panic, he knew he had to fight the fire, however much he wanted to find his wife and daughter. Controlling the flames would give them the best chance of getting out.

'There's good men up in that gallery,' Harry muttered to the next man in line as he swapped his empty bucket for a full one. 'They'll get 'em out.'

The man, Edward Stutterghyll, the proprietor of Haworth's largest ironmongery, nodded, and shouted, 'Happen it'll be all right.' He couldn't have heard Harry's mutter, but didn't need to, to understand the mason's distress.

Everyone in the village knew of Martha's deal with Old Dan Walker, and whilst few approved, no one could argue it didn't make sense for them to share the loom, it was too much for either Dan or Martha to work at for a full day. Besides, fool be the man who denied Martha Sutcliffe anything she'd set her mind on. Including her husband.

Harry swapped another empty pail for a full one, stepped forward and launched the water. They were making progress.

He cursed Martha for insisting on weaving here. Aye, he knew they couldn't yet manage on his wage alone, not with a growing family, but still. Barraclough was getting on now; Harry couldn't see him yet and wondered if he'd managed to shuffle down Church Lane to help out.

He'd have to ask for a raise. He did most of the work now anyway, forty years of working the chisel had left the old man's scarred hands with a never-ending tremble, and he stuck to facing the stones, while issuing a stream of advice to his protégé.

Harry threw another bucket load. *Blasted woolcombers!* This shed, shack really, had been a fire waiting to happen for years. The combers stoked their charcoal fires till they could have forged new combs, never mind heating their existing ones so they slid easier through the greasy wool fibres, pulling at noils and neps to leave the long fibres needed for spinning into worsted yarn.

'Leave shed, leave shed,' Stutterghyll's shout penetrated Harry's thoughts. 'It's gone. Save cottages!'

Harry redirected the path of the water he was throwing on to the stone wall of the first weaver's cottage.

Not afore time, he thought, as steam rose from the stone of his neighbour's home, before being overcome by smoke.

He took a few steps to his right, to better direct the flow of water, and flung his next bucketful.

He noticed more folk had joined the firefighting effort, including Barraclough, and more and more buckets and ewers were being emptied on the cottages. There was barely anything left of the woolcombing shed now, and the steps leading down the stone wall from the gallery were open to the sky for the first time in years.

'Harry, Harry!'

He turned and stared at Edward Stutterghyll. The ironmonger jerked his head, indicating Martha, standing and staring at her workplace, Edna on her hip. Safe and well the pair of them.

'Praise the Lord.' Harry raised his eyes skyward, thrust his bucket at Edward, and rushed to take his wife and child in his arms. Whatever else had been lost this day, he still had them.

3.

'After three,' John Brown said. 'One, two, three, heave!'

Harry and the sexton bent their backs to the altar gravestone. It shifted three inches.

'And again. One, two, three, heave!'

Six feet long and three wide, the heavy memorial shifted another few inches, and the two men strained their backs to lift it enough so that they could slide it on to the neighbouring slab.

'Thanks for giving me a hand, Harry,' John panted while they took a breather.

'It's nay bother, glad to help,' Harry replied. 'It's that busy with the smallpox, I may as well just set up shop in churchyard, especially now Barraclough's succumbed an'all.'

'Aye, there's half a dozen graves left open after funerals with so many ill. Can't be shifting these things backwards and forwards every time the pox takes another, not when there's whole families taken out at times.'

'I reckon some of graves'll need to be dug deeper,' Harry said. 'And I'm running out of space to add names on the older ones.' He indicated the older, lower part of the churchyard, abutting the Black Bull.

'How do, Miss Emily,' the sexton called. 'Watch thy footing there, there's open graves by path.'

'Will do, Mr Brown, thank you. Morning, Harry.'

Harry returned Emily's greeting and watched her pick her way down the path from the parsonage, the graves so close, her skirts brushed the flat stones clear of dead leaves and twigs. The cleanest graves in the churchyard were those regularly swept clean by Brontë skirts.

'She's a rum 'un, that lass,' John said. 'Can't get two words out of her normally, in a world of her own she is, but her and her sisters have been out every day taking food and water to the worst-hit families.'

'Aye, I just hope they don't catch it themselves.'

'Aye, our Tabitha has them burning their gloves at end of day, and she's constantly washing gowns. The Reverend's torn; it's their duty to call on the sick, but he don't want to lose any more daughters. He ain't even complaining about buying so many gloves, though they're making do with shoddy.'

'They won't be bothered about that, not them lasses,' Harry said, nodding after Emily. 'They've got more important things going on in their heads.'

'What, poems and them tiny magazines they make? Have you seen 'em then?'

Harry nodded. He still didn't quite know what to make of Emily and her siblings' fascination with Branwell's toy soldiers, or why they wasted their time making inch-long 'magazines' for the toys to 'read'.

'So have you moved into Barraclough's cottage?' the sexton said as he indicated they should resume lifting.

'Aye. Martha's burnt every scrap of fabric and scrubbed every surface, but at last she's happy and Edna's allowed out of her basket.' Harry laughed. He hadn't wanted to move in quite so quickly after Mr Barraclough's passing, he thought it unseemly, but Martha had waved aside his objections.

'And how's new bairn coming on?' John asked, puffing after another heave.

Harry frowned. 'Martha's not carrying this one so well,' he confided. 'I don't mind telling thee I'm concerned about her, but Martha won't ruddy listen.'

John grimaced and shook his head. He'd had his run-ins with Martha Sutcliffe over the years, he knew exactly how forthright she could be. 'Here she is now,' he warned, spotting the newly large figure making her way into the churchyard.

'Lord above, what now?' Harry muttered. 'Let's take five, John.' He turned to meet his wife.

'I've just seen that Emily Brontë,' she said before he had chance to greet her. 'Rushing off with her baskets, doing God's work, that ruddy dog at her heels.'

Martha hated Emily's new pet, an enormous mastiff called Keeper. And to be fair, he was a beast; Emily was the only one able to control him.

'Well she's Reverend's daughter,' Harry said, trying to mollify her. 'She has pastoral duties.' He winked at Edna, who had just peeked out at him from behind her mother's skirts. She hid again as soon as she'd seen her father take notice of her.

'Pastoral duties?' Martha screeched and Harry winced as he realised his mistake. 'Thee's been talking to her again, hasn't thee? Using her fancy words!'

'Martha, calm down. It's unavoidable, she's been helping people sort funerals and what wording they want on stones.'

'Hmph.'

'Martha, love. I keep telling thee, thee's nowt to worry about.' He winked as Edna peeped out a second time. She ducked behind Martha again with a giggle.

'That had better be true, Harry Sutcliffe. God help thee if it ain't.'

'Martha!' Harry was shocked she'd cursed him out in this of all places, and in front of the sexton too.

'Aye, well,' she said, embarrassed, but too proud to take it back.

'Anyroad, I'm off to see Sarah Butterworth.'

'Nay! I've told thee afore, Martha. Thee's not to visit any house where there's smallpox.'

'I'll be all reet, Harry.'

'Nay, thee won't. I won't have thee risking thyself nor our child.' Harry stroked her belly and she softened.

'Thee does love me, don't thee?'

'Aye, 'course I do, thee daft apeth.'

Harry ran his hand around her waist, and squeezed. Her answering squeal told him he'd won this one, at least. 'Now get thee back home and get the weight off thy feet. I'll be late with all this work on, but I'll be home as soon as I can.'

'Aye, all reet then. I'll make sure there's some supper left for thee. Come on, Edna, say ta ta to thy papa.'

The little girl peeped again from her mother's skirts, face beaming. Harry picked her up, swung her round, carefully, then sent her on her way with her mother, both his girls receiving a pat on the rump in farewell.

Harry watched them go, concerned. Martha was hiding it from him, but he knew her too well, and the child she was carrying was paining her; far more than Edna, or Baby John before her. He swallowed his grief for his firstborn, buried just two rows over, and was overwhelmed with concern for his wife and next-born.

Would she tell me if owt serious were wrong? he thought, *Or just refuse to believe it were happening?*

4.

Martha clung to Harry's arm as they negotiated the treacherous lane. Half-frozen slush and leather soles, her first pair of proper shoes rather than her usual wooden-soled clogs, did not mix well and she'd nearly been over three times already, even on this short walk homeward from the church.

Harry's hobnailed boots, which she was now glad he'd insisted on wearing to early morning Christmas Mass, were far better suited, and he was as steady on his feet as a newly shod horse.

They still had to hurry though, slush or no slush. It was their first Christmas in the big house. *Well, it's small next to the parsonage,* Martha thought. *But bigger than any I ever had any reet to expect.* She blessed Mr Barraclough yet again for making Harry his heir, then her thoughts returned to the day ahead. Most of her family and Harry's were coming to be fed and were expecting a Christmas feast.

She shuddered at the thought of all the coins and notes she'd handed over to the butcher in exchange for ham and beef. Not to mention the raisins and brandy for the Christmas pudding. But Harry had insisted on 'doing things proper'.

Haworth's winter had been terrible, upwards of four hundred folk dead of the smallpox on top of the usual winter maladies, and there wasn't a family in the Worth Valley who hadn't lost someone. A couple of families, the Hardys and the Slaters, had been wiped out; there was simply no one left to continue the name.

Those that were left were in a right state: one minute grieving, then euphoric for those left alive, then remembering once more. Harry was determined that today, at least, the Sutcliffes and the Earnshaws would be celebrating. And he could afford to with all the work he had on.

He was looking at taking on another apprentice too. Martha's nephew, Charlie, couldn't keep up, and Harry's own nephew, Georgie, was coming up to an age where he could be of use.

I could do with an apprentice in house, she mused. *Or an housekeeper.* She smiled up at her husband; she was still working on that one, but was confident she'd get a kitchen maid at least. Especially once the new babby was here.

She put a hand to her belly and winced.

'Aw reet, love?'

'Aye, I'm fine. Just a twinge, probably just the cold air.'

'Aye, well. Happen thee's got too much on today.'

Martha said naught.

'That's why our Mary'll be joining us a bit later.'

Mary was his elder sister's girl. Nice enough, but a bit lazy, Martha judged.

'What does thee mean?'

'She'll be giving thee an hand. And living in an'all; she can have the small room next to the kitchen.'

'Thee means—'

'Aye. Merry Christmas, love. We have an housekeeper.'

'Oh Harry!' Martha swung into his arms, nearly knocking them both off her feet in her joy. She'd soon cure Mary of her sloth.

Martha looked around her dining table and could have cried. This was the first time both families had come together since her wedding three and a half years before.

Despite the latest additions, Edna amongst them, they were less than half in number. She and Harry had grieved each and every death, but the sum total of their losses hit her.

She looked across at Harry and knew he felt the same, as did everyone around the table; those of an age to understand, anyway.

Both her and Harry's parents had gone now, as had near half a dozen of their own generation, plus twice more little ones. All in three years.

It felt too much to bear at times, and now she did not feel like celebrating this Christmas after all.

Harry brought out the crowning glory of their feast, a huge joint of roasted beef, to a round of diminished yet still heartfelt applause. He picked up the carving set, then put them down again. He looked around the table, tears in his eyes, and Martha knew without doubt that he felt the same way as she.

'It's aw reet, love,' she said, placing a hand on his forearm in a rare public gesture of affection. 'We all know, we all understand, and we all miss them.'

'Hear, hear,' Thomas, Harry's sole remaining brother, said, raising his glass. 'Truer words may not be spoken.'

Harry lifted his own glass. 'To them no longer with us, may thy spirits soar, and thy memory live long.'

The Sutcliffe-Earnshaw clan drank as one, and a rare silence descended over them, deep enough to include even the youngest members; then, as one, conversation broke out: compliments about the house and feast; enquiries over the various trades represented around the table; and news of a more homely nature.

Harry reclaimed his carving knife and meat fork, then dropped them once more as Martha screamed in agony.

***

'Reet then, lass, that's the last of 'em gone home. Gave 'em all a reet scare thee did.'

'I scared mesen, love. Thought me insides were ripping apart.'

'So where's pain?'

'Round me hips and in front.'

'But babby's not coming?'

'Nay, not yet. Pain's been coming on awhile, but nowt as bad as that afore.'

'Thee should have said, love. Thee's been overdoing it. Thee should have been resting.'

'Too much to do to rest.'

'How's thee really feeling though?' Harry did not want to start arguing, not now.

'I've been better, Harry, and that's the truth, but pain's lessening now.'

'Lizzie says it happens sometimes if babby's lying wrong.'

'Hmm. Lizzie's no midwife,' Martha pointed out.

'Nay, but she's had bairns of her own.'

'So have I.' Martha glanced at the ceiling where, in the room above, Edna had finally been put down to sleep after watching her mother's collapse and the near hysteria of her relatives.

'I'll be reet,' she said, her voice softer. 'Don't take on so, Harry.'

He perched on the side of her armchair and chucked her under her chin. 'Don't ask the impossible, love. I'll allus fret over thee.'

Martha leant her head against his strong shoulder. 'Lizzie does have a point though,' she allowed. 'Plenty of women have pains like this in run up to a birth. I'll just have to take it easy, tha's all.'

'Well, thee can now that Mary's here. She's moving in tomorrow.'

'What? On Boxing Day? She'll have to sort all Christmas boxes out. Thee'll have to make sure she gives reet ones to butcher and baker, we can't have them getting mixed up.'

'Aye, we'll sort it, Martha. Thee needs looking after, lass, and she's family, she's happy to do it.'

There was silence for a moment, then Harry rose, crossed to the sideboard and awkwardly poured himself a brandy. After only three weeks in this house, it still did not feel like his, and nor did the style of life that went with his new position.

'One for thee an'all, Martha?'

'Aye, it'll dull pain a bit,' she said and held out her hand for the half-full glass.

5.

Harry dropped his chisel with a curse as another scream from Martha speared through the cottage wall and into his workshop. She'd been at this for hours already and the shrieks had only increased in their intensity.

He listened but heard no more, so picked up his chisel and examined the stone. It pained him that there was naught he could do for his wife at present, but that was the truth of it and he had to accept it as did every other father-to-be.

Uttering another oath, he ran his hand over the F in *WIFE*. Or what was supposed to read *WIFE*. It looked more like a P now. He offered the late Florence Butterworth a heartfelt apology, knowing it would be the living he would have to answer to for the grave error. Her son, Robert.

Poor woman; it was bad enough her name did not appear on her own memorial stone, now it read: RICHARD BUTTERWORTH AND HIS WIP with only the husband's dates below.

He would do what he could to correct it, and he chiselled away the offending stone to inscribe the correct F, deeper than the other letters, but at least her station in life would be spelled correctly. He pondered whether Robert Butterworth's wife, Martha's friend Sarah, would suffer the same fate.

Martha would not, he knew that, and once more he stared at the wall in the direction of their bedchamber as the volume of her screams rose again. If, God forbid, she did not survive this birth, he would ensure she'd be named properly, her name on their family memorial clear for all to see.

More likely, 'twill read MARTHA SUTCLIFFE RELICT OF HENRY SUTCLIFFE, Harry thought with a stray smile. Despite her current distress, she was strong, much stronger than he, and apt to outlive him. *Would she be proud of me enough to be known as my relict, my widow? Or would even that be an indignity too far for her?*

More screams prevented him from answering his own question, and he threw down his chisel before he could make any more errors upon the Butterworths' gravestone.

'Harry.'

He looked up to see Emily at the door.

'It don't sound as if the child comes easy.'

'Nay, Emily, 'tis a hard birthing for sure. No surprise considering how hard she's been carrying this bairn these past months.'

'If anyone can do it, Martha Earnshaw can.'

'Sutcliffe.'

'Aye, of course. I meant nothing by it.' Emily stepped aside and returned the harsh glare of the new arrival.

'Sarah, what news?' Harry asked.

Sarah glanced at the gravestone Harry was carving for her in-laws, then stared back at Emily, though she elicited no further reaction.

'I think thee should come, Harry.'

'What?' Harry blanched and another scream answered him. His wife had not passed.

'Just to be close by, offer her comfort,' Sarah qualified. 'Old Peg is with her now, but this is an hard one. Martha needs to know you're near. Though be warned, she'll not show thee much appreciation till the birthing is complete.'

And mayhap not even then, Harry thought as he nodded his understanding and followed Sarah to the cottage. He did not pause as Emily placed a brief hand on his arm as he passed; nonetheless, he felt and appreciated the comfort she offered him.

Sarah slipped through the bedchamber door, careful to open it no wider than necessary; she did not want to give Harry any larger a view than necessary from his vantage point in the corridor.

'He's just outside the door, Martha.'

'Oh, sitting comfortably is he?' Martha yelled between grunts, each one crescendoing to a hoarse scream. Sarah forbore to point out the heavy tread of Harry's hobnailed books as he paced the boards outside.

'Well he might! He'll never get near me again. If he tries, I'll make sure I pass on every ounce of this agony.' The last word was barely recognisable from a shriek, but everyone within hearing understood. Including Harry. His pacing stopped and both Sarah and Peg heard the crunch of his chair back against the wall as he dropped into the seat. Martha was oblivious.

'Can thee not widen thy legs any further, lass?' Peg had been encouraging her to do this since she'd arrived an hour ago, but to no avail.

'I've already told thee, no I ruddy well can't!' Martha screamed. 'There's summat wrong, has been for months, thee knows that.'

'Her legs and hips just ain't working right,' Sarah interrupted before Martha could resume her earlier name calling. Peg had nearly left five minutes after her arrival due to the filth that had spewed from Martha's lips. 'Is there another way?'

Peg stared at the stricken woman on the bed for a moment, then accepted these were not the usual insults of a woman in the throes of childbirth. 'Aye, mebbe so. Help me roll her on to her side, Sarah, then we'll get her on to her knees, see if that'll help.'

'It'd better, thee awd carlin, else I'll have thee hanged for witchcraft.'

'Martha!' Sarah was horrified. That was not something to be joked about. A couple of hundred years before, near a dozen people, most of them women from just over the hill at Pendle, had been hanged for the same, possibly another in her own house on West Lane.

'What's thee dawdling at, lass?' Peg broke into Sarah's thoughts. ' 'Tis an idle threat, she knows I'd have her turned into a toad afore she could even blink at constable.'

Sarah laughed, even Martha made a strangled, gurgling sound that passed for a moment of mirth, then screamed anew as her two attendants manhandled Martha into a crouch.

The next pain elicited such a shriek, even Peg blanched, and Harry banged on the door, demanding to know what torture they were inflicting upon his wife. He obeyed Peg's sharp instruction to remain where he was.

Peg, who still had the strength of a farmer's wife despite being near seventy, grabbed hold of Martha's midsection, pulled, and dropped the mother's knees to the floor. Martha's head and shoulders collapsed on the bed in a temporary relief. Sarah leapt on to the soiled coverlet and grabbed her friend's hands, desperate to offer support; to do *anything* to help.

'Push reet hard now, lass,' Peg instructed, one hand buried in Martha's nether regions. 'I can feel the head. Thee's nearly there.'

Harry winced at the curses emanating from his bedchamber, and uttered a quick prayer that the parson would not hear his wife's profanities, then hung his head in shame at his disloyalty.

He sprang to his feet and recommenced his pacing of the corridor. 'Twas not lengthy enough to ease his fears, and his hobnailed boots did the floorboards no good at all. *Martha'll have my guts for garters,* he thought when he spotted the scuffmarks occasioned by his turns at the window and stairtop. *I hope.*

He winced at another scream, even put his hands to his ears in an attempt to block out the sounds, then slumped back down on to his chair, head in hands. *How can anyone survive this? Mother or child?*

After a few moments of silence, he raised his head. *Why is she not screaming?* Then a new cry, a babe's. But relief did not come, Martha was too quiet.

Sarah emerged from the room, her eyes downcast.

'Look at me, woman! What is the news?'

She crouched beside his chair. 'Thee has a son, Harry Sutcliffe. A fine boy.'

'And Martha?'

'She'll recover.'

Harry eased his back with a sigh of relief. 'She lives?'

Sarah nodded. 'Aye, she does, but she's weak. She'll be abed for some time.'

'But she lives, she'll recover?'

Sarah said naught.

'Sarah Butterworth, tell me!'

'Walking will allus be difficult, and she'll bear thee no more children.'

'But she lives?'

'Aye, Harry, she does.'

'Can I see her? And the boy?'

Sarah glanced at the closed door. 'Not yet, it's been an ordeal, let her rest. I'll bring the bairn out when he's fed. Oh, and best Edna stays with Lizzie a while longer, till Martha regains some strength.'

6.

Martha stared down the flight of stairs and gritted her teeth. A woman's laugh echoed up the dark stairwell and Martha turned sideways on to the steps, thumped her gnarled hawthorn walking stick on to the top tread and grasped the bannister with her free hand. Grunting, she forced her right foot down a step, then her left joined it.

A deep breath, then she jammed her stick on to the next step and she repeated the process.

She was greeted at the bottom by Emily Brontë. 'Good morn to you, Martha. I was just about to come up and help you.'

'Aye, so I heard,' Martha muttered as she brushed past the parson's daughter and thunked her way to the kitchen. She sank into her prized rattan chair by the fire with a sigh and eyed with distaste the basket on the table.

'Where's that been? I'd better not have to scrub the tabletop when she's gone.'

'Good morn, Martha,' Harry said, refusing to let his wife's sour temper spoil the day so soon. He was becoming well-practiced at this particular trick. 'How did thee sleep?'

'Like I were lying on a bed of thorns.'

'Better than nest of wasps the night afore.' Harry tried a smile to no avail.

'Hmph,' was Martha's only response.

'I've brought you fresh-baked baps.' Emily bustled into the kitchen and removed the cloth from atop her basket. 'And some new honey from the sexton's hives.' She placed the goods on the tabletop.

'Thank thee, Miss Emily, that's much appreciated. The sexton's honey is best in village, ain't it, Martha?'

'Hmph.'

'My pleasure. But I must hurry, I'd like to get the rest of these to Weaver's Row while they're still warm.'

'Pass my regards to Lizzie and rest of 'em, will thee?' Harry said.

'They appreciate thy charity do they? Hardworking men and women the lot of 'em, earning their way, then you turn up to dole out the scraps from thy kitchen.'

'Martha!'

Emily held up a hand to forestall Harry's protest. 'You may call it charity, Martha Sutcliffe, but no one turns down Tabby's baking nor John Brown's honey.'

'Aye well, Tabitha Aykroyd must be into her seventies now, barely able to walk she is, and you and your family still have her keeping house as if she were a young lass.'

'Now look here, Martha Sutcliffe.' Emily planted both hands on the tabletop and leaned forward to glare at Martha. 'Tabby is as much a part of the family as I, Charlotte, Anne or Branwell. And you've never heard her complain, have you?'

Martha looked away and stared into the fire.

'Papa is the parson of this village, and we all know however hard everyone works, there isn't enough food for all the hungry mouths. So Tabby and I turn what we can from the collection plate into flour, and we bake; all ruddy week we bake, so everyone in this godforsaken rookery of a village can eat!'

'Just making an observation. No need to get het up.' Martha glared at Emily. 'Bet the wives of this "godforsaken rookery of a village" love you calling on their husbands. Choosing which one to take for thyself is thee? Or has thee already chosen?' She looked at Harry, her accusation clear.

'You bitter old witch!'

'Now, now, that's no way for a parson's daughter to speak.'

Emily's colour rose further, her cheeks flaming red with her ire.

'That's enough, Martha!' Harry thundered. 'Emily has been nowt but friend to us. It ain't her fault thee's in pain.' He bent to pick up their son, Thomas, now a year old. 'Ain't his fault neither, and he needs his ma. Thee barely even looks at him.'

'Hmph.'

Harry sighed, walked over to his wife and placed their son in her lap. He glanced at Emily, whose temper, he saw, was not yet under her control. *If it ever were,* he thought ruefully. 'Come on, lass, there's no talking sense to her these days. Thank thee for bread and honey, and my regards to thy father. I'll see thee out.'

Emily re-covered her basket with the cloth, gave Martha a parting glare, which was returned in full, then turned and made her way to the front door, Harry close behind.

'I'm sorry, lass. Mornings ain't a good time for her. She's still in so much pain, has been since birth, but at least she's getting about easier now than she were.'

'But the birth was over a year ago, Harry.'

'Aye, and don't I ruddy know it.'

Emily touched his arm. 'Don't give up hope. I have some more of the preparation Mrs Hardaker makes.' She gave him a small bottle. 'She's still not happy about making it up without seeing Martha, you know what druggists are like, but she trusts me. And knows Martha of old.'

'Thank thee, Emily. It does help, even though she won't admit it and I have to sneak it into her food.'

'Just take care, Harry, she'll have you in the gaolhouse for trying to poison her.'

Harry grunted. 'Nay, she won't.' He cheered up as the thought struck him. 'Without it, she'd never get upstairs on her own. Happen laudanum's the only thing ever gives either of us a bit of peace.' He laughed. 'Anyway, she needs me to earn our living. She wouldn't want to rely on alms or you for her bread, even if I really were poisoning her.'

'That won't be an issue after next week.'

'What do you mean?'

'I'm departing with Charlotte for Brussels on Tuesday next.'

'What?' Harry's mouth dropped open in shock. 'You're leaving? *You*? But—'

'I know, I know, but we're serious about founding this school, and Charlotte is convinced a few months studying in Brussels at the Pensionnat Heger will give us vital experience and make it much more likely to succeed.'

'A few months?'

'Weeks if I can help it.' Emily smiled. 'You know how I get if I'm too long from the moors.'

'Aye, 'tis like a sickness in you.'

'So you know I won't be away long.' She glanced at the house. 'Martha should be cheered, at least. She hates the very sight of me, it seems.'

'Don't thee mind her. She's a jealous woman, in all things. Allus has been. And pain's making her worse.'

'Mrs Hardaker has upped the amount of laudanum.' Emily indicated the bottle that Harry still held in his hand. 'That should ease the pain; the pain in her body anyway. Branwell swears it heals pain in the mind an'all. Maybe my absence will help to heal the pain in her heart.'

'I'll miss thee, Emily,' Harry whispered.

'Aye, I know. I'll miss you too. All of you.' She turned to encompass the dogs, duck and pheasant that patiently awaited her. 'Wish I could take all my friends with me.'

Harry knew he was excluded from that sentiment, it was only the company of animals and birds that Emily craved.

7.

Edna grasped hold of her mother's skirts, trying to hide in the folds as a dray cart, laden with casks, thundered down West Lane, barely a foot away.

'Oh don't fret, lass,' Martha scolded as she knocked on the door. ' 'Tis only a drayman. Scared of owt, thee is.'

'How do, Martha, thank thee for coming,' Sarah Butterworth said as she opened the door.

Edna shrank even further into the protection of Martha's skirts. Sarah had only just survived the outbreak of smallpox a couple of years before. Glad of her life, she nonetheless rued the loss of her looks; her face now a patchwork of disfiguring scars left behind by the foul pustules.

'Aye, well, sorry for thy troubles,' Martha said. 'What else are friends for?' She followed Sarah into the house and deposited Edna and Thomas into the care of Sarah's eldest girl, Betty. Aged seven years, she'd be following her elder brother's footsteps on to the mill floor any day now.

'He's upstairs,' Sarah said. She lit a candle and led the way up, solicitously walking slowly to give Martha time to climb the stairs.

'In here.' She pushed open the door to a small, dim room and used her flame to light two more.

'Ain't this the haunted room?' Martha asked.

'Aye, none of kids'll sleep in it for fear of the Pendle witch. He has no choice now, though.' Sarah nodded to a trestle table under the shuttered window.

Martha walked over to the small, still figure of Edward, and crossed herself. 'Such a shame, and him only seven.'

'Eight,' Sarah corrected. 'He turned eight last month.'

'Of course he did, damn fine day it were too. Strapping lad he were, such a shame,' she repeated.

'Aye, he were a good worker. Old Man Rook thought highly of him up at mill. He had a good future ahead; family won't be same without him.'

They stood in silence a moment, regarding the child's body. Betty could only look forward to a spinner's wage, Edward could have had his own loom in a few years and earned a decent wage weaving pieces for the Rooks. *Ain't going to happen now.*

'Aye, a right shame,' Martha said again.

'Aye.'

'Reet, so what needs doing?' Martha had had enough of sentimentality and got down to the business at hand.

'The lot, I'm afraid. Wash him, dress him, then sew him into his shroud. Our Robert's gone to see Tobias Webster about coffin boards, then parson will bury him next week.'

'Next week? Why so long?'

'He has his own bereavement, ain't you heard? His sister passed last night. All funerals have to wait.'

'Miss Branwell's passed?'

'Aye. That's why we're doing this. Doris is up at parsonage, laying out Miss Branwell, and I'll not have my Edward lying here still with mill dust on him. Bad enough it killed him, he'll not suffer it in death an'all.'

'It were the mill lung?'

'Aye. Either that or the consumption. Result's the same, anyroad.'

Sarah bent her head to her son. 'He's loosening up now.' She eased his left arm out of his jacket and Martha limped round to take care of his right.

Sarah lifted him to remove the woollen garment, folded it neatly, and placed it on the seat of a wooden chair. 'It'll do for our lass's boy, Stephen. He's growing fast that one.'

'Aye, 'tis a good jacket,' Martha said.

'Sewed it mesen,' Sarah said unnecessarily. Almost everyone in the village made their own clothes.

She untied his shirt, then moved the body into a sitting position so she could lift it over his head.

Next were his breeks, then his long johns, and soon the eight-year-old boy lay pale and mottled with blue on the makeshift table.

Sarah fetched a bowl of water and placed it on the wooden boards by his feet. Both women wrung out rags and started to wipe away the dirt from Edward's skin.

'So if Miss Branwell's passed, the sisters will no doubt be returning home,' Martha said.

'Aye, more than likely. They'll want to be here for their aunt's funeral, no matter how far they have to travel. She more or less raised them after their ma died so young.'

'Hmm.'

'Thee still fretting about Emily and Harry?'

Martha shrugged.

'They're just pals, Martha, allus have been, ever since they were little. Thee knows that.'

'She allus hangs about him.'

Sarah tsked. 'No she don't. She stops by to say how do, the workshop and house is right by the parsonage. 'Twould be an insult if she didn't.'

'Far too ruddy often if thee asks me.'

'She ain't got no eyes for anyone, 'cept them animals that follow her around everywhere.'

'She's a rum 'un.'

'Aye, that she is. And so's thee, Martha Sutcliffe, if thee can't see that Harry only has eyes for thee.'

Martha screwed up her face in a scowl.

'He still ain't touched thee? Not since . . .' Sarah knew better than to mention Thomas's birth, even though she'd lived every agonising minute with Martha.

'Won't let him.' Martha shrugged. 'Last bairn all but crippled me. I ain't chancing another.'

Sarah said naught, but stroked the cheek of her son.

'I'd love more, but Robert won't come near me now.' She indicated her face. 'Hardly ever here, either. It's just me and the girls now.'

'Well, what a pair of misery guts we are!'

Sarah managed a slight smile, then looked up at her lifelong friend, expecting her to have more words of wisdom. She was unprepared for the look of horror on Martha's white face.

Slowly, Sarah turned to see what had frightened Martha so.

A figure, a woman, hanged from the rafters in the middle of the room, little more than a foot away. She slowly rotated on the rope that encircled her neck, creating deep purple welts, her tongue protruding from her swollen face, cocked to one side. Inch by inch, the head straightened, and Sarah later swore she saw that grotesque mouth stretch in a smile.

She would see no more though; with a piercing shriek, she bolted from the room.

Sarah's scream broke Martha's paralysis, and she limped around the room, as far away from the apparition as she could manage, and followed her friend.

As she approached the top of the stairs, Sarah had reached the bottom, flung the door open, and charged into the street.

Straight into the path of a heavily laden wool cart.

The horse's shriek matched Sarah's and the drayman's for intensity, and the animal reared up as Sarah floundered beneath its pawing hoofs.

Robert Butterworth, returning from his meeting with Tobias Webster, was quick enough in mind to grab hold of her, and he hauled her away from the descending horseflesh.

'What the Devil do you think you're doing, woman? Scaring the horse like that! Get back inside with you. All this carry on and our son lying dead upstairs!' He shoved her back into the house.

'I'll take care of him, Robert, you look after Sarah,' Martha said with a gulp. 'It's too much for her.'

She glared at Sarah, warning her not to mention the phantom they had both seen. Robert would not appreciate such tales. She made her slow way back to the room, pushed open the door, and sighed in relief. The only occupant was Edward.

8.

'Good morn to you, Harry Sutcliffe.'

Emily received no response bar the rhythmic clanging of Harry's mallet upon his chisel.

'How do, Harry?' she shouted, then laughed as the master stonemason jumped and dropped his tools.

He glared at Emily then inspected the stone he was working on. 'Lucky for thee, there's no damage done,' he said. 'Good morning to thee.'

Emily grinned at him. 'You're in a world of your own when you're carving.'

'This is the last impact the dead have on this world,' Harry said, indicating the stones. 'Each name and date should be my best work. Though it were almost my own name that needed carving today. I wish thee'd take more care when thee discharges thy father's pistol of a morning, Emily.'

She shrugged. 'I can't point it at the moors, I might hit a hare or lapwing. Papa jests he'd almost be safer firing it himself, even with his sight failing the way it is.'

'At least he's never pointed the damned thing towards village, and I were never scared of morning's shot afore!'

Another of Emily's rare smiles graced him. 'I'd never hit you, Harry Sutcliffe.'

'I'm surprised he still keeps it by his bedside at night, it's been many years now. Branwell must take more care on his way home from Black Bull on his visits home too; any noisier and he'll have his father mistaking him for a rioter.'

'Aye, Charlotte's said the same thing. Papa will never lose his fear of the Luddites, though, and the riots he bore witness to in Hartshead.'

'But he's safe now surely? It's only mills and their owners that are being targeted.'

'True, but feeling still runs high. So many children are maimed or worse, and so many families starving now their work can be done faster by machine. 'Tis not only spinners now, there are new contraptions for carding, gilling and winding. If they devise a loom that runs on steam instead of manpower, many more will starve.'

'People have it tough round here, and no mistake,' Harry said. 'Thank the Lord for thy father, if he hadn't had old Mr Barraclough take me on as apprentice all them years back, Lord only knows where I'd be now;

and family an'all.' He shuddered at the thought of little Edna and Thomas going to the mill every day to slave over spinning mules from dawn until dusk and beyond.

'Aye, Haworth's nowt but one large rookery as it is,' Emily said, staring downhill at the village spewing coal smoke from every chimney. 'Reduced to a slum, nowt more.'

'Surely 'tis not so bad as that,' Harry protested.

'Oh it is. I've seen more places than you, Harry Sutcliffe, and Haworth does not measure well. The water stinks, effluent soaks the streets, and sickness thrives. Papa conducts so many funerals, he's exhausted with it, they each take a toll. 'Tis not right, Harry. Folk should live better.'

'Aye, that they should.' Harry struggled to order his thoughts. 'But who shall make it so? The men are so knackered by their work, they have neither time nor heart to fight for better, and 'tis not in the interests of those who are idle to fight.'

Emily dropped a copy of *The Fleet Papers* on to the stone on which Harry had been working. She said naught, trusting Harry to know they were the work of the anti-Yorkshire-slavery activist, Richard Oastler, who continued to campaign, despite his ongoing incarceration in The Fleet prison for his debts.

It took Harry a moment, but then he understood. Emily had talked of him before. He picked up the publication.

The Fleet Papers; being Letters to Thomas Thornhill Esquire of Riddlesworth from Richard Oastler his prisoner in the Fleet With occasional Communications from Friends.

'Read it,' she said. 'Tell people about it. He speaks true.'

'Aye, I'll spread the word,' Harry said after scanning the article, his head spinning in dismay with details of corn laws, poor laws and diatribe against the long working days of the mills. 'I'll need time to take this in, but I'll help Oaster's cause if I can, small as my part may be, if it helps the poor sods who still have to send their nippers to mill instead of school.'

Emily nodded and opened her mouth to say something more, but the ringing of a bell forestalled her.

'It's mill,' Harry said. 'Summat's up, come on, lass, there's summat wrong at mill!'

He took off running down Church Lane, then up West Lane and on to Lord Lane to Rook's Mill. Emily's mastiff, Keeper, kept pace with him, so he knew Emily was not far behind. And, apart from a few souls ahead, he knew the rest of the village not already working in the mills would be there too. All fretting over who was hurt, and praying it was no one of their kin.

The bell continued its toll.

9.

'What's gone on?' Harry asked Bartholomew Grange, who stood at the mill door, blocking the way.

Everyone stopped for a moment as the constant rumble of spinning jennies and mules faded into silence. Even Big Bart looked uneasy.

'One of little 'uns got trapped in mule,' he said, his voice like thunder in the unaccustomed silence.

'Who? Let us in, man! What's happening?' A chorus of voices at Harry's back echoed his own words.

'Let us in, man!' Harry shouted at Bart, and reached for his lapels. Bart was big, and he was hard, but Harry worked with rock every day, and was likely the only one in the village who could take him on, and Big Bart knew it.

He stared at him in silence a moment, then flicked his gaze to Harry's feet. 'No hobnails on mill floor, Harry.'

'What? Someone's hurt, and you want me to take me boots off afore I come in? This ain't the big house thee knows, Bart!'

'No hobnails on mill floor,' Bart repeated, no expression on his face. 'Place is full of wool fluff; any spark from nails could have whole place going up in flames.'

'Come off it, Bart,' Harry said and tried to push past him. 'They need our help. Someone could be dying in there.'

Bart lifted Dasher, his alley strap, and Harry stared at him in shock. Bart was a big man, yes, and a hard man, but he'd never been a cruel man.

He met Harry's stare. 'Only takes a second,' he said. 'Me brother were killt that way over at Beckhead Mill. One pair of hobnailed boots, one spark, and whole mill floor were engulfed with flame afore any bugger could get out. Happened in a second and three hundred dead. No hobnails on mill floor.'

Harry nodded. Bart was right. He bent to free his feet of his boots while Bart repeated his words to the rest of the villagers. 'Boots off. No hobnails on mill floor.' He had no need to shout; he was used to making his words heard over machines, no one had any trouble hearing him when the machines were quiet.

Finally in stockinged feet, he let Harry pass, the others following as quickly as they could.

The stonemason ran down the main gangway, coughing on the wool fibres in the air, so thick it gave the impression of a snowstorm. He pushed his way through the gaggle of women and children, then stopped short at the sight of his sister, Lizzie. She had a little 'un in her arms.

Harry couldn't see who it was and part of him didn't want to know. By the amount of blood streaked over them both and the floor, there was no helping the child.

He looked the machine over. One of the new mules; the low horizontal carriage would normally be unrelenting, pulling and spinning the wool fibres through rollers until it reached the end of its traverse, clanging against the support stanchion before travelling back to the main body of the machine to wrap the yarn on to spindles.

He gulped as he saw white flecks of bone amidst the blood on the second stanchion.

Harry knelt by his sister. 'Give her to me, lass.'

Lizzie slowly turned her head to him and he gasped. Her normally rosy cheeks were stark white, her eyes dark and wide, looking like caves in her normally pretty face.

'Lizzie?'

'She's hurt too. Her hand. Getting Betty out. Ain't spoken since.' Harry didn't see who had spoken, his full attention was on the two before him.

'Betty?'

'Aye, Betty Butterworth.'

Harry recognised the dress then, the poor lass was Martha's friend, Sarah's girl. Eight years old.

'Lizzie,' Harry said again and this time thought he saw a glimmer of recognition in her eyes. 'Lizzie, it's me, Harry. Give Betty to me, I'll look after her.'

'It's all right, Lizzie,' Emily said from beside him, and Harry looked at her in relief. She'd know what to do.

He bent to take Betty from Lizzie, and gasped at the state of Lizzie's hand. The mule had crushed it as she'd tried to get Betty out. He couldn't look at Betty, or what was left of her. *Even her mother won't recognise her*, he thought with dismay. *Only the dress, the one she'd made herself and were so proud of, told of her identity now.*

'I'll take care of Lizzie, Harry,' Emily said.

Harry nodded, stood, and turned to see Martha and Sarah at the front of the crowd of bootless men and women. Sarah stared at Harry. She must have heard, but hadn't taken note yet.

'Sarah,' Harry said. 'Best thee don't look, love.'

'No.' The word was quiet, desperate, and she collapsed against Martha. Harry met Martha's eyes and knew she was thinking the exact same thing he was.

Thank God Edna don't have to do this work.

'Give her to me.' Robert Butterworth ignored his wife as he pushed past her, making both Sarah and Martha stumble in his wake.

He glared at Harry, who stared back. He saw no compassion in Butterworth's face and wondered how deep it was buried. Too many in this village had simply lost too much.

He took his daughter, and Harry noticed his hands shook. But he showed no other sign of his distress. The villagers parted to let him through, and Sarah and Martha followed, Martha's stick thumping a funereal tattoo as they went.

Harry turned back to Lizzie and Emily, and knelt back down beside them.

'How bad is it?'

Emily didn't look up at him, but carried on her work. She'd torn strips from her petticoat, but didn't even blush as she did so. 'Don't tell Papa, he can't afford another, and I don't need it, not really.'

Harry smiled at her, then flinched at a particularly loud thump from Martha's stick at the other end of the mill floor. 'How bad?' he asked again.

'It ain't going to be much use no more,' Lizzie said, staring at the misshapen clump on the end of her wrist. She screamed as Emily wrapped one of the lengths of cotton around it.

'Sorry Lizzie, we've got to stem the bleeding. Doctor Ingram's on his way, he'll set the bones and do what he can for thee. He'll give thee summat for the pain too.'

'It'll have to be downstairs,' Bart said. 'Need to clear the floor; get machines up and running again.'

'You can't be serious!' Harry looked up at him, then noticed a child even younger than Betty scrubbing the blood away from the spinning mule.

'Make sure thee gets into all them cracks and crannies,' Bart directed the boy. 'We don't want no blood on new yarn.'

He looked back at Harry and shrugged. 'Mill got to run, Harry. Mill got to run.'

Harry nodded. He had to look after Lizzie now, and Bart weren't the problem here, the Rooks were. If anyone were going to take *them* on, they'd need to think it through first.

Harry opened the door to the Black Bull and a riotous fug of shouts and odours assaulted him. He smiled ruefully; after tending to Lizzie all day, and quieting Martha's fears about Emily once more, he had hoped for a quiet drink. That was clearly not to be.

A slap on his shoulder sent him reeling towards the bar and he ordered ale, then tried to make sense of the arguments. Big Bart seemed to be taking the brunt of the men's tempers, and Harry made his way through the throng of his neighbours, all of whom seemed to hold the overlooker responsible for today's disaster.

'There were nowt I could do,' Big Bart said, his roar easily heard over the din. 'It all happened in a second. Everything were well, and then, then...'

Harry stood before him and placed his hand on Bart's shaking shoulder.

'And then what?' A new voice was raised. A strident voice, full of grief and anger, which silenced the pub. 'Then your mule crushed the head of my little girl. My little Betty. We've none left now. No more Butterworths. All gone. Taken. By your damnable machinery!'

Bart looked Robert Butterworth in the eye and calmed. 'Thee sent her to work there.'

'What did thee say?'

'Thee heard. I do me best for them lasses, whatever age they are when they're sent out to work. She were too young to be on mill floor, and thee knew it, but thee'd had her working there ower a year already.'

Men stepped back, leaving the way clear for the two men squaring up to each other.

Harry moved between them. Robert Butterworth wasn't soft, but he was no match for Bart; and no amount of fury would give him enough strength to hurt the overlooker. If he tried, Bart would fight. He needed to hit out. And Bart would beat the living daylights out of the man, grieving father or no.

'Move aside, Harry.'

'No. This is not the answer. This does not honour any of the mill youngsters.'

'Too right,' Will Sugden, the innkeeper of the Black Bull, put in. 'Take it outside or drown it in ale, them's thy choices.'

'They'll drown it in ale, on my tab, Will.'

As one, the men of Haworth turned to the man who had walked into the middle of this. Zemeraim Rook, his father and brother at his shoulders.

'I mean it. Tonight's ale is on the Rooks. Tonight we commiserate, we remember, and we talk. Tomorrow we take steps to stop this happening again.'

'And how does thee intend to do that?' Butterworth sneered.

'We'll enforce the twelve-hour rule, there'll be no more exceptions, no matter how much you plead for more hours for pay. No woman or child will work more than that per day. And they'll take an hour and a half of rest during the day.'

'It's still twelve hours though! What about the ten-hour rule?

'Aye, it is, but only nine on Sundays. There's a new act going through Parliament as we speak, which means machinery will soon have to be fenced in, and we've already started on that. As for the ten-hour rule, we'll have to see what Parliament says about that in time.'

'Too late for my Betty,' Butterworth snarled as he stepped up to Zem Rook. 'Eight year old and her life crushed out of her.'

To his credit, Zem did not flinch, even when the spittle from Butterworth's words hit his cheek. 'Eight, Mr Butterworth? You insisted she was nine when she started with us last year. You know full well children under nine should not be on our workforce.'

'Thee knew damn well she were seven when she started, just like most of others crawling under thy machinery.'

'I distinctly remembering asking you to swear to her age of nine. I have your thumbprint on her record of work to prove it.'

Men shuffled away, eager to drown the truth in free ale. They all knew the law that forbade anyone eight or younger from working. But they also knew that births had only been registered since the queen came to the throne. No one over the age of six had a birth certificate, and when it came to feeding too many mouths on not enough coin, the Butterworths were not the only family in Haworth who had claimed their daughter to be 'small for her age'. Most of the men now guzzling their ale had done the same thing, and their shame was beginning to overcome their sympathy.

Butterworth looked around at them, recognising he would get no further. He looked back at Bart who stepped up to him, placed his brawny hands on the smaller man's shoulders, and said, 'I did all I could. Thee did all thee could. We can do no more. Come, drink with me.'

Friends once more, the two men turned to the bar, where a space was cleared for them. They sat on a couple of upturned casks and were handed tankards of best porter. Those tankards would not be empty until both men were passed out on the filthy floor; sorrows well and truly drowned. At least for the night.

Harry turned to the Rooks, just as they were about to leave. 'There is more that can be done.'

Zem met his gaze and raised an eyebrow.

'Making life easier in mill is one thing, but what about at home?'

'What do you mean?'

'Thy weavers and woolcombers. Does thee know how many men, women and children are crammed into them cottages thee rents out? Most of space is given over to looms and the woolcombers' charcoal fires. As thy mill grows, so does thy workforce. They all need to live somewhere. I bet fewer would be taken by smallpox and the other plagues if they weren't so crowded in. That's what Reverend says, anyroad.'

Zem regarded Harry for a moment, then looked around the room, sensing the charge in the atmosphere, before turning to his father and brother. Harry could not hear what was said, but could see they had a decision when Zem turned back to face the room, head high.

'What do you have in mind, Mr Sutcliffe?'

'The site of the old woolcomber's shed, the one that burned down a few years ago, next to Weaver's Row. I can build thee four cottages on that scrap of land. And me family needs the extra work now that Lizzie's hand were maimed in that machine of thine.'

Zem nodded. 'We'll give thought to where else to build.' As one, all three Rooks bowed their heads once, exited the Black Bull, then replaced their top hats for the short walk to their carriage.

10.

Martha dipped her rag into the water bowl beside her, wrung it out and put the cooled fabric to her daughter's brow. She stroked Edna's cheek, whispering encouragement to the eight-year-old. 'Come on, lass, look at thy ma, let me see them beautiful eyes of thine.'

She dripped water on to Edna's lips in the hope that some drops would find their way into the girl's mouth, but there was no response, and tears filled Martha's eyes as she looked down at her daughter. Wrinkled, blue-grey skin and dark circles around her eyes, hot to the touch, and heart beating double time, there was no mistaking the signs of the cholera. Half the village was down with it.

Edna groaned as cramps took hold of her again and expelled what little sustenance, and liquid, remained in the small body.

'Doctor Ingram's with the Rooks,' Harry said from the doorway, and Martha jumped. 'Whole village is suffering; there are so many shutters closed on Main Street, it's heartbreaking.'

Martha looked at him and said nothing, then turned back to her daughter. There was nothing to say.

'I'll go get Emily, mebbe she can help.'

'She's here again, that ruddy basket over her arm,' Sarah announced as she entered Lizzie's cottage on Weaver's Row.

'What, Emily? Where is she?' Martha paused, turning away from Lizzie and dropping her cloth into the bowl of cool, murky water.

'Where do you think? Talking to thy Harry.'

Martha's colour rose. Since Edna had died, she had spent most of her time with Lizzie, looking after her and her husband Thomas, and Sarah had taken to coming to help. It was no secret that since Betty's death, Robert had been finding comfort in arms other than his wife's and she could not bear to stay home in an empty house.

'I wish he'd never suggested building them cottages. She's there every ruddy day, and he laps it up!'

'Thee'll have to watch him better, Martha. Thee knows what men are like.'

'Not our Harry,' Lizzie croaked. 'Not him.'

Martha wrung the cloth out, and stroked her sister-in-law's burning face. 'Hush now, Lizzie, keep thy strength.'

'He's a good man is Harry,' Lizzie whispered before sinking back into sleep.

'Martha.'

She looked up at Sarah, who had gone to check on Thomas. Heart sinking, she struggled to her feet and crossed the small room to Thomas's bed as Sarah passed her hand over his face to shut his unseeing eyes.

Martha sighed. 'I'll go tell Harry. He can sort coffin boards out while we lay him out. Will thee watch Little Thomas while I'm gone?'

'Aye. They'll be running out of ground in that churchyard at this rate.'

Sarah got to her feet, and closed the shutters, then she checked on Lizzie again, before making her way to the kitchen to search out black ribbon; it would be needed for the family to wear, and to cover the doorknob to warn visitors. She'd make a wreath for the front door as well from laurel and yew, and wind the ribbon around that. She couldn't collect the greenery yet, though, first she needed to ensure there would only be the one wreath to make.

'It seems I only see thee when there's a funeral on these days, Martha,' Harry said as he watched his wife dress their remaining child, Little Thomas, in his Sunday best.

'Aye, well.'

'I thought I'd be seeing more of thee while I were working on them new cottages, what with thee spending so much time at Lizzie's.'

'Aye well, her brood keep us busy, especially with her only having one hand.'

'But Sarah seems to be there every day too, can she not do more?'

'Thee spends thy time talking with thy friends, I'll spend my time with me own.'

Harry stared at her, then understood. 'Not this again. Emily *is* a friend, no more. If thee don't believe it of me, thee should believe it of her.'

'Hmph.'

'Martha, please, not again, I don't know what else to tell thee. There's nowt going on, all she does is pass the time of day.'

'Several times a day from what I hear.'

'Martha!'

She stopped what she was doing as Harry raised his voice, and sent Little Thomas waddling out of the room, then stood to face her husband, her face set.

'Not today. Not when I'm burying me daughter and me brother. Just give it a rest, will thee?'

Martha said naught, but her eyes prickled as she watched her husband give up on her and go to find his son.

She followed them down the stairs to the front parlour where

Thomas and Edna were laid out ready for the funeral.

'It's right that he's here,' Harry said. 'I know it's more work for thee, Martha, but Lizzie couldn't have coped well on her own.'

'I'd have managed fine, Harry,' Lizzie said from the door.

He sighed and turned to deal with the living. 'It weren't a disservice, Lizzie, I know thee'd have managed, I just want to make it easier for thee, that's all. Thee's me brother's widow, he'd want me to look after thee.'

Lizzie softened as her gaze went to her husband's coffin, three times the size of Edna's. 'Aye, I know, Harry, and I thank thee for that. There ain't many folk who'd take on a crippled widow and her brood.' She raised her gloved stump of a hand.

'Stop talking of thysen like that,' Martha scolded. 'Thee's got another hand, and it ain't slowing thee down much.'

'That's true enough.' Lizzie crossed the room, and strewed more flowers in both coffins. 'They look peaceful don't they? As if they're sleeping.'

'Aye. Harry's had a photograph took of 'em. They won't be forgot.'

Lizzie nodded.

'Reet then, is there anything else that needs doing afore the parson gets here?' Harry asked.

Martha and Lizzie examined the room: the coffins were placed against the back wall, draped in black and white ribbon with a multitude of flowers; and as many chairs as could be crammed into the room were arranged in rows. 'No, we're ready,' Martha said, with a nod from Lizzie.

Harry grimaced, nodded and strode to the front door to prop it open for their guests and allow them to view Thomas and Edna before the service began.

Harry, Martha and Lizzie followed the parson and pallbearers past their friends and neighbours, and out into the sunshine. All three were numb, and barely aware of the service they had just sat through to commemorate their lost family.

The youngsters: Georgie, Little Thomas, and Stephen followed behind, pleased to be out in the fresh air again instead of the stuffy room, and leading the rest of the mourners out of the house and down Church Lane.

From the back of the procession, the large pine box and smaller white casket seemed to be moving on a sea of black crêpe and ribbon. At the gate, only those closest to Thomas and Edna entered the churchyard, everybody else continued to the King's Arms to make a start on the ale and food that Harry was laying on for them.

The family, plus Sarah and one or two other close friends gathered around the Sutcliffe family grave as Reverend Brontë began the rite of committal.

Harry stared at the elaborate memorial stone he had carved after Baby John's death five years before. Elaborate scrolls and a frieze carved around the edge, he'd also carved a statue of a young child into one of the supports that would carry the altar stone. He had a second one to put into place when they replaced the stone. Harry stared at the names already on there, and gulped as he remembered carving Edna's name two days before in preparation.

He had thought himself hardened to it by now; he'd carved so many of his friends' names, and their children's as well as his own kin, but none had been as hard as carving his daughter's.

He caught the hand of Little Thomas, his sole surviving child, and was pleased to feel Martha's hand creep into his other, then realised Lizzie clasped Martha's free hand. Their numbers may be diminished, but they were family, and they would make the best of the days to come; together.

II.

'How's our Mary doing?' Lizzie asked.

'Thee could at least let me in and sit down afore thee grills me,' Martha grumbled.

Lizzie stepped back to allow her friend to clump past her into the kitchen and settle down in the most comfortable chair.

'She's on the mend, stop fretting, Lizzie. The coughing's subsiding and doctor's happy that it ain't consumption after all. Probably her lungs are weak from mills and soot. She'll be on her feet again by end of week.'

'That's good news,' Lizzie said, and put some water on to boil. 'Will thee have some dandelion tea?'

'Aye, that'd do me reet,' Martha said. 'Has thee heard about Bart Grange?'

'Aye, dead of the consumption last week.'

'Aye, but that's not all. He were the last in line, and instead of burying him in family plot near church, Rooks have bought Granges' grave.'

'They never have! What about bones? And where'll they put Big Bart?'

'Up top of new bit – alongside parsonage by field wall.'

'That's terrible – they should be left to rest in peace.'

'Aye, Harry's livid. Reckons it's too disrespectful, even though there's no bugger left to mourn them. He's shocked at parson for allowing it.'

'Well, I hope he's making Rooks pay through nose for it. Oh that'll be Sarah.' Lizzie bustled to the door to let her in. 'I wonder if she's heard about it.'

'Were that Emily's voice I heard?' Martha queried when the two women joined her.

'Aye,' Sarah said with a glance at Lizzie.

'She's been there every ruddy morning, and afternoon too. What the ruddy hell is she playing at?'

'Oh Martha, hush. There's nowt going on, thee can trust Harry, he ain't one to fool around on thee.'

'Thee can never tell,' Sarah disagreed. 'It were months afore I realised my Robert were playing away.'

'Well, I've had enough. I'm going to find out what's going on, and if I don't like it I'm putting a stop to it. I'll be up in weaver's gallery, I'll be able to see what they're saying from top of steps.'

Lizzie and Sarah shared another glance as Martha heaved herself up from her chair and clumped towards the internal stairs to the gallery above.

Lizzie shouted after her, 'No good'll come of it, Martha. You'd do better staying down here with us.'

She received only a harrumph for answer, accompanied by the thumping of Martha's stick as she scaled the treads.

'How do, Ellis.'

'What did you call me?' Emily Brontë turned on Harry, her face twisted into her fiercest scowl.

Despite himself, Harry took a step backwards, nearly falling over the stone behind him waiting to be faced. He held his hands up, still clasping hammer and chisel, to ward her off. 'Steady on, Emily. I'm reet then, am I? It is thee that wrote that book, thee's Ellis Bell?'

'No! No, I am not!' Emily stamped her foot to further stress her denials.

Harry ignored her. 'Aye, thee is. It's thee that wrote it. "I wish I were a girl again, half savage and hardy, and free . . . Why am I so changed? I'm sure I should be myself were I once among the heather on those hills." Them's thy words, Emily, no matter what's written on cover.'

Emily glared at him, her fists clenched, and Harry wondered if her basket would hold up to the force of her fingers, but he wasn't going to let his advantage go now.

'Anyroad, ain't Bell one of the curate's names? And if thee's Ellis, I'm guessing Currer is Charlotte, and Acton, Anne. I'm not daft thee knows. Anyroad, no bugger else could write about the moors like that – reading *Wuthering Heights* were like seeing the moors through thine eyes.'

'Does Martha know?'

'Ha! I knew it! And no she don't. I weren't sure mesen till just now. I've been teaching her letters, and she's reading it at moment, though I doubt she'll work it out. She don't know thee like I do.'

'You can't tell her, Harry Sutcliffe, you have to promise me. It'd be all round the village by noon.'

'I don't keep secrets from me wife, Emily.'

She scowled again, and Harry gave in. 'All right, I won't tell her, I'll keep thy secret.'

Emily relaxed and Harry grinned at her.

'So, who's Heathcliff based on, anyone we know?'

'No.'

'The only lad daft enough to scrabble around moors with thee were mesen.'

'Don't flatter yourself, Harry Sutcliffe.'

'I can't help but notice there's a similarity in the name an'all.'

'There's similarities to most names in village. It doesn't mean folk are in the book. It's just a story, with characters not neighbours.'

Harry raised his eyebrows, and Emily shrugged.

'Well, happen I did get some inspiration from the goings on in Haworth.'

'I knew it!' Harry grinned at her.

Emily shook her head at him, opened her mouth, then with a glance upward, shut it again and began to climb the stairs to the weaver's gallery, basket over her arm. Halfway up, she paused, started to turn, then changed her mind and continued upward.

Martha stepped forward into the doorway, blocking Emily's entry to the gallery. She smiled at the smaller woman, who was further disadvantaged by having to pause on a lower step as Martha loomed over her.

Emily glared at her, but Martha did not move aside.

The background noise of the looms working softened then tailed away as the weavers realised something was happening and they paused in their work to watch and listen.

'I can't get past.'

Martha made no reply, but crossed her arms, strengthening her position.

'Please stand aside.'

'It's time we had a little chat, Miss Brontë. Thee's spending far too much time with my husband and I would prefer it if you would desist.' Martha looked at her in triumph at her well-worded demand. No one would be able to say she wasn't polite.

Emily flushed a deep red, and moved forward until there was just one step between them. Martha did not move, but Emily was not one to be cowed.

'There's nowt improper happening, you know that well, just as everyone else does. If you don't like Harry talking to folk, maybe you should try talking to him yourself.'

It was Martha's turn to colour, but she was aware she had an audience and stood her ground.

'I can still lip-read from me days in the mill, thee knows. Comes in reet handy it does.' Martha grinned at Emily. 'I've read that book an'all. Some of it, anyroad, I'm not quick with me letters like thee and Harry.'

Emily gasped. 'Martha, no!'

'Harry's *my* husband; he ain't *thy* Heathcliff. Thee's made me a laughing stock with that ruddy book!'

'Then stop talking and don't tell anyone,' Emily hissed. 'I don't want folk to know. As far as the world knows, Mr Ellis Bell wrote that book, and that's the way it can stay.'

'Well.' Martha uncrossed her arms and rested her hands on her hips. 'If it's privacy thee wants to keep, thee'll have to do summat for me to keep me mouth shut. Stay away from my Harry!'

'Martha!' Harry had noticed the quarrel and rushed up the steps.

Emily took advantage of Martha's momentary distraction, and pushed by the larger woman, then hurried through the gallery.

'What the ruddy hell's going on here?' Harry stared after his friend as she reached the far steps and scurried down them.

'Is Martha reet? Did Miss Emily write that book everyone's been on about?' Alf Thackray asked.

Harry turned to his wife. 'What has thee done? What was thee thinking? Thee's full of spite, Martha Sutcliffe, and there's nowt worse than a spiteful woman!'

'She's writing ruddy love stories about thee!' Martha protested. 'And having whole world read 'em. The pair of thee have humiliated me! Even Robert Butterworth *tried* to keep his dalliances private – thine are ruddy *published*. Ruddy Heathcliff, my arse!'

Harry stared at his wife, barely recognising her as the woman he'd fallen in love with ten years ago. Now he felt only disgust at the woman she'd grown into, and grieved for the woman she could have been had life been kinder; or if she'd chosen different words and actions over the years.

'Well, if I started out as Heathcliff, I reckon thee's the inspiration for the monster he becomes at end. That there lass,' he indicated the direction in which Emily had rushed, 'has more kindness, more sense, and an hell of a lot more goddamned plain *decency* than you ever had. And she sees people true; she sees me, and she ruddy well sees thee for who thee is!'

Martha gasped in shock as his words ignited lightning in her heart that tore her apart, setting fires of rage, jealousy and humiliation burning through her, consuming her. The emotion exploded from her and she screamed as the world spun; she couldn't make sense of what she saw: stone steps, the still looms, and Harry's face, spinning away from her.

Part Four

April 2017

"He's more myself than I am. Whatever our souls are made of, his and mine are the same."

Wuthering Heights
Emily Brontë, 1847
Haworth, West Yorkshire

I.

The shrill staccato shriek spears through my skull, accompanied by a dull, throbbing roar. Over and over, piercing the darkness; the sound a lightning strike on my brain; the roar the thunder of my pulse. The storm isn't just overhead, it's *in* my head. Gratefully, I sink back down into dark, silent oblivion.

A new lightning strike shocks me back into awareness. I lie still, trying to make sense of the sounds. Regular, clipped, like the piping call of a lapwing, only much louder.

There are more, beyond the loud one – quieter birds calling their rhythm. *That's right,* I commend myself on the realisation. *It's a rhythm – this is no song. So why are they singing so drearily?*

I rise from the darkness once more, cognisance seeping into me like the dawning sun's rays – gentle at first, then more insistent. *It's quiet! No lapwings!* Instead, a new pain; my eyes now. In place of darkness, all is red; a bright, resolute red – not like the dawning sun at all but a setting one the night before a glorious summer day.

I squeeze my eyes tight against the unrelenting light. *That's better.*

'Verity? Verity are you awake?'

My breath freezes. *Who's here?*

'Lara, I think the light's too bright, will you close the curtains?'

Movement, the scrape of a chair, then the redness dims and I relax my eyelids.

That name again – *Verity.* It sounds familiar, but I can't place it. *Who is Verity?*

'Can you open your eyes?'

All of a sudden, it feels imperative that I do so. At least two people – strangers – are sitting over me as I lie here helpless. I need to see; to assess the danger.

I try to lift my lids, without success. *They're stuck! What's happening to me?* Again – some small success – a chink of light. *Too bright.* I squeeze my eyes shut again.

'Come on, Verity, you can do it. Come back to us.'

A hand strokes my arm, another my face. *Don't touch me!*

I draw in a breath, gather my determination around me and force my lids open. It's like prizing apart two woolcombs.

The lids on my right eye give way and I immediately shut them again. I can feel my breath coming faster, as if I'd walked up Main Street. *Just from opening an eye for a second?* I think with terror. *What's happened to me?*

As my breath calms, I try to make sense of the indistinct image my eye records before snapping shut. It's no use, everything's blurred.

I flinch when a cool cloth is placed over my eyes, then gently drawn away.

'There, that's better,' one of the voices says. 'Wiped the sleep away, it should be easier now. Try again, Verity.'

My fear eases. There is gentleness in that voice and action; concern.

Obediently, I try again. Now they open, the cloth has done its work. I slam them shut again, but this time in a blink; a series of blinks as I allow light into my world and thoughts, giving my eyes time to get used to it.

Two heads appear over me. Strange heads. Women, but not women. *Angels?* No, angels would not have such blood-red lips and blackened eyes. *Devils.*

A small cry escapes me and the darkness rushes back to claim me, then a child's voice, following me down: 'What's wrong with her, Mummy? Why isn't she Auntie Verity anymore?'

'Welcome back.'

It's one of the she-devils. I slowly turn my head to look at her.

'Sorry we crowded you yesterday. It was too much, overwhelming. We were just so pleased to see you awake.'

These are not the words of a devil. I blink, then blink again, trying to focus on her features.

'Jayne's taken Hannah to get a cup of hot chocolate, it's only me here now,' the woman says. 'It's quiet now, they've muted the machines – finally, all that beeping was driving me mad!' I flinch as she laughs, showing teeth.

'It was worse on the ward, a dozen of the things, all going off – a right racket. But they moved you into a side room when you started to show signs of waking. It's much better in here. Sorry, I'm babbling.'

The woman laughs again, this time without showing her teeth. I realise she's holding my hand. I stare into her face. She looks familiar somehow. *But who . . .*

'We've been so scared, Verity. When you and William collapsed like that, and then just lay here, day after day. Thank God you're awake. Oh Verity—' She breaks off, tears running down her face, leaving strange, dirty lines. *Coal dust?*

'Who . . .' I try to say, but my throat is so dry no words emerge.

'Here, have some water.' The other woman's back. And the child. 'Support her head for me, Lara, that's right. There, drink.'

She's pushing a cold tube between my lips.

'It's okay, it's water, just suck.'

I do as I'm bid, and cold fresh liquid floods my mouth. I close my eyes in pleasure as I swallow the liquid, then suck again.

'That's enough,' the second woman says, pulling the strange tube from my mouth. 'The nurse said just a little bit, your body needs to get used to it again.'

I stare at her. 'Who . . .' An audible sound this time. I try again. 'Who's Verity?'

Silence. Before I receive an answer, I sink back into sleep – the effort of waking too much for me.

My eyes open, gently this time. The light is dim and the room silent, and I relax back into the bedding in relief. I'm alone.

But where am I? I wrinkle my nose at the strange, harsh smell as I look around the room. The walls are smooth and plain; no stonework visible, no wallpaper either. The curtains at the window are so thin and flimsy, I struggle to think of them as curtains; they're far too short as well, finishing almost a leg's length above the floor.

And what kind of bed is this? I grasp the metal rails to each side. *'Tis half cage, and not big enough to share, even with a bairn!* Yet it's so soft and comfortable. I rub the blanket between thumb and forefinger. Thin again, but warm enough and with some kind of loose covering. Clean too – not a speck of coal dust or fluff.

The pillows, though! I move my head from side to side. I have never rested on anything so fine and soft.

I wrinkle my nose again. *What is that smell?* Sharp, stringent. *Caustic soda? Lye?* No, not quite. I've never smelled anything like it.

Disinfectant.

Of course. But what's disinfectant?

Brow wrinkling as well as my nose now, I jump as the door opens and a man walks in. Tall, clean-shaven and with no hat, he wears the plainest frockcoat I have ever seen. It's white! How can a gentleman walk the streets in a white frock coat? It will grey with soot and coal in seconds!

He wears numerous strange ornamentations in his top pocket. And the coat itself is too short for him. *Why on earth can he not fasten his buttons? Or wear a neck tie? He's walking into a lady's private room half undressed!*

'Ah, good, you're awake,' he says, with no greeting or manners at all.

The doctor, I think – though I know not why. This is certainly not Doctor Ingram.

He says no more, but moves to the foot of my bed, takes the clipboard hanging there and flicks through the pages.

I furrow my brow further in consternation. *Clipboard?*

Still silent, the man – this *doctor* – moves to the side of my bed, takes one of his ornamentations from his pocket and points it at me.

I scream at the unexpected, blinding light.

'Nothing to worry about, just look past my shoulder while I check your eyes.' He flicks the light left and right, thoroughly confusing me. I've never known a doctor, or even a druggist, do such a thing. *And how on earth is he fuelling the light? It cannot be candle nor gas.*

Batteries, I think, then frown again.

'Watch my finger.'

I stare at the man. *Is he mad? Am I in Bedlam?*

'Just follow it with your eyes.'

I decide to humour him, and watch his finger move left, right, up, down.

'Hmm,' he says, making a note on his – *what is it? Ah yes, clipboard.* Then he takes a seat. *He is sitting on my bed!* I stare at him in outrage.

'Do you know where you are?'

I continue to stare at the strange man who finds it appropriate to sit on a lady's bed.

'You're in hospital,' he says.

Hospital? I look about me again. Bright, clean, too large, and this strange, rude doctor. *So it is the madhouse then.*

'You've been in a coma for three months.' He looks at me carefully and I stare back in shock.

Three months? I've been in the madhouse these past three months? How is Harry coping without me? Did he put me here? What of Little Thomas?

'We've run MRIs and CAT scans, but can find no reason why both you and your friend have been afflicted in this way.' He pauses. 'Can you tell me what you remember?'

I look at him blankly.

He sighs, then smiles. 'I'm rushing you – I'm anxious to work out the puzzle and am getting carried away. Let's start at the beginning. Can you tell me your name?'

'Martha Sutcliffe.' I know that at least. Or do I? The name seems wrong now that I've uttered it, and the doctor has a strange look on his face. Worried.

'Martha Sutcliffe,' he repeats.

'Yes. No.' I realise I don't know. I'm certain now. That isn't my name. I stare at the man, feeling helpless. Tears prickle at my eyes and my breathing quickens. *Who am I?*

'Don't worry.' He pats my arm. 'You've only just woken, things are bound to be confusing at first. It's nothing to worry about, we'll just give it a bit of time. I'll come back and see you tomorrow.'

The door opens. 'Are you ready for us?' A woman's voice.

'Ah, I'm not sure. Are you up for a visitor? It might jog your memory.'

I say nothing. A woman dressed in a strange blue smock pushes someone into the room.

I stare at the man in the wheeled contraption.

'Harry!'

'Martha! God, please no, get me out of here! Get her away from me!'

Darkness rushes back to claim me and I gratefully spin away from the image of the husband I killed. I know now, this is the madhouse, and Harry the devil that will plague me for the rest of my days and beyond. But I'm not in Bedlam, no. I must have died too, I'm in Hell.

2.

'Here you go, Jayne, coffee,' one voice says.

'Double shot?' says the other.

'Of course. I don't know how you sleep at night, the amount of caffeine you consume.'

It's the she-devils with the red lips, I realise. I keep my eyes closed.

'Any sign of waking?'

'No. I wondered a minute or two ago, but nothing.'

'We should swap her water for your coffee, Jayne, that would keep her awake.'

The two women laugh. *Are they talking about poisoning me?* I focus on keeping my breathing steady so they won't realise I'm listening to their plans.

'Vikram says The Rookery is nearly ready,' one of them says – the one called Jayne, I think.

'Yes, it's looking great. Mo is just finishing off the tiling in the en-suites and he's decorating Verity's apartment too.'

'There's nothing in the budget for that.'

'He's doing it as a favour for me.'

'Ah, so that's going well, is it? Good, I'm glad. You deserve to be happy, Lara.'

'Happy? With Verity just lying here?'

'You know what I mean.'

A sigh. 'Yes, 'course I do. I'm just remembering how excited Verity was about The Rookery, and meeting William. Then that *stupid* séance! Oh why did I do it?'

'We were trying to help, Lara. Nobody could have predicted Verity and William reacting like this – and if we'd even thought it *could* happen . . . Well, to be honest, none of us would have believed it and we'd have carried on anyway.'

Silence. I imagine the one called Lara nodding and hear her sniff.

'Too much was happening in that building, it was freaking us all out.'

'Yes, and escalating too. Those birds, and then when I saw the Grey Lady.'

'I know, Lara. And I'm sorry I ridiculed you when you first talked about orbs and spirits.'

'It's fine, Jayne. You need to see or experience something to believe, otherwise it's all claptrap. I understand.'

'Well, I know better now, and it was all centred round Verity and William.'

'I wonder who Martha and Harry are. Were.'

My ears prick up. *Were?*

'I've been doing some research,' Jayne says, her voice quiet and careful. 'They're both mentioned in the parish records – their marriage is recorded anyway: April 1837.

'So they definitely lived in Haworth.'

'Yes, and died there.'

Died?

'Maybe they're trying to talk through Verity and William, send a message. It's strange that they both woke at the same time, spouting the same names. It's got the nurses in a right state. Some won't even come into their rooms, and the doctors are befuddled too; nobody knows what to make of it all.'

'Has anything else happened at The Rookery while you've been staying there, Lara? Anything at all?'

'No, nothing. I've told you already. Even those awful birds have gone since Vikram put those rubber spikes on the window ledges and guttering.'

'Good, he said they'd do the trick. If there's nowhere for them to perch, they'll move on.'

'You really like him, don't you, Jayne? How's it going?'

Silence. *What's she doing?*

A clap. 'That's wonderful! And about time, you've been on your own for far too long!'

'It doesn't seem right with Verity . . .'

'Verity won't mind a bit. She's only ever wanted you to be happy, you know that.'

'Yes.'

I open my eyes and stare at them both. 'Who's Mo?' I croak.

They stare at me, then slowly smile, and both lean forward. Jayne grabs my arm, Lara my hand, and I notice she's scraped most of the nail varnish off her finger nails.

'Verity?'

'Yes.' I nod. 'Yes, it's me.'

'Ah, Ms Earnshaw, back with us I see, good, good.'

I blink until the blob of pale colours coalesce into a man. The doctor. I say nothing. I don't quite know what to make of him.

He looks down at his clipboard, turns over a few pages, then puts it down and clears his throat.

'Your case is . . . most perplexing.'

I raise my eyebrows.

'We can find no sign of any kind of injury, nothing to explain why you've been unconscious for three months.'

I stare at him, it seems I can do no more.

'And . . . well . . . I'm afraid we have so far been unable to determine the cause.' He wrinkles his forehead, clearly expecting me to make a comment, then continues when I remain mute.

'What is even more perplexing is that your, er, friend, passed into unconsciousness at the same time, and, er, well, appears to have woken at exactly the same moment as yourself. As you know, he also suffered the same delusions as yourself, although unfortunately, has not come out of it the way you have. He still thinks himself to be somebody called Harry.'

'What?' The news shakes me out of my stupor. *Is William still stuck in the nightmare?*

'As I say, we can find no physical cause, so I have asked a colleague from Psychiatry to come and talk to you both. Although I will still want to see you regularly as well in case any symptoms re-emerge, or you experience any other, well, strange behaviours or beliefs.'

'Strange behaviours or beliefs?' I question.

He shrugs his shoulders. 'How else would you put it?'

The door bangs open, followed by an immediate apology as Lara spots the doctor. I realise I don't know his name, then another thought grips me.

'Lara – William still thinks he's Harry.'

'Yes, I know, Mo and Vikram have been trying to get through to him, but haven't managed it yet. His sister, Rebekah will be back at the weekend, hopefully she'll be able to help.'

'I'll deal with Harry,' I say. I pull off the sensor clamped to my finger, and fling the blankets back.

'Ms Earnshaw, I really must caution you—'

He's too late. I've swung my legs over the side of the hospital bed and placed my feet on the floor. I crumple as I put my weight on them, just as he says, '—to stay in bed.'

Lara helps me back up – neither she nor I would wait for a nurse – and I look at the doctor, my eyes wide with fright.

'As I was trying to explain,' he begins, then glances at Lara and softens under her furious glare. 'You have been in bed for three months. Muscles lose their condition very quickly, and I'm afraid it's going to take some work to build your strength back up.'

'What do you mean, some work?' Lara asks.

I lie in the bed, out of breath and terrified. *If I can't stand or walk, how on earth am I going to live in and run a three-storey guesthouse?*

'Physio,' the doctor says. 'Somebody will be along shortly to get you started, but if you're determined enough, you'll be back on your feet and running in a few weeks.'

I've had enough. I close my eyes and will oblivion to take me away. Just for a little while. Then I'll concentrate on learning to walk again.

3.

'I need to see William,' I say after the doctor has gone and I feel stronger again.

'Verity, no, you heard what the doctor said. You need to concentrate on getting your strength back,' Jayne says.

I glare at her. 'I've been *asleep* for three months. During that time, I lived another person's life. It sounds like William still is. I've got to help him out of it.'

'I grant you it's strange you had the same dreams—'

'It was *not* a dream!' I stop, realising my voice has risen into a shout. 'It wasn't a dream,' I repeat more calmly. 'I *was* Martha, I wasn't dreaming about her, I was living her life, feeling her emotions, walking in her shoes.'

'And William still thinks he's Harry,' Lara says.

'Exactly – he's still trapped. I've got to help him. Maybe the sight of me will shock him out of it.'

'*Shock* him out of it?' Lara questions. 'Exactly how does this story end?'

I shake my head. I can't tell my two best friends that I killed Harry. No, that *Martha* killed Harry. I shake my head again, this time in confusion, trying to make sense of the last image of my dream. *Did Martha kill him, or have I just* assumed *she did?* I'm no longer sure what is real and what isn't.

'I'll go get you a wheelchair,' Lara says.

'But the nurses,' Jayne protests. 'They'll stop us – you heard the doctor.'

'The nurses are freaked out by the pair of them – haven't you noticed they won't come in here or into William's room unless they have to?'

'I just thought they were busy,' Jayne says. 'They're run off their feet.'

'Well, that too.' Lara smiles at Jayne. 'Either way, they won't stop us. I won't be long.'

She slips out of the door and is gone before Jayne can say anything more.

'It'll be okay, Jayne. I have to do this. I have to help him get back to himself.'

Jayne sighs, then sits down by the bed and takes my hand. 'I know you do, Verity, and I'd do the same. We just don't know what we're dealing with and I'm scared that you confronting William, or Harry – or whatever's doing this to him – will only make things worse.'

I squeeze her hand with a small smile in reply.

* * *

Jayne approaches the door of my room, checks both ways, then beckons us forward.

Lara pushes with rather more enthusiasm than I expect, and I grip the armrests of the wheelchair as it careens through a ninety-degree angle between the doorway and corridor.

A stern-looking nurse in a dark blue uniform looks at us in surprise, then frowns. 'And just what, exactly, is going on here?'

I feel like a schoolgirl again, caught running in the corridor by a teacher.

'She's feeling very cooped up,' Jayne says. 'We thought we'd take her out and about for a change of scenery.'

'I see.'

I regard the woman, doing my best to keep my face blank. I wonder if I imagine her shudder when she meets my eyes.

'Very well. Don't be too long. The physiotherapist is due in an hour to start,' she glances at me, then looks back at Jayne before continuing, 'Ms Earnshaw's rehab.'

I narrow my eyes. *Why doesn't she speak directly to me?*

She bustles past, still refusing to look at me.

'I think you're right, Lara. That woman looked terrified!'

Neither Jayne nor Lara say anything, and I don't blame them. What is there to say?

Lara starts pushing again, and my wheelchair trundles forwards. For the first time I wonder if Jayne's right, and I should let William find his own way out of the past.

I open my mouth to tell Lara to halt, but instead she tells me, 'Here we are. This is his room,' as Jayne pushes open the door.

I see Vikram and another man first – Mo, I guess from the way his eyes light up when he sees Lara. Vikram looks at Jayne in just the same way. They're both half-standing, half-sitting on the windowsill and I wonder why they aren't using the chairs by the bed.

I look at him then, William, and recoil at the look of horror on his face.

'It's okay, William,' I say, hoping at least a part of the real him is awake and can hear me. 'It's me, Verity, you're safe.'

The others in the room stare at me in confusion.

'Harridan!' William – no, Harry – shouts. 'Murderer! Get thee away from me! I have no wish to see thee!'

Lara gasps from behind me. I ignore her. I *have* to get through to William.

'That was Martha, William. And a long time ago. She didn't mean to do it.'

'Thee broke me neck!' Harry screams. 'Killed me after I loved and cared for thee!'

'No. Martha killed Harry, William.' I struggle to keep my voice calm. 'You're alive, you're William Sutcliffe. Harry and Martha lived a long time ago – they're both long gone.'

'Get away, get away, get away from me, thee hear?'

'What on earth is going on in here?' The door bursts open and the nurse in the dark blue tunic we'd seen in the corridor bustles into the room.

She looks at me – glares. 'I might have known.' Then she turns her gaze on Lara and Jayne. 'A change of scenery, you said. Get her back to her room, while we calm Mr Sutcliffe. He needs to rest.'

I realise another nurse has entered behind the bossy one, and she's already at William's bedside, syringe in hand.

'Sorry,' I whisper. 'I thought I could get through to him.'

'Just get her back to her room. Everybody out. Now.'

We obey, Vikram now pushing my chair as Lara – tears threatening – walks with Mo's comforting arm around her. No one speaks.

4.

The physio helps me stagger back to the bed and fall on to it. I lie there for a few moments, out of breath, waiting for the hot trembling in my legs to calm down.

They begin to feel less like jelly and more like flesh and blood appendages of my body, and I heave myself fully on to the bed with a grunt.

Another rest, then I turn and manage to get myself under, and the blanket over. I lie back on the pillows panting with effort. This is ridiculous, I've only walked a few yards to the bathroom and back! *How am I going to manage all the stairs at The Rookery?*

It'll be months at this rate, yet they're sending me home in a couple of days.

A knock at the door, and I force my features into a smile as Lara's head pops round it. 'Are you up for visitors?'

'Always,' I say, my smile turning genuine as Hannah bursts into the room, runs to the bed and jumps up to give me one of the most welcome hugs of my life.

I squeeze back, holding her tight, although even that hurts and tears are threatening. Not of sadness, but a jumble of emotions. Relief, joy at being loved, fear and love of my own for the little girl in my arms, her mother, and her other 'aunt'.

'It's good to see you,' I say.

'Let Auntie Verity breathe, Hans,' Lara says. 'You're suffocating her.'

I shuffle over a little to make some room. 'Here, you stay up here with me, Hans.'

'How are you feeling?' Jayne says as she takes one of the chairs and Lara the other.

I frown, then catch myself. I've come to hate that question in the last few days, but I know Jayne is asking out of genuine concern.

'I'm okay – getting there, anyway. Is there any news of William?'

Lara narrows her eyes at me, knowing I'm avoiding telling them how I really feel, but Jayne answers before she can say anything.

'He's coming out of it, but is still quite confused. Occasionally he talks as if he's Harry still, but Vikram says he can see more and more of William every day.'

'Do you think he'll see me?'

'Not yet, Verity, sorry.' Jayne leans over and grasps my hand. 'He's still very confused, and after last time . . . well, best to give him some space; he'll come to you when he's ready.'

I nod, unsure what to say. I was feeling so sorry for myself only minutes ago, yet William is still struggling to free himself from the nightmare of Harry and Martha.

'How about you?' Lara asks. 'Are you still aware of Martha?'

I consider her question. 'Not in the same way as when I woke up. I can still remember everything, even how she felt – I felt it all myself and it's like a memory. But I know I'm Verity, I *think* Martha's gone.'

'Think?' Jayne pounces on the word.

I shrug and give Hannah a squeeze. 'How can I know for sure? All I can tell you is that while I have her memories, I'm fully cognisant that she's a third party.'

'Fully cognisant,' Lara repeats. 'You've seen the psychiatrist then.'

I give a small laugh. 'Yes. Not that she was any help. She has no real idea of what happened, and the best she can say is that it was some kind of mental break.'

'But William having the exact same one at the same time,' Jayne says. 'How does she explain that?'

I shrug again. 'Mass hysteria.'

'Mass? It only happened to the two of you,' she protests, 'and whilst I don't know William, judging by his friends he's not the hysterical type, and I know you're not.'

'As I said – no real idea.'

'Is she going to keep you in?' Lara asks.

'No.' I try to smile. 'No, she's happy that whatever the episode was, it's over and I can go home on Monday.'

'That's fantastic news!' Lara and Jayne say together, beaming as Hannah says, 'Yay!' and snuggles into me.

'Isn't it?' Lara asks, seeing right through my fake smile.

'Of course it is, I just—' I pause and take a deep breath to prevent new tears forming before admitting, 'I don't know how I'll manage. All those stairs and all that work. I can barely get myself to the bathroom and back.' I wave in the direction of the en-suite bathroom door and lose my battle with the tears.

'How am I going to get around The Rookery? It could take weeks, even months before I'm fit again – my muscle strength has just, just *gone*.'

'Don't worry, Auntie Verity, it's because you've been lying down so long. Your muscles will come back, you'll see.'

I smile at Hannah as she accompanies her assertion with a rather impressive bicep curl, then I glance at Lara – I know those are her words.

'You heard the physio,' she responds. 'Walk a little further every day. Keep pushing yourself, but rest when you need to. You're the only one who can rebuild your strength, and I know you can and will do it.'

'And you're not alone,' Jayne adds. 'Lara and I will be with you as much as possible, and the boys have been brilliant. I can't wait for you to see how The Rookery looks now, you'll be amazed.'

I stare at them. 'What do you mean? Have they carried on working? What have they done?' I start to panic, my breathing becoming faster as I think about all the decisions I should have been there to make. All the plans I'd made being taken over by others. *What have they done to my home?* I'm struggling to take in enough air, and Hannah looks alarmed.

'Calm down, Verity, and don't worry. Everything's okay,' Lara says.

'It looks really cool, Auntie Verity, I can't wait for you to see it!'

I look back at my friends and my breathing slows as trust reasserts itself at the smiles on their faces. 'Tell me.'

5.

I gape at my friends in amazed wonder. Lara has overseen the build every day in between taking Hannah to school and back, and all three of them have spent every weekend there to help get things ready.

Once my prepayment to Keighley Builders was used up, Jayne put up her own money to fund the rest, and has waited until now to ask me to sign the necessary paperwork for me to reimburse her.

On top of that, she's managed both builders and Lara to ensure the build will come in near or even on budget.

'Vikram has been an absolute star,' she says. 'You owe him big time. He's been joining us at the weekends – on his own time – to help with cleaning and buying furniture and stuff. All you have left to do is trial the toiletries to decide what to put in the guest bathrooms – and I'm afraid Lara's ordered you quite a few to test.'

Lara shrugs. 'Gotta get it right – who doesn't love those little bottles of gorgeousness when you go away? It's such a disappointment if it's nasty, cheap stuff.'

I grin at Lara. 'Quite right – we can all test them, then compare results.' I turn my smile on Jayne. 'Vikram seems very keen,' I say with arched eyebrow.

'He's Aunt Jayne's boyfriend,' Hannah informs me. 'And Mo is Mum's.'

'Hans!'

'Well he is. You're not very good at keeping secrets, Mum. I have eyes and ears, you know.'

The three of us stare at Hannah, Lara's face turning a very unflattering shade of beetroot, then Jayne and I can no longer contain our laughter.

'Is William still your boyfriend, Auntie Verity?'

I sober and we all fall silent.

'No, Hannah. He's poorly at the moment, and I don't know what will happen, or if we'll still be friends.'

'You're sure to be when he's himself again,' the child asserts. 'Everyone says so.'

'Hannah, why don't you go and get a drink? You know where the machine is.'

'Coke?'

'Diet Coke. And one for me too. Would you like one, Verity?'

Suddenly I have a monumental craving for sweet fizz. 'Yes, please, full-strength for me though, Hannah, I haven't had any sugar for three months!'

She raises her eyebrows at Lara, waiting for her mother's permission. After receiving the required nod, she looks at Jayne, who holds up a travel mug. 'I'm okay, thanks Hans. I still have coffee.'

She collects some coins and skips out of the room, delighted at the prospect of pop.

'Now she's gone, you two – spill. I haven't had a chance to ask you properly. When did you and Vikram get together, Jayne? Exactly who is Mo, and how long have you been seeing him, Lara?'

'Short answer, a couple of months now,' Jayne says. 'We've all been spending a lot of time both here and at your place. We just clicked.' She waves a hand, embarrassed.

I smile, it's been too long since she's been interested in a man, and Vikram is a decent one. A bit abrupt at times if I remember correctly, but then so is Jayne. They're a good match.

I turn my attention to Lara, my smile widening at the grin on her face.

'Mo works with Vikram. He's a tiler, in fact he's there now, working on the en-suites.'

'Tiling?' I'm shocked. The last time I saw The Rookery, it was a building site, and I'm still struggling to fully comprehend the length of time I've been in hospital.

'It really is nearly ready, Verity,' Lara says, taking my hand. 'I know it must be hard, but you've been here a long time. You can still open for Easter if you want to.'

'Easter?'

'Yes, it's in a couple of weeks.'

'Two weeks?' I'm stunned. We only just celebrated Christmas.

Lara squeezes my hand, and Jayne moves to sit on the bed. 'It'll take a while to orient yourself,' she says, ever practical. 'We haven't done anything about guests yet. No advertising, and while we've registered you with the online booking sites, we've not made the listings live.'

'We wanted to wait until you were home and well again,' Lara puts in. 'You should be the one to click those buttons.'

'And we wanted to help but not take over,' Jayne finishes.

'Have we done right?' Lara asks.

Tears are pouring down my face, and I grasp both their hands in mine. 'I don't know how to thank you both,' I manage to say. 'I could have lost everything, have nowhere to go.'

'You'll always have somewhere to go,' Jayne says as they both embrace me.

'What's happened?'

Lara turns. 'Nothing, Hans. We've just been telling Auntie Verity about all the work that's been done at The Rookery. She's only crying because she's happy.'

'Oh.' Hannah thinks a moment. 'If Auntie Verity's going home, does that mean we won't live there anymore?'

A shaft of horror spears my heart, and I glance at Lara, then Jayne, then back again.

'How am I going to manage all those stairs?'

'Don't worry, Verity, we've thought of that,' Jayne says. 'You mentioned to Vikram about having the downstairs doorways wide enough for wheelchairs and pushchairs, and we realised it would take you a while to get your strength back.'

'We've made it a fully disabled-accessible room,' Lara interrupts. 'Grab handles in the bathroom, walk-in shower with a drop-down seat, all the necessary rails everywhere.'

'We thought you could use it until you were strong enough to live upstairs again. You'd have everything you needed.'

'What about a kitchen?' I break in.

Jayne continues, 'The kitchen for guest breakfasts is all ready. You can use that for yourself too, and you can get around every area downstairs in a wheelchair if you need to.'

'At least at first,' Lara adds. 'And when you're ready for guests, you can send them up to their rooms and maybe hire one of the local girls as chambermaid, or . . .' She pauses to wave her open palms in a gesture similar to jazz hands. '*Or*, during the Easter holidays, Hannah and I can stay in your apartment, and I can take guests up and help with their rooms.'

Tears overwhelm me yet again. 'I don't know what to say,' I gasp. 'Thank you.'

'Stop doing that with your hands, Mum, it's weird.'

This time, Hannah is part of the group hug.

6.

'Ready?' Lara asks.

'Definitely,' I say and smile, although I'm far from sure about it. On the one hand I can't wait to get out of the hospital. But on the other, I'm nervous about returning to The Rookery. And my trepidation is not just about managing a three-storey guesthouse in hilly, cobblestoned Haworth while dependant on crutches and a wheelchair.

What would I find there? And, more importantly, what would find me?

'Can I push?' Hannah asks.

'Only if you're careful and don't go too fast.'

'Okay!' She gets behind my wheelchair, grabs the handles, and throws her weight behind her push, but I don't budge.

'You need to take the brake off, Hans. Here, now try.'

'Thanks, Mum.' She squeals as we career across the room.

'Yeah, thanks Lara,' I say, hanging on for dear life.

'Don't worry, Auntie Verity, I won't crash you, I'm getting the hang of it!'

'Oof,' I say as my knees bang into the door. 'Maybe let Mum get me out of the room, then you can do the straight bits.'

'Okay.'

'Sorry, Verity,' Lara whispers in my ear as she manoeuvres the chair on to a more productive course.

'It's fine,' I say, uncontrollable laughter spilling out of me. 'I haven't ridden the dodgems for years!'

'They're not that easy to control, you know.' Lara just manages to avoid another bump.

'Me now!' Hannah says.

'Verity?'

'Why not? This is the most fun I've had in months!'

'Don't encourage her, Verity. We've got a long walk to get out of here.'

I clutch the armrests again, as Lara grabs the handles to help Hannah retain control and avoid us crashing into the nurses' station.

'Whoa,' the man sitting there says. 'Looks like you've got an awkward one there.'

'She's doing her best,' Lara defends her daughter.

The nurse smiles. 'I meant the chair. Let's see if I can find you a better one.'

'Oh. Yes please. Thank you.'

I don't have to see Lara to know she's bright red and refusing to look at Hannah. She won't hear the end of this for a very long time.

'Here, try this one. Do you need a hand transferring?'

'No, I should be okay, thanks,' I say and use one of my crutches to lever myself up to my feet, then back down to sit in the new chair.

'This one's much better, thank you!' Hannah sings out as she pushes me – now in a straight line – down the corridor.

Lara is strangely quiet as I hang on, and I breathe a sigh of relief when we reach the lift doors with no further mishap.

'I said not so fast, Hans,' Lara pants as she catches us up.

'This isn't an awkward one, Mum. I didn't bump Auntie Verity into *anything* with this one,' Hannah replies as the lift pings and the doors open.

I'm face-to-face with William. His face drains of colour but he tries to smile.

'Hi,' I say.

He nods.

'Hello Verity,' Vikram says from his position at the controls of William's wheelchair. 'How are you feeling?'

They both glance at Lara and Hannah, then look back at me in my chair, trying to hold on to my crutches as well as the armrests.

I shrug. 'Getting there. Well, you know.'

William nods. 'Going home?' he asks.

'Yes, not quite sure how I'll get on though.' I smile and nudge the crutches. 'You?'

'Not yet.' He lapses back into silence and the lift doors start to close.

'Oops,' Lara says and William sticks his leg out to halt the doors.

'Come on, William, we're holding them up.'

William doesn't look at me again as Vikram pushes him past us and we take their place in the lift.

'Well, that was awkward,' Lara says once we start our descent.

'He's still not the proper William,' Hannah says.

'What do you mean, Hans?'

Hannah lifts her shoulders exaggeratedly then drops them again in response to her mother's question, but remains silent.

I remain quiet on the journey home. Lara does her best to distract me, but I can't forget the way William's face paled at the sight of me, nor the stilted words – I can't call it conversation. At least I saw William rather than Harry, but who did *he* see? Me or Martha?

'Verity.'

I startle out of my reveries and look at Lara, then out of the window – we're parked outside The Rookery.

'Sorry, Lara, lost in thought.'

For answer, she smiles, lays a gentle hand on my forearm, then gets out of the car and walks around to open my door and hand me my crutches.

'Thanks.' I haul myself out of the car and catch hold of Lara as one of my crutches slips on the wet cobbles.

'Welcome home. What do you think?'

I look up at the new voice. 'Jayne, what are you doing here?'

'I've taken a week off work so I can help you settle back in.'

I smile at her then look up at the façade of The Rookery and freeze.

'Don't you like it?'

'I told you we should have waited until she was home,' Lara says.

'It's supposed to be a surprise – a welcome home, but if you don't like it, we can get it redone,' Jayne says.

I stare at the signage, at the three rooks above the lettering. 'Three for a funeral,' I say.

'What?'

'One for sorrow, two for mirth, three for a funeral.'

'No Verity. It's one for sorrow, two for joy, three for a girl,' Lara says.

'I'll google it,' Jayne says, ever practical. 'Come inside and sit down. I know you have to keep walking, but you're also not supposed to overdo it.'

'I thought Vikram put those pigeon spikes on all the window ledges,' I say.

'Only upstairs and the roof edge,' Jayne says. 'He says no birds will roost on the ground-floor window ledges, there are too many people about. Now come on, stop worrying, and come inside before you fall.'

I force a smile on to my face.' I can't wait to see what you've done inside,' I say as I negotiate my way up the steps and through the front door.

'There's wheelchair access at the side,' Lara says, 'but this is what most people will see when they come in for the first time. We wanted to give you the full effect.'

I stop as the feeling of foreboding that overtook me outside diminishes. To my relief, the reception area is laid out exactly as I'd envisaged and arranged with the build team, with desk before me, a lounge area to my left, and open-plan dining room to my right.

The wallpaper is a tasteful gold and pale blue pattern; classy without being chintzy, and I grin at Jayne, already looking quite at home behind the reception desk.

Before I can speak, Lara has bustled me to the new downstairs guest room, and I sit on the bed in relief.

'You look exhausted, Verity.'

I nod. 'That trip took a lot out of me.'

'Your strength will come back.' Lara rubs my arm in reassurance. 'Have a rest and come back out when you're ready. We've ordered you a wheelchair from Amazon, and it should arrive tomorrow, will you be all right on crutches for today?'

'I'll manage. Thanks, Lara,' I say as she leaves me in peace to recover, and I look round to take in the room.

They've done a fantastic job, and have stuck to my visions for the décor, but it doesn't feel quite right.

I haven't chosen the wallpaper or the furniture. I haven't placed it. Nor have I chosen the curtains, bedding, carpet – even though I may well have made the same choices as my friends.

I sigh. I'm being ungrateful and know it.

Jayne and Lara have done an amazing job and I'm extremely lucky to have them. If they hadn't taken it on, the build would have stopped, I'd have nowhere habitable to stay and would not be able to start renting rooms out to guests for months yet.

I give myself a mental shake, then clump to the bathroom on my crutches. I eye the grab handles and rails with a mixture of relief and distaste; hating that I need them, yet grateful that they're there.

It's only temporary.

I turn to exit, and see rows of small toiletry bottles arranged neatly on the windowsill and shelf above the sink. The samples to test. I peek into the shower cubicle. Yep, at least a dozen bottles of shower gel, shampoo and conditioner. I giggle to myself – Lara clearly enjoyed that job!

When I'm ready, I make my way back to Reception, where my friends are waiting for me. I give them a big grin. 'I don't know how to thank you both.'

'Do you like it?'

I nod. 'It's perfect. You even remembered what I said about wallpapers.'

'Of course we did.'

'It was ages ago.'

'You know our Jayne,' Lara says. 'Never forgets anything, just files it away in that head of hers.'

'And you've been grateful for it on more than one occasion,' Jayne retorts as she taps a computer keyboard. 'Ah, here we are.' She scans the screen. 'You might want to sit down.'

My heart sinks. *What now?* But a seat is a good idea at this moment and I limp to the nearest armchair as Lara dashes around the desk to check out the screen for herself.

I catch a look between the two women as I sit. 'Just tell me,' I say. 'Whatever it is, just say it.'

'Well, you're both right. About the rooks. The modern version of the nursery rhyme is one for sorrow, two for joy, three for a girl, and four for a boy, and it counts the birds you see, whether magpies, rooks or crows.'

'But,' I prompt.

'But there's an earlier version. The one you quoted outside, Verity.'

'How much earlier?'

'Do you know any other lines?' Jayne asks in lieu of answering my question.

'Er, let me see. One for sorrow, two for mirth, three for a funeral, four for birth. Umm, five for Heaven, six for Hell, seven for the Devil, his own self.'

'If seven's for the Devil, what's a whole flock of them for?' Lara asks.

'Parliament,' I correct. They ignore me.

'Well,' Jayne says. 'There are a couple of older versions as well, but that one ... That one, according to Wikipedia ...' she tails off.

'Just say it, Jayne.' I think I know what she's going to say and feel almost resigned to it.

'The one you just recited was published in a book of proverbs and popular sayings—'

'When?'

'1846.'

'When Harry and Martha lived,' I say.

'Hmm.'

'It means nothing,' Lara says, hugging a tearful Hannah. 'It's coincidence, that's all. It's a common verse and there are all sorts of versions.'

'Yes, well said, Lara,' Jayne says. 'We're letting fear and imagination take over. Enough of that. Lara, will you get the champagne? It's time to celebrate Verity's homecoming, not worry about creepy old nursery rhymes.'

7.

'Off to bed now, Hans,' Lara says. 'They'll be here soon.'

'Aw, can't I stay up a bit longer, Mummy? Say goodnight to Mo and Vikram too?'

Lara rests her hands on her hips and regards her daughter with pursed lips. 'All right. But just half an hour.'

Jayne and I exchange a glance at the theatre of Hannah's bedtime routine.

'An hour.'

'Half.'

'Half an hour, then TV.' Hannah grins, knowing she's won when the knock at the door interrupts negotiations and her mother winks at her.

'I'll get it,' Jayne motions at me to stay on my chair. She's been warning me all day not to overdo it. And whilst frustrating, I'm beginning to appreciate her concern. We've been preparing for tonight all day, and every muscle in my body hurts. I'm looking forward to a fun, relaxing evening with my friends.

'Evening,' I say, greeting Vikram and Mo with a smile.

Mo crosses the room to Lara to give her a quick kiss, then crouches in front of Hannah.

I crane my neck to look behind Vikram, but no one else is with them. I'm not surprised at his absence, only at the sense of loss I feel.

I glance back at Mo as Hannah erupts into giggles, and my smile becomes genuine once again as I catch the glance that passes between Mo and Lara. I haven't seen Lara look so happy for a very long time.

I turn my attention back to Jayne as she asks Vikram, 'No William?'

He shrugs. 'We invited him, and he may turn up.'

'Or he may not,' Mo butts in.

Vikram pushes his lower lip up in a scowl. 'Aye. It's hard to know with him at the moment. But if he don't turn up, he'll be missing out by the smell of it.'

'A proper roast,' I say, trying to ignore the subject of William. 'Roast Yorkshire lamb, veg and potatoes, homemade mint sauce, the works. What would you like to drink?'

'Don't you dare wait on them, Verity. They know where the kitchen is, they can help themselves.'

'Should do, we built it,' Vikram jokes and points Mo toward the kitchen door.

'You're not the boss tonight, Vik, it's your turn to get the drinks in,'

Mo retorts. The uneasy formality collapses and the atmosphere lightens.

Jayne goes with him to choose a bottle of wine for us and I wonder if they're trying to hide something from me. I give myself a mental shake – being stuck inside for so long is playing with my head, they probably just want a moment alone.

'I've basted the lamb,' Jayne says when they emerge laden with glasses and bottles. 'It's nearly there so I've taken it out to rest while the veg and spuds finish off.'

'Thanks, Jayne,' I say as I accept a glass of red.

'How are you feeling, Verity?' Vikram asks. 'I can't see any crutches, are you getting about easier?'

'Yes, thank goodness! I still need crutches on the stairs, but I can walk on the flat now without too much pain. I just need a stick by afternoon, and I'm getting stronger every day.'

'You'll be back to normal in no time,' Lara says.

'Yes, it's scary, though, just how quickly muscles deteriorate, and how hard it is to get back into condition.'

'You'll be fine once you're open,' Mo says. 'Running up and down all those stairs all day will get and keep you fit.'

I laugh. 'You can say that again!'

'Have you had any more thoughts about when to open?' Vikram asks. 'You were hoping to be up and running soon.' He flinches at Jayne's elbow jab then realises what he's said and gives me an embarrassed smile with gritted teeth. 'So to speak.'

I laugh again. 'Very true – in all sorts of ways! I'm taking up Lara's offer of help, and am planning on a soft opening just after Easter, no fuss. Hopefully if I start slowly and build, I'll be able to manage.'

'That sounds sensible. Shame though, I was looking forward to a big opening party.'

'We can always have one of those later in the year – midsummer or something,' Lara says.

'Has anything else . . . odd . . . happened?' Mo asks.

'No, thank goodness. All quiet.'

'That's good,' Vikram says. 'Maybe it's over.'

'Maybe,' I say. 'Hope so.'

'I'm going up to my room now, Mum. 'Night, everyone,' Hannah says.

'Of course, Hans. Just remember, half an hour of TV, then lights out.'

Hannah nods, wends her way around the room to bestow goodnight kisses, then disappears up the staircase.

'Is she all right?' Vikram asks.

Lara sighs. 'Not really. She was scared when Verity and William were in the hospital, but she's dealing with it. I'll go up and check on her in a few minutes.'

No one knows what to say, and we all jump at a knock on the door.

Vikram shoots to his feet. 'I'll get it.'

'Mate, you made it!' he exclaims, then stands aside to allow William access.

He moves a few steps forwards, then stops, looking unnerved at being the centre of attention. 'Hi,' he says. 'I-I thought it was time . . . and with the lads being here too . . .' he tails off again after glancing at Vikram and Mo.

'Welcome, William,' I say and get to my feet. 'It's good to see you. What would you like to drink?'

'Black Sheep if you've got it, please.'

'I'll get it,' Jayne says. 'I need to check on the veg anyway.'

'Come and sit down, mate,' Vikram says. 'What's that?'

'Oh, I thought, well . . .' William stops, then looks at me. 'It's a housewarming present. I started working on it months ago, before . . . well, you know. Before you even bought this place. I-I'm sorry I didn't tell you about it before, but, well, you know . . .'

He turns the large picture frame and I gasp, then stare at the painting. I'm standing at the top of a stone flight of steps. Steps I recognise. Steps that are no longer there, but once rose up the wall to my back to the weaver's gallery. The last image Harry would have seen.

8.

'That was delicious,' Vikram says as he pushes his chair away from the table to give his belly a bit more room. 'Can't beat a proper homemade apple pie.'

I catch the glance between Jayne and Lara and hide my smile. I wonder which supermarket it came from, whichever one it was would be seeing a sharp rise in apple pie sales.

'Would anyone like coffee or are you happy on wine?'

I catch another glance between my two best friends and my heart sinks. *Now what are they planning?*

'Let's stick to alcohol,' Lara says. 'At least till we show you this.'

'Show me what?'

'You remember the CCTV Sparkly had such fun and games installing?' Vikram asks.

I nod, though in truth had forgotten all about it until now.

'While you were in the hospital we—'

'We watched it,' Lara cuts Vikram off. 'We needed to find any clues at all about what happened, why both of you fell unconscious that night.'

'And you found something?'

'I'll say we did,' Mo butts in.

'It's all set up behind reception to play back,' Jayne adds. 'Do you want to see it?'

I glance at William as he flicks his gaze to me, and as one we push our chairs back and move towards Reception.

'I think that's a yes,' Vikram says, smiling at Jayne.

Our friends gather around us, and I take hold of the mouse.

'You just need to click there.' Vikram points to the arrow icon.

Lara leads the way out of my living area into camera shot, Jayne hot on her heels, Vikram doing his best to protect them with the chair.

'Where's Verity?'

'And William?'

The three look at each other in terror, then Vikram draws a deep breath, warns Lara and Jayne to stay back and opens the door a crack.

Squinting, peering into the dim room, he steps back in surprise and the door swings open, presenting a view of the living and dining area.

The birds have all found a perch, covering almost every surface – except for one area around the table, an area they all seem to be watching; maybe guarding.

William and I are in a heap on the floor, clutching each other, neither moving, with two orbs spinning and dancing above us.

'Will? Will, mate, can you hear me?' Vikram edges into the room, but the birds hold their perches.

Jayne and Lara follow, calling my name.

I don't answer, and the birds don't take flight.

'Rewind that, will you?' William says, leaning forward on his seat. 'What just happened there?'

'Did you see it too, Verity?' Lara asks.

Shocked into silence by what I saw, I nod.

Jayne rewinds the footage, saying, 'Lara saw it straight away, I had to rewatch it a couple of times before I could see.'

She clicks on Play, and we lean forward as far as we can to get the best view of the screen.

The orbs whirling and dancing above us part, then disappear. One zooms into William's chest, and the other into my forehead. They do not reappear.

Vikram reaches our prone bodies and shakes William's shoulder.

No reaction.

He places two fingers on William's neck.

'There's a pulse. Verity too, but they're not responding. I think you'd better call for an ambulance.'

9.

'Well that was less than subtle,' William says as the two couples make their excuses and go upstairs.

'Not really.' I laugh.

'No,' he agrees. 'Well, at least things are starting to make sense now, kind of.'

'Yes, that footage is pretty unequivocal. Those orbs were Harry and Martha.'

'Must have been. But why would they do this to us?'

I have no answer for that, and we sit in awkward silence while we both scrabble for something to say.

'She did finish *Wuthering Heights*, you know. Martha,' I say, at last.

'Did she?'

'She knew she got it wrong, jumped to false conclusions. That you, that Harry, wasn't Heathcliff.'

'Hmm.'

'She never forgave herself.'

'Good.'

'She was terrified of losing Harry; of what might be. Life was so fragile back then.'

'Still is.'

I pause, wondering how to draw William out and get him talking. 'Who do you think it was?'

'What?'

'That Emily loved so fiercely.'

William smiled. 'Emily did everything fiercely, why not love too?'

'But who?' I persist.

'I reckon it wasn't a who at all, she certainly didn't love Harry like that. I reckon it was a what, a where.'

Confused, I pull a face. 'What are you talking about?'

'I mean, that's how she loved the moors: intensely, passionately, with deep abandon, even when the weather closed in, and when they turned on her and nearly killed her. Remember the bog burst?'

I nod.

'It never stopped her going back up there. The animals she helped – saved from the moors – they hurt her sometimes, bit or clawed her, but she never minded.'

'And when she was away from the moors, she got ill,' I say, remembering.

'Aye, she used to say that if she was ever forced to live anywhere else, she would die.'

'No wonder she never married.'

'She was only thirty when she died, she had time yet.'

'Not in those days,' I remind him. 'People married young 'cause they died young too, especially in Haworth.'

'Aye, you've a point there.'

'Heath,' I say. 'It's another word for moor.'

'Aye, and there are a few cliffs up there too.' William grins. 'She did things her own way, did Emily. One of a kind, that girl, always was.'

We lapse into silence.

I regard him for a few moments, but he doesn't meet my gaze. I decide to tackle this head on.

'You're scared to be alone with me, aren't you?'

'No. Well, yes, a little bit. I look at you and can see Martha, standing at the top of those stairs, staring after me. It's . . . bewildering, and frightening. History has a habit of repeating itself.'

'It's already tried, and failed,' I admit. 'It's done, history is history.'

'What do you mean?'

'Antony.' I reply, then heave a breath to bolster my resolve. 'When I found out about what he was up to . . .' I falter, and William reaches out to take my hand. He meets my eyes, and I decide to believe in the encouragement and reassurance I see there.

'When I found out about the other women, the catfishing.' I pause again, then sigh. I have to do this or it will never go away. 'I was so hurt, so angry. I felt so betrayed, so humiliated, I *wanted* to kill him. No!' I reach out to keep hold of William's suddenly withdrawn hand. 'Hear me out.'

I take another deep breath, then caress the back of William's hand with my thumb.

'I didn't. He was right there, at the top of the stairs, just like Harry and Martha.'

'But you didn't push?' William interrupts.

I meet his eyes again. 'Not only that, but I used every ounce of willpower I possessed to *not* push him.'

'Is that supposed to reassure me?'

'Yes. Don't you see? I'm not Martha. I haven't lived her life. I fought against the hurt and betrayal. I fought the instinct to push. I am not a killer.'

William gazes into my face, unnerving me with his close scrutiny. 'But you were scared you could be.'

My features crumple and tears spill. 'Terrified,' I confess. 'For an instant, for one terrible instant, I really considered doing it. I could have said he'd tripped and no one would have known I had it in me to kill.

He's a clumsy bastard, I could have got away with it.' My voice had reduced to a whisper.

'But you didn't, did you?'

No. Not said, just a shape formed by my lips.

'Then you're *not* a killer.'

I can't speak or meet his eyes any longer.

He grasps my hand now. Hard.

'Don't you see, Verity?'

'What?'

'That's what this is all about. We know from your father's name that you're related to Martha somehow.'

'So I have a murder gene, is that what you're saying?'

'No, dammit!' William takes a calming breath, sits back down after his explosive words, and places his hands on his knees after I pull away from him.

'You were given the same test, don't you see? And you passed. Where Martha didn't. You've just not accepted that because the "could have" is so strong in your conscience; it stopped you accepting that the important thing is that you *didn't* push.'

'What?' I'm thoroughly confused now.

'You didn't kill Antony, despite what he did and how much you wanted to,' William explains. 'You didn't kill him, Verity, you are not a killer.'

'But I came so close!'

'And didn't do it. And Martha came back to make you understand that.'

I stare at him, starting to accept what he's saying.

'You're not a killer, Verity,' he repeats.

'No. No, I'm not am I?' I laugh – a strange, strangled sound, but a laugh of relief all the same. 'I didn't kill him. I really, *really* wanted to, but – I didn't,' I add quickly, seeing the alarm in William's eyes. 'I didn't push.'

William smiles at me, and I sit back, my body feeling weak, as if I would crumple.

The fear and self-loathing that has been keeping me upright since that morning suddenly drains away. 'I'm not a killer, I'm not that person.'

William moves closer, tentatively it has to be said, but forward propulsion all the same. He pulls his chair along, until he's as close as he can be without sitting on my lap, and wraps his arms around me.

I pull back.

'I understand now why Martha came, why she's been here, but what about Harry? He's been with you – there were definitely two orbs – why? And why did they push Jayne and attack Antony?'

'My guess is it was Martha who did both of those – she was the one who let anger get the better of her, who lashed out.' William takes my hand as he speaks and rubs his thumb over my skin.

'That does actually make sense. She was frustrated, unable to communicate, and trying to do so in the only way she could.'

'Jayne, and especially Antony, were getting in the way of us meeting.'

'But why was Harry with her?'

'To keep her in check maybe?'

'Or to warn you to stay away from me?'

William laughs. 'Just the opposite. He's forgiven her, don't you see? He came here now to help Martha communicate her message. Whatever she did—'

'Whatever she did? She pushed him down the stairs and broke his neck!'

'But he's forgiven her – he understands, he still loves her and wants to be with her. The only one who can't forgive her is Martha herself, and Harry wants her to understand that. And he's letting us know too.'

I stare at him. *Does he really believe that?* I remember my dreams when I first arrived in Haworth, Harry had been with Emily, not Martha.

He recognises the scepticism in my eyes and sighs, grins, then says, 'All right, fair enough, that's unlikely. He's probably punishing her still, won't ever forget it or stop hating her, but is making sure we get it right while he's at it.'

'Now *that* I can believe,' I say with a small smile.

'It's only been a hundred and eighty years or so,' William adds. 'She still has millennia to repent.'

I eye him cautiously. '*You're* not going to hold a grudge, are you?'

He smiles properly and shrugs. 'Well, it does kind of run in the family . . .'

The humour evaporates.

'In the family,' I repeat. 'We're related!'

'I guess so.'

We stare at each other, stricken.

'But only very, very, *very* distantly,' he adds, then leans forward and kisses me.

I pull back. 'One more thing.'

'What?' He sounds exasperated.

'The Grey Lady. How does she fit in?'

He opens his mouth, then closes it again with a frown. 'I'm not sure. Emily was there, wasn't she? I mean here.' He points at the wall between The Rookery and Weaver's Row.

'Yes. And Lara said something–' I pause, trying to remember.

'What?'

'That the Grey Lady is an, an *imprint*, like a recording in time.

Repeating the same action over and over again.'

'So ... what? She's repeating that final climb up the steps before Harry's death, and has done for all these years?'

'I guess so.' I shrug. 'Although the last time I saw her, she turned and looked at me.'

'Maybe she has resolution too, now, and can finally rest in peace.'

'I hope so.'

10.

Two Weeks Later

'Morning, Verity,' Lara says as she enters Reception. 'Are you ready for the big day?'

I pull my lips into a tortured smile and Lara laughs.

'Don't look so worried. We're ready, and Hannah and I will stay for the rest of the Easter holidays – by that time you'll be able to cope with the stairs much better and you can vacate the downstairs room and let it out. You're not on your own, you know.'

I give her a proper smile and relax. 'Thank you so much for giving up your holidays to help me out.'

'Are you kidding? This is an adventure – we have our own apartment for three weeks, and in a guesthouse.' She pointed upwards to indicate my quarters. 'And we're spending the holidays with good friends. Hannah loves exploring the village and moors, and there's always something to do. She thinks she *is* on holiday, don't you, Hans?'

Hannah looks confused, then shrugs. 'I guess so. Can I take Grasper out later?'

'You'll have to ask Aunt Jayne when she gets here.'

'Okay.'

'Speak of the Devil,' I say at a knock at the door, and go to let Jayne in.

'Morning,' she sings out as she enters The Rookery.

Lara giggles. 'Looks like you had a good night.'

Jayne blushes, then shrugs. 'I'd forgotten what it was like to wake up next to someone in the morning.'

'You and Vikram getting on well then?' Lara asks.

Jayne nods, her face still red, and I give her a hug. 'It's great to see you so happy.'

'Yes, yes, okay,' Jayne says, embarrassed. 'Have you got the coffee on?'

Lara laughs, walks to the sideboard and gestures at the freshly made pot of coffee waiting for us.

'Well pour it then,' Jayne says, laughing, 'don't just show it off, you're not hosting a game show.'

'I hope Vikram knows what he's getting into,' I say with a chuckle.

Jayne gives an embarrassed grimace. 'The first thing he does in the morning is get me a coffee,' she admits.

'Aunt Jayne, where's Grasper?'

'He's at Vikram's house, Hannah. With it being Auntie Verity's big opening, he's better off out of the way.'

'Oh.' Hannah's face falls in disappointment.

'Don't worry, we can go and get him later and you can take him out for a walk.'

'Okay.'

'Right, well, shall we have breakfast, then we can get on with the day?'

'Just what I was thinking,' I say. 'Come on through to the dining room.'

'Well, that went pretty smoothly,' I say, pleased with myself, 'despite all your different orders.'

'It was a test run, Verity. When guests are here, they'll all be ordering different things, and you need to serve everyone at the same table at the same time,' Jayne says. 'Whether you still need that walking stick or not.'

'I'm not talking to you for ordering poached eggs. That was just cruel.'

'But delicious and perfectly cooked.'

Lara smiles and tops up our coffees. 'What's up, Verity? You seem a bit out of sorts this morning.'

I sip my drink, then place my cup carefully on its saucer. 'I think I understand the orbs and the Grey Lady.' I pause.

'Yes,' Lara encourages. 'For what it's worth, I think you and William are right about them, and I don't think any of them will be seen again. They've done what they needed to do, and are at peace now.'

'That's not it, though, is it, Verity?' Jayne presses.

'No. It's the birds. Why did they congregate here? Why were they tapping the windows and breaking them?'

'Yes, Mum, I've been thinking about that too,' Hannah says. 'What were the birds doing?'

Lara sips her coffee. 'To be honest, I don't think we'll ever know for sure. It could be that the old tale about graveyard rooks being the souls of the dead, or maybe the souls of children who died before being christened, are true, and Harry and Martha being here made it easier for them to interact with us.'

'Or?' I push.

'Or Martha and Harry were trying to use them to communicate.'

'But it was Emily Brontë who had the connection with animals and birds,' Jayne points out. 'Could she have been trying to warn Verity?

Trying to prevent Martha taking her over?'

'That does make sense, Jayne, I'm impressed,' Lara says with a proud grin. 'Emily saw Martha at her worst, and was also invested in the village and doing what she could to ease suffering – whether animal or human. It makes sense she would or could use the birds to stop Martha causing more harm.'

I nod, the words whirling around my head.

'Have you been dreaming again?' Lara asks.

'No. Well, no dreams of Harry and Martha anyway, although I have been having nightmares. Probably just thinking about the opening.'

'It's no good just thinking about it, you've got to do it an'all, you know.'

'William!' I stand with a smile, unsure whether I should greet him with a kiss. Before I decide, the moment is over.

'What's that?' I ask instead, indicating the large, slim parcel he's carrying.

'Well, when we first met, I promised a certain somebody a painting.'

Hannah squeals. 'Is it my portrait? Have you painted me, Uncle William?'

I glance at William in consternation at the word uncle, but he's smiling broadly and offers the parcel to Hannah. As she takes it and all attention is on her, he leans over and kisses me.

I glance up, meet his eyes, and smile. My heart flips as he grins back down at me. At last, I only see William when I look at him and, as far as I can tell, he no longer sees Martha in me.

'William, that . . . that's amazing!' Lara says. 'I can't thank you enough. What do you think, Hans?'

Hannah is gobsmacked and stares at the painting. 'You've painted Grasper too.'

'Is that okay?'

'It-it's perfect! I love it! Thank you, Uncle William.' She leaves the painting on the tabletop and runs over to give him a hug. The smile on William's face expands further, and I step over to the painting to have a proper look.

He has really caught Hannah, not only superficially, but something in her expression that is simply . . . Hannah. She's cuddling Grasper, who is looking at her in adoration; they're alone on the moors, with a reservoir in the background and a hovering kestrel above.

I glance up at Lara and see she is close to tears. Jayne gives her a squeeze and grins at her, but doesn't tease her. I can see Jayne is moved too.

'I'm going to hang it in my room, I can, can't I, Mum?'

'Yes, of course you can. Or we can hang it in the lounge if you want, so everyone can see it.'

'Umm, I'll think about it,' Hannah says, and I realise how much she's matured over the months I was absent. Physically she's still the same Hans, but she seems much older now somehow. *She's growing up*, I realise. *Fast*.

'Has everything gone live?'

I glance up at William, aghast. With the excitement of Opening Day, I'd completely forgotten to look.

'Let's check now then.'

I nod and cross to the reception desk to boot up the computer, while Jayne and Lara clear the breakfast things. Hannah is fixated, staring at her picture, exclaiming every time she notices a new detail.

I check my own website first, and make sure the booking page is now working as my web designer promised it would, then go to booking.com to check The Rookery's listing is live. William peers over my shoulder and rests his hands on my hips.

'Congratulations, Verity,' he whispers. 'You're officially open.'

I turn to check the others are still otherwise engaged, and wrap my arms around his neck. 'Thank you,' I whisper back.

'What for?'

'Well, you know. Sticking around and helping me after everything, well, after Martha—'

'Shh. That's all over, stop worrying. We're Verity and William. Martha and Harry have gone. Or has something happened?'

'No.' I shake my head. 'These days I only dream about you.' I stretch towards him and he meets my lips in a lingering kiss.

'No time for that, you've got a business to run.' Jayne's voice breaks the spell, and I pull back from him with a rueful grin.

I turn to admonish her, but am surprised to see her proffering two champagne flutes.

'Bucks fizz,' she clarifies, as Lara appears behind her with two more glasses.

'To The Rookery,' Jayne toasts. 'May God bless her and all who stay in her.'

I grin at the parody of the queen's ship-launch blessing, and sip the orange juice and champagne.

'To good friends.' It is my turn to toast.

'And to success and happiness – in all things,' Lara adds.

'I'll drink to that,' William says. 'And I have another gift, I think now is the ideal moment.' He fishes out a brown-paper-wrapped, flat package from his back pocket and hands it to me.

I glance up at him in question.

'Open it.'

I pull the paper away to reveal a flat board attached to a chain. *Vacancies* I read, then turn it over. *No Vacancies*. It's hand-painted, with a moor-landscape background, and the lettering is picked out in black. I look closer. Each stroke of each letter is styled as a feather.

'It's perfect, thank you, William.' I grin up at him and give him another kiss. A short one this time. 'I'd completely forgotten about a sign.'

He reaches into another pocket, pulls out a hook attached to a sucker, takes back the sign, and hangs it on the large window next to the front door.

'Now what?' Lara says. 'Is there anything that needs doing?'

I shake my head. 'Now we wait.'

'Well, I'll leave you to it,' William says. 'I need to open the gallery, but I'll pop back at lunchtime.' He gives me a peck on the cheek and waves to Lara, Jayne and Hannah. 'Have a good day – I'll put the word out on Main Street too, let people know you're open.'

'That would be great, thanks.'

11.

'Anything?' Jayne asks when she returns with Grasper, ready for his walk with Hannah.

I shake my head. 'Nothing. Five hours open and not a single enquiry.'

'Don't look so down, it's only the first day, it'll take time for word to get out, we just need to be patient.'

'Or maybe not,' Lara says, nodding at the window.

I glance out to see Vikram and Mo walking alongside a young couple and gesturing at The Rookery.

'Have you any rooms free?' Mo asks, throwing a wink to Lara. 'We met Carole and Bob here in the Bull. They've come out for the day and have decided to stay on, but haven't booked anywhere, can you help?'

'We certainly can,' I say. 'Welcome to The Rookery. How long would you like to stay?'

'A couple of nights,' Bob says. 'We didn't realise how much there is to do around here, and Carole really wants to go to an event at the museum tomorrow.'

'Oh, the Branwell Brontë talk?'

'Yes, and Bob wants to see the Flying Scotsman.'

'Oh yes, that's very popular – do you have tickets?'

'Yes, we bought them this morning.'

'Great – I hope you enjoy it. It's £100 per double room per night with full, home-cooked breakfast. Can I ask you to fill out a registration form, and also an authorisation for your credit card? You won't be charged until you check out.'

'That sounds fine,' Bob says, and Carole picks up the pen to fill in their details.

'We also include a complimentary bottle of wine – there's red in the room, or if you prefer we can change it for white.'

'Oh that's a nice touch. Red's fine, thank you.'

'You're in Emily's Room, which is at the back, so you have a view of the parsonage, and Lara will take you up. I hope you enjoy your stay.'

'Thank you.'

Lara ushers them to the stairs and upward, and I turn to thank Vikram and Mo, but realise Jayne has already taken care of them.

'You realise Will's been up and down Main Street telling everyone about this place,' Vikram says. 'Don't be surprised if you get busy.'

'Aye, but you'd better let him know when you're full, else you'll be turning people away.' Mo chuckles. 'The man's on a mission!'

I colour as they laugh, but can't help a big grin spread over my face at the thought of William herding tourists up the hill to The Rookery.

'Must want this place to be a success for some reason.' Vikram winks at me, then steps out of the way as another couple enter.

'Is this the place run by a real Earnshaw?' the man asks.

My colour deepens. 'It is, yes. I'm Verity Earnshaw, welcome to The Rookery.'

'The man in the art gallery said you could trace your family back to the Brontë era, his too.'

'That's right, yes.'

'And between them, they inspired at least one of Emily's characters,' Vikram put in.

I don't answer, but fill in the paperwork and send them upstairs with Lara as soon as she returns.

When we're alone again, I turn to Vikram. 'Don't do that, please.'

'What?'

'Use Harry and Martha like that, after what happened. Just let them rest in peace.'

'The best way you can ensure they rest is by getting things right. You *and* William,' Jayne says. 'And that includes filling this place. After what you went through, why wouldn't you take whatever advantage comes from it too?'

'And anyway, it's not like it's a lie, is it?' Vikram says.

'See, it pays to get in with the locals,' Jayne says as Lara shepherds another couple up to their room. 'I don't think you're going to have any trouble filling the rooms, not with Vikram and William on the case. You'll need more rooms at this rate!'

'Calm down, Jayne, it's only the first day, and we're not booked up yet. I'm still taking up the downstairs guest room, and the single room is still free.'

'Perfect, just what I was going to ask you.'

I turn to see a woman of my own age standing in the foyer, William behind her. *I need to install a bell on that door.*

'Welcome to The Rookery,' I say, and flash a smile at William. 'I see you've met our local artist.'

The woman and William burst out laughing.

'You could say that,' he says eventually, oblivious to my discomfort. 'Let me introduce you. Verity, this is my sister, Rebekah. Rebekah, Verity.'

'Oh!' I turn bright red with embarrassment. 'I'm so sorry. It's good to meet you.'

'And you. I missed you when I came up to visit William in hospital, but I've heard a lot about you. Hello, Jayne, nice to see you again,' she adds.

I'm confused for a moment but realise they must have met when I was unconscious.

'So how are you? I keep quizzing this one,' she links her arm with William's, 'but getting information is like dragging blood out of a stone.'

'It's a bit difficult to explain over the phone,' William defends himself.

'Why don't you come for dinner tonight? We'll fill you in on all the details, and we can get to know each other too.'

'Sounds perfect.'

I check her in, just in time for Lara's reappearance.

I turn the sign over to read: *No Vacancies*.

'Full already? See, nowt to worry about,' William says and embraces me. Stick with me, lass, we'll be reet.'

I nod. 'Will you stay tonight?'

'Sure?'

'Aye.' I'm aware of the silly grin on my face but can't do anything about it.

'Then there'll be no keeping me away.'

I grab William's arm at a tapping sound, and we turn to see a familiar black shape perching on the stone ledge outside the window. The rook pecks the glass again and both of us freeze. It holds my gaze for a few frenzied heartbeats then flaps away.

The End

If you enjoyed any of the books in the *Ghosts of Yorkshire* Boxed Set please consider leaving a rating and review on the site where you bought it. Reviews are incredibly important – they give the author valuable feedback, and help steer other readers/listeners towards books they would enjoy. Thank you.

"Writing can be an isolating occupation (apart from the characters marauding through my head!), and readers' opinions are the best motivator out there – to keep writing, to keep learning, to keep experimenting, and above all, to keep pouring my heart and soul into every story I write, but it's you – the reader – who give those characters life.
Thank you."

– Karen Perkins
North Yorkshire

**For more information on the full range of Karen Perkins' fiction, please go to her website:
www.karenperkinsauthor.com/**

**If you would like to contact Karen and/or join Karen's mailing list to be kept updated with news, upcoming releases and special offers, please go to:
www.karenperkinsauthor.com/contact**

Books by Karen Perkins include:

Yorkshire Ghost Stories

Parliament of Rooks: Haunting Brontë Country (Ghosts of Haworth, Book 1)
Knight of Betrayal: A Medieval Haunting (Ghosts of Knaresborough, Book 1)
The Haunting of Thores-Cross: A Yorkshire Ghost Story (Ghosts of Thores-Cross, Book 1)
Cursed (A Ghosts of Thores-Cross Short Story)

Expected late 2018:
Jennet: A Novel (Ghosts of Thores-Cross, Book 2)

To find out more about the full range of books in the Yorkshire Ghost Series, including upcoming titles, please visit:
www.karenperkinsauthor.com/yorkshire-ghosts

Valkyrie Series

Look Sharpe!
Ill Wind
Dead Reckoning

The Valkyrie Series: The First Fleet (Look Sharpe!, Ill Wind & Dead Reckoning)

Where Away – a Valkyrie short story (see below)

To find out more about the full range of books in the Valkyrie Series, including upcoming titles, please visit:
www.karenperkinsauthor.com/valkyrie

Where Away is being offered FREE for readers of the Valkyrie Series and will not be released separately—if you would like to read it, please go to: www.karenperkinsauthor.com/contact--special-offers

About the Author – Karen Perkins

Karen Perkins is the author of seven fiction titles in the Valkyrie Series of Caribbean pirate adventures and the Yorkshire Ghosts Stories.

All of her fiction titles have appeared at the top of bestseller lists on both sides of the Atlantic, including the top 50 in the UK Kindle Store.

Her first Yorkshire Ghosts novel – THE HAUNTING OF THORES-CROSS – won the silver medal for European fiction in the prestigious 2015 Independent Publisher Book Awards in New York, whilst her Valkyrie novel, DEAD RECKONING, was long-listed in the 2011 MSLEXIA novel competition.

Upcoming Release:
Jennet (The Ghosts of Thores-Cross #2) – Expected 2018

See more about Karen Perkins, including contact details and sign up to her newsletter, on her website:
www.karenperkinsauthor.com

Karen is on Social Media:

Facebook:
www.facebook.com/karenperkinsauthor
www.facebook.com/Yorkshireghosts
www.facebook.com/ValkyrieSeries

Twitter:
@LionheartG

Glossary of Yorkshire Terms

Addled	Confused, muddled
Allus	Always
An'all	As well
Anyroad	Anyway
Apeth	Idiot/fool
Aw reet	All right
Awd Carlin	Sharp old woman
Ey up	Greeting
Barguest	Evil spirit in form of an animal
Besom	A broom made from heather or twigs tied round a stick
Breeks	Breeches
Canny	Astute
Fret	Worry
Frit	Frightened
Gimmer	Young female sheep
Ken	Know
Mesen	Myself
Mithering	Fussing, pestering
Neps	Clusters and knots of wool fibres
Nithered	Cold/frozen
Noils	Short wool fibres
Nowt	Nothing
Ower 'ere	Over here
Owt	Anything
Poddy Lamb	Orphaned lamb
Reet	Right
Shoddy	Lowest quality wool, made from recycled garments and/or the sweepings from the mill floor
Spain	Separate lambs and ewes
Stook	Sheaves of grain stood up in field
Summat	Something
Tup	Breeding male sheep/ram
Watter	Water
Wether	Castrated lamb
Whiskybae	Whisky
Witchpost	Carved wooden post used as protection against witchcraft.

Lightning Source UK Ltd.
Milton Keynes UK
UKHW01n1943250718
326295UK00003B/7/P